Erotic Works of D.H. Lawrence

Erotic Works of D.H. Lawrence

EDITED BY CLAIRE BOOSS
AND CHRISTOPHER BUSA

Introduction by Christopher Busa

ILLUSTRATED IN COLOR WITH
THE EROTIC PAINTINGS OF
D.H. LAWRENCE

AVENEL BOOKS
New York

This volume contains the complete and unabridged texts of the original editions. They have been completely reset for this volume.

Note: the spelling and punctuation of the original works have been retained for this edition.

This 1989 edition is published by Avenel Books, distributed by Crown Publishers, Inc., 225 Park Avenue South, New York, New York 10003.

The paintings by D. H. Lawrence have been reproduced courtesy of the Rare Books and Manuscripts Division of the New York Public Library, Astor, Lenox, and Tilden Foundations.

Printed and bound in the United States of America

Library of Congress Cataloging-in-Publication Data

Lawrence, D. H. (David Herbert), 1885–1930.
    Erotic works of D. H. Lawrence / edited by Claire Booss and Christopher Busa ; introduction by Christopher Busa ; illustrated in color with the erotic paintings of D. H. Lawrence.
        p. cm.
    Contents: The trespasser—Honour and arms—Sun—Lady Chatterley's lover—A propos of Lady Chatterley's lover—Pornography and obscenity—The virgin and the gipsy—Love among the haystacks—Selected poems.
    ISBN 0-517-64304-9
    1. Erotic literature, English. I. Booss, Claire. II. Busa, Christopher. III. Title.
PR6023.A93A6 1989
823′.912—dc19   88-28328
                                                       CIP

Book design by Cynthia Dunne

h g f e d c b a

Contents

*I*llustrations in Color

About the Paintings

Although D. H. Lawrence did not create these paintings specifically for any of the works in this volume, they express so strongly the spirit of freedom and lyrical eroticism that it seems highly appropriate to reproduce them here.

When the paintings were first exhibited in London in 1929, the public shock and outcry was so great that the police closed the exhibit shortly thereafter. Lawrence deplored the then-current "horror of sexual life" characterized by an attitude to life "paralysed by fear . . . the most intimate fear and hate of one's own instinctive, intuitive body, and fear and hate of every other man's and every other woman's warm, procreative body and imagination." And he went on to observe the result this would have on the plastic arts "which depend entirely on the representation of substantial bodies [that] can only be perceived by the imagination . . . a kindled state of consciousness in which intuitive awareness predominates."

The plastic arts are all imagery, and imagery is the body of our imaginative life, and our imaginative life is a great joy and fulfilment to us, for the imagination is a more powerful and more comprehensive flow of consciousness than our ordinary flow. In the flow of true imagination we know in full, mentally and physically, at once, in a greater, enkindled awareness. At the maximum of our imagination we are religious. And if we deny our imagination, and have no imaginative life, we are poor worms who have never lived.

All the paintings which follow were executed in oil, with the exception of *Leda, Renascence of Men,* and *Under the Haystack,* which were done in watercolor. The phoenix motif was Lawrence's own design of the legendary bird that he took as his personal symbol.

CLAIRE BOOSS

The Myth of the Phoenix

"Beneath a hill in Elysium lies a verdant meadow shaded by dark-leaved ilex trees, where the moist earth grows ever green with undying grass. If we can trust in questionable beliefs, this is said to be the dwelling place of the sacred winged creatures, where profane birds are forbidden to go. There, far and wide, the innocent swans graze, and the long-lived phoenix, a bird always alone of its kind." *Et vivax phoenix, unica semper avis, the long-lived phoenix, a bird always alone of its kind,* wrote the Roman poet Ovid in a finely honed line that weighs immortality against eternal solitude.

The myth of the phoenix tells of its scarce sightings, rumored to be once every five hundred years. Lacking an eyewitness account, Herodotus, the Greek historian, based his description of the phoenix on paintings he had seen, and decreed that its plumage was "partly gold, partly red, and in shape and size exactly like an eagle." At the end of five hundred years, the phoenix builds its nest at the top of a palm tree—a funeral pyre of perfumed barks and yellow myrrh—and consumes itself in flames. From this nest of death a young phoenix emerges, flame from flame, life from death, to live alone another five hundred years and to bury its father's body in the temple of the Sun.

D. H. Lawrence first created his famous illustration of the phoenix burning in its nest for the 1928 edition of *Lady Chatterley's Lover.* As a symbol of his personal mythology, the phoenix is a figure rich with the conflicting imagery of Lawrence's writing. For he sensed the great forces that surge through our lives, separating and colliding, polarizing industrialization against nature, captivity against freedom, frigidity against sexuality. His sensuality was of flamelike intensity; his writing scented with the perfumed wood of the phoenix's funeral pyre. Like the phoenix, he transformed matter into being with the mastery of his craft; like the phoenix, he is unique—alone of his kind.

LOIS HILL

Introduction

Sex surely has a specific meaning. Sex means the being divided into male and female; and the magnetic drive or impulse which puts male apart from female, in a negative or sundering magnetism, but which also draws male and female together in a long and infinitely varied approach toward the critical act of coition. Sex without the consummating act of coition is never quite sex, in human relationships, just as a eunuch is never quite a man.

—D. H. Lawrence, from *Fantasia of the Unconscious*

This collection of writings by D. H. Lawrence emphasizes the erotic element, quite justifiably so, for Lawrence was the writer who penned "the best descriptions of sexual experience which have yet been done in English," as the eminent literary critic, Edmund Wilson, said of *Lady Chatterley's Lover* in a review he wrote at the time of its publication in the late 1920s. Lawrence was not competing with pornography. Deeply consumed by a powerful love for his wife, Frieda, he knew no such thing as bad sex, or rather knew that even when sex is bad, it is good. And Frieda said, "Considering sex is the very root of our existence, without which we would not walk on this earth, it seems worthy of any mature man's thought as much as any atom bomb."

Born in 1885, Lawrence grew up in the English Midlands as the beauty of the rural countryside was becoming blighted by machinery and smoke from newly mechanized industries. Nearby were the city of Nottingham and the Sherwood Forest of Robin Hood, the legendary outlaw who poached the king's deer, stole from the rich and gave to the poor, and who treated women well. As he grew up, Lawrence saw his own mother regret her choice of husband. His father was a warm, crude, passionate, black-bearded miner whose face and hands were perpetually stained with coal dust. Underground labor in the mines gave him the swarthy aspect of someone from an alien world, like a criminal or gipsy. He was almost illiterate and he read the newspaper by pointing to one letter at a time until he could spell out one word and move on to the next. Suspicious of the written word, he was astonished that his son should be paid a healthy sum for his first book, *The White Peacock*: "Fifty pounds! An' tha's never done a day's work in thy life!"

Lawrence's mother, a former schoolteacher and the daughter of an engineer, was more refined and had a love of books. Indeed, she valued the word above the flesh, the spirit more than the body. Her idea of a pleasant afternoon was to drink tea with the minister, Lawrence's godfather, discoursing on the meaning of Christ's miracle at Cana where He changed water into wine. Lawrence's mother was something of a snob, feeling superior to her husband. Perhaps she was justified in her irritation when she heard him in the lane, drunk, late for dinner, singing "Lead, Kindly Light," one of the hymns the congregation sang at the church on Sunday, as he lurched home in the dark after drinking with fellow miners in the pub.

For Lawrence, his father became associated with the demonic, the unconscious, and the animal way of knowing through one's senses, especially the sense of touch. Years later, in his essay "Nottingham and the Mining Countryside," Lawrence recalled his father's job as a "butty," a kind of foreman in charge of a face of coal and a gang of men: "Under the butty system, the miners worked underground as a sort of intimate community, they knew each other practically naked, and with curious close intimacy, and the darkness and the underground remoteness of the pit 'stall,' and the continual presence of danger, made the physical, instinctive, and intuitional contact between men very highly developed, a contact almost as close as touch, very real and very powerful." Despite the subjugation of his father to a life underground, Lawrence nevertheless esteemed the mode of knowledge that that life offered. In contrast, he believed that the civilizing process, leading to intellectual knowledge, took us further and further from intimate contact.

Lawrence was abnormally close to his mother. Their relationship is the theme of his autobiographical novel, *Sons and Lovers,* in which mother and son sleep together during a sickness, because "sleep is still most perfect, in spite of hygienists, when it is shared with a beloved. The warmth, the security and peace of soul, the utter comfort from the touch of the other, knits the sleep, so that it takes the body and soul completely in its healing." Lawrence absorbed his mother's traits—her yearning to be elsewhere; her prideful sense of being wellborn, of being in some sense aristocratic; her intellectual enthusiasm.

Sons and Lovers was published in 1913, shortly after the appearance of Sigmund Freud's essay, "The Most Prevalent Form of Degradation in Erotic Life," which treated analytically what Lawrence depicted with a vividness so exact as to be brutal. He showed the truth of Freud's statement that a man who is beloved as an infant will always retain the confidence of a conqueror. Of his mother, Lawrence wrote in the novel, "How she serves him, how she stimulates him, how her true female self is his, is wife-submissive to him as never, never it could be to a husband."

In *Sons and Lovers,* mother stimulates son to become an artist at the same time that she interferes with his developing love life, dividing his ability to feel affection and erotic desire for the same girl. Freud observed that this was one aspect of the Oedipal complex that was seldom resolved, causing men to become impotent with lovers who strike them as too "pure," too like their mothers, and to prefer sex with women who can be degraded in some way. Freud said that "some degree of this condition does in fact characterize the erotic life of civilized people," and Lawrence declared that it was "the tragedy of thousands of young men in England."

When he began publishing his work Lawrence was a scholarship student, and then became a teacher. The headmaster of the school where he taught, in the suburbs of London, remembered that "He used to say that boys ought to learn love poems at school, as a preparation for love in real life." Lawrence's first poems were almost botanical in their insistence that flowers are the sexual organs of plants. His second novel, *The Trespasser* (which appears in this collection), is an exceptionally fine, but less well-known, novel that shows the youthful Lawrence imagining himself as an older alter ego who has failed at love.

Although Lawrence's last novel, *Lady Chatterley's Lover,* attempted to show that adultery under certain circumstances is legitimate, the theme of the earlier *The Trespasser* treated adultery as a major moral transgression. The novel was based on a true story told to Lawrence by his friend and fellow schoolteacher, Helen Corke. Despondent and numb, she told Lawrence how her lover had hanged himself some months earlier. Using a diary she provided, Lawrence rewrote the story, imaginatively putting himself in the place of the dead lover, a thirty-nine-year-old music teacher and concert violinist named Siegmund. Siegmund hangs himself because "Helena" (as Helen is called in the novel) will not make love to him. They have "trespassed" by going away together to the Isle of Wight for a five-day idyll; he is married, with children. (Most departures from social morality in Lawrence take the form of trips, most often to foreign places.) There, Siegmund learns the bitter truth that "the best sort of women—the most interesting—are the worst for us. By instinct they aim at suppressing the gross and animal in us." Such a woman is a "dreaming woman whose passion exhausts itself at the mouth," meaning her lips manipulate her breath in the clever arts of talking and kissing, but she withholds herself sexually, exquisitely frustrating the man. As rule-breakers, Siegmund and Helena are failures; they fail to sin. Lawrence would later read Thomas Hardy and criticize Hardy for letting society win out in the end and punish the individual who trespasses. Here the risk taker is punished for risking, yet not risking enough.

Just prior to the publication of *The Trespasser,* Lawrence met Frieda von Richthofen. It was the great, transforming event of his life. With her he would spend the eighteen years that remained to him. When Lawrence first met Frieda, he was twenty-six and virtually penniless. Forced to stop teaching after becoming ill with pneumonia, he consulted, upon his recovery, Professor Weekley, a language instructor at Nottingham University (with whom he had studied French) about the possibility of going to Germany, where he hoped to obtain a position as *Lektor* or a "foreign teacher of his mother tongue." The professor had married a German woman during his own teaching period in Germany a dozen years earlier, and it was his wife, Frieda, who answered the door when Lawrence arrived for lunch at their house. In her memoir, *"Not I, But the Wind,"* Frieda relates, "The half hour before lunch the two of us talked in my room, French windows open, curtains fluttering in the spring wind, my children playing on the lawn." Lawrence said in his high-pitched, penetrating voice, "You are quite unaware of your husband, you take no notice of him."

This was true. Frieda was the bored wife of a dull professor. She was six years older than Lawrence, and had had three children during her marriage. She made frequent trips alone to Germany to visit her family and to meet with a circle of bohemian intellectual friends. After Frieda eloped with Lawrence, in explanation of her action she sent her husband letters she had received from her friend Otto Gross, who wrote that he dreamed of Frieda as "the woman of the future . . . this miracle, you, golden child" who managed to keep "the dirt of two gloomy millennia from your soul with your laughter and love." Gross believed that to make such a woman happy was to give the world a sun.

Lawrence, too, connected sun worship with the sexual pleasure of women, as is evident in the beautiful short story, "Sun." In this story about the liberating powers of the sun, a woman is ordered by her doctor to leave her northern city and seek the sun. She takes her child with her, so "he shall not grow up like his father, like a worm that the sun has never seen." She remembers that the Greeks had said, "A white, unsunned body was unhealthy, and fishy." The woman becomes sexually receptive through an almost biochemical process of exposure to the sun, which begins to seem almost a lover to her. The story is provocative in championing the woman's desire for pleasure against her husband's inhibitions. This is uniquely characteristic of Lawrence, who once promised "to do my work for women, better than suffrage." And it is also modern in the woman's revelations of body consciousness.

Six weeks after Lawrence spent that half hour talking with Frieda in her room, with the spring wind fluttering the curtains, the pair eloped to the continent. Henceforth, Lawrence boldly opted to live by his pen. The honeymooners tramped through the Alps under pale blue skies, living on black bread, fresh eggs, and berries. As she confesses in her memoir, Frieda was a lazy housekeeper and had never washed sheets until she lived with Lawrence. When she stumbled on a path and broke a strap on her shoe, she took off the other shoe and tossed it away. Lawrence lectured her: "A pair of shoes takes a long time to make and you should respect the labor somebody's put into those shoes," to which she retorted, "Things are there for me and not I for them, so when they are a nuisance I throw them away." Lawrence was also disgusted with the coffee she made, telling her, "Any common woman can do lots of things you can't do."

They were to become a legendary couple. When Frieda spilled coffee on a pillow, she would merely turn the pillow over. A visitor, David Garnett, reminisced in his memoirs on how Lawrence made washing dishes an occasion for a good time. He recalled that "His writing did not affect our daily life. It never occurred to me, or I think to Frieda, not to interrupt him, and we spent all the day together in one room, while he scribbled away at odd moments in the corner, jumping up continually to look after the cooking." After dinner they played charades. Lawrence had a phenomenal memory and an uncanny psychological insight into people. He was also a natural mimic, and one friend remembers that "He had a genius for 'taking people off,' and could reproduce voice and manner exactly. He told you that he had once seen Yeats or Ezra Pound for half an hour in a drawing-room, and straightaway Yeats or Ezra appeared before you. The slightest affectation of manner or social pretence was seized on mercilessly."

Lawrence's first editor, Ford Madox Ford, was an important British author when he befriended the as yet unpublished writer. In his book *Portraits from Life* he recalled the strong impression that Lawrence's writing made on him: "Each time that I have opened one of his books, or merely resumed reading one of his novels, I have had a feeling of disturbance—not so much as if something odd was going to happen to me but as if I myself might be going to do something eccentric." He wondered if this was the same sort of "disturbing emotion caused in manufacturers and bankers by seeing, in a deep woodland, the God Pan—or Priapus—peeping round beside the trunk of an ancient oak."

This glimpse into the uncanny and alien Lawrence called his "demon." When he found a blue gentian in the mountains, Frieda said, "I remember feeling as if he had a strange communion with it, as if the gentian yielded up its blueness, its essence to him." Lawrence did not think this detachment was extraordinary. In "Nottingham and the Mining Countryside" he wrote, "I've seen many a collier stand in his back garden looking down at a flower with that odd, remote sort of contemplation which shows a *real* awareness of the presence of beauty. It would not even be admiration, or joy, or delight, or any of those things which so often have a root in the possessive instinct. It would be a sort of contemplation: which shows the incipient artist."

In his writing Lawrence attempted to achieve a quality that he found in some paintings, which he described thus: "as if I'd painted the shimmering protoplasm in the leaves and everywhere, and not the stiffness of the shape." (Significantly, Lawrence spent most of his late adolescence painting, rather than writing, and late in life he returned seriously to painting.) Much of the splendid animation in Lawrence's writing comes from the way his images and situations and the cadences of his phrasing set up patterns of repetition, with mounting tensions that create excitement over slight modifications, so the words "shimmer" with additional meaning. If one can imagine this pleasurable tension transformed into sexual excitement, then it is easy to understand why Lawrence's critics were made uncomfortable by his very style. He defended himself, saying, "In point of style, fault is often found with the continual, slightly modified repetition. The only answer is that it is natural to the author; and that every natural crisis in emotion or passion or understanding comes from this pulsing, frictional to-and-fro which works up to culmination."

With Frieda, Lawrence claimed he had been transported into a condition of blessedness. Perhaps too stridently, he boasted, "I really believe in marriage. I have proved it." He countered Frieda's despair over her abandoned children with sharp anger. In a travel essay (published in the collection *Twilight in Italy*) written while living with Frieda in Italy, Lawrence described a man he had met who had been unable to produce children, a man who stood annulled and ashamed, "nothing, a shadow that vanishes into nothing." He wrote, "I was startled. This then is the secret of Italy's attraction for us, this phallic worship. To the Italians the phallus is the symbol of individual creative immortality, to each man his own Godhead. The child is but the evidence of the Godhead." He continued, "The substratum of Italy has always been pagan, sensuous, the most potent symbol the sexual symbol. The child is really a non-Christian symbol: it is the symbol of man's triumph of eternal life in procreation." Lawrence and Frieda went childless, and Lawrence declared, "The children are not the future. The living truth is the future."

Lawrence had begun the writing that led to *The Rainbow* and *Women in Love,* both novels considered to be masterpieces of English literature for their probings, especially into the psychology of women. He wrote to one of his editors, "I don't so much care what the woman *feels*—in the ordinary sense of the word. That presumes an *ego* to feel with." He likened the ego to a diamond and elemental woman to carbon, declaring, "The ordinary novel would trace the history of the diamond—but I say, Diamond, what! This is carbon!"

Lawrence and Frieda spent extended sojourns in Italy, France, India, Australia, the southwestern United States, and Mexico. Often they met other writers and painters in some remote spot on the globe, such as Capri (at that time). Lawrence had a gift for remaining friends with those whom he brilliantly insulted. His ridicule could be lethal, but he was also unsparing of himself. He created an intense and necessary atmosphere of intimacy, where truth had to be spoken before politeness could be observed. It was as if truth itself were nothing personal, but rather a third, impersonal thing, a holy ghost surrounding any relationship of significance.

Something of a priest for truth, Lawrence argued for a frank and healthy openness about sex. In his essay "Pornography and Obscenity" (included in this collection) he wrote, "Masturbation is the one thoroughly secret act of the human being, more secret even than excrementation." For Lawrence perceived that erotic excitement, if it were operating erotically and not merely as a thought in the head of the thinker, was not self-conscious. Lawrence condemned all inducements to masturbation, which he called "sex in the head," as they encouraged self-consciousness rather than a confrontation with the unknown. The range of his sexual sympathy is remarkable. As a novelist, he explored the sexual power of women from the point of view of women, and he imagined the sexual power of men from the viewpoint of men, making him alternately vulnerable to charges of male chauvinism as well as homosexuality. Yet Lawrence's shifts of perspective can be so dizzying that it is impossible to pin him down. As he himself said, "Trust the tale, not the teller."

Lawrence and Frieda returned to England prior to World War I, staying until the end of the war, when they left on what one biographer, Catherine Carswell, has called a "savage pilgrimage." They never again returned to England permanently. Frieda finally obtained her divorce and married Lawrence, but she was still prevented from seeing her children.

England and Germany were at war while Lawrence and Frieda lived alongside the English Channel in Cornwall, hidden away in a stone cottage on the bleak coast, like "creatures in a cave." Frieda's cousin was the ace German pilot known as the "Red Baron." Her father was Baron Friedrich von Richthofen, an officer who had fought in the Franco-Prussian war. He kept a diary which showed that he beat his orderly much in the way Lawrence described the Prussian officer's behavior in "Honour and Arms" (also known as "The Prussian Officer"), one of his most powerful stories.

While in Germany before the war, Lawrence had met Frieda's father at their house, and in her memoirs Frieda recalled that "They looked at each other fiercely—my father, the pure aristocrat, Lawrence, the miner's son. My father, hostile, offered a cigarette to Lawrence. That night I dreamt that they had a fight, and that Lawrence defeated my father." In "Honour and Arms" some of this hostility appears as seethingly repressed sexuality. The story seemed particularly significant to Lawrence, Frieda said. "He wrote it before the war but as if he had sensed it. The unhappy, conscious man, the superior in authority envying the other man his simple, satisfied nature. I felt as if he himself were both those people. They seemed to represent the split in his soul, the split between the conscious and unconscious man."

The man from the working class was now a poor, persecuted writer married to an aristocratic woman whose country was at war with his own. Maintaining intermittent contact with an elite, influential circle of friends, Lawrence developed plans for a utopian colony he called *Rananim,* a sanctuary where the chosen few would go and where he would be their leader. In a sense, he already lived in *Rananim,* that mythic place where people had rid themselves of the idea of money, and where "a rich man with a beautiful house is like a jewel on a leper's body."

The energy of Lawrence's spleen during the war could only have heightened the irony of his celebrated marriage, which was as explosive as war. At the country house of Lady Ottoline Morrell, Lawrence argued with Bertrand Russell and other figures of Bloomsbury, while back at Cornwall he tarred the chimney to seal the bricks against the crumbling mortar, an action observed by the authorities who saw the Lawrences as spies sending signals to enemy boats. Lawrence kept sane by singing German folk songs while the British police crouched within earshot under the hedges. His published work was banned at the time, as later *Lady Chatterley's Lover* would be.

In that work, Lawrence addresses the issue of the couple who placed extraordinary importance on the satisfaction of their erotic drives. If they were genuinely fulfilled sexually, Connie and Mellors, the principals of *Lady Chatterley's Lover,* were also fulfilled inwardly, and therefore could live happily "in the chinks" of society, away from politics and commerce and war.

For a time after the war, as an alternative to monogamy, Lawrence experimented with the theme of male friendship, which was intimate without being sexual. He also considered how man might live alone, without a partner, and returned to this solitude in the diary-like poems (some of which are included here) that he wrote near the end of his life. In "There are No Gods," he asks:

> Who is it smooths the bed-sheets like the cool
> smooth ocean when the fishes rest on edge
> in their own dream?

and he answers himself, "I tell you, it is no woman, it is no man, for I am alone."

Lawrence was weakening with tuberculosis, despite his efforts to live in hot, dry climates. Increasingly, he complained of his "bronchials," while ignoring the fact that he was doomed by what Kafka called "the germ of death itself." Yet Lawrence maintained an incredible level of literary production: novels, stories, essays, poems, plays, letters, translations, and reviews. Since he lived by his pen, publication was important, and in this context it is interesting that "Love Among the Haystacks" (also included here) was not published during Lawrence's lifetime. It is a haunting story of two misfits who fall in love: an oaf of a man and a female tramp. Each confronts the loneliness of the other. While they sit on the hay in the shed, he massages her feet, which are sore and cold from tramping after her husband who goes from town to town. "He reckons he's looking for a job. But he doesn't like work in any shape or form," she says. Much of Lawrence's power as a writer comes from the way he implicitly incorporates potential absurdities, such as that under certain circumstances a certain man will fall in love with a female tramp. And even the tramp, when soothed by love, is transformed: "Her bitter disillusionment with life, her unalleviated shame and degradation during the last four years, had driven her into loneliness, and hardened her till a large part of her nature was caked and sterile. Now she softened again, and her spring might be beautiful." This is a story of fulfillment that ignores the class conflict between farmer and tramp, exposing all the more effectively the power of the desire to find satisfaction in love.

After the war Lawrence said, "I shall say goodbye to England, forever, and set off in quest of our *Rananim*." He attempted to persuade several of his friends to follow him in his travels, but they preferred to visit at their leisure. During the 1920s, Lawrence spent considerable time near Taos, New Mexico, where he owned a ranch, the only property he ever possessed. (Frieda gave Mable Dodge Luhan the manuscript of *Sons and Lovers* in payment for the ranch when Lawrence refused to accept it as a gift.)

By the mid–1920s Lawrence had returned to Italy, where he wrote "Sun" and "The Virgin and the Gipsy" almost upon his arrival. "Italy feels very familiar: almost too familiar, like the ghost of one's own self," he confided in a letter.

Before he returned to Italy, he had stopped in England for one month. He drove through his native Midlands, and through nearby Derbyshire, the setting for "The Virgin and the Gipsy," where industrial blue smoke hung in dead, damp air, making Lawrence cough and causing the landscape to look dreary. In this novella, the characters of the region are stunted, twisted, or dwarfish. The virgin's father is a church rector, mean-spirited from a scandal years past "when the vicar's wife ran off with a young and penniless man," leaving him "with the inferiority of a heart which has no core of warm belief in it." The book is dedicated to Frieda. At the time it was written, in Italy, Frieda's two daughters were visiting for the first time in their lives. In the novella, the virgin, approaching womanhood, wants to know of her absent mother, "Why did she do it?" As if in answer, she meets the gipsy: "One of the black, loose-bodied handsome sort." Charmingly, after he saves her life from the flash flood that destroys the rectory, and after they have made love, she learns the gipsy's name. It is a small detail, like the tip of a dart, but it sticks to its meaning. The gipsy, "being of a race that exists only to be harrying the outskirts of our society, forever hostile and living only by spoil," rescues the virgin. And he rescues her as much from the cold nunnery of her virginity as he does from the "strange, uncanny mass of water" that wells up at the book's climax, rather like an ejaculation that occurs unconsciously at night in a dream. On the last page, the girl reads a note from the gipsy, sees he has signed his name, and learns only then that he has a name. Identity follows being: and the name is the last thing you need to know about your lover, Lawrence suggests.

Toward the end of his short life Lawrence became quite sick. His writing took on a quality of essentiality, at times becoming too bluntly assertive, at other times reaching a simplicity that was as magisterial as the arch of a rainbow bursting with bright colors. Some of his works employ elements of the fable, in which a moral is expressed through the behavior of animals. As with the gipsy of "The Virgin and the Gipsy," an obstinate, irrational, animal-like consciousness is present in Lawrence's writing the way the eyes of a fox might be present in a child's drawing, gleaming and red.

Thinking of death, Lawrence toured the Etruscan tombs in central Italy. In some of the tombs the walls were painted with banquet scenes, "honouring the dead with wine," as Lawrence wrote in a fine essay on the Etruscan afterlife. He studied these paintings under torchlight and he saw that the Etruscans affirmed life in the presence of death. Soon Lawrence began to paint again, mixing his paints on a pane of glass, painting with his fingers, even with the palm of his hand, as well as with brushes. He painted slant-eyed Etruscan figures squinting at each other's genitals. One picture showed the Lord God being pelted by apples, thrown by Adam and Eve, to keep Him away.

Lawrence's oil paintings and watercolors, some of which are reproduced for this edition, convey the warm and spontaneous expression of sexuality that also runs throughout his writing. Phallic reality is not only a theme, it is also a form of visionary philosophy that links sexuality and life to form an ideal, organic whole. Incredibly, the year before Lawrence's death, at an exhibition of these paintings in London to which 20,000 people swarmed during the three weeks it was open, the police impounded his "wicked" paintings. They also took a portfolio of William Blake's drawings, but returned them when they learned Blake had been dead a hundred years.

Lawrence envisioned sex as an opportunity for a man and a woman to ritualize their lovemaking, so that it would take on something of the sacred glow of ritual. In his essay "A Propos of *Lady Chatterley's Lover*," (included here), Lawrence wrote, "We *must* get back into relation, vivid and nourishing relation to the cosmos and the universe. The way is through daily ritual." An example of such a ritual would be Mellors' address to his penis, "John Thomas," in *Lady Chatterley's Lover,* Lawrence's most celebrated novel and the last he wrote. " 'John Thomas! Dost want *her?* Dost want my lady Jane? Tha's dipped in me again tha hast. Ay, an'tha comes up smilin'." Of this book, which he rewrote three times from start to finish, Lawrence said, "I always labor at the same thing, to make the sex relation valid and precious, instead of shameful. And this novel is the furthest I've gone."

Lady Chatterley's Lover is something of a love poem to Frieda. Lawrence has profoundly split himself into the characters of the crippled writer, who is cuckolded, and the gamekeeper, who did the poaching. Lady Chatterley is Frieda, married to the dying Lawrence, who, threatened with impotence, yet retains the wit to know that "if a woman hasn't got a tiny streak of the harlot in her, she's a dry stick as a rule." In "A Propos of *Lady Chatterley's Lover*," Lawrence revealed, "I have been asked many times if I intentionally made Clifford paralyzed, if it is symbolic. . . . Certainly not in the beginning, when Clifford was created. When I created Clifford and Connie, I had no idea what they were or why they were." The novel is structured around the satisfaction of Connie's desire. Mellors was created to become the man of her dreams, were she to have had the power of Lawrence's invention.

Scholars have shown that in the course of the composition of the novel, during the successive rewritings, Lawrence developed Mellors' character until he ceased to be a brute from the lower classes, becoming instead a man much like his creator, "a collier's son," educated and eloquent in both the King's English and the Midland dialect, which he speaks as a sexual language with Connie. Indeed, Mellors belongs to that "classless class" to which Lawrence belonged. Is the ending absurd? Like the couple in "Love Among the Haystacks," Mellors and Connie plan to live in Canada after their baby is born. They consider the prospects of their romance in the real world, elsewhere. The possibilities would be slim for the ordinary couple, but they remain strong for those who would become extraordinary through the force of their desire. Often for Lawrence the rigidity of class structure was the evil to be overcome. In this novel of the lady and the gamekeeper, Lawrence's class conflict clearly persisted to the end, and one scholar has wittily remarked that *Lady Chatterley* represents the initiation of the upper classes into proletarian sex. But where does the Laurentian couple live? In Canada? In *Rananim*? The question remains open today, and each reader must answer for his or her self.

Knowing that the novel would be banned in England, Lawrence published it himself. It was typeset in a little print shop in Florence, Italy, where "not a soul knew English." As Lawrence wrote in "A Propos of *Lady Chatterley's Lover*," the men who did the work were told the contents of the book, and that the descriptions of the sex act were explicit. The men shrugged, "O! *ma!* but we do it every day!" One of the poems reprinted in this volume, "To Pino," is addressed to Lawrence's Florentine printer, who shared Lawrence's chuckle at the outraged moralism of the Great British Public, as he calls his censors in another squiblike poem.

Lady Chatterley's Lover was banned in the United States until 1959, when a New York court ruled that the book as a whole appealed to more than just prurient interests. Like the gipsy in "The Virgin and the Gipsy," Lawrence was outside the law, but, like Mellors the gamekeeper, he was not without law. Something of a priest, Lawrence was also something of a pirate. From Florence, under secret wrappers with false titles printed on the book jacket, he mailed copies of *Lady Chatterley's Lover* past the eyes of customs officers and postal inspectors.

For his personal symbol, Lawrence took the image of the immortal phoenix, the legendary bird of scarlet and gold that is supposed to live 500 years, then fly to the sun at the time of its death, in order to be reborn. Lawrence drew his own design for the phoenix and emblazoned it on the cover of both *Lady Chatterley's Lover* and a special bound edition of the short story "Sun" (rarely read in the unexpurgated version that is included here). The phoenix, burning in its nest, is sex—libido aflame. "Far be it from me to suggest that all women should go running after gamekeepers," Lawrence cautioned, even as he urged them into awareness of their desires, so that they would become, like the men who loved them, excited by truth, as if truth itself were erotic.

CHRISTOPHER BUSA

Provincetown
1989

Acknowledgments

I and my coeditor would like to thank our mutual friend, Dr. Michael A. Sperber, for first bringing us together—an introduction that eventually resulted in this book. We would also like to thank Cynthia Sternau, Editor, for her splendid and dedicated in-house editing; Naomi Kleinberg, Executive Editor, for illumination and lucid guidance in matters of word, art, and style; Eli Hausknecht, Production Supervisor, for her skillful and thorough production work and her patience; and not least, Cynthia Dunne, for her beautiful design for this book.

CHRISTOPHER BUSA

The Trespasser

I

Take off that mute, do!" cried Louisa, snatching her fingers from the piano keys, and turning abruptly to the violinist.

Helena looked slowly from her music.

"My dear Louisa," she replied, "it would be simply unendurable." She stood tapping her white skirt with her bow in a kind of a pathetic forbearance.

"But I can't understand it," cried Louisa, bouncing on her chair with the exaggeration of one who is indignant with a beloved. "It is only lately you would even submit to muting your violin. At one time you would have refused flatly, and no doubt about it."

"I have only lately submitted to many things," replied Helena, who seemed weary and stupefied, but still sententious. Louisa drooped from her bristling defiance.

"At any rate," she said, scolding in tones too naked with love, "I don't like it."

"Go on from *Allegro*," said Helena, pointing with her bow to the place on Louisa's score of the Mozart sonata. Louisa obediently took the chords, and the music continued.

A young man, reclining in one of the wicker armchairs by the fire, turned luxuriously from the girls to watch the flames poise and dance with the music. He was evidently at his ease, yet he seemed a stranger in the room.

It was the sitting-room of a mean house standing in line with hundreds of others of the same kind, along a wide road in South London. Now and again the trams hummed by, but the room was foreign to the trams and to the sound of the London traffic. It was Helena's room, for which she was responsible. The walls were of the dead-green colour of August foliage; the green carpet, with its border of polished floor, lay like a square of grass in a setting of black loam. Ceiling and frieze and fireplace were smooth white. There was no other colouring.

The furniture, excepting the piano, had a transitory look; two light wicker armchairs by the fire, the two frail stands of dark, polished wood, the couple of flimsy chairs, and the case of books in the recess—all seemed uneasy, as if they

3

might be tossed out to leave the room clear, with its green floor and walls, and its white rim of skirting-board, serene.

On the mantelpiece were white lustres, and a small soapstone Buddha from China, grey, impassive, locked in his renunciation. Besides these, two tablets of translucent stone, beautifully clouded with rose and blood, and carved with Chinese symbols; then a litter of mementoes, rock-crystals, and shells and scraps of seaweed.

A stranger, entering, felt at a loss. He looked at the bare wall-spaces of dark green, at the scanty furniture, and was assured of his unwelcome. The only objects of sympathy in the room were the white lamp that glowed on a stand near the wall, and the large, beautiful fern, with narrow fronds, which ruffled its cloud of green within the gloom of the window-bay. These only, with the fire, seemed friendly.

The three candles on the dark piano burned softly, the music fluttered on, but, like numbed butterflies, stupidly. Helena played mechanically. She broke the music beneath her bow, so that it came lifeless, very hurting to hear. The young man frowned, and pondered. Uneasily, he turned again to the players.

The violinist was a girl of twenty-eight. Her white dress, high-waisted, swung as she forced the rhythm, determinedly swaying to the time as if her body were the white stroke of a metronome. It made the young man frown as he watched. Yet he continued to watch. She had a very strong, vigorous body. Her neck, pure white, arched in strength from the fine hollow between her shoulders as she held the violin. The long white lace of her sleeve swung, floated, after the bow.

Byrne could not see her face, more than the full curve of her cheek. He watched her hair, which at the back was almost of the colour of the soapstone idol, take the candle-light into its vigorous freedom in front and glisten over her forehead.

Suddenly Helena broke off the music, and dropped her arm in irritable resignation. Louisa looked round from the piano, surprised.

"Why," she cried, "wasn't it all right?"

Helena laughed wearily.

"It was all wrong," she answered, as she put her violin tenderly to rest.

"Oh, I'm sorry I did so badly," said Louisa in a huff. She loved Helena passionately.

"You didn't do badly at all," replied her friend, in the same tired, apathetic tone. "It was I."

When she had closed the black lid of her violin case, Helena stood a moment as if at a loss. Louisa looked up with eyes full of affection, like a dog that did not dare to move to her beloved. Getting no response, she drooped over the piano. At length Helena looked at her friend, then slowly closed her eyes. The burden of this excessive affection was too much for her. Smiling faintly, she said, as if she were coaxing a child:

"Play some Chopin, Louisa."

"I shall only do that all wrong, like everything else," said the elder plaintively. Louisa was thirty-five. She had been Helena's friend for years.

"Play the mazurkas," repeated Helena calmly.

Louisa rummaged among the music. Helena blew out her violin candle, and came to sit down on the side of the fire opposite to Byrne. The music began. Helena pressed her arms with her hands, musing.

"They are inflamed still!" said the young man.

She glanced up suddenly, her blue eyes, usually so heavy and tired, lighting up with a small smile.

"Yes," she answered, and she pushed back her sleeve, revealing a fine, strong arm, which was scarlet on the outer side from shoulder to wrist, like some long, red-burned fruit. The girl laid her cheek on the smarting, soft flesh caressively.

"It is quite hot," she smiled, again caressing her sun-scalded arm with peculiar joy.

"Funny to see a sunburn like that in mid-winter," he replied, frowning. "I can't think why it should last all these months. Don't you ever put anything on to heal it?"

She smiled at him again, almost pitying, then put her mouth lovingly on the burn.

"It comes out every evening like this," she said softly, with curious joy.

"And that was August, and now it's February!" he exclaimed. "It must be psychological, you know. You make it come—the smart; you invoke it."

She looked up at him, suddenly cold.

"I! I never think of it," she answered briefly, with a kind of sneer.

The young man's blood ran back from her at her acid tone. But the mortification was physical only. Smiling quickly, gently—

"Never?" he re-echoed.

There was silence between them for some moments, whilst Louisa continued to play the piano for their benefit. At last:

"Drat it!" she exclaimed, flouncing round on the piano-stool.

The two looked up at her.

"Ye did run well—what hath hindered you?" laughed Byrne.

"You!" cried Louisa. "Oh, I can't play any more," she added, dropping her arms along her skirt pathetically. Helena laughed quickly.

"Oh, I can't, Helen!" pleaded Louisa.

"My dear," said Helena, laughing briefly, "you are really under *no* obligation *whatever.*"

With the little groan of one who yields to a desire contrary to her self-respect, Louisa dropped at the feet of Helena, laid her arm and her head languishingly on the knee of her friend. The latter gave no sign, but continued to gaze in the fire. Byrne, on the other side of the hearth, sprawled in his chair, smoking a reflective cigarette.

The room was very quiet, silent even of the tick of a clock. Outside, the traffic swept by, and feet pattered along the pavement. But this vulgar storm of life seemed shut out of Helena's room, that remained indifferent, like a church. Two candles burned dimly as on an altar, glistening yellow on the dark piano. The lamp was blown out, and the flameless fire, a red rubble, dwindled in the grate, so that the yellow glow of the candles seemed to shine even on the embers. Still no one spoke.

At last Helena shivered slightly in her chair, though did not change her position. She sat motionless.

"Will you make coffee, Louisa?" she asked. Louisa lifted herself, looked at her friend, and stretched slightly.

"Oh!" she groaned voluptuously. "This is so comfortable!"

"Don't trouble then, I'll go. No, don't get up," said Helena, trying to disengage herself. Louisa reached and put her hands on Helena's wrists.

"I will go," she drawled, almost groaning with voluptuousness and appealing love.

Then, as Helena still made movements to rise, the elder woman got up slowly, leaning as she did so all her weight on her friend.

"Where is the coffee?" she asked, affecting the dulness of lethargy. She was full of small affectations, being consumed with uneasy love.

"I think, my dear," replied Helena, "it is in its usual place."

"Oh—o-o-oh!" yawned Louisa, and she dragged herself out.

The two had been intimate friends for years, had slept together, and played together, and lived together. Now the friendship was coming to an end.

"After all," said Byrne, when the door was closed, "if you're alive you've got to live."

Helena burst into a titter of amusement at this sudden remark.

"Wherefore?" she asked indulgently.

"Because there's no such thing as passive existence," he replied, grinning.

She curled her lip in amused indulgence of this very young man.

"I don't see it at all," she said.

"You can't," he protested, "any more than a tree can help budding in April— it can't help itself, if it's alive; same with you."

"Well, then"—and again there was the touch of a sneer—"if I can't help myself, why trouble, my friend?"

"Because—because I suppose *I* can't help myself—if it bothers me, it does. You see, I"—he smiled brilliantly—"am April."

She paid very little attention to him, but began, in a peculiar reedy, metallic tone, that set his nerves quivering:

"But I am not a bare tree. All my dead leaves, they hang to me—and—and go through a kind of *danse macabre*——"

"But you bud underneath—like beech," he said quickly.

"Really, my friend," she said coldly, "I am too tired to bud."

"No," he pleaded, "no!" With his thick brows knitted, he surveyed her anxiously. She had received a great blow in August, and she still was stunned. Her face, white and heavy, was like a mask, almost sullen. She looked in the fire, forgetting him.

"You want March," he said—he worried endlessly over her—"to rip off your old leaves. I s'll have to be March," he laughed.

She ignored him again because of his presumption. He waited awhile, then broke out once more.

"You must start again—you must. Always you rustle your red leaves of a blasted summer. You are not dead. Even if you want to be, you're not. Even if it's a bitter thing to say, you have to say it: you are not dead. . . ."

Smiling a peculiar, painful smile, as if he hurt her, she turned to gaze at a photograph that hung over the piano. It was the profile of a handsome man in the prime of life. He was leaning slightly forward, as if yielding beneath a burden of life, or to the pull of fate. He looked out musingly, and there was no hint of rebellion in the contours of the regular features. The hair was brushed back, soft and thick, straight from his fine brow. His nose was small and shapely, his chin rounded, cleft, rather beautifully moulded. Byrne gazed also at the photo. His look became distressed and helpless.

"You cannot say you are dead with Siegmund," he cried brutally. She shuddered, clasped her burning arms on her breast, and looked into the fire. "You are not dead with Siegmund," he persisted, "so you can't say you live with him. You may live with his memory. But Siegmund is dead, and his memory is not he—himself." He made a fierce gesture of impatience. "Siegmund now—he is not a memory—he is not your dead red leaves—he is Siegmund Dead! And you do not know him, because you are alive, like me, so Siegmund Dead is a stranger to you."

With her head bowed down, cowering like a sulky animal, she looked at him under her brows. He stared fiercely back at her, but beneath her steady, glowering gaze he shrank, then turned aside.

"You stretch your hands blindly to the dead; you look backwards. No, you never touch the living," he cried.

"I have the arms of Louisa always round my neck," came her voice, like the cry of a cat. She put her hands on her throat as if she must relieve an ache. He saw her lip raised in a kind of disgust, a revulsion from life. She was very sick after the tragedy.

He frowned, and his eyes dilated.

"Folk are good; they are good for one. You never have looked at them. You would linger hours over a blue weed, and let all the people down the road go by. Folks are better than a garden in full blossom——"

She watched him again. A certain beauty in his speech, and his passionate way, roused her when she did not want to be roused, when moving from her torpor was painful. At last—

"You are merciless, you know, Cecil," she said.

"And I will be," protested Byrne, flinging his hand at her. She laughed softly, wearily.

For some time they were silent. She gazed once more at the photograph over the piano, and forgot all the present. Byrne, spent for the time being, was busy hunting for some life-interest to give her. He ignored the simplest—that of love—because he was even more faithful than she to the memory of Siegmund, and blinder than most to his own heart.

"I do wish I had Siegmund's violin," she said quietly, but with great intensity. Byrne glanced at her, then away. His heart beat sulkily. His sanguine, passionate spirit dropped and slouched under her contempt. He, also, felt the jar, heard the discord. She made him sometimes pant with her own horror. He waited, full of hate and tasting of ashes, for the arrival of Louisa with the coffee.

II

Siegmund's violin, desired of Helena, lay in its case beside Siegmund's lean portmanteau in the white dust of the lumber-room in Highgate. It was worth twenty pounds, but Beatrice had not yet roused herself to sell it; she kept the black case out of sight.

Siegmund's violin lay in the dark, folded up, as he had placed it for the last time, with hasty, familiar hands, in its red silk shroud. After two dead months the first string had snapped, sharply striking the sensitive body of the instrument. The second string had broken near Christmas, but no one had heard the faint moan of its going. The violin lay mute in the dark, a faint odour of must creeping over the smooth, soft wood. Its twisted, withered strings lay crisped from the anguish of breaking, smothered under the silk folds. The fragrance of Siegmund himself, with which the violin was steeped, slowly changed into an odour of must.

Siegmund died out even from his violin. He had infused it with his life, till its fibres had been as the tissue of his own flesh. Grasping his violin, he seemed to have his fingers on the strings of his heart and of the heart of Helena. It was his little beloved that drank his being and turned it into music. And now Siegmund was dead; only an odour of must remained of him in his violin.

It lay folded in silk in the dark, waiting. Six months before it had longed for rest; during the last nights of the season, when Siegmund's fingers had pressed too hard, when Siegmund's passion, and joy, and fear had hurt, too, the soft body of his little beloved, the violin had sickened for rest. On that last night of opera, without pity Siegmund had struck the closing phrases from the fiddle, harsh in his impatience, wild in anticipation.

The curtain came down, the great singers bowed, and Siegmund felt the spattering roar of applause quicken his pulse. It was hoarse, and savage, and startling on his inflamed soul, making him shiver with anticipation, as if something had brushed his hot nakedness. Quickly, with hands of habitual tenderness, he put his violin away.

The theatre-goers were tired, and life drained rapidly out of the opera-house. The members of the orchestra rose, laughing, mingling their weariness with good wishes for the holiday, with sly warning and suggestive advice, pressing hands warmly ere they disbanded. Other years Siegmund had lingered, unwilling to take the long farewell of his associates of the orchestra. Other years he had left the opera-house with a little pain of regret. Now he laughed, and took his comrade's hands, and bade farewells, all distractedly, and with impatience. The theatre, awesome now in its emptiness, he left gladly, hastening like a flame stretched level on the wind.

With his black violin-case he hurried down the street, then halted to pity the flowers massed pallid under the gaslight of the market-hall. For himself, the sea and the sunlight opened great spaces tomorrow. The moon was full above the river. He looked at it as a man in abstraction watches some clear thing; then he came to a standstill. It was useless to hurry to his train. The traffic swung past, the lamplight shone warm on all the golden faces; but Siegmund had already left the city. His face was silver and shadows to the moon; the river, in its soft grey, shaking golden sequins among the folds of its shadows, fell open like a garment before him, to reveal the white moon-glitter brilliant as living flesh. Mechanically, overcast with the reality of the moonlight, he took his seat in the train, and watched the moving of things. He was in a kind of trance, his consciousness seeming suspended. The train slid out amongst lights and dark places. Siegmund watched the endless movement, fascinated.

This was one of the crises of his life. For years he had suppressed his soul, in a kind of mechanical despair doing his duty and enduring the rest. Then his soul had been softly enticed from its bondage. Now he was going to break free altogether, to have at least a few days purely for his own joy. This, to a man of his integrity, meant a breaking of bonds, a severing of blood-ties, a sort of new birth. In the excitement of this last night his life passed out of his control, and he sat at the carriage-window, motionless, watching things move.

He felt busy within him a strong activity which he could not help. Slowly the body of his past, the womb which had nourished him in one fashion for so many years, was casting him forth. He was trembling in all his being, though he knew not with what. All he could do now was to watch the lights go by, and to let the translation of himself continue.

When at last the train ran out into the full, luminous night, and Siegmund saw the meadows deep in moonlight, he quivered with a low anticipation. The elms' great grey shadows, seemed to loiter in their cloaks across the pale fields. He had not seen them so before. The world was changing.

The train stopped, and with a little effort he rose to go home. The night air was cool and sweet. He drank it thirstily. In the road again he lifted his face to the moon. It seemed to help him; in its brilliance amid the blonde heavens it seemed to transcend fretfulness. It would front the waves with silver as they slid to the shore, and Helena, looking along the coast, waiting, would lift her white hands with sudden joy. He laughed, and the moon hurried laughing alongside, through the black masses of the trees.

He had forgotten he was going home for this night. The chill wetness of his little white garden-gate reminded him, and a frown came on his face. As he closed the door, and found himself in the darkness of the hall, the sense of his fatigue came fully upon him. It was an effort to go to bed. Nevertheless, he went very quietly into the drawing-room. There the moonlight entered, and he thought the whiteness was Helena. He held his breath and stiffened, then breathed again. "To-morrow," he thought, as he laid his violin-case across the arms of a wicker chair. But he had a physical feeling of the presence of Helena: in his shoulders he seemed to be aware of her. Quickly, half lifting his arms, he turned to the moonshine. "To-morrow!" he exclaimed quietly; and he left the room stealthily, for fear of disturbing the children.

In the darkness of the kitchen burned a blue bud of light. He quickly turned up the gas to a broad yellow flame, and sat down at table. He was tired, excited, and vexed with misgiving. As he lay in his arm-chair, he looked round with disgust.

The table was spread with a dirty cloth that had great brown stains betokening children. In front of him was a cup and saucer, and a small plate with a knife laid across it. The cheese, on another plate, was wrapped in a red-bordered, fringed cloth, to keep off the flies, which even then were crawling round, on the sugar, on the loaf, on the cocoa-tin. Siegmund looked at his cup. It was chipped, and a stain had gone under the glaze, so that it looked like the mark of a dirty mouth. He fetched a glass of water.

The room was drab and dreary. The oil-cloth was worn into a hole near the door. Boots and shoes of various sizes were scattered over the floor, while the sofa was littered with children's clothing. In the black stove the ash lay dead; on the range were chips of wood, and newspapers, and rubbish of papers, and crusts of bread, and crusts of bread-and-jam. As Siegmund walked across the floor, he crushed two sweets underfoot. He had to grope under sofa and dresser to find his slippers; and he was in evening dress.

It would be the same, while ever Beatrice was Beatrice and Seigmund her husband. He ate his bread and cheese mechanically, wondering why he was miserable, why he was not looking forward with joy to the morrow. As he ate, he closed his eyes, half wishing he had not promised Helena, half wishing he had no to-morrow.

Leaning back in his chair, he felt something in the way. It was a small teddy-bear and half of a strong white comb. He grinned to himself. This was the summary of his domestic life—a broken, coarse comb, a child crying because her hair was lugged, a wife who had let the hair go till now, when she had got into a temper to see the job through; and then the teddy-bear, pathetically cocking a black worsted nose, and lifting absurd arms to him.

He wondered why Gwen had gone to bed without her pet. She would want the silly thing. The strong feeling of affection for his children came over him, battling with something else. He sank in his chair, and gradually his baffled mind went dark. He sat, overcome with weariness and trouble, staring blankly into the space. His own stifling roused him. Straightening his shoulders, he took a deep breath, then relaxed again. After a while he rose, took the teddy-bear, and went slowly to bed.

Gwen and Marjory, aged nine and twelve, slept together in a small room. It was fairly light. He saw his favourite daughter lying quite uncovered, her wilful head thrown back, her mouth half open. Her black hair was tossed across the pillow: he could see the action. Marjory snuggled under the sheet. He placed the teddy-bear between the two girls.

As he watched them, he hated the children for being so dear to him. Either he himself must go under, and drag on an existence he hated, or they must suffer. But he had agreed to spend this holiday with Helena, and meant to do so. As he turned, he saw himself like a ghost cross the mirror. He looked back; he peered at himself. His hair still grew thick and dark from his brow: he could not see the grey at the temples. His eyes were dark and tender, and his mouth, under the black moustache, was full with youth.

He rose, looked at the children, frowned, and went to his own small room. He was glad to be shut alone in the little cubicle of darkness.

Outside the world lay in a glamorous pallor, casting shadows that made the farm, the trees, the bulks of villas, look like live creatures. The same pallor went through all the night, glistening on Helena as she lay curled up asleep at the core of the glamour, like the moon; on the sea rocking backwards and forwards till it rocked her island as she slept. She was so calm and full of her own assurance. It was a great rest to be with her. With her, nothing mattered but love and the beauty of things. He felt parched and starving. She had rest and love, like water and manna for him. She was so strong in her self-possession, in her love of beautiful things and of dreams.

The clock downstairs struck two.

"I must get to sleep," he said.

He dragged his portmanteau from beneath the bed and began to pack it. When at last it was finished, he shut it with a snap. The click sounded final. He stood up, stretched himself, and sighed.

"I am fearfully tired," he said.

But that was persuasive. When he was undressed he sat in his pyjamas for some time, rapidly beating his fingers on his knee.

"Thirty-eight years old," he said to himself, "and disconsolate as a child!" He began to muse of the morrow.

When he seemed to be going to sleep, he woke up to find thoughts labouring over his brain, like bees in a hive. Recollections, swift thoughts, flew in and alighted upon him, as wild geese swing down and take possession of a pond. Phrases from the opera tyrannized over him; he played the rhythm with all his blood. As he turned over in this torture, he sighed, and recognized a movement of the De Beriot concerto which Helena had played for her last lesson. He found himself watching her as he had watched then, felt again the wild impatience when she was wrong, started again as, amid the dipping and sliding of her bow, he realized where his thoughts were going. She was wrong, he was hasty; and he felt her blue eyes looking intently at him.

Both started as his daughter Vera entered suddenly. She was a handsome girl of nineteen. Crossing the room, brushing Helena as if she were a piece of furniture in the way, Vera had asked her father a question, in a hard, insulting tone, then had gone out again, just as if Helena had not been in the room.

Helena stood fingering the score of "Pelléas." When Vera had gone, she asked, in the peculiar tone that made Siegmund shiver:

"Why do you consider the music of 'Pelléas' cold?"

Siegmund had struggled to answer. So they passed everything off, without mention, after Helena's fashion, ignoring all that might be humiliating; and to her much was humiliating.

For years she had come as pupil to Siegmund, first as a friend of the household. Then she and Louisa went occasionally to whatever hall or theatre had Siegmund in the orchestra, so that shortly the three formed the habit of coming home together. Then Helena had invited Siegmund to her home; then the three friends went walks together; then the two went walks together, whilst Louisa sheltered them.

Helena had come to read his loneliness and the humiliation of his lot. He had felt her blue eyes, heavily, steadily gazing into his soul, and he had lost himself to her.

That day, three weeks before the end of the season, when Vera had so insulted Helena, the latter had said, as she put on her coat, looking at him all the while with heavy blue eyes: "I think, Siegmund, I cannot come here any more. Your home is not open to me any longer." He had writhed in confusion and humiliation. As she pressed his hand, closely and for a long time, she said: "I will write to you." Then she left him.

Siegmund had hated his life that day. Soon she wrote. A week later, when he lay resting his head on her lap in Richmond Park, she said:

"You are so tired, Siegmund." She stroked his face, and kissed him softly. Siegmund lay in the molten daze of love. But Helena was, if it is not to debase the word, virtuous: an inconsistent virtue, cruel and ugly for Siegmund.

"You are so tired, dear. You must come away with me and rest, the first week in August."

His blood had leapt, and whatever objections he raised, such as having no money, he allowed to be overridden. He was going to Helena, to the Isle of Wight, to-morrow.

Helena, with her blue eyes so full of storm, like the sea, but, also like the sea, so eternally self-sufficient, solitary; with her thick white throat, the strongest and most wonderful thing on earth, and her small hands, silken and light as wind-flowers, would be his to-morrow, along with the sea and the downs. He clung to the exquisite flame which flooded him. . . .

But it died out, and he thought of the return to London, to Beatrice, and the children. How would it be? Beatrice, with her furious dark eyes, and her black hair loosely knotted back, came to his mind as she had been the previous day, flaring with temper when he said to her:

"I shall be going away to-morrow for a few days' holiday."

She asked for detail, some of which he gave. Then, dissatisfied and inflamed, she broke forth in her suspicion and her abuse, and her contempt, while two large-eyed children stood listening by. Siegmund hated his wife for drawing on him the grave, cold looks of condemnation from his children.

Something he had said touched Beatrice. She came of good family, had been brought up like a lady, educated in a convent school in France. He evoked her old pride. She drew herself up with dignity, and called the children away. He wondered if he could bear a repetition of that degradation. It bled him of his courage and self-respect.

In the morning Beatrice was disturbed by the sharp sneck of the hall-door. Immediately awake, she heard his quick, firm step hastening down the gravel path. In her impotence, discarded like a worn out object, she lay for the moment stiff with bitterness.

"I am nothing, I am nothing," she said to herself. She lay quite rigid for a time.

There was no sound anywhere. The morning sunlight pierced vividly through the slits of the blind. Beatrice lay rocking herself, breathing hard, her fingernails pressing into her palm. Then came the sound of a train slowing down in the station, and directly the quick "chuff-chuff-chuff" of its drawing out. Beatrice imagined the sunlight on the puffs of steam, and the two lovers, her husband and Helena, rushing through the miles of morning sunshine.

"God strike her dead! Mother of God, strike her down!" she said aloud, in a low tone. She hated Helena.

Irene, who lay with her mother, woke up and began to question her.

III

In the miles of morning sunshine, Siegmund's shadows, his children, Beatrice, his sorrow, dissipated like mist, and he was elated as a young man setting forth to travel. When he had passed Portsmouth Town everything had vanished but the old gay world of romance. He laughed as he looked out at the carriage window.

Below, in the street, a military band passed glittering. A brave sound floated up, and again he laughed, loving the tune, the clash and glitter of the band, the movement of scarlet, blithe soldiers beyond the park. People were drifting brightly from church. How could it be Sunday! It was no time; it was Romance, going back to Tristan.

Women, like crocus-flowers, in white and blue and lavender, moved gaily. Everywhere fluttered the small flags of holiday. Every form danced lightly in the sunshine.

And beyond it all were the silent hillsides of the island, with Helena. It was so wonderful, he could bear to be patient. She would be all in white, with her cool, thick throat left bare to the breeze, her face shining, smiling as she dipped her head because of the sun, which glistened on her uncovered hair.

He breathed deeply, stirring at the thought. But he would not grow impatient. The train had halted over the town, where scarlet soldiers, and ludicrous blue sailors, and all the brilliant women from church shook like a kaleidoscope down the street. The train crawled on, drawing near to the sea, for which Siegmund waited breathless. It was so like Helena, blue, beautiful, strong in its reserve.

Another moment they were in the dirty station. Then the day flashed out, and Siegmund mated with joy. He felt the sea heaving below him. He looked round, and the sea was blue as a periwinkle flower, while gold and white and blood-red sails lit here and there upon the blueness. Standing on the deck, he gave himself to the breeze and to the sea, feeling like one of the ruddy sails—as if he were part of it all. All his body radiated amid the large, magnificent sea-moon like a piece of colour.

The little ship began to pulse, to tremble. White with the softness of a bosom, the water rose up frothing and swaying gently. Ships drew near like inquisitive birds; the old *Victory* shook her myriad pointed flags of yellow and scarlet; the straight old houses of the quay passed by.

Outside the harbour, like fierce creatures of the sea come wildly up to look, the battleships laid their black snouts on the water. Siegmund laughed at them. He felt the foam on his face like a sparkling, felt the blue sea gathering round.

On the left stood the round fortress, quaintly chequered, and solidly alone in the walk of water, amid the silent flight of the golden and crimson winged boats.

Siegmund watched the bluish bulk of the island. Like the beautiful women in the myths, his love hid in its blue haze. It seemed impossible. Behind him, the white wake trailed myriads of daisies. On either hand the grim and wicked battleships watched along their sharp noses. Beneath him the clear green water swung and puckered as if it were laughing. In front, Sieglinde's island drew near and nearer, creeping towards him, bringing him Helena.

Meadows and woods appeared, houses crowded down to the shore to meet him; he was in the quay, and the ride was over. Siegmund regretted it. But Helena was on the island, which rode like an anchored ship under the fleets of cloud that had launched whilst Siegmund was on water. As he watched the end of the pier loom higher, large ponderous trains of cloud cast over him the shadows of their bulk, and he shivered in the chill wind.

His travelling was very slow. The sky's dark shipping pressed closer and closer, as if all the clouds had come to harbour. Over the flat lands near Newport the wind moaned like the calling of many violoncellos. All the sky was grey. Siegmund waited drearily on Newport Station, where the wind swept coldly. It was Sunday, and the station and the island were desolate, having lost their purposes.

Seigmund put on his overcoat and sat down. All his morning's blaze of elation was gone, though there still glowed a great hope. He had slept only two hours of the night. An empty man, he had drunk joy, and now the intoxication was dying out.

At three o'clock of the afternoon he sat alone in the second-class carriage, looking out. A few raindrops struck the pane, then the blurred dazzle of a shower came in a burst of wind, and hid the downs and the reeds that shivered in the marshy places. Siegmund sat in a chilly torpor. He counted the stations. Beneath his stupor his heart was thudding heavily with excitement, surprising him, for his brain felt dead.

The train slowed down: Yarmouth! One more station, then. Siegmund watched the platform, shiny with rain, slide past. On the dry grey under the shelter, one white passenger was waiting. Suddenly Siegmund's heart leaped up, wrenching wildly. He burst open the door, and caught hold of Helena. She dilated, gave a palpitating cry as he dragged her into the carriage.

"You *here!*" he exclaimed, in a strange tone. She was shivering with cold. Her almost naked arms were blue. She could not answer Siegmund's question, but lay clasped against him, shivering away her last chill as his warmth invaded her. He laughed in his heart as she nestled in to him.

"Is it a dream now, dear?" he whispered. Helena clasped him tightly, shuddering because of the delicious suffusing of his warmth through her.

Almost immediately they heard the grinding of the brakes.

"Here we are, then!" exclaimed Helena, dropping into her conventional, cheerful manner at once. She put straight her hat, while he gathered his luggage.

Until teatime there was a pause in their progress. Siegmund was tingling with an exquisite vividness, as if he had taken some rare stimulant. He wondered at himself. It seemed that every fibre in his body was surprised with joy, as each tree in a forest at dawn utters astonished cries of delight.

When Helena came back, she sat opposite to him to see him. His naïve look of joy was very sweet to her. His eyes were dark blue, showing the fibrils, like a purple veined flower at twilight, and somehow, mysteriously, joy seemed to quiver in the iris. Helena appreciated him, feature by feature. She liked his clear forehead, with its thick black hair, and his full mouth, and his chin. She loved his hands, that were small, but strong and nervous, and very white. She liked his breast, that breathed so strong and quietly, and his arms, and his thighs, and his knees.

For him, Helena was a presence. She was ambushed, fused in an aura of his love. He only saw she was white, and strong, and full fruited, he only knew her blue eyes were rather awful to him.

Outside, the sea-mist was travelling thicker and thicker inland. Their lodging was not far from the bay. As they sat together at tea, Siegmund's eyes dilated, and he looked frowning at Helena.

"What is it?" he asked, listening uneasily.

Helena looked up at him, from pouring out the tea. His little anxious look of distress amused her.

"The noise, you mean? Merely the fog-horn, dear—not Wotan's wrath, nor Siegfried's dragon. . . ."

The fog was white at the window. They sat waiting. After a few seconds the sound came low, swelling, like the mooing of some great sea-animal, alone, the last of the monsters. The whole fog gave off the sound for a second or two, then it died down into an intense silence. Siegmund and Helena looked at each other. His eyes were full of trouble. To see a big, strong man anxious-eyed as a child because of a strange sound amused her. But he was tired.

"I assure you, it *is* only a fog-horn," she laughed.

"Of course. But it is a depressing sort of sound."

"Is it?" she said curiously. "Why? Well—yes—I think I can understand it's being so to some people. It's something like the call of the horn across the sea to Tristan."

She hummed softly, then three times she sang the horn-call. Siegmund, with his face expressionless as a mask, sat staring out at the mist. The boom of the siren broke in upon them. To him, the sound was full of fatality. Helena waited till the noise died down, then she repeated her horn-call.

"Yet it is very much like the fog-horn," she said, curiously interested.

"This time next week, Helena!" he said.

She suddenly went heavy, and stretched across to clasp his hand as it lay upon the table.

"I shall be calling to you from Cornwall," she said.

He did not reply. So often she did not take his meaning, but left him alone with his sense of tragedy. She had no idea how his life was wrenched from its roots, and when he tried to tell her, she balked him, leaving him inwardly quite lonely.

"There is *no* next week," she declared, with great cheerfulness. "There is only the present."

At the same moment she rose and slipped across to him. Putting her arms round his neck, she stood holding his head to her bosom, pressing it close, with her hand among his hair. His nostrils and mouth were crushed against her breast. He smelled the silk of her dress and the faint, intoxicating odour of her person. With shut eyes he owned heavily to himself again that she was blind to him. But some other self urged with gladness, no matter how blind she was, so that she pressed his face upon her.

She stroked and caressed his hair, tremblingly clasped his head against her breast, as if she would never release him; then she bent to kiss his forehead. He took her in his arms, and they were still for awhile.

Now he wanted to blind himself with her, to blaze up all his past and future in a passion worth years of living.

After tea they rested by the fire, while she told him all the delightful things she had found. She had a woman's curious passion for details, a woman's peculiar attachment to certain dear trifles. He listened, smiling, revived by her delight, and forgetful of himself. She soothed him like sunshine, and filled him with pleasure; but he hardly attended to her words.

"Shall we go out, or are you too tired? No, you are tired—you are very tired," said Helena.

She stood by his chair, looking down on him tenderly.

"No," he replied, smiling brilliantly at her, and stretching his handsome limbs in relief—"no, not at all tired now."

Helena continued to look down on him in quiet, covering tenderness. But she quailed before the brilliant, questioning gaze of his eyes.

"You must go to bed early to-night," she said, turning aside her face, ruffling his soft black hair. He stretched slightly, stiffening his arms, and smiled without answering. It was a very keen pleasure to be thus alone with her and in her charge. He rose, bidding her wrap herself up against the fog.

"You are sure you're not too tired?" she reiterated.

He laughed.

Outside, the sea-mist was white and woolly. They went hand in hand. It was cold, so she thrust her hand with his into the pocket of his overcoat, while they walked together.

"I like the mist," he said, pressing her hand in his pocket.

"I don't dislike it," she replied, shrinking nearer to him.

"It puts us together by ourselves," he said. She plodded alongside, bowing her head, not replying. He did not mind her silence.

"It couldn't have happened better for us than this mist," he said.

She laughed curiously, almost with a sound of tears.

"Why?" she asked, half tenderly, half bitterly.

"There is nothing else but you, and for you there is nothing else but me—look!"

He stood still. They were on the downs, so that Helena found herself quite alone with the man in a world of mist. Suddenly she flung herself sobbing against his breast. He held her closely, tenderly, not knowing what it was all about, but happy and unafraid.

In one hollow place the siren from the Needles seemed to bellow full in their ears. Both Siegmund and Helena felt their emotion too intense. They turned from it.

"What is the pitch?" asked Helena.

"Where it is horizontal? It slides up a chromatic scale," said Siegmund.

"Yes, but the settled pitch—is it about E?"

"E!" exclaimed Siegmund. "More like F."

"Nay, listen!" said Helena.

They stood still and waited till there came the long booing of the fog-horn.

"There!" exclaimed Siegmund, imitating the sound. "That is not E." He repeated the sound. "It is F."

"Surely it is E," persisted Helena.

"Even F sharp," he rejoined, humming the note.

She laughed, and told him to climb the chromatic scale.

"But you agree?" he said.

"I do not," she replied.

The fog was cold. It seemed to rob them of their courage to talk.

"What is the note in 'Tristan?'" Helena made an effort to ask.

"That is not the same," he replied.

"No, dear, that is not the same," she said in low, comforting tones. He quivered at the caress. She put her arms round him, reached up her face yearningly for a kiss. He forgot they were standing in the public footpath, in daylight, till she drew hastily away. She heard footsteps down the fog.

As they climbed the path the mist grew thinner, till it was only a grey haze at the top. There they were on the turfy lip of the land. The sky was fairly clear overhead. Below them the sea was singing hoarsely to itself.

Helena drew him to the edge of the cliff. He crushed her hand, drawing slightly back. But it pleased her to feel the grip on her hand becoming unbearable. They stood right on the edge, to see the smooth cliff slope into the mist, under which the sea stirred noisily.

"Shall we walk over, then?" said Siegmund, glancing downwards. Helena's heart stood still a moment at the idea, then beat heavily. How could he play with the idea of death, and the five great days in front? She was afraid of him just then.

"Come away, dear," she pleaded.

He would, then, forego the few consummate days! It was bitterness to her to think so.

"Come away, dear!" she repeated, drawing him slowly to the path.

"You are not afraid?" he asked.

"Not afraid, no. . . ." Her voice had that peculiar, reedy, harsh quality that made him shiver.

"It is too easy a way," he said satirically.

She did not take in his meaning.

"And five days of our own before us, Siegmund!" she scolded. "The mist is Lethe. It is enough for us if its spell lasts five days."

He laughed, and took her in his arms, kissing her very closely.

They walked on joyfully, locking behind them the doors of forgetfulness.

As the sun set, the fog dispersed a little. Breaking masses of mist went flying from cliff to cliff, and far away beyond the cliffs the western sky stood dimmed with gold. The lovers wandered aimlessly over the golf-links to where green mounds and turfed banks suggested to Helena that she was tired, and would sit down. They faced the lighted chamber of the west, whence, behind the torn, dull-gold curtains of fog, the sun was departing with pomp.

Siegmund sat very still, watching the sunset. It was a splendid, flaming bridal chamber where he had come to Helena. He wondered how to express it; how other men had borne this same glory.

"What is the music of it?" he asked.

She glanced at him. His eyelids were half lowered, his mouth slightly open, as if in ironic rhapsody.

"Of what, dear?"

"What music do you think holds the best interpretation of sunset?"

His skin was gold, his real mood was intense. She revered him for a moment.

"I do not know," she said quietly; and she rested her head against his shoulder, looking out west.

There was a space of silence, while Siegmund dreamed on.

"A Beethoven symphony—the one——" and he explained to her.

She was not satisfied, but leaned against him, making her choice. The sunset hung steady; she could scarcely perceive a change.

"The Grail music in 'Lohengrin,' " she decided.

"Yes," said Siegmund. He found it quite otherwise, but did not trouble to dispute. He dreamed by himself. This displeased her. She wanted him for herself. How could he leave her alone while he watched the sky? She almost put her two hands over his eyes.

IV

The gold march of sunset passed quickly, the ragged curtains of mist closed to. Soon Siegmund and Helena were shut alone within the dense wide fog. She shivered with the cold and the damp. Startled, he took her in his arms, where she lay and clung to him. Holding her closely, he bent forward, straight to her lips. His moustache was drenched cold with fog, so that she shuddered slightly after his kiss, and shuddered again. He did not know why the strong tremor passed through her. Thinking it was with fear and with cold, he undid his overcoat, put her close on his breast, and covered her as best he could. That she feared him at that moment was half pleasure, half shame to him. Pleadingly he hid his face on her shoulder, held her very tightly, till his face grew hot, buried against her soft strong throat.

"You are so big I can't hold you," she whispered plaintively, catching her breath with fear. Her small hands grasped at the breadth of his shoulders ineffectually.

"You will be cold. Put your hands under my coat," he whispered.

He put her inside his overcoat and his coat. She came to his warm breast with a sharp intaking of delight and fear; she tried to make her hands meet in the warmth of his shoulders, tried to clasp him.

"See! I can't," she whispered.

He laughed short, and pressed her closer.

Then, tucking her head in his breast, hiding her face, she timidly slid her hands along his sides, pressing softly, to find the contours of his figure. Softly her hands crept over the silky back of his waistcoat, under his coats, and as they stirred, his blood flushed up, and up again, with fire, till all Siegmund was hot blood, and his breast was one great ache.

He crushed her to him—crushed her in upon the ache of his chest. His muscles set hard and unyielding; at that moment he was a tense, vivid body of flesh, without a mind; his blood, alive and conscious, running towards her. He remained perfectly still, locked about Helena, conscious of nothing.

She was hurt and crushed, but it was pain delicious to her. It was marvellous to her how strong he was, to keep up that grip of her like steel. She swooned in a kind of intense bliss. At length she found herself released, taking a great breath, while Siegmund was moving his mouth over her throat, something like a dog snuffing her, but with his lips. Her heart leaped away in revulsion. His moustache thrilled her strangely. His lips, brushing and pressing her throat beneath the ear, and his warm breath flying rhythmically upon her, made her vibrate through all her body. Like a violin under the bow, she thrilled beneath his mouth, and shuddered from his moustache. Her heart was like fire in her breast.

Suddenly she strained madly to him, and, drawing back her head, placed her lips on his, close, till at the mouth they seemed to melt and fuse together. It was the long, supreme kiss, in which man and woman have one being. Two-in-one, the only Hermaphrodite.

When Helena drew away her lips, she was exhausted. She belonged to that class of "dreaming women" with whom passion exhausts itself at the mouth. Her desire was accomplished in a real kiss. The fire, in heavy flames, had poured through her to Siegmund, from Siegmund to her. It sank, and she felt herself flagging. She had not the man's brightness and vividness of blood. She lay upon his breast, dreaming how beautiful it would be to go to sleep, to swoon unconscious there, on that rare bed. She lay still on Siegmund's breast, listening to his heavily beating heart.

With her the dream was always more than the actuality. Her dream of Siegmund was more to her than Siegmund himself. He might be less than her dream, which is as it may be. However, to the real man she was very cruel.

He held her close. His dream was melted in his blood, and his blood ran bright for her. His dreams were the flowers of his blood. Hers were more detached and inhuman. For centuries a certain type of woman has been rejecting the "animal" in humanity, till now her dreams are abstract, and full of fantasy, and her blood runs in bondage, and her kindness is full of cruelty.

Helena lay flagging upon the breast of Siegmund. He folded her closely, and his mouth and his breath were warm on her neck. She sank away from his caresses, passively, subtly drew back from him. He was far too sensitive not to be aware of this, and far too much of a man not to yield to the woman. His heart sank, his blood grew sullen at her withdrawal. Still he held her; the two were motionless and silent for some time.

She became distressedly conscious that her feet, which lay on the wet grass, were aching with cold. She said softly, gently, as if he was her child whom she must correct and lead:

"I think we ought to go home, Siegmund." He made a small sound, that might mean anything, but did not stir or release her. His mouth, however, remained motionless on her throat, and the caress went out of it.

"It is cold and wet, dear; we ought to go," she coaxed determinedly.

"Soon," he said thickly.

She sighed, waited a moment, then said very gently, as if she were loath to take him from his pleasure:

"Siegmund, I am cold."

There was a reproach in this which angered him.

"Cold!" he exclaimed. "But you are warm with me——"

"But my feet are out on the grass, dear, and they are like wet pebbles."

"Oh dear!" he said. "Why didn't you give them me to warm?" He leaned forward, and put his hand on her shoes.

"They are very cold," he said. "We must hurry and make them warm."

When they rose, her feet were so numbed she could hardly stand. She clung to Siegmund, laughing.

"I wish you had told me before," he said. "I ought to have known. . . ."

Vexed with himself, he put his arm round her, and they set off home.

V

*T*hey found the fire burning brightly in their room. The only other person in the pretty, stiffly-furnished cottage was their landlady, a charming old lady who let this sitting-room more for the change, for the sake of having visitors, than for gain.

Helena introduced Siegmund as "My friend." The old lady smiled upon him. He was big, and good-looking, and embarrassed. She had had a son years back. . . . And the two were lovers. She hoped they would come to her house for their honeymoon.

Siegmund sat in his great horse-hair chair by the fire, while Helena attended to the lamp. Glancing at him over the glowing globe, she found him watching her with a small, peculiar smile of irony, and anger, and bewilderment. He was not quite himself. Her hand trembled so, she could scarcely adjust the wicks.

Helena left the room to change her dress.

"I shall be back before Mrs. Curtiss brings in the tray. There is the Nietzsche I brought——"

He did not answer as he watched her go. Left alone, he sat with his arms along his knees, perfectly still. His heart beat heavily, and all his being felt sullen, watchful, aloof, like a balked animal. Thoughts came up in his brain like bubbles— random, hissing out aimlessly. Once, in the startling inflammability of his blood, his veins ran hot, and he smiled.

When Helena entered the room his eyes sought hers swiftly, as sparks lighting on the tinder. But her eyes were only moist with tenderness. His look instantly changed. She wondered at his being so silent, so strange.

Coming to him in her unhesitating, womanly way—she was only twenty-six to his thirty-eight—she stood before him, holding both his hands and looking down on him with almost gloomy tenderness. She wore a white dress that showed her throat gathering like a fountain-jet of solid foam to balance her head. He could see the full white arms passing clear through the dripping spume of lace, towards the rise of her breasts. But her eyes bent down upon him with such gloom of tenderness that he dared not reveal the passion burning in him. He could not look at her. He strove almost pitifully to be with her sad, tender, but he could not put out his fire. She held both his hands firm, pressing them in appeal for her dream love. He glanced at her wistfully, then turned away. She waited for him. She wanted his caresses and tenderness. He would not look at her.

"You would like supper now, dear?" she asked, looking where the dark hair ended, and his neck ran smooth, under his collar, to the strong setting of his shoulders.

"Just as you will," he replied.

Still she waited, and still he would not look at her. Something troubled him, she thought. He was foreign to her.

"I will spread the cloth, then," she said, in deep tones of resignation. She pressed his hands closely, and let them drop. He took no notice, but, still with his arms on his knees, he stared into the fire.

In the golden glow of lamplight she set small bowls of white and lavender sweet-peas, and mignonette, upon the round table. He watched her moving, saw the stir of her white, sloping shoulders under the lace, and the hollow of her shoulders firm as marble, and the slight rise and fall of her loins as she walked. He felt as if his breast were scalded. It was a physical pain to him.

Supper was very quiet. Helena was sad and gentle; he had a peculiar, enigmatic look in his eyes, between suffering and mockery and love. He was quite intractable; he would not soften to her, but remained there aloof. He was tired, and the look of weariness and suffering was evident to her through his strangeness. In her heart she wept.

At last she tinkled the bell for supper to be cleared. Meanwhile, restlessly, she played fragments of Wagner on the piano.

"Will you want anything else?" asked the smiling old landlady.

"Nothing at all, thanks," said Helena, with decision.

"Oh! Then I think I will go to bed when I've washed the dishes. You will put the lamp out, dear?"

"I am well used to a lamp," smiled Helena. "We use them always at home."

She had had a day before Siegmund's coming, in which to win Mrs. Curtiss' heart, and she had been successful. The old lady took the tray.

"Good-night, dear—good-night, sir. I will leave you. You will not be long, dear?"

"No, we shall not be long. Mr. MacNair is very evidently tired out."

"Yes—yes. It is very tiring, London."

When the door was closed, Helena stood a moment undecided, looking at Siegmund. He was lying in his armchair in a dispirited way, and looking in the fire. As she gazed at him with troubled eyes, he happened to glance to her, with the same dark, curiously searching, disappointed eyes.

"Shall I read to you?" she asked bitterly.

"If you will," he replied.

He sounded so indifferent, she could scarcely refrain from crying. She went and stood in front of him, looking down on him heavily.

"What is it, dear?" she said.

"You," he replied, smiling with a little grimace.

"Why me?"

He smiled at her ironically, then closed his eyes. She slid into his arms with a little moan. He took her on his knee, where she curled up like a heavy white cat. She let him caress her with his mouth, and did not move, but lay there curled up and quiet and luxuriously warm.

He kissed her hair, which was beautifully fragrant of itself, and time after time drew between his lips one long, keen thread, as if he would ravel out with his mouth her vigorous confusion of hair. His tenderness of love was like a soft flame lapping her voluptuously.

After a while they heard the old lady go upstairs. Helena went very still, and seemed to contract. Siegmund himself hesitated in his love-making. All was very quiet. They could hear a faint breathing of the sea. Presently the cat, which had been sleeping in a chair, rose and went to the door.

"Shall I let her out?" said Siegmund.

"Do!" said Helena, slipping from his knee. "She goes out when the nights are fine."

Siegmund rose to set free the tabby. Hearing the front door open, Mrs. Curtiss called from upstairs: "Is that you, dear?"

"I have just let Kitty out," said Siegmund.

"Ah, thank you. Good-night!" They heard the old lady lock her bedroom door.

Helena was kneeling on the hearth. Siegmund softly closed the door, then waited a moment. His heart was beating fast.

"Shall we sit by firelight?" he asked tentatively.

"Yes—if you wish," she replied, very slowly, as if against her will. He carefully turned down the lamp, then blew out the light. His whole body was burning and surging with desire.

The room was black and red with firelight. Helena shone ruddily as she knelt, a bright, bowed figure, full in the glow. Now and then red stripes of firelight leapt across the walls. Siegmund, his face ruddy, advanced out of the shadows.

He sat in the chair beside her, leaning forward, his hands hanging like two scarlet flowers listless in the fire glow, near to her, as she knelt on the hearth, with head bowed down. One of the flowers awoke and spread towards her. It asked for her mutely. She was fascinated, scarcely able to move.

"Come," he pleaded softly.

She turned, lifted her hands to him. The lace fell back, and her arms, bare to the shoulder, shone rosily. He saw her breasts raised towards him. Her face was bent between her arms as she looked up at him afraid. Lit up by the firelight, in her white, clinging dress, cowering between her uplifted arms, she seemed to be offering him herself to sacrifice.

In an instant he was kneeling, and she was lying on his shoulder, abandoned to him. There was a good deal of sorrow in his joy.

*   *   *   *   *

It was eleven o'clock when Helena at last loosened Siegmund's arms, and rose from the armchair where she lay beside him. She was very hot, feverish, and restless. For the last half-hour he had lain absolutely still, with his heavy arms about her, making her hot. If she had not seen his eyes blue and dark, she would have thought him asleep. She tossed in restlessness on his breast.

"Am I not uneasy?" she had said, to make him speak. He had smiled gently.

"It is wonderful to be as still as this," he said. She had lain tranquil with him, then, for a few moments. To her there was something sacred in his stillness and peace. She wondered at him; he was so different from an hour ago. How could he be the same! Now he was like the sea, blue and hazy in the morning, musing by itself. Before, he was burning, volcanic, as if he would destroy her.

She had given him this new soft beauty. She was the earth in which his strange flowers grew. But she herself wondered at the flowers produced of her. He was so strange to her, so different from herself. What next would he ask of her, what new blossom would she rear in him then. He seemed to grow and flower involuntarily. She merely helped to produce him.

Helena could not keep still; her body was full of strange sensations, of involuntary recoil from shock. She was tired, but restless. All the time Siegmund lay with his hot arms over her, himself so incomprehensible in his haze of blue, open-eyed slumber, she grew more breathless and unbearable to herself.

At last she lifted his arm, and drew herself out of the chair. Siegmund looked at her from his tranquillity. She put the damp hair from her forehead, breathed deep, almost panting. Then she glanced hauntingly at her flushed face in the mirror. With the same restlessness, she turned to look at the night. The cool, dark, watery sea called to her. She pushed back the curtain.

The moon was wading deliciously through shallows of white cloud. Beyond the trees and the few houses was the great concave of darkness, the sea, and the moonlight. The moon was there to put a cool hand of absolution on her brow.

"Shall we go out a moment, Siegmund?" she asked fretfully.

"Ay, if you wish to," he answered, altogether willing. He was filled with an easiness that would comply with her every wish.

They went out softly, walked in silence to the bay. There they stood at the head of the white, living moonpath, where the water whispered at the casement of the land seductively.

"It's the finest night I have seen," said Siegmund. Helena's eyes suddenly filled with tears, at his simplicity of happiness.

"I like the moon on the water," she said.

"I can hardly tell the one from the other," he replied simply. "The sea seems to be poured out of the moon, and rocking in the hands of the coast. They are all one, just as your eyes and hands and what you say, are all you."

"Yes," she answered, thrilled. This was the Siegmund of her dream, and she had created him. Yet there was a quiver of pain. He was beyond her now, and did not need her.

"I feel at home here," he said; "as if I had come home where I was bred."

She pressed his hand hard, clinging to him.

"We go an awful long way round, Helena," he said, "just to find we're all right." He laughed pleasantly. "I have thought myself such an outcast! How can one be outcast in one's own night, and the moon always naked to us, and the sky half her time in rags? What do we want?"

Helena did not know. Nor did she know what he meant. But she felt something of the harmony.

"Whatever I have or haven't from now," he continued, "the darkness is a sort of mother, and the moon a sister, and the stars children, and sometimes the sea is a brother: and there's a family in one house, you see."

"And I, Siegmund?" she said softly, taking him in all seriousness. She looked up at him piteously. He saw the silver of tears among the moonlit ivory of her face. His heart tightened with tenderness, and he laughed, then bent to kiss her.

"The key of the castle," he said. He put his face against hers, and felt on his cheek the smart of her tears.

"It's all very grandiose," he said comfortably, "but it does for to-night, all this that I say."

"It is true for ever," she declared.

"In so far as to-night is eternal," he said.

He remained, with the wetness of her cheek smarting on his, looking from under his brows at the white transport of the water beneath the moon. They stood folded together, gazing into the white heart of the night.

VI

Siegmund woke with wonder in the morning. "It is like the magic tales," he thought, as he realized where he was; "and I am transported to a new life, to realize my dream. Fairy-tales are true, after all."

He had slept very deeply, so that he felt strangely new. He issued with delight from the dark of sleep into the sunshine. Reaching out his hand, he felt for his watch. It was seven o'clock. The dew of a sleep-drenched night glittered before his eyes. Then he laughed and forgot the night.

The creeper was tapping at the window, as a little wind blew up the sunshine. Siegmund put out his hands for the unfolding happiness of the morning. Helena was in the next room, which she kept inviolate. Sparrows in the creeper were shaking shadows of leaves among the sunshine; a milk-white shallop of cloud stemmed bravely across the bright sky; the sea would be blossoming with a dewy shimmer of sunshine.

Siegmund rose to look, and it was so. Also the houses, like white, and red, and black cattle, were wandering down the bay, with a mist of sunshine between him and them. He leaned with his hands on the window-ledge looking out of the casement. The breeze ruffled his hair, blew down the neck of his sleeping-jacket upon his chest. He laughed, hastily threw on his clothes, and went out.

There was no sign of Helena. He strode along, singing to himself, and spinning his towel rhythmically. A small path led him across a field and down a zig-zag in front of the cliffs. Some nooks, sheltered from the wind, were warm with sunshine, scented of honeysuckle and of thyme. He took a sprig of woodbine that was coloured of cream and butter. The grass wetted his brown shoes and his flannel trousers. Again, a fresh breeze put the scent of the sea in his uncovered hair. The cliff was a tangle of flowers above and below, with poppies at the lip being blown out like red flame, and scabious leaning inquisitively to look down, and pink and white rest-harrow everywhere, very pretty.

Siegmund stood at a bend where heath blossomed in shaggy lilac, where the sunshine but no wind came. He saw the blue bay curl away to the far-off headland. A few birds, white and small, circled, dipped by the thin foam-edge of the water; a few ships dimmed the sea with silent travelling; a few small people, dark or naked-white, moved below the swinging birds.

He chose his bathing-place where the incoming tide had half covered a stretch of fair, bright sand that was studded with rocks resembling square altars, hollowed on top. He threw his clothes on a high rock. It delighted him to feel the fresh, soft fingers of the wind touching him and wandering timidly over his nakedness. He ran laughing over the sand to the sea, where he waded in, thrusting his legs noisily through the heavy green water.

It was cold, and he shrank. For a moment he found himself thigh-deep, watching the horizontal stealing of a ship through the intolerable glitter, afraid to plunge. Laughing, he went under the clear green water.

He was a poor swimmer. Sometimes a choppy wave swamped him, and he rose gasping, wringing the water from his eyes and nostrils, while he heaved and sank with the rocking of the waves that clasped his breast. Then he stooped again to resume his game with the sea. It is splendid to play, even at middle age, and the sea is a fine partner.

With his eyes at the shining level of the water, he liked to peer across, taking a seal's view of the cliffs as they confronted the morning. He liked to see the ships standing up on a bright floor; he liked to see the birds come down.

But in his playing he drifted towards the spur of rock, where, as he swam, he caught his thigh on a sharp, submerged point. He frowned at the pain, at the sudden cruelty of the sea; then he thought no more of it, but ruffled his way back to the clear water, busily continuing his play.

When he ran out on to the fair sand his heart, and brain, and body were in a turmoil. He panted, filling his breast with the air that was sparkled and tasted of the sea. As he shuddered a little, the wilful palpitation of his flesh pleased him, as if birds had fluttered against him. He offered his body to the morning, glowing with the sea's passion. The wind nestled in to him, the sunshine came on his shoulders like warm breath. He delighted in himself.

The rock before him was white and wet, like himself; it had a pool of clear water, with shells and one rose anemone.

"She would make so much of this little pool," he thought. And as he smiled, he saw, very faintly, his own shadow in the water. It made him conscious of himself, seeming to look at him. He glanced at himself, at his handsome, white maturity. As he looked he felt the insidious creeping of blood down his thigh, which was marked with a long red slash. Siegmund watched the blood travel over the bright skin. It wound itself redly round the rise of his knee.

"That is I, that creeping red, and this whiteness I pride myself on is I, and my black hair, and my blue eyes are I. It is a weird thing to be a person. What makes me myself, among all these?"

Feeling chill, he wiped himself quickly.

"I am at my best, at my strongest," he said proudly to himself. "She ought to be rejoiced at me, but she is not; she rejects me as if I were a baboon under my clothing."

He glanced at his whole handsome maturity, the firm plating of his breasts, the full thighs, creatures proud in themselves. Only he was marred by the long raw scratch, which he regretted deeply.

"If I was giving her myself, I wouldn't want that blemish on me," he thought.

He wiped the blood from the wound. It was nothing.

"She thinks ten thousand times more of that little pool, with a bit of pink anemone and some yellow weed, than of me. But, by Jove! I'd rather see her shoulders and breast than all heaven and earth put together could show. . . . Why doesn't she like me?" he thought as he dressed. It was his physical self thinking.

After dabbling his feet in a warm pool, he returned home. Helena was in the dining-room arranging a bowl of purple pansies. She looked up at him rather heavily as he stood radiant on the threshold. He put her at her ease. It was a gay, handsome boy she had to meet, not a man, strange and insistent. She smiled on him with tender dignity.

"You have bathed?" she said, smiling, and looking at his damp, ruffled black hair. She shrank from his eyes, but he was quite unconscious.

"You have not bathed!" he said; then bent to kiss her. She smelt the brine in his hair.

"No; I bathe later," she replied. "But what——"

Hesitating, she touched the towel, then looked up at him anxiously.

"It *is* blood?" she said.

"I grazed my thigh—nothing at all," he replied.

"Are you sure?"

He laughed.

"The towel looks bad enough," she said.

"It's an alarmist," he laughed.

She looked in concern at him, then turned aside.

"Breakfast is quite ready," she said.

"And I for breakfast—but shall I do?"

She glanced at him. He was without a collar, so his throat was bare above the neck-band of his flannel shirt. Altogether she disapproved of his slovenly appearance. He was usually so smart in his dress.

"I would not trouble," she said almost sarcastically.

Whistling, he threw the towel on a chair.

"How did you sleep?" she asked gravely, as she watched him beginning to eat.

"Like the dead—solid," he replied. "And you?"

"Oh, pretty well, thanks," she said, rather piqued that he had slept so deeply, whilst she had tossed, and had called his name in a torture of sleeplessness.

"I haven't slept like that for years," he said enthusiastically. Helena smiled gently on him. The charm of his handsome, healthy zest came over her. She liked his naked throat and his shirt-breast, which suggested the breast of the man beneath it. She was extraordinarily happy, with him so bright. The dark-faced pansies, in a little crowd, seemed gaily winking a golden eye at her.

After breakfast, while Siegmund dressed, she went down to the sea. She dwelled, as she passed, on all tiny, pretty things—on the barbaric yellow ragwort, and pink convolvuli; on all the twinkling of flowers, and dew, and snail-tracks drying in the sun. Her walk was one long lingering. More than the spaces, she loved the nooks, and fancy more than imagination.

She wanted to see just as she pleased, without any of humanity's previous vision for spectacles. So she knew hardly any flower's name, nor perceived any of the relationships, nor cared a jot about an adaptation or a modification. It pleased her that the lowest browny florets of the clover hung down; she cared no more. She clothed everything in fancy.

"That yellow flower hadn't time to be brushed and combed by the fairies before dawn came. It is towzled . . ." so she thought to herself. The pink convolvuli were fairy horns or telephones from the day fairies to the night fairies. The rippling sunlight on the sea was the Rhine maidens spreading their bright hair to the sun. That was her favourite form of thinking. The value of all things was in the fancy they evoked. She did not care for people; they were vulgar, ugly, and stupid, as a rule.

Her sense of satisfaction was complete as she leaned on the low sea-wall, spreading her fingers to warm on the stones, concocting magic out of the simple morning. She watched the indolent chasing of wavelets round the small rocks, the curling of the deep blue water round the water-shadowed reefs.

"This is very good," she said to herself. "This is eternally cool, and clean and fresh. It could never be spoiled by satiety."

She tried to wash herself with the white and blue morning, to clear away the soiling of the last night's passion.

The sea played by itself, intent on its own game. Its aloofness, its self-sufficiency, are its great charm. The sea does not give and take, like the land and the sky. It has no traffic with the world. It spends its passions upon itself. Helena was something like the sea, self-sufficient and careless of the rest.

Siegmund came bareheaded, his black hair ruffling to the wind, his eyes shining warmer than the sea—like cornflowers rather, his limbs swinging backward and forward like the water. Together they leaned on the wall, warming the four white hands upon the grey bleached stone as they watched the water playing.

When Siegmund had Helena near, he lost the ache, the yearning towards something, which he always felt otherwise. She seemed to connect him with the beauty of things, as if she were the nerve through which he received intelligence of the sun, and wind, and sea, and of the moon and the darkness. Beauty she never felt herself came to him through her. It is that makes love. He could always sympathize with the wistful little flowers, and trees lonely in their crowds, and wild, sad sea-birds. In these things he recognized the great yearning, the ache outwards towards something, with which he was ordinarily burdened. But with Helena, in this large sea-morning, he was whole and perfect as the day.

"Will it be fine all day?" he asked, when a cloud came over.

"I don't know," she replied, in her gentle, inattentive manner, as if she did not care at all. "I think it will be a mixed day—cloud and sun—more sun than cloud."

She looked up gravely to see if he agreed. He turned from frowning at the cloud to smile at her. He seemed so bright, teeming with life.

"I like a bare blue sky," he said; "sunshine that you seem to stir about as you walk."

"It is warm enough here, even for you," she smiled.

"Ah, here!" he answered, putting his face down to receive the radiation from the stone, letting his fingers creep towards Helena's. She laughed, and captured his fingers, pressing them into her hand. For nearly an hour they remained thus in the still sunshine by the sea-wall, till Helena began to sigh, and to lift her face to the little breeze that wandered down from the west. She fled as soon from warmth as from cold. Physically, she was always so; she shrank from anything extreme. But psychically she was an extremist, and a dangerous one.

They climbed the hill to the fresh-breathing west. On the highest point of land stood a tall cross, railed in by a red iron fence. They read the inscription.

"That's all right—but a vilely ugly railing!" exclaimed Siegmund.

"Oh, they'd have to fence in Lord Tennyson's white marble," said Helena, rather indefinitely.

He interpreted her according to his own idea.

"Yes, he did belittle great things, didn't he?" said Siegmund.

"Tennyson!" she exclaimed.

"Not peacocks and princesses, but the bigger things."

"I shouldn't say so," she declared.

"Ha-a!"

He sounded indeterminate, but was not really so.

They wandered over the downs westward, among the wind. As they followed the headland to the Needles, they felt the breeze from the wings of the sea brushing them, and heard restless, poignant voices screaming below the cliffs. Now and again a gull, like a piece of spume flung up, rose over the cliff's edge, and sank again. Now and again, as the path dipped in a hollow, they could see the low, suspended intertwining of the birds passing in and out of the cliff shelter.

These savage birds appealed to all the poetry and yearning in Helena. They fascinated her, they almost voiced her. She crept nearer and nearer the edge, feeling she must watch the gulls thread out in flakes of white above the weed-black rocks. Siegmund stood away back, anxiously. He would not dare to tempt Fate now, having too strong a sense of death to risk it.

"Come back, dear. Don't go so near," he pleaded, following as close as he might. She heard the pain and appeal in his voice. It thrilled her, and she went a little nearer. What was death to her but one of her symbols, the death of which the sagas talk—something grand, and sweeping, and dark.

Leaning forward, she could see the line of grey sand and the line of foam broken by black rocks, and over all the gulls, stirring round like froth on a pot, screaming in chorus.

She watched the beautiful birds, heard the pleading of Siegmund, and she thrilled with pleasure, toying with his keen anguish.

Helena came smiling to Siegmund, saying:

"They look so fine down there."

He fastened his hands upon her, as a relief from his pain. He was filled with a keen, strong anguish of dread, like a presentiment. She laughed as he gripped her.

They went searching for a way of descent. At last Siegmund inquired of the coastguard the nearest way down the cliff. He was pointed to the "Path of the Hundred Steps."

"When is a hundred not a hundred?" he said sceptically, as they descended the dazzling white chalk. There were sixty-eight steps. Helena laughed at his exactitude.

"It must be a love of round numbers," he said.

"No doubt," she laughed. He took the thing so seriously.

"Or of exaggeration," he added.

There was a shelving beach of warm white sand, bleached soft as velvet. A sounding of gulls filled the dark recesses of the headland; a low chatter of shingle came from where the easy water was breaking; a confused, shell-like murmur of the sea between the folded cliffs. Siegmund and Helena lay side by side upon the dry sand, small as two resting birds, while thousands of gulls whirled in a white-flaked storm above them, and the great cliffs towered beyond, and high up over the cliffs the multitudinous clouds were travelling, a vast caravan *en route*. Amidst the journeying of oceans and clouds and the circling flight of heavy spheres, lost to sight in the sky, Siegmund and Helena, two grains of life in the vast movement, were travelling a moment side by side.

They lay on the beach like a grey and a white sea-bird together. The lazy ships that were idling down the Solent observed the cliffs and the boulders, but Siegmund and Helena were too little. They lay ignored and insignificant, watching through half-closed fingers the diverse caravan of Day go past. They lay with their latticed fingers over their eyes, looking out at the sailing of ships across their vision of blue water.

"Now, that one with the greyish sails——" Siegmund was saying.

"Like a housewife of forty going placidly round with the duster—yes?" interrupted Helena.

"That is a schooner. You see her four sails, and——"

He continued to classify the shipping, until he was interrupted by the wicked laughter of Helena.

"That is right, I am sure," he protested.

"I won't contradict you," she laughed, in a tone which showed him he knew even less of the classifying of ships than she did.

"So you have lain there amusing yourself at my expense all the time?" he said, not knowing in the least why she laughed. They turned and looked at one another, blue eyes smiling and wavering as the beach wavers in the heat. Then they closed their eyes with sunshine.

Drowsed by the sun, and the white sand, and the foam, their thoughts slept like butterflies on the flowers of delight. But cold shadows startled them up.

"The clouds are coming," he said regretfully.

"Yes; but the wind is quite strong enough for them," she answered.

"Look at the shadows—like blots floating away. Don't they devour the sunshine?"

"It is quite warm enough here," she said, nestling in to him.

"Yes; but the sting is missing. I like to feel the warmth biting in."

"No, I do not. To be cosy is enough."

"I like the sunshine on me, real, and manifest, and tangible. I feel like a seed that has been frozen for ages. I want to be bitten by the sunshine."

She leaned over and kissed him. The sun came bright-footed over the water, leaving a shining print on Siegmund's face. He lay, with half-closed eyes, sprawled loosely on the sand. Looking at his limbs, she imagined he must be heavy, like the boulders. She sat over him, with her finger stroking his eyebrows, that were broad and rather arched. He lay perfectly still, in a half-dream.

Presently she laid her head on his breast, and remained so, watching the sea, and listening to his heartbeats. The throb was strong and deep. It seemed to go through the whole island and the whole afternoon, and it fascinated her: so deep, unheard, with its great expulsions of life. Had the world a heart? Was there also deep in the world a great God thudding out waves of life, like a great heart, unconscious? It frightened her. This was the God she knew not, as she knew not this Siegmund. It was so different from the half-shut eyes with black lashes, and the winsome, shapely nose. And the heart of the world, as she heard it, could not be the same as the curling splash and retreat of the little sleepy waves. She listened for Siegmund's soul, but his heart overbeat all other sound, thudding powerfully.

VII

Siegmund woke to the muffled firing of guns on the sea. He looked across at the shaggy grey water in wonder. Then he turned to Helena.

"I suppose," he said, "they are saluting the Czar. Poor beggar!"

"I was afraid they would wake you," she smiled.

They listened again to the hollow, dull sound of salutes from across the water and the downs.

The day had gone grey. They decided to walk, down below, to the next bay.

"The tide is coming in," said Helena.

"But this broad strip of sand hasn't been wet for months. It's as soft as pepper," he replied.

They laboured along the shore, beside the black, sinuous line of shrivelled fucus. The base of the cliff was piled with chalk débris. On the other side was the level plain of the sea. Hand in hand, alone and overshadowed by huge cliffs, they toiled on. The waves staggered in, and fell, overcome at the end of the race.

Siegmund and Helena neared a headland, sheer as the side of a house, its base weighted with a tremendous white mass of boulders, that the green sea broke amongst with a hollow sound, followed by a sharp hiss of withdrawal. The lovers had to cross this desert of white boulders, that glistened in smooth skins uncannily. But Siegmund saw the waves were almost at the wall of the headland. Glancing back, he saw the other headland white-dashed at the base with foam. He and Helena must hurry, or they would be prisoned on the thin crescent of strand still remaining between the great wall and the water.

The cliffs overhead oppressed him—made him feel trapped and helpless. He was caught by them in a net of great boulders, while the sea fumbled for him. But he had Helena. She laboured strenuously beside him, blinded by the skin-like glisten of the white rock.

"I think I will rest awhile," she said.

"No, come along," he begged.

"My dear," she laughed, "there is tons of this shingle to buttress us from the sea."

32

He looked at the waves curving and driving maliciously at the boulders. It would be ridiculous to be trapped.

"Look at this black wood," she said. "Does the sea really char it?"

"Let us get round the corner," he begged.

"Really, Siegmund, the sea is not so anxious to take us," she said ironically.

When they rounded the first point, they found themselves in a small bay jutted out to sea; the front of the headland was, as usual, grooved. This bay was pure white at the base, from its great heaped mass of shingle. With the huge concave of the cliff behind, the foothold of massed white boulders, and the immense arc of the sea in front, Helena was delighted.

"This is fine, Siegmund!" she said, halting and facing west.

Smiling ironically, he sat down on a boulder. They were quite alone, in this great white niche thrust out to sea. Here, he could see, the tide would beat the base of the wall. It came plunging not far from their feet.

"Would you really like to travel beyond the end?" he asked.

She looked round quickly, thrilled, then answered as if in rebuke:

"This is a fine place. I should like to stay here an hour."

"And then where?"

"Then? Oh, then, I suppose, it would be tea-time."

"Tea on brine and pink anemones, with Daddy Neptune."

She looked sharply at the outjutting capes. The sea did foam perilously near their bases.

"I suppose it *is* rather risky," she said; and she turned, began silently to clamber forwards.

He followed; she should set the pace.

"I have no doubt there's plenty of room, really," he said. "The sea only looks near."

But she toiled on intently. Now it was a question of danger, not of inconvenience, Siegmund felt elated. The waves foamed up, as it seemed, against the exposed headland, from which the massive shingle had been swept back. Supposing they could not get by. He began to smile curiously. He became aware of the tremendous noise of waters, of the slight shudder of the shingle when a wave struck it, and he always laughed to himself. Helena laboured on in silence; he kept just behind her. The point seemed near, but it took longer than they thought. They had against them the tremendous cliff, the enormous weight of shingle, and the swinging sea. The waves struck louder, booming fearfully; wind, sweeping round the corner, wet their faces. Siegmund hoped they were cut off, and hoped anxiously the way was clear. The smile became set on his face.

Then he saw there was a ledge or platform at the base of the cliff, and it was against this the waves broke. They climbed the side of this ridge, hurried round to the front. There the wind caught them, wet and furious; the water raged below. Between the two Helena shrank, wilted. She took hold of Siegmund. The great, brutal water flung itself at the rock, then drew back for another heavy spring. Fume and spray were spun on the wind like smoke. The roaring thud of the waves reminded Helena of a beating heart. She clung closer to him, as her hair was blown out damp, and her white dress flapped in the wet wind. Always, against the rock, came the slow thud of the waves, like a great heart beating under the breast. There was something brutal about it that she could not bear. She had no weapon against brute force.

She glanced up at Siegmund. Tiny drops of mist greyed his eyebrows. He was looking out to sea, screwing up his eyes, and smiling brutally. Her face became heavy and sullen. He was like the heart and the brute sea, just here; he was not her Siegmund. She hated the brute in him.

Turning suddenly, she plunged over the shingle towards the wide, populous bay. He remained alone, grinning at the smashing turmoil, careless of her departure. He would easily catch her.

When at last he turned from the wrestling water, he had spent his savagery, and was sad. He could never take part in the great battle of action. It was beyond him. Many things he had let slip by. His life was whittled down to only a few interests, only a few necessities. Even here, he had but Helena, and through her the rest. After this week—well, that was vague. He left it in the dark, dreading it.

And Helena was toiling over the rough beach alone. He saw her small figure bowed as she plunged forward. It smote his heart with the keenest tenderness. She was so winsome, a playmate with beauty and fancy. Why was he cruel to her because she had not his own bitter wisdom of experience? She was young and naïve, and should he be angry with her for that? His heart was tight at the thought of her. She would have to suffer also, because of him.

He hurried after her. Not till they had nearly come to a little green mound, where the downs sloped and the cliffs were gone, did he catch her up. Then he took her hand as they walked.

They halted on the green hillock beyond the sand, and, without a word, he folded her in his arms. Both were out of breath. He clasped her close, seeming to rock her with his strong panting. She felt his body lifting into her, and sinking away. It seemed to force a rhythm, a new pulse, in her. Gradually, with a fine, keen thrilling, she melted down on him, like metal sinking on a mould. He was sea and sunlight mixed, heaving, warm, deliciously strong.

Siegmund exulted. At last she was moulded to him in pure passion.

They stood folded thus for some time. Then Helena raised her burning face, and relaxed. She was throbbing with strange elation and satisfaction.

"It might as well have been the sea as any other way, dear," she said, startling both of them. The speech went across their thoughtlessness like a star flying into the night, from nowhere. She had no idea why she said it. He pressed his mouth on hers. "Not for you," he thought, by reflex. "You can't go that way yet." But he said nothing, strained her very tightly, and kept her lips.

They were roused by the sound of voices. Unclasping, they went to walk at the fringe of the water. The tide was creeping back. Siegmund stooped, and from among the water's combings picked up an electric-light bulb. It lay in some weed at the base of a rock. He held it in his hand to Helena. Her face lighted with a curious pleasure. She took the thing delicately from his hand, fingered it with her exquisite softness.

"Isn't it remarkable!" she exclaimed joyously. "The sea must be very, very gentle—and very kind."

"Sometimes," smiled Siegmund.

"But I did not think it could be so fine-fingered," she said. She breathed on the glass bulb till it looked like a dim magnolia bud; she inhaled its fine savour.

"It would not have treated *you* so well," he said. She looked at him with heavy eyes. Then she returned to her bulb. Her fingers were very small and very pink. She had the most delicate touch in the world, like a faint feel of silk. As he watched her lifting her fingers from off the glass, then gently stroking it, his blood ran hot. He watched her, waited upon her words and movements attentively.

"It is a graceful act on the sea's part," she said. "Wotan is so clumsy—he knocks over the bowl, and flap-flap-flap go the gasping fishes, *pizzicato!*—but the sea——"

Helena's speech was often difficult to render into plain terms. She was not lucid.

"But life's so full of anti-climax," she concluded. Siegmund smiled softly at her. She had him too much in love to disagree or to examine her words.

"There's no reckoning with life, and no reckoning with the sea. The only way to get on with both is to be as near a vacuum as possible, and float," he jested. It hurt her that he was flippant. She proceeded to forget he had spoken.

There were three children on the beach. Helena had handed him back the senseless bauble, not able to throw it away. Being a father:

"I will give it to the children," he said.

She looked up at him, loved him for the thought.

Wandering hand in hand, for it pleased them both to own each other publicly, after years of conventional distance, they came to a little girl who was bending over a pool. Her black hair hung in long snakes to the water. She stood up, flung back her locks to see them as they approached. In one hand she clasped some pebbles.

"Would you like this? I found it down there," said Siegmund, offering her the bulb.

She looked at him with grave blue eyes and accepted his gift. Evidently she was not going to say anything.

"The sea brought it all the way from the mainland without breaking it," said Helena, with the interesting intonation some folk use to children.

The girl looked at her.

"The waves put it out of their lap on to some seaweed with such careful fingers——"

The child's eyes brightened.

"The tide-line is full of treasures," said Helena, smiling.

The child answered her smile a little.

Siegmund had walked away.

"What beautiful eyes she had!" said Helena.

"Yes," he replied.

She looked up at him. He felt her searching him tenderly with her eyes. But he could not look back at her. She took his hand and kissed it, knowing he was thinking of his own youngest child.

VIII

*T*he way home lay across country, through deep little lanes where the late foxgloves sat seriously, like sad hounds; over open downlands, rough with gorse and ling, and through pocketed hollows of bracken and trees.

They came to a small Roman Catholic church in the fields. There the carved Christ looked down on the dead whose sleeping forms made mounds under the coverlet. Helena's heart was swelling with emotion. All the yearning and pathos of Christianity filled her again.

The path skirted the churchyard wall, so that she had on the one hand the sleeping dead, and on the other Siegmund, strong and vigorous, but walking in the old, dejected fashion. She felt a rare tenderness and admiration for him. It was unusual for her to be so humble-minded, but this evening she felt she must minister to him, and be submissive.

She made him stop to look at the graves. Suddenly, as they stood, she kissed him, clasped him fervently, roused him till his passion burned away his heaviness, and he seemed tipped with life, his face glowing as if soon he would burst alight. Then she was satisfied, and could laugh.

As they went through the fir copse, listening to the birds like a family assembled and chattering at home in the evening, listening to the light swish of the wind, she let Siegmund predominate; he set the swing of their motion; she rested on him like a bird on a swaying bough.

They argued concerning the way. Siegmund, as usual, submitted to her. They went quite wrong. As they retraced their steps, stealthily, through a poultry farm whose fowls were standing in forlorn groups, once more dismayed by evening, Helena's pride battled with her new subjugation to Siegmund. She walked head down, saying nothing. He also was silent, but his heart was strong in him. Somewhere in the distance a band was playing "The Watch on the Rhine."

As they passed the beeches and were near home, Helena said, to try him, and to strike a last blow for her pride:

"I wonder what next Monday will bring us."

"Quick curtain," he answered joyously. He was looking down and smiling at her with such careless happiness that she loved him. He was wonderful to her.

She loved him, was jealous of every particle of him that evaded her. She wanted to sacrifice to him, make herself a burning altar to him, and she wanted to possess him.

The hours that would be purely their own came too slowly for her.

That night she met his passion with love. It was not his passion she wanted, actually. But she desired that he should want *her* madly, and that he should have all—everything. It was a wonderful night to him. It restored in him the full "will to live." But she felt it destroyed her. Her soul seemed blasted.

At seven o'clock in the morning Helena lay in the deliciously cool water, while small waves ran up the beach full and clear and foamless, continuing perfectly in their flicker the rhythm of the night's passion. Nothing, she felt, had ever been so delightful as this cool water running over her. She lay and looked out on the shining sea. All things, it seemed, were made of sunshine more or less soiled. The cliffs rose out of the shining waves like clouds of strong, fine texture, and rocks along the shore were the dapplings of a bright dawn. The coarseness was fused out of the world, so that sunlight showed in the veins of the morning cliffs and the rocks. Yea, everything ran with sunshine, as we are full of blood, and plants are tissued from green-gold, glistening sap. Substance and solidity were shadows that the morning cast round itself to make itself tangible: as she herself was a shadow, cast by that fragment of sunshine, her soul, over its inefficiency.

She remembered to have seen the bats flying low over a burnished pool at sunset, and the web of their wings had burned in scarlet flickers, as they stretched across the light. Winged momentarily on bits of tissued flame, threaded with blood, the bats had flickered a secret to her.

Now the cliffs were like wings uplifted, and the morning was coming dimly through them. She felt the wings of all the world upraised against the morning in a flashing, multitudinous flight. The world itself was flying. Sunlight poured on the large round world till she fancied it a heavy bee humming on its iridescent atmosphere across a vast air of sunshine.

She lay and rode the fine journey. Sunlight liquid in the water made the waves heavy, golden, and rich with a velvety coolness like cowslips. Her feet fluttered in the shadowy underwater. Her breast came out bright as the breast of a white bird.

Where was Siegmund? she wondered. He also was somewhere among the sea and the sunshine, white and playing like a bird, shining like a vivid, restless speck of sunlight. She struck the water, smiling, feeling alone with him. They two were the owners of this morning, as a pair of wild, large birds inhabiting an empty sea.

Siegmund had found a white cave welling with green water, brilliant and full of life as mounting sap. The white rock glimmered through the water, and soon Siegmund shimmered also in the living green of the sea, like pale flowers trembling upward.

"The water," said Siegmund, "is as full of life as I am," and he pressed forward his breast against it. He swam very well that morning; he had more wilful life than the sea, so he mastered it laughingly with his arms, feeling a delight in his triumph over the waves. Venturing recklessly in his new pride, he swam round the corner of the rock, through an archway, lofty and spacious, into a passage where the water ran like a flood of green light over the skin-white bottom. Suddenly he emerged in the brilliant daylight of the next tiny scoop of a bay.

There he arrived like a pioneer, for the bay was inaccessible from the land. He waded out of the green, cold water on to sand that was pure as the shoulders of Helena, out of the shadow of the archway into the sunlight, on to the glistening petal of this blossom of a sea-bay.

He did not know till he felt the sunlight how the sea had drunk with its cold lips deeply of his warmth. Throwing himself down on the sand that was soft and warm as white fur, he lay glistening wet, panting, swelling with glad pride at having conquered also this small, inaccessible sea-cave, creeping into it like a white bee into a white virgin blossom that had waited, how long, for its bee.

The sand was warm to his breast, and his belly, and his arms. It was like a great body he cleaved to. Almost, he fancied, he felt it heaving under him in its breathing. Then he turned his face to the sun, and laughed. All the while, he hugged the warm body of the sea-bay beneath him. He spread his hands upon the sand; he took it in handfuls, and let it run smooth, warm, delightful, through his fingers.

"Surely," he said to himself, "it is like Helena;" and he laid his hands again on the warm body of the shore, let them wander, discovering, gathering all the warmth, the softness, the strange wonder of smooth warm pebbles, then shrinking from the deep weight of cold his hand encountered as he burrowed under the surface wrist-deep. In the end he found the cold mystery of the deep sand also thrilling. He pushed in his hands again and deeper, enjoying the almost hurt of the dark, heavy coldness. For the sun and the white flower of the bay were breathing and kissing him dry, were holding him in their warm concave, like a bee in a flower, like himself on the bosom of Helena, and flowing like the warmth of her breath in his hair came the sunshine, breathing near and lovingly: yet, under all, was this deep mass of cold, that the softness and warmth merely floated upon.

Siegmund lay and clasped the sand, and tossed it in handfuls till over him he was all hot and cloyed. Then he rose and looked at himself and laughed. The water was swaying reproachfully against the steep pebbles below, murmuring like a child that it was not fair—it was not fair he should abandon his playmate. Siegmund laughed, and began to rub himself free of the clogging sand. He found himself strangely dry and smooth. He tossed more dry sand, and more, over himself, busy and intent like a child playing some absorbing game with itself. Soon his body was dry and warm and smooth as a camomile flower. He was, however, greyed and smeared with sand-dust. Siegmund looked at himself with disapproval, though his body was full of delight and his hands glad with the touch of himself. He wanted himself clean. He felt the sand thick in his hair, even in his moustache. He went painfully over the pebbles till he found himself on the smooth rock bottom. Then he soused himself, and shook his head in the water, and washed and splashed and rubbed himself with his hands assiduously.

He must feel perfectly clean and free—fresh, as if he had washed away all the years of soilure in this morning's sea and sun and sand. It was the purification. Siegmund became again a happy priest of the sun. He felt as if all the dirt of misery were soaked out of him, as he might soak clean a soiled garment in the sea, and bleach it white on the sunny shore. So white and sweet and tissue-clean he felt—full of lightness and grace.

The garden in front of their house, where Helena was waiting for him, was long and crooked, with a sunken flagstone pavement running up to the door by the side of the lawn. On either hand the high fence of the garden was heavy with wild clematis and honeysuckle. Helena sat sideways, with a map spread out on her bench under the bushy little labur-num-tree, tracing the course of their wanderings. It was very still. There was just a murmur of bees going in and out the brilliant little porches of nasturtium flowers. The nasturtium leaf-coins stood cool and grey; in their delicate shade, underneath in the green twilight, a few flowers shone their submerged gold and scarlet. There was a faint scent of mignonette. Helena, like a white butterfly in the shade, her two white arms for antennae stretching firmly to the bench, leaned over her map. She was busy, very busy, out of sheer happiness. She traced word after word, and evoked scene after scene. As she discovered a name, she conjured up the place. As she moved to the next mark she imagined the long path lifting and falling happily.

She was waiting for Siegmund, yet his hand upon the latch startled her. She rose suddenly, in agitation. Siegmund was standing in the sunshine at the gate. They greeted each other across the tall roses.

When Siegmund was holding her hand, he said, softly laughing:

"You have come out of the water very beautiful this morning."

She laughed. She was not beautiful, but she felt so at that moment. She glanced up at him, full of love and gratefulness.

"And you," she murmured, in a still tone, as if it were almost sacrilegiously unnecessary to say it.

Siegmund was glad. He rejoiced to be told he was beautiful. After a few moments of listening to the bees and breathing the mignonette, he said:

"I found a little white bay, just like you—a virgin bay. I had to swim there."

"Oh!" she said, very interested in him, not in the fact.

"It seemed just like you. Many things seem like you," he said.

She laughed again in her joyous fashion, and the reed-like vibration came into her voice.

"I saw the sun through the cliffs, and the sea, and you," she said.

He did not understand. He looked at her searchingly. She was white and still and inscrutable. Then she looked up at him; her earnest eyes, that would not flinch, gazed straight into him. He trembled, and things all swept into a blur. After she had taken away her eyes he found himself saying:

"You know, I felt as if I were the first man to discover things: like Adam when he opened the first eyes in the world."

"I saw the sunshine in you," repeated Helena quietly, looking at him with her eyes heavy with meaning.

He laughed again, not understanding, but feeling she meant love.

"No, but you have altered everything," he said.

The note of wonder, of joy, in his voice touched her almost beyond self-control. She caught his hand and pressed it; then quickly kissed it. He became suddenly grave.

"I feel as if it were right—you and me, Helena—so, even righteous. It is so, isn't it? And the sea and everything, they all seem with us. Do you think so?"

Looking at her, he found her eyes full of tears. He bent and kissed her, and she pressed his head to her bosom. He was very glad.

IX

The day waxed hot. A few little silver tortoises of cloud had crawled across the desert of sky, and hidden themselves. The chalk roads were white, quivering with heat. Helena and Siegmund walked eastward bareheaded under the sunshine. They felt like two insects in the niche of a hot hearth as they toiled along the deep road. A few poppies here and there among the wild rye floated scarlet in sunshine like blood-drops on green water. Helena recalled Francis Thompson's poems, which Siegmund had never read. She repeated what she knew, and laughed, thinking what an ineffectual pale shadow of a person Thompson must have been. She looked at Siegmund, walking in large easiness beside her.

"Artists are supremely unfortunately persons," she announced.

"Think of Wagner," said Siegmund, lifting his face to the hot bright heaven, and drinking the heat with his blinded face. All states seemed meagre, save his own. He recalled people who had loved, and he pitied them—dimly, drowsily, without pain.

They came to a place where they might gain access to the shore by a path down a landslip. As they descended through the rockery, yellow with ragwort, they felt themselves dip into the inert, hot air of the bay. The living atmosphere of the uplands was left overhead. Among the rocks of the sand, white as if smelted, the heat glowed and quivered. Helena sat down and took off her shoes. She walked on the hot, glistening sand till her feet were delightfully, almost intoxicatingly scorched. Then she ran into the water to cool them. Siegmund and she paddled in the light water, pensively watching the haste of the ripples, like crystal beetles, running over the white outline of their feet; looking out on the sea that rose so near to them, dwarfing them by its far reach.

For a short time they flitted silently in the water's edge. Then there settled down on them a twilight of sleep, the little hush that closes the doors and draws

A HOLY FAMILY

CLOSE-UP (KISS)

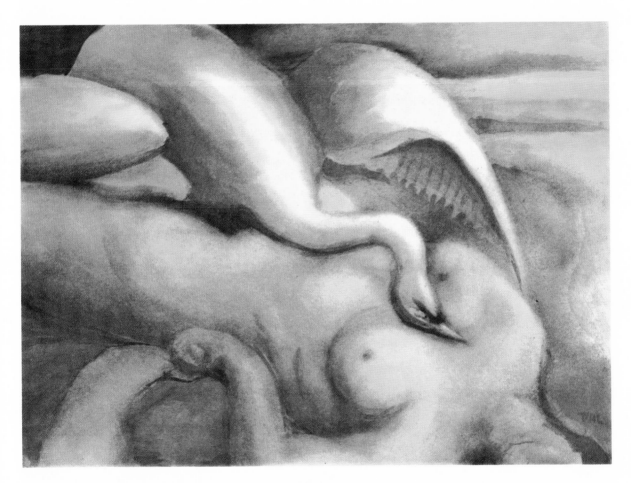

LEDA

RENASCENCE OF MEN

UNDER THE HAYSTACK

FAMILY ON A VERANDAH

CONTADINI

THE LAWRENCE PHOENIX

the blinds of the house after a festival. They wandered out across the beach above high-water mark, where they sat down together on the sand, leaning back against a flat brown stone, Siegmund with the sunshine on his forehead, Helena drooping close to him, in his shadow. Then the hours ride by unnoticed, making no sound as they go. The sea creeps nearer, nearer, like a snake which watches two birds asleep. It may not disturb them, but sinks back, ceasing to look at them with its bright eyes.

Meanwhile the flowers of their passion were softly shed, as poppies fall at noon, and the seed of beauty ripened rapidly within them. Dreams came like a wind through their souls, drifting off with the seed-dust of beautiful experience which they had ripened, to fertilize the souls of others withal. In them the sea and the sky and ships had mingled and bred new blossoms of the torrid heat of their love. And the seed of such blossoms was shaken as they slept, into the hand of God, who held it in his palm preciously; then scattered it again, to produce new splendid blooms of beauty.

A little breeze came down the cliffs. Sleep lightened the lovers of their experience; new buds were urged in their souls as they lay in a shadowed twilight, at the porch of death. The breeze fanned the face of Helena; a coolness wafted on her throat. As the afternoon wore on she revived. Quick to flag, she was easy to revive, like a white pansy flung into water. She shivered lightly and rose.

Strange, it seemed to her, to rise from the brown stone into life again. She felt beautifully refreshed. All around was quick as a garden wet in the early morning of June. She took her hair and loosened it, shook it free from sand, spread, and laughed like a fringed poppy that opens itself to the sun. She let the wind comb through its soft fingers the tangles of her hair. Helena loved the wind. She turned to it, and took its kisses on her face and throat.

Siegmund lay still, looking up at her. The changes in him were deeper, like alteration in his tissue. His new buds came slowly, and were of a fresh type. He lay smiling at her. At last he said:

"You look now as if you belonged to the sea."

"I do; and some day I shall go back to it," she replied.

For to her at that moment the sea was a great lover, like Siegmund, but more impersonal, who would receive her when Siegmund could not. She rejoiced momentarily in the fact. Siegmund looked at her and continued smiling. His happiness was budded firm and secure.

"Come!" said Helena, holding out her hand.

He rose somewhat reluctantly from his large, fruitful inertia.

X

Siegmund carried the boots and the shoes while they wandered over the sand to the rocks. There was a delightful sense of risk in scrambling with bare feet over the smooth irregular jumble of rocks. Helena laughed suddenly from fear as she felt herself slipping. Siegmund's heart was leaping like a child's with excitement as he stretched forward, himself very insecure, to succour her. Thus they travelled slowly. Often she called to him to come and look in the lovely little rock-pools, dusky with blossoms of red anemones and brown anemones that seemed nothing but shadows, and curtained with green of finest sea-silk. Siegmund loved to poke the white pebbles, and startle the little ghosts of crabs in a shadowy scuttle through the weed. He would tease the expectant anemones, causing them to close suddenly over his finger. But Helena liked to watch without touching things. Meanwhile the sun was slanting behind the cross far away to the west, and the light was swimming in silver and gold upon the lacquered water. At last Siegmund looked doubtfully at two miles more of glistening, gilded boulders. Helena was seated on a stone, dabbling her feet in a warm pool, delicately feeling the wet sea-velvet of the weeds.

"Don't you think we had better be mounting the cliffs?" he said.

She glanced up at him, smiling with irresponsible eyes. Then she lapped the water with her feet, and surveyed her pink toes. She was absurdly, childishly happy.

"Why should we?" she asked lightly.

He watched her. Her child-like indifference to consequences touched him with a sense of the distance between them. He himself might play with the delicious warm surface of life, but always he recked of the relentless mass of cold beneath—the mass of life which has no sympathy with the individual, no cognizance of him.

She loved the trifles and the toys, the mystery and the magic of things. She would not own life to be relentless. It was either beautiful, fantastic, or weird, or unscrutable, or else mean and vulgar, below consideration. He had to get a sense of the anemone and a sympathetic knowledge of its experience, into his blood, before he was satisfied. To Helena an anemone was one more fantastic pretty figure in her kaleidoscope.

So she sat dabbling her pink feet in the water, quite unconscious of his gravity. He waited on her, since he never could capture her.

"Come," he said very gently. "You are only six years old to-day."

She laughed as she let him take her. Then she nestled up to him, smiling in a brilliant, child-like fashion. He kissed her with all the father in him sadly alive.

"Now put your stockings on," he said.

"But my feet are wet." She laughed.

He kneeled down and dried her feet on his handkerchief, while she sat tossing his hair with her fingertips. The sunlight grew more and more golden.

"I envy the savages their free feet," she said.

"There is no broken glass in the wilderness—or there used not to be," he replied.

As they were crossing the sands, a whole family entered by the cliff track. They descended in single file, unequally, like the theatre: two boys, then a little girl, the father, another girl, then the mother. Last of all trotted the dog, warily, suspicious of the descent. The boys emerged into the bay with a shout; the dog rushed, barking, after them. The little one waited for her father, calling shrilly:

"Tiss can't fall now, can she, dadda? Shall I put her down?"

"Ay, let her have a run," said the father.

Very carefully she lowered the kitten which she had carried clasped to her bosom. The mite was bewildered and scared. It turned round pathetically.

"Go on, Tissie; you're all right," said the child.

"Go on; have a run on the sand."

The kitten stood dubious and unhappy. Then, perceiving the dog some distance ahead, it scampered after him, a fluffy, scurrying mite. But the dog had already raced into the water. The kitten walked a few steps, turning its small face this way and that, and mewing piteously. It looked extraordinarily tiny as it stood, a fluffy handful, staring away from the noisy water, its thin cry floating over the plash of waves.

Helena glanced at Siegmund, and her eyes were shining with pity. He was watching the kitten and smiling.

"Crying because things are too big, and it can't take them in," he said.

"But look how frightened it is," she said.

"So am I." He laughed. "And if there are any gods looking on and laughing at me, at least they won't be kind enough to put me in their pinafores. . . ."

She laughed very quickly.

"But why?" she exclaimed. "Why should you want putting in a pinafore?"

"I don't," he laughed.

On the top of the cliff they were between two bays, with darkening blue water on the left, and on the right gold water smoothing to the sun. Siegmund seemed to stand waist-deep in shadow, with his face bright and glowing. He was watching earnestly.

"I want to absorb it all," he said.

When at last they turned away:

"Yes," said Helena slowly; "one can recall the details, but never the atmosphere."

He pondered a moment.

"How strange!" he said. "I can recall the atmosphere, but not the detail. It is a moment to me, not a piece of scenery. I should say the picture was in me, not out there."

Without troubling to understand—she was inclined to think it verbiage—she made a small sound of assent.

"That is why you want to go again to a place, and I don't care so much, because I have it with me," he concluded.

XI

They decided to find their way through the lanes to Alum Bay, and then, keeping the Cross in sight, to return over the downs, with the moon-path broad on the water before them. For the moon was rising late. Twilight, however, rose more rapidly than they had anticipated. The lane twisted among meadows and wild lands and copses—a wilful little lane, quite incomprehensible. So they lost their distant landmark, the white cross.

Darkness filtered through the daylight. When at last they came to a signpost, it was almost too dark to read it. The fingers seemed to withdraw into the dusk the more they looked.

"We must go to the left," said Helena.

To the left rose the downs, smooth and grey near at hand, but higher black with gorse, like a giant lying asleep with a bearskin over his shoulders.

Several pale chalk-tracks ran side by side through the turf. Climbing, they came to a disused chalk-pit, which they circumvented. Having passed a lonely farmhouse, they mounted the side of the open down, where was a sense of space and freedom.

"We can steer by the night," said Siegmund, as they trod upwards pathlessly. Helena did not mind whither they steered. All places in that large fair night were home and welcome to her. They drew nearer to the shaggy cloak of furze.

"There will be a path through it," said Siegmund.

But when they arrived there was no path. They were confronted by a tall, impenetrable growth of gorse, taller than Siegmund.

"Stay here," said he, "while I look for a way through. I am afraid you will be tired."

She stood alone by the walls of gorse. The lights that had flickered into being during the dusk grew stronger, so that a little farmhouse down the hill glowed with great importance on the night, while the far-off invisible sea became like a roadway, large and mysterious, its specks of light moving slowly, and its bigger lamps stationed out amid the darkness. Helena wanted the day-wanness to be quite wiped off the west. She asked for the full black night, that would obliterate everything save Siegmund. Siegmund it was that the whole world meant. The darkness, the gorse, the downs, the specks of light, seemed only to bespeak him. She waited for him to come back. She could hardly endure the condition of intense waiting.

He came, in his grey clothes almost invisible. But she felt him coming.

"No good," he said, "no vestige of a path. Not a rabbit-run."

"Then we will sit down awhile," said she calmly.

" 'Here on this mole-hill' " he quoted mockingly.

They sat down in a small gap in the gorse, where the turf was very soft, and where the darkness seemed deeper. The night was all fragrance, cool odour of darkness, keen, savoury scent of the downs, touched with honey-suckle and gorse and bracken scent.

Helena turned to him, leaning her hand on his thigh.

"What day is it, Siegmund?" she asked, in a joyous, wondering tone. He laughed, understanding, and kissed her.

"But really," she insisted, "I would not have believed the labels could have fallen off everything like this."

He laughed again. She still leaned towards him, her weight on her hand stopping the flow in the artery down his thigh.

"The days used to walk in procession like seven marionettes, each in order and costume, going endlessly round." She laughed, amused at the idea.

"It is very strange," she continued, "to have the days and nights smeared into one piece, as if the clock-hand only went round once in a lifetime."

"That is how it is," he admitted, touched by her eloquence. "You have torn the labels off things, and they all are so different. This morning! It does seem absurd to talk about this morning. Why should I be parcelled up into mornings and evenings and nights? *I* am not made up of sections of time. Now, nights and days go racing over us like cloud-shadows and sunshine over the sea, and all the time we take no notice."

She put her arms round his neck. He was reminded by a sudden pain in his leg how much her hand had been pressing on him. He held his breath from pain. She was kissing him softly over his eyes. They lay cheek to cheek, looking at the stars. He felt a peculiar tingling sense of joy, a keenness of perception, a fine, delicate tingling as of music.

"You know," he said, repeating himself, "it is true. You seem to have knit all things in a piece for me. Things are not separate; they are all in a symphony. They go moving on and on. You are the motive in everything."

Helena lay beside him, half upon him, sad with bliss.

"You must write a symphony of this—of us," she said, prompted by a disciple's vanity.

"Some time," he answered. "Later, when I have time."

"Later," she murmured—"later than what?"

"I don't know," he replied. "This is so bright we can't see beyond." He turned his face to hers and through the darkness smiled into her eyes that were so close to his. Then he kissed her long and lovingly. He lay, with her head on his shoulder, looking through her hair at the stars.

"I wonder how it is you have such a fine natural perfume," he said, always in the same abstract, inquiring tone of happiness.

"Haven't all women?" she replied, and the peculiar penetrating twang of a brass reed was again in her voice.

"I don't know," he said, quite untouched. "But you are scented like nuts, new kernels of hazel-nuts, and a touch of opium. . . ." He remained abstractedly breathing her with his open mouth, quite absorbed in her.

"You are so strange," she murmured tenderly, hardly able to control her voice to speak.

"I believe," he said slowly, "I can see the stars moving through your hair. No, keep still, *you* can't see them." Helena lay obediently very still. "I thought I could watch them travelling, crawling like gold flies on the ceiling," he continued in a slow sing-song. "But now you make your hair tremble, and the stars rush about." Then, as a new thought struck him: "Have you noticed that you can't recognize the constellations lying back like this. I can't see one. Where is the north, even?"

She laughed at the idea of his questioning her concerning these things. She refused to learn the names of the stars or of the constellations, as of the wayside plants. "Why should I want to label them?" she would say. "I prefer to look at them, not to hide them under a name." So she laughed when he asked her to find Vega or Arcturus.

"How full the sky is!" Siegmund dreamed on—"like a crowded street. Down here it is vastly lonely in comparison. We've found a place far quieter and more private than the stars, Helena. Isn't it fine to be up here, with the sky for nearest neighbour?"

"I did well to ask you to come?" she inquired wistfully. He turned to her.

"As wise as God for the minute," he replied softly. "I think a few furtive angels brought us here—smuggled us in."

"And you are glad?" she asked. He laughed.

"Carpe diem," he said. "We have plucked a beauty, my dear. With this rose in my coat I dare go to hell or anywhere."

"Why hell, Siegmund?" she asked in displeasure.

"I suppose it is the *postero*. In everything else I'm a failure, Helena. But," he laughed, "this day of ours is a rose not many men have plucked."

She kissed him passionately, beginning to cry in a quick, noiseless fashion.

"What does it matter, Helena?" he murmured. "What does it matter? We are here yet."

The quiet tone of Siegmund moved her with a vivid passion of grief. She felt she should lose him. Clasping him very closely, she burst into uncontrollable sobbing. He did not understand, but he did not interrupt her. He merely held her very close, while he looked through her shaking hair at the motionless stars. He bent his head to hers, he sought her face with his lips, heavy with pity. She grew a little quieter. He felt his cheek all wet with her tears, and, between his cheek and hers, the ravelled roughness of her wet hair that chafed and made his face burn.

"What is it, Helena?" he asked at last. "Why should you cry?"

She pressed her face in his breast, and said in a muffled, unrecognizable voice: "You won't leave me, will you, Siegmund?"

"How could I? How should I?" he murmured soothingly. She lifted her face suddenly and pressed on him a fierce kiss.

"How could I leave you?" he repeated, and she heard his voice waking, felt the grip coming into his arms, and she was glad.

An intense silence came over everything. Helena almost expected to hear the stars moving, everything below was so still. She had no idea what Siegmund was thinking. He lay with his arms strong around her. Then she heard the beating of his heart, like the muffled sound of salutes, she thought. It gave her the same thrill of dread and excitement, mingled with a sense of triumph. Siegmund had changed again, his mood was gone, so that he was no longer wandering in a night of thoughts, but had become different, incomprehensible to her. She had no idea what she thought or felt. All she knew was that he was strong, and was knocking urgently with his heart on her breast, like a man who wanted something and who dreaded to be sent away. How he came to be so concentratedly urgent she could not understand. It seemed an unreasonable, an incomprehensible obsession to her. Yet she was glad, and she smiled in her heart, feeling triumphant and restored. Yet again, dimly, she wondered where was the Siegmund of ten minutes ago, and her heart lifted slightly with yearning, to sink with a dismay. This Siegmund was so incomprehensible. Then again, when he raised his head and found her mouth, his lips filled her with a hot flush like wine, a sweet, flaming flush of her whole body, most exquisite, as if she were nothing but a soft rosy flame of fire against him for a moment or two. That, she decided, was supreme, transcendental.

The lights of the little farmhouse below had vanished, the yellow specks of ships were gone. Only the pier-light, far away, shone in the black sea like the broken piece of a star. Overhead was a silver-greyness of stars; below was the velvet blackness of the night and the sea. Helena found herself glimmering with fragments of poetry, as she saw the sea, when she looked very closely, glimmered dustily with a reflection of stars.

> "Tiefe Stille herrscht im Wasser
> Ohne Regung ruht das Meer . . ."

She was fond of what scraps of German verse she knew. With French verse she had no sympathy; but Goethe and Heine and Uhland seemed to speak her language.

> "Die Luft ist kühl, und es dunkelt,
> Und ruhig fliesst der Rhein."

She liked Heine best of all:

> "Wie Träume der Kindheit seh'ich es flimmern
> Auf deinen wogenden Wellengebiet,
> Und alte Errinnrung erzählt mir auf's Neue
> Von all dem lieben herrlichen Spielzeug,
> Von all den blinkenden Weihnachtsgaben . . ."

As she lay in Siegmund's arms again, and he was very still, dreaming she knew not what, fragments such as these flickered and were gone, like the gleam of a falling star over water. The night moved on imperceptibly across the sky. Unlike the day, it made no sound and gave no sign, but passed unseen, unfelt, over them. Till the moon was ready to step forth. Then the eastern sky blenched, and there was a small gathering of clouds round the opening gates:

> "Aus alten Märchen winkt es
> Hervor mit weisser Hand,
> Da singt es und da klingt es
> Von einem Zauberland."

Helena sang this to herself as the moon lifted herself slowly among the clouds. She found herself repeating them aloud in a forgetful singsong, as children do.

"What is it?" said Siegmund. They were both of them sunk in their own stillness, therefore it was a moment or two before she repeated her singsong, in a little louder tone. He did not listen to her, having forgotten that he had asked her a question.

"Turn your head," she told him, when she had finished the verse, "and look at the moon."

He pressed back his head, so that there was a gleaming pallor on his chin and his forehead and a deep black shadow over his eyes and his nostrils. This thrilled Helena with a sense of mystery and magic.

" 'Die grosse Blumen schmachten,' " she said to herself, curiously awake and joyous. "The big flowers open with black petals and silvery ones, Siegmund. You are the big flowers, Siegmund; yours is the bridegroom face, Siegmund, like a black and glistening flesh-petalled flower, Siegmund, and it blooms in the Zauberland, Siegmund—this is the magic land."

Between the phrases of this whispered ecstasy she kissed him swiftly on the throat, in the shadow, and on his faintly gleaming cheeks. He lay still, his heart beating heavily; he was almost afraid of the strange ecstasy she concentrated on him. Meanwhile she whispered over him sharp, breathless phrases in German and English, touching him with her mouth and her cheeks and her forehead.

" 'Und Liebesweisen tönen'—not to-night, Siegmund. They are all still—gorse and the stars and the sea and the trees, are all kissing, Siegmund. The sea has its mouth on the earth, and the gorse and the trees press together, and they all look up at the moon, they put up their faces in a kiss, my darling. But they haven't you—and it all centres in you, my dear, all the wonder-love is in you, more than in them all, Siegmund—Siegmund!"

He felt the tears falling on him as he lay with heart beating in slow heavy drops under the ecstasy of her love. Then she sank down and lay prone on him, spent, clinging to him, lifted up and down by the beautiful strong motion of his breathing. Rocked thus on his strength, she swooned lightly into unconsciousness.

When she came to herself she sighed deeply. She woke to the exquisite heaving of his life beneath her.

"I have been beyond life. I have been a little way into death!" she said to her soul, with wide-eyed delight. She lay dazed, wondering upon it. That she should come back into a marvellous, peaceful happiness astonished her.

Suddenly she became aware that she must be slowly weighing down the life of Siegmund. There was a long space between the lift of one breath and the next. Her heart melted with sorrowful pity. Resting herself on her hands, she kissed him—a long, anguished kiss, as if she would fuse her soul into his for ever. Then she rose, sighing, sighing again deeply. She put up her hands to her head and looked at the moon. "No more," said her heart, almost as if it sighed to—"no more!"

She looked down at Seigmund. He was drawing in great heavy breaths. He lay still on his back, gazing up at her, and she stood motionless at his side, looking down at him. He felt stunned, half-conscious. Yet as he lay helplessly looking up at her some other consciousness inside him murmured: "Hawwa—Eve—Mother!" She stood compassionate over him. Without touching him she seemed to be yearning over him like a mother. Her compassion, her benignity, seemed so different from his little Helena. This woman, tall and pale, drooping with the strength of her compassion, seemed stable, immortal, not a fragile human being, but a personification of the great motherhood of woman.

"I am her child, too," he dreamed, as a child murmurs unconscious in sleep. He had never felt her eyes so much as now, in the darkness, when he looked only into deep shadow. She had never before so entered and gathered his plaintive masculine soul to the bosom of her nurture.

"Come," she said gently, when she knew he was restored. "Shall we go?"

He rose, with difficulty gathering his strength.

XII

Siegmund made a great effort to keep the control of his body. The hillside, the gorse, when he stood up, seemed to have fallen back into shadowed vagueness about him. They were meaningless dark heaps at some distance, very great, it seemed.

"I can't get hold of them," he said distractedly to himself. He felt detached from the earth, from all the near, concrete, beloved things; as if these had melted away from him, and left him, sick and unsupported, somewhere alone on the edge of an enormous space. He wanted to lie down again, to relieve himself of the sickening effort of supporting and controlling his body. If he could lie down again perfectly still he need not struggle to animate the cumbersome matter of his body, and then he would not feel thus sick and outside himself.

But Helena was speaking to him, telling him they would see the moon path. They must set off downhill. He felt her arm clasped firmly, joyously, round his waist. Therein was his stability and warm support. Siegmund felt a keen flush of pitiful tenderness for her as she walked with buoyant feet beside him, clasping him so happily, all unconscious. This pity for her drew him nearer to life.

He shuddered lightly now and again, as they stepped lurching down the hill. He set his jaws hard to suppress this shuddering. It was not in his limbs, or even on the surface of his body, for Helena did not notice it. Yet he shuddered almost in anguish internally.

"What is it?" he asked himself in wonder.

His thought consisted of these detached phrases, which he spoke verbally to himself. Between whiles he was conscious only of an almost insupportable feeling of sickness, as a man feels who is being brought from under an anæsthetic; also he was vaguely aware of a teeming stir of activity, such as one may hear from a closed hive, within him.

They swung rapidly downhill. Siegmund still shuddered, but not so uncontrollably. They came to a stile which they must climb. As he stepped over it needed a concentrated effort of will to place his foot securely on the step. The effort was so great that he became conscious of it.

"Good Lord!" he said to himself. "I wonder what it is."

He tried to examine himself. He thought of all the organs of his body—his brain, his heart, his liver. There was no pain, and nothing wrong with any of them, he was sure. His dim searching resolved itself into another detached phrase. "There is nothing the matter with me," he said.

Then he continued vaguely wondering, recalling the sensation of wretched sickness which sometimes follows drunkenness, thinking of the times when he had fallen ill.

"But I am not like that," he said, "because I don't feel tremulous. I am sure my hand is steady."

Helena stood still to consider the road. He held out his hand before him. It was as motionless as a dead flower on this silent night.

"Yes, I think this is the right way," said Helena, and they set off again, as if gaily.

"It certainly feels rather deathly," said Siegmund to himself. He remembered distinctly, when he was a child and had diphtheria, he had stretched himself in the horrible sickness, which he felt was—and here he chose the French word—"l'agonie." But his mother had seen and had cried aloud, which suddenly caused him to struggle with all his soul to spare her her suffering.

"Certainly it is like that," he said. "Certainly it is rather deathly. I wonder how it is."

Then he reviewed the last hour.

"I believe we are lost!" Helena interrupted him.

"Lost! What matter!" he answered indifferently, and Helena pressed him tighter, nearer to her in a kind of triumph. "But did we not come this way?" he added.

"No. See"—her voice was reeded with restrained emotion—"we have certainly not been along this bare path which dips up and down."

"Well, then, we must merely keep due eastward, towards the moon pretty well, as much as we can," said Siegmund, looking forward over the down, where the moon was wrestling heroically to win free of the pack of clouds which hung on her like wolves on a white deer. As he looked at the moon he felt a sense of companionship. Helena, not understanding, left him so much alone; the moon was nearer.

Siegmund continued to review the last hours. He had been so wondrously happy. The world had been filled with a new magic, a wonderful, stately beauty which he had perceived for the first time. For long hours he had been wandering in another—a glamorous, primordial world.

"I suppose," he said to himself, "I have lived too intensely. I seem to have had the stars and moon and everything else for guests, and now they've gone my house is weak."

So he struggled to diagnose his case of splendour and sickness. He reviewed his hour of passion with Helena.

"Surely," he told himself, "I have drunk life too hot, and it has hurt my cup. My soul seems to leak out—I am half here, half gone away. That's why I understand the trees and the night so painfully."

Then he came to the hour of Helena's strange ecstasy over him. That, somehow, had filled him with passionate grief. It was happiness concentrated one drop too keen, so that what should have been vivid wine was like a pure poison scathing him. But his consciousness, which had been unnaturally active, now was dulling. He felt the blood flowing vigorously along the limbs again, and stilling his brain, sweeping away his sickness, soothing him.

"I suppose," he said to himself for the last time, "I suppose living too intensely kills you, more or less."

Then Siegmund forgot. He opened his eyes and saw the night about him. The moon had escaped from the cloud-pack, and was radiant behind a fine veil which glistened to her rays, and which was broidered with a lustrous halo, very large indeed, the largest halo Siegmund had ever seen. When the little lane turned full towards the moon, it seemed as if Siegmund and Helena would walk through a large Moorish arch of horse-shoe shape, the enormous white halo opening in front of them. They walked on, keeping their faces to the moon, smiling with wonder and a little rapture, until once more the little lane curved wilfully, and they were walking north. Helena observed three cottages crouching under the hill and under trees to cover themselves from the magic of the moonlight.

"We certainly did not come this way before," she said triumphantly. The idea of being lost delighted her.

Siegmund looked round at the grey hills smeared over with a low, dim glisten of moon-mist. He could not yet fully realize that he was walking along a lane in the Isle of Wight. His surroundings seemed to belong to some state beyond ordinary experience—some place in romance, perhaps, or among the hills where Brünhild lay sleeping in her large bright halo of fire. How could it be that he and Helena were two children of London wandering to find their lodging in Freshwater? He sighed, and looked again over the hills where the moonlight was condensing in mist ethereal, frail, and yet substantial, reminding him of the way the manna must have condensed out of the white moonlit mists of Arabian deserts.

"We may be on the road to Newport," said Helena presently, "and the distance is ten miles."

She laughed, not caring in the least whither they wandered, exulting in this wonderful excursion! She, and Siegmund alone in a glistening wilderness of night at the back of habited days and nights! Siegmund looked at her. He by no means shared her exultation, though he sympathized with it. He walked on alone in his deep seriousness, of which she was not aware. Yet when he noticed her abandon, he drew her nearer, and his heart softened with protecting tenderness towards her, and grew heavy with responsibility.

The fields breathed off a scent as if they were come to life with the night, and were talking with fragrant eagerness. The farms huddled together in sleep, and pulled the dark shadow over them to hide from the supernatural white night; the cottages were locked and darkened. Helena walked on in triumph through this wondrous hinterland of night, actively searching for the spirits, watching the cottages they approached, listening, looking for the dreams of those sleeping inside, in the darkened rooms. She imagined she could see the frail dream-faces at the windows; she fancied they stole out timidly into the gardens, and went running away among the rabbits on the gleamy hillside. Helena laughed to herself, pleased with her fancy of wayward little dreams playing with weak hands and feet among the large, solemn-sleeping cattle. This was the first time, she told herself, that she had ever been out among the grey-frocked dreams and white-armed fairies. She imagined herself lying asleep in her room, while her own dreams slid out down the moon-beams. She imagined Siegmund sleeping in his room, while his dreams, dark-eyed, their blue eyes very dark and yearning at night-time, came wandering over the grey grass seeking her dreams.

So she wove her fancies as she walked, until for very weariness she was fain to remember that it was a long way—a long way. Siegmund's arm was about her to support her; she rested herself upon it. They crossed a stile and recognized, on the right of the path, the graveyard of the Catholic chapel. The moon, which the days were paring smaller with envious keen knife, shone upon the white stones in the burial-ground. The carved Christ upon his cross hung against a silver-grey sky. Helena looked up wearily, bowing to the tragedy. Siegmund also looked, and bowed his head.

"Thirty years of earnest love; three years' life like a passionate ecstasy—and it was finished. He was very great and very wonderful. I am very insignificant, and shall go out ignobly. But we are the same; love, the brief ecstasy, and the end. But mine is one rose, and His all the white beauty in the world."

Siegmund felt his heart very heavy, sad, and at fault, in presence of the Christ. Yet he derived comfort from the knowledge that life was treating him in the same manner as it had treated the Master, though his compared small and despicable with the Christ-tragedy. Siegmund stepped softly into the shadow of the pine copse.

"Let me get under cover," he thought. "Let me hide in it; it is good, the sudden intense darkness. I am small and futile: my small, futile tragedy!"

Helena shrank in the darkness. It was almost terrible to her, and the silence was like a deep pit. She shrank to Siegmund. He drew her closer, leaning over her as they walked, trying to assure her. His heart was heavy, and heavy with a tenderness approaching grief, for his small, brave Helena.

"Are you sure this is the right way?" he whispered to her.

"Quite, quite sure," she whispered confidently in reply. And presently they came out into the hazy moonlight, and began stumbling down the steep hill. They were both very tired, both found it difficult to go with ease or surety this sudden way down. Soon they were creeping cautiously across the pasture and the poultry farm. Helena's heart was beating, as she imagined what a merry noise there would be should they wake all the fowls. She dreaded any commotion, any questioning, this night, so she stole carefully along till they issued on the highroad not far from home.

XIII

*I*n the morning, after bathing, Siegmund leaned upon the sea wall in a kind of reverie. It was late, towards nine o'clock, yet he lounged, dreamily looking out on the turquoise blue water, and the white haze of morning, and the small, fair shadows of ships slowly realizing before him. In the bay were two battleships, uncouth monsters, lying as naïve and curious as sealions strayed afar.

Siegmund was gazing oversea in a half-stupid way, when he heard a voice beside him say:

"Where have they come from; do you know, sir?"

He turned, saw a fair, slender man of some thirty-five years standing beside him and smiling faintly at the battleships.

"The men of war? There are a good many at Spithead," said Siegmund.

The other glanced negligently into his face.

"They look rather incongruous, don't you think? We left the sea empty and shining, and when we come again, behold, these objects keeping their eye on us!"

Siegmund laughed.

"You are not an Anarchist, I hope?" he said jestingly.

"A Nihilist, perhaps," laughed the other. "But I am quite fond of the Czar, if pity is akin to love. No; but you can't turn round without finding some policeman or other at your elbow—look at them, abominable ironmongery!—ready to put his hand on your shoulder."

The speaker's grey-blue eyes, always laughing with mockery, glanced from the battleships and lit on the dark blue eyes of Siegmund. The latter felt his heart lift in a convulsive movement. This stranger ran so quickly to a perturbing intimacy.

"I suppose we are in the hands of—God," something moved Siegmund to say. The stranger contracted his eyes slightly as he gazed deep at the speaker.

"Ah!" he drawled curiously. Then his eyes wandered over the wet hair, the white brow, and the bare throat of Siegmund, after which they returned again to the eyes of his interlocutor. "Does the Czar sail this way?" he asked at last.

"I do not know," replied Siegmund, who, troubled by the other's penetrating, gaze, had not expected so trivial a question.

"I suppose the newspaper will tell us?" said the man.

"Sure to," said Siegmund.

"You haven't seen it this morning?"

"Not since Saturday."

The swift blue eyes of the man dilated. He looked curiously at Siegmund.

"You are not alone on your holiday?"

"No." Siegmund did not like this—he gazed over the sea in displeasure.

"I live here—at least for the present—name, Hampson——"

"Why, weren't you one of the first violins at the Savoy fifteen years back?" asked Siegmund.

They chatted awhile about music. They had known each other, had been fairly intimate, and had since become strangers. Hampson excused himself for having addressed Siegmund:

"I saw you with your nose flattened against the window," he said, "and as I had mine in the same position too, I thought we were fit to be re-acquainted."

Seigmund looked at the man in astonishment.

"I only mean you were staring rather hard at nothing. It's a pity to try and stare out of a beautiful blue day like this, don't you think?"

"Stare beyond it, you mean?" asked Siegmund.

"Exactly!" replied the other, with a laugh of intelligence. "I call a day like this 'the blue room.' It's the least draughty apartment in all the confoundedly draughty House of Life."

Siegmund look at him very intently. This Hampson seemed to express something in his own soul.

"I mean," the man explained, "that after all, the great mass of life that washes unidentified, and that we call death, creeps through the blue envelope of the day, and through our white tissue, and we can't stop it, once we've begun to leak."

"What do you mean by 'leak?' " asked Siegmund.

"Goodness knows—I talk through my hat. But once you've got a bit tired of the house, you glue your nose to the window pane, and stare for the dark—as you were doing."

"But, to use your metaphor, I'm not tired of the House—if you mean Life," said Siegmund.

"Praise God! I've met a poet who's not afraid of having his pocket picked—or his soul, or his brain!" said the stranger, throwing his head back in a brilliant smile, his eyes dilated.

"I don't know what you mean, sir," said Siegmund, very quietly, with a strong fear and a fascination opposing each other in his heart.

"You're not tired of the House, but of your own particular room—say, suite of rooms——"

"To-morrow I am turned out of this 'blue room,' " said Siegmund with a wry smile. The other looked at him seriously.

"Dear Lord!" exclaimed Hampson; then: "Do you remember Flaubert's saint, who laid naked against a leper? I could *not* do it."

"Nor I," shuddered Siegmund.

"But you've got to—or something near it!"

Siegmund looked at the other with frightened, horrified eyes.

"What of yourself?" he said, resentfully.

"I've funked—ran away from my leper, and now am eating my heart out, and staring from the window at the dark."

"But can't you *do* something?" said Siegmund.

The other man laughed with amusement, throwing his head back and showing his teeth.

"I won't ask you what *your* intentions are," he said, with delicate irony in his tone. "You know, I am a tremendously busy man. I earn five hundred a year by hard work; but it's no good. If you have acquired a liking for intensity in life, you can't do without it. I mean vivid soul experience. It takes the place, with us, of the old adventure, and physical excitement."

Siegmund looked at the other man with baffled, anxious eyes.

"Well, and what then?" he said.

"What then? A craving for intense life is nearly as deadly as any other craving. You become a 'concentré'; you feed your normal flame with oxygen, and it devours your tissue. The soulful ladies of romance are always semi-transparent."

Siegmund laughed.

"At least, I am quite opaque," he said.

The other glanced over his easy, mature figure and strong throat.

"Not altogether," said Hampson. "And you, I should think, are one whose flame goes nearly out, when the stimulant is lacking."

Siegmund glanced again at him, startled.

"You haven't much reserve. You're like a tree that'll flower till it kills itself," the man continued. "You'll run till you drop, and then you won't get up again. You've no dispassionate intellect to control you and economize."

"You're telling me very plainly what I am and am not," said Siegmund, laughing rather sarcastically. He did not like it.

"Oh, it's only what I think," replied Hampson. "We're a good deal alike, you see, and have gone the same way. You married and I didn't; but women have always done as they liked with me."

"That's hardly so in my case," said Siegmund.

Hampson eyed him critically.

"Say one woman; it's enough," he replied.

Siegmund gazed, musing, over the sea.

"The best sort of women—the most interesting—are the worst for us," Hampson resumed. "By instinct they aim at suppressing the gross and animal in us. Then they are supersensitive—refined a bit beyond humanity. We, who are as little gross as need be, become their instruments. Life is grounded in them, like electricity in the earth; and we take from them their unrealized life, turn it into light or warmth or power for them. The ordinary woman is, alone, a great potential force, an accumulator, if you like, charged from the source of life. In us her force becomes evident.

"She can't live without us, but she destroys us. These deep, interesting women don't want *us;* they want the flowers of the spirit they can gather of us. We, as natural men, are more or less degrading to them and to their love of us; therefore they destroy the natural man in us—that is, us altogether."

"You're a bit downright, are you not?" asked Siegmund, deprecatingly. He did not disagree with what his friend said, nor tell him such statements were arbitrary.

"That's according to my intensity," laughed Hampson. "I can open the blue heaven with looking, and push back the doors of day a little, and see—God knows what! One of these days I shall slip through. Oh, I am perfectly sane; I only strive beyond myself!"

"Don't you think it's wrong to get like it?" asked Siegmund.

"Well, I do, and so does everybody; but the crowd profits by us in the end. When they understand my music, it will be an education to them; and the whole aim of mankind is to render life intelligible."

Siegmund pondered a little.

"You make me feel—as if I were loose, and a long way off from myself," he said slowly.

The young man smiled, then looked down at the wall, where his own hands lay white and fragile, showing the blue veins.

"I can scarcely believe they are me," he said. "If they rose up and refused me, I should not be surprised. But aren't they beautiful?"

He looked, with a faint smile, at Siegmund.

Siegmund glanced from the stranger's to his own hands, which lay curved on the sea-wall as if asleep. They were small for a man of his stature, but, lying warm in the sun, they looked particularly secure in life. Instinctively, with a wave of self-love, he closed his fists over his thumbs.

"I wonder," said Hampson softly, with strange bitterness, "that she can't see it; I wonder she doesn't cherish you. You are full and beautiful enough in the flesh—why will she help to destroy you, when she loved you to such extremity?"

Siegmund looked at him with awe-stricken eyes. The frail, swift man, with his intensely living eyes, laughed suddenly.

"Fools—the fools, these women!" he said. "Either they smash their own crystal, or it revolts, turns opaque, and leaps out of their hands. Look at me, I am whittled down to the quick; but your neck is thick with compressed life; it is a stem so tense with life that it will hold up by itself. I am very sorry."

All at once he stopped. The bitter despair in his tone was the voice of a heavy feeling of which Siegmund had been vaguely aware for some weeks. Siegmund felt a sense of doom. He laughed, trying to shake it off.

"I wish I didn't go on like this," said Hampson piteously. "I wish I could be normal. How hot it is already! You should wear a hat. It is really hot." He pulled open his flannel shirt.

"I like the heat," said Siegmund.

"So do I."

Directly the young man dashed the long hair on his forehead into some sort of order, bowed, and smiling in his gay fashion, walked leisurely to the village.

Siegmund stood awhile as if stunned. It seemed to him only a painful dream. Sighing deeply to relieve himself of the pain, he set off to find Helena.

XIV

*I*n the garden of tall rose-trees and nasturtiums Helena was again waiting. It was past nine o'clock, so she was growing impatient. To herself, however, she professed a great interest in a little book of verses she had bought in St. Martin's Lane for twopence.

> "A late, harsh blackbird smote him with her wings,
> As through the glade, dim in the dark, she flew. . . ."

So she read. She made a curious, pleased sound, and remarked to herself that she thought these verses very fine. But she watched the road for Siegmund.

> "And now she takes the scissors on her thumb . . .
> Oh then, no more unto my lattice come."

"H'm!" she said, "I really don't know whether I like that or not."

Therefore she read the piece again before she looked down the road.

"He really is very late. It is absurd to think he may have got drowned; but if he were washing about at the bottom of the sea, his hair loose on the water!"

Her heart stood still as she imagined this.

"But what nonsense! I like these verses *very* much. I will read them as I walk along the side path, where I shall hear the bees, and catch the flutter of a butterfly among the words. That will be a very fitting way to read this poet."

So she strolled to the gate, glancing up now and again. There, sure enough, was Siegmund coming, the towel hanging over his shoulder, his throat bare, and his face bright. She stood in the mottled shade.

"I have kept you waiting," said Siegmund.

"Well, I was reading, you see."

She would not admit her impatience.

"I have been talking," he said.

"Talking!" she exclaimed in slight displeasure. "Have you found an acquaintance even here?"

"A fellow who was quite close friends in Savoy days; he made me feel queer—sort of Doppelgänger, he was."

Helena glanced up swiftly and curiously.

"In what way?" she said.

"He talked all the skeletons in the cupboard—such piffle it seems, now! The sea is like a hare-bell, and there are two battleships lying in the bay. You can hear the voices of the men on deck distinctly. Well, have you made the plans for to-day?"

They went into the house to breakfast. She watched him helping himself to the scarlet and green salad.

"Mrs. Curtiss," she said, in rather reedy tone, "has been very motherly to me this morning; "oh, very motherly!"

Siegmund, who was in a warm, gay mood, shrank up.

"What, has she been saying something about last night?" he asked.

"She was very much concerned for me—was afraid something dreadful had happened," continued Helena, in the same keen, sarcastic tone, which showed she was trying to rid herself of her own mortification.

"Because we weren't in till about eleven?" said Siegmund, also with sarcasm.

"I mustn't do it again. Oh no, I mustn't do it again, really."

"For fear of alarming the old lady?" he asked.

" 'You know, dear, it troubles *me* a good deal . . . but if I were your *mother,* I don't know *how* I should feel,' " she quoted.

"When one engages rooms one doesn't usually stipulate for a step-mother to nourish one's conscience," said Siegmund. They laughed, making jest of the affair; but they were both too thin-skinned. Siegmund writhed within himself with mortification, while Helena talked as if her teeth were on edge.

"I don't *mind* in the least," she said. "The poor old woman has her opinions, and I mine."

Siegmund brooded a little.

"I know I'm a moral coward," he said bitterly.

"Nonsense!" she replied. Then, with a little heat: "But you *do* continue to try so hard to justify yourself, as if *you* felt you needed justification."

He laughed bitterly.

"I tell you—a little thing like this—it remains tied tight round something inside me, reminding me for hours—well, what everybody else's opinion of me is."

Helena laughed rather plaintively.

"I thought you were so sure we were right," she said.

He winced again.

"In myself I am. But in the eyes of the world——"

"If you feel so in yourself, is not that enough?" she said brutally.

He hung his head, and slowly turned his serviette ring.

"What is myself?" he asked.

"Nothing very definite," she said, with a bitter laugh.

They were silent. After a while she rose, went lovingly over to him, and put her arms round his neck.

"This is our last clear day, dear," she said.

A wave of love came over him, sweeping away all the rest. He took her in his arms. . . .

"It will be hot to-day," said Helena, as they prepared to go out.

"I felt the sun steaming in my hair as I came up," he replied.

"I shall wear a hat—you had better do so too."

"No," he said. "I told you I wanted a sunsoaking; now I think I shall get one."

She did not urge or compel him. In these matters he was old enough to choose for himself.

This morning they were rather silent. Each felt the tarnish on their remaining day.

"I think, dear," she said, "we ought to find the little path that escaped us last night."

"We were lucky to miss it," he answered. "You don't get a walk like that twice in a lifetime, in spite of the old ladies."

She glanced up at him with a winsome smile, glad to hear his words.

They set off, Siegmund bare-headed. He was dressed in flannels and a loose canvas shirt, but he looked what he was—a Londoner on holiday. He had the appearance, the diffident bearing, and the well-cut clothes of a gentleman. He had a slight stoop, a strong-shouldered stoop, and as he walked he looked unseeing in front of him.

Helena belonged to the unclassed. She was not ladylike, nor smart, nor assertive. One could not tell whether she were of independent means or a worker. One thing was obvious about her: she was evidently educated.

Rather short, of strong figure, she was much more noticeably a *concentrée* than was Siegmund. Unless definitely looking at something she always seemed coiled within herself.

She wore a white voile dress made with the waist just below her breasts, and the skirt dropping straight and clinging. On her head was a large, simple hat of burnt straw.

Through the open-worked sleeves of her dress she could feel the sun bite vigorously.

"I wish you had put on a hat, Siegmund," she said.

"Why?" he laughed. "My hair is like a hood." He ruffled it back with his hand. The sunlight glistened on his forehead.

On the higher paths a fresh breeze was energetically chasing the butterflies and driving the few small clouds disconsolate out of the sky. The lovers stood for some time watching the people of the farm in the down below dip their sheep on this sunny morning. There was a ragged noise of bleating from the flock penned in a corner of the yard. Two red-armed men seized a sheep, hauled it to a large bath that stood in the middle of the yard, and there held it, more or less in the bath, whilst a third man baled a dirty yellow liquid over its body. The white legs of the sheep twinkled as it butted this way and that to escape the yellow douche, the blue-shirted men ducked and struggled. There was a faint splashing and shouting to be heard even from a distance. The farmer's wife and children stood by ready to rush in with assistance if necessary.

Helena laughed with pleasure.

"That is really a very quaint and primitive proceeding," she said. "It is cruder than Theocritus."

"In an instant it makes me wish I were a farmer," he laughed. "I think every man has a passion for farming at the bottom of his blood. It would be fine to be plain-minded, to see no further than the end of one's nose, and to own cattle and land."

"Would it?" asked Helena sceptically.

"If I had a red face, and went to sleep as soon as I sat comfortable, I should love it," he said.

"It amuses me to hear you long to be stupid," she replied.

"To have a simple, slow-moving mind and an active life is the desideratum."

"Is it?" she asked ironically.

"I would give anything to be like that," he said.

"That is, not to be yourself," she said pointedly.

He laughed without much heartiness.

"Don't they seem a long way off?" he said, staring at the bucolic scene. "They are farther than Theocritus—down there is farther than Sicily, and more than twenty centuries from us. I wish it weren't."

"Why do you?" she cried, with curious impatience.

He laughed.

Crossing the down, scattered with dark bushes, they came directly opposite the path through the furze.

"There it is!" she cried. "How could we miss it?"

"Ascribe it to the fairies," he replied, whistling the bird music out of *Siegfried,* then pieces of *Tristan.* They talked very little.

She was tired. When they arrived at a green, naked hollow near the cliff's edge, she said:

"This shall be our house to-day."

"Welcome home!" said Siegmund.

He flung himself down on the high, breezy slope of the dip, looking out to sea. Helena sat beside him. It was absolutely still, and the wind was slackening more and more. Though they listened attentively, they could hear only an indistinct breathing sound, quite small, from the water below: no clapping nor hoarse conversation of waves. Siegmund lay with his hands beneath his head, looking over the sparkling sea. To put her page in the shadow, Helena propped her book against him and began to read.

Presently the breeze, and Siegmund, dropped asleep. The sun was pouring with dreadful persistence. It beat and beat on Helena, gradually drawing her from her book in a confusion of thought. She closed her eyes wearily, longing for shade. Vaguely she felt a sympathy with Adama in "Adam Cast Forth." Her mind traced again the tumultuous, obscure strugglings of the two, forth from Eden through the primitive wildernesses, and she felt sorrowful. Thinking of Adam blackened with struggle, she looked down at Siegmund. The sun was beating him upon the face and upon his glistening brow. His two hands, which lay out on the grass, were full of blood, the veins of his wrists purple and swollen with heat. Yet he slept on, breathing with a slight, panting motion. Helena felt deeply moved. She wanted to kiss him as he lay helpless, abandoned to the charge of the earth and the sky. She wanted to kiss him, and shed a few tears. She did neither, but instead, moved her position so that she shaded his head. Cautiously putting her hand on his hair, she found it warm, quite hot, as when you put your hand under a sitting hen, and feel the hot-feathered bosom.

"It will make him ill," she whispered to herself, and she bent over to smell the hot hair. She noticed where the sun was scalding his forehead. She felt very pitiful and helpless when she saw his brow becoming inflamed with the sun-scalding.

Turning weariedly away, she sought relief in the landscape. But the sea was glittering unbearably, like a scaled dragon wreathing. The houses of Freshwater slept, as cattle sleep motionless in the hollow valley. Green Ffarringford on the slope, was drawn over with a shadow of heat and sleep. In the bay below the hill the sea was hot and restless. Helena was sick with sunshine and the restless glitter of water.

" 'And there shall be no more sea,' " she quoted to herself, she knew not wherefrom.

"No more sea, no more anything," she thought dazedly, as she sat in the midst of this fierce welter of sunshine. It seemed to her as if all the lightness of her fancy and her hope were being burned away in this tremendous furnace, leaving her, Helena, like a heavy piece of slag seamed with metal. She tried to imagine herself resuming the old activities, the old manner of living.

"It is impossible," she said; "it is impossible! What shall I be when I come out of this? I shall not come out, except as metal to be cast in another shape. No more the same Siegmund, no more the same life. What will become of us—what will happen?"

She was roused from these semi-delirious speculations in the sun furnace by Siegmund's waking. He opened his eyes, took a deep breath, and looked smiling at Helena.

"It is worth while to sleep," said he, "for the sake of waking like this. I was dreaming of huge ice-crystals."

She smiled at him. He seemed unconscious of fate, happy and strong. She smiled upon him almost in condescension.

"I should like to realize your dream," she said. "This is terrible!"

They went to the cliff's edge, to receive the cool up-flow of air from the water. She drank the travelling freshness eagerly with her face, and put forward her sunburnt arms to be refreshed.

"It is really a very fine sun," said Siegmund lightly. "I feel as if I were almost satisfied with heat."

Helena felt the chagrin of one whose wretchedness must go unperceived, while she affects a light interest in another's pleasure. This time, when Siegmund "failed to follow her," as she put it, she felt she must follow him.

"You are having your satisfaction complete this journey," she said, smiling; "even a sufficiency of me."

"Ay!" said Siegmund drowsily. "I think I am. I think this is about perfect, don't you?"

She laughed.

"I want nothing more and nothing different," he continued; "and that's the extreme of a decent time, I should think."

"The extreme of a decent time!" she repeated.

But he drawled on lazily:

"I've only rubbed my bread on the cheese-board until now. Now I've got all the cheese—which is you, my dear."

"I certainly feel eaten up," she laughed, rather bitterly. She saw him lying in a royal ease, his eyes naïve as a boy's, his whole being careless. Although very glad to see him thus happy, for herself, she felt very lonely. Being listless with sun-weariness, and heavy with a sense of impending fate, she felt a great yearning for his sympathy, his fellow-suffering. Instead of receiving this, she had to play to his buoyant happiness, so as not to shrivel one petal of his flower, or spoil one minute of his consummate hour.

From the high point of the cliff where they stood, they could see the path winding down to the beach, and broadening upwards towards them. Slowly approaching up the slight incline came a black invalid's chair, wheeling silently over the short dry grass. The invalid, a young man, was so much deformed that already his soul seemed to be wilting in his pale sharp face, as if there were not enough life-flow in the distorted body to develop the fair bud of the spirit. He turned his pain-sunken eyes towards the sea, whose meaning, like that of all things, was half obscure to him. Siegmund glanced, and glanced quickly away, before he should see. Helena looked intently for two seconds. She thought of the torn, shrivelled seaweed flung above the reach of the tide—"the life tide," she said to herself. The pain of the invalid overshadowed her own distress. She was fretted to her soul.

"Come!" she said quietly to Siegmund, no longer resenting the completeness of his happiness, which left her unnecessary to him.

"We will leave the poor invalid in possession of our green hollow—so quiet," she said to herself.

They sauntered downwards towards the bay. Helena was brooding on her own state, after her own fashion.

"The Mist Spirit," she said to herself. "The Mist Spirit draws a curtain round us—it is very kind. A heavy gold curtain sometimes; a thin, torn curtain sometimes. I want the Mist Spirit to close the curtain again. I do not want to think of the outside. I am afraid of the outside, and I am afraid when the curtain tears open in rags. I want to be in our own fine world inside the heavy gold mist-curtain."

As if in answer or in protest to her thoughts, Siegmund said:

"Do you want anything better than this, dear? Shall we come here next year, and stay for a whole month?"

"If there be any next year," said she.

Siegmund did not reply.

She wondered if he had really spoken in sincerity, or if he, too, were mocking fate. They walked slowly through the broiling sun towards their lodging.

"There will be an end to this," said Helena, communing with herself. "And when we come out of the mist-curtain, what will it be? No matter—let come what will. All along Fate has been resolving, from the very beginning, resolving obvious discords, gradually, by unfamiliar progressions; and out of original combinations weaving wondrous harmonies with our lives. Really, the working out has been wondrous, is wondrous now. The Master-Fate, is too great an artist to suffer an anti-climax. I am sure the Master Musician is too great an artist to allow a bathetic anti-climax."

XV

*T*he afternoon of the blazing day passed drowsily. Lying close together on the beach, Siegmund and Helena let the day exhale its hours like perfume, unperceived. Siegmund slept, a light evanescent sleep irised with dreams and with suffering: nothing definite, the colour of dreams without shape. Helena, as usual, retained her consciousness much more clearly. She watched the far-off floating of ships, and the near wading of children through the surf. Endless trains of thought, like little waves, rippled forward and broke on the shore of her drowsiness. But each thought-ripple, though it ran lightly, was tinged with copper-coloured gleams as from a lurid sunset. Helena felt that the sun was setting on her and Siegmund. The hour was too composed, spellbound, for grief or anxiety or even for close perception. She was merely aware that the sun was wheeling down, tangling Siegmund and her in the traces, like overthrown charioteers. So the hours passed.

After tea they went eastwards on the downs. Siegmund was animated, so that Helena caught his mood. It was very rare that they spoke of the time preceding their acquaintance. Helena knew little or nothing of Siegmund's life up to the age of thirty, whilst he had never learned anything concerning her childhood. Somehow she did not encourage him to self-discovery. To-day, however, the painful need of lovers for self-revelation took hold on him.

"It is awfully funny," he said. "I was *so* gone on Beatrice when I married her. She had only just come back from Egypt. Her father was an army officer, a very handsome man, and, I believe, a bit of a rake. Beatrice is really well connected, you know. But old FitzHerbert ran through all his money, and through everything else. He was too hot for the rest of the family, so they dropped him altogether.

"He came to live at Peckham when I was sixteen. I had just left school, and was to go into father's business. Mrs. FitzHerbert left cards, and very soon we were acquainted. Beatrice had been a good time in a French convent school. She had only knocked about with the army a little while, but it had brought her out. I remember I thought she was miles above me—which she was. She wasn't bad-looking, either, and you know men all like her. I bet she'd marry again, in spite of the children.

"At first I fluttered round her. I remember I'd got a little, silky moustache. They all said I looked older than sixteen. At that time I was mad on the violin, and she played rather well. Then FitzHerbert went off abroad somewhere, so Beatrice and her mother half lived at our house. The mother was an invalid.

"I remember I nearly stood on my head one day. The conservatory opened off the smoking-room, so when I came in the room, I heard my two sisters and Beatrice talking about good-looking men.

" 'I consider Bertram will make a handsome man,' said my younger sister.

" 'He's got beautiful eyes,' said my other sister.

" 'And a real darling nose and chin!' cried Beatrice. 'If only he was more *solide!* He is like a windmill, all limbs.'

" 'He will fill out. Remember, he's not quite seventeen,' said my elder sister.

" 'Ah, he is *doux*—he is *câlin,'* said Beatrice.

" 'I think he is rather *too* spoony for his age,' said my elder sister.

" 'But he's a fine boy for all that. See how thick his knees are,' my younger sister chimed in.

" 'Ah, *si, si!'* cried Beatrice.

"I made a row against the door, then walked across.

" 'Hello, is somebody in here?' I said, as I pushed into the little conservatory.

"I looked straight at Beatrice, and she at me. We seemed to have formed an alliance in that look: she was the other half of my consciousness, I of hers. Ha, ha! there were a lot of white narcissus, and little white hyacinths, Roman hyacinths, in the conservatory. I can see them now, great white stars, and tangles of little ones, among a bank of green; and I can recall the keen, fresh scent on the warm air; and the look of Beatrice . . . her great dark eyes.

"It's funny, but that Beatrice is as dead—ay, far more dead—than Dante's. And I am not that young fool, not a bit.

"I was very romantic, fearfully emotional, and the soul of honour. Beatrice said nobody cared a thing about her. FitzHerbert was always jaunting off, the mother was a fretful invalid. So I was seventeen, earning half a guinea a week, and she was eighteen, with no money, when we ran away to Brighton and got married. Poor old Pater, he took it awfully well. I have been a frightful drag on him, you know.

"There's the romance. I wonder how it will all end."

Helena laughed, and he did not detect her extreme bitterness of spirit.

They walked on in silence for some time. He was thinking back, before Helena's day. This left her very much alone, and forced on her the idea that, after all, love, which she chose to consider as single and wonderful a thing in a man's life as birth, or adolescence, or death, was temporary, and formed only an episode. It was her hour of disillusion.

"Come to think of it," Siegmund continued, "I have always shirked. Whenever I've been in a tight corner I've gone to Pater."

"I think," she said, "marriage has been a tight corner you couldn't get out of to go to anybody."

"Yet I'm here," he answered simply.

The blood suffused her face and neck.

"And some men would have made a better job of it. When it's come to sticking out against Beatrice, and sailing the domestic ship in spite of her, I've always funked. I tell you I'm something of a moral coward."

He had her so much on edge she was inclined to answer, "So be it." Instead, she ran back over her own history: it consisted of petty discords in contemptible surroundings, then of her dreams and fancies, finally—Siegmund.

"In my life," she said, with the fine, grating discord in her tones, "I might say *always,* the real life has seemed just outside—brownies running and fairies peeping— just beyond the common, ugly place where I am. I seem to have been hedged in by vulgar circumstances, able to glimpse outside now and then, and see the reality."

"You are so hard to get at," said Siegmund. "And so scornful of familiar things."

She smiled, knowing he did not understand. The heat had jaded her, so that physically she was full of discord, of dreariness that set her teeth on edge. Body and soul, she was out of tune.

A warm, noiseless twilight was gathering over the downs and rising darkly from the sea. Fate, with wide wings, was hovering just over her. Fate, ashen grey and black, like a carrion crow, had her in its shadow. Yet Siegmund took no notice. He did not understand. He walked beside her, whistling to himself, which only distressed her the more.

They were alone on the smooth hills to the east. Helena looked at the day melting out of the sky, leaving the permanent structure of the night. It was her turn to suffer the sickening detachment which comes after moments of intense living.

The rosiness died out of the sunset as embers fade into thick ash. In herself, too, the ruddy glow sank and went out. The earth was a cold dead heap, coloured drearily, the sky was dark with flocculent grey ash, and she herself an upright mass of soft ash.

She shuddered slightly with horror. The whole face of things was to her livid and ghastly. Being a moralist rather than an artist, coming of fervent Wesleyan stock, she began to scourge herself. She had done wrong again. Looking back, no one had she touched without hurting. She had a destructive force; anyone she embraced she injured. Faint voices echoed back from her conscience. The shadows were full of complaint against her. It was all true, she was a harmful force, dragging Fate to petty, mean conclusions.

Life and hope were ash in her mouth. She shuddered with discord. Despair grated between her teeth. This dreariness was worse than any her dreary, lonely life had known. She felt she could bear it no longer.

Siegmund was there. Surely he could help? He would rekindle her. But he was straying ahead, carelessly whistling the Spring Song from *Die Walküre*. She looked at him, and again shuddered with horror. Was that really Siegmund, that stooping, thick-shouldered, indifferent man? Was that the Siegmund who had seemed to radiate joy into his surroundings, the Siegmund whose coming had always changed the whole weather of her soul? Was that the Siegmund whose touch was keen with bliss for her, whose face was a panorama of passing God? She looked at him again. His radiance was gone, his aura had ceased. She saw him a stooping man, past the buoyancy of youth, walking and whistling rather stupidly—in short, something of the "clothed animal on end," like the rest of men.

She suffered an agony of disillusion. Was this the real Siegmund, and her own ony a projection of her soul? She took her breath sharply. Was he the real clay, and that other, her beloved, only the breathing of her soul upon this. There was an awful blank before her.

"Siegmund!" she said in despair.

He turned sharply at the sound of her voice. Seeing her face pale and distorted in the twilight, he was filled with dismay. She mutely lifted her arms to him, watching him in despair. Swiftly he took her in his arms, and asked in a troubled voice:

"What is it, dear? Is something wrong?"

His voice was nothing to her—it was stupid. She felt his arms round her, felt her face pressed against the cloth of his coat, against the beating of his heart. What was all this? This was not comfort or love. He was not understanding or helping, only chaining her, hurting. She did not want his brute embrace—she was most utterly alone, gripped so in his arms. If he could not save her from herself, he must leave her free to pant her heart out in free air. The secret thud, thud of his heart, the very self of that animal in him she feared and hated, repulsed her. She struggled to escape.

"What is it? Won't you tell me what is the matter?" he pleaded.

She began to sob, dry wild sobs, feeling as if she would go mad. He tried to look at her face, for which she hated him. And all the time he held her fast, all the time she was imprisoned in the embrace of this brute, blind creature, whose heart confessed itself in thud, thud, thud.

"Have you heard anything against us? Have I done anything? Have I said anything? Tell me—at any rate tell me, Helena."

Her sobbing was like the chattering of dry leaves. She grew frantic to be free. Stifled in that prison any longer, she would choke and go mad. His coat chafed her face; as she struggled she could see the strong working of his throat. She fought against him; she struggled in panic to be free.

"Let me go!" she cried. "Let me go! Let me go!" He held her in bewilderment and terror. She thrust her hands in his chest and pushed him apart. Her face, blind to him, was very much distorted by her suffering. She thrust him furiously away with great strength.

His heart stood still with wonder. She broke from him and dropped down, sobbing wildly, in the shelter of the tumuli. She was bunched in a small, shaken heap. Siegmund could not bear it. He went on one knee beside her, trying to take her hand in his, and pleading:

"Only tell me, Helena, what it is. Tell me what it is. At least tell me, Helena; tell me what it is. Oh, but this is dreadful!"

She had turned convulsively from him. She shook herself, as if beside herself, and at last covered her ears with her hands, to shut out this unreasoning pleading of his voice.

Seeing her like this, Siegmund at last gave in. Quite still, he knelt on one knee beside her, staring at the late twilight. The intense silence was crackling with the sound of Helena's dry, hissing sobs. He remained silenced, stunned by the unnatural conflict. After waiting a while, he put his hand on her. She winced convulsively away.

Then he rose, saying in his heart, "It is enough." He went behind the small hill, and looked at the night. It was all exposed. He wanted to hide, to cover himself from the openness, and there was not even a bush under which he could find cover.

He lay down flat on the ground, pressing his face into the wiry turf, trying to hide. Quite stunned, with a death taking place in his soul, he lay still, pressed against the earth. He held his breath for a long time before letting it go, then again he held it. He could scarcely bear, even by breathing, to betray himself. His consciousness was dark.

Helena had sobbed and struggled the life animation back into herself. At length, weary but comfortable, she lay still to rest. Almost she could have gone to sleep. But she grew chilly, and a ground insect tickled her face. Was somebody coming?

It was dark when she rose. Siegmund was not in sight. She tidied herself, and, rather frightened, went to look for him. She saw him like a thick shadow on the earth. Now she was heavy with tears good to shed. She stood in silent sorrow, looking at him.

Suddenly she became aware of someone passing and looking curiously at them.

"Dear!" she said softly, stooping and touching his hair. He began to struggle with himself to respond. At that minute he would rather have died than face anyone. His soul was too much uncovered.

"Dear, someone is looking," she pleaded.

He drew himself up from cover. But he kept his face averted. They walked on.

"Forgive me, dear," she said softly.

"Nay, it's not you," he answered, and she was silenced. They walked on till the night seemed private. She turned to him, and "Siegmund!" she said, in a voice of great sorrow and pleading.

He took her in his arms, but did not kiss her, though she lifted her face. He put his mouth against her throat, below the ear, as she offered it, and stood looking out through the ravel of her hair, dazed, dreamy.

The sea was smoking with darkness under half-luminous heavens. The stars, one after another, were catching alight. Siegmund perceived first one, and then another dimmer one, flicker out in the darkness over the sea. He stood perfectly still, watching them. Gradually he remembered how, in the cathedral, the tapers of the choir-stalls would tremble and set steadily to burn, opening the darkness point after point with yellow drops of flame, as the acolyte touched them, one by one, delicately with his rod. The night was religious, then, with its proper order of service. Day and night had their ritual, and passed in uncouth worship.

Siegmund found himself in an abbey. He looked up the nave of the night, where the sky came down on the sea-like arches, and he watched the stars catch fire. At least it was all sacred, whatever the God might be. Helena herself, the bitter bread, was stuff of the ceremony, which he touched with his lips as part of the service.

He had Helena in his arms, which was sweet company, but in spirit he was quite alone. She would have drawn him back to her, and on her woman's breast have hidden him from fate, and saved him from searching the unknown. But this night he did not want comfort. If he were "an infant crying in the night," it was crying that a woman could not still. He was abroad seeking courage and faith for his own soul. He, in loneliness, must search the night for faith.

"My fate is finely wrought out," he thought to himself. "Even damnation may be finely imagined for me in the night. I have come so far. Now I must get clarity and courage to follow out the theme. I don't want to botch and bungle even damnation."

But he needed to know what was right, what was the proper sequence of his acts. Staring at the darkness, he seemed to feel his course, though he could not see it. He bowed in obedience. The stars seemed to swing softly in token of submission.

XVI

*F*eeling him abstract, withdrawn from her, Helena experienced the dread of losing him. She was in his arms, but his spirit ignored her. That was insufferable to her pride. Yet she dared not disturb him— she was afraid. Bitterly she repented her of the giving way to her revulsion a little space before. Why had she not smothered it and pretended? Why had she, a woman, betrayed herself so flagrantly? Now perhaps she had lost him for good. She was consumed with uneasiness.

At last she drew back from him, held him her mouth to kiss. As he gently, sadly kissed her she pressed him to her bosom. She must get him back, whatever else she lost. She put her hand tenderly on his brow.

"What are you thinking of?" she asked.

"I?" he replied. "I really don't know. I suppose I was hardly thinking anything."

She waited a while, clinging to him, then, finding some difficulty in speech, she asked:

"Was I very cruel, dear?"

It was so unusual to hear her grieved and filled with humility that he drew her close into him.

"It was pretty bad, I suppose," he replied. "But I should think neither of us could help it."

She gave a little sob, pressed her face into his chest, wishing she had helped it. Then, with Madonna love, she clasped his head upon her shoulder, covering her hands over his hair. Twice she kissed him softly in the nape of the neck, with fond, reassuring kisses. All the while, delicately, she fondled and soothed him, till he was child to her Madonna.

They remained standing with his head on her shoulder for some time, till at last he raised himself to lay his lips on hers in a long kiss of healing and renewal—long, pale kisses of after-suffering.

Someone was coming along the path. Helena let him go, shook herself free, turned sharply aside, and said:

"Shall we go down to the water?"

"If you like," he replied, putting out his hand to her. They went thus with clasped hands down the cliff path to the beach.

There they sat in the shadow of the uprising island, facing the restless water. Around them the sand and shingle were grey; there stretched a long pale line of surf, beyond which the sea was black and smeared with star-reflections. The deep, velvety sky shone with lustrous stars.

As yet the moon was not risen. Helena proposed that they should lie on a tuft of sand in a black cleft of the cliff to await its coming. They lay close together without speaking. Each was looking at a low, large star which hung straight in front of them, dripping its brilliance in a thin streamlet of light along the sea almost to their feet. It was a star-path fine and clear, trembling in its brilliance, but certain upon the water. Helena watched it with delight. As Siegmund looked at the star, it seemed to him a lantern hung at the gate to light someone home. He imagined himself following the thread of the star-track. What was behind the gate?

They heard the wash of a steamer crossing the bay. The water seemed populous in the night-time, with dark, uncanny comings and goings.

Siegmund was considering.

"What *was* the matter with you?" he asked.

She leaned over him, took his head in her lap, holding his face between her two hands as she answered in a low, grave voice, very wise and old in experience:

"Why, you see, dear, you won't understand. But there was such a greyish darkness, and through it—the crying of lives I have touched. . . ."

His heart suddenly shrank and sank down. She acknowledged, then, that she also had helped to injure Beatrice and his children. He coiled with shame.

". . . A crying of lives against me, and I couldn't silence them, nor escape out of the darkness. I wanted you—I saw you in front, whistling the Spring Song, but I couldn't find you—it was not you—I couldn't find you."

She kissed his eyes and his brows.

"No, I don't see it," he said. "You would always be you. I could think of hating you, but you'd still be yourself."

She made a moaning, loving sound. Full of passionate pity, she moved her mouth on his face, as a woman does on her child that has hurt itself.

"Sometimes," she murmured, in a low, grieved confession, "you lose me."

He gave a brief laugh.

"I lose you!" he repeated. "You mean I lose my attraction for you, or my hold over you, and then you——?"

He did not finish. She made the same grievous murmuring noise over him.

"It shall not be any more," she said.

"All right," he replied, "since you decide it."

She clasped him round the chest and fondled him, distracted with pity.

"You mustn't be bitter," she murmured.

"Four days is enough," he said. "In a fortnight I should be intolerable to you. I am not masterful."

"It is not so, Siegmund," she said sharply.

"I give way always," he repeated. "And then—to-night!"

"To-night, to-night!" she cried in wrath. "To-night I have been a fool!"

"And I?" he asked.

"You—what of you?" she cried. Then she became sad. "I have little perverse feelings," she lamented.

"And I can't bear to compel anything, for fear of hurting it. So I'm always pushed this way and that, like a fool."

"You don't know how you hurt me, talking so," she said.

He kissed her. After a moment he said:

"You are not like other folk. 'Ihr Lascheks seid ein anderes Geschlecht.' I thought of you when we read it."

"Would you rather have me more like the rest, or more unlike, Siegmund? Which is it?"

"Neither," he said. "You are *you*."

They were quiet for a space. The only movement in the night was the faint gambolling of starlight on the water. The last person had passed in black silhouette between them and the sea.

He was thinking bitterly. She seemed to goad him deeper and deeper into life. He had a sense of despair, a preference of death. The German she read with him—she loved its loose and violent romance—came back to his mind: "Der Tod geht einem zur Seite, fast sichtbarlich, und jagt einen immer tiefer ins Leben."

Well, the next place he would be hunted to, like a hare run down, was home. It seemed impossible the morrow would take him back to Beatrice.

"This time to-morrow night," he said.

"Siegmund!" she implored.

"Why not?" he laughed.

"Don't, dear," she pleaded.

"All right, I won't."

Some large steamer crossing the mouth of the bay made the water clash a little as it broke in accentuated waves. A warm puff of air wandered in on them now and again.

"You won't be tired when you go back?" Helena asked.

"Tired!" he echoed.

"You know how you were when you came," she reminded him, in tones full of pity. He laughed.

"Oh, that is gone," he said.

With a slow, mechanical rhythm she stroked his cheek.

"And will you be sad?" she said, hesitating.

"Sad!" he repeated.

"But will you be able to take the old life up, happier, when you go back?"

"The old life will take me up, I suppose," he said.

There was a pause.

"I think, dear," she said, "I have done wrong."

"Good Lord—you have not!" he replied sharply, pressing back his head to look at her, for the first time.

"I shall have to send you back to Beatrice and the babies—to-morrow—as you are now. . . ."

" 'Take no thought for the morrow.' Be quiet, Helena!" he exclaimed as the reality bit him. He sat up suddenly.

"Why?" she asked, afraid.

"Why!" he repeated. He remained sitting, leaning forward on the sand, staring intently at Helena. She looked back in fear at him. The moment terrified her, and she lost courage.

With a fluttered motion she put her hand on his, which was pressed hard on the sand as he leaned forward. At once he relaxed his intensity, laughed, then became tender.

Helena yielded herself like a forlorn child to his arms, and there lay, half crying, whilst he smoothed her brow with his fingers, and grains of sand fell from his palm on her cheek. She shook with dry, withered sobs, as a child does when it snatches itself away from the lancet of the doctor and hides in the mother's bosom, refusing to be touched.

But she knew the morrow was coming, whether or not, and she cowered down on his breast. She was wild with fear of the parting and the subsequent days. They must drink, after to-morrow, separate cups. She was filled with vague terror of what it would be. The sense of the oneness and unity of their fates was gone.

Siegmund also was cowed by the threat of separation. He had more definite knowledge of the next move than had Helena. His heart was certain of calamity, which would overtake him directly. He shrank away. Wildly he beat about to find a means of escape from the next day and its consequences. He did not want to go. Anything rather than go back.

In the midst of their passion of fear the moon rose. Siegmund started to see the rim appear ruddily beyond the sea. His struggling suddenly ceased, and he watched, spell-bound, the oval horn of fiery gold come up, resolve itself. Some golden liquor dripped and spilled upon the far waves, where it shook in ruddy splashes. The gold-red cup rose higher, looming before him very large, yet still not all discovered. By degrees the horn of gold detached itself from the darkness at back of the waves. It was immense and terrible. When would the tip be placed upon the table of the sea?

It stood at last, whole and calm, before him; then the night took up this drinking-cup of fiery gold, lifting it with majestic movement overhead, letting stream forth the wonderful unwasted liquor of gold over the sea—a libation.

Siegmund looked at the shaking flood of gold and paling gold spread wider as the night upraised the blanching crystal, poured out further and further the immense libation from the whitening cup, till at last the moon looked frail and empty.

And there, exhaustless in the night, the white light shook on the floor of the sea. He wondered how it would be gathered up. "I gather it up into myself," he said. And the stars and the cliffs and a few trees were watching, too. "If I have spilled my life," he thought, "the unfamiliar eyes of the land and sky will gather it up again."

Turning to Helena, he found her face white and shining as the empty moon.

XVII

*T*oward morning, Siegmund went to sleep. For four hours, until seven o'clock, the womb of sleep received him and nourished him again.

"But it is finest of all to wake," he said, as the bright sunshine of the window, and the lumining green sunshine coming through the lifted hands of the leaves, challenged him into the open.

The morning was exceedingly fair, and it looked at him so gently that his blue eyes trembled with self-pity. A fragment of scarlet geranium glanced up at him as he passed, so that amid the vermilion tyranny of the uniform it wore he could see the eyes of the flower, wistful, offering him love, as one sometimes sees the eyes of a man beneath the brass helmet of a soldier, and is startled. Everything looked at him with the same eyes of tenderness, offering him, timidly, a little love.

"They are all extraordinarily sweet," said Siegmund to the full-mouthed scabious and the awkward, downcast ragwort. Three or four butterflies fluttered up and down in agitated little leaps, around him. Instinctively Siegmund put his hand forward to touch them.

"The careless little beggars!" he said.

When he came to the cliff tops there was the morning, very bravely dressed, rustling forward with a silken sound and much silken shining to meet him. The battleships had gone; the sea was blue with a *panier* of diamonds; the sky was full with a misty tenderness like love. Siegmund had never recognized before the affection that existed between him and everything. We do not realize how tremendously dear and indispensable to us are the hosts of common things, till we must leave them, and we break our hearts.

"We have been very happy together," everything seemed to say.

Siegmund looked up into the eyes of the morning with a laugh.

"It is very lovely," he said, "whatever happens."

So he went down to the beach; his dark blue eyes, darker from last night's experience, smiled always with the pride of love. He undressed by his usual altarstone.

"How closely familiar everything is," he thought. "It seems almost as if the curves of this stone were rounded to fit in my soul."

He touched the smooth white slope of the stone gently with discovering fingers, in the same way as he touched the cheek of Helena, or of his own babies. He found great pleasure in this feeling of intimacy with things. A very soft wind, shy as a girl, put its arms round him, and seemed to lay its cheek against his chest. He placed his hands beneath his arms, where the wind was caressing him, and his eyes opened with wondering pleasure.

"They find no fault with me," he said. "I suppose they are as fallible as I, and so don't judge," he added, as he waded thigh-deep into the water, thrusting it to hear the mock-angry remonstrance.

"Once more," he said, and he took the sea in his arms. He swam very quietly. The water buoyed him up, holding him closely clasped. He swam towards the white rocks of the headlands; they rose before him like beautiful buttressed gates, so glistening that he half expected to see fantail pigeons puffing like white irises in the niches, and white peacocks with dark green feet stepping down the terraces, trailing a sheen of silver.

"Helena is right," he said to himself as he swam, scarcely swimming, but moving upon the bosom of the tide; "she is right, it is all enchanted. I have got into her magic at last. Let us see what it is like."

He determined to visit again his little bay. He swam carefully round the terraces, whose pale shadows through the swift-spinning emerald facets of the water seemed merest fancy. Siegmund touched them with his foot; they were hard, cold, dangerous. He swam carefully. As he made for the archway, the shadows of the headland chilled the water. There under water, clamouring in a throng at the base of the submerged walls, were sea-women with dark locks, and young sea-girls, with soft hair, vividly green, striving to climb up out of the darkness into the morning, their hair swirling in abandon. Siegmund was half afraid of their frantic efforts.

But the tide carried him swiftly through the high gate into the porch. There was exultance in this sweeping entry. The skin-white, full-fleshed walls of the archway were dappled with green lights that danced in and out among themselves. Siegmund was carried along in an invisible chariot, beneath the jewel-stained walls. The tide swerved, threw him as he swam against the inward-curving white rock; his elbow met the rock, and he was sick with pain. He held his breath, trying to get back the joy and magic. He could not believe that the lovely, smooth side of the rock, fair as his own side with its ripple of muscles, could have hurt him thus. He let the water carry him till he might climb out on to the shingle. There he sat upon a warm boulder, and twisted to look at his arm. The skin was grazed, not very badly, merely a ragged scarlet patch no bigger than a carnation petal. The bruise, however, was painful, especially when, a minute or two later, he bent his arm.

"No," said he pitiably to himself, "it is impossible it should have hurt me. I suppose I was careless."

Nevertheless, the aspect of the morning changed. He sat on the boulder looking out on the sea. The azure sky and the sea laughed on, holding a bright conversation one with another. The two headlands of the tiny bay gossiped across the street of water. All the boulders and pebbles of the seashore played together.

"Surely," said Siegmund, "they take no notice of me; they do not care a jot or a tittle for me. I am a fool to think myself one with them."

He contrasted this with the kindness of the morning as he had stood on the cliffs.

"I was mistaken," he said. "It was an illusion."

He looked wistfully out again. Like neighbours leaning from opposite windows of an overhanging street, the headlands were occupied one with another. White rocks strayed out to sea, followed closely by other white rocks. Everything was busy, interested, occupied with its own pursuit and with its own comrades. Siegmund alone was without pursuit or comrade.

"They will all go on the same; they will be just as gay. Even Helena, after a while, will laugh and take interest in others. What do I matter?"

Siegmund thought of the futility of death:

> "We are not long for music and laughter,
>   Love and desire and hate;
> I think we have no portion in them after
>   We pass the gate."

"Why should I be turned out of the game?" he asked himself, rebelling. He frowned, and answered: "Oh, Lord!—the old argument!"

But the thought of his own expunging from the picture was very bitter.

"Like the puff from the steamer's funnel, I should be gone."

He looked at himself, at his limbs and his body in the pride of his maturity. He was very beautiful to himself.

"Nothing, in the place where I am," he said. "Gone, like a puff of steam that melts on the sunshine."

Again Siegmund looked at the sea. It was glittering with laughter as at a joke.

"And I," he said, lying down in the warm sand, "I am nothing. I do not count; I am inconsiderable."

He set his teeth with pain. There were no tears, there was no relief. A convulsive gasping shook him as he lay on the sands. All the while he was arguing with himself.

"Well," he said, "if I am nothing dead I am nothing alive."

But the vulgar proverb arose—"Better a live dog than a dead lion," to answer him. It seemed an ignominy to be dead. It meant, to be overlooked, even by the smallest creature of God's earth. Surely that was a great ignominy.

Helena, meanwhile, was bathing, for the last time, by the same seashore with him. She was no swimmer. Her endless delight was to explore, to discover small treasures. For her the world was still a great wonder-box which hid innumerable sweet toys for surprises in all its crevices. She had bathed in many rock-pools' tepid baths, trying first one, then another. She had lain on the sand where the cold arms of the ocean lifted her and smothered her impetuously, like an awful lover.

"The sea is a great deal like Siegmund," she said, as she rose panting, trying to dash her nostrils free from water. It was true; the sea as it flung over her filled her with the same uncontrollable terror as did Siegmund when he sometimes grew silent and strange in a tide of passion.

She wandered back to her rock-pools; they were bright and docile; they did not fling her about in a game of terror. She bent over watching the anemone's fleshy petals shrink from the touch of her shadow, and she laughed to think they should be so needlessly fearful. The flowing tide trickled noiselessly among the rocks, widening and deepening insidiously her little pools. Helena retreated towards a large cave round the bend. There the water gurgled under the bladder-wrack of the large stones; the air was cool and clammy. She pursued her way into the gloom, bending, though there was no need, shivering at the coarse feel of the seaweed beneath her naked feet. The water came rustling up beneath the fucus as she crept along on the big stones; it returned with a quiet gurgle which made her shudder, though even that was not disagreeable. It needed, for all that, more courage than was easy to summon before she could step off her stone into the black pool that confronted her. It was festooned thick with weeds that slid under her feet like snakes. She scrambled hastily upwards towards the outlet.

Turning, the ragged arch was before her, brighter than the brightest window. It was easy to believe the light-fairies stood outside in a throng, excited with fine fear, throwing handfuls of light into the dragon's hole.

"How surprised they will be to see me!" said Helena, scrambling forward, laughing.

She stood still in the archway, astounded. The sea was blazing with white fire, and glowing with azure as coals glow red with heat below the flames. The sea was transfused with white burning, while over it hung the blue sky in a glory, like the blue smoke of the fire of God. Helena stood still and worshipped. It was a moment of astonishment, when she stood breathless and blinded, involuntarily offering herself for a thank-offering. She felt herself confronting God at home in His white incandescence, His fire settling on her like the Holy Spirit. Her lips were parted in a woman's joy of adoration.

The moment passed, and her thoughts hurried forward in confusion.

"It is good," said Helena; "it is very good." She looked again, and saw the waves like a line of children racing hand in hand, the sunlight pursuing, catching hold of them from behind, as they ran wildly till they fell, caught, with the sunshine dancing upon them like a white dog.

"It is really wonderful here!" said she; but the moment had gone, she could not see again the grand burning of God among the waves. After a while she turned away.

As she stood dabbling her bathing dress in a pool, Siegmund came over the beach to her.

"You are not gone, then?" he said.

"Siegmund!" she exclaimed, looking up at him with radiant eyes, as if it could not be possible that he had joined her in this rare place. His face was glowing with the sun's inflaming, but Helena did not notice that his eyes were full of misery.

"I, actually," he said, smiling.

"I did not expect you," she said, still looking at him in radiant wonder. "I could easier have expected"—she hesitated, struggled, and continued—"Eros walking by the sea. But you are like him," she said, looking radiantly up into Siegmund's face. "Isn't it beautiful this morning?" she added.

Siegmund endured her wide, glad look for a moment, then he stooped and kissed her. He remained moving his hand in the pool, ashamed, and full of contradiction. He was at the bitter point of farewell; could see, beyond the glamour around him, the ugly building of his real life.

"Isn't the sea wonderful this morning?" asked Helena, as she wrung the water from her costume.

"It is very fine," he answered. He refrained from saying what his heart said: "It is my last morning; it is not yours. It is my last morning, and the sea is enjoying the joke, and you are full of delight."

"Yes," said Siegmund, "the morning is perfect."

"It is," assented Helena warmly. "Have you noticed the waves? They are like a line of children chased by a white dog."

"Ay!" said Siegmund.

"Didn't you have a good time?" she asked, touching with her finger-tips the nape of his neck as he stooped beside her.

"I swam to my little bay again," he replied.

"Did you?" she exclaimed, pleased.

She sat down by the pool, in which she washed her feet free from sand, holding them to Siegmund to dry.

"I am very hungry," she said.

"And I," he agreed.

"I feel quite established here," she said gaily, something in his position having reminded her of their departure.

He laughed.

"It seems another eternity before the three forty-five train, doesn't it?" she insisted.

"I wish we might never go back," he said.

Helena sighed.

"It would be too much for life to give. We have had something, Siegmund," she said.

He bowed his head, and did not answer.

"It has been something, dear," she repeated.

He rose and took her in his arms.

"Everything," he said, his face muffled in the shoulder of her dress. He could smell her fresh and fine from the sea. "Everything!" he said.

She pressed her two hands on his head.

"I did well, didn't I, Siegmund?" she asked. Helena felt the responsibility of this holiday. She had proposed it; when he had withdrawn, she had insisted, refusing to allow him to take back his word, declaring that she should pay the cost. He permitted her at last.

"Wonderfully well, Helena," he replied.

She kissed his forehead.

"You are everything," he said.

She pressed his head on her bosom.

XVIII

Siegmund had shaved and dressed, and come down to breakfast. Mrs. Curtiss brought in the coffee. She was a fragile little woman, of delicate, gentle manner.

"The water would be warm this morning," she said, addressing no one in particular.

Siegmund stood on the hearthrug with his hands behind him, swaying from one leg to the other. He was embarrassed always by the presence of the amiable little woman; he could not feel at ease before strangers, in his capacity of accepted swain of Helena.

"It was," assented Helena. "It was as warm as new milk."

"Ay, it would be," said the old lady, looking in admiration upon the experience of Siegmund and his beloved. "And did ye see the ships of war?" she asked.

"No, they had gone," replied Helena.

Siegmund swayed from foot to foot, rythmically.

"You'll be coming in to dinner to-day?" asked the old lady.

Helena arranged the matter.

"I think ye both look better," Mrs. Curtiss said. She glanced at Siegmund.

He smiled constrainedly.

"I thought ye looked so worn when you came," she said sympathetically.

"He had been working hard," said Helena, also glancing at him.

He bent his head, and was whistling without making any sound.

"Ay," sympathized the little woman. "And it's a very short time for you. What a pity ye can't stop for the fireworks at Cowes on Monday. They are grand, so they say."

Helena raised her eyebrows in polite interest. "Have you never seen them?" she asked.

"No," replied Mrs. Curtiss. "I've never been able to get; but I hope to go yet."

"I hope you may," said Siegmund.

The little woman beamed on him. Having won a word from him, she was quite satisfied.

"Well," she said brightly, "the eggs must be done by now."

She tripped out, to return directly.

"I've brought you," she said, "some of the Island cream, and some white currants, if ye'll have them. You must think well of the Island, and come back."

"How could we help?" laughed Helena.

"We will," smiled Siegmund.

When finally the door was closed on her Siegmund sat down in relief. Helena looked in amusement at him. She was perfectly self-possessed in presence of the delightful little lady.

"This is one of the few places that has ever felt like home to me," she said. She lifted a tangled bunch of fine white currants.

"Ah!" exclaimed Siegmund, smiling at her.

"One of the few places where everything is friendly," she said. "And everybody."

"You have made so many enemies?" he asked, with gentle irony.

"Strangers," she replied. "I seem to make strangers of all the people I meet."

She laughed in amusement at this *mot*. Siegmund looked at her intently. He was thinking of her left alone amongst strangers.

"Need we go—need we leave this place of friends?" he said, as if ironically. He was very much afraid of tempting her.

She looked at the clock on the mantelpiece and counted: "One, two, three, four, five hours, thirty-five minutes. It is an age yet," she laughed.

Siegmund laughed too, as he accepted the particularly fine bunch of currants she had extricated for him.

XIX

The air was warm and sweet in the little lane, remote from the sea, which led them along their last walk. On either side the white path was a grassy margin thickly woven with pink convolvuli. Some of the reckless little flowers, so gay and evanescent, had climbed the trunk of an old yew-tree, and were looking up pertly at their rough host.

Helena walked along, watching the flowers, and making fancies out of them.

"Who called them 'fairies' telephones?' " she said to herself. "They are tiny children in pinafores. How gay they are! They are children dawdling along the pavement of a morning. How fortunate they are! See how they take a wind-thrill! See how wide they are set to the sunshine! And when they are tired, they will curl daintily to sleep, and some fairies in the dark will gather them away. They won't be here in the morning, shrivelled and dowdy. . . . If only we could curl up and be gone, after our day . . ."

She looked at Siegmund. He was walking moodily beside her.

"It is good when life holds no anti-climax," she said.

"Ay!" he answered. Of course, he could not understand her meaning.

She strayed into the thick grass, a sturdy white figure that walked with bent head, abstract, but happy.

"What is she thinking?" he asked himself. "She is sufficient to herself—she doesn't want me. She has her own private way of communing with things, and is friends with them."

"The dew has been very heavy," she said, turning and looking up at him from under her brows, like a smiling witch.

"I see it has," he answered. Then to himself he said: "She can't translate herself into language. She is incommunicable; she can't render herself to the intelligence. So she is alone and a law unto herself: she only wants me to explore me, like a rock pool, and to bathe in me. After a while, when I am gone, she will see I was not indispensable. . . ."

The lane led up to the eastern down. As they were emerging, they saw on the left hand an extraordinarily spick and span red bungalow. The low roof of dusky red sloped down towards the coolest green lawn, that was edged and ornamented with scarlet, and yellow, and white flowers brilliant with dew.

A stout man in an alpaca jacket and panama hat was seated on the bare lawn, his back to the sun, reading a newspaper. He tried in vain to avoid the glare of the sun on his reading. At last he closed the paper and looked angrily at the house—not at anything in particular.

He irritably read a few more lines, then jerked up his head in sudden decision, glared at the open door of the house, and called:

"Amy! Amy!"

No answer was forthcoming. He flung down the paper and strode off indoors, his mien one of wrathful resolution. His voice was heard calling curtly from the dining-room. There was a jingle of crockery as he bumped the table leg in sitting down.

"He is in a bad temper," laughed Siegmund.

"Breakfast is late," said Helena with contempt.

"Look!" said Siegmund.

An elderly lady in black and white striped linen, a young lady in holland, both carrying some wild flowers, hastened towards the garden gate. Their faces were turned anxiously to the house. They were hot with hurrying, and had no breath for words. The girl pressed forward, opened the gate for the lady in striped linen, who hastened over the lawn. Then the daughter followed, and vanished also under the shady veranda.

There was a quick sound of women's low, apologetic voices, overridden by the resentful abuse of the man.

The lovers moved out of hearing.

"Imagine that breakfast table!" said Siegmund.

"I feel," said Helena, with a keen twang of contempt in her voice, "as if a fussy cock and hens had just scuffled across my path."

"There are many such roosts," said Siegmund pertinently.

Helena's cold scorn was very disagreeable to him. She talked to him winsomely and very kindly as they crossed the open down to meet the next incurving of the coast, and Siegmund was happy. But the sense of humiliation, which he had got from her the day before, and which had fixed itself, bled him secretly, like a wound. This hæmorrhage of self-esteem tortured him to the end.

Helena had rejected him. She gave herself to her fancies only. For some time she had confused Siegmund with her god. Yesterday she had cried to her ideal lover, and found only Siegmund. It was the spear in the side of his tortured self-respect.

"At least," he said, in mortification of himself—"at least, someone must recognize a strain of God in me—and who does? I don't believe in it myself."

And, moreover, in the intense joy and suffering of his realized passion, the island, with its sea and sky, had fused till, like a brilliant bead, all their beauty ran together out of the common ore, and Siegmund saw it naked, saw the beauty of everything naked in the shifting magic of this bead. The island would be gone to-morrow: he would look for the beauty and find the dirt. What was he to do?"

"You know, Domine," said Helena—it was his old nickname she used—"you look quite stern to-day."

"I feel anything but stern," he laughed. "Weaker than usual, in fact."

"Yes, perhaps so, when you talk. Then you are really surprisingly gentle. But when you are silent, I am even afraid of you—you seem so grave."

He laughed.

"And shall I not be grave?" he said. "Can't you smell *Fumum et opes strepitumque Romæ?* He turned quickly to Helena. "I wonder if that's right," he said. "It's years since I did a line of Latin, and I thought it had all gone."

"In the first place, what does it mean?" said Helena calmly, "for I can only half translate. I have thrown overboard all my scrap-books of such stuff."

"Why," said Siegmund, rather abashed, "only 'the row and the smoke of Rome.' But it is remarkable, Helena"—here the peculiar look of interest came on his face again—"it is really remarkable that I should have said that."

"Yes, you look surprised," smiled she.

"But it must be twenty"—he counted—"twenty-two or three years since I learned that, and I forgot it—goodness knows how long ago. Like a drowning man, I have these memories before . . ." He broke off, smiling mockingly, to tease her.

"Before you go back to London," said she, in a matter-of-fact, almost ironical tone. She was inscrutable. This morning she could not bear to let any deep emotion come uppermost. She wanted rest. "No," she said, with calm distinctness, a few moments after, when they were climbing the rise to the cliff's edge. "I can't say that I smell the smoke of London. The mist-curtain is thick yet. There it is"—she pointed to the heavy, purple-grey haze that hung like arras on a wall, between the sloping sky and the sea. She thought of yesterday morning's mist-curtain, thick and blazing gold, so heavy that no wind could sway its fringe.

They lay down in the dry grass, upon the gold bits of bird's-foot trefoil of the cliff's edge, and looked out to sea. A warm, drowsy calm drooped over everything.

"Six hours," thought Helena, "and we shall have passed the mist-curtain. Already it is thinning. I could break it open with waving my hand. I will not wave my hand."

She was exhausted by the suffering of the last night, so she refused to allow any emotion to move her this morning, till she was strong. Siegmund was also exhausted; but his thoughts laboured like ants, in spite of himself, striving towards a conclusion.

Helena had rejected him. In his heart he felt that in this love affair also he had been a failure. No matter how he contradicted himself, and said it was absurd to imagine he was a failure as Helena's lover, yet he felt a physical sensation of defeat, a kind of knot in his breast which reason, nor dialectics, nor circumstance, not even Helena, could untie. He had failed as lover to Helena.

It was not surprising his marriage with Beatrice should prove disastrous. Rushing into wedlock as he had done, at the ripe age of seventeen, he had known nothing of his woman, nor she of him. When his mind and soul set to develop, as Beatrice could not sympathize with his interests, he naturally inclined away from her, so that now, after twenty years, he was almost a stranger to her. That was not very surprising.

But why should he have failed with Helena?

The bees droned fitfully over the scented grass, aimlessly swinging in the heat. Siegmund watched one gold and amber fellow lazily let go a white cloverhead, and boom in a careless curve out to sea, humming softer and softer as he reeled along in the giddy space.

"The little fool!" said Siegmund, watching the black dot swallowed into the light.

No ship sailed the curving sea. The light danced in a whirl upon the ripples. Everything else watched with heavy eyes of heat entrancement the wild spinning of the lights.

"Even if I were free," he continued to think, "we should only grow apart, Helena and I. She would leave me. This time I should be the laggard. She is young and vigorous; I am beginning to set.

"Is that why I have failed? I ought to have had her in love sufficiently to keep her these few days. I am not quick. I do not follow her or understand her swiftly enough. And I am always timid of compulsion. I cannot compel anybody to follow me.

"So we are here. I am out of my depth. Like the bee, I was mad with the sight of so much joy, such a blue space, and now I shall find no footing to alight on. I have flown out into life beyond my strength to get back. What can I set my feet on when this is gone?"

The sun grew stronger. Slower and more slowly went the hawks of Siegmund's mind, after the quarry of conclusion. He lay bare-headed, looking out to sea. The sun was burning deeper into his face and head.

"I feel as if it were burning into me," thought Siegmund abstractedly. "It is certainly consuming some part of me. Perhaps it is making me ill." Meanwhile, perversely, he gave his face and his hot black hair to the sun.

Helena lay in what shadow he afforded. The heat put out all her thought-activity. Presently she said:

"This heat is terrible, Siegmund. Shall we go down to the water?"

They climbed giddily down the cliff path. Already they were somewhat sun-intoxicated. Siegmund chose the hot sand, where no shade was, on which to lie.

"Shall we not go under the rocks?" said Helena.

"Look!" he said, "the sun is beating on the cliffs. It is hotter, more suffocating, there."

So they lay down in the glare, Helena watching the foam retreat slowly with a cool splash; Siegmund thinking. The naked body of heat was dreadful.

"My arms, Siegmund," said she. "They feel as if they were dipped in fire."

Siegmund took them, without a word, and hid them under his coat.

"Are you sure it is not bad for you—your head, Siegmund? Are you sure?"

He laughed stupidly.

"That is all right," he said. He knew that the sun was burning through him, and doing him harm, but he wanted the intoxication.

As he looked wistfully far away over the sea at Helena's mist-curtain, he said:

"I *think* we should be able to keep together if"—he faltered—"if only I could have you a little longer. I have never had you . . ."

Some sound of failure, some tone telling her it was too late, some ring of despair in his quietness, made Helena cling to him wildly, with a savage little cry as if she were wounded. She clung to him, almost beside herself. She could not lose him, she could not spare him. She would not let him go. Helena was, for the moment, frantic.

He held her safely, saying nothing until she was calmer, when, with his lips on her cheek, he murmured:

"I should be able, shouldn't I, Helena?"

"You are always able!" she cried. "It is I who play with you at hiding."

"I have really had you so little," he said.

"Can't you forget it, Siegmund?" she cried. "Can't you forget it? It was only a shadow, Siegmund. It was a lie, it was nothing real. Can't you forget it, dear?"

"You can't do without me?" he asked.

"If I lose you I am lost," answered she with swift decision. She had no knowledge of weeping, yet her tears were wet on his face. He held her safely; her arms were hidden under his coat.

"I will have no mercy on those shadows the next time they come between us," said Helena to herself. "They may go back to hell."

She still clung to him, craving so to have him that he could not be reft away.

Siegmund felt very peaceful. He lay with his arms about her, listening to the backward-creeping tide. All his thoughts, like bees, were flown out to sea and lost.

"If I had her more, I should understand her through and through. If we were side by side we should grow together. If we could stay here, I should get stronger and more upright."

This was the poor heron of quarry the hawks of his mind had struck.

Another hour fell like a foxglove bell from the stalk. There were only two red blossoms left. Then the stem would have set to seed. Helena leaned her head upon the breast of Siegmund, her arms clasping, under his coat, his body, which swelled and sank gently, with the quiet of great power.

"If," thought she, "the whole clock of the world could stand still now, and leave us thus, me with the lift and fall of the strong body of Siegmund in my arms. . . ."

But the clock ticked on in the heat, the seconds marked off by the falling of the waves, repeated so lightly, and in such fragile rhythm, that it made silence sweet.

"If now," prayed Siegmund, "death would wipe the sweat from me, and it were dark . . ."

But the waves softly marked the minutes, retreating farther, leaving the bare rocks to bleach and the weed to shrivel.

Gradually, like the shadow on a dial, the knowledge that it was time to rise and go crept upon them. Although they remained silent, each knew that the other felt the same weight of responsibility, the shadow-finger of the sundial travelling over them. The alternative was, not to return, to let the finger travel and be gone. But then . . . Helena knew she must not let the time cross her; she must rise before it was too late, and travel before the coming finger. Siegmund hoped she would not get up. He lay in suspense, waiting.

At last she sat up abruptly.

"It is time, Siegmund," she said.

He did not answer, he did not look at her, but lay as she had left him. She wiped her face with her handkerchief, waiting. Then she bent over him. He did not look at her. She saw his forehead was swollen and inflamed with the sun. Very gently she wiped from it the glistening sweat. He closed his eyes, and she wiped his cheeks and his mouth. Still he did not look at her. She bent very close to him, feeling her heart crushed with grief for him.

"We must go, Siegmund," she whispered.

"All right," he said, but still he did not move.

She stood up beside him, shook herself, and tried to get a breath of air. She was dazzled blind by the sunshine.

Siegmund lay in the bright light, with his eyes closed, never moving. His face was inflamed, but fixed like a mask.

Helena waited, until the terror of the passing of the hour was too strong for her. She lifted his hand, which lay swollen with heat on the sand, and she tried gently to draw him.

"We shall be too late," she said in distress.

He sighed and sat up, looking out over the water.

Helena could not bear to see him look so vacant and expressionless. She put her arm round his neck, and pressed his head against her skirt.

Siegmund knew he was making it unbearable for her. Pulling himself together, he bent his head from the sea, and said:

"Why, what time is it?"

He took out his watch, holding it in his hand. Helena still held his left hand, and had one arm round his neck.

"I can't see the figures," he said. "Everything is dimmed, as if it were coming dark."

"Yes," replied Helena, in that reedy, painful tone of hers. "My eyes were the same. It is the strong sunlight."

"I can't," he repeated, and he was rather surprised—"I can't see the time. Can you?"

She stooped down and looked.

"It is half-past one," she said.

Siegmund hated her voice as she spoke. There was still sufficient time to catch the train. He stood up, moved inside his clothing, saying: "I feel almost stunned by the heat. I can hardly see, and all my feeling in my body is dulled."

"Yes," answered Helena, "I am afraid it will do you harm."

"At any rate," he smiled as if sleepily, "I have had enough. If it's too much— what *is* too much?"

They went unevenly over the sand, their eyes sun-dimmed.

"We are going back—we are going back!" the heart of Helena seemed to run hot, beating these words.

They climbed the cliff path toilsomely. Standing at the top, on the edge of the grass, they looked down the cliffs at the beach and over the sea. The strand was wide, forsaken by the sea, forlorn with rocks bleaching in the sun, and sand and sea-weed breathing off their painful scent upon the heat. The sea crept smaller, further away; the sky stood still. Siegmund and Helena looked hopelessly out on their beautiful, incandescent world. They looked hopelessly at each other. Siegmund's mood was gentle and forbearing. He smiled faintly at Helena, then turned, and, lifting his hand to his mouth in a kiss for the beauty he had enjoyed, "Addio!" he said.

He turned away, and, looking from Helena landwards, he said, smiling peculiarly:

"It reminds me of Traviata—an 'Addio' at every verse-end."

She smiled with her mouth in acknowledgment of his facetious irony; it jarred on her. He was pricked again by her supercilious reserve.

"Addi-i-i-i-o, Addi-i-i-o!" he whistled between his teeth, hissing out the Italian's passion-notes in a way that made Helena clench her fists.

"I suppose," she said, swallowing, and recovering her voice to check this discord—"I suppose we shall have a fairly easy journey—Thursday."

"I don't know," said Siegmund.

"There will not be very many people," she insisted.

"I think," he said, in a very quiet voice, "you'd better let me go by the South-Western from Portsmouth while you go on by the Brighton."

"But why?" she exclaimed in astonishment.

"I don't want to sit looking at you all the way," he said.

"But why should you?" she exclaimed.

He laughed.

"Indeed no!" she said. "We shall go together."

"Very well," he answered.

They walked on in silence towards the village. As they drew near the little post-office he said:

"I suppose I may as well wire them that I shall be home to-night."

"You haven't sent them any word?" she asked.

He laughed. They came to the open door of the little shop. He stood still, not entering. Helena wondered what he was thinking.

"Shall I?" he asked, meaning, should he wire to Beatrice. His manner was rather peculiar.

"Well, I should think so," faltered Helena, turning away to look at the postcards in the window. Siegmund entered the shop. It was dark and cumbered with views, cheap china ornaments, and toys. He asked for a telegraph form.

"My God!" he said to himself bitterly as he took the pencil. He could not sign the abbreviated name his wife used towards him. He scribbled his surname, as he would have done to a stranger. As he watched the amiable, stout woman counting up his words carefully, pointing with her finger, he felt sick with irony.

"That's right," she said, picking up the sixpence and taking the form to the instrument. "What beautiful weather!" she continued. "It will be making you sorry to leave us."

"There goes my warrant," thought Siegmund, watching the flimsy bit of paper under the postmistress's heavy hand.

"Yes—it is too bad, isn't it," he replied, bowing and laughing to the woman.

"It is, sir," she answered pleasantly. "Good-morning."

He came out of the shop still smiling, and when Helena turned from the postcards to look at him the lines of laughter remained over his face like a mask. She glanced at his eyes for a sign; his facial expression told her nothing; his eyes were just as inscrutable, which made her falter with dismay.

"What is he thinking of?" she asked herself. Her thoughts flashed back. "And why did he ask me so peculiarly whether he should wire them at home?"

"Well," said Siegmund, "are there any postcards?"

"None that I care to take," she replied. "Perhaps you would like one of these?"

She pointed to some faded-looking cards which proved to be imaginary views of Alum Bay done in variegated sand. Siegmund smiled.

"I wonder if they dribbled the sand on with a fine glass tube," he said.

"Or a brush," said Helena.

"She does not understand," said Siegmund to himself. "And whatever I do I must not tell her. I should have thought she would understand."

As he walked home beside her there mingled with his other feelings resentment against her. Almost he hated her.

XX

*A*t first they had a carriage to themselves. They sat opposite each other with averted faces, looking out of the windows and watching the houses, the downs dead asleep in the sun, the embankments of the railway with exhausted hot flowers go slowly past out of their reach. They felt as if they were being dragged away like criminals. Unable to speak or think, they stared out of the windows, Helena struggling in vain to keep back her tears, Siegmund labouring to breathe normally.

At Yarmouth the door was snatched open, and there was a confusion of shouting and running; a swarm of humanity, clamouring, attached itself at the carriage doorway, which was immediately blocked by a stout man who heaved a leathern bag in front of him as he cried in German that here was room for all. Faces innumerable—hot, blue-eyed faces—strained to look over his shoulders at the shocked girl and the amazed Siegmund.

There entered eight Germans into the second-class compartment, five men and three ladies. When at last the luggage was stowed away they sank into the seats. The last man on either side to be seated lowered himself carefully, like a wedge, between his two neighbours. Siegmund watched the stout man, the one who had led the charge, settling himself between his large lady and the small Helena. The latter crushed herself against the side of the carriage. The German's hips came down tight against her. She strove to lessen herself against the window, to escape the pressure of his flesh, whose heat was immediately transmitted to her. The man squeezed in the opposite direction.

"I am afraid I press you," he said, smiling in his gentle, chivalric German fashion. Helena glanced swiftly at him. She liked his grey eyes, she liked the agreeable intonation, and the pleasant sound of his words.

"Oh no," she answered. "You do not crush me."

Almost before she had finished the words she turned away to the window. The man seemed to hesitate a moment, as if recovering himself from a slight rebuff, before he could address his lady with the good-humoured remark in German: "Well, and have we not managed it very nicely, eh?"

The whole party began to talk in German with great animation. They told each other of the quaint ways of this or the other; they joked loudly over "Billy"— this being a nickname discovered for the German Emperor—and what he would be saying of the Czar's trip; they questioned each other, and answered each other concerning the places they were going to see, with great interest, displaying admirable knowledge. They were pleased with everything; they extolled things English.

Helena's stout neighbour, who, it seemed, was from Dresden, began to tell anecdotes. He was a *raconteur* of the naïf type: he talked with face, hands, with his whole body. Now and again he would give little spurts in his seat. After one of these he must have become aware of Helena—who felt as if she were enveloped by a soft stove—struggling to escape his compression. He stopped short, lifted his hat, and, smiling beseechingly, said in his persuasive way:

"I am sorry. I am sorry. I compress you!" He glanced round in perplexity, seeking some escape or remedy. Finding none, he turned to her again, after having squeezed hard against his lady to free Helena, and said:

"Forgive me, I am sorry."

"You are forgiven," replied Helena, suddenly smiling into his face with her rare winsomeness. The whole party, attentive, relaxed into a smile at this. The good-humour was complete.

"Thank you," said the German gratefully.

Helena turned away. The talk began again like the popping of corn; the *raconteur* resumed his anecdote. Everybody was waiting to laugh. Helena rapidly wearied of trying to follow the tale. Siegmund had made no attempt. He had watched, with the others, the German's apologies, and the sight of his lover's face had moved him more than he could tell.

She had a peculiar, childish wistfulness at times, and with this an intangible aloofness that pierced his heart. It seemed to him he should never know her.

There was a remoteness about her, an estrangement between her and all natural daily things, as if she were of an unknown race that never can tell its own story. This feeling always moved Siegmund's pity to its deepest, leaving him poignantly helpless. This same foreignness, revealed in other ways, sometimes made him hate her. It was as if she would sacrifice him rather than renounce her foreign birth. There was something in her he could never understand, so that never, never could he say he was master of her as she was of him the mistress.

As she smiled and turned away from the German, mute, uncomplaining, like a child wise in sorrow beyond its years. Siegmund's resentment against her suddenly took fire, and blazed him with sheer pain of pity. She was very small. Her quiet ways, and sometimes her impetuous clinging made her seem small; for she was very strong. But Siegmund saw her now, small, quiet, uncomplaining, living for him who sat and looked at her. But what would become of her when he had left her, when she was alone, little foreigner as she was, in this world, which apologizes when it has done the hurt, too blind to see beforehand? Helena would be left behind; death was no way for her. She could not escape thus with him from this house of strangers which she called "life." She had to go on alone, like a foreigner who cannot learn the strange language.

"What will she do?" Siegmund asked himself, "when her loneliness comes upon her like a horror, and she has no one to go to. She will come to the memory of me for a while, and that will take her over till her strength is established. But what then?"

Siegmund could find no answer. He tried to imagine her life. It would go on, after his death, just in the same way, for a while, and then? He had not the faintest knowledge of how she would develop. What would she do when she was thirty-eight, and as old as himself? He could not conceive. Yet she would not die, of that he was certain.

Siegmund suddenly realized that he knew nothing of her life, her real inner life. She was a book written in characters unintelligible to him and to everybody. He was tortured with the problem of her till it became acute, and he felt as if his heart would burst inside him. As a boy he had experienced the same sort of feeling after wrestling for an hour with a problem in Euclid, for he was capable of great concentration.

He felt Helena looking at him. Turning, he found her steady, unswerving eyes fixed on him, so that he shrank confused from them. She smiled: by an instinctive movement she made him know that she wanted him to hold her hand. He leaned forward and put his hand over hers. She had peculiar hands, small, with a strange, delightful silkiness. Often they were cool or cold; generally they lay unmoved within his clasp, but then they were instinct with life, not inert. Sometimes he would feel a peculiar jerking in his pulse, very much like electricity, when he held her hand. Occasionally it was almost painful, and felt as if a little virtue were passing out of his blood. But that he dismissed as nonsense.

The Germans were still rattling away, perspiring freely, wiping their faces with their handkerchiefs as they laughed, moving inside their clothing, which was sticking to their sides. Siegmund had not noticed them for some time, he was so much absorbed. But Helena, though she sympathized with her fellow-passengers, was tormented almost beyond endurance by the noise, the heat of her neighbour's body, the atmosphere of the crowded carriage, and her own emotion. The only thing that could relieve her was the hand of Siegmund soothing her in its hold.

She looked at him with the same steadiness which made her eyes feel heavy upon him, and made him shrink. She wanted his strength of nerve to support her, and he submitted at once, his one aim being to give her out of himself whatever she wanted.

XXI

The tall white yachts in a throng were lounging off the roads of Ryde. It was near the regatta time, so these proud creatures had flown loftily together, and now flitted hither and thither among themselves, like a concourse of tall women, footing the waves with superb touch. To Siegmund they were very beautiful, but removed from him, as dancers crossing the window lights are removed from the man who looks up from the street. He saw the Solent and the world of glamour flying gay as snow outside, where inside was only Siegmund, tired, dispirited, without any joy.

He and Helena had climbed among coils of rope on to the prow of their steamer, so they could catch a little spray of speed on their faces to stimulate them. The sea was very bright and crowded. White sails leaned slightly and filed along the roads; two yachts with sails of amber floated, it seemed without motion, amid the eclipsed blue of the day; small boats with red and yellow flags fluttered quickly, trailing the sea with colour; a pleasure steamer coming from Cowes swung her soft stout way among the fleeting ships; high in the background were men-of-war, a long line, each one threading tiny triangles of flags through a sky dim with distance.

"It is all very glad," said Siegmund to himself, "but it seems to me fanciful."

He was out of it. Already he felt detached from life. He belonged to his destination. It is always so: we have no share in the beauty that lies between us and our goal.

Helena watched with poignant sorrow all the agitation of colour on the blue afternoon.

"We must leave it; we must pass out of it," she lamented, over and over again. Each new charm she caught eagerly.

"I like the steady purpose of that brown-sailed tramp," she said to herself, watching a laden coaster making for Portsmouth.

They were still among the small shipping of Ryde. Siegmund and Helena, as they looked out, became aware of a small motor-launch heading across their course towards a yacht whose tall masts were drawn clean on the sky. The eager launch, its nose up as if to breathe, was racing over the swell like a coursing dog. A lady, in white, and a lad with dark head and white jersey were leaning in the bows; a gentleman was bending over some machinery in the middle of the boat, while the sailor in the low stern was also stooping forward attending to something. The steamer was sweeping onwards, huge above the water; the dog of a boat was coursing straight across her track. The lady saw the danger first. Stretching forward, she seized the arm of the lad and held him firm, making no sound, but watching the forward menace of the looming steamer.

"Look!" cried Helena, catching hold of Siegmund. He was already watching. Suddenly the steamer bell clanged. The gentleman looked up, with startled, sunburned face; then he leaped to the stern. The launch veered. It and the steamer closed together like a pair of scissors. The lady, still holding the boy, looked up with an expressionless face at the high sweeping chisel of the steamer's bows; the husband stood rigid, staring ahead. No sound was to be heard save the rustling of water under the bows. The scissors closed, the launch skelped forward like a dog from in front of the traffic. It escaped by a yard or two. Then, like a dog, it seemed to look round. The gentleman in the stern glanced back quickly. He was a handsome, dark-haired man with dark eyes. His face was as if carven out of oak, set and grey-brown. Then he looked to the steering of his boat. No one had uttered a sound. From the tiny boat coursing low on the water, not a sound, only tense waiting. The launch raced out of danger towards the yacht. The gentleman, with a brief gesture, put his man in charge again, whilst he himself went forward to the lady. He was a handsome man, very proud in his movements; and she, in her bearing, was prouder still. She received him almost with indifference.

Helena turned to Siegmund. He took both her hands and pressed them, whilst she looked at him with eyes blind with emotion. She was white to the lips, and heaving like the buoy in the wake of the steamer. The noise of life had suddenly been hushed, and each heart had heard for a moment the noiselessness of death. How everyone was white and gasping! They strove, on every hand, to fill the day with noise and the colour of life again.

"By Jove, that was a near thing!"

"Ah, that has made me feel bad!" said a woman.

"A French yacht," said somebody.

Helena was waiting for the voice of Siegmund. But he did not know what to say. Confused, he repeated:

"That was a close shave."

Helena clung to him, searching his face. She felt his difference from herself. There was something in his experience that made him different, quiet, with a peculiar expression as if he were pained.

"Ah, dear Lord!" he was saying to himself. "How bright and whole the day is for them! If God had suddenly put His hand over the sun, and swallowed us up in a shadow, they could not have been more startled. That man, with his fine, white-flannelled limbs and his dark head, has no suspicion of the shadow that supports it all. Between the blueness of the sea and the sky he passes easy as a gull, close to the fine white sea-mew of his mate, amid red flowers of flags, and soft birds of ships, and slow moving monsters of steamboats.

"For me the day is transparent and shrivelling. I can see the darkness through its petals. But for him it is a fresh bell-flower, in which he fumbles with delights like a bee.

"For me, quivering in the interspaces of the atmosphere, is the darkness the same that fills in my soul. I can see death urging itself into life, the shadow supporting the substance. For my life is burning an invisible flame. The glare of the light of myself, as I burn on the fuel of death, is not enough to hide from me the source and the issue. For what is a life but a flame that bursts off the surface of darkness, and tapers into the darkness again. But the death that issues differs from the death that was the source. At least, I shall enrich death with a potent shadow, if I do not enrich life."

"Wasn't that woman fine!" said Helena.

"So perfectly still," he answered.

"The child realized nothing," she said.

Siegmund laughed, then leaned forward impulsively to her.

"I am always so sorry," he said, "that the human race is urged inevitably into a deeper and deeper realization of life."

She looked at him, wondering what provoked such a remark.

"I guess," she said slowly, after a while, "that the man, the sailor, will have a bad time. He was abominably careless."

"He was careful of something else just then," said Siegmund, who hated to hear her speak in cold condemnation. "He was attending to the machinery or something."

"That was scarcely his first business," said she, rather sarcastic.

Siegmund looked at her. She seemed very hard in judgment—very blind. Sometimes his soul surged against her in hatred.

"Do you think the man *wanted* to drown the boat?" he asked.

"He nearly succeeded," she replied.

There was antagonism between them. Siegmund recognized in Helena the world sitting in judgment, and he hated it. But, after all," he thought, "I suppose it is the only way to get along, to judge the event and not the person. I have a disease of sympathy, a vice of exoneration."

Nevertheless, he did not love Helena as a judge. He thought rather of the woman in the boat. She was evidently one who watched the sources of life, saw it great and impersonal.

"Would the woman cry, or hug and kiss the boy when she got on board?" he asked.

"I rather think not. Why?" she replied.

"I hope she didn't," he said.

Helena sat watching the water spurt back from the bows. She was very much in love with Siegmund. He was suggestive; he stimulated her. But to her mind he had not his own dark eyes of hesitation; he was swift and proud as the wind. She never realized his helplessness.

Siegmund was gathering strength from the thought of that other woman's courage. If she no so much restraint as not to cry out, or alarm the boy, if she had so much grace not to complain to her husband, surely he himself might refrain from revealing his own fear to Helena, and from lamenting his hard fate.

They sailed on past the chequered round towers. The sea opened, and they looked out to eastward into the sea-space. Siegmund wanted to flee. He yearned to escape down the open ways before him. Yet he knew he would be carried on to London. He watched the sea-ways closing up. The shore came round. The high old houses stood flat on the right hand. The shore swept round in a sickle, reaping them into the harbour. There the old *Victory,* gay with myriad pointed pennons, was harvested, saved for a trophy.

"It is a dreadful thing," thought Siegmund, "to remain as a trophy when there is nothing more to do." He watched the landing-stage swooping nearer. There were the trains drawn up in readiness. At the other end of the train was London.

He could scarcely bear to have Helena before him for another two hours. The suspense of that protracted farewell, while he sat opposite her in the beating train, would cost too much. He longed to be released from her.

They had got their luggage, and were standing at the foot of the ladder, in the heat of the engines and the smell of hot oil, waiting for the crowd to pass on, so that they might ascend and step off the ship on to the mainland.

"Won't you let me go by the South-Western, and you by the Brighton?" asked Siegmund, hesitating, repeating the morning's question.

Helena looked at him, knitting her brows with misgiving and perplexity.

"No," she replied. "Let us go together."

Siegmund followed her up the iron ladder to the quay.

There was no great crowd on the train. They easily found a second-class compartment without occupants. He swung the luggage on the rack and sat down, facing Helena.

"Now," said he to himself, "I wish I were alone."

He wanted to think and prepare himself.

Helena, who was thinking actively, leaned forward to him to say:

"Shall I not go down to Cornwall?"

By her soothing willingness to do anything for him, Siegmund knew that she was dogging him closely. He could not bear to have his anxiety protracted.

"But you have promised Louisa, have you not?" he replied.

"Oh, well!" she said, in the peculiar slighting tone she had when she wished to convey the unimportance of affairs not touching him.

"Then you must go," he said.

"But," she began, with harsh petulance, "I do not want to go down to Cornwall with *Louisa* and *Olive*"—she accentuated the two names—"after *this,*" she added.

"Then Louisa will have no holiday—and you have promised," he said gravely.

Helena looked at him. She saw he had decided that she should go.

"Is my promise so *very* important?" she asked. She glanced angrily at the three ladies who were hesitating in the doorway. Nevertheless, the ladies entered, and seated themselves at the opposite end of the carriage. Siegmund did not know whether he were displeased or relieved by their intrusion. If they had stayed out, he might have held Helena in his arms for still another hour. As it was, she could not harass him with words. He tried not to look at her, but to think.

The train at last moved out of the station. As it passed through Portsmouth, Siegmund remembered his coming down, on the Sunday. It seemed an indefinite age ago. He was thankful that he sat on the side of the carriage opposite from the one he had occupied five days before. The afternoon of the flawless sky was ripening into evening. The chimneys and the sides of the houses of Portsmouth took on that radiant appearance which transfigures the end of day in town. A rich bloom of light appears on the surfaces of brick and stone.

"It will go on," thought Siegmund, "being gay of an evening, for ever. And I shall miss it all!"

But as soon as the train moved into the gloom of the Town Station, he began again:

"Beatrice will be proud, and silent as steel when I get home. She will say nothing, thank God—nor shall I. That will expedite matters: there will be no interruptions . . .

"But we cannot continue together after this. Why should I discuss reasons for and against? We cannot. She goes to a cottage in the country. Already I have spoken of it to her. I allow her all I can of my money, and on the rest I manage for myself in lodgings in London. Very good.

"But when I am comparatively free I cannot live alone. I shall want Helena; I shall remember the children. If I have the one, I shall be damned by the thought of the other. This bruise on my mind will never get better. Helena says she would never come to me; but she would, out of pity for me. I know she would.

"But then, what then? Beatrice and the children in the country, and me not looking after the children. Beatrice is thriftless. She would be in endless difficulty. It would be a degradation to me. She would keep a red sore inflamed against me; I should be a shameful thing in her mouth. Besides, there would go all her strength. She would not make any efforts. 'He has brought it on us,' she would say; 'let him see what the result is.' And things would go from bad to worse with them. It would be a gangrene of shame.

"And Helena—I should have nothing but mortification. When she was asleep I could not look at her. She is such a strange, incongruous creature. But I should be responsible for her. She believes in me as if I had the power of God. What should I think of myself?"

Siegmund leaned with his head against the window, watching the country whirl past, but seeing nothing. He thought imaginatively, and his imagination destroyed him. He pictured Beatrice in the country. He sketched the morning—breakfast haphazard at a late hour; the elder children rushing off without food, miserable and untidy, the youngest bewildered under her swift, indifferent preparations for school. He thought of Beatrice in the evening, worried and irritable, her bills unpaid, the work undone, declaiming lamentably against the cruelty of her husband, who had abandoned her to such a burden of care while he took his pleasure elsewhere.

This line exhausted or intolerable, Siegmund switched off to the consideration of his own life in town. He would go to America; the agreement was signed with the theatre manager. But America would be only a brief shutting of the eyes and closing of the mouth. He would wait for the home-coming to Helena, and she would wait for him. It was inevitable; then would begin—what? He would never have enough money to keep Helena, even if he managed to keep himself. Their meetings would then be occasional and clandestine. Ah, it was intolerable!

"If I were rich," said Siegmund, "all would be plain. I would give each of my children enough, and Beatrice, and we would go away; but I am nearly forty; I have no genius; I shall never be rich." Round and round went his thoughts like oxen over a threshing floor, treading out the grain. Gradually the chaff flew away; gradually the corn of conviction gathered small and hard upon the floor.

As he sat thinking, Helena leaned across to him, and laid her hand on his knee.

"If I have made things more difficult," she said, her voice harsh with pain, "you will forgive me."

He started. This was one of the cruel cuts of pain that love gives, filling the eyes with blood. Siegmund stiffened himself; slowly he smiled, as he looked at her childish, plaintive lips, and her large eyes haunted with pain.

"Forgive you?" he repeated. "Forgive you for five days of perfect happiness; the only real happiness I have ever known!"

Helena tightened her fingers on his knee. She felt herself stinging with painful joy; but one of the ladies was looking at her curiously. She leaned back in her place, and turned to watch the shocks of corn strike swiftly, in long rows, across her vision.

Siegmund, also quivering, turned his face to the window, where the rotation of the wide sea-flat helped the movement of his thought. Helena had interrupted him. She had bewildered his thoughts from their hawking, so that they struck here and there, wildly, among small, pitiful prey that was useless, conclusions which only hindered the bringing home of the final convictions.

"What will she do?" cried Siegmund. "What will she do when I am gone? What will become of her? Already she has no aim in life; then she will have no object. Is it any good my going if I leave her behind? What an inextricable knot this is! But what will she do?"

It was a question she had aroused before, a question which he could never answer; indeed, it was not for him to answer.

They wound through the pass of the south downs. As Siegmund, looking backward, saw the northern slope of the downs swooping smoothly, in a great, broad bosom of sward, down to the body of the land, he warmed with sudden love for the earth; there the great downs were, naked like a breast, leaning kindly to him. The earth is always kind; it loves us, and would foster us like a nurse. The downs were big and tender and simple. Siegmund looked at the farm, folded in a hollow, and he wondered what fortunate folk were there, nourished and quiet, hearing the vague roar of the train that was carrying him home.

Up towards Arundel the cornfields of red wheat were heavy with gold. It was evening, when the green of the trees went out, leaving dark shapes proud upon the sky; but the red wheat was forged in the sunset, hot and magnificent. Siegmund almost gloated as he smelled the ripe corn, and opened his eyes to its powerful radiation. For a moment he forgot everything, amid the forging of red fields of gold in the smithy of the sunset. Like sparks, poppies blew along the railway banks, a crimson train. Siegmund waited, through the meadows, for the next wheat-field. It came like the lifting of yellow-hot metal out of the gloom of darkened grass-lands.

Helena was reassured by the glamour of evening over ripe Sussex. She breathed the land now and then, while she watched the sky. The sunset was stately. The blue-eyed day, with great limbs, having fought its victory and won, now mounted triumphant on its pyre, and with white arms uplifted took the flames, which leaped like blood about its feet. The day died nobly, so she thought.

One gold cloud, as an encouragement tossed to her, followed the train.

"Surely that cloud is for us," said she, as she watched it anxiously. Dark trees brushed between it and her, while she waited in suspense. It came, unswerving, from behind the trees.

"I am sure it is for us," she repeated. A gladness came into her eyes. Still the cloud followed the train. She leaned forward to Siegmund and pointed out the cloud to him. She was very eager to give him a little of her faith.

"It has come with us quite a long way. Doesn't it seem to you to be travelling with us? It is the golden hand; it is the good omen."

She then proceeded to tell him the legend from "Aylwin."

Siegmund listened, and smiled. The sunset was handsome on his face.

Helena was almost happy.

"I am right," said he to himself. "I am right in my conclusions, and Helena will manage by herself afterwards. I am right; there is the hand to confirm it."

The heavy train settled down to an easy, unbroken stroke, swinging like a greyhound over the level northwards. All the time Siegmund was mechanically thinking the well-known movement from the Valkyrie Ride, his whole self beating to the rhythm. It seemed to him there was a certain grandeur in this flight, but it hurt him with its heavy insistance of catastrophe. He was afraid; he had to summon his courage to sit quiet. For a time he was reassured; he believed he was going on towards the right end. He hunted through the country and the sky, asking of everything, "Am I right? am I right?" He did not mind what happened to him, so long as he felt it was right. What he meant by "right" he did not trouble to think, but the question remained. For a time he had been reassured; then a dullness came over him, when his thoughts were stupid, and he merely submitted to the rhythm of the train, which stamped him deeper and deeper with a brand of catastrophe.

The sun had gone down. Over the west was a gush of brightness as the fountain of light bubbled lower. The stars, like specks of froth from the foaming of the day, clung to the blue ceiling. Like spiders they hung overhead, while the hosts of the gold atmosphere poured out of the hive by the western low door. Soon the hive was empty, a hollow dome of purple, with here and there on the floor a bright brushing of wings—a village; then, overhead, the luminous star-spiders began to run.

"Ah, well!" thought Siegmund—he was tired—"if one bee dies in a swarm, what is it, so long as the hive is all right? Apart from the gold light, and the hum and the colour of day, what was I? Nothing! Apart from these rushings out of the hive, along with swarm, into the dark meadows of night, gathering God knows what, I was a pebble. Well, the day will swarm in golden again, with colour on the wings of every bee, and humming in each activity. The gold and the colour and sweet smell and the sound of life, they exist, even if there is no bee; it only happens we see the iridescence on the wings of a bee. It exists whether or not, bee or no bee. Since the iridescence and the humming of life *are* always, and since it was they who made me, then I am not lost. At least, I do not care. If the spark goes out, the essence of the fire is there in the darkness. What does it matter? Besides, I *have* burned bright; I have laid up a fine cell of honey somewhere—I wonder where? We can never point to it; but it *is* so—what does it matter, then!"

They had entered the north downs, and were running through Dorking towards Leatherhead. Box Hill stood dark in the dusky sweetness of the night. Helena remembered that here she and Siegmund had come for their first walk together. She would like to come again. Presently she saw the quick stilettos of stars on the small, baffled river; they ran between high embankments. Siegmund recollected that these were covered with roses of Sharon—the large golden St. John's wort of finest silk. He looked, and could just distinguish the full-blown, delicate flowers, ignored by the stars. At last he had something to say to Helena:

"Do you remember," he asked, "the roses of Sharon all along here?"

"I do," replied Helena, glad he spoke so brightly. "Weren't they pretty?"

After a few moments of watching the bank, she said:

"Do you know, I have never gathered one? I think I should like to; I should like to feel them, and they should have an orangy smell."

He smiled, without answering.

She glanced up at him, smiling brightly.

"But shall we come down here in the morning, and find some?" she asked. She put the question timidly. "Would you care to?" she added.

Siegmund darkened and frowned. Here was the pain revived again.

"No," he said gently; "I think we had better not." Almost for the first time he did not make apologetic explanation.

Helena turned to the window, and remained, looking out at the spinning of the lights of the towns without speaking, until they were near Sutton. Then she rose and pinned on her hat, gathering her gloves and her basket. She was, in spite of herself, slightly angry. Being quite ready to leave the train, she sat down to wait for the station. Siegmund was aware that she was displeased, and again, for the first time, he said to himself, "Ah, well, it must be so."

She looked at him. He was sad, therefore she softened instantly.

"At least," she said doubtfully, "I shall see you at the station."

"At Waterloo?" he asked.

"No, at Wimbledon," she replied, in her metallic tone.

"But——" he began.

"It will be the best way for us," she interrupted, in the calm tone of conviction. "Much better than crossing London from Victoria to Waterloo."

"Very well," he replied.

He looked up a train for her in his little timetable.

"You will get in Wimbledon 10.5—leave 10.40—leave Waterloo 11.30," he said.

"Very good," she answered.

The brakes were grinding. They waited in a burning suspense for the train to stop.

"If only she will soon go!" thought Siegmund. It was an intolerable minute. She rose; everything was a red blur. She stood before him, pressing his hand; then he rose to give her the bag. As he leaned upon the window-frame and she stood below on the platform, looking up at him, he could scarcely breathe. "How long will it be?" he said to himself, looking at the open carriage doors. He hated intensely the lady who could not get a porter to remove her luggage; he could have killed her; he could have killed the dilatory guard. At last the doors slammed and the whistle went. The train started imperceptibly into motion.

"Now I lose her," said Siegmund.

She looked up at him; her face was white and dismal.

"Goodbye, then!" she said, and she turned away.

Siegmund went back to his seat. He was relieved, but he trembled with sickness. We are all glad when intense moments are done with; but why did she fling round in that manner, stopping the keen note short; what would she do?

XXII

Siegmund went up to Victoria. He was in no hurry to get down to Wimbledon. London was warm and exhausted after the hot day, but this peculiar lukewarmness was not unpleasant to him. He chose to walk from Victoria to Waterloo.

The streets were like polished gun-metal glistened over with gold. The taxi-cabs, the wild cats of the town, swept over the gleaming floor swiftly, soon lessening in the distance, as if scornful of the other clumsy-footed traffic. He heard the merry click-clock of the swinging hansoms, then the excited whirring of the motor-buses as they charged full-tilt heavily down the road, their hearts, as it seemed, beating with trepidation; they drew up with a sigh of relief by the kerb, and stood there panting—great, nervous, clumsy things. Siegmund was always amused by the headlong, floundering career of the buses. He was pleased with this scampering of the traffic; anything for distraction. He was glad Helena was not with him, for the streets would have irritated her with their coarse noise. She would stand for a long time to watch the rabbits pop and hobble along on the common at night; but the tearing along of the taxis and the charge of a great motor-bus was painful to her. "Discords," she said, "after the trees and sea." She liked the glistening of the streets; it seemed a fine alloy of gold laid down for pavement, such pavement as drew near to the pure gold streets of Heaven; but this noise could not be endured near any wonderland.

Siegmund did not mind it; it drummed out his own thoughts. He watched the gleaming magic of the road, raced over with shadows, project itself far before him into the night. He watched the people. Soldiers, belted with scarlet, went jauntily on in front. There was a peculiar charm in their movement. There was a soft vividness of life in their carriage; it reminded Siegmund of the soft swaying and lapping of a poised candle-flame. The women went blithely alongside. Occasionally, in passing, one glanced at him; then, in spite of himself, he smiled; he knew not why. The women glanced at him with approval, for he was ruddy; besides, he had that carelessness and abstraction of despair. The eyes of the women said: "You are comely, you are lovable," and Siegmund smiled.

When the street opened, at Westminster, he noticed the city sky, a lovely deep purple, and the lamps in the Square steaming out a vapour of grey-gold light.

"It is a wonderful night," he said to himself. "There are not two such in a year."

He went forward to the Embankment, with a feeling of elation in his heart. This purple and gold-grey world, with the fluttering flame-warmth of soldiers and the quick brightness of women, like lights that clip sharply in a draught, was a revelation to him.

As he leaned upon the Embankment parapet the wonder did not fade, but rather increased. The trams, one after another, floated loftily over the bridge. They went like great burning bees in an endless file into a hive, past those which were drifting dreamily out, while below, on the black, distorted water, golden serpents flashed and twisted to and fro.

"Ah!" said Siegmund to himself; "it is far too wonderful for me. Here, as well as by the sea, the night is gorgeous and uncouth. Whatever happens, the world is wonderful."

So he went on amid all the vast miracle of movement in the city night, the swirling of water to the sea, the gradual sweep of the stars, the floating of many lofty, luminous cars through the bridged darkness, like an army of angels filing past on one of God's campaigns, the purring haste of the taxis, the slightly dancing shadows of people. Siegmund went on slowly, like a slow bullet winging into the heart of life. He did not lose this sense of wonder, not in the train, nor as he walked home in the moonless dark.

When he closed the door behind him and hung up his hat he frowned. He did not think definitely of anything, but his frown meant to him: "Now for the beginning of Hell!"

He went towards the dining-room, where the light was, and the uneasy murmur. The clock, with its deprecating, suave chime, was striking ten. Siegmund opened the door of the room. Beatrice was sewing, and did not raise her head. Frank, a tall, thin lad of eighteen, was bent over a book. He did not look up. Vera had her fingers thrust in among her hair, and continued to read the magazine that lay on the table before her. Siegmund looked at them all. They gave no sign to show they were aware of his entry; there was only that unnatural tenseness of people who cover their agitation. He glanced round to see where he should go. His wicker armchair remained empty by the fireplace; his slippers were standing under the sideboard, as he had left them. Siegmund sat down in the creaking chair; he began to feel sick and tired.

"I suppose the children are in bed," he said.

His wife sewed on as if she had not heard him; his daughter noisily turned over a leaf and continued to read, as if she were pleasantly interested and had known no interruption. Siegmund waited, with his slipper dangling from his hand, looking from one to another.

"They've been gone two hours," said Frank at last, still without raising his eyes from his book. His tone was contemptuous, his voice was jarring, not yet having developed a man's fulness.

Siegmund put on his slipper, and began to unlace the other boot. The slurring of the lace through the holes and the snacking of the tag seemed unnecessarily loud. It annoyed his wife. She took a breath to speak, then refrained, feeling suddenly her daughter's scornful restraint upon her. Siegmund rested his arms upon his knees, and sat leaning forward, looking into the barren fireplace, which was littered with paper, and orange-peel, and a banana-skin.

"Do you want any supper?" asked Beatrice, and the sudden harshness of her voice startled him into looking at her.

She had her face averted, refusing to see him. Siegmund's heart went down with weariness and despair at the sight of her.

"Aren't *you* having any?" he asked.

The table was not laid. Beatrice's work-basket, a little wicker fruit-skep, overflowed scissors, and pins, and scraps of holland, and reels of cotton on the green serge cloth. Vera leaned both her elbows on the table.

Instead of replying to him, Beatrice went to the sideboard. She took out a tablecloth, pushed her sewing litter aside, and spread the cloth over one end of the table. Vera gave her magazine a little knock with her hand.

"Have you read this tale of a French convent school in here, mother?" she asked.

"In where?" said Beatrice.

"In this month's *Nash's.*"

"No," replied Beatrice. "What time have I for reading, much less for anything else?"

"You should think more of yourself, and a little less of other people, then," said Vera, with a sneer at the "other people." She rose. "Let me do this. You sit down; you are tired, mother," she said.

Her mother, without replying, went out to the kitchen. Vera followed her. Frank, left alone with his father, moved uneasily, and bent his thin shoulders lower over his book. Siegmund remained with his arms on his knees, looking into the grate. From the kitchen came the chinking of crockery, and soon the smell of coffee. All the time Vera was heard chatting with affected brightness to her mother, addressing her in fond tones, using all her wits to recall bright little incidents to retail to her. Beatrice answered rarely, and then with utmost brevity.

Presently Vera came in with the tray. She put down a cup of coffee, a plate with boiled ham, pink and thin, such as is bought from a grocer, and some bread-and-butter. Then she sat down, noisily turning over the leaves of her magazine. Frank glanced at the table; it was laid solely for his father. He looked at the bread and the meat, but restrained himself, and went on reading, or pretended to do so. Beatrice came in with the small cruet; it was conspicuously bright.

Everything was correct: knife and fork, spoon, cruet, all perfectly clean, the crockery fine, the bread and butter thin—in fact, it was just as it would have been for a perfect stranger. This scrupulous neatness, in a household so slovenly and easygoing, where it was an established tradition that something should be forgotten or wrong, impressed Siegmund. Beatrice put the serving knife and fork by the little dish of ham, saw that all was proper, then went and sat down. Her face showed no emotion; it was calm and proud. She began to sew.

"What do you say, mother?" said Vera, as if resuming a conversation. "Shall it be Hampton Court or Richmond on Sunday?"

"I say, as I said before," replied Beatrice: "I cannot afford to go out."

"But you must begin, my dear, and Sunday shall see the beginning. Dîtes donc!"

"There are other things to think of," said Beatrice.

"Now, maman, nous avons changé tout cela! We are going out—a jolly little razzle!" Vera, who was rather handsome, lifted up her face and smiled at her mother gaily.

"I am afraid there will be no *razzle*"—Beatrice accented the word, smiling slightly—"for me. You are slangy, Vera."

"Un doux argot, ma mère. You look tired."

Beatrice glanced at the clock.

"I will go to bed when I have cleared the table," she said.

Siegmund winced. He was still sitting with his head bent down, looking in the grate. Vera went on to say something more. Presently Frank looked up at the table, and remarked in his grating voice:

"There's your supper, father."

The women stopped and looked round at this. Siegmund bent his head lower. Vera resumed her talk. It died out, and there was silence.

Siegmund was hungry.

"Oh, good Lord, good Lord! bread of humiliation to-night!" he said to himself

before he could muster courage to rise and go to the table. He seemed to be
shrinking inwards. The women glanced swiftly at him and away from him as his
chair creaked and he got up. Frank was watching from under his eyebrows.

Siegmund went through the ordeal of eating and drinking in presence of his
family. If he had not been hungry, he could not have done it, despite the fact
that he was content to receive humiliation this night. He swallowed the coffee
with effort. When he had finished he sat irresolute for some time; then he arose
and went to the door.

"Good-night!" he said.

Nobody made any reply. Frank merely stirred in his chair. Siegmund shut the
door and went.

There was absolute silence in the room till they heard him turn on the tap in
the bathroom; then Beatrice began to breathe spasmodically, catching her breath
as if she would sob. But she restrained herself. The faces of the two children set
hard with hate.

"He is not worth the flicking of your little finger, mother," said Vera.

Beatrice moved about with pitiful, groping hands, collecting her sewing and
her cottons.

"At any rate, he's come back red enough," said Frank, in his grating tone of
contempt. "He's like boiled salmon."

Beatrice did not answer anything. Frank rose, and stood with his back to the
grate, in his father's characteristic attitude.

"I *would* come slinking back in a funk!" he said, with a young man's sneer.

Stretching forward, he put a piece of ham between two pieces of bread, and
began to eat the sandwich in large bites. Vera came to the table at this, and
began to make herself a more dainty sandwich. Frank watched her with jealous
eye.

"There is a little more ham, if you'd like it," said Beatrice to him. "I kept
you some."

"All right, ma," he replied. "Fetch it in."

Beatrice went out to the kitchen.

"And bring the bread-and-butter, too, will you?" called Vera after her.

"The damned coward! Ain't he a rotten funker?" said Frank, *sotto voce,* while
his mother was out of the room.

Vera did not reply, but she seemed tacitly to agree.

They petted their mother, while she waited on them. At length Frank yawned.
He fidgeted a moment or two, then he went over to his mother, and, putting his
hand on her arm—the feel of his mother's round arm under the black silk sleeve
made his tears rise—he said, more gratingly than ever:

"Ne'er mind, ma; we'll be all right to you." Then he bent and kissed her.
"Good-night, mother," he said awkwardly, and he went out of the room.

Beatrice was crying.

XXIII

I shall never re-establish myself," said Siegmund as he closed behind him the dining-room door and went upstairs in the dark. "I am a family criminal. Beatrice might come round, but the children's insolent judgment is too much. And I am like a dog that creeps round the house from which it escaped with joy. I have nowhere else to go. Why did I come back? But I am sleepy. I will not bother to-night."

He went into the bathroom and washed himself. Everything he did gave him a grateful sense of pleasure, notwithstanding the misery of his position. He dipped his arms deeper into the cold water, that he might feel the delight of it a little farther. His neck he swilled time after time, and it seemed to him he laughed with pleasure as the water caught him and fell away. The towel reminded him how sore were his forehead and his neck, blistered both to a state of rawness by the sun. He touched them very cautiously to dry them, wincing, and smiling at his own childish touch-and-shrink.

Though his bedroom was very dark he did not light the gas. Instead, he stepped out into the small balcony. His shirt was open at the neck and wrists. He pulled it farther apart, baring his chest to the deliciously soft night. He stood looking out at the darkness for some time. The night was as yet moonless, but luminous with a certain atmosphere of light. The stars were small. Near at hand, large shapes of trees rose up. Farther, lamps like little mushroom groups shone amid an undergrowth of darkness. There was a vague hoarse noise filling the sky, like the whispering in a shell, and this breathing of the summer night occasionally swelled into a restless sigh as a train roared across the distance.

"What a big night!" thought Siegmund. "The night gathers everything into a oneness. I wonder what is in it."

He leaned forward over the balcony, trying to catch something out of the night. He felt his soul like tendrils stretched out anxiously to grasp a hold. What could he hold to in this great, hoarse-breathing night? A star fell. It seemed to burst into sight just across his eyes with a yellow flash. He looked up, unable to make up his mind whether he had seen it or not. There was no gap in the sky.

"It is a good sign—a shooting star," he said to himself. "It is a good sign for me. I know I am right. That was my sign."

Having assured himself, he stepped indoors, unpacked his bag, and was soon in bed.

"This is a good bed," he said. "And the sheets are very fresh."

He lay for a little while with his head bending forwards, looking from his pillow out at the stars, then he went to sleep.

At half-past six in the morning he suddenly opened his eyes.

"What is it?" he asked, and almost without interruption answered: "Well, I've got to go through it."

His sleep had shaped him perfect premonition, which, like a dream, he forgot when he awoke. Only this naïve question and answer betrayed what had taken place in his sleep. Immediately he awoke this subordinate knowledge vanished.

Another fine day was striding in triumphant. The first thing Siegmund did was to salute the morning, because of its brightness. The second thing was to call to mind the aspect of that bay in the Isle of Wight. "What would it just be like now?" said he to himself. He had to give his heart some justification for the peculiar pain left in it from his sleep activity, so he began poignantly to long for the place which had been his during the last mornings. He pictured the garden with roses and nasturtiums; he remembered the sunny way down the shore, and all the expanse of sea hung softly between the tall white cliffs.

"It is impossible it is gone!" he cried to himself. "It can't be gone. I looked forward to it as if it never would come. It can't be gone now. Helena is not lost to me, surely." Then he began a long pining for the departed beauty of his life. He turned the jewel of memory, and facet by facet it wounded him with its brilliant loveliness. This pain, though it was keen, was half pleasure.

Presently he heard his wife stirring. She opened the door of the room next to his, and he heard her:

"Frank, it's a quarter to eight. You *will* be late."

"All right, mother. Why didn't you call me sooner?" grumbled the lad.

"I didn't wake myself. I didn't go to sleep till morning, and then I slept."

She went downstairs. Siegmund listened for his son to get out of bed. The minutes passed.

"The young donkey, why doesn't he get out?" said Siegmund angrily to himself. He turned over, pressing himself upon the bed in anger and humiliation, because now he had no authority to call to his son and keep him to his duty. Siegmund waited, writhing with anger, shame, and anxiety. When the suave, velvety "Pan-n-n! pan-n-n-n!" of the clock was heard striking, Frank stepped with a thud on to the floor. He could be heard dressing in clumsy haste. Beatrice called from the bottom of the stairs:

"Do you want any hot water?"

"You know there isn't time for me to shave now," answered her son, lifting his voice to a kind of broken falsetto.

The scent of the cooking of bacon filled the house. Siegmund heard his second daughter, Marjory, aged nine, talking to Vera, who occupied the same room with her. The child was evidently questioning, and the elder girl answered briefly. There was a lull in the household noises, broken suddenly by Marjory, shouting from the top of the stairs:

"Mam!" She waited. "Mam!" Still Beatrice did not hear her. "Mam! Mamma!" Beatrice was in the scullery. "Mamma-a!" The child was getting impatient. She lifted her voice and shouted: "Mam? Mamma!" Still no answer. "Mam-mee-e!" she squealed.

Siegmund could hardly contain himself.

"Why don't you go down and ask?" Vera called crossly from the bedroom.

And at the same moment Beatrice answered, also crossly: "What do you want?"

"Where's my stockings?" cried the child at the top of her voice.

"Why do you ask me? Are they down here?" replied her mother. "What are you shouting for?"

The child podded downstairs. Directly she returned, and as she passed into Vera's room, she grumbled: "And now they're not mended."

Siegmund heard a sound that made his heart beat. It was the crackling of the sides of the crib, as Gwen, his little girl of five, climbed out. She was silent for a space. He imagined her sitting on the white rug and pulling on her stockings. Then there came the quick little thud of her feet as she went downstairs.

"Mam," Siegmund heard her say as she went down the hall, "has dad come?"

The answer and the child's further talk were lost in the distance of the kitchen. The small, anxious question, and the quick thudding of Gwen's feet, made Siegmund lie still with torture. He wanted to hear no more. He lay shrinking within himself. It seemed that his soul was sensitive to madness. He felt that he could not, come what might, get up and meet them all.

The front door banged, and he heard Frank's hasty call: "Good-bye!" Evidently the lad was in an ill-humour. Siegmund listened for the sound of the train; it seemed an age; the boy would catch it. Then the water from the wash-hand bowl in the bathroom ran loudly out. That, he supposed, was Vera, who was evidently not going up to town. At the thought of this, Siegmund almost hated her. He listened for her to go downstairs. It was nine o'clock.

The footsteps of Beatrice came upstairs. She put something down in the bathroom—his hot water. Siegmund listened intently for her to come to his door. Would she speak? She approached hurriedly, knocked, and waited. Siegmund, startled, for the moment could not answer. She knocked loudly.

"All right," said he.

Then she went downstairs.

He lay probing and torturing himself for another half-hour, till Vera's voice said coldly, beneath his window outside:

"You should clear away, then. We don't want the breakfast things on the table for a week."

Siegmund's heart set hard. He rose, with a shut mouth, and went across to the bathroom. There he started. The quaint figure of Gwen stood at the bowl, her back was towards him; she was sponging her face gingerly. Her hair, all blowsed from the pillow, was tied in a stiff little pigtail, standing out from her slender, childish neck. Her arms were bare to the shoulder. She wore a bodiced petticoat of pink flannelette, which hardly reached her knees. Siegmund felt slightly amused to see her stout little calves planted so firmly close together. She carefully sponged her cheeks, her pursed-up mouth, and her neck, soaping her hair, but not her ears. Then, very deliberately, she squeezed out the sponge and proceeded to wipe away the soap.

For some reason or other she glanced round. Her startled eyes met his. She, too, had beautiful dark blue eyes. She stood, with the sponge at her neck, looking full at him. Siegmund felt himself shrinking. The child's look was steady, calm, inscrutable.

"Hello!" said her father. "Are you here!"

The child, without altering her expression in the slightest, turned her back on him, and continued wiping her neck. She dropped the sponge in the water and took the towel from off the side of the bath. Then she turned to look again at Siegmund, who stood in his pyjamas before her, his mouth shut hard, but his eyes shrinking and tender. She seemed to be trying to discover something in him.

"Have you washed your ears?" he said gaily.

She paid no heed to this, except that he noticed her face now wore a slight constrained smile as she looked at him. She was shy. Still she continued to regard him curiously.

"There is some chocolate on my dressing-table," he said.

"Where have you been to?" she asked suddenly.

"To the seaside," he answered, smiling.

"To Brighton?" she asked. Her tone was still condemning.

"Much farther than that," he replied.

"To Worthing?" she asked.

"Farther—in a steamer," he replied.

"But who did you go with?" asked the child.

"Why, I went all by myself," he answered.

"Twuly?" she asked.

"Weally and twuly," he answered, laughing.

"Couldn't you take me?" she asked.

"I will next time," he replied.

The child still looked at him, unsatisfied.

"But what did you go for?" she asked, goading him suspiciously.

"To see the sea and the ships and the fighting ships with cannons——"

"You *might* have taken me," said the child reproachfully.

"Yes, I ought to have done, oughtn't I?" he said, as if regretful.

Gwen still looked full at him.

"You *are* red," she said.

He glanced quickly in the glass, and replied:

"That is the sun. Hasn't it been hot?"

"Mm! It made my nose all peel. Vera said she would scrape me like a new potato." The child laughed and turned shyly away.

"Come here," said Siegmund. "I believe you've got a tooth out, haven't you?"

He was very cautious and gentle. The child drew back. He hesitated, and she drew away from him, unwilling.

"Come and let me look," he repeated.

She drew farther away, and the same constrained smile appeared on her face, shy, suspicious, condemning.

"Aren't you going to get your chocolate?" he asked, as the child hesitated in the doorway.

She glanced into his room, and answered:

"I've got to go to mam and have my hair done."

Her awkwardness and her lack of compliance insulted him. She went downstairs without going into his room.

Siegmund, rebuffed by the only one in the house from whom he might have expected friendship, proceeded slowly to shave, feeling sick at heart. He was a long time over his toilet. When he stripped himself for the bath, it seemed to him he could smell the sea. He bent his head and licked his shoulder. It tasted decidedly salt.

"A pity to wash it off," he said.

As he got up dripping from the cold bath, he felt for the moment exhilarated. He rubbed himself smooth. Glancing down at himself, he thought: "I look young. I look as young as twenty-six."

He turned to the mirror. There he saw himself a mature, complete man of forty, with grave years of experience on his countenance.

"I used to think that, when I was forty," he said to himself, "I should find everything straight as the nose on my face, walking through my affairs as easily as you like. Now I am no more sure of myself, have no more confidence than a boy of twenty. What can I do? It seems to me a man needs a mother all his life. I don't feel much like a lord of creation."

Having arrived at this cynicism, Siegmund prepared to go downstairs. His sensitiveness had passed off; his nerves had become callous. When he was dressed he went down to the kitchen without hesitation. He was indifferent to his wife and children. No one spoke to him as he sat to the table. That was as he liked it; he wished for nothing to touch him. He ate his breakfast alone, while his wife bustled about upstairs and Vera bustled about in the dining-room. Then he retired to the solitude of the drawing-room. As a reaction against his poetic activity, he felt as if he were gradually becoming more stupid and blind. He remarked nothing, not even the extravagant bowl of grasses placed where he would not have allowed it—on his piano; nor his fiddle, laid cruelly on the cold, polished floor near the window. He merely sat down in an armchair, and felt sick.

All his unnatural excitement, all the poetic stimulation of the past few days, had vanished. He sat flaccid, while his life struggled slowly through him. After an intoxication of passion and love, and beauty, and of sunshine, he was prostrate. Like a plant that blossoms gorgeously and madly, he had wasted the tissue of his strength, so that now his life struggled in a clogged and broken channel.

Siegmund sat with his head between his hands, leaning upon the table. He

would have been stupidly quiescent in his feeling of loathing and sickness had
not an intense irritability in all his nerves tormented him into consciousness.

"I suppose this is the result of the sun—a sort of sunstroke," he said, realizing
an intolerable stiffness of his brain, a stunned condition in his head.

"This is hideous!" he said. His arms were quivering with intense irritation. He
exerted all his will to stop them, and then the hot irritability commenced in his
belly. Siegmund fidgeted in his chair without changing his position. He had not
the energy to get up and move about. He fidgeted like an insect pinned down.

The door opened. He felt violently startled; yet there was no movement
perceptible. Vera entered, ostensibly for an autograph album into which she was
going to copy a drawing from the *London Opinion,* really to see what her father
was doing. He did not move a muscle. He only longed intensely for his daughter
to go out of the room, so that he could let go. Vera went out of the drawing-
room humming to herself. Apparently she had not even glanced at her father.
In reality, she had observed him closely.

"He is sitting with his head in his hands," she said to her mother.

Beatrice replied: "I'm glad he's nothing else to do."

"I should think he's pitying himself," said Vera.

"He's a good one at it," answered Beatrice.

Gwen came forward and took hold of her mother's skirt, looking up anxiously.

"What is he doing, mam?" she asked.

"Nothing," replied her mother—"nothing; only sitting in the drawing-room."

"But what has he *been* doing?" persisted the anxious child.

"Nothing—nothing that I can tell *you.* He's only spoilt all our lives."

The little girl stood regarding her mother in the greatest distress and perplexity.

"But what will he do, mam?" she asked.

"Nothing. Don't bother. Run and play with Marjory now. Do you want a nice
plum?"

She took a yellow plum from the table. Gwen accepted it without a word. She
was too much perplexed.

"What do you say?" asked her mother.

"Thank you," replied the child, turning away.

Siegmund sighed with relief when he was again left alone. He twisted in his
chair, and sighed again, trying to drive out the intolerable clawing irritability
from his belly.

"Ah, this is horrible!" he said.

He stiffened his muscles to quieten them.

"I've never been like this before. What is the matter?" he asked himself.

But the question died out immediately. It seemed useless and sickening to try
and answer it. He began to cast about for an alleviation. If he could only do
something, or have something he wanted, it would be better.

"What do I want?" he asked himself, and he anxiously strove to find this out.

Everything he suggested to himself made him sicken with weariness or distaste:
the seaside, a foreign land, a fresh life that he had often dreamed of, farming in
Canada.

"I should be just the same there," he answered himself. "Just the same sickening feeling there that I want nothing."

"Helena!" he suggested to himself, trembling.

But he only felt a deeper horror. The thought of her made him shrink convulsively.

"I can't endure this," he said. "If this is the case I had better be dead. To have no want, no desire—that is death, to begin with."

He rested awhile after this. The idea of death alone seemed entertaining. Then "Is there really nothing I could turn to?" he asked himself.

To him, in that state of soul, it seemed there was not.

"Helena!" he suggested again, appealingly testing himself. "Ah, no!" he cried, drawing sharply back, as from an approaching touch upon a raw place.

He groaned slightly as he breathed, with a horrid weight of nausea. There was a fumbling upon the door-knob. Siegmund did not start. He merely pulled himself together. Gwen pushed open the door, and stood holding on to the door-knob looking at him.

"Dad, mam says dinner's ready," she announced.

Siegmund did not reply. The child waited, at a loss for some moments, before she repeated, in a hesitating tone:

"Dinner's ready."

"All right," said Siegmund. "Go away."

The little girl returned to the kitchen with tears in her eyes, very crestfallen.

"What did he say?" asked Beatrice.

"He shouted at me," replied the little one, breaking into tears.

Beatrice flushed. Tears came into her own eyes. She took the child in her arms and pressed her to her, kissing her forehead.

"Did he?" she said very tenderly. "Never mind, then, dearie—never mind."

The tears in her mother's voice made the child sob bitterly. Vera and Marjory sat silent at table. The steak and mashed potatoes steamed and grew cold.

XXIV

When Helena arrived home on the Thursday evening she found everything repulsive. All the odours of the sordid street through which she must pass hung about the pavement, having crept out in the heat. The house was bare and narrow. She remembered children sometimes to have brought her moths shut up in matchboxes. As she knocked at the door she felt like a numbed moth which a boy is pushing off its leaf-rest into his box.

The door was opened by her mother. She was a woman whose sunken mouth, ruddy cheeks, and quick brown eyes gave her the appearance of a bird which walks about pecking suddenly here and there. As Helena reluctantly entered the mother drew herself up, and immediately relaxed, seeming to peck forwards as she said:

"Well?"

"Well, here we are!" replied the daughter in a matter-of-fact tone.

Her mother was inclined to be affectionate, therefore she became proportionately cold.

"So I see," exclaimed Mrs. Verden, tossing her head in a peculiar jocular manner. "And what sort of a time have you had?"

"Oh, very good," replied Helena, still more coolly.

"H'm!"

Mrs. Verden looked keenly at her daughter. She recognized the peculiar sulky, childish look she knew so well, therefore, making an effort, she forbore to question.

"You look well," she said.

Helena smiled ironically.

"And are you ready for your supper?" she asked, in the playful, affectionate manner she had assumed.

"If the supper is ready I will have it," replied her daughter.

"Well, it's not ready." The mother shut tight her sunken mouth, and regarded her daughter with playful challenge. "Because," she continued, "I didn't know when you were coming." She gave a jerk with her arm, like an orator who utters the incontrovertible. "But," she added, after a tedious dramatic pause, "I can soon have it ready. What will you have?"

"The full list of your capacious larder," replied Helena.

Mrs. Verden looked at her again, and hesitated.

"Will you have cocoa or lemonade?" she asked, coming to the point curtly.

"Lemonade," said Helena.

Presently Mr. Verden entered—a small, white-bearded man with a gentle voice.

"Oh, so you are back, Nellie!" he said, in his quiet, reserved manner.

"As you see, Pater," she answered.

"H'm!" he murmured, and he moved about at his accounts.

Neither of her parents dared to question Helena. They moved about her on tiptoe, stealthily. Yet neither subserved her. Her father's quiet "H'm!" her mother's curt question, made her draw inwards like a snail which can never retreat far enough from condemning eyes. She made a careless pretence of eating. She was like a child which has done wrong, and will not be punished, but will be left with the humiliating smear of offence upon it.

There was a quick, light palpitating of the knocker. Mrs. Verden went to the door.

"Has she come?"

And there were hasty steps along the passage. Louisa entered. She flung herself upon Helena and kissed her.

"How long have you been in?" she asked, in a voice trembling with affection.

"Ten minutes," replied Helena.

"Why didn't you send me the time of the train, so that I could come and meet you?" Louisa reproached her.

"Why?" drawled Helena.

Louisa looked at her friend without speaking. She was deeply hurt by this sarcasm.

As soon as possible Helena went upstairs. Louisa stayed with her that night. On the next day they were going to Cornwall together for their usual mid-summer holiday. They were to be accompanied by a third girl—a minor friend of Louisa, a slight acquaintance of Helena.

During the night neither of the two friends slept much. Helena made confidences to Louisa, who brooded on these, on the romance and tragedy which enveloped the girl she loved so dearly. Meanwhile, Helena's thoughts went round and round, tethered amid the five days by the sea, pulling forwards as far as the morrow's meeting with Siegmund, but reaching no further.

Friday was an intolerable day of silence, broken by little tender advances and playful, affectionate sallies on the part of the mother, all of which were rapidly repulsed. The father said nothing, and avoided his daughter with his eyes. In his humble reserve there was a dignity which made his disapproval far more difficult to bear than the repeated flagrant questionings of the mother's eyes. But the day wore on. Helena pretended to read, and sat thinking. She played her violin a little, mechanically. She went out into the town, and wandered about.

At last the night fell.

"Well," said Helena to her mother, "I suppose I'd better pack."

"Haven't you done it?" cried Mrs. Verden, exaggerating her surprise. "You'll never have it done. I'd better help you. What time does the train go?"

Helena smiled.

"Ten minutes to ten."

Her mother glanced at the clock. It was only half-past eight. There was ample time for everything.

"Nevertheless, you'd better look sharp," Mrs. Verden said.

Helena turned away, weary of this exaggeration.

"I'll come with you to the station," suggested Mrs. Verden. "I'll see the last of you. We shan't see much of you just now."

Helena turned round in surprise.

"Oh, I wouldn't bother," she said, fearing to make her disapproval too evident.

"Yes—I will—I'll see you off."

Mrs. Verden's animation and indulgence were remarkable. Usually she was curt and undemonstrative. On occasions like these, however, when she was reminded of the ideal relations between mother and daughter, she played the part of the affectionate parent, much to the general distress.

Helena lit a candle and went to her bedroom. She quickly packed her dress-basket. As she stood before the mirror to put on her hat her eyes, gazing heavily, met her heavy eyes in the mirror. She glanced away swiftly as if she had been burned.

"How stupid I look!" she said to herself. "And Siegmund, how is he, I wonder?"

She wondered how Siegmund had passed the day, what had happened to him, how he felt, how he looked. She thought of him protectively.

Having strapped her basket, she carried it downstairs. Her mother was ready, with a white lace scarf round her neck. After a short time Louisa came in. She dropped her basket in the passage, and then sank into a chair.

"I don't want to go, Nell," she said, after a few moments of silence.

"Why, how is that?" asked Helena, not surprised, but condescending, as to a child.

"Oh, I don't know; I'm tired," said the other petulantly.

"Of course you are. What do you expect, after a day like this?" said Helena.

"And rushing about packing," exclaimed Mrs. Verden, still in an exaggerated manner, this time scolding playfully.

"Oh, I don't know. I don't think I want to go, dear," repeated Louisa dejectedly.

"Well, it is time we set out," replied Helena, rising. "Will you carry the basket or the violin, Mater?"

Louisa rose, and with a forlorn expression took up her light luggage.

The west opposite the door was smouldering with sunset. Darkness is only smoke that hangs suffocatingly over the low red heat of the sunken day. Such was Helena's longed-for night. The tramcar was crowded. In one corner Olive, the third friend, rose excitedly to greet them. Helena sat mute, while the car swung through the yellow, stale lights of a third-rate street of shops. She heard Olive remarking on her sunburned face and arms; she became aware of the renewed inflammation in her blistered arms; she heard her own curious voice answering. Everything was in a maze. To the beat of the car, while the yellow blur of the shops passed over her eyes, she repeated: "Two hundred and forty miles—two hundred and forty miles."

XXV

Siegmund passed the afternoon in a sort of stupor. At teatime Beatrice, who had until then kept herself in restraint, gave way to an outburst of angry hysteria.

"When does your engagement at the Comedy Theatre commence?" she had asked him coldly.

He knew she was wondering about money.

"To-morrow—if ever," he had answered.

She was aware that he hated the work. For some reason or other her anger flashed out like sudden lightning at his "if ever."

"What do you think you *can* do?" she cried. "For I think you have done enough. We can't do as we like altogether—indeed, indeed we cannot. You have had your fling, haven't you? You have had your fling, and you want to keep on. But there's more than one person in the world. Remember that. But there are your children, let me remind you. Whose are they? You talk about shirking the engagement, but who is going to be responsible for your children, do you think?"

"I said nothing about shirking the engagement," replied Siegmund, very coldly.

"No, there was no need to say. I know what it means. You sit there sulking all day. What do you think *I* do? I have to see to the children, I have to work and slave, I go on from day to day. I tell you *I'll* stop, I tell you *I'll* do as I like. *I'll* go as well. No, I wouldn't be such a coward, you know that. You know *I* wouldn't leave little children—to the workhouse or anything. They're my children; they mightn't be yours."

"There is no need for this," said Siegmund contemptuously.

The pressure in his temples was excruciating, and he felt loathsomely sick.

Beatrice's dark eyes flashed with rage.

"Isn't there!" she cried. "Oh, isn't there? No, there is need for a great deal more. I don't know what you think I am. How much farther do you think you can go? No, you don't like reminding of us. You sit moping, sulking, because you have to come back to your own children. I wonder how much you think I shall stand? What do you think I am, to put up with it? What do you think I am? Am I a servant to eat out of your hand?"

"Be quiet!" shouted Siegmund. "Don't I know what you are? Listen to yourself!"

Beatrice was suddenly silenced. It was the stillness of white-hot wrath. Even Siegmund was glad to hear her voice again. She spoke low and trembling.

"You coward—you miserable coward! It is I, is it, who am wrong? It is I who am to blame, is it? You miserable thing! I have no doubt you know what I am."

Siegmund looked up at her as her words died off. She looked back at him with dark eyes loathing his cowed, wretched animosity. His eyes were bloodshot and furtive, his mouth was drawn back in a half-grin of hate and misery. She was goading him, in his darkness whither he had withdrawn himself like a sick dog, to die or recover as his strength should prove. She tortured him till his sickness was swallowed by anger, which glared redly at her as he pushed back his chair to rise. He trembled too much, however. His chin dropped again on his chest. Beatrice sat down in her place, hearing footsteps. She was shuddering slightly, and her eyes were fixed.

Vera entered with the two children. All three immediately, as if they found themselves confronted by something threatening, stood arrested. Vera tackled the situation.

"Is the table ready to be cleared yet?" she asked in an unpleasant tone.

Her father's cup was half emptied. He had come to tea late, after the others had left the table. Evidently he had not finished, but he made no reply, neither did Beatrice. Vera glanced disgustedly at her father. Gwen sidled up to her mother, and tried to break the tension.

"Mam, there was a lady had a dog, and it ran into a shop, and it licked a sheep, mam, what was hanging up."

Beatrice sat fixed, and paid not the slightest attention. The child looked up at her, waited, then continued softly:

"Mam, there was a lady had a dog——"

"Don't bother!" snapped Vera sharply.

The child looked, wondering and resentful, at her sister. Vera was taking the things from the table, snatching them, and thrusting them on the tray. Gwen's eyes rested a moment or two on the bent head of her father; then deliberately she turned again to her mother, and repeated in her softest and most persuasive tones:

"Mam, I saw a dog, and it ran in a butcher's shop and licked a piece of meat. Mam, mam!"

There was no answer. Gwen went forward and put her hand on her mother's knee.

"Mam!" she pleaded timidly.

No response.

"Mam!" she whispered.

She was desperate. She stood on tiptoe, and pulled with little hands at her mother's breast.

"Mam!" she whispered shrilly.

Her mother, with an effort of self-denial, put off her investment of tragedy, and, laying her arm round the child's shoulders, drew her close. Gwen was somewhat reassured, but not satisfied. With an earnest face upturned to the impassive countenance of her mother, she began to whisper, sibilant, coaxing, pleading:

"Mam, there was a lady, she had a dog——"

Vera turned sharply to stop this whispering, which was too much for her nerves, but the mother forestalled her. Taking the child in her arms, she averted her face, put her cheek against the baby cheek, and let the tears run freely. Gwen was too much distressed to cry. The tears gathered very slowly in her eyes, and fell without her having moved a muscle in her face. Vera remained in the scullery, weeping tears of rage, and pity, and shame into the towel. The only sound in the room was the occasional sharp breathing of Beatrice. Siegmund sat without the trace of a movement, almost without breathing. His head was ducked low; he dared never lift it, he dared give no sign of his presence.

Presently Beatrice put down the child, and went to join Vera in the scullery. There came the low sound of women's talking—an angry, ominous sound. Gwen followed her mother. Her little voice could be heard cautiously asking:

"Mam, is dad cross—is he? What did he do?"

"Don't bother!" snapped Vera. "You *are* a little nuisance! Here, take this into the dining-room, and don't drop it."

The child did not obey. She stood looking from her mother to her sister. The latter pushed a dish into her hand.

"Go along," she said, gently thrusting the child forth.

Gwen departed. She hesitated in the kitchen. Her father still remained unmoved. The child wished to go to him, to speak to him, but she was afraid. She crossed the kitchen slowly, hugging the dish; then she came slowly back, hesitating. She sidled into the kitchen; she crept round the table inch by inch, drawing nearer her father. At about a yard from his chair she stopped. He, from under his bent brows, could see her small feet in brown slippers, nearly kicked through at the toes, waiting and moving nervously near him. He pulled himself together, as a man does who watches the surgeon's lancet suspended over his wound. Would the child speak to him? Would she touch him with her small hands? He held his breath, and, it seemed, held his heart from beating. What he should do he did not know.

He waited in a daze of suspense. The child shifted from one foot to another. He could just see the edge of her white-frilled drawers. He wanted, above all things, to take her in his arms, to have something against which to hide his face. Yet he was afraid. Often, when all the world was hostile, he had found her full of love, he had hidden his face against her, she had gone to sleep in his arms, she had been like a piece of apple-blossom in his arms. If she should come to him now—his heart halted again in suspense—he knew not what he would do. It would open, perhaps, the tumour of his sickness. He was quivering too fast with suspense to know what he feared, or wanted, or hoped.

"Gwen!" called Vera, wondering why she did not return. "Gwen!"

"Yes," answered the child, and slowly Siegmund saw her feet lifted, hesitate, move, then turn away.

She had gone. His excitement sank rapidly, and the sickness returned stronger, more horrible and wearying than ever. For a moment it was so bad that he was afraid of losing consciousness. He recovered slightly, pulled himself up, and went upstairs. His fists were tightly clenched, his fingers closed over his thumbs, which were pressed bloodless. He lay down on the bed.

For two hours he lay in a dazed condition resembling sleep. At the end of that time the knowledge that he had to meet Helena was actively at work—an activity quite apart from his will or his consciousness, jogging and pulling him awake. At eight o'clock he sat up. A cramped pain in his thumbs made him wonder. He looked at them, and mechanically shut them again under his fingers into the position they sought after two hours of similar constraint. Siegmund opened his hands again, smiling.

"It is said to be the sign of a weak, deceitful character," he said to himself.

His head was peculiarly numbed; at the back it felt heavy, as if weighted with lead. He could think only one detached sentence at intervals. Between whiles there was a blank, grey sleep or swoon.

"I have got to go and meet Helena at Wimbledon," he said to himself, and instantly he felt a peculiar joy, as if he had laughed somewhere. "But I must be getting ready. I can't disappoint her," said Siegmund.

The idea of Helena woke a craving for rest in him. If he should say to her, "Do not go away from me; come with me somewhere," then he might lie down somewhere beside her, and she might put her hands on his head. If she could hold his head in her hands—for she had fine, silken hands that adjusted themselves with a rare pressure, wrapping his weakness up in life—then his head would gradually grow healed, and he could rest. This was the one thing that remained for his restoration—that she should with long, unwearying gentleness put him to rest. He longed for it utterly—for the hands and the restfulness of Helena.

"But it is no good," he said, starting like a drunken man from sleep. "What time is it?"

It was ten minutes to nine. She would be in Wimbledon by 10.10. It was time he should be getting ready. Yet he remained sitting on the bed.

"I am forgetting again," he said. "But I do not want to go. What is the good? I have only to tie a mask on for the meeting. It is too much."

He waited and waited; his head dropped forward in a sort of sleep. Suddenly he started awake. The back of his head hurt severely.

"Goodness," he said, "it's getting quite dark!"

It was twenty minutes to ten. He went bewildered into the bathroom to wash in cold water and bring back his senses. His hands were sore, and his face blazed with sun inflammation. He made himself neat as usual. It was ten minutes to ten. He would be very late. It was practically dark, though these bright days were endless. He wondered whether the children were in bed. It was too late, however, to wonder.

Siegmund hurried downstairs and took his hat. He was walking down the path when the door was snatched open behind him, and Vera ran out crying:

"Are you going out? Where are you going?"

Siegmund stood still and looked at her.

"She is frightened," he said to himself, smiling ironically.

"I am only going a walk. I have to go to Wimbledon. I shall not be very long."

"Wimbledon, at this time!" said Vera sharply, full of suspicion.

"Yes, I am late. I shall be back in an hour."

He was sorry for her. She knew he gave her an honourable promise.

"You need not keep us sitting up," she said.

He did not answer, but hurried to the station.

XXVI

Helena, Louisa, and Olive climbed the steps to go to the South-Western platform. They were laden with dress-baskets, umbrellas, and little packages. Olive and Louisa, at least, were in high spirits. Olive stopped before the indicator.

"The next train for Waterloo," she announced, in her contralto voice, "is 10.30. It is now 10.12."

"We go by the 10.40; it is a better train," said Helena.

Olive turned to her with a heavy-arch manner.

"Very well, dear. There is a parting to be got through, I am told. We sympathize, dear, but we regret it. Starting for a holiday is always a prolonged agony. But I am strong to endure it."

"You look it. You look as if you could tackle a bull," cried Louisa, skittish.

"My dear Louisa," rang out Olive's contralto, "don't judge me by appearances. You're sure to be taken in. With me it's a case of

"'Oh, the gladness of her gladness when she's sad,
    And the sadness of her sadness when she's glad!'"

She looked round to see the effect of this. Helena, expected to say something, chimed in sarcastically:

"'They are nothing to her madness——'"

"When she's going for a holiday, dear," cried Olive.

"Oh, go on being mad," cried Louisa.

"What, do you like it? I thought you'd be thanking Heaven that sanity was given me in large doses."

"And holidays in small," laughed Louisa. "Good! No, I like your madness, if you call it such. You are always so serious."

"'It's ill talking of halters in the house of the hanged,' dear," boomed Olive.

She looked from side to side. She felt triumphant. Helena smiled, acknowledging the sarcasm.

"But," said Louisa, smiling anxiously, "I don't quite see it. What's the point?"

"Well, to be explicit, dear," replied Olive, "it is hardly safe to accuse me of sadness and seriousness in *this* trio."

Louisa laughed and shook herself.

"Come to think of it, it isn't," she said.

Helena sighed, and walked down the platform. Her heart was beating thickly; she could hardly breathe. The station lamps hung low, so they made a ceiling of heat and dusty light. She suffocated under them. For a moment she beat with hysteria, feeling, as most of us feel when sick on a hot summer night, as if she must certainly go crazed, smothered under the grey, woolly blanket of heat. Siegmund was late. It was already twenty-five minutes past ten.

She went towards the booking-office. At that moment Siegmund came on to the platform.

"Here I am!" he said. "Where is Louisa?"

Helena pointed to the seat without answering. She was looking at Siegmund. He was distracted by the excitement of the moment, so she could not read him.

"Olive is there, too," she explained.

Siegmund stood still, straining his eyes to see the two women seated amidst pale wicker dress-baskets and dark rugs. The stranger made things more complex.

"Does she—your other friend—does she know?" he asked.

"She knows nothing," replied Helena in a low tone, as she led him forward to be introduced.

"How do you do?" replied Olive in most mellow contralto. "Behold the dauntless three, with their traps! You will see us forth on our perils?"

"I will, since I may not do more," replied Siegmund, smiling, continuing; "And how is Sister Louisa?"

"She is very well, thank you. It is *her* turn now," cried Louisa, vindictive, triumphant.

There was always a faint animosity in her bearing towards Siegmund. He understood, and smiled at her enmity, for the two were really good friends.

"It is your turn now," he repeated, smiling, and he turned away.

He and Helena walked down the platform.

"How did you find things at home?" he asked her.

"Oh, as usual," she replied indifferently. "And you?"

"Just the same," he answered. He thought for a moment or two, then added: "The children are happier without me."

"Oh, you mustn't say that kind of thing!" protested Helena miserably. "It's not true."

"It's all right, dear," he answered. "So long as they are happy, it's all right." After a pause he added: "But I feel pretty bad to-night."

Helena's hand tightened on his arm. He had reached the end of the platform. There he stood, looking up the line which ran dark under a haze of lights. The high red signal-lamps hung aloft in a scarlet swarm; farther off, like spangles shaking downwards from a burst sky-rocket, was a tangle of brilliant red and green signal-lamps settling. A train with the warm flare on its thick column of smoke came thundering upon the lovers. Dazed, they felt the yellow bar of carriage-windows brush in vibration across their faces. The ground and the air rocked. Then Siegmund turned his head to watch the red and the green lights in the rear of the train swiftly dwindle on the darkness. Still watching the distance where the train had vanished, he said:

"Dear, I want you to promise that, whatever happens to me, you will go on. Remember, dear, two wrongs don't make a right."

Helena swiftly, with a movement of terror, faced him, looking into his eyes. But he was in the shadow, she could not see him. The flat sound of his voice, lacking resonance—the dead, expressionless tone—made her lose her presence of mind. She stared at him blankly.

"What do you mean? What has happened? Something has happened to you. What has happened at home? What are you going to do?" she said sharply. She palpitated with terror. For the first time she felt powerless. Siegmund was beyond her grasp. She was afraid of him. He had shaken away her hold over him.

"There is nothing fresh the matter at home," he replied wearily. He was to be scourged with emotion again. "I swear it," he added. "And I have not made up my mind. But I can't think of life without you—and life must go on."

"And I swear," she said wrathfully, turning at bay, "that I won't live a day after you."

Siegmund dropped his head. The dead spring of his emotion swelled up scalding hot again. Then he said, almost inaudibly: "Ah, don't speak to me like that, dear. It is late to be angry. When I have seen your train out to-night there is nothing left."

Helena looked at him, dumb with dismay, stupid, angry.

They became aware of the porters shouting loudly that the Waterloo train was to leave from another platform.

"You'd better come," said Siegmund, and they hurried down towards Louisa and Olive.

"We've got to change platforms," cried Louisa, running forward and excitedly announcing the news.

"Yes," replied Helena, pale and impassive.

Siegmund picked up the luggage.

"I say," cried Olive, rushing to catch Helena and Louisa by the arm, "look— look—both of you—look at that hat!" A lady in front was wearing on her hat a wild and dishevelled array of peacock feathers. "It's the sight of a lifetime. I wouldn't have you miss it," added Olive in hoarse *sotto voce.*

"Indeed not!" cried Helena, turning in wild exasperation to look. "Get a good view of it, Olive. Let's have a good mental impression of it—one that will last."

"That's right, dear," said Olive, somewhat nonplussed by this outburst.

Siegmund had escaped with the heaviest two bags. They could see him ahead, climbing the steps. Olive readjusted herself from the wildly animated to the calmly ironical.

"After all, dear," she said, as they hurried in the tail of the crowd, "it's not half a bad idea to get a man on the job."

Louisa laughed aloud at this vulgar conception of Siegmund.

"Just now, at any rate," she rejoined.

As they reached the platform the train ran in before them. Helena watched anxiously for an empty carriage. There was not one.

"Perhaps it is as well," she thought. "We needn't talk. There will be three-quarters of an hour at Waterloo. If we were alone, Olive would make Siegmund talk."

She found a carriage with four people, and hastily took possession. Siegmund followed her with the bags. He swung these on the rack, and then quickly received the rugs, umbrellas, and packages from the other two. These he put on the seats or anywhere, while Helena stowed them. She was very busy for a moment or two; the racks were full. Other people entered; their luggage was troublesome to bestow.

When she turned round again she found Louisa and Olive seated, but Siegmund was outside on the platform, and the door was closed. He saw her face move as if she would cry to him. She restrained herself, and immediately called:

"You are coming? Oh, you are coming to Waterloo?"

He shook his head.

"I cannot come," he said.

She stood looking blankly at him for some moments, unable to reach the door because of the portmanteau thrust through with umbrellas and sticks, which stood on the floor between the knees of the passengers. She was helpless. Siegmund was repeating deliriously in his mind:

"Oh—go—go—go—when will she go?"

He could not bear her piteousness. Her presence made him feel insane.

"Would you like to come to the window?" a man asked of Helena kindly.

She smiled suddenly in his direction, without perceiving him. He pulled the portmanteau under his legs, and Helena edged past. She stood by the door, leaning forward with some of her old protective grace, her "Hawwa" spirit evident. Benign and shielding, she bent forward, looking at Siegmund. But her face was blank with helplessness, with misery of helplessness. She stood looking at Siegmund, saying nothing. His forehead was scorched and swollen, she noticed sorrowfully, and beneath one eye the skin was blistered. His eyes were bloodshot and glazed in a kind of apathy; they filled her with terror. He looked up at her because she wished it. For himself, he could not see her; he could only recoil from her. All he wished was to hide himself in the dark, alone. Yet she wanted him, and so far he yielded. But to go to Waterloo he could not yield.

The people in the carriage, made uneasy by this strange farewell, did not speak. There were a few taut moments of silence. No one seems to have strength to interrupt these spaces of irresolute anguish. Finally, the guard's whistle went. Siegmund and Helena clasped hands. A warm flush of love and healthy grief came over Siegmund for the last time. The train began to move, drawing Helena's hand from his.

"Monday," she whispered—"Monday," meaning that on Monday she should receive a letter from him. He nodded, turned, hesitated, looked at her, turned and walked away. She remained at the window watching him depart.

"Now, dear, we are manless," said Olive in a whisper. But her attempt at a joke fell dead. Everybody was silent and uneasy.

XXVII

He hurried down the platform, wincing at every stride, from the memory of Helena's last look of mute, heavy yearning. He gripped his fists till they trembled; his thumbs were again closed under his fingers. Like a picture on a cloth before him he still saw Helena's face, white, rounded, in feature quite mute and expressionless, just made terrible by the heavy eyes, pleading dumbly. He thought of her going on and on, still at the carriage window looking out; all through the night rushing west and west to the land of Isolde. Things began to haunt Siegmund like a delirium. He knew not where he was hurrying. Always in front of him, as on a cloth, was the face of Helena, while somewhere behind the cloth was Cornwall, a far-off lonely place where darkness came on intensely. Sometimes he saw a dim, small phantom in the darkness of Cornwall, very far off. Then the face of Helena, white, inanimate as a mask, with heavy eyes, came between again.

He was almost startled to find himself at home, in the porch of his house. The door opened. He remembered to have heard the quick thud of feet. It was Vera. She glanced at him, but said nothing. Instinctively she shrank from him. He passed without noticing her. She stood on the door-mat, fastening the door, striving to find something to say to him.

"You have been over an hour," she said, still more troubled when she found her voice shaking. She had no idea what alarmed her.

"Ay," returned Siegmund.

He went into the dining-room and dropped into his chair, with his head between his hands. Vera followed him nervously.

"Will you have anything to eat?" she asked.

He looked up at the table, as if the supper laid there were curious and incomprehensible. The delirious lifting of his eyelids showed the whole of the dark pupils and the blood-shot white of his eyes. Vera held her breath with fear. He sank his head again and said nothing. Vera sat down and waited. The minutes ticked slowly off. Siegmund neither moved nor spoke. At last the clock struck midnight. She was weary with sleep, querulous with trouble.

"Aren't you going to bed?" she asked.

Siegmund heard her without paying any attention. He seemed only to half hear. Vera waited awhile, then repeated plaintively:

"Aren't you going to bed, father?"

Siegmund lifted his head and looked at her. He loathed the idea of having to move. He looked at her confusedly.

"Yes, I'm going," he said, and his head dropped again. Vera knew he was not asleep. She dared not leave him till he was in his bedroom. Again she sat waiting.

"Father!" she cried at last.

He started up, gripping the arms of his chair, trembling.

"Yes, I'm going," he said.

He rose, and went unevenly upstairs. Vera followed him close behind.

"If he reels and falls backwards he will kill me," she thought, but he did not fall. From habit he went into the bathroom. While trying to brush his teeth he dropped the tooth-brush on to the floor.

"I'll pick it up in the morning," he said, continuing deliriously: "I must go to bed—I must go to bed—I am very tired." He stumbled over the door-mat into his own room.

Vera was standing behind the unclosed door of her room. She heard the sneck of his lock. She heard the water still running in the bathroom, trickling with the mysterious sound of water at dead of night. Screwing up her courage, she went and turned off the tap. Then she stood again in her own room, to be near the companionable breathing of her sleeping sister, listening. Siegmund undressed quickly. His one thought was to get into bed.

"One must sleep," he said as he dropped his clothes on the floor. He could not find the way to put on his sleeping-jacket, and that made him pant. Any little thing that roused or thwarted his mechanical action aggravated his sickness till his brain seemed to be bursting. He got things right at last, and was in bed.

Immediately he lapsed into a kind of unconsciousness. He would have called it sleep, but such it was not. All the time he could feel his brain working ceaselessly, like a machine running with unslackening rapidity. This went on, interrupted by little flickerings of consciousness, for three or four hours. Each time he had a glimmer of consciousness he wondered if he made any noise.

"What am I doing? What is the matter? Am I unconscious? Do I make any noise? Do I disturb them?" he wondered, and he tried to cast back to find the record of mechanical sense impression. He believed he could remember the sound of inarticulate murmuring in his throat. Immediately he remembered, he could feel his throat producing the sounds. This frightened him. Above all things, he was afraid of disturbing the family. He roused himself to listen. Everything was breathing in silence. As he listened to this silence he relapsed into his sort of sleep.

He was awakened finally by his own perspiration. He was terribly hot. The pillow, the bedclothes, his hair, all seemed to be steaming with hot vapour, whilst his body was bathed in sweat. It was coming light. Immediately he shut his eyes again and lay still. He was now conscious, and his brain was irritably active, but his body was a separate thing, a terrible, heavy, hot thing over which he had slight control.

Siegmund lay still, with his eyes closed, enduring the exquisite torture of the trickling of drops of sweat. First it would be one gathering and running its irregular, hesitating way into the hollow of his neck. His every nerve thrilled to it, yet he felt he could not move more than to stiffen his throat slightly. While yet the nerves in the track of this drop were quivering, raw with sensitiveness, another drop would start from off the side of his chest, and trickle downwards among the little muscles of his side, to drip on to the bed. It was like the running of a spider over his sensitive, moveless body. Why he did not wipe himself he did not know. He lay still and endured this horrible tickling, which seemed to bite deep into him, rather than make the effort to move, which he loathed to do. The drops ran off his forehead down his temples. Those he did not mind: he was blunt there. But they started again, in tiny, vicious spurts, down the sides of his chest, from under his armpits, down the inner sides of his thighs, till he seemed to have a myriad quivering tracks of a myriad running insects over his hot, wet, highly-sensitized body. His nerves were trembling, one and all, with outrage and vivid suspense. It became unbearable. He felt that, if he endured it another moment, he would cry out, or suffocate and burst.

He sat up suddenly, threw away the bedclothes, from which came a puff of hot steam, and began to rub his pyjamas against his sides and his legs. He rubbed madly for a few moments. Then he sighed with relief. He sat on the side of the bed, moving from the hot dampness of the place where he had lain. For a moment he thought he would go to sleep. Then, in an instant his brain seemed to click awake. He was still as loath as ever to move, but his brain was no longer clouded in hot vapour: it was clear. He sat, bowing forward on the side of the bed, his sleeping jacket open, the dawn stealing into the room, the morning air entering fresh through the wide-flung window-door. He felt a peculiar sense of guilt, of wrongness, in thus having jumped out of bed. It seemed to him as if he ought to have endured the heat of his body, and the infernal trickling of the drops of sweat. But at the thought of it he moved his hands gratefully over his sides, which now were dry, and soft, and smooth; slightly chilled on the surface perhaps, for he felt a sudden tremor of shivering from the warm contact of his hands.

Siegmund sat up straight: his body was re-animated. He felt the pillow and the groove where he had lain. It was quite wet and clammy. There was a scent of sweat on the bed, not really unpleasant, but he wanted something fresh and cool.

Siegmund sat in the doorway that gave on to the small veranda. The air was beautifully cool. He felt his chest again to make sure it was not clammy. It was smooth as silk. This pleased him very much. He looked out on the night again, and was startled. Somewhere the moon was shining duskily, in a hidden quarter of sky; but straight in front of him, in the north-west, silent lightning was fluttering. He waited breathlessly to see if it were true. Then, again, the pale lightning jumped up into the dome of the fading night. It was like a white bird stirring restlessly on its nest. The night was drenching thinner, greyer. The lightning, like a bird that should have flown before the arm of day, moved on its nest in the boughs of darkness, raised itself, flickered its pale wings rapidly, then sank again, loath to fly. Siegmund watched it with wonder and delight.

The day was pushing aside the boughs of darkness, hunting. The poor moon would be caught when the net was flung. Siegmund went out on the balcony to look at it. There it was, like a poor white mouse, a half-moon, crouching on the mound of its course. It would run nimbly over to the western slope, then it would be caught in the net, and the sun would laugh, like a great yellow cat, as it stalked behind playing with its prey, flashing out its bright paws. The moon, before making its last run, lay crouched, palpitating. The sun crept forth, laughing to itself as it saw its prey could not escape. The lightning, however, leaped low off the nest like a bird decided to go, and flew away. Siegmund no longer saw it opening and shutting its wings in hesitation amid the disturbance of the dawn. Instead there came a flush, the white lightning gone. The brief pink butterflies of sunrise and sunset rose up from the mown fields of darkness, and fluttered low in a cloud. Even in the west they flew in a narrow, rosy swarm. They separated, thinned, rising higher. Some, flying up, became golden. Some flew rosy gold across the moon, the mouse-moon motionless with fear. Soon the pink butterflies had gone, leaving a scarlet stretch like a field of poppies in the fens. As a wind, the light of day blew in from the east, puff after puff filling with whiteness the space which had been the night. Siegmund sat watching the last morning blowing in across the mown darkness, till the whole field of the world was exposed, till the moon was like a dead mouse which floats on water.

When the few birds had called in the August morning, when the cocks had finished their crowing, when the minute sounds of the early day were astir, Siegmund shivered disconsolate. He felt tired again, yet he knew he could not sleep. The bed was repulsive to him. He sat in his chair at the open door, moving uneasily. What should have been sleep was an ache and a restlessness. He turned and twisted in his chair.

"Where is Helena?" he asked himself, and he looked out on the morning.

Everything out of doors was unreal, like a show, like a peep-show. Helena was an actress somewhere in the brightness of this view. He alone was out of the piece. He sighed petulantly, pressing back his shoulders as if they ached. His arms, too, ached with irritation, while his head seemed to be hissing with angry irritability. For a long time he sat with clenched teeth, merely holding himself in check. In his present state of irritability everything that occurred to his mind stirred him with dislike or disgust. Helena, music, the pleasant company of friends, the sunshine of the country, each, as it offered itself to his thoughts, was met by an angry contempt, was rejected scornfully. As nothing could please or distract him, the only thing that remained was to support the discord. He felt as if he were a limb out of joint from the body of life: there occurred to his imagination a disjointed finger, swollen and discoloured, racked with pains. The question was, How should he reset himself into joint? The body of life for him meant Beatrice, his children, Helena, the Comic Opera, his friends of the orchestra. How could he set himself again into joint with these? It was impossible. Towards his family he would henceforward have to bear himself with humility. That was a cynicism. He would have to leave Helena, which he could not do. He would have to play strenuously, night after night, the music of "The Saucy Little Switzer," which was absurd. In fine, it was all absurd and impossible. Very well, then, that being so, what remained possible? Why, to depart. "If thine hand offend thee, cut it off." He could cut himself off from life. It was plain and straightforward.

But Beatrice, his young children, without him! He was bound by an agreement which there was no discrediting to provide for them. Very well, he must provide for them. And then what? Humiliation at home, Helena forsaken, musical comedy night after night. That was insufferable—impossible! Like a man tangled up in a rope, he was not strong enough to free himself. He could not break with Helena and return to a degrading life at home; he could not leave his children and go to Helena.

Very well, it was impossible! Then there remained only one door which he could open in this prison corridor of life. Siegmund looked round the room. He could get his razor, or he could hang himself. He had thought of the two ways before. Yet now he was unprovided. His portmanteau stood at the foot of the bed, its straps flung loose. A portmanteau strap would do. Then it should be a portmanteau strap!

"Very well!" said Siegmund, "it is finally settled. I had better write to Helena, and tell her, and say to her she must go on. I'd better tell her."

He sat for a long time with his notebook and a pencil, but he wrote nothing. At last he gave up.

"Perhaps it is just as well," he said to himself. "She said she would come with me—perhaps that is just as well. She will go to the sea. When she knows, the sea will take her. She must know."

He took a card, bearing her name and her Cornwall address, from his pocket-book, and laid it on the dressing-table.

"She will come with me," he said to himself, and his heart rose with elation.

"That is a cowardice," he added, looking doubtfully at the card, as if wondering whether to destroy it.

"It is in the hands of God. Beatrice may or may not send word to her at Tintagel. It is in the hands of God," he concluded.

Then he sat down again.

" 'But for that fear of something after-death,' " he quoted to himself.

"It is not fear," he said. "The act itself will be horrible and fearsome, but the after-death—it's no more than struggling awake when you're sick with a fright of dreams. 'We are such stuff as dreams are made of.' "

Siegmund sat thinking of the after-death, which to him seemed so wonderfully comforting, full of rest, and reassurance, and renewal. He experienced no mystical ecstasies. He was sure of a wonderful kindness in death, a kindness which really reached right through life, though here he could not avail himself of it. Siegmund had always inwardly held faith that the heart of life beat kindly towards him. When he was cynical and sulky he knew that in reality it was only a waywardness of his.

The heart of life is implacable in its kindness. It may not be moved to fluttering of pity; it swings on uninterrupted by cries of anguish or of hate.

Siegmund was thankful for this unfaltering sternness of life. There was no futile hesitation between doom and pity. Therefore, he could submit and have faith. If each man by his crying could swerve the slow, sheer universe, what a doom of guilt he might gain. If Life could swerve from its orbit for pity, what terror of vacillation; and who would wish to bear the responsibility of the deflection?

Siegmund thanked God that life was pitiless, strong enough to take his treasures out of his hands, and to thrust him out of the room; otherwise, how could he go with any faith to death; otherwise, he would have felt the helpless disillusion of a youth who finds his infallible parents weaker than himself.

"I know the heart of life is kind," said Siegmund, "because I feel it. Otherwise I would live in defiance. But Life is greater than me or anybody. We suffer, and we don't know why, often. Life doesn't explain. But I can keep faith in it, as a dog has faith in his master. After all, Life is as kind to me as I am to my dog. I have, proportionally, as much zest. And my purpose towards my dog is good. I need not despair of Life."

It occurred to Siegmund that he was meriting the old gibe of the atheists. He was shirking the responsibility of himself, turning it over to an imaginary god.

"Well," he said, "I can't help it. I do not feel altogether self-responsible."

The morning had waxed during these investigations. Siegmund had been vaguely aware of the rousing of the house. He was finally startled into a consciousness of the immediate present by the calling of Vera at his door.

"There are two letters for you, father."

He looked about him in bewilderment; the hours had passed in a trance, and he had no idea of his time or place.

"Oh, all right," he said, too much dazed to know what it meant. He heard his daughter going downstairs. Then swiftly returned over him the throbbing ache of his head and his arms, the discordant jarring of his body.

"What made her bring me the letters?" he asked himself. It was a very unusual attention. His heart replied, very sullen and shameful: "She wanted to know; she wanted to make sure I was all right."

Siegmund forgot all his speculations on a divine benevolence. The discord of his immediate situation overcame every harmony. He did not fetch in the letters.

"Is it so late?" he said. "Is there no more time for me?"

He went to look at his watch. It was a quarter to nine. As he walked across the room he trembled, and a sickness made his bones feel rotten. He sat down on the bed.

"What am I going to do?" he asked himself.

By this time he was shuddering rapidly. A peculiar feeling, as if his belly were turned into nothingness, made him want to press his fists into his abdomen. He remained shuddering drunkenly, like a drunken man who is sick, incapable of thought or action.

A second knock came at the door. He started with a jolt.

"Here is your shaving-water," said Beatrice in cold tones. "It's half-past nine."

"All right," said Siegmund, rising from the bed, bewildered.

"And what time shall you expect dinner?" asked Beatrice. She was still contemptuous.

"Any time. I'm not going out," he answered.

He was surprised to hear the ordinary cool tone of his own voice, for he was shuddering uncontrollably, and was almost sobbing. In a shaking, bewildered, disordered condition he set about fulfilling his purpose. He was hardly conscious of anything he did; try as he would, he could not keep his hands steady in the violent spasms of shuddering, nor could he call his mind to think. He was one shuddering turmoil. Yet he performed his purpose methodically and exactly. In every particular he was thorough, as if he were the servant of some stern will. It was a mesmeric performance, in which the agent trembled with convulsive sickness.

XXVIII

Siegmund's lying late in bed made Beatrice very angry. The later it became, the more wrathful she grew. At half-past nine she had taken up his shaving-water. Then she proceeded to tidy the dining-room, leaving the breakfast spread in the kitchen.

Vera and Frank were gone up to town; they would both be home for dinner at two o'clock. Marjory was despatched on an errand, taking Gwen with her. The children had no need to return home immediately, therefore it was highly probable they would play in the field or in the lane for an hour or two. Beatrice was alone downstairs. It was a hot, still morning, when everything out-doors shone brightly, and all indoors was dusked with coolness and colour. But Beatrice was angry. She moved rapidly and determinedly about the dining-room, thrusting old newspapers and magazines between the cupboard and the wall, throwing the litter in the grate, which was clear, Friday having been charwoman's day, passing swiftly, lightly over the front of the furniture with the duster. It was Saturday, when she did not spend much time over the work. In the afternoon she was going out with Vera. That was not, however, what occupied her mind as she brushed aside her work. She had determined to have a settlement with Siegmund, as to how matters should continue. She was going to have no more of the past three years' life; things had come to a crisis, and there must be an alteration. Beatrice was going to do battle, therefore she flew at her work, thus stirring herself up to a proper heat of blood. All the time, as she thrust things out of sight or straightened a cover, she listened for Siegmund to come downstairs.

He did not come, so her anger waxed.

"He can lie skulking in bed!" she said to herself. "Here I've been up since seven, broiling at it. I should think he's pitying himself. He ought to have something else to do. He ought to have to go out to work every morning, like another man, as his son has to do. He has had too little work. He has had too much his own way. But it's come to a stop now. I'll servant-housekeeper him no longer."

Beatrice went to clean the step of the front door. She clanged the bucket loudly, every minute becoming more and more angry. That piece of work finished, she

went into the kitchen. It was twenty past ten. Her wrath was at ignition point.
She cleared all the things from the table and washed them up. As she was so
doing, her anger, having reached full intensity without bursting into flame, began
to dissipate in uneasiness. She tried to imagine what Siegmund would do and
say to her. As she was wiping a cup, she dropped it, and the smash so unnerved
her that her hands trembled almost too much to finish drying the things and
putting them away. At last it was done. Her next piece of work was to make the
beds. She took her pail and went upstairs. Her heart was beating so heavily in
her throat that she had to stop on the landing to recover breath. She dreaded
the combat with him. Suddenly controlling herself, she said loudly at Siegmund's
door, her voice coldly hostile:

"Aren't you going to get up?"

There was not the faintest sound in the house. Beatrice stood in the gloom of
the landing, her heart thudding in her ears.

"It's after half-past ten—aren't you going to get up?" she called.

She waited again. Two letters lay unopened on a small table. Suddenly she put
down her pail and went into the bathroom. The pot of shaving-water stood
untouched on the shelf, just as she had left it. She returned and knocked swiftly
at her husband's door, not speaking. She waited, then she knocked again, loudly,
a long time. Something in the sound of her knocking made her afraid to try
again. The noise was dull and thudding: it did not resound through the house
with a natural ring, so she thought. She ran downstairs in terror, fled out into
the front garden, and there looked up at his room. The window-door was open—
everything seemed quiet.

Beatrice stood vacillating. She picked up a few tiny pebbles and flung them in
a handful at his door. Some spattered on the panes sharply; some dropped dully
in the room. One clinked on the wash-hand bowl. There was no response. Beatrice
was terribly excited. She ran, with her black eyes blazing, and wisps of her black
hair flying about her thin temples, out on to the road. By a mercy she saw the
window-cleaner just pushing his ladder out of the passage of a house a little
further down the road. She hurried to him.

"Will you come and see if there's anything wrong with my husband?" she
asked wildly.

"Why, mum?" answered the window-cleaner, who knew her, and was humbly
familiar. "Is he taken bad or something? Yes, I'll come."

He was a tall thin man with a brown beard. His clothes were all so loose, his
trousers so baggy, that he gave one the impression his limbs must be bone, and
his body a skeleton. He pushed at his ladders with a will.

"Where is he, mum?" he asked officiously, as they slowed down at the side
passage.

"He's in his bedroom, and I can't get an answer from him."

"Then Is'll want a ladder," said the window-cleaner, proceeding to lift one off
his trolley. He was in a very great bustle. He knew which was Siegmund's room:
he had often seen Siegmund rise from some music he was studying and leave
the drawing-room when the window-cleaning began, and afterwards he had found

him in the small front bedroom. He also knew there were matrimonial troubles: Beatrice was not reserved.

"Is it the least of the front rooms he's in?" asked the window-cleaner.

"Yes, over the porch," replied Beatrice.

The man bustled with his ladder.

"It's easy enough," he said. "The door's open, and we're soon on the balcony."

He set the ladder securely. Beatrice cursed him for a slow, officious fool. He tested the ladder, to see it was safe, then he cautiously clambered up. At the top he stood leaning sideways, bending over the ladder to peer into the room. He could see all sorts of things, for he was frightened.

"I say there!" he called loudly.

Beatrice stood below in horrible suspense.

"Go in!" she cried. "Go in! Is he there?"

The man stepped very cautiously with one foot on to the balcony, and peered forward. But the glass door reflected into his eyes. He followed slowly with the other foot, and crept forward, ready at any moment to take flight.

"Hie, hie!" he suddenly cried in terror, and he drew back.

Beatrice was opening her mouth to scream, when the window-cleaner exclaimed weakly, as if dubious:

"I believe 'e's 'anged 'imself from the door-'ooks!"

"No!" cried Beatrice. "No, no, no!"

"I believe 'e 'as!" repeated the man.

"Go in and see if he's dead!" cried Beatrice.

The man remained in the doorway, peering fixedly.

"I believe he is," he said doubtfully.

"No—go and see!" screamed Beatrice.

The man went into the room, trembling, hesitating. He approached the body as if fascinated. Shivering, he took it round the loins and tried to lift it down. It was too heavy.

"I know!" he said to himself, once more bustling now he had something to do. He took his clasp-knife from his pocket, jammed the body between himself and the door so that it should not drop, and began to saw his way through the leathern strap. It gave. He started, and clutched the body, dropping his knife. Beatrice, below in the garden, hearing the scuffle and the clatter, began to scream in hysteria. The man hauled the body of Siegmund, with much difficulty, on to the bed, and with trembling fingers tried to unloose the buckle in which the strap ran. It was bedded in Siegmund's neck. The window-cleaner tugged at it frantically, till he got it loose. Then he looked at Siegmund. The dead man lay on the bed with swollen, discoloured face, with his sleeping-jacket pushed up in a bunch under his arm-pits, leaving his side naked. Beatrice was screaming below. The window-cleaner, quite unnerved, ran from the room and scrambled down the ladder. Siegmund lay heaped on the bed, his sleeping-suit twisted and bunched up about him, his face hardly recognizable.

XXIX

Helena was dozing down in the cove at Tintagel. She and Louisa and Olive lay on the cool sands in the shadow, and steeped themselves in rest, in a cool, sea-fragrant tranquillity.

The journey down had been very tedious. After waiting for half an hour in the midnight turmoil of an August Friday in Waterloo Station, they had seized an empty carriage, only to be followed by five north-countrymen, all of whom were affected by whisky. Olive, Helena, Louisa, occupied three corners of the carriage. The men were distributed between them. The three women were not alarmed. Their tipsy travelling companions promised to be tiresome, but they had a frank honesty of manner that placed them beyond suspicion. The train drew out westward. Helena began to count the miles that separated her from Siegmund. The north-countrymen began to be jolly: they talked loudly in their uncouth English; they sang the music-hall songs of the day; they furtively drank whisky. Through all this they were polite to the girls. As much could hardly be said in return of Olive and Louisa. They leaned forward whispering one to another. They sat back in their seats laughing, hiding their laughter by turning their backs on the men, who were a trifle disconcerted by this amusement.

The train spun on and on. Little homely clusters of lamps, suggesting the quiet of country life, turned slowly round through the darkness. The men dropped into a doze. Olive put a handkerchief over her face and went to sleep. Louisa gradually nodded and jerked into slumber. Helena sat weariedly and watched the rolling of the sleeping travellers and the dull blank of the night sheering off outside. Neither the men nor the women looked well asleep. They lurched and nodded stupidly. She thought of Bazarof in "Fathers and Sons," endorsing his opinion on the appearance of sleepers: all but Siegmund. Was Siegmund asleep? She imagined him breathing regularly on the pillows; she could see the under arch of his eyebrows, the fine shape of his nostrils, the curve of his lips, as she bent in fancy over his face.

The dawn came slowly. It was rather cold. Olive wrapped herself in rugs and went to sleep again. Helena shivered, and stared out of the window. There appeared a wanness in the night, and Helena felt inexpressibly dreary. A rosiness spread out far away. It was like a flock of flamingoes hovering over a dark lake. The world vibrated as the sun came up.

Helena waked the tipsy men at Exeter, having heard them say that there they must change. Then she walked the platform, very jaded. The train rushed on again. It was a most, most wearisome journey. The fields were very flowery, the morning was very bright, but what were these to her? She wanted dimness, sleep, forgetfulness. At eight o'clock, breakfast time, the "dauntless three" were driving in a waggonette amid blazing, breathless sunshine, over country naked of shelter, ungracious and harsh.

"Why am I doing this?" Helena asked herself.

The three friends, washed, dressed, and breakfasted. It was too hot to rest in the house, so they trudged down to the coast, silently, each feeling in an ill humour.

When Helena was really rested, she took great pleasure in Tintagel. In the first place, she found that the cove was exactly, almost identically the same as the Walhalla scene in "Walküre"; in the second place, "Tristan" was here, in the tragic country filled with the flowers of a late Cornish summer, an everlasting reality; in the third place, it was a sea of marvellous, portentous sunsets, of sweet morning baths, of pools blossomed with life, of terrible suave swishing of foam which suggested the Anadyomene. In sun it was the enchanted land of divided lovers. Helena for ever hummed fragments of "Tristan." As she stood on the rocks she sang, in her little, half-articulate way, bits of Isolde's love, bits of Tristan's anguish, to Siegmund.

She had not received her letter on Sunday. That had not very much disquieted her, though she was disappointed. On Monday she was miserable because of Siegmund's silence, but there was so much of enchantment in Tintagel, and Olive and Louisa were in such high spirits, that she forgot most whiles.

On Monday night, towards two o'clock, there came a violent storm of thunder and lightning. Louisa started up in bed at the first clap, waking Helena. The room palpitated with white light for two seconds; the mirror on the dressing-table glared supernaturally. Louisa clutched her friend. All was dark again, the thunder clapping directly.

"There, wasn't that lovely!" cried Louisa, speaking of the lightning. "Oo, wasn't it magnificent!—glorious!"

The door clicked and opened: Olive entered in her long white nightgown. She hurried to the bed.

"I say, dear!" she exclaimed, "may I come into the fold? I prefer the shelter of your company, dear, during this little lot."

"Don't you like it?" cried Louisa. "I think it's *lovely*—lovely!"

There came another slash of lightning. The night seemed to open and shut. It was a pallid vision of a ghost-world between the clanging shutters of darkness. Louisa and Olive clung to each other spasmodically.

"There!" exclaimed the former, breathless. "That was fine! Helena, did you see that?"

She clasped ecstatically the hand of her friend, who was lying down. Helena's answer was extinguished by the burst of thunder.

"There's no accounting for tastes," said Olive, taking a place in the bed. "I can't say I'm struck on lightning. What about you, Helena?"

"I'm not struck yet," replied Helena, with a sarcastic attempt at a jest.

"Thank you, dear," said Olive; "you do me the honour of catching hold."

Helena laughed ironically.

"Catching what?" asked Louisa, mystified.

"Why, dear," answered Olive, heavily condescending to explain, "I offered Helena the handle of a pun, and she took it. What a flash! You know, it's not that I'm afraid. . . ."

The rest of her speech was overwhelmed in thunder.

Helena lay on the edge of the bed, listening to the ecstatics of one friend and to the impertinences of the other. In spite of her ironical feeling, the thunder impressed her with a sense of fatality. The night opened, revealing a ghostly landscape, instantly to shut again with blackness. Then the thunder crashed. Helena felt as if some secret were being disclosed too swiftly and violently for her to understand. The thunder exclaimed horribly on the matter. She was sure something had happened.

Gradually the storm drew away. The rain came down with a rush, persisted with a bruising sound upon the earth and the leaves.

"What a deluge!" exclaimed Louisa.

No one answered her. Olive was falling asleep, and Helena was in no mood to reply. Louisa, disconsolate, lay looking at the black window, nursing a grievance, until she, too, drifted into sleep. Helena was awake; the storm had left her with a settled sense of calamity. She felt bruised. The sound of the heavy rain bruising the ground outside represented her feeling; she could not get rid of the bruised sense of disaster.

She lay wondering what it was, why Siegmund had not written, what could have happened to him. She imagined all sorts of tragedy, all of them terrible, and endued with grandeur, for she had kinship with Hedda Gabler.

"But no," she said to herself, "it is impossible anything should have happened to him—I should have known. I should have known the moment his spirit left his body; he would have come to me. But I slept without dreams last night, and to-day I am sure there has been no crisis. It is impossible it should have happened to him: I should have known."

She was very certain that in event of Siegmund's death, she would have received intelligence. She began to consider all the causes which might arise to prevent his writing immediately to her.

"Nevertheless," she said at last, "if I don't hear to-morrow I will go and see."

She had written to him on Monday. If she should receive no answer by Wednesday morning she would return to London. As she was deciding this she went to sleep.

The next day passed without news. Helena was in a state of distress. Her wistfulness touched the other two women very keenly. Louisa waited upon her, was very tender and solicitous. Olive, who was becoming painful by reason of her unsatisfied curiosity, had to be told in part the state of affairs.

Helena looked up a train. She was quite sure by this time that something fatal awaited her.

The next morning she bade her friends a temporary good-bye, saying she would return in the evening. Immediately the train had gone, Louisa rushed into the little waiting-room of the station and wept. Olive shed tears for sympathy and self-pity. She pitied herself that she should be let in for so dismal a holiday. Louisa suddenly stopped crying and sat up:

"Oh, I know I'm a pig, dear, am I not?" she exclaimed. "Spoiling your holiday. But I couldn't help it, dear, indeed I could not."

"My dear Lou!" cried Olive in tragic contralto, "Don't refrain for my sake. The bargain's made; we can't help what's in the bundle."

The two unhappy women trudged the long miles back from the station to their lodging. Helena sat in the swinging express revolving the same thought like a prayer-wheel. It would be difficult to think of anything more trying than thus sitting motionless in the train, which itself is throbbing and bursting its heart with anxiety, while one waits hour after hour for the blow which falls nearer as the distance lessens. All the time Helena's heart and her consciousness were with Siegmund in London, for she believed he was ill and needed her.

"Promise me," she had said, "if ever I were sick and wanted you, you would come to me."

"I would come to you from hell!" Siegmund had replied.

"And if you were ill—you would let me come to you?" she had added.

"I promise," he answered.

Now Helena believed he was ill, perhaps very ill, perhaps she only could be of any avail. The miles of distance were like hot bars of iron across her breast, and against them it was impossible to strive. The train did what it could.

That day remains as a smear in the record of Helena's life. In it there is no spacing of hours, no lettering of experience, merely a smear of suspense.

Towards six o'clock she alighted at Surbiton Station, deciding that this would be the quickest way of getting to Wimbledon. She paced the platform slowly, as if resigned, but her heart was crying out at the great injustice of delay. Presently the local train came in. She had planned to buy a local paper at Wimbledon, and if from that source she could learn nothing, she would go on to his house and inquire. She had pre-arranged everything minutely.

After turning the newspaper several times she found what she sought.

"The funeral took place at two o'clock to-day at Kingston Cemetery, of——. Deceased was a professor of music, and had just returned from a holiday on the South Coast. . . ."

The paragraph, in a bald twelve lines, told her everything.

"Jury returned a verdict of suicide during temporary insanity. Sympathy was expressed for the widow and children."

Helena stood still on the station for some time, looking at the print. Then she dropped the paper and wandered into the town, not knowing where she was going.

"That was what I got," she said, months afterwards; "and it was like a brick, it was like a brick."

She wandered on and on, until suddenly she found herself in the grassy lane with only a wire fence bounding her from the open fields on either side, beyond which fields, on the left, she could see Siegmund's house standing florid by the road, catching the western sunlight. Then she stopped, realizing where she had come. For some time she stood looking at the house. It was no use her going there; it was of no use her going anywhere; the whole wide world was opened, but in it she had no destination, and there was no direction for her to take. As if marooned in the world, she stood desolate, looking from the house of Siegmund over the fields and the hills. Siegmund was gone; why had he not taken her with him?

The evening was drawing on; it was nearly half-past seven when Helena looked at her watch, remembering Louisa, who would be waiting for her to return to Cornwall.

"I must either go to her, or wire to her. She will be in a fever of suspense," said Helena to herself, and straightway she hurried to catch a tram-car to return to the station. She arrived there at a quarter to eight; there was no train down to Tintagel that night. Therefore she wired the news:

"Siegmund dead. No train to-night. Am going home."

This done, she took her ticket and sat down to wait. By the strength of her will everything she did was reasonable and accurate. But her mind was chaotic.

"It was like a brick," she reiterated, and that brutal simile was the only one she could find, months afterwards, to describe her condition. She felt as if something had crashed into her brain, stunning and maiming her.

As she knocked at the door of home she was apparently quite calm. Her mother opened to her.

"What, are you alone?" cried Mrs. Verden.

"Yes. Louisa did not come up," replied Helena, passing into the dining-room. As if by instinct she glanced on the mantel-piece to see if there was a letter. There was a newspaper cutting. She went forward and took it. It was from one of the London papers.

"Inquest was held to-day upon the body of——."

Helena read it, read it again, folded it up and put it in her purse. Her mother stood watching her, consumed with distress and anxiety.

"How did you get to know?" she asked.

"I went to Wimbledon and bought a paper," replied the daughter, in her muted, toneless voice.

"Did you go to the house?" asked the mother sharply.

"No," replied Helena.

"I was wondering whether to send you that paper," said her mother hesitatingly.

Helena did not answer her. She wandered about the house mechanically, looking for something. Her mother followed her, trying very gently to help her.

For some time Helena sat at table in the dining-room staring before her. Her parents moved restlessly in silence, trying not to irritate her by watching her, praying for something to change the fixity of her look. They acknowledged themselves helpless; like children, they felt powerless and forlorn, and were very quiet.

"Won't you go to rest, Nellie?" asked the father at last. He was an unobtrusive, obscure man, whose sympathy was very delicate, whose ordinary attitude was one of gentle irony.

"Won't you go to rest, Nellie?" he repeated.

Helena shivered slightly.

"Do, my dear," her mother pleaded. "Let me take you to bed."

Helena rose. She had a great horror of being fussed or petted, but this night she went dully upstairs, and let her mother help her to undress. When she was in bed the mother stood for some moments looking at her, yearning to beseech her daughter to pray to God; but she dared not. Helena moved with a wild impatience under her mother's gaze.

"Shall I leave you the candle?" said Mrs. Verden.

"No, blow it out," replied the daughter. The mother did so, and immediately left the room, going downstairs to her husband. As she entered the dining-room he glanced up timidly at her. She was a tall, erect woman. Her brown eyes, usually so swift and searching, were haggard with tears that did not fall. He bowed down, obliterating himself. His hands were tightly clasped.

"Will she be all right if you leave her?" he asked.

"We must listen," replied the mother abruptly.

The parents sat silent in their customary places. Presently Mrs. Verden cleared the supper table, sweeping together a few crumbs from the floor in the place where Helena had sat, carefully putting her pieces of broken bread under the loaf to keep moist. Then she sat down again. One could see she was keenly alert to every sound. The father had his hand to his head; he was thinking and praying.

Mrs. Verden suddenly rose, took a box of matches from the mantel-piece, and hurrying her stately, heavy tread, went upstairs. Her husband followed in much trepidation, hovering near the door of his daughter's room. The mother tremblingly lit the candle. Helena's aspect distressed and alarmed her. The girl's face was masked as if in sleep, but occasionally it was crossed by a vivid expression of fear or horror. Her wide eyes showed the active insanity of her brain. From time to time she uttered strange, inarticulate sounds. Her mother held her hands and soothed her. Although she was hardly aware of the mother's presence, Helena was more tranquil. The father went downstairs and turned out the light. He brought his wife a large shawl, which he put on the bedrail, and silently left the room. Then he went and kneeled down by his own bedside, and prayed.

Mrs. Verden watched her daughter's delirium, and all the time, in a kind of mental chant, invoked the help of God. Once or twice the girl came to herself, drew away her hand on recognizing the situation, and turned from her mother, who patiently waited until, upon relapse, she could soothe her daughter again. Helena was glad of her mother's presence, but she could not bear to be looked at.

Towards morning the girl fell naturally asleep. The mother regarded her closely, lightly touched her forehead with her lips, and went away, having blown out the candle. She found her husband kneeling in his nightshirt by the bed. He muttered a few swift syllables, and looked up as she entered.

"She is asleep," whispered the wife hoarsely.

"Is it a—a natural sleep?" hesitated the husband.

"Yes. I think it is. I think she will be all right."

"Thank God!" whispered the father, almost inaudibly.

He held his wife's hand as she lay by his side. He was the comforter. She felt as if now she might cry and take comfort and sleep. He, the quiet, obliterated man, held her hand, taking the responsibility upon himself.

XXX

*B*eatrice was careful not to let the blow of Siegmund's death fall with full impact upon her. As it were, she dodged it. She was afraid to meet the accusation of the dead Siegmund, with the sacred jury of memories. When the event summoned her to stand before the bench of her own soul's understanding, she fled, leaving the verdict upon herself eternally suspended.

When the neighbours had come, alarmed by her screaming, she had allowed herself to be taken away from her own house into the home of a neighbour. There the children were brought to her. There she wept, and stared wildly about, as if by instinct seeking to cover her mind with confusion. The good neighbour controlled matters in Siegmund's house, sending for the police, helping to lay out the dead body. Before Vera and Frank came home, and before Beatrice returned to her own place, the bedroom of Siegmund was locked.

Beatrice avoided seeing the body of her husband; she gave him one swift glance, blinded by excitement; she never saw him after his death. She was equally careful to avoid thinking of him. Whenever her thoughts wandered towards a consideration of how he must have felt, what his inner life must have been, during the past six years, she felt herself dilate with terror, and she hastened to invoke protection.

"The children!" she said to herself—"the children. I must live for the children; I must think for the children."

This she did, and with much success. All her tears and her wildness rose from terror and dismay rather than from grief. She managed to fend back a grief that would probably have broken her. Vera was too practical-minded, she had too severe a notion of what ought to be and what ought not, ever to put herself in her father's place and try to understand him. She concerned herself with judging him sorrowfully, exonerating him in part because Helena, that other, was so much more to blame. Frank, as a sentimentalist, wept over the situation, not over the personæ. The children were acutely distressed by the harassing behaviour of the elders, and longed for a restoration of equanimity. By common consent no word was spoken of Siegmund. As soon as possible after the funeral Beatrice moved from South London to Harrow. The memory of Siegmund began to fade rapidly.

Beatrice had had all her life a fancy for a more open, public form of living than that of a domestic circle. She liked strangers about the house; they stimulated her agreeably. Therefore, nine months after the death of her husband, she determined to carry out the scheme of her heart, and take in boarders. She came of a well-to-do family, with whom she had been in disgrace owing to her early romantic but degrading marriage with a young lad who had neither income nor profession. In the tragic, but also sordid, event of his death, the Waltons returned again to the aid of Beatrice. They came hesitatingly, and kept their gloves on. They inquired what she intended to do. She spoke highly and hopefully of her future boarding-house. They found her a couple of hundred pounds, glad to salve their consciences so cheaply. Siegmund's father, a winsome old man with a heart of young gold, was always ready further to diminish his diminished income for the sake of his grandchildren. So Beatrice was set up in a fairly large house in High-gate, was equipped with two maids, and gentlemen were invited to come and board in her house. It was a huge adventure, wherein Beatrice was delighted. Vera was excited and interested; Frank was excited, but doubtful and grudging; the children were excited, elated, wondering. The world was big with promise.

Three gentlemen came, before a month was out, to Beatrice's establishment. She hoped shortly to get a fourth or a fifth. Her plan was to play hostess, and thus bestow on her boarders the inestimable blessing of family life. Breakfast was at eight-thirty, and everyone attended. Vera sat opposite Beatrice, Frank sat on the maternal right hand; Mr. MacWhirter, who was *superior,* sat on the left hand; next him sat Mr. Allport, whose opposite was Mr. Holiday. All were young men of less than thirty years. Mr. MacWhirter was tall, fair, and stoutish; he was very quietly spoken, was humorous and amiable, yet extraordinarily learned. He never, by any chance, gave himself away, maintaining always an absolute reserve amid all his amiability. Therefore Frank would have done anything to win his esteem, while Beatrice was deferential to him. Mr. Allport was tall and broad, and thin as a door; he had also a remarkably small chin. He was naïve, inclined to suffer in the first pangs of disillusionment; nevertheless, he was waywardly humorous, sometimes wistful, sometimes petulant, always gentle and gallant. Therefore Vera liked him, whilst Beatrice mothered him. Mr. Holiday was short, very stout, very ruddy, with black hair. He had a disagreeable voice, was vulgar in the grain, but officiously helpful if appeal were made to him. Therefore Frank hated him. Vera liked his handsome, lusty appearance, but resented bitterly his behaviour. Beatrice was proud of the superior and skilful way in which she handled him, clipping him into shape without hurting him.

One evening in July, eleven months after the burial of Siegmund, Beatrice went into the dining-room and found Mr. Allport sitting with his elbow on the window-sill, looking out on the garden. It was half-past seven. The red rents between the foliage of the trees showed the sun was setting; a fragrance of evening-scented stocks filtered into the room through the open window; towards the south the moon was budding out of the twilight.

"What, you here all alone!" exclaimed Beatrice, who had just come from putting the children to bed. "I thought you had gone out."

"No—o! What's the use," replied Mr. Allport, turning to look at his landlady, "of going out? There's nowhere to go."

"Oh, come! There's the Heath, and the City—and you must join a tennis club. Now I know just the thing—the club to which Vera belongs."

"Ah, yes! You go down to the City—but there's nothing there—what I mean to say—you want a pal—and even then—well"—he drawled the word—"we-ell, it's merely escaping from yourself—killing time."

"Oh, don't say that!" exclaimed Beatrice. "You want to enjoy life."

"Just so! Ah, just so!" exclaimed Mr. Allport. "But all the same—it's like this— you only get up to the same thing to-morrow. What I mean to say—what's the good, after all? It's merely living because you've got to."

"You are too pessimistic altogether for a young man. I look at it differently myself; yet I'll be bound I have more cause for grumbling. What's the trouble now?"

"We-ell—you can't lay your finger on a thing like that! What I mean to say— it's nothing very definite. But, after all—what is there to do but to hop out of life as quick as possible? That's the best way."

Beatrice became suddenly grave.

"You talk in that way, Mr. Allport," she said. "You don't think of the others."

"I don't know," he drawled. "What does it matter? Look here—who'd care? What I mean to say—for long?"

"That's all very easy, but it's cowardly," replied Beatrice gravely.

"Nevertheless," said Mr. Allport, "it's true—isn't it?"

"It is not—and I *should* know," replied Beatrice, drawing a cloak of reserve ostentatiously over her face. Mr. Allport looked at her and waited. Beatrice relaxed towards the pessimistic young man.

"Yes," she said, "I call it very cowardly to want to get out of your difficulties in that way. Think what you inflict on other people. You men, you're all selfish. The burden is always left for the woman."

"Ah, but, then," said Mr. Allport very softly and sympathetically, looking at Beatrice's black dress, "I've no one depending on *me*."

"No—you haven't—but you've a mother and sister. The women always have to bear the brunt."

Mr. Allport looked at Beatrice, and found her very pathetic.

"Yes, they do rather," he replied sadly, tentatively waiting.

"My husband——" began Beatrice. The young man waited. "My husband was one of your sort: he ran after trouble, and when he'd found it—he couldn't carry it off—and left it—to me."

Mr. Allport looked at her very sympathetically.

"You don't mean it!" he exclaimed softly. "Surely he didn't——?"

Beatrice nodded, and turned aside her face.

"Yes," she said. "I know what it is to bear that kind of thing—and it's no light thing, I can assure you."

There was a suspicion of tears in her voice.

"And when was this, then—that he——?" asked Mr. Allport, almost with reverence.

"Only last year," replied Beatrice.

Mr. Allport made a sound expressing astonishment and dismay. Little by little Beatrice told him so much: "Her husband had got entangled with another woman. She herself had put up with it for a long time. At last she had brought matters to a crisis, declaring what she should do. He had killed himself—hanged himself— and left her penniless. Her people, who were very wealthy, had done for her as much as she would allow them. She and Frank and Vera had done the rest. She did not mind for herself; it was for Frank and Vera, who should be now enjoying their careless youth, that her heart was heavy."

There was silence for a time. Mr. Allport murmured his sympathy, and sat overwhelmed with respect for this little woman who was unbroken by tragedy. The bell rang in the kitchen. Vera entered.

"Oh, what a nice smell! Sitting in the dark, mother?"

"I was just trying to cheer up Mr. Allport; he is very despondent."

"Pray do not overlook me," said Mr. Allport, rising and bowing.

"Well! I did not see you! Fancy your sitting in the twilight chatting with the mater. You must have been an unscrupulous bore, maman."

"On the contrary," replied Mr. Allport, "Mrs. MacNair has been so good as to bear with me making a fool of myself."

"In what way?" asked Vera sharply.

"Mr. Allport is so despondent. I think he must be in love," said Beatrice playfully.

"Unfortunately, I am not—or at least I am not yet aware of it," said Mr. Allport, bowing slightly to Vera.

She advanced and stood in the bay of the window, her skirt touching the young man's knees. She was tall and graceful. With her hands clasped behind her back she stood looking up at the moon, now white upon the richly darkening sky.

"Don't look at the moon, Miss MacNair, it's all rind," said Mr. Allport in melancholy mockery. "Somebody's bitten all the meat out of our slice of moon, and left us nothing but peel."

"It certainly does look like a piece of melon-shell—one portion," replied Vera.

"Never mind, Miss MacNair," he said. "Whoever got the slice found it raw, I think."

"Oh, I don't know," she said. "But isn't it a beautiful evening? I will just go and see if I can catch the primroses opening."

"What! primroses?" he exclaimed.

"Evening primroses—there are some."

"Are there?" he said in surprise. Vera smiled to herself.

"Yes, come and look," she said.

The young man rose with alacrity.

Mr. Holiday came into the dining-room whilst they were down the garden.

"What, nobody in!" they heard him exclaim.

"There is Holiday," murmured Mr. Allport resentfully.

Vera did not answer. Holiday came to the open window, attracted by the fragrance.

"Ho! that's where you are!" he cried in his nasal tenor, which annoyed Vera's trained ear. She wished she had not been wearing a white dress to betray herself.

"What have you got?" he asked.

"Nothing in particular," replied Mr. Allport.

Mr. Holiday sniggered.

"Oh, well, if it's nothing particular and private——" said Mr. Holiday, and with that he leaped over the window-sill and went to join them.

"Curst fool!" muttered Mr. Allport. "I beg your pardon," he added swiftly to Vera.

"Have you ever noticed, Mr. Holiday," asked Vera, as if very friendly, "how awfully tantalizing these flowers are? They won't open while you're looking."

"No," sniggered he, "I don't blame 'em. Why should they give themselves away any more than you do? You won't open while you're watched." He nudged Allport facetiously with his elbow.

After supper, which was late and badly served, the young men were in poor spirits. Mr. MacWhirter retired to read. Mr. Holiday sat picking his teeth; Mr. Allport begged Vera to play the piano.

"Oh, the piano is not my instrument; mine was the violin, but I do not play now," she replied.

"But you will begin again," pleaded Mr. Allport.

"No, never!" she said decisively. Allport looked at her closely. The family tragedy had something to do with her decision, he was sure. He watched her interestedly.

"Mother used to play——" she began.

"Vera!" said Beatrice reproachfully.

"Let us have a song," suggested Mr. Holiday.

"Mr. Holiday wishes to sing, mother," said Vera, going to the music-rack.

"Nay—I—it's not me," Holiday began.

" 'The Village Blacksmith,' " said Vera, pulling out the piece. Holiday advanced. Vera glanced at her mother.

"But I have not touched the piano for—for years, I am sure," protested Beatrice.

"You can play beautifully," said Vera.

Beatrice accompanied the song. Holiday sang atrociously. Allport glared at him. Vera remained very calm.

At the end Beatrice was overcome by the touch of the piano. She went out abruptly.

"Mother has suddenly remembered that to-morrow's jellies are not made," laughed Vera.

Allport looked at her, and was sad.

When Beatrice returned, Holiday insisted she should play again. She would have found it more difficult to refuse than to comply.

Vera retired early, soon to be followed by Allport and Holiday. At half-past ten Mr. MacWhirter came in with his ancient volume. Beatrice was studying a cookery-book.

"You, too, at the midnight lamp!" exclaimed MacWhirter politely.

"Ah, I am only looking for a pudding for tomorrow," Beatrice replied.

"We shall feel hopelessly in debt if you look after us so well," smiled the young man ironically.

"I must look after you," said Beatrice.

"You do—wonderfully. I feel that we owe you large debts of gratitude." The meals were generally late, and something was always wrong.

"Because I scan a list of puddings?" smiled Beatrice uneasily.

"For the puddings themselves, and all your good things. The piano, for instance. That was very nice indeed." He bowed to her.

"Did it disturb you? But one does not hear very well in the study."

"I opened the door," said MacWhirter, bowing again.

"It is not fair," said Beatrice. "I am clumsy now—clumsy. I once could play."

"You play excellently. Why that 'once could'?" said MacWhirter.

"Ah, you are amiable. My old master would have said differently," she replied.

"We," said MacWhirter, "are humble amateurs, and to us you are more than excellent."

"Good old Monsieur Fannière, how he would scold me! He said I would not take my talent out of the napkin. He would quote me the New Testament. I always think Scripture sounds false in French, do not you?"

"Er—my acquaintance with modern languages is not extensive, I regret to say."

"No? I was brought up at a convent school near Rouen."

"Ah—that would be very interesting."

"Yes, but I was there six years, and the interest wears off everything."

"Alas!" assented MacWhirter, smiling.

"Those times were very different from these," said Beatrice.

"I should think so," said MacWhirter, waxing grave and sympathetic.

XXXI

*I*n the same month of July, not yet a year after Siegmund's death, Helena sat on the top of the tramcar with Cecil Byrne. She was dressed in blue linen, for the day had been hot. Byrne was holding up to her a yellow-backed copy of "Einsame Menschen," and she was humming the air of the Russian folk-song printed on the front page, frowning, nodding with her head, and beating time with her hand to get the rhythm of the song. She turned suddenly to him, and shook her head, laughing.

"I can't get it—it's no use. I think it's the swinging of the car prevents me getting the time," she said.

"These little outside things always come a victory over you," he laughed.

"Do they?" she replied, smiling, bending her head against the wind. It was six o'clock in the evening. The sky was quite overcast, after a dim, warm day. The tramcar was leaping along southwards. Out of the corners of his eyes Byrne watched the crisp morsels of hair shaken on her neck by the wind.

"Do you know," she said, "it feels rather like rain."

"Then," said he calmly, but turning away to watch the people below on the pavement, "you certainly ought not to be out."

"I ought not," she said, "for I'm totally unprovided."

Neither, however, had the slightest intention of turning back.

Presently they descended from the car, and took a road leading uphill off the highway. Trees hung over one side, whilst on the other side stood a few villas with lawns upraised. Upon one of these lawns two great sheep-dogs rushed and stood at the brink of the grassy declivity, at some height above the road, barking and urging boisterously. Helena and Byrne stood still to watch them. One dog was grey, as is usual, the other pale fawn. They raved extravagantly at the two pedestrians. Helena laughed at them.

"They are——" she began, in her slow manner.

"Villa sheep-dogs baying us wolves," he continued.

"No," she said, "they remind me of Fasner and Fasolt."

"Fasolt? They *are* like that. I wonder if they really dislike us."

"It appears so," she laughed.

"Dogs generally chum up to me," he said.

Helena began suddenly to laugh. He looked at her inquiringly.

"I remember," she said, still laughing, "at Knockholt—you—a half-grown lamb—a dog—in procession." She marked the position of the three with her finger.

"What an ass I must have looked!" he said.

"Sort of silent Pied Piper," she laughed.

"Dogs do follow me like that, though," he said.

"They did Siegmund," she said.

"Ah!" he exclaimed.

"I remember they had for a long time a little brown dog that followed him home."

"Ah!" he exclaimed.

"I remember, too," she said, "a little black-and-white kitten that followed me. Mater *would not* have it in—she would not. And I remember finding it, a few days after, dead in the road. I don't think I ever quite forgave my mater that."

"More sorrow over one kitten brought to destruction than over all the sufferings of men," he said.

She glanced at him and laughed. He was smiling ironically.

"For the latter, you see," she replied, "I am not responsible."

As they neared the top of the hill a few spots of rain fell.

"You know," said Helena, "if it begins it will continue all night. Look at that!" She pointed to the great dark reservoir of cloud ahead.

"Had we better go back?" he asked.

"Well, we will go on and find a thick tree; then we can shelter till we see how it turns out. We are not far from the cars here."

They walked on and on. The raindrops fell more thickly, then thinned away.

"It is exactly a year to-day," she said, as they walked on the round shoulder of the down with an oak-wood on the left hand. "Exactly!"

"What anniversary is it, then?" he inquired.

"Exactly a year to-day, Siegmund and I walked here—by the day, Thursday. We went through the larch-wood. Have you ever been through the larch-wood?"

"No."

"We will go, then," she said.

"History repeats itself," he remarked.

"How?" she asked calmly.

He was pulling at the heads of the cocksfoot grass as he walked.

"I see no repetition," she added.

"No," he exclaimed bitingly; "you are right!"

They went on in silence. As they drew near a farm they saw the men unloading a last waggon of hay on to a very brown stack. He sniffed the air. Though he was angry, he spoke.

"They got that hay rather damp," he said. "Can't you smell it—like hot tobacco and sandal-wood?"

"What, is that the stack?" she asked.

"Yes, it's always like that when it's picked damp."

The conversation was restarted, but did not flourish. When they turned on to
a narrow path by the side of the field he went ahead. Leaning over the hedge,
he pulled three sprigs of honeysuckle, yellow as butter, full of scent; then he
waited for her. She was hanging her head, looking in the hedge-bottom. He
presented her with the flowers without speaking. She bent forward, inhaled the
rich fragrance, and looked up at him over the blossoms with her beautiful,
beseeching blue eyes. He smiled gently to her.

"Isn't it nice?" he said. "Aren't they fine bits?"

She took them without answering, and put one piece carefully in her dress. It
was quite against her rule to wear a flower. He took his place by her side.

"I always like the gold-green of cut fields," he said. "They seem to give off
sunshine even when the sky's greyer than a tabby cat."

She laughed, instinctively putting out her hand towards the glowing field on
her right.

They entered the larch-wood. There the chill wind was changed into sound.
Like a restless insect he hovered about her, like a butterfly whose antennæ flicker
and twitch sensitively as they gather intelligence, touching the aura, as it were,
of the female. He was exceedingly delicate in his handling of her.

The path was cut windingly through the lofty, dark, and closely serried trees,
which vibrated like chords under the soft bow of the wind. Now and again he
would look down passages between the trees—narrow pillared corridors, dusky
as if webbed across with mist. All around was a twilight, thickly populous with
slender, silent trunks. Helena stood still, gazing up at the tree-tops where the
bow of the wind was drawn, causing slight, perceptible quivering. Byrne walked
on without her. At a bend in the path he stood, with his hand on the roundness
of a larch-trunk, looking back at her, a blue fleck in the brownness of congregated
trees. She moved very slowly down the path.

"I might as well not exist, for all she is aware of me," he said to himself
bitterly. Nevertheless, when she drew near he said brightly:

"Have you noticed how the thousands of dry twigs between the trunks make
a brown mist, a brume?"

She looked at him suddenly as if interrupted.

"H'm? Yes, I see what you mean."

She smiled at him, because of his bright boyish tone and manner.

"That's the larch fog," he laughed.

"Yes," she said, "you see it in pictures. I had not noticed it before."

He shook the tree on which his hand was laid.

"It laughs through its teeth," he said, smiling, playing with everything he
touched.

As they went along she caught swiftly at her hat; then she stooped, picking up
a hat-pin of twined silver. She laughed to herself as if pleased by a coincidence.

"Last year," she said, "the larch-fingers stole both my pins—the same ones."

He looked at her, wondering how much he was filling the place of a ghost
with warmth. He thought of Siegmund, and seemed to see him swinging down
the steep bank out of the wood exactly as he himself was doing at the moment,

with Helena stepping carefully behind. He always felt a deep sympathy and kinship with Siegmund; sometimes he thought he hated Helena.

They had emerged at the head of a shallow valley—one of those wide hollows in the North Downs that are like a great length of tapestry held loosely by four people. It was raining. Byrne looked at the dark blue dots rapidly appearing on the sleeves of Helena's dress. They walked on a little way. The rain increased. Helena looked about for shelter.

"Here," said Byrne—"here is our tent—a black tartar's—ready pitched."

He stooped under the low boughs of a very large yew-tree that stood just back from the path. She crept after him. It was really a very good shelter. Byrne sat on the ledge of a root, Helena beside him. He looked under the flap of the black branches down the valley. The grey rain was falling steadily; the dark hollow under the tree was immersed in the monotonous sound of it. In the open, where the bright young corn shone intense with wet green, was a fold of sheep. Exposed in a large pen on the hillside, they were moving restlessly; now and again came the "tong-ting-tong" of a sheep-bell. First the grey creatures huddled in the high corner, then one of them descended and took shelter by the growing corn lowest down. The rest followed, bleating and pushing each other in their anxiety to reach the place of desire, which was no whit better than where they stood before.

"That's like us all," said Byrne whimsically. "We're all penned out on a wet evening, but we think, if only we could get where someone else is, it would be deliciously cosy."

Helena laughed swiftly, as she always did when he became whimsical and fretful. He sat with his head bent down, smiling with his lips, but his eyes melancholy. She put her hand out to him. He took it without apparently observing it, folding his own hand over it, and unconsciously increasing the pressure.

"You are cold," he said.

"Only my hands, and they usually are," she replied gently.

"And mine are generally warm."

"I know that," she said. "It's almost the only warmth I get now—your hands. They really are wonderfully warm and close-touching."

"As good as a baked potato," he said.

She pressed his hand, scolding him for his mockery.

"So many calories per week—isn't that how we manage it?" he asked. "On credit?"

She put her other hand on his, as if beseeching him to forego his irony, which hurt her. They sat silent for some time. The sheep broke their cluster, and began to straggle back to the upper side of the pen.

"Tong-tong, tong," went the forlorn bell. The rain waxed louder.

Byrne was thinking of the previous week. He had gone to Helena's home to read German with her as usual. She wanted to understand Wagner in his own language.

In each of the armchairs, reposing across the arms, was a violin-case. He had sat down on the edge of one seat in front of the sacred fiddle. Helena had come quickly and removed the violin.

"I shan't knock it—it is all right," he had said, protesting.

This was Siegmund's violin, which Helena had managed to purchase, and Byrne was always ready to yield its precedence.

"It was all right," he repeated.

"But you were not," she had replied gently.

Since that time his heart had beat quick with excitement. Now he sat in a little storm of agitation, of which nothing was betrayed by his gloomy, pondering expression, but some of which was communicated to Helena by the increasing pressure of his hand, which adjusted itself delicately in a stronger and stronger stress over her fingers and palm. By some movement he became aware that her hand was uncomfortable. He relaxed. She sighed, as if restless and dissatisfied. She wondered what he was thinking of. He smiled quietly.

"The Babes in the Wood," he teased.

Helena laughed, with a sound of tears. In the tree overhead some bird began to sing, in spite of the rain, a broken evening song.

"That little beggar sees it's a hopeless case, so he reminds us of heaven. But if he's going to cover us with yew-leaves, he's set himself a job."

Helena laughed again, and shivered. He put his arm round her, drawing her nearer his warmth. After this new and daring move neither spoke for a while.

"The rain continues," he said.

"And will do," she added, laughing.

"Quite content," he said.

The bird overhead chirruped loudly again.

" 'Strew on us roses, roses,' " quoted Byrne, adding after a while, in wistful mockery: " 'And never a sprig of yew'—eh?"

Helena made a small sound of tenderness and comfort for him, and weariness for herself. She let herself sink a little closer against him.

"Shall it not be so—no yew?" he murmured.

He put his left hand, with which he had been breaking larch-twigs, on her chilled wrist. Noticing that his fingers were dirty, he held them up.

"I shall make marks on you," he said.

"They will come off," she replied.

"Yes, we come clean after everything. Time scrubs all sorts of scars off us."

"Some scars don't seem to go," she smiled.

And she held out her other arm, which had been pressed warm against his side. There, just above the wrist, was the red sun-inflammation from last year. Byrne regarded it gravely.

"But it's wearing off—even that," he said wistfully.

Helena put her arms round him under his coat. She was cold. He felt a hot wave of joy suffuse him. Almost immediately she released him, and took off her hat.

"That is better," he said.

"I was afraid of the pins," said she.

"I've been dodging them for the last hour," he said, laughing, as she put her arms under his coat again for warmth.

She laughed, and, making a small, moaning noise, as if of weariness and helplessness, she sank her head on his chest. He put down his cheek against hers.

"I want rest and warmth," she said, in her dull tones.

"All right!" he murmured.

Honour
and
Arms

I

They had marched more than thirty kilometres since dawn, along the white, hot road where occasional thickets of trees threw a moment of shade, then out into the glare again. On either hand, the valley, wide and shallow, glittered with heat; dark green patches of rye, pale young corn, fallow and meadow and black pine woods spread in a dull, hot diagram under a glistening sky. But right in front the mountains ranged across, pale blue and very still, snow gleaming gently out of the deep atmosphere. And towards the mountains, on and on, the regiment marched between the rye fields and the meadows, between the ruined fruit-trees set regularly on either side the high road. The burnished, dark green rye threw off a suffocating heat, the mountains drew gradually nearer and more distinct. While the feet of the soldiers grew hotter, sweat ran through their hair under their helmets, and their knapsacks could burn no more in contact with their shoulders, but seemed instead to give off a cold, prickly sensation.

He could now walk almost without pain. At the start, he had determined not to limp. It had made him sick to take the first steps, and during the first mile or so, he had held his breath, and the cold drops of sweat had stood on his forehead. But he had walked it off. What were they after all but bruises! He had looked at them, as he was getting up: deep bruises on the backs of his thighs. And since he had made his first step in the morning, he had been conscious of them, till now he had a tight, hot place in his chest, with suppressing the pain, and holding himself in. There seemed no air when he breathed. But he walked almost lightly.

The Captain's hand had trembled at taking his coffee at dawn: his orderly saw it again. And he saw the fine figure of the Captain wheeling on horseback at the farm-house ahead, a handsome figure in pale blue uniform with facings of scarlet, and the metal gleaming on the black helmet and the sword-scabbard, and dark streaks of sweat coming on the silky bay horse. The orderly felt he was connected with that figure moving so suddenly on horseback: he followed it like a shadow, mute and inevitable and damned by it. And the officer was always aware of the tramp of the company behind, the march of his orderly among the men.

The Captain was a tall man of about forty, grey at the temples. He had a handsome, finely-knit figure, and was one of the best horsemen in the West. His orderly, having to rub him down, admired the amazing riding-muscles of his loins.

For the rest, the orderly scarcely noticed the officer any more than he noticed himself. It was rarely he saw his master's face: he did not look at it. The Captain had reddish-brown, stiff hair, that he wore short and well brushed. His moustache was also cut short and bristly over a full, brutal mouth. His face was rather rugged, the cheeks thin. Perhaps the man was the more handsome for the deep lines in his face, the irritable tension of his brow, which gave him the look of a man who fights with life. His fair eye-brows stood bushy over light blue eyes that were always flashing with cold fire. He was a Prussian aristocrat, haughty and overbearing. Having made too many gambling debts when he was young, he had ruined his prospects in the Army, and remained an infantry captain. He had never married: his position did not allow of it, and no woman had ever moved him to it. His time he spent riding—occasionally on one of his own horses at the races—and at the officers' club. Now and then he took himself a mistress. But after such an event, he returned to duty with his brow still more tense, his eyes still more hostile and irritable.

The orderly was a youth of about twenty-two, of medium height, and well built. He had strong, heavy limbs, was swarthy, with a soft, black, young moustache. There was something altogether warm and young about him. He had firmly-marked eyebrows over dark, expressionless eyes, that seemed never to have thought, only to have received life direct through his senses, as if he acted straight from instinct.

Gradually the officer had become aware of his servant's young, vigorous, unconscious presence about him. He could not get away from the sense of the youth's person, while he was in attendance. There was something so free and self-contained about him, and something in the young fellow's movement, that made the elder man glance at him. And this irritated the Prussian. To see the soldier's young, brown, shapely peasant's hand grasp the loaf or the wine-bottle sent a flash of hate or of anger through the other man's blood. It was not that the youth was clumsy: it was rather the blind, instinctive sureness of movement of an unhampered young animal that irritated the officer to such a degree.

He had served the Captain for more than a year, and so knew his duty. This he performed easily, as if it were natural to him. The officer and his commands he took for granted, as he took the sun and the rain, and he served as a matter of course. It did not implicate him personally.

But in spite of himself, the Captain could not regain his neutrality of feeling towards his orderly. Nor could he leave the man alone. In spite of himself, he watched him, gave him sharp orders, tried to take up as much of his time as possible. Sometimes he flew into a rage with the young soldier, and bullied him. Then the orderly shut himself off, as it were out of earshot, and waited, with sullen, flushed face for the end of the noise. The words never pierced to his intelligence, and he made himself, protectively, impervious to the feelings of his master.

He had a scar on his left thumb, a deep seam going across the knuckle. The officer had long suffered from it, and wanted to do something to it. Still it was there, ugly and brutal on the young, brown hand. At last the Captain's reserve gave way. One day, as the orderly was smoothing out the tablecloth, the officer pinned down his thumb with a pencil, asking:

"How did you come by that?"

The young man winced and drew back at attention.

"A wood axe, Sir," he answered.

The officer waited for further explanation. None came. The orderly went about his duties. The elder man was sullenly angry. His servant avoided him. And the next day he had to use all his will-power to avoid seeing the scarred thumb. He wanted to get hold of it and——. A hot flame ran in his blood.

He knew his servant would soon be free, and would be glad. As yet, the soldier had held himself off from the elder man. The Captain grew madly irritable. He could not rest when the soldier was away, and when he was present, he glared at him with tormented eyes. He hated those fine, black brows over the reserved, dark eyes, he was infuriated by the free movement of the handsome limbs, which no military discipline could make stiff. And he became harsh and cruelly bullying, using contempt and satire. The young soldier only grew more mute and expressionless.

"What scum were you bred by, that you can't keep straight eyes? Look at me when I speak to you."

And the soldier turned his dark eyes to the other's face, but there was no sight in them: he stared with the slightest possible cast, holding back his sight, perceiving the blue of his master's eyes, but receiving no look from them. And the elder man went pale with fury, and his reddish eyebrows twitched. He gave his order, barrenly.

But there were only two months more. The youth tried to keep himself intact: he tried to serve the officer as if the latter were an abstract authority and not a man. All his instinct was to avoid personal contact, even definite hate. But in spite of himself the hate grew, responsive to the officer's passion. However, he would keep it in the background. When he had left the Army he could vent it in expression. By nature he was active, and had many friends. But there was always some part of himself that had been apart from his comrades, they had ranged themselves on their own side, left him alone on his. Now this solitariness was intensified. It would carry him through his term. But the officer seemed to be going irritably insane, and the youth was deeply frightened.

The soldier had a sweetheart, a girl from the mountains, independent and primitive. The two walked together, rather silently. He went with her, not to talk, but to have his arm round her, and for the physical contact. This eased him, made it easier for him to ignore the Captain; for he could rest with her held fast against his chest. And she, in some unbroken fashion, was there for him.

But the Captain perceived it, and was mad with mortification. He kept the young man engaged all the evenings long, and took pleasure in the dark look that came on his face. Occasionally, the eyes of the two men met, those of the younger sullen and reserved, waiting doggedly, those of the elder sneering with restless contempt.

The officer tried hard not to acknowledge the passion that had got hold of him. He would not admit that his feeling for his orderly was anything but that of a man incensed by a stupid, perverse servant. So, keeping quite justified and conventional in his consciousness, he let the other thing run on. His nerves, however, were suffering. At last he slung the end of a belt in his servant's face. When he saw the youth start back, the pain-tears in his eyes and the blood on his mouth, he had felt at once a thrill of deep pleasure and of shame.

But this, he acknowledged to himself, was a thing he had never done before. The fellow was too exasperating. But his own nerves must be going to pieces. He went away for some days with a woman.

It was a mockery of pleasure. He simply did not want the woman. But he hung on for his time. At the end of it, he came back in an agony of irritation, torment, and misery. He rode all the evening, then came straight in to supper. His orderly was out. The officer sat with his long, fine hands lying on the table, perfectly still, and all his blood seemed to be corroding.

At last his servant entered. He watched the strong, easy young figure, the fine eyebrows, the thick black hair. In a week's time the youth had got back his old well-being. The hands of the officer twitched and seemed to be full of mad flame. The young man stood at attention, unmoving, shut off.

The meal went in silence. But the orderly seemed eager. He made a clatter with the dishes.

"Are you in a hurry?" asked the officer, watching the intent, warm face of his servant. The other did not reply.

"Will you answer my question?" said the Captain.

"Yes, Sir," replied the orderly, standing with his pile of deep Army plates. The Captain waited, looked at him, then asked again:

"Are you in a hurry?"

"Yes, Sir," came the answer, that sent a flash through the listener.

"For what?"

"I was going out, Sir."

"I want you this evening."

There was a moment's hesitation. The officer had a curious stiffness of countenance.

"Yes, Sir," replied the servant, in his throat.

"I want you to-morrow evening also—in fact, you may consider your evenings occupied, unless I give you leave."

The mouth with the young moustache set close.

"Yes, Sir," answered the orderly, through shut teeth.

He again turned to the door.

"And why have you a piece of pencil in your ear?"

The orderly hesitated, then continued on his way without answering. He set the plates in a pile outside the door, took the stump of pencil from his ear, and put it in his pocket. Having had a sentimental impulse, he had been copying a verse for his sweetheart's birthday card. He returned to finish clearing the table. The officer's eyes were dancing, he had a little, eager smile.

"Why have you a piece of pencil in your ear?" he asked.

The orderly took his hands full of dishes. His master was standing near the great green stove, a little smile on his face, his chin thrust forward. When the young soldier saw him his heart suddenly ran hot. He felt blind. Instead of answering, he turned dazedly to the door. As he was crouching to set down the dishes, he was pitched forward by a kick from behind. The pots went in a stream down the stairs, he clung to the pillar of the bannisters. And as he was rising he was kicked heavily again, and again, so that he clung sickly to the post for some moments. His master had gone swiftly into the room and closed the door. The maid-servant downstairs looked up the staircase and made a mocking face at the crockery disaster.

The officer's heart was plunging.

"Schöner!" he said.

The soldier was a little slower in coming to attention.

"Yes, Sir!"

The youth stood before him, with pathetic young moustache, and fine eyebrows very distinct on his forehead of dark marble.

"I asked you a question."

"Yes, Sir."

The officer's tone bit like acid.

"Why had you a pencil in your ear?"

Again the servant's heart ran hot, and he could not breathe. With dark, strained eyes, he looked at the officer as if fascinated. And he stood there sturdily planted, unconscious. The withering smile came into the Captain's eyes, and he lifted his foot.

"I—I forgot it—Sir," panted the soldier, his dark eyes fixed on the other man's dancing blue ones.

"What was it doing there?"

He saw the young man's breast heaving as he panted for words.

"I had been writing."

"Writing what?"

Again the soldier looked him up and down. The officer could hear him panting. The smile came into the blue eyes. The soldier worked his dry throat, but could not speak. Suddenly the smile lit like a flame on the officer's face, and a kick came heavily against the orderly's thigh. The youth moved a pace sideways. His face went dead, with two black, staring eyes.

"Well?" said the officer.

The orderly's mouth had gone dry, and his tongue rubbed in it as on dry brown paper. He worked his throat. The officer raised his foot. The servant went stiff.

"Some poetry, Sir," came the crackling, unrecognisable sound of his voice.

"Poetry, to whom?" asked the Captain, with a sickly smile.

Again there was the working in the throat. The Captain's heart had suddenly gone down heavily, and he stood sick and tired.

"My girl, Sir," he heard the dry, inhuman sound.

"Oh!" he said, turning away. "Clear the table."

"Click" went the soldier's throat; then again, "click!"; and then the half-articulate: "Yes, Sir."

The young soldier was gone, looking old, and walking heavily.

The officer, left alone, held himself rigid, to prevent himself from thinking. His instinct warned him that he must not think. Deep inside him was the intense gratification of his passion, still working powerfully. Then there was a counter-action, a horrible breaking down of something inside him, a whole agony of reaction. He stood there for an hour motionless, a chaos of sensations, but rigid with a will to keep blank his consciousness, to prevent his mind grasping. And he held himself so until the worst of the stress had passed, when he began to drink, drank himself to an intoxication, till he slept obliterated.

The orderly had gone about in a stupor all the evening. He drank some beer because he was parched, but not much, the alcohol made his feeling come back, and he could not bear it. He was dulled, as if nine-tenths of the ordinary man in him were killed. He crawled about disfigured. Still, when he thought of the kicks, he went sick, and when he thought of the threat of more kicking, in the room afterwards, his heart went hot and faint, and he panted, remembering the one that had come. He had been forced to say, "To my girl." He was much too done even to want to cry.

In the morning were the manœuvres. But he woke even before the bugle sounded. The painful ache in his chest, the dryness of his throat, the awful steady feeling of misery made his eyes come awake and dreary at once. But he knew, without thinking, what had happened. And he knew that the day had come again, when he must go on with his round. The last bit of darkness was being pushed out of the room. He would have to drag up his inert body and go on. He was so young, and had known so little trouble, that he was bewildered. He only wished it would stay night, so that he could lie still, covered up by the darkness. And yet nothing would prevent the day from coming, nothing would save him from having to get up and saddle the Captain's horse, and make the Captain's coffee. It was there, inevitable. And then, he thought, it was impossible. Yet they would not leave him alone. He must go and take the coffee to the Captain. He was too stunned to understand it. He only knew it was inevitable—inevitable, however long he lay inert.

At last, after heaving at himself, for he seemed to be a mass of inertia, he got up. But he had to force every one of his movements from behind, with his will. He felt lost, and dazed, and helpless. Then he clutched hold of the bed, the pain was so keen. And looking at his thighs, he saw the darker bruises on his swarthy flesh and he knew that, if he pressed one of his fingers on one of the bruises, he should faint. But he did not want to faint—he did not want anybody to know. No one should ever know. It was between him and the Captain. There were only the two people in the world now—himself and the Captain.

Slowly, economically, he got dressed and forced himself to walk. Everything was obscure, except just what he had his hands on. But he managed to get through his work. The very pain revived his dull senses. The worst remained yet. He took the tray and went up to the Captain's room. The officer, pale and heavy, sat at the table. The orderly, as he saluted, felt himself put out of existence. He stood still for a moment submitting to his own nullification—then he gathered himself, on the rebound, and then the Captain seemed to grow vague, unreal, and the young soldier's heart beat up with pride. He clung to this sensation— that the Captain did not exist—so that he himself might live. But when he saw his officer's hand tremble as he took the coffee, he felt everything falling shattered. And he went away, feeling as if he himself were coming to pieces, disintegrated. And when the Captain was there on horseback, giving orders, while he himself stood, with rifle and knapsack, sick with pain, he felt as if he must shut his eyes and be gone—as if he must shut his eyes on his own existence. It was only the long agony of marching with a parched throat that filled him with one single, sleep-heavy intention: to get away, to save himself.

II

He was getting used even to his parched throat. That the snowy peaks were radiant among the sky, that the whitey-green glacier-river twisted through its pale shoals, in the valley below, seemed almost supernatural. But he was going mad with fever and thirst. He plodded on, uncomplaining. He did not want to complain, not to anybody. There were two gulls, like flakes of water and snow, over the river. The scent of green rye soaked in sunshine came like a sickness. And the march continued, monotonously, almost like a bad sleep.

At the next farm-house, which stood low and broad near the high road, tubs of water had been put out. The soldiers clustered round to drink. They took off their helmets, and the steam mounted from their wet hair. The Captain sat on horseback, watching. He needed to see his orderly. His helmet threw a dark shadow over his light, fierce eyes, but his moustache and mouth and chin were distinct in the sunshine. The orderly could scarcely move in the presence of the figure of the horseman. It was not that he was afraid, or cowed. It was as if he was disembowelled, made empty, like an empty shell. He felt himself as nothing, a shadow creeping under the sunshine. And, thirsty as he was, he could scarcely drink, feeling the Captain near him. He would not take off his helmet to wipe his wet hair. He wanted to efface himself, not to be forced into consciousness. Starting, he saw the light heel of the officer prick the belly of the horse; the Captain cantered away, and he himself could relapse into vacancy.

Nothing, however, could give him back his living place in the hot, bright morning. He felt like a gap among it all. Whereas the Captain was prouder and fuller. A hot flash went through the young servant's body. The Captain was firmer and prouder with life, he himself was empty as a shadow. Again the flash went through him, dazing him out. But his heart ran a little firmer.

The company turned up the hill, to make a loop for the return. Below, from among the trees, the farm-bell clanged. He saw the labourers, mowing bare-foot at the thick grass, leave off their work and go down hill, their scythes hanging over their shoulders, like long, bright claws curving down behind them. They seemed like dream-people, as if they had no relation to himself. He felt as he felt in a blackish dream: as if all the other things were there and had form, but he himself was only a consciousness, a gap that could think and perceive.

At last there was the halt. They stacked rifles in a conical stack, put down their kit in a scattered circle around it, and dispersed a little, sitting on a small knoll high on the hill-side. The chatter began. The soldiers were steaming with heat, but were lively. He sat still, seeing the blue mountains rising upon the land, twenty kilometres away.

Suddenly something moved into the coloured mirage before his eyes. The Captain, a small, light-blue and scarlet figure, was trotting evenly between the strips of corn, along the level brow of the hill. And the man making flag-signals was coming on. Proud and sure moved the horseman's figure, the quick, bright thing, in which was concentrated all the light of this morning, which for the rest lay a fragile, shining shadow. Submissive, apathetic, the young soldier sat and stared. But as the horse slowed to a walk, coming up the last steep path, the great flash flared over the body and soul of the orderly. He sat waiting. The back of his head felt as if it were weighted with a heavy piece of fire. He did not want to eat. His hands trembled slightly as he moved them. Meanwhile the officer on horseback was approaching slowly and proudly. The tension grew in the orderly's soul. Then again, seeing the Captain ease himself on the saddle, the flash blazed through him.

The Captain looked at the patch of light-blue and scarlet, and dark heads, scattered closely on the hill-side. It pleased him. The command pleased him. And he was feeling proud. His orderly was among them in common subjection. The officer rose a little on his stirrups to look. The young soldier sat with averted, dumb face. The Captain relaxed on to his seat. His slim-legged, beautiful horse, brown as a beech-nut, walked proudly uphill. The Captain passed into the zone of the company's atmosphere: a hot smell of men, of sweat, of leather. He knew it very well. After a word with the lieutenant, he went a few paces higher, and sat there, a dominant figure, his sweat-marked horse swishing its tail, while he looked down on his men, on his orderly, a nonentity among the crowd.

The young soldier's heart was like fire in his chest, and he breathed with difficulty. The officer, looking down-hill, saw three of the young soldiers, two pails of water between them, staggering across a sunny green field. A table had been set up under a tree, and there the slim lieutenant stood, importantly busy. Then the Captain summoned himself to an act of courage. He called his orderly.

The flame leapt into the young soldier's throat as he heard the command, and he rose blindly, stifled. He saluted, standing below the officer. He did not look up. But there was the flicker in the Captain's voice.

"Go to the inn and fetch me. . . ." the officer gave his commands. "Quick!" he added.

At the last word, the heart of the servant leapt with a flash, and he felt the strength come over his body. But he turned in mechanical obedience, and set off at a heavy run down-hill, looking almost like a bear, his trousers bagging over his military boots. And the officer watched this blind, plunging run all the way.

But it was only the outside of the orderly's body that was obeying so humbly and mechanically. Inside had gradually accumulated a core into which all the energy of that young life was compact and concentrated. He executed his commission, and plodded quickly back up-hill. There was a pain in his head, as he walked, that made him twist his features unknowingly. But hard there in the centre of his chest was himself, himself, firm, and not to be plucked to pieces.

The Captain had gone up into the wood. The orderly plodded through the hot, powerfully-smelling zone of the company's atmosphere. He had a curious mass of energy inside him now. The Captain was less real than himself. He approached the green entrance to the wood. There, in the half-shade, he saw the horse standing, the sunshine and the flickering shadow of leaves dancing over his brown body. There was a clearing where timber had lately been felled. Here, in the gold-green shade beside the brilliant cup of sunshine, stood two figures, blue and pink, the bits of pink showing out plainly. The Captain was talking to his lieutenant.

The orderly stood on the edge of the bright clearing, where great trunks of trees, supple and glistening, lay stretched like naked, brown-skinned bodies. Chips of wood littered the trampled floor, and the bases of the felled trees rose here and there, with their raw, level tops. Beyond was the brilliant, sunlit green of a beech.

"Then I will ride forward," the orderly heard his Captain say. The lieutenant saluted and strode away. He himself went forward. A hot flash passed through his belly, as he tramped towards his officer.

The Captain watched the rather heavy figure of the young soldier stumble forward, and his veins, too, ran hot. This was to be another man to man encounter. He yielded before the solid, stumbling figure with bent head. The orderly stooped and put the food on a level-sawn tree-base. The Captain watched the glistening, sun-inflamed, naked hands. He wanted to speak to the young soldier, but could not. The servant propped a bottle against his thigh, pressed open the cork, and poured out the beer into the mug. He kept his head bent. The Captain accepted the mug.

"Hot!" he said, as if amiably.

The flame sprang out of the orderly's heart, nearly suffocating him.

"Yes, Sir," he replied, between shut teeth.

And he heard the sound of the Captain's drinking, and he clenched his fists, such a strong torment came into his wrists. Then came the faint clang of the closing of the pot-lid. He looked up. The Captain was watching him. He glanced swiftly away. Then he saw the officer stoop and take a piece of bread from the tree-base. Again the flash of flame went through the young soldier, seeing the proud body stoop beneath him, and his hands jerked. He looked away. He could feel the officer was nervous. The bread fell as it was being broken. The officer ate the other piece. The two men stood tense and still, the master laboriously chewing his bread, the servant staring with averted face, his fists clenched.

Then the young soldier started. The officer had pressed open the lid of the pot again. The orderly watched the lid of the mug, and the white hand that clenched the handle, as if he were fascinated. It was raised. The youth followed it with his eyes. And then he saw the thin, strong throat of the elder man moving up and down as he drank, the strong jaw working. And the instinct which had been jerking at the young man's wrists suddenly jerked free. He jumped, feeling as if he were rent in two by a strong flame. He had lost his normal consciousness.

The spur of the officer caught in a tree-root, he went down backwards with a crash, the middle of his back thudding sickeningly against a sharp-edged tree-base, the pot flying away. And in a second his orderly, with serious, earnest young face, and underlip between his teeth, had got his knee in his chest and was pressing the chin backward over the farther edge of the tree stump, pressing, with all his heart behind in a passion of relief, the tension of his wrists exquisite with relief. And with the base of his palms he shoved at the chin, with all his might. And it was pleasant, too, to have that chin, that hard jaw already slightly rough with beard, in his hands. He did not relax one hair's breadth, but, all the force of all his blood exulting in his thrust, he shoved back the head of the other man, till there was a little "cluck" and a crunching sensation. Then he felt as if his head went to vapour. Heavy convulsions shook the body of the officer, frightening and horrifying the young soldier. Yet it pleased him, too, to repress them. It pleased him to keep his hands pressing back the chin, to feel the chest of the other man yield in expiration to the weight of his strong, young knees, to feel the hard twitchings of the prostrate body jerking his own whole frame, which was pressed down on it.

But it went still. He could look into the nostrils of the other man, the eyes he could scarcely see. How curiously the mouth was pushed out, exaggerating the full lips, and the moustache bristling up from them. Then, with a start, he noticed the nostrils gradually filled with blood. The red brimmed, hesitated, ran over, and went in a thin trickle down the face to the eyes.

It shocked and distressed him. Slowly, he got up. The body twitched and sprawled there, inert. He stood and looked at it in silence. It was a pity *it* was broken. It represented more than the thing which had kicked and bullied him. He was afraid to look at the eyes. They were hideous now, only the whites showing, and the blood running to them. The face of the orderly was drawn with horror at the sight. Well, it was so. In his heart he was satisfied. He had hated the face of the Captain, It was extinguished now. There was a heavy relief in the orderly's soul. That was as it should be. But he could not bear to see the long, military body lying broken over the tree-base, the fine fingers crisped. He wanted to hide it away.

Quickly, busily, he gathered it up and laid it under the felled tree trunks, which rested their beautiful, smooth length either end on logs. The face was horrible with blood. He covered it with the helmet. Then he put the limbs straight and decent, and brushed the dead leaves off the fine cloth of the uniform. So, it lay quite still in the shadow under there. A little strip of sunshine ran along the breast, from a chink between the logs. The orderly sat by it for a few moments. Here his own life also ended.

Then, through his daze, he heard the lieutenant, in a loud voice, explaining to the men outside the wood, that they were to suppose the bridge on the river below was held by the enemy. Now they were to march to the attack in such and such a manner. The lieutenant had no gift of expression. The orderly, listening from habit, got muddled. And when the lieutenant began it all again, he ceased to hear.

He knew he must go. He stood up. It surprised him that the leaves were glittering in the sun, and the chips of wood reflecting white from the ground. For him a change had come over the world. But for the rest it had not—all the world seemed the same. Only he had left it. And he could not go back. It was his duty to return with the beer-pot and the bottle. He could not. He had left all that. The lieutenant was still hoarsely explaining. He must go, or they would overtake him. And he could not bear contact with anyone now.

He drew his fingers over his eyes, trying to find out where he was. Then he turned away. He saw the horse standing in the path. He went up to it and mounted. It hurt him to sit in the saddle. The pain of keeping his seat occupied him as they cantered through the wood. He would not have minded anything, but he could not get away from the sense of being cut off from the others. The path led out of the trees. On the edge of the wood he pulled up and stood watching. There in the spacious sunshine of the valley soldiers were moving in a little swarm. Every now and then, a man harrowing on a strip of fallow shouted to his oxen, at the turn. The village and the white-towered church was small in the sunshine. And he no longer belonged to it—he sat there, beyond, like a man outside in the dark. He had gone out from every-day life into the unknown, and he could not, he even did not want to go back.

Turning from the sun-blazing valley, he rode deep into the wood. Tree-trunks, like people standing grey and still, took no notice as he went. A doe, herself a moving bit of sunshine and shadow, went running through the flecked shade. There were bright green rents in the foliage. Then it was all pinewood, dark and cool. And he was sick with pain, he had an intolerable great pulse in his head, and he was sick. He had never been ill in his life. He felt lost, quite dazed with all this.

Trying to get down from the horse, he fell, astonished at the pain and his lack of balance. The horse shifted uneasily. He jerked its bridle and sent it cantering jerkily away. It was his last connection with the rest of things.

But he only wanted to lie down and not be disturbed. Stumbling through the trees, he came on a quiet place where beeches and pine trees grew on a slope. Immediately he had lain down and closed his eyes, his consciousness went racing on without him. A big pulse of sickness beat in him as if it throbbed through the whole earth. He was burning with dry heat. But he was too busy, too tearingly active in the incoherent race of delirium to observe.

III

*H*e came to with a start. His mouth was dry and hard, his heart beat heavily, but he had not the energy to get up. His heart beat heavily. Where was he?—the barracks—at home? There was something knocking. And, making an effort, he looked round—trees, and litter of greenery, and reddish, bright, still pieces of sunshine on the floor. He did not believe he was himself, he did not believe what he saw. Something was knocking. He made a struggle towards consciousness, but relapsed. Then he struggled again. And gradually his surroundings fell into relationship with himself. He knew, and a great pang of fear went through his heart. Somebody was knocking. He could see the heavy, black rags of a fir-tree overhead. Then everything went black. Yet he did not believe he had closed his eyes. He had not. Out of the blackness sight slowly emerged again. And someone was knocking. Quickly, he saw the blood-disfigured face of his Captain, which he hated. And he held himself still with horror. Yet, deep inside him, he knew that it was so, the Captain should be dead. But the physical delirium got hold of him. Someone was knocking. He lay perfectly still, as if dead, with fear. And he went unconscious.

When he opened his eyes again, he started, seeing something creeping swiftly up a tree-trunk. It was a little bird. And a bird was whistling overhead. Tap-tap-tap—it was the small, quick bird rapping the tree-trunk with its beak, as if its head were a little round hammer. He watched it curiously. It shifted sharply, in its creeping fashion. Then, like a mouse, it slid down the bare trunk. Its swift creeping sent a flash of revulsion through him. He raised his head. It felt a great weight. Then, the little bird ran out of the shadow across a still patch of sunshine, its little head bobbing swiftly, its white legs twinkling brightly for a moment. How neat it was, in its build, so compact, with pieces of white on its wings. There were several of them. They were so pretty—but they crept like swift, erratic mice, running here and there among the beech-mast.

He lay down again, exhausted, and his consciousness lapsed. He had a horror of the little creeping birds. All his blood seemed to be darting and creeping.

Struggling to his feet, he lurched away. He went on walking, walking, looking for something—for a drink. His brain felt hot and inflamed for want of water. He stumbled on. Then he did not know anything. He went unconscious as he walked. Yet he stumbled on, his mouth open.

When, to his dumb wonder, he opened his eyes on the world again, he no longer tried to remember what it was. There was thick, golden light behind golden-green glitterings, and tall, grey-purple shafts, and darknesses further off, surrounding him, growing deeper. He was conscious of a sense of arrival. He was amid the truth. But there was the thirst burning a hole in his brain. He felt lighter, not so heavy. He supposed it was newness. The air was muttering with thunder. He thought he was walking wonderfully swiftly and was coming straight to relief—or to water to drink.

Suddenly he stood still with fear. There was a tremendous flare of deep gold, immense—just a few dark trunks like bars between him and it. All the young level wheat was burnished, gold glaring on its silky green. A woman, full-skirted, a black cloth on her head for head-dress, was passing like a block of shadow through the glistening, green corn, into the full glare. There was a farm, too, pale blue in shadow, and the timber black. And there was a church-spire, nearly fused away in the gold. The woman moved on, away from him. He had no language with which to speak to her. His connection with her was gone. She would make a noise of words that would confuse him, and her eyes would look at him without seeing him. She was crossing there to the other side. He stood leaning against a tree.

When at last he turned, looking down the long, bare groove whose flat bed was already filling dark, he saw the mountains in a wonder-light, not far away, and radiant. Behind the soft, grey ridge of the nearest range the further mountains stood golden and pale grey, the snow all radiant like pure, soft gold. So still, gleaming in the sky, fashioned pure out of the ore of the sky, they shone in their silence. He stood and looked at them, his face illuminated. And like the golden, lustrous gleaming of the snow he felt his own thirst bright in him. He stood and gazed, leaning against a tree. And then everything slid away into space.

During the night the lightning fluttered perpetually, making the whole sky white. He must have walked again. The world hung livid round him for moments, fields a level sheen of grey-green light, trees in dark bulk, and the range of clouds black across a white sky. Then the darkness fell like a shutter, and the night was whole. A faint flutter of a half-revealed world, that could not quite leap out of the darkness!—Then there again stood a sweep of pallor for the land, dark shapes looming, a range of clouds hanging overhead. The world was a ghostly shadow, thrown for a moment upon the pure darkness, which returned ever whole and complete.

And the mere delirium of sickness and fever went on inside him—his brain opening and shutting like the night—then sometimes convulsions of terror from something with great eyes that stared round a tree—then the long agony of the march, and the sun decomposing his blood—then the pang of hate for the Captain, followed by the pang of tenderness and ease. But everything was distorted, born of an ache and resolving into an ache.

In the morning he came definitely awake. Then his brain flamed with the sole horror of thirstiness! The sun was on his face, the dew was steaming from his wet clothes. Like one possessed, he got up. There, straight in front of him, blue and cool and tender, the mountains ranged across the pale edge of the morning sky. He wanted them—he wanted them alone—he wanted to leave himself, to be identified with them. They did not move, they were still and soft, with white, gentle markings of snow. He stood still, mad with suffering, his hands crisping and clutching. Then he was twisting in a paroxysm on the grass.

He lay still, in a kind of dream of anguish. His thirst seemed to have separated itself from him, and to stand apart, a single demand. Then the pain he felt was another single self. Then there was the clog of his body, another separate thing. He was divided among all kinds of separate beings. There was some strange, agonised connection between them, but they were drawing further apart. Then they would all split. The sun, drilling down on him, was drilling through the bond. Then they would all fall, fall through the everlasting lapse of space.

Then again, his consciousness reasserted itself. He roused on to his elbow and stared at the gleaming mountains. There they ranked, all still and wonderful between earth and heaven. He stared till his eyes went black, and the mountains, as they stood in their beauty, so clean and cool, seemed to have it, that which was lost in him.

IV

When the soldiers found him, three hours later, he was lying with his face over his arm, his black hair giving off heat under the sun. But he was still alive. Seeing the open, black mouth the young soldiers started from him in horror.

He died in the hospital at night without having seen again.

The doctors saw the bruises on his legs, behind, and were silent. On this account the affair was hushed up.

The bodies of the two men lay together, side by side, in the mortuary, the one white and slender, but laid rigidly at rest, the other looking as if every moment it must rouse into life again, so young and unused, from a slumber.

Sun

*T*ake her away, into the sun," the doctor said. She herself was sceptical of the sun, but she permitted herself to be carried away, with her child, and a nurse, and her mother, over the sea.

The ship sailed at midnight. And for two hours her husband stayed with her, while the child was put to bed, and the passengers came on board. It was a black night, the Hudson swayed with heaving blackness; shaken over with spilled dribbles of light. She leaned over the rail, and looking down thought: this is the sea; it is deeper than one imagines, and fuller of memories. At that moment the sea seemed to heave like the serpent of chaos that has lived for ever.

"These partings are no good, you know," her husband was saying, at her side. "They're no good. I don't like them."

His tone was full of apprehension, misgiving, and there was a certain clinging to the last straw of hope.

"No, neither do I," she responded in a flat voice.

She remembered how bitterly they wanted to get away from one another, he and she. The emotion of parting gave a slight tug at her emotions, but only caused the iron that had gone into her soul to gore deeper.

So, they looked at their sleeping son, and the father's eyes were wet. But it is not the wetting of the eyes that counts, it is the deep iron rhythm of habit, the year-long, life-long habits; the deepset stroke of power.

And in their two lives, the stroke of power was hostile, his and hers. Like two engines running at variance, they shattered one another.

"All ashore! All ashore!"

"Maurice, you must go."

And she thought to herself: For him it is All Ashore! For me it is Out to Sea!

Well, he waved his hanky on the midnight dreariness of the pier, as the boat inched away; one among a crowd. One among a crowd! C'est ca!

The ferry-boats, like great dishes piled with rows of lights, were still slanting across the Hudson. That black mouth must be the Lackawanna Station.

The ship ebbed on between the lights, the Hudson seemed interminable. But at last they were round the bend, and there was the poor harvest of lights at the Battery. Liberty flung up her torch in a tantrum. There was the wash of the sea.

And though the Atlantic was grey as lava, they did come at last into the sun. Even she had a house above the bluest of seas, with a vast garden, or vineyard, all vines and olives, dropping steeply in terrace after terrace, to the strip of coast plain; and the garden full of secret places, deep groves of lemon far down in the cleft of earth, and hidden, pure green reservoirs of water; then a spring issuing out of a little cavern, where the old Sicules had drunk before the Greeks came; and a grey goat bleating, stabled in an ancient tomb with the niches empty. There was the scent of mimosa, and beyond, the snow of the volcano.

She saw it all, and in a measure it was soothing. But it was all external. She didn't really care about it. She was herself just the same, with all her anger and frustration inside her, and her incapacity to feel anything real. The child imitated her, and preyed on her peace of mind. She felt so horribly, ghastly responsible for him: as if she must be responsible for every breath he drew. And that was torture to her, to the child, and to everybody else concerned.

"You know, Juliet, the doctor told you to lie in the sun, without your clothes. Why don't you?" said her mother.

"When I am fit to do so, I will. Do you want to kill me?" Juliet flew at her.

"To kill you, no! Only to do you good."

"For God's sake, leave off wanting to do me good."

The mother at last was so hurt and incensed, she departed.

The sea went white, and then invisible. Pouring rain fell. It was cold, in the house built for the sun.

Again a morning when the sun lifted himself molten and sparkling, naked over the sea's rim. The house faced south-east, Juliet lay in her bed and watched him rise. It was as if she had never seen the sun rise before. She had never seen the naked sun stand up pure upon the sea-line, shaking the night off himself, like wetness. And he was full and naked. And she wanted to come to him.

So the desire sprang secretly in her, to be naked to the sun. She cherished her desire like a secret. She wanted to come together with the sun.

But she would have to go away from the house—away from people. And it is not easy, in a country where every olive tree has eyes, and every slope is seen from afar, to go hidden, and have intercourse with the sun.

But she found a place: a rocky bluff shoved out to the sea and sun, and overgrown with the large cactus called prickly pear. Out of this thicket of cactus rose one cypress tree, with a pallid, thick trunk, and a tip that leaned over, flexible, in the blue. It stood like a guardian looking to sea; or a candle whose huge flame was darkness against light: the long tongue of darkness licking up at the sky.

Juliet sat down by the cypress tree, and took off her clothes. The contorted cactus made a forest, hideous yet fascinating, about her. She sat and offered her bosom to the sun, sighing, even now, with a certain hard pain, against the cruelty of having to give herself: but exulting that at last it was no human lover.

But the sun marched in blue heaven and sent down his rays as he went. She felt the soft air of the sea on her breasts, that seemed as if they would never ripen. But she hardly felt the sun. Fruits that would wither and not mature, her breasts.

Soon, however, she felt the sun inside them, warmer than ever love had been, warmer than milk or the hands of her baby. At last, at last her breasts were like long white grapes in the hot sun.

She slid off all her clothes, and lay naked in the sun, and as she lay she looked up through her fingers at the central sun, his blue pulsing roundness, whose outer edges streamed brilliance. Pulsing with marvellous blue, and alive, and streaming white fire from his edges, the Sun! He faced down to her with blue body of fire, and enveloped her breasts and her face, her throat, her tired belly, her knees, her thighs and her feet.

She lay with shut eyes, the colour of rosy flame through her lids. It was too much. She reached and put leaves over her eyes. Then she lay again, like a long gourd in the sun, green that must ripen to gold.

She could feel the sun penetrating into her bones; nay, further, even into her emotions and thoughts. The dark tensions of her emotion began to give way, the cold dark clots of her thoughts began to dissolve. She was beginning to be warm right through. Turning over, she let her shoulders lie in the sun, her loins, the backs of her thighs, even her heels. And she lay half stunned with the strangeness of the thing that was happening to her. Her weary, chilled heart was melting, and in melting, evaporating. Only her womb remained tense and resistant, the eternal resistance. It would resist even the sun.

When she was dressed again she lay once more and looked up at the cypress tree, whose crest, a filament, fell this way and that in the breeze. Meanwhile, she was conscious of the great sun roaming in heaven, and of her own resistance.

So, dazed, she went home, only half-seeing, sun-blinded and sun-dazed. And her blindness was like a richness to her, and her dim, warm, heavy half-consciousness was like wealth.

"Mummy! Mummy!" her child came running towards her, calling in that peculiar bird-like little anguish of want, always wanting her. She was surprised that her drowsed heart for once felt none of the anxious love-tension in return. She caught the child up in her arms, but she thought: He should not be such a lump! If he had any sun in him, he would spring up.—And she felt again the unyielding resistance of her womb, against him and everything.

She resented, rather, his little hands clutching at her, especially her neck. She pulled her throat away. She did not want him getting hold of it. She put the child down.

"Run!" she said. "Run in the sun!"

And there and then she took off his clothes and set him naked on the warm terrace.

"Play in the sun!" she said.

He was frightened and wanted to cry. But she, in the warm indolence of her body, and the complete indifference of her heart, and the resistance of her womb, rolled him an orange across the red tiles, and with his soft, unformed little body he toddled after it. Then, immediately he had it, he dropped it because it felt strange against his flesh. And he looked back at her, wrinkling his face to cry, frightened because he was stark.

"Bring me the orange," she said, amazed at her own deep indifference to his trepidation. "Bring Mummy the orange."

"He shall not grow up like his father," she said to herself. "Like a worm that the sun has never seen."

II

She had had the child so much on her mind, in a torment of responsibility, as if, having borne him, she had to answer for his whole existence. Even if his nose were running, it had been repulsive and a goad in her vitals, as if she must say to herself: Look at the thing you brought forth!

Now a change took place. She was no longer vitally consumed about the child, she took the strain of her anxiety and her will from off him. And he thrived all the more for it.

She was thinking inside herself, of the sun in his splendour, and his entering into her. Her life was now a secret ritual. She always lay awake, before dawn, watching for the grey to colour to pale gold, to know if clouds lay on the sea's edge. Her joy was when he rose all molten in his nakedness, and threw off blue-white fire, into the tender heaven.

But sometimes he came ruddy, like a big, shy creature. And sometimes slow and crimson red, with a look of anger, slowly pushing and shouldering. Sometimes again she could not see him, only the level cloud threw down gold and scarlet from above, as he moved behind the wall.

She was fortunate. Weeks went by, and though the dawn was sometimes clouded, and afternoon was sometimes grey, never a day passed sunless, and most days, winter though it was, streamed radiant. The thin little wild crocuses came up mauve and striped, the wild narcissus hung their winter stars.

Every day, she went down to the cypress tree, among the cactus grove on the knoll with yellowish cliffs at the foot. She was wiser and subtler now, wearing only a dove-grey wrapper, and sandals. So that in an instant, in any hidden niche, she was naked to the sun. And the moment she was covered again she was grey and invisible.

Every day, in the morning towards noon, she lay at the foot of the powerful, silver-pawed cypress tree, while the sun strode jovial in heaven. By now she knew the sun in every thread of her body. Her heart of anxiety, that anxious, straining heart, had disappeared altogether, like a flower that falls in the sun, and leaves only a little ripening fruit. And her tense womb, though still closed, was slowly unfolding, slowly, slowly, like a lily bud under water, as the sun mysteriously touched it. Like a lily bud under water it was slowly rising to the sun, to expand at last, to the sun, only to the sun.

She knew the sun in all her body, the blue-molten with his white fire edges, throwing off fire. And, though he shone on all the world, when she lay unclothed he focussed on her. It was one of the wonders of the sun, he could shine on a million people, and still be the radiant, splendid, unique sun, focussed on her alone.

With her knowledge of the sun, and her conviction that the sun was gradually penetrating her to know her, in the cosmic carnal sense of the word, came over her a feeling of detachment from people, and a certain contemptuous tolerance for human beings altogether. They were so un-elemental, so un-sunned. They were so like graveyard worms.

Even the peasants passing up the rocky, ancient little road with their donkeys, sun-blackened as they were, were not sunned right through. There was a little soft white core of fear, like a snail in a shell, where the soul of the man cowered in fear of the natural blaze of life. He dared not quite see the sun: always innerly cowed. All men were like that.

Why admit men!

With her indifference to people, to men, she was not now so cautious about being seen. She had told Marinina, who went shopping for her in the village, that the doctor had ordered sun-baths. Let that suffice.

Marinina was a woman of sixty or more, tall, thin, erect, with curling dark-grey hair, and dark-grey eyes that had the shrewdness of thousands of years in them, with the laugh, half mockery, that underlies all long experience. Tragedy is lack of experience.

"It must be beautiful to go naked in the sun," said Marinina, with a shrewd laugh in her eyes, as she looked keenly at the other woman. Juliet's fair, bobbed hair curled in a little cloud at her temples. Marinina was a woman of Magna Graecia, and had far memories. She looked again at Juliet.

"But when a woman is beautiful, she can show herself to the sun? eh? isn't it true?" she added, with that queer, breathless little laugh of the women of the past.

"Who knows if I am beautiful!" said Juliet.

But beautiful or not, she felt that by the sun she was appreciated. Which is the same.

When, out of the sun at noon, sometimes she stole down over the rocks and past the cliff-edge, down to the deep gully where the lemons hung in cool eternal shadow; and in the silence slipped off her wrapper to wash herself quickly at one of the deep, clear green basins, she would notice, in the bare green twilight under the lemon leaves, that all her body was rosy, rosy and turning to gold. She was like another person. She was another person.

So she remembered that the Greeks had said a white unsunned body was unhealthy, and fishy.

And she would rub a little olive oil into her skin, and wander a moment in the dark underworld of the lemons, balancing a lemon-flower in her navel, laughing to herself. There was just a chance some peasant might see her. But if he did, he would be more afraid of her than she of him. She knew the white core of fear in the clothed bodies of men.

She knew it even in her little son. How he mistrusted her, now that she laughed at him, with the sun in her face! She insisted on his toddling naked in the sunshine, every day. And now his little body was pink too, his blond hair was pushed thick from his brow, his cheeks had a pomegranate scarlet, in the delicate gold of the sunny skin. He was bonny and healthy, and the servants, loving his gold and red and blue, called him an angel from heaven.

But he mistrusted his mother: she laughed at him. And she saw, in his wide blue eyes, under the little frown, that centre of fear, misgiving, which she believed was at the centre of all male eyes, now. She called it fear of the sun. And her womb stayed shut against all men, sun-fearers.

"He fears the sun," she would say to herself, looking down into the eyes of the child.

And as she watched him toddling, swaying, tumbling in the sunshine, making his little bird-like noises, she saw that he held himself tight and hidden from the sun, inside himself, and his balance was clumsy, his movements a little gross. His spirit was like a snail in a shell, in a damp, cold crevice inside himself. It made her think of his father. And she wished she could make him come forth, break out in a gesture of recklessness, a salutation to the sun.

She determined to take him with her, down to the cypress tree among the cactus. She would have to watch him, because of the thorns. But surely in that place he would come forth from the little shell, deep inside him. That little civilised tension would disappear off his brow.

She spread a rug for him and sat down. Then she slid off her wrapper and lay down herself, watching a hawk high in the blue, and the tip of the cypress hanging over.

The boy played with stones on the rug. When he got up to toddle away, she got up too. He turned and looked at her. Almost, from his blue eyes, it was the challenging, warm look of the true male. And he was handsome, with the scarlet in the golden blond of his skin. He was not really white. His skin was gold-dusky.

"Mind the thorns, darling," she said.

"Thorns!" re-echoed the child, in a birdy chirp, still looking at her over his shoulder, like some naked *putto* in a picture, doubtful.

"Nasty prickly thorns."

"Ickly thorns!"

He staggered in his little sandals over the stones, pulling at the dry mint. She was quick as a serpent, leaping to him, when he was going to fall against the prickles. It surprised even herself. "What a wild cat I am, really!" she said to herself.

She brought him every day, when the sun shone, to the cypress tree.

"Come!" she said, "Let us go to the cypress tree."

And if there was a cloudy day, with the tramontana blowing, so that she could not go down, the child would chirp incessantly: "Cypress tree! Cypress tree!"

He missed it as much as she did.

It was not just taking sun-baths. It was much more than that. Something deep inside her unfolded and relaxed, and she was given to a cosmic influence. By some mysterious will inside her, deeper than her known conciousness and her known will, she was put into connection with the sun, and the stream of the sun flowed through her, round her womb. She herself, her conscious self, was secondary, a secondary person, almost an onlooker. The true Juliet lived in the dark flow of the sun within her deep body, like a river of dark rays circling, circling dark and violet round the sweet, shut bud of her womb.

She had always been mistress of herself, aware of what she was doing, and held tense in her own command. Now she felt inside her quite another sort of power, something greater than herself, darker and more savage, the element flowing upon her. Now she was vague, in the spell of a power beyond herself.

III

The end of February was suddenly very hot. Almond blossom was falling like pink snow, in the touch of the smallest breeze. The mauve, silky little anemones were out, the asphodels tall in bud, and the sea was corn-flower blue.

Juliet had ceased to care about anything. Now, most of the day, she and the child were naked in the sun, and it was all she wanted. Sometimes she went down to the sea to bathe: often she wandered in the gullies where the sun shone in, and she was out of sight. Sometimes she saw a peasant with an ass, and he saw her. But she went so simply and quietly with her child; and the fame of the sun's healing power, for the soul as well as for the body, had already spread among the people; so that there was no excitement.

The child and she were now both tanned with a rosy-golden tan, all over. "I am another being," she said to herself, as she looked at her red-gold breasts and thighs.

The child, too, was another creature, with a peculiar, quiet, sun-darkened absorption. Now he played by himself in silence, and she need hardly notice him. He seemed no longer to notice when he was alone.

There was not a breeze, and the sea was ultramarine. She sat by the great silver paw of the cypress tree, drowsed in the sun, but her breasts alert, full of sap. She was becoming aware of an activity rousing in her, an activity which would bring another self awake in her. Still she did not want to be aware. The new rousing would mean a new contact, and this she did not want. She knew well enough the vast cold apparatus of civilisation, and what contact with it meant; and how difficult it was to evade.

The child had gone a few yards down the rocky path, round the great sprawling of a cactus. She had seen him, a real gold-brown infant of the winds, with burnt gold hair and red cheeks, collecting the speckled pitcher-flowers and laying them in rows. He could balance now, and was quick for his own emergencies, like an absorbed young animal playing.

Suddenly she heard him speaking: *Look, Mummy! Mummy look!* A note in his bird-like voice made her lean forward sharply.

Her heart stood still. He was looking over his naked little shoulder at her, and pointing with a loose little hand at a snake which had reared itself up a yard away from him, and was opening its mouth so that its forked, soft tongue flickered black like a shadow, uttering a short hiss.

"Look! Mummy!"

"Yes, darling, it's a snake!" came the slow deep voice. He looked at her, his wide blue eyes uncertain whether to be afraid or not. Some stillness of the sun in her reassured him.

"Snake!" he chirped.

"Yes, darling! Don't touch it, it can bite."

The snake had sunk down, and was reaching away from the coils in which it had been basking asleep, and slowly was easing its long, gold-brown body into the rocks, with slow curves. The boy turned and watched it in silence. Then he said:

"Snake going!"

"Yes! Let it go. It likes to be alone."

He still watched the slow, easing length as the creature drew itself apathetic out of sight.

"Snake gone back," he said.

"Yes, it is gone back. Come to Mummy a moment."

He came and sat with his plump, naked little body on her naked lap, and she smoothed his burnt, bright hair. She said nothing, feeling that everything was past. The curious careless power of the sun filled her, filled the whole place like a charm, and the snake was part of the place, along with her and the child.

Another day, in the dry stone wall of one of the olive terraces, she saw a black snake horizontally creeping.

"Marinina," she said, "I saw a black snake. Are they harmful?"

"Ah, the black snakes, no! But the yellow ones, yes! If the yellow one bites you, you die. But they frighten me, they frighten me, even the black ones, when I see one."

Juliet still went to the cypress tree with the child. But she always looked carefully round, before she sat down, examining everywhere the child might go. Then she would lie and turn to the sun again, her tanned, pear-shaped breasts pointing up. She would take no thought for the morrow. She refused to think outside the garden, and she could not write letters. She would tell the nurse to write. So she lay in the sun, but not for long, for it was getting strong, fierce. And in spite of herself, the bud that had been tight and deep immersed in the innermost gloom of her, was rearing, rearing and straightening its curved stem, to open its dark tips and show a gleam of rose. Her womb was coming open wide with rosy ecstasy, like a lotus flower.

IV

Spring was becoming summer, in the south of the sun, and the rays were very powerful. In the hot hours she would lie in the shade of trees, or she would even go down to the depths of the cool lemon grove. Or sometimes she went in the shadowy deeps of the gullies, at the bottom of the little ravine, towards home. The child fluttered around in silence, like a young animal absorbed in life.

Going slowly home in her nakedness down among the bushes of the dark ravine, one noon, she came round a rock suddenly upon the peasant of the next *podere,* who was stooping binding up a bundle of brush-wood he had cut, his ass standing near. He was wearing summer cotton trousers, and stooping his buttocks towards her. It was utterly still and private down in the dark bed of the little ravine. A weakness came over her, for a moment she could not move. The man lifted the bundle of wood with powerful shoulders, and turned to the ass. He started and stood transfixed as he saw her, as if it were a vision. Then his eyes met hers, and she felt the blue fire running through her limbs to her womb, which was spreading in the helpless ecstasy. Still they looked into each other's eyes, and the fire flowed between them, like the blue, streaming fire from the heart of the sun. And she saw the phallus rise under his clothing, and knew he would come towards her.

"Mummy, a man! Mummy!" The child had put a hand against her thigh. "Mummy, a man!"

She heard the note of fear and swung round.

"It's all right, boy!" she said, and taking him by the hand, she led him back round the rock again, while the peasant watched her naked, retreating buttocks lift and fall.

She put on her wrap, and taking the boy in her arms, began to stagger up a steep goat-track through the yellow-flowering tangle of shrubs, up to the level of day, and the olive trees below the house. There she sat down to collect herself.

The sea was blue, very blue and soft and still-looking, and her womb inside her was wide open, wide open like a lotus flower, or a cactus flower, in a radiant sort of eagerness. She could feel it, and it dominated her consciousness. And a biting chagrin burned in her breast, against the child, against the complication of frustration.

She knew the peasant by sight: a man something over thirty, broad and very powerfully set. She had many times watched him from the terrace of her house: watched him come with his ass, watched him trimming the olive trees, working alone, always alone and physically powerful, with a broad red face and a quiet self-possession. She had spoken to him once or twice, and met his big blue eyes, dark and southern hot. And she knew his sudden gestures, a little violent and over-generous. But she had never thought of him. Save she had noticed that he was always very clean and well-cared for: and then she had seen his wife one day, when the latter had brought the man's meal, and they sat in the shade of a carob tree, on either side the spread white cloth. And then Juliet had seen that the man's wife was older than he, a dark, proud, gloomy woman. And then a young woman had come with a child, and the man had danced with the child, so young and passionate. But it was not his own child: he had no children. It was when he danced with the child, in such a sprightly way, as if full of suppressed passion, that Juliet had first really noticed him. But even then, she had never thought of him. Such a broad red face, such a great chest, and rather short legs. Too much a crude beast for her to think of, a peasant.

But now the strange challenge of his eyes had held her, blue and overwhelming like the blue sun's heart. And she had seen the fierce stirring of the phallus under his thin trousers: for her. And with his red face, and with his broad body, he was like the sun to her, the sun in its broad heat.

She felt him so powerfully, that she could not go further from him. She continued to sit there under the tree. Then she heard nurse tinkling a bell at the house, and calling. And the child called back. She had to rise and go home.

In the afternoon she sat on the terrace of her house, that looked over the olive slopes to the sea. The man came and went, came and went to the little hut on his *podere,* on the edge of the cactus grove. And he glanced again at her house, at her sitting on the terrace. And her womb was open to him.

Yet she had not the courage to go down to him. She was paralysed. She had tea, and still sat there on the terrace. And the man came and went, and glanced, and glanced again. Till the evening bell had jangled from the capuchin church at the village gate, and the darkness came on. And still she sat on the terrace. Till at last in the moonlight she saw him load his ass and drive it sadly along the path to the little road. She heard him pass on the stones of the road behind her house. He was gone—gone home to the village, to sleep, to sleep with his wife, who would want to know why he was so late. He was gone in dejection.

Juliet sat late on into the night, watching the moon on the sea. The sun had opened her womb, and she was no longer free. The trouble of the open lotus blossom had come upon her, and now it was she who had not the courage to take the steps across the gully.

But at last she slept. And in the morning she felt better. Her womb seemed to have closed again: the lotus flower seemed back in bud again. She wanted so much that it should be so. Only the immersed bud, and the sun! She would never think of that man.

She bathed in one of the great tanks away down in the lemon-grove, down in the far ravine, far as possible from the other wild gully, and cool. Below, under the lemons, the child was wading among the yellow oxalis flowers of the shadow, gathering fallen lemons, passing with his tanned little body into flecks of light, moving all dappled. She sat in the sun on the steep bank in the gully, feeling almost free again, the flower drooping in shadowy bud, safe inside her.

Suddenly, high over the land's edge, against the full-lit pale blue sky, Marinina appeared, a black cloth tied round her head, calling quietly: *Signora! Signora Giulietta!*

Juliet faced round, standing up. Marinina paused a moment, seeing, the naked woman standing alert, her sun-faded fair hair in a little cloud. Then the swift old woman came down the slant of the steep, sun-blazed track.

She stood a few steps, erect, in front of the sun-coloured woman, and eyed her shrewdly.

"But how beautiful you are, you!" she said cooly, almost cynically. "Your husband has come."

"What husband?" cried Juliet.

The old woman gave a shrewd bark of a little laugh, the mockery of the woman of the past.

"Haven't you got one, a husband, you?" she said, taunting.

"How? Where? In America," said Juliet.

The old woman glanced over her shoulder, with another noiseless laugh.

"No America at all. He was following me here. He will have missed the path." And she threw back her head in the noiseless laugh of women.

The paths were all grown high with grass and flowers and nepitella, till they were like bird-tracks in an eternally wild place. Strange, the vivid wildness of the old classic places, that have known men so long.

Juliet looked at the Sicilian woman with meditating eyes.

"Oh very well," she said at last. "Let him come."

And a little flame leaped in her. It was the opening flower. At least he was a man.

"Bring him here? Now?" asked Marinina, her mocking, smoke-grey eyes looking with laughter into Juliet's eyes. Then she gave a little jerk of her shoulders.

"All right! As you wish! But for him it is a rare one!" She opened her mouth with a noiseless laugh of amusement then she pointed down to the child, who was heaping lemons against his little chest. "Look how beautiful the child is? An angel from heaven! That certainly will please him, poor thing. Then I shall bring him?"

"Bring him," said Juliet.

The old woman scrambled rapidly up the track again, and found Maurice at a loss among the vine terraces, standing there in his grey felt hat and dark-grey city suit. He looked pathetically out of place, in that resplendent sunshine and the grace of the old Greek world; like a blot of ink on the pale, sun-glowing slope.

"Come!" said Marinina to him. "She is down here."

And swiftly she led the way, striding with a long stride, marking the way through the grasses. Suddenly she stopped on the brow of the slope. The tops of the lemon trees were dark, away below.

"You, you go down here," she said to him, and he thanked her, glancing up at her swiftly.

He was a man of forty, clean-shaven, grey-faced, very quiet and really shy. He managed his own business carefully without startling success, but efficiently. And he confided in nobody. The old woman of Magna Graecia saw him at a glance: he is good, she said to herself, but not a man, poor thing.

"Down there is the Signora," said Marinina, pointing like one of the Fates.

And again he said "Thank you! Thank you!" without a twinkle, and stepped carefully into the track. Marinina lifted her chin with a joyful wickedness. Then she strode off towards the house.

Maurice was watching his step, through the tangle of Mediterranean herbage, so he did not catch sight of his wife till he came round a little bend, quite near her. She was standing erect and nude by the jutting rock, glistening with the sun and the warm life. Her breasts seemed to be lifting up, alert, to listen, her thighs looked brown and fleet. Inside her, the lotus of her womb was wide open, spread almost gaping in the violet rays of the sun, like a great lotus flower. And she thrilled helplessly: a man was coming. Her glance on him, as he came gingerly, like ink on blotting-paper, was swift and nervous.

Maurice, poor fellow, hesitated and glanced away from her, turning his face aside.

"Hello, Julie!" he said, with a little nervous cough. "Splendid! Splendid!"

He advanced with his face averted, shooting further glances at her, furtively, as she stood with the peculiar satiny gleam of the sun on her tanned skin. Somehow she did not seem so terribly naked. It was the golden-rose of the sun that clothed her.

"Hello Maurice!" she said, hanging back from him, and a cold shadow falling on the open flower of her womb. "I wasn't expecting you so soon."

"No," he said. "No! I managed to slip away a little earlier."

And again he coughed unawares. Furtively, purposely he had taken her by surprise. They stood several yards away from one another, and there was silence. But this was a new Julie to him, with the sun-tanned, wind-stroked thighs: not that nervous New York woman.

"Well!" he said, "er - this is splendid-splendid! You are - er - splendid! Where is the boy?"

He felt, in his far-off depths, the desire stirring in him for the limbs and sun-wrapped flesh of the woman: the woman of flesh. It was a new desire in his life, and it hurt him. He wanted to side-track.

"There he is," she said, pointing down to where a naked urchin in the deep shade was piling fallen lemons together.

The father gave an odd little laugh, almost neighing.

"Ah! yes! There he is! So there's the little man! Fine!" His nervous, suppressed soul was thrilling with violent thrills, he clung to the straw of his upper consciousness. "Hello, Johnny!" he called, and it sounded rather feeble. "Hello Johnny!"

The child looked up, spilling lemons from his chubby arms, but did not respond.

"I guess we'll go down to him," said Juliet, as she turned and went striding down the path. In spite of herself, the cold shadow was lifting off the open flower of her womb, and every petal was thrilling again. Her husband followed, watching the rosy, fleet-looking lifting and sinking of her quick hips, as she swayed a little in the socket of her waist. He was dazed with admiration, but also at a deadly loss. He was used to her as a person. And this was no longer a person, but a fleet sun-strong body, soulless and alluring as a nymph, twinkling its haunches. What would he do with himself? He was utterly out of the picture, in his dark grey suit and pale grey hat, and his grey, monastic face of a shy business man, and his grey mercantile mentality. Strange thrills shot through his loins and his legs. He was terrified, and he felt he might give a wild whoop of triumph, and jump towards that woman of tanned flesh.

"He looks all right, doesn't he," said Juliet, as they came through the deep sea of yellow-flowering oxalis, under the lemon-trees.

"Ah! - yes! yes! Splendid! Splendid! - Hello Johnny! Do you know Daddy? Do you know Daddy, Johnny?"

He squatted down, forgetting his trouser-crease, and held out his hands.

"Lemons!" said the child, birdily chirping. "Two lemons!"

"Two lemons!" replied the father. "Lots of lemons!"

The infant came and put a lemon in each of his father's open hands. Then he stood back to look.

"Two lemons!" repeated the father. "Come, Johnny! Come and say Hello! to Daddy."

"Daddy going back?" said the child.

"Going back? Well - well - not today."

And he took his son in his arms.

"Take a coat off! Daddy take a coat off!" said the boy, squirming debonair away from the cloth.

"All right, son! Daddy take a coat off."

He took off his coat and laid it carefully aside, then looked at the creases in his trousers, hitched them a little, and crouched down and took his son in his arms. The child's warm naked body against him made him feel faint. The naked woman looked down at the rosy infant in the arms of the man in his shirt-sleeves. The boy had pulled off his father's hat, and Juliet looked at the sleek black-and-grey hair of her husband, not a hair out of place. And utterly, utterly sunless! The cold shadow was over the flower of her womb again. She was silent for a long time, while the father talked to the child, who had been fond of his Daddy.

"What are you going to do about it, Maurice?" she said suddenly. He looked at her swiftly, sideways, hearing her abrupt American voice. He had forgotten her.

"Er - about what, Julie?"

"Oh, everything! About this! I can't go back into East Forty-Seventh."

"Er -," he hesitated, "no, I suppose not—Not just now, at least."

"Never!" she said abruptly, and there was a silence.

"Well - er - I don't know," he said.

"Do you think you can come out here?" she said savagely.

"Yes! - I can stay for a month. I think I can manage a month," he hesitated. Then he ventured a complicated, shy peep at her, and turned away his face again.

She looked down at him, her alert breasts lifted with a sigh, as if she would impatiently shake the cold shadow of sunlessness off her.

"I can't go back," she said slowly, "I can't go back on this sun. If you can't come here—"

She ended on an open note. But the voice of the abrupt, personal American woman had died out, and he heard the voice of the woman of flesh, the sun-ripe body. He glanced at her again and again, with growing desire and lessening fear.

"No!" he said. "This kind of thing suits you. You are splendid. - No, I don't think you can go back."

And at the caressive sound of his voice, in spite of her, her womb-flower began to open and thrill its petals.

He was thinking visionarily of her in the New York flat, pale, silent, oppressing him terribly. He was the soul of gentle timidity in his human relations, and her silent, awful hostility after the baby was born had frightened him deeply. Because he had realized that she could not help it. Women were like that. Their feelings took a reverse direction, even against their own selves, and it was awful—devastating. Awful, awful to live in the house with a woman like that, whose feelings were reversed even against herself. He had felt himself borne down under the stream of her heavy hostility. She had ground even herself down to the quick, and the child as well. No, anything rather than that. Thank God, that menacing ghost-woman seemed to be sunned out of her now.

"But what about you?" she asked.

"I? Oh, I! - I can carry on in the business, and - er come over here for long holidays - so long as you like to stay here. You stay as long as you wish—" He looked down a long time at the earth. He was so frightened of rousing that menacing, avenging spirit of womanhood in her, he did so hope she might stay as he had seen her now, like a naked, ripening strawberry, a female like a fruit. He glanced up at her with a touch of supplication in his uneasy eyes.

"Even for ever?" she said.

"Well - er - yes, if you like. For ever is a long time. One can't set a date."

"And can I do anything I like?" She looked him straight in the eyes, challenging. And he was powerless against her rosy, wind-hardened nakedness, in his fear of arousing that other woman in her, the personal American woman, spectral and vengeful.

"Er - yes! - I suppose so! So long as you don't make yourself unhappy—or the boy."

Again he looked up at her with a complicated, uneasy appeal—thinking of the child, but hoping for himself.

"I won't," she said quickly.

"No!" he said, "No! I don't think you will."

There was a pause. The bells of the village were hastily clanging mid-day. That meant lunch.

She slipped into her grey crêpe kimono, and fastened a broad green sash round her waist. Then she slipped a little blue shirt over the boy's head, and they went up to the house.

At table she watched her husband, his grey city face, his glued, grey-black hair, his very precise table manners, and his extreme moderation in eating and drinking. Sometimes he glanced at her furtively, from under his black lashes. He had the uneasy, gold-grey eyes of a creature that has been caught young, and reared entirely in captivity, strange and cold, knowing no warm hopes. Only his black eye-brows and eye-lashes were nice. She did not take him in. She did not realize him. Being so sunned, she could not see him, his sunlessness was like nonentity.

They went on to the balcony for coffee, under the rosy mass of the bougainvillea. Below, beyond, on the next podere, the peasant and his wife were sitting under the carob tree, near the tall green wheat, sitting facing one another across a little white cloth spread on the ground. There was still a huge piece of bread—but they had finished eating and sat with dark wine in their glasses.

The peasant looked up at the terrace, as soon as the American emerged. Juliet put her husband with his back to the scene. Then she sat down, and looked back at the peasant. Until she saw his dark-visaged wife turn to look too.

V

*T*he man was hopelessly in love with her. She saw his broad, rather short red face gazing up at her fixedly: till his wife turned too to look, then he picked up his glass and tossed the wine down his throat. The wife stared long at the figures on the balcony. She was handsome and rather gloomy, and surely older than he, with that great difference that lies between a rather overwhelming, superior woman over forty, and her more irresponsible husband of thirty-five or so. It seemed like the difference of a whole generation. "He is my generation," thought Juliet, "and she is Maurice's generation." Juliet was not yet thirty.

The peasant in his white cotton trousers and pale pink shirt, and battered old straw hat, was attractive, so clean, and full of the cleanliness of health. He was stout and broad, and seemed shortish, but his flesh was full of vitality, as if he were always about to spring up into movement, to work, even, as she had seen him with the child, to play. He was the type of Italian peasant that wants to make an offering of himself, passionately wants to make an offering of himself, of his powerful flesh and thudding blood-stroke. But he was also completely a peasant, in that he would wait for the woman to make the move. He would hang round in a long, consuming passivity of desire, hoping, hoping for the woman to come for him. But he would never try to advance to her: never. She would have to make the advance. Only he would hang round, within reach.

Feeling her look at him, he flung off his old straw hat, showing his round, close-cropped brown head, and reached out with a large brown-red hand for the great loaf, from which he broke a piece and started chewing with bulging cheek. He knew she was looking at him. And she had such power over him, the hot, inarticulate animal, with such a hot, massive blood-stream down his great veins! He was hot through with countless suns, and mindless as noon. And shy with a violent, farouche shyness, that would wait for her with consuming wanting, but would never, never move towards her.

With him, it would be like bathing in another kind of sunshine, heavy and big and perspiring: and afterwards one would forget. Personally, he would not exist. It would be just a bath of warm, powerful life—then separating and forgetting. Then again, the procreative bath, like sun.

But would that not be good! She was so tired of personal contacts, and having to talk with the man afterwards. With that healthy creature, one would just go satisfied away, afterwards. As she sat there, she felt the life streaming from him to her, and her to him. She knew by his movements he felt her even more than she felt him. It was almost a definite pain of consciousness in the body of each of them, and each sat as if distracted, watched by a keen-eyed spouse, possessor.

And Juliet thought: Why shouldn't I go to him! Why shouldn't I bear his child! It would be like bearing a child to the unconscious sun and the unconscious earth, a child like a fruit. - And the flower of her womb radiated. It did not care about sentiment or possession. It wanted man-dew only, utterly improvident. But her heart was clouded with fear. She dare not! She dare not! If only the man would find some way! But he would not. He would only hover and wait, hover in endless desire, waiting for her to cross the gully. And she dare not, she dare not. And he would hang round.

"You are not afraid of people seeing you when you take your sun-baths?" said her husband, turning round and looking across at the peasants. The saturnine wife over the gully, turned also to stare at the Villa. It was a kind of battle.

"No! One needn't be seen. Will you do it too? Will you take sun-baths?" said Juliet to him.

"Why - er - yes! I think I should like to, while I am here."

There was a gleam in his eyes, a desperate kind of courage of desire to taste this new fruit, this woman with rosy, sun-ripening breasts tilting within her wrapper. And she thought of him with his blanched, etiolated little city figure, walking in the sun in the desperation of a husband's rights. And her mind swooned again. The strange, branded little fellow, the good citizen, branded like a criminal in the naked eye of the sun. How he would hate exposing himself!

And the flower of her womb went dizzy, dizzy. She knew she would take him. She knew she would bear his child. She knew it was for him, the branded little city man, that her womb was open radiating like a lotus, like the purple spread of a daisy anemone, dark at the core. She knew she would not go across to the peasant; she had not enough courage, she was not free enough. And she knew the peasant would never come for her, he had the dogged passivity of the earth, and would wait, wait, only putting himself in her sight, again and again, lingering across her vision, with the persistency of animal yearning.

She had seen the flushed blood in the peasant's burnt face, and felt the jetting, sudden blue heat pouring over her from his kindled eyes, and the rousing of his big penis against his body - for her, surging for her. Yet she would never come to him - she daren't, she daren't, so much was against her. And the little etiolated body of her husband, city-branded, would possess her, and his little, frantic penis would beget another child in her. She could not help it. She was bound to the vast, fixed wheel of circumstance, and there was no Perseus in the universe to cut the bonds.

Lady
Chatterley's
Lover

Chapter One

Ours is essentially a tragic age, so we refuse to take it tragically. The cataclysm has happened, we are among the ruins, we start to build up new little habits, to have new little hopes. It is rather hard work: there is now no smooth road into the future: but we go round, or scramble over the obstacles. We've got to live, no matter how many skies have fallen.

This was more or less Constance Chatterley's position. The war had brought the roof down over her head. And she had realized that one must live and learn.

She married Clifford Chatterley in 1917, when he was home for a month on leave. They had a month's honeymoon. Then he went back to Flanders: to be shipped over to England again six months later, more or less in bits. Constance, his wife, was then twenty-three years old, and he was twenty-nine.

His hold on life was marvellous. He didn't die, and the bits seemed to grow together again. For two years he remained in the doctor's hands. Then he was pronounced a cure, and could return to life again, with the lower half of his body, from the hips down, paralyzed for ever.

This was in 1920. They returned, Clifford and Constance, to his home, Wragby Hall, the family "seat." His father had died, Clifford was now a baronet, Sir Clifford, and Constance was Lady Chatterley. They came to start housekeeping and married life in the rather forlorn home of the Chatterleys on a rather inadequate income. Clifford had a sister, but she had departed. Otherwise there were no near relatives. The elder brother was dead in the war. Crippled for ever, knowing he could never have any children, Clifford came home to the smoky Midlands to keep the Chatterley name alive while he could.

He was not really downcast. He could wheel himself about in a wheeled chair, and he had a bath-chair with a small motor attachment, so he could drive himself slowly round the garden and into the fine melancholy park, of which he was really so proud, though he pretended to be flippant about it.

Having suffered so much, the capacity for suffering had to some extent left him. He remained strange and bright and cheerful, almost, one might say, chirpy, with his ruddy, healthy-looking face, and his pale-blue, challenging bright eyes. His shoulders were broad and strong, his hands were very strong. He was expensively dressed, and wore handsome neckties from Bond Street. Yet still in his face one saw the watchful look, the slight vacancy of a cripple.

He had so very nearly lost his life, that what remained was wonderfully precious to him. It was obvious in the anxious brightness of his eyes, how proud he was, after the great shock, of being alive. But he had been so much hurt that something inside him had perished, some of his feelings had gone. There was a blank of insentience.

Constance, his wife, was a ruddy, country-looking girl with soft brown hair and sturdy body, and slow movements, full of unusual energy. She had big, wondering eyes, and a soft mild voice, and seemed just to have come from her native village. It was not so at all. Her father was the once well-known R.A., old Sir Malcolm Reid. Her mother had been one of the cultivated Fabians in the palmy, rather pre-Raphaelite days. Between artists and cultured socialists, Constance and her sister Hilda had had what might be called an aesthetically unconventional upbringing. They had been taken to Paris and Florence and Rome to breathe in art, and they had been taken also in the other direction, to the Hague and Berlin, to great Socialist conventions, where the speakers spoke in every civilized tongue, and no one was abashed.

The two girls, therefore, were from an early age not the least daunted by either art or ideal politics. It was their natural atmosphere. They were at once cosmopolitan and provincial, with the cosmopolitan provincialism of art that goes with pure social ideals.

They had been sent to Dresden at the age of fifteen, for music among other things. And they had had a good time there. They lived freely among the students, they argued with the men over philosophical, sociological and artistic matters, they were just as good as the men themselves: only better, since they were women. And they tramped off to the forests with sturdy youths bearing guitars, twang-twang! They sang the Wandervogel songs, and they were free. Free! That was the great word. Out in the open world, out in the forests of the morning, with lusty and splendid-throated young fellows, free to do as they liked, and—above all—to say what they liked. It was the talk that mattered supremely: the impassioned interchange of talk. Love was only a minor accompaniment.

Both Hilda and Constance had had their tentative love-affairs by the time they were eighteen. The young men with whom they talked so passionately and sang so lustily and camped under the trees in such freedom wanted, of course, the love connection. The girls were doubtful, but then the thing was so much talked about, it was supposed to be so important. And the men were so humble and craving. Why couldn't a girl be queenly, and give the gift of herself?

So they had given the gift of themselves, each to the youth with whom she had the most subtle and intimate arguments. The arguments, the discussions were the great thing: the love-making and connection were only a sort of primitive reversion and a bit of an anti-climax. One was less in love with the boy afterwards, and a little inclined to hate him, as if he had trespassed on one's privacy and inner freedom. For, of course, being a girl, one's whole dignity and meaning in life consisted in the achievement of an absolute, a perfect, a pure and noble freedom. What else did a girl's life mean? To shake off the old and sordid connections and subjections.

And however one might sentimentalize it, this sex business was one of the most ancient, sordid connections and subjections. Poets who glorified it were mostly men. Women had always known there was something better, something higher. And now they knew it more definitely than ever. The beautiful pure freedom of a woman was infinitely more wonderful than any sexual love. The only unfortunate thing was that men lagged so far behind women in the matter. They insisted on the sex thing like dogs.

And a woman had to yield. A man was like a child with his appetites. A woman had to yield him what he wanted, or like a child he would probably turn nasty and flounce away and spoil what was a very pleasant connection. But a woman could yield to a man without yielding her inner, free self. That the poets and talkers about sex did not seem to have taken sufficiently into account. A woman could take a man without really giving herself away. Certainly she could take him without giving herself into his power. Rather she could use this sex thing to have power over him. For she only had to hold herself back in sexual intercourse, and let him finish and expend himself without herself coming to the crisis: and then she could prolong the connection and achieve her orgasm and her crisis while he was merely her tool.

Both sisters had had their love experience by the time the war came, and they were hurried home. Neither was ever in love with a young man unless he and she were verbally very near: that is unless they were profoundly interested, TALKING to one another. The amazing, the profound, the unbelievable thrill there was in passionately talking to some really clever young man by the hour, resuming day after day for months . . . this they had never realized till it happened! The paradisal promise: Thou shalt have men to talk to!—had never been uttered. It was fulfilled before they knew what a promise it was.

And if after the roused intimacy of these vivid and soul-enlightened discussions the sex thing became more or less inevitable, then let it. It marked the end of a chapter. It had a thrill of its own too: a queer vibrating thrill inside the body, a final spasm of self-assertion, like the last word, exciting, and very like the row of asterisks that can be put to show the end of a paragraph, and a break in the theme.

When the girls came home for the summer holidays of 1913, when Hilda was twenty and Connie eighteen, their father could see plainly that they had had the love experience.

L'amour avait passé par là, as somebody puts it. But he was a man of experience himself, and let life take its course. As for the mother, a nervous invalid in the last few months of her life, she only wanted her girls to be "free," and to "fulfill themselves." She herself had never been able to be altogether herself: it had been denied her. Heaven knows why, for she was a woman who had her own income and her own way. She blamed her husband. But as a matter of fact, it was some old impression of authority on her own mind or soul that she could not get rid of. It had nothing to do with Sir Malcolm, who left his nervously hostile, high-spirited wife to rule her own roost, while he went his own way.

So the girls were "free," and went back to Dresden, and their music, and the university and the young men. They loved their respective young men, and the respective young men loved them with all the passion of mental attraction. All the wonderful things the young men thought and expressed and wrote, they thought and expressed and wrote for the young women. Connie's young man was musical, Hilda's was technical. But they simply lived for their young women. In their minds and their mental excitements, that is. Somewhere else they were a little rebuffed, though they did not know it.

It was obvious in them too that love had gone through them: that is, the physical experience. It is curious what a subtle but unmistakable transmutation it makes, both in the body of men and women: the women more blooming, more subtly rounded, her young angularities softened, and her expression either anxious or triumphant: the man much quieter, more inward, the very shapes of his shoulders and his buttocks less assertive, more hesitant.

In the actual sex-thrill within the body, the sisters nearly succumbed to the strange male power. But quickly they recovered themselves, took the sex-thrill as a sensation, and remained free. Whereas the men, in gratitude to the women for the sex experience, let their souls go out to her. And afterwards looked rather as if they had lost a shilling and found sixpence. Connie's man could be a bit sulky, and Hilda's a bit jeering. But that is how men are! Ungrateful and never satisfied. When you don't have them they hate you because you won't; and when you do have them they hate you again, for some other reason. Or for no reason at all, except that they are discontented children, and can't be satisfied whatever they get, let a woman do what she may.

However, came the war, Hilda and Connie were rushed home again after having been home already in May, to their mother's funeral. Before Christmas of 1914 both their German young men were dead: whereupon the sisters wept, and loved the young men passionately, but underneath forgot them. They didn't exist any more.

Both sisters lived in their father's, really their mother's, Kensington house, and mixed with the young Cambridge group, the group that stood for "freedom" and flannel trousers, and flannel shirts open at the neck, and a well-bred sort of emotional anarchy, and a whispering, murmuring sort of voice, and an ultra-sensitive sort of manner. Hilda, however, suddenly married a man ten years older than herself, an elder member of the same Cambridge group, a man with a fair amount of money, and a comfortable family job in the government: he also wrote philosophical essays. She lived with him in a smallish house in Westminster, and moved in that good sort of society of people in the government who are not tip-toppers, but who are, or would be, the real intelligent power in the nation: people who know what they're talking about, or talk as if they did.

Connie did a mild form of war-work, and consorted with the flannel-trousered Cambridge intransigeants, who gently mocked at everything, so far. Her "friend" was a Clifford Chatterley, a young man of twenty-two, who had hurried home from Bonn, where he was studying the technicalities of coal-mining. He had previously spent two years at Cambridge. Now he had become a first lieutenant in a smart regiment, so he could mock at everything more becomingly in uniform.

Clifford Chatterley was more upper-class than Connie. Connie was well-to-do intelligentsia, but he was aristocracy. Not the big sort, but still *it*. His father was a baronet, and his mother had been a viscount's daughter.

But Clifford, while he was better bred than Connie, and more "society," was in his own way more provincial and more timid. He was at his ease in the narrow "great world," that is, landed aristocracy society, but he was shy and nervous of all that other big world which consists of the vast hordes of the middle and lower classes, and foreigners. If the truth must be told, he was a little bit frightened of middle and lower class humanity, and of foreigners not of his own class. He was, in some paralyzing way, conscious of his own defenselessness, though he had all the defense of privilege. Which is curious, but a phenomenon of our day.

Therefore the peculiar soft assurance of a girl like Constance Reid fascinated him. She was so much more mistress of herself in that outer world of chaos than he was master of himself.

Nevertheless he too was a rebel: rebelling even against his class. Or perhaps rebel is too strong a word; far too strong. He was only caught in the general, popular recoil of the young against convention and against any sort of real authority. Fathers were ridiculous: his own obstinate one supremely so. And governments were ridiculous: our own wait-and-see sort especially so. And armies were ridiculous, and old buffers of generals altogether, the red-faced Kitchener supremely. Even the war was ridiculous, though it did kill rather a lot of people.

In fact everything was a little ridiculous, or very ridiculous: certainly everything connected with authority, whether it were in the army or the government or the universities, was ridiculous to a degree. And as far as the governing class made any pretensions to govern, they were ridiculous too. Sir Geoffrey, Clifford's father, was intensely ridiculous, chopping down his trees, and weeding men out of his colliery to shove them into the war: and himself being so safe and patriotic; but, also, spending more money on his country than he'd got.

When Miss Chatterley—Emma—came down to London from the Midlands to do some nursing work, she was very witty in a quiet way about Sir Geoffrey and his determined patriotism. Herbert, the elder brother and heir, laughed outright, though it was his trees that were falling for trench props. But Clifford only smiled a little uneasily. Everything was ridiculous, quite true. But when it came too close and oneself became ridiculous too . . .? At least people of a different class, like Connie, were earnest about something. They believed in something.

They were rather earnest about the Tommies, and the threat of conscription, and the shortage of sugar and toffee for the children. In all these things, of course, the authorities were ridiculously at fault. But Clifford could not take it to heart. To him the authorities were ridiculous *ab ovo*, not because of toffee or Tommies.

And the authorities felt ridiculous, and behaved in a rather ridiculous fashion, and it was all a mad hatter's tea-party for a while. Till things developed over there, and Lloyd George came to save the situation over here. And this surpassed even ridicule, the flippant young laughed no more.

In 1916 Herbert Chatterley was killed, so Clifford became heir. He was terrified even of this. His importance as son of Sir Geoffrey and child of Wragby was so ingrained in him, he could never escape it. And yet he knew that this too, in the eyes of the vast seething world, was ridiculous. Now he was heir and responsible for Wragby. Was that not terrible? And also splendid and at the same time, perhaps, purely absurd?

Sir Geoffrey would have none of the absurdity. He was pale and tense, withdrawn into himself, and obstinately determined to save his country and his own position, let it be Lloyd George or who it might. So cut off he was, so divorced from the England that was really England, so utterly incapable, that he even thought well of Horatio Bottomley. Sir Geoffrey stood for England and Lloyd George as his forebears had stood for England and St. George: and he never knew there was a difference. So Sir Geoffrey felled timber and stood for Lloyd George and England, England and Lloyd George.

And he wanted Clifford to marry and produce an heir. Clifford felt his father was a hopeless anachronism. But wherein was he himself any further ahead, except in a wincing sense of the ridiculousness of everything, and the paramount ridiculousness of his own position? For willy-nilly he took his baronetcy and Wragby with the last seriousness.

The gay excitement had gone out of the war . . . dead. Too much death and horror. A man needed support and comfort. A man needed to have an anchor in the safe world. A man needed a wife.

The Chatterleys, two brothers and a sister, had lived curiously isolated, shut in with one another at Wragby, in spite of all their connections. A sense of isolation intensified the family tie, a sense of the weakness of their position, a sense of defenselessness, in spite of, or because of the title and the land. They were cut off from those industrial Midlands in which they passed their lives. And they were cut off from their own class by the brooding, obstinate, shut-up nature of Sir Geoffrey, their father, whom they ridiculed but whom they were so sensitive about.

The three had said they would all live together always. But now Herbert was dead, and Sir Geoffrey wanted Clifford to marry. Sir Geoffrey barely mentioned it: he spoke very little. But his silent, brooding insistence that it should be so was hard for Clifford to bear up against.

But Emma said No! She was ten years older than Clifford, and she felt his marrying would be a desertion and a betrayal of what the young ones of the family had stood for.

Clifford married Connie, nevertheless, and had his month's honeymoon with her. It was the terrible year 1917, and they were intimate as two people who stand together on a sinking ship. He had been virgin when he married: and the sex part did not mean much to him. They were so close, he and she, apart from that. And Connie exulted a little in this intimacy which was beyond sex, and beyond a man's "satisfaction." Clifford anyhow was not just keen on his "satisfaction," as so many men seemed to be. No, the intimacy was deeper, more personal than that. And sex was merely an accident, or an adjunct, one of the curious obsolete, organic processes which persisted in its own clumsiness, but was not really necessary. Though Connie did want children: if only to fortify her against her sister-in-law Emma.

But early in 1918 Clifford was shipped home smashed, and there was no child. And Sir Geoffrey died of chagrin.

Chapter Two

Connie and Clifford came home to Wragby in the autumn of 1920. Miss Chatterley, still disgusted at her brother's defection, had departed and was living in a little flat in London.

Wragby was a long low old house in brown stone, begun about the middle of the eighteenth century, and added on to, till it was a warren of a place without much distinction. It stood on an eminence in a rather fine old park of oak trees, but alas, one could see in the near distance the chimney of Tevershall pit, with its clouds of stream and smoke, and on the damp, hazy distance of the hill the raw straggle of Tevershall village, a village which began almost at the park gates, and trailed in utter hopeless ugliness for a long and gruesome mile: houses, rows of wretched, small, begrimed, brick houses, with black slate roofs for lids, sharp angles and wilful, blank dreariness.

Connie was accustomed to Kensington or the Scottish hills or the Sussex downs: that was her England. With the stoicism of the young she took in the utter, soulless ugliness of the coal-and-iron Midlands at a glance, and left it at what it was: unbelievable and not to be thought about. From the rather dismal rooms at Wragby she heard the rattle-rattle of the screens at the pit, the puff of the winding-engine, the clink-clink of shunting trucks, and the hoarse little whistle of the colliery locomotives. Tevershall pit-bank was burning, had been burning for years, and it would cost thousands to put it out. So it had to burn. And when the wind was that way, which was often, the house was full of the stench of this sulphurous combustion of the earth's excrement. But even on windless days the air always smelt of something under-earth: sulphur, iron, coal, or acid. And even on the Christmas roses the smuts settled persistently, incredible, like black manna from skies of doom.

Well, there it was: fated like the rest of things! It was rather awful, but why kick? You couldn't kick it away. It just went on. Life, like all the rest! On the low dark ceiling of cloud at night red blotches burned and quavered, dappling and swelling and contracting, like burns that give pain. It was the furnaces. At first they fascinated Connie with a sort of horror; she felt she was living underground. Then she got used to them. And in the morning it rained.

Clifford professed to like Wragby better than London. This country had a grim will of its own, and the people had guts. Connie wondered what else they had: certainly neither eyes nor minds. The people were as haggard, shapeless, and dreary as the countryside, and as unfriendly. Only there was something in their deep-mouthed slurring of the dialect, and the thresh-thresh of their hob-nailed pit-boots as they trailed home in gangs on the asphalt from work, that was terrible and a bit mysterious.

There had been no welcome home for the young squire, no festivities, no deputation, not even a single flower. Only a dank ride in a motor-car up a dark, damp drive, burrowing through gloomy trees, out to the slope of the park where grey damp sheep were feeding, to the knoll where the house spread its dark brown façade, and the housekeeper and her husband were hovering, like unsure tenants on the face of the earth, ready to stammer a welcome.

There was no communication between Wragby Hall and Tevershall village, none. No caps were touched, no curtseys bobbed. The colliers merely stared; the tradesmen lifted their caps to Connie as to an acquaintance, and nodded awkwardly to Clifford; that was all. Gulf impassable, and a quiet sort of resentment on either side. At first Connie suffered from the steady drizzle of resentment that came from the village. Then she hardened herself to it, and it became a sort of tonic, something to live up to. It was not that she and Clifford were unpopular, they merely belonged to another species altogether from the colliers. Gulf impassable, breach indescribable, such as is perhaps non-existent south of the Trent. But in the Midlands and the industrial North gulf impassable, across which no communication could take place. You stick to your side, I'll stick to mine! A strange denial of the common pulse of humanity.

Yet the village sympathized with Clifford and Connie in the abstract. In the flesh it was—You leave me alone!—on either side.

The rector was a nice man of about sixty, full of his duty, and reduced, personally, almost to a nonentity by the silent—You leave me alone!—of the village. The miners' wives were nearly all Methodists. The miners were nothing. But even so much official uniform as the clergyman wore was enough to obscure entirely the fact that he was a man like any other man. No, he was Mester Ashby, a sort of automatic preaching and praying concern.

This stubborn, instinctive—We think ourselves as good as you, if you *are* Lady Chatterley!—puzzled and baffled Connie at first extremely. The curious, suspicious, false amiability with which the miners' wives met her overtures; the curiously offensive tinge of—Oh dear me! I *am* somebody now, with Lady Chatterley talking to me! But she needn't think I'm not as good as her for all that!—which she always heard twanging in the women's half-fawning voices, was impossible. There was no getting past it. It was hopelessly and offensively nonconformist.

Clifford left them alone, and she learnt to do the same: she just went by without looking at them, and they stared as if she were a walking wax figure. When he had to deal with them, Clifford was rather haughty and contemptuous; one could no longer afford to be friendly. In fact he was altogether rather supercilious and contemptuous of anyone not in his own class. He stood his ground, without any attempt at conciliation. And he was neither liked nor disliked by the people; he was just part of things, like the pit-bank and Wragby itself.

But Clifford was really extremely shy and self-conscious now he was lamed. He hated seeing anyone except just the personal servants. For he had to sit in a wheeled chair or a sort of bath-chair. Nevertheless he was just as carefully dressed as ever, by his expensive tailors, and he wore the careful Bond Street neckties just as before, and from the top he looked just as smart and impressive as ever. He had never been one of the modern ladylike young men: rather bucolic even, with his ruddy face and broad shoulders. But his very quiet, hesitating voice, and his eyes, at the same time bold and frightened, assured and uncertain, revealed his nature. His manner was often offensively supercilious, and then again modest and self-effacing, almost tremulous.

Connie and he were attached to one another, in the aloof modern way. He was much too hurt in himself, the great shock of his maiming, to be easy and flippant. He was a hurt thing. And as such Connie stuck to him passionately.

But she could not help feeling how little connection he really had with people. The miners were, in a sense, his own men; but he saw them as objects rather than men, parts of the pit rather than parts of life, crude raw phenomena rather than human beings along with him. He was in some way afraid of them, he could not bear to have them look at him now he was lame. And their queer, crude life seemed as unnatural as that of hedgehogs.

He was remotely interested; but like a man looking down a microscope, or up a telescope. He was not in touch. He was not in actual touch with anybody, save, traditionally, with Wragby, and, through the close bond of family defense, with Emma. Beyond this nothing really touched him. Connie felt that she herself didn't really, not really touch him; perhaps there was nothing to get at ultimately; just a negation of human contact.

Yet he was absolutely dependent on her, he needed her every moment. Big and strong as he was, he was helpless. He could wheel himself about in a wheeled chair, and he had a sort of bath-chair with a motor attachment, in which he could puff slowly round the park. But alone he was like a lost thing. He needed Connie to be there, to assure him he existed at all.

Still he was ambitious. He had taken to writing stories; curious, very personal stories about people he had known. Clever, rather spiteful, and yet, in some mysterious way, meaningless. The observation was extraordinary and peculiar. But there was no touch, no actual contact. It was as if the whole thing took place in a vacuum. And since the field of life is largely an artificially-lighted stage today, the stories were curiously true to modern life, to the modern psychology, that is.

Clifford was almost morbidly sensitive about these stories. He wanted everyone to think them good, of the best, *ne plus ultra*. They appeared in the most modern magazines, and were praised and blamed as usual. But to Clifford the blame was torture, like knives goading him. It was as if the whole of his being were in his stories.

Connie helped him as much as she could. At first she was thrilled. He talked everything over with her monotonously, insistently, persistently, and she had to respond with all her might. It was as if her whole soul and body and sex had to rouse up and pass into these stories of his. This thrilled her and absorbed her.

Of physical life they lived very little. She had to superintend the house. But the housekeeper had served Sir Geoffrey for many years, and the dried-up, elderly, superlatively correct female . . . you could hardly call her a parlor-maid, or even a woman . . . who waited at table, had been in the house for forty years. Even the very housemaids were no longer young. It was awful! What could you do with such a place, but leave it alone! All these endless rooms that nobody used, all the Midlands routine, the mechanical cleanliness and the mechanical order! Clifford had insisted on a new cook, an experienced woman who had served him in his rooms in London. For the rest the place seemed run by mechanical anarchy. Everything went on in pretty good order, strict cleanliness, and strict punctuality; even pretty strict honesty. And yet, to Connie, it was a methodical anarchy. No warmth of feeling united it organically. The house seemed as dreary as a disused street.

What could she do but leave it alone . . . ? So she left it alone. Miss Chatterley came sometimes, with her aristocratic thin face, and triumphed, finding nothing altered. She would never forgive Connie for ousting her from her union in consciousness with her brother. It was she, Emma, who should be bringing forth the stories, these books, with him; the Chatterley stories, something new in the world, that *they*, the Chatterleys, had put there. There was no other standard. There was no organic connection with the thought and expression that had gone before. Only something new in the world: the Chatterley books, entirely personal.

Connie's father, when he paid a flying visit to Wragby, said in private to his daughter: As for Clifford's writing, it's smart, but there's nothing in it. It won't last! . . . Connie looked at the burly Scottish knight who had done himself well all his life, and her eyes, her big, still-wondering blue eyes became vague. Nothing in it! What did he mean by *nothing in it?* If the critics praised it, and Clifford's name was almost famous, and it even brought in money . . . what did her father mean by saying there was nothing in Clifford's writing? What else could there be?

For Connie had adopted the standard of the young: what there was in the moment was everything. And moments followed one another without necessarily belonging to one another.

It was in her second winter at Wragby her father said to her: "I hope, Connie, you won't let circumstances force you into being a *demi-vierge*."

A *demi-vierge!*" replied Connie vaguely. "Why? Why not?"

"Unless you like it, of course!" said her father hastily. To Clifford he said the same, when the two men were alone: "I'm afraid it doesn't quite suit Connie to be a *demi-vierge*."

"A half-virgin!" replied Clifford, translating the phrase to be sure of it.

He thought for a moment, then flushed very red. He was angry and offended.

"In what way doesn't it suit her?" he asked stiffly.

"She's getting thin . . . angular. It's not her style. She's not the pilchard sort of little slip of a girl, she's a bonny Scotch trout."

"Without the spots, of course!" said Clifford.

He wanted to say something later to Connie about the demi-vierge business . . . the half-virgin state of her affairs. But he could not bring himself to do it. He was at once too intimate with her and not intimate enough. He was so very much at one with her, in his mind and hers, but bodily they were non-existent to one another, and neither could bear to drag in the corpus delicti. They were so intimate, and utterly out of touch.

Connie guessed, however, that her father had said something, and that something was in Clifford's mind. She knew that he didn't mind whether she were demi-vierge or demi-monde, so long as he didn't absolutely know, and wasn't made to see. What the eye doesn't see and the mind doesn't know, doesn't exist.

Connie and Clifford had now been nearly two years at Wragby, living their vague life of absorption in Clifford and his work. Their interests had never ceased to flow together over his work. They talked and wrestled in the throes of composition, and felt as if something were happening, really happening, really in the void.

And thus far it was a life: in the void. For the rest it was non-existence. Wragby was there, the servants . . . but spectral, not really existing. Connie went for walks in the park, and in the woods that joined the park, and enjoyed the solitude and the mystery, kicked the brown leaves of autumn, and picked the primroses of spring. But it was all a dream; or rather it was like the simulacrum of reality. The oak-leaves were to her like oak-leaves seen ruffling in a mirror, she herself was a figure somebody had read about, picking primroses that were only shadows or memories, or words. No substance to her or anything . . . no touch, no contact! Only this life with Clifford, this endless spinning of webs of yarn, of the minutiae of consciousness, these stories Sir Malcolm said there was nothing in, and they wouldn't last. Why should there be anything in them, why should they last? Sufficient unto the day is the evil thereof. Sufficient unto the moment is the *appearance* of reality.

Clifford had quite a number of friends, acquaintances really, and he invited them to Wragby. He invited all sorts of people, critics and writers, people who would help to praise his books. And they were flattered at being asked to Wragby, and they praised. Connie understood it all perfectly. But why not? This was one of the fleeting patterns in the mirror. What was wrong with it?

She was hostess to these people . . . mostly men. She was hostess also to Clifford's occasional aristocratic relations. Being a soft, ruddy, country-looking girl, inclined to freckles, with big blue eyes, and curling, brown hair, and a soft voice and rather strong, female loins she was considered a little old-fashioned and "womanly." She was not a "little pilchard sort of fish," like a boy. She was too feminine to be quite smart.

So the men, especially those no longer young, were very nice to her indeed. But, knowing what torture poor Clifford would feel at the slightest sign of flirting on her part, she gave them no encouragement at all. She was quiet and vague, she had no contact with them and intended to have none. Clifford was extraordinarily proud of himself.

His relatives treated her quite kindly. She knew that the kindliness indicated a lack of fear, and that these people had no respect for you unless you could frighten them a little. But again she had no contact. She let them be kindly and disdainful, she let them feel they had no need to draw their steel in readiness. She had no real connection with them.

Time went on. Whatever happened, nothing happened, because she was so beautifully out of contact. She and Clifford lived in their ideas and his books. She entertained . . . there were always people in the house. Time went on as the clock does, half-past eight instead of half-past seven.

Chapter Three

Connie was aware, however, of a growing restlessness. Out of her disconnection, a restlessness was taking possession of her like madness. It twitched her limbs when she didn't want to twitch them, it jerked her spine when she didn't want to jerk upright but preferred to rest comfortably. It thrilled inside her body, in her womb, somewhere, till she felt she must jump into water and swim to get away from it; a mad restlessness. It made her heart beat violently for no reason. And she was getting thinner.

It was just restlessness. She would rush off across the park, and abandon Clifford, and lie prone in the bracken. To get away from the house . . . she must get away from the house and everybody. The wood was her one refuge, her sanctuary.

But it was not really a refuge, a sanctuary, because she had no connection with it. It was only a place where she could get away from the rest. She never really touched the spirit of the wood itself . . . if it had any such nonsensical thing.

Vaguely she knew herself that she was going to pieces in some way. Vaguely she knew she was out of connection: she had lost touch with the substantial and vital world. Only Clifford and his books, which did not exist . . . which had nothing in them! Void to void. Vaguely she knew. But it was like beating her head against a stone.

Her father warned her again: "Why don't you get yourself a beau, Connie? Do you all the good in the world."

That winter Michaelis came for a few days. He was a young Irishman who had already made a large fortune by his plays in America. He had been taken up quite enthusiastically for a time by smart society in London, for he wrote smart society plays. Then gradually smart society realized that it had been made ridiculous at the hands of a down-at-heel Dublin street-rat, and revulsion came. Michaelis was the last word in what was caddish and bounderish. He was discovered to be anti-English, and to the class that made this discovery this was worse than the dirtiest crime. He was cut dead, and his corpse thrown into the refuse-can.

Nevertheless Michaelis had his apartment in Mayfair, and walked down Bond Street the image of a gentleman, for you cannot get even the best tailors to cut their low-down customers, when the customers pay.

Clifford was inviting the young man of thirty at an inauspicious moment in that young man's career. Yet Clifford did not hesitate. Michaelis had the ear of a few million people, probably; and, being a hopeless outsider, he would no doubt be grateful to be asked down to Wragby at this juncture, when the rest of the smart world was cutting him. Being grateful, he would no doubt do Clifford "good" over there in America. Kudos! A man gets a lot of kudos, whatever that may be, by being talked about in the right way, especially "over there." Clifford was a coming man; and it was remarkable what a sound publicity instinct he had. In the end Michaelis did him most nobly in a play, and Clifford was a sort of popular hero. Till the reaction, when he found he had been made ridiculous.

Connie wondered a little over Clifford's blind, imperious instinct to become known: known, that is, to the vast amorphous world he did not himself know, and of which he was uneasily afraid; known as a writer, as a first-class modern writer. Connie was aware from successful, old, hearty, bluffing Sir Malcolm, that artists did advertise themselves, and exert themselves to put their goods over. But her father used channels ready-made, used by all the other R.A.'s who sold their pictures. Whereas Clifford discovered new channels of publicity, all kinds. He had all kinds of people at Wragby, without exactly lowering himself. But, determined to build himself a monument of a reputation quickly, he used any handy rubble in the making.

Michaelis arrived duly, in a very neat car, with a chauffeur and a manservant. He was absolutely Bond Street! But at sight of him something in Clifford's country soul recoiled. He wan't exactly . . . not exactly . . . in fact, he wasn't at all, well, what his appearance intended to imply. To Clifford this was final and enough. Yet he was very polite to the man; to the amazing success in him. The bitch-goddess, as she is called, of Success, roamed, snarling and protective, round the half-humble, half-defiant Michaelis' heels, and intimidated Clifford completely: for he wanted to prostitute himself to the bitch-goddess Success also, if only she would have him.

Michaelis obviously wasn't an Englishman, in spite of all the tailors, hatters, barbers, booters of the very best quarter of London. No, no, he obviously wasn't an Englishman: the wrong sort of flattish, pale face and bearing; and the wrong sort of grievance. He had a grudge and a grievance: that was obvious to any true-born English gentleman, who would scorn to let such a thing appear blatant in his own demeanor. Poor Michaelis had been much kicked, so that he had a slightly tail-between-the-legs look even now. He had pushed his way by sheer instinct and sheerer effrontery on to the stage and to the front of it, with his plays. He had caught the public. And he had thought the kicking days were over. Alas, they weren't. . . . They never would be. For he, in a sense, asked to be kicked. He pined to be where he didn't belong . . . among the English upper classes. And how they enjoyed the various kicks they got at him! And how he hated them!

Nevertheless he traveled with his manservant and his very neat car, this Dublin mongrel.

There was something about him that Connie liked. He didn't put on airs to himself; he had no illusions about himself. He talked to Clifford sensibly, briefly, practically about all the things Clifford wanted to know. He didn't expand or let himself go. He knew he had been asked down to Wragby to be made use of, and like an old, shrewd, almost indifferent business man, or big-business man, he let himself be asked questions, and he answered with as little waste of feeling as possible.

"Money!" he said. "Money is a sort of instinct. It's a sort of property of nature in a man to make money. It's nothing you do. It's no trick you play. It's a sort of permanent accident of your own nature; once you start, you make money, and you go on; up to a point, I suppose."

"But you've got to begin," said Clifford.

"Oh, quite! You've got to get in. You can do nothing if you are kept outside. You've got to beat your way in. Once you've done that, you can't help it!"

"But could you have made money except by plays?" asked Clifford.

"Oh, probably not! I may be a good writer or I may be a bad one, but a writer and a writer of plays is what I am, and I've got to be. There's no question of that."

"And you think it's a writer of popular plays that you've got to be?" asked Connie.

"There, exactly!" he said, turning to her in a sudden flash. "There's nothing in it! There's nothing in popularity. There's nothing in the public, if it comes to that. There's nothing really in my plays to *make* them popular. It's not that. They just are, like the weather . . . the sort that will *have* to be . . . for the time being."

He turned his slow, rather full eyes, that had been drowned in such fathomless disillusion, on Connie, and she trembled a little. He seemed so old . . . endlessly old, built up of layers of disillusion, going down in him generation after generation, like geological strata; and at the same time he was forlorn like a child. An outcast, in a certain sense; but with the desperate bravery of his rat-like existence.

"At least it's wonderful what you've done at your time of life," said Clifford contemplatively.

"I'm thirty . . . yes, I'm thirty!" said Michaelis, sharply and suddenly, with a curious laugh; hollow, triumphant, and bitter.

"And are you alone?" asked Connie.

"How do you mean? Do I live alone? I've got my servant. He's a Greek, so he says, and quite incompetent. But I keep him. And I'm going to marry. Oh, yes, I must marry."

"It sounds like going to have your tonsils cut," laughed Connie. "Will it be an effort?"

He looked at her admiringly. "Well, Lady Chatterley, somehow it will! I find . . . excuse me . . . I find I can't marry an Englishwoman, not even an Irishwoman. . . ."

"Try an American," said Clifford.

"Oh, American!" he laughed a hollow laugh. "No, I've asked my man if he will find me a Turk or something . . . something nearer to the Oriental."

Connie really wondered at this queer, melancholy specimen of extraordinary success; it was said he had an income of fifty thousand dollars from America alone. Sometimes he was handsome: sometimes as he looked sideways, downwards, and the light fell on him, he had the silent, enduring beauty of a carved ivory negro mask, with his rather full eyes, and the strong queerly-arched brows, the immobile compressed mouth; that momentary but revealed immobility, an immobility, a timelessness which the Buddha aims at, and which negroes express sometimes without even aiming at it; something old, old, and acquiescent in the race! Aeons of acquiescence in race destiny, instead of our individual resistance. And then a swimming through, like rats in a dark river. Connie felt a sudden, strange leap of sympathy for him, a leap mingled with compassion, and tinged with repulsion, amounting almost to love. The outsider! The outsider! And they called him a bounder! How much more bounderish and assertive Clifford looked! How much stupider!

Michaelis knew at once he had made an impression on her. He turned his full, hazel, slightly prominent eyes on her in a look of pure detachment. He was estimating her, and the extent of the impression he had made. With the English nothing could save him from being the eternal outsider, not even love. Yet women sometimes fell for him. . . . Englishwomen too.

He knew just where he was with Clifford. They were two alien dogs which would have liked to snarl at one another, but which smiled instead, perforce. But with the woman he was not quite so sure.

Breakfast was served in the bedrooms; Clifford never appeared before lunch, and the dining-room was a little dreary. After coffee Michaelis, restless and ill-sitting soul, wondered what he should do. It was a fine November day . . . fine for Wragby. He looked over the melancholy park. My God! What a place!

He sent a servant to ask, could he be of any service to Lady Chatterley: he thought of driving into Sheffield. The answer came, would he care to go up to Lady Chatterley's sitting-room?

Connie had a sitting-room on the third floor, the top floor of the central portion of the house. Clifford's rooms were on the ground floor, of course. Michaelis was flattered by being asked up to Lady Chatterley's own parlor. He followed blindly after the servant . . . he never noticed things, or had contact with his surroundings.

In her room he did glance vaguely round at the fine German reproductions of Renoir and Cézanne.

"It's very pleasant up here," he said, with his queer smile, as if it hurt him to smile, showing his teeth. "You are wise to get up to the top."

"Yes, I think so," she said.

Her room was the only gay, modern one in the house, the only spot in Wragby where her personality was at all revealed. Clifford had never seen it, and she asked very few people up.

Now she and Michaelis sat on opposite sides of the fire and talked. She asked him about himself, his mother and father, his brothers . . . other people were always something of a wonder to her, and when her sympathy was awakened she was quite devoid of class feeling. Michaelis talked frankly about himself, quite frankly, without affectation, simply revealing his bitter, indifferent, stray-dog's soul, then showing a gleam of revengeful pride in his success.

"But why are you such a lonely bird?" Connie asked him; and again he looked at her, with his full, searching, hazel look.

"Some birds *are* that way," he replied. Then, with a touch of familiar irony: "But, look here, what about yourself? Aren't you by way of being a lonely bird yourself?" Connie, a little startled, thought about it for a few moments, and then she said: "Only in a way! Not altogether, like you!"

"Am I altogether a lonely bird?" he asked, with his queer grin of a smile, as if he had toothache; it was so wry, and his eyes were so perfectly unchangingly melancholy, or stoical, or disillusioned, or afraid.

"Why?" she said, a little breathless, as she looked at him. "You are, aren't you?"

She felt a terrible appeal coming to her from him, that made her almost lose her balance.

"Oh, you're quite right!" he said, turning his head away, and looking sideways, downwards, with that strange immobility of an old race that is hardly here in our present day. It was that that really made Connie lose her power to see him detached from herself.

He looked up at her with the full glance that saw everything, registered everything. At the same time, the infant crying in the night was crying out of his breast to her, in a way that affected her very womb.

"It's awfully nice of you to think of me," he said laconically.

"Why shouldn't I think of you?" she exclaimed, with hardly breath to utter it.

He gave the wry, quick hiss of a laugh.

"Oh, in that way! . . . May I hold your hand for a minute?" he asked suddenly, fixing his eyes on her with almost hypnotic power, and sending out an appeal that affected her direct in the womb.

She stared at him, dazed and transfixed, and he went over and kneeled beside her, and took her two feet close in his two hands, and buried his face in her lap, remaining motionless. She was perfectly dim and dazed, looking down in a sort of amazement at the rather tender nape of his neck, feeling his face pressing against her. In all her burning dismay, she could not help putting her hand, with tenderness and compassion, on the defenseless nape of his neck, and he trembled, with a deep shudder.

Then he looked up at her with that awful appeal in his full, glowing eyes. She was utterly incapable of resisting it. From her breast flowed the answering, immense yearning over him; she must give him anything, anything.

He was a curious and very gentle lover, very gentle with the woman, trembling uncontrollably, and yet at the same time detached, aware, aware of every sound outside.

To her it meant nothing except that she gave herself to him. And at length he ceased to quiver any more, and lay quite still, quite still. Then, with dim, compassionate fingers, she stroked his head, that lay on her breast.

When he rose, he kissed both her hands, then both her feet, in their suede slippers, and in silence went away to the end of the room, where he stood with his back to her. There was silence for some minutes. Then he turned and came to her again as she sat in her old place by the fire.

"And now, I suppose you'll hate me!" he said in a quiet, inevitable way. She looked up at him quickly.

"Why should I?" she asked.

"They mostly do," he said; then he caught himself up. "I mean . . . a woman is supposed to."

"This is the last moment when I ought to hate you," she said resentfully.

"I know! I know! It should be so! You're *frightfully* good to me . . ." he cried miserably.

She wondered why he should be miserable. "Won't you sit down again?" she said. He glanced at the door.

"Sir Clifford!" he said, "won't he . . . won't he be . . .?"

She paused a moment to consider. "Perhaps!" she said. And she looked up at him. "I don't want Clifford to know . . . not even to suspect. It would hurt him so much. But I don't think it's wrong, do you?"

"Wrong! Good God, no! You're only too infinitely good to me. . . . I can hardly bear it."

He turned aside, and she saw that in another moment he would be sobbing.

"But we needn't let Clifford know, need we?" she pleaded. "It *would* hurt him so. And if he never knows, never suspects, it hurts nobody."

"Me!" he said, almost fiercely; "he'll know nothing from me! You see if he does. Me give myself away! Ha! Ha!" he laughed hollowly, cynically at such an idea. She watched him in wonder. He said to her: "May I kiss your hand and go? I'll run into Sheffield I think, and lunch there, if I may, and be back to tea. May I do anything for you? May I be sure you don't hate me—and that you won't?"—he ended with a desperate note of cynicism.

"No, I don't hate you," she said. "I think you're nice."

"Ah!" he said to her fiercely, "I'd rather you said that to me than that you love me! It means such a lot more. . . . Till afternoon then. I've plenty to think about till then." He kissed her hands humbly and was gone.

"I don't think I can stand that young man," said Clifford at lunch.

"Why?" asked Connie.

"He's such a bounder underneath his veneer . . . just waiting to bounce us."

"I think people have been so unkind to him," said Connie.

"Do you wonder? And do you think he employs his shining hours doing deeds of kindness?"

"I think he has a certain sort of generosity."

"Towards whom?"

"I don't quite know."

"Naturally you don't. I'm afraid you mistake unscrupulousness for generosity."

Connie paused. Did she? It was just possible. Yet the unscrupulousness of Michaelis had a certain fascination for her. He went whole lengths where Clifford only crept a few timid paces. In his way he had conquered the world, which was what Clifford wanted to do. Ways and means . . . ? Were those of Michaelis more despicable than those of Clifford? Was the way the poor outsider had shoved and bounced himself forward in person, and by the back doors, any worse than Clifford's way of advertising himself into prominence? The bitch-goddess, Success, was trailed by thousands of gasping dogs with lolling tongues. The one that got her first was the real dog among dogs, if you go by success! So Michaelis could keep his tail up.

The queer thing was, he didn't. He came back towards tea-time with a large handful of violets and lilies, and the same hang-dog expression. Connie wondered sometimes if it were a sort of mask to disarm opposition, because it was almost too fixed. Was he really such a sad dog?

His sad-dog sort of extinguished self persisted all the evening, though through it Clifford felt the inner effrontery. Connie didn't feel it, perhaps because it was not directed against woman; only against men, and their presumptions and assumptions. That indestructible, inward effrontery in the meager fellow was what made men so down on Michaelis. His very presence was an affront to a man of society, cloak it as he might in an assumed good manner.

Connie was in love with him, but she managed to sit with her embroidery and let the men talk, and not give herself away. As for Michaelis, he was perfect; exactly the same melancholic, attentive, aloof young fellow of the previous evening, millions of degrees remote from his hosts, but laconically playing up to them to the required amount, and never coming forth to them for a moment. Connie felt he must have forgotten the morning. He had not forgotten. But he knew where he was . . . in the same old place outside, where the born outsiders are. He didn't take the love-making altogether personally. He knew it would not change him from an ownerless dog, whom everybody begrudges its golden collar, into a comfortable society dog.

The final fact being that at the very bottom of his soul he *was* an outsider, and anti-social, and he accepted the fact inwardly, no matter how Bond-Streety he was on the outside. His isolation was a necessity to him; just as the appearance of conformity and mixing-in with the smart people was also a necessity.

But occasional love, as a comfort and soothing, was also a good thing, and he was not ungrateful. On the contrary, he was burningly, poignantly grateful for a piece of natural, spontaneous kindness: almost to tears. Beneath his pale, immobile, disillusioned face, his child's soul was sobbing with gratitude to the woman, and burning to come to her again; just as his outcast soul was knowing he would keep really clear of her.

He found an opportunity to say to her, as they were lighting the candles in the hall:

"May I come?"

"I'll come to you," she said.

"Oh, good!"

He waited for her a long time . . . but she came.

He was the trembling excited sort of lover, whose crisis soon came, and was finished. There was something curiously childlike and defenseless about him. His defenses were all in his wits and cunning, his very instincts of cunning, and when these were in abeyance he seemed doubly naked and like a child, of unfinished, tender flesh, and somehow struggling helplessly.

He aroused in the woman a wild sort of compassion and yearning, and a wild, craving physical desire. The physical desire he did not satisfy in her; he was always come and finished so quickly, then shrinking down on her breast, and recovering somewhat his effrontery while she lay dazed, disappointed, lost.

But then she soon learnt to hold him, to keep him there inside her when his crisis was over. And there he was generous and curiously potent; he stayed firm inside her, given to her, while she was active . . . wildly, passionately active, coming to her own crisis. And as he felt the frenzy of her achieving her own orgasmic satisfaction from his hard, erect passivity, he had a curious sense of pride and satisfaction.

"Ah, how good!" she whispered tremulously, and she became quite still, clinging to him. And he lay there in his own isolation, but somehow proud.

He stayed that time only the three days, and to Clifford was exactly the same as on the first evening; to Connie also. There was no breaking down his external man.

He wrote to Connie with the same plaintive melancholy note as ever, sometimes witty, and touched with a queer, sexless affection. A kind of hopeless affection he seemed to feel for her, and the essential remoteness remained the same. He was hopeless at the very core of him, and he wanted to be hopeless. He rather hated hope. *"Une immense espérance an traversé la terre,"* he read somewhere, and his comment was: "—and it's darned-well drowned everything worth having."

Connie never really understood him, but in her way, she loved him. And all the time she felt the reflection of his hopelessness in her. She couldn't quite, quite love in hopelessness. And he, being hopeless, couldn't ever quite love at all.

So they went on for quite a time, writing, and meeting occasionally in London. She still wanted the physical, sexual thrill she could get with him by her own activity, his little orgasm being over. And he still wanted to give it her. Which was enough to keep them connected.

And enough to give her a subtle sort of self-assurance, something blind and a little arrogant. It was an almost mechanical confidence in her own powers, and went with a great cheerfulness.

She was terrifically cheerful at Wragby. And she used all her aroused cheerfulness and satisfaction to stimulate Clifford, so that he wrote his best at this time, and was almost happy in his strange blind way. He really reaped the fruits of the sensual satisfaction she got out of Michaelis' male passivity erect inside her. But of course he never knew it, and, if he had, he wouldn't have said thank-you!

Yet when those days of her grand joyful cheerfulness and stimulus were gone, quite gone, and she was depressed and irritable, how Clifford longed for them again! Perhaps if he'd known he might even have wished to get her and Michaelis together again.

Chapter Four

Connie always had a foreboding of the hopelessness of her affair with Mick, as people called him. Yet other men seemed to mean nothing to her. She was attached to Clifford. He wanted a good deal of her life and she gave it to him. But she wanted a good deal from the life of a man, and this Clifford did not give her; could not. There were occasional spasms of Michaelis. But, as she knew by foreboding, that would come to an end. Mick *couldn't* keep anything up. It was part of his very being that he must break off any connection, and be loose, isolated, absolutely lone dog again. It was his major necessity, even though he always said: She turned me down!

The world is supposed to be full of possibilities, but they narrow down to pretty few in most personal experience. There's lots of good fish in the sea . . . maybe . . . but the vast masses seem to be mackerel or herring, and if you're not mackerel or herring yourself, you are likely to find very few good fish in the sea.

Clifford was making strides into fame, and even money. People came to see him. Connie nearly always had somebody at Wragby. But if they weren't mackerel they were herring, with an occasional cat-fish, or conger-eel.

There were a few regular men, constants; men who had been at Cambridge with Clifford. There was Tommy Dukes, who had remained in the army, and was a Brigadier-General. "The army leaves me time to think, and saves me from having to face the battle of life," he said.

There was Charles May, an Irishman, who wrote scientifically about stars. There was Hammond, another writer. All were about the same age as Clifford; the young intellectuals of the day. They all believed in the life of the mind. What you did apart from that was your private affair, and didn't much matter. No one thinks of enquiring of another person at what hour he retires to the privy. It isn't interesting to anyone but the person concerned.

And so with most of the matters of ordinary life . . . how you make your money, or whether you love your wife, or if you have "affairs." All these matters concern only the person concerned, and, like going to the privy, have no interest for anyone else.

"The whole point about the sexual problem," said Hammond, who was a tall thin fellow with a wife and two children, but much more closely connected with a typewriter, "is that there is no point to it. Strictly there is no problem. We don't want to follow a man into the W.C., so why should we want to follow him into bed with a woman? And therein lies the problem. If we took no more notice of the one thing than the other, there'd be no problem. It's all utterly senseless and pointless; a matter of misplaced curiosity."

"Quite, Hammond, quite! But if someone starts making love to Julia, you begin to simmer; and if he goes on, you are soon at boiling point." . . . Julia was Hammond's wife.

"Why, exactly! So I should be if he began to urinate in a corner of my drawing-room. There's a place for all these things."

"You mean you wouldn't mind if he made love to Julia in some discreet alcove?"

Charlie May was slightly satirical, for he had flirted a very little with Julia, and Hammond had cut up very roughly.

"Of course I should mind. Sex is a private thing between me and Julia; and of course I should mind anyone else trying to mix in."

"As a matter of fact," said the lean and freckled Tommy Dukes, who looked much more Irish than May, who was pale and rather fat: "as a matter of fact, Hammond, you have a strong property instinct, and a strong will to self-assertion, and you want success. Since I've been in the army definitely, I've got out of the way of the world, and now I see how inordinately strong the craving for self-assertion and success is in men. It is enormously over-developed. All our individuality has run that way. And of course men like you think you'll get through better with a woman's backing. That's why you're so jealous. That's what sex is to you . . . a vital little dynamo between you and Julia to bring success. If you began to be unsuccessful you'd begin to flirt, like Charlie, who isn't successful. Married people like you and Julia have labels on you, like travellers' trunks. Julia is labelled *Mrs. Arnold B. Hammond* . . . just like a trunk on the railway that belongs to somebody. And you are labelled Arnold B. Hammond, c/o *Mrs. Arnold B. Hammond.* Oh, you're quite right, you're quite right! The life of the mind needs a comfortable house and decent cooking. You're quite right. It even needs posterity. But it all hinges on the instinct for success. That is the pivot on which all things turn."

Hammond looked rather piqued. He was rather proud of the integrity of his mind, and of his *not* being a time-server. None the less, he did want success.

"It's quite true, you can't live without cash," said May. "You've got to have a certain amount of it to be able to live and get along . . . even to be free to *think* you must have a certain amount of money, or your stomach stops you. But it seems to me you might leave the labels off sex. We're free to talk to anybody; so why shouldn't we be free to make love to any woman who inclines us that way?"

"There speaks the lascivious Celt," said Clifford.

"Lascivious! Well, why not? I can't see I do a woman any more harm by sleeping with her than by dancing with her . . . or even talking to her about the weather. It's just an interchange of sensations instead of ideas, so why not?"

"Be as promiscuous as the rabbits!" said Hammond.

"Why not? What's wrong with rabbits? Are they any worse than a neurotic, revolutionary humanity, full of nervous hate?"

"But we're not rabbits, even so," said Hammond.

"Precisely! I have my mind: I have certain calculations to make in certain astronomical matters that concern me almost more than life or death. Sometimes indigestion interferes with me. Hunger would interfere with me disastrously. In the same way starved sex interferes with me. What then?"

"I should have thought sexual indigestion from surfeit would have interfered with you more seriously," said Hammond satirically.

"Not it! I don't over-eat myself, and I don't over-fuck myself. One has a choice about eating too much. But you would absolutely starve me."

"Not at all. You can marry."

"How do you know I can? It may not suit the process of my mind. Marriage might . . . and would . . . stultify my mental processes. I'm not properly pivoted that way . . . and so must I be chained in a kennel like a monk? All rot and funk, my boy. I must live and do my calculations. I need women sometimes. I refuse to make a mountain of it, and I refuse anybody's moral condemnation or prohibition. I'd be ashamed to see a woman walking around with my name-label on her, address and railway station, like a wardrobe trunk."

These two men had not forgiven each other about the Julia flirtation.

"It's an amusing idea, Charlie," said Dukes, "that sex is just another form of talk, where you act the words instead of saying them. I suppose it's quite true. I suppose we might exchange as many sensations and emotions with women as we do ideas about the weather, and so on. Sex might be a sort of normal, physical conversation between a man and a woman. You don't talk to a woman unless you have ideas in common: that is you don't talk with any interest. And in the same way, unless you had some emotion or sympathy in common with a woman you wouldn't sleep with her. But if you had. . . ."

"If you *have* the proper sort of emotion or sympathy with a woman, you *ought* to sleep with her," said May. "It's the only decent thing to do with her. Just as, when you are interested talking to someone, the only decent thing is to have the talk out. You don't prudishly put your tongue between your teeth and bit it. You just say out your say. And the same the other way."

"No," said Hammond. "It's wrong. You, for example, May, you squander half your force with women. You'll never really do what you should do, with a fine mind such as yours. Too much of you goes the other way."

"Maybe it does. . . . and too little of you goes that way, Hammond, my boy, married or not. You can keep the purity and integrity of your mind, but it's going damned dry. Your pure mind is going as dry as fiddlesticks, from what I see of it. You're simply talking it down."

Tommy Dukes burst into a laugh.

"Go it, you two minds!" he said. "Look at me . . . I don't do any high and pure mental work, nothing but jot down a few ideas. And yet I neither marry nor run after women. I think Charlie's quite right; if he wants to run after the women, he's quite free not to run too often. But I wouldn't prohibit him from running. As for Hammond, he's got a property instinct, so naturally the straight road and the narrow gate are right for him. You'll see he'll be an English Man of Letters before he's done, A. B. C. from top to toe. Then there's me. I'm nothing. Just a squib. And what about you, Clifford? Do you think sex is a dynamo to help a man on to success in the world?"

Clifford rarely talked much at these times. He never held forth; his ideas were really not vital enough for it, he was too confused and emotional. Now he blushed and looked uncomfortable.

"Well!" he said, "being myself *hors de combat,* I don't see I've anything to say on the matter."

"Not at all," said Dukes; "the top of you's by no means *hors de combat.* You've got the life of the mind sound and intact. So let us hear your ideas."

"Well," stammered Clifford, "even then I don't suppose I have much idea. . . . I suppose marry-and-have-done-with-it would pretty well stand for what I think. Though of course between a man and woman who care for one another, it is a great thing."

"What sort of great thing?" said Tommy.

"Oh, . . . it perfects the intimacy," said Clifford, uneasy as a woman in such talk.

"Well, Charlie and I believe that sex is a sort of communication like speech. Let any woman start a sex conversation with me, and it's natural for me to go to bed with her to finish it, all in due season. Unfortunately no woman makes any particular start with me, so I go to bed by myself; and am none the worse for it. . . . I hope so anyway, for how should I know? Anyhow I've no starry calculations to be interfered with, and no immortal works to write. I'm merely a fellow skulking in the army. . . ."

Silence fell. The four men smoked. And Connie sat there and put another stitch in her sewing. . . . Yes, she sat there! She had to sit mum. She had to be quiet as a mouse, not to interfere with the immensely important speculations of these highly-mental gentlemen. But she had to be there. They didn't get on so well without her; their ideas didn't flow so freely. Clifford was much more edgy and nervous, he got cold feet much quicker in Connie's absence, and the talk didn't run. Tommy Dukes came off best; he was a little inspired by her presence. Hammond she didn't really like; he seemed so selfish in a mental way. And Charles May, though she liked something about him, seemed a little distasteful and messy, in spite of his stars.

How many evenings had Connie sat and listened to the manifestations of these four men! these, and one or two others. That they never seemed to get anywhere didn't trouble her deeply. She liked to hear what they had to say, especially when Tommy was there. It was fun. Instead of men kissing you, and touching you, they revealed their minds to you. It was great fun! But what cold minds!

And also it was a little irritating. She had more respect for Michaelis, on whose name they all poured such withering contempt, as a little mongrel arriviste, and uneducated bounder of the worst sort. Mongrel and bounder or not, he jumped to his own conclusions. He didn't merely walk round them with millions of words, in the parade of the life of the mind.

Connie quite liked the life of the mind, and got a great thrill out of it. But she did think it overdid itself a little. She loved being there, amidst the tobacco smoke of those famous evenings of the cronies, as she called them privately to herself. She was infinitely amused, and proud too, that even their talking they could not do without her silent presence. She had an immense respect for thought . . . and these men, at least, tried to think honestly. But somehow there was a cat, and it wouldn't jump. They all alike talked at something, though what it was, for the life of her she couldn't say. It was something that Mick didn't clear, either.

But then Mick wasn't trying to do anything, but just get through his life, and put as much across other people as they tried to put across him. He was really anti-social, which was what Clifford and his cronies had against him. Clifford and his cronies were not anti-social; they were more or less bent on saving mankind, or on instructing it, to say the least.

There was a gorgeous talk on Sunday evening, when the conversation drifted again to love.

>   "Blest be the tie that binds
>   Our hearts in kindred something-or-other"—

said Tommy Dukes. "I'd like to know what the tie is. . . . The tie that binds *us* just now is mental friction on one another. And, apart from that, there's damned little tie between us. We bust apart, and say spiteful things about one another, like all the other damned intellectuals in the world. Damned everybodies, as far as that goes, for they all do it. Else we bust apart, and cover up the spiteful things we feel against one another by saying false sugaries. It's a curious thing that the mental life seems to flourish with its roots in spite, ineffable and fathomless spite. Always has been so! Look at Socrates, in Plato, and his bunch round him! The sheer spite of it all, just sheer joy in pulling somebody else to bits. . . . Protagoras, or whoever it was! And Alcibiades, and all the other little disciple dogs joining in the fray! I must say it makes one prefer Buddha, quietly sitting under a bo-tree, or Jesus, telling his disciples little Sunday stories, peacefully, and without any mental fireworks. No, there's something wrong with the mental life, radically. It's rooted in spite and envy, envy and spite. Ye shall know the tree by its fruit."

"I don't think we're altogether so spiteful," protested Clifford.

"My dear Clifford, think of the way we talk each other over, all of us. I'm rather worse than anybody else, myself. Because I infinitely prefer the spontaneous spite to the concocted sugaries; now they *are* poison; when I begin saying what a fine fellow Clifford is, etc.,etc., then poor Clifford is to be pitied. For God's sake, all of you, say spiteful things about me, then I shall know I mean something to you. Don't say sugaries, or I'm done."

"Oh, but I do think we honestly like one another," said Hammond.

"I tell you we must . . . we say such spiteful things to one another, about one another, behind our backs! I'm the worst."

"And I do think you confuse the mental life with the critical activity. I agree with you, Socrates gave the critical activity a grand start, but he did more than that," said Charlie May, rather magisterially. The cronies had such a curious pomposity under their assumed modesty. It was all so *ex cathedra,* and it all pretended to be so humble.

Dukes refused to be drawn out about Socrates.

"That's quite true, criticism and knowledge are not the same thing," said Hammond.

"They aren't, of course," chimed in Berry, a brown, shy young man, who had called to see Dukes, and was staying the night.

They all looked at him as if the ass had spoken.

"I wasn't talking about knowledge. . . . I was talking about the mental life," laughed Dukes. "Real knowledge comes out of the whole corpus of the consciousness; out of your belly and your penis as much as out of your brain and mind. The mind can only analyze and rationalize. Set the mind and the reason to cock it over the rest, and all they can do is criticize, and make a deadness. I say *all* they can do. It is vastly important. My God, the world needs criticizing to death. Therefore let's live the mental life, and glory in our spite, and strip the rotten old show. But, mind you, it's like this; while you *live* your life, you are in some way an organic whole with all life. But once you start the mental life you pluck the apple. You've severed the connection between the apple and the tree: the organic connection. And if you've got nothing in your life *but* the mental life, then you yourself are a plucked apple . . . you've fallen off the tree. And then it is a logical necessity to be spiteful, just as it's a natural necessity for a plucked apple to go bad."

Clifford made big eyes: it was all stuff to him. Connie secretly laughed to herself.

"Well then, we're all plucked apples," said Hammond, rather acidly and petulantly.

"So let's make cider of ourselves," said Charlie.

"But what do you think of Bolshevism?" put in the brown Berry, as if everything had led up to it.

"Bravo!" roared Charlie. "What do you think of Bolshevism?"

"Come on! Let's make hay of Bolshevism!" said Dukes.

"I'm afraid Bolshevism is a large question," said Hammond, shaking his head seriously.

"Bolshevism, it seems to me," said Charlie, "is just a superlative hatred of the thing they call the bourgeois; and what the bourgeois is, isn't quite defined. It is Capitalism, among other things. Feelings and emotions are also so decidedly bourgeois that you have to invent a man without them.

"Then the individual, especially the *personal* man, is bourgeois: so he must be suppressed. You must submerge yourselves in the great thing, the Soviet-social thing. Even an organism is bourgeois: so the ideal must be mechanical. The only thing that is a unit, non-organic, composed of many different, and equally essential parts, is the machine. Each man a machine-part, and the driving power of the machine, hate . . . hate of the bourgeois. That, to me, is Bolshevism."

"Absolutely!" said Tommy. "But also, it seems to me a perfect description of the whole of the industrial ideal. It's the factory-owner's ideal in a nut-shell; except that he would deny that the driving power was hate. Hate it is, all the same: hate of life itself. Just look at these Midlands, if it isn't plainly written up . . . but it's all part of the life of the mind, it's a logical development."

"I deny that Bolshevism is logical, it rejects the major part of the premises," said Hammond.

"My dear man, it allows the material premise; so does the pure mind . . . exclusively."

"At least Bolshevism has got down to rock bottom," said Charlie.

"Rock bottom! The bottom that has no bottom! The Bolshevists will have the finest army in the world in a very short time, with the finest mechanical equipment."

"But this thing can't go on . . . this hate business. There must be a reaction . . ." said Hammond.

"Well, we've been waiting for years . . . we wait longer. Hate's a growing thing like anything else. It's the inevitable outcome of forcing ideas on to life, of forcing one's deepest instincts; our deepest feelings we force according to certain ideas. We drive ourselves with a formula, like a machine. The logical mind pretends to rule the roost, and the roost turns into pure hate. We're all Bolshevists, only we are hypocrites. The Russians are Bolshevists without hypocrisy."

"But there are many other ways," said Hammond, "than the Soviet way. The Bolshevists aren't really intelligent."

"Of course not. But sometimes it's intelligent to be half-witted: if you want to make your end. Personally, I consider Bolshevism half-witted; but so do I consider our social life in the west half-witted. So I even consider our far-famed mental life half-witted. We're all as cold as crétins, we're all as passionless as idiots. We're all of us Bolshevists, only we give it another name. We think we're gods . . . men like gods! It's just the same as Bolshevism. One has to be human, and have a heart and a penis, if one is going to escape being either a god or a bolshevist . . . for they are the same thing: they're both too good to be true."

Out of the disapproving silence came Berry's anxious question:

"You do believe in love then, Tommy, don't you?"

"You lovely lad!" said Tommy. "No, my cherub, nine times out of ten, no!

Love's another of those half-witted performances to-day. Fellows with swaying waists fucking little jazz girls with small-boy buttocks, like two collar studs! Do you mean that sort of love? Or the joint-property, make-a-success-of-it, My-husband-my-wife sort of love? No, my fine fellow, I don't believe in it at all!"

"But you do believe in something?"

"Me? Oh, intellectually I believe in having a good heart, a chirpy penis, a lively intelligence, and the courage to say 'shit!' in front of a lady."

"Well, you've got them all," said Berry.

Tommy Dukes roared with laughter. "You angel boy! If only I had! If only I had! No; my heart's as numb as a potato, my penis droops and never lifts its head up, I dare rather cut him clean off than say 'shit!' in front of my mother or my aunt . . . they are real ladies, mind you; and I'm not really intelligent, I'm only a 'mental-lifer.' It would be wonderful to be intelligent: then one would be alive in all the parts mentioned and unmentionable. The penis rouses his head and says: How do you do? to any really intelligent person. Renoir said he painted his pictures with his penis . . . he did too, lovely pictures! I wish I did something with mine. God! when one can only talk! Another torture added to Hades! And Socrates started it."

"There are nice women in the world," said Connie, lifting her head up and speaking at last.

The men resented it . . . she should have pretended to hear nothing. They hated her admitting she had attended so closely to such talk.

"My God!—*'If they be not nice to me*
What care I how nice they be?'—

No, it's hopeless! I just simply can't vibrate in unison with a woman. There's no woman I can really want when I'm faced with her, and I'm not going to start forcing myself to it . . . My God, no! I'll remain as I am, and lead the mental life. It's the only honest thing I can do. I can be quite happy *talking* to women; but it's all pure, hopelessly pure. Hopelessly pure! What do you say, Hildebrand, my chicken?"

"It's much less complicated if one stays pure," said Berry.

"Yes, life is all too simple!"

Chapter Five

On a frosty morning with a little February sun, Clifford and Connie went for a walk across the park to the wood. That is, Clifford chuffed in his motor-chair, and Connie walked beside him.

The hard air was still sulphurous, but they were both used to it. Round the near horizon went the haze, opalescent with frost and smoke, and on the top lay the small blue sky; so that it was like being inside an enclosure, always inside. Life always a dream or a frenzy, inside an enclosure.

The sheep coughed in the rough, sere grass of the park, where frost lay bluish in the sockets of the tufts. Across the park ran a path to the wood-gate, a fine ribbon of pink. Clifford had had it newly gravelled with sifted gravel from the pit-bank. When the rock and refuse of the underworld had burned and given off its sulphur, it turned bright pink, shrimp-colored on dry days, darker, crab-colored on wet. Now it was pale shrimp-color, with a bluish-white hoar of frost. It always pleased Connie, this underfoot of sifted, bright pink. It's an ill-wind that brings nobody good.

Clifford steered cautiously down the slope of the knoll from the hall, and Connie kept her hand on the chair. In front lay the wood, the hazel thicket nearest, the purplish density of oaks beyond. From the wood's edge rabbits bobbed and nibbled. Rooks suddenly rose in a black train, and went trailing off over the little slope.

Connie opened the wood-gate, and Clifford puffed slowly through into the broad riding that ran up an incline between the clean-whipped thickets of the hazel. The wood was a remnant of the great forest where Robin Hood hunted, and this riding was an old, old thoroughfare coming across country. But now, of course, it was only a riding through the private wood. The road from Mansfield swerved round to the north.

In the wood everything was motionless, the old leaves on the ground keeping the frost on their underside. A jay called harshly, many little birds fluttered. But there was no game; no pheasants. They had been killed off during the war, and the wood had been left unprotected, till now Clifford had got his gamekeeper again.

Clifford loved the wood; he loved the old oak trees. He felt they were his own through generations. He wanted to protect them. He wanted this place inviolate, shut off from the world.

The chair chuffed slowly up the incline, rocking and jolting on the frozen clods. And suddenly, on the left, came a clearing where there was nothing but a ravel of dead bracken, a thin and spindling sapling leaning here and there, big sawn stumps showing their tops and their grasping roots, lifeless. And patches of blackness where the woodmen had burned the brushwood and rubbish.

This was one of the places that Sir Geoffrey had cut during the war for trench timber. The whole knoll, which rose softly on the right of the riding, was denuded and strangely forlorn. On the crown of the knoll where the oaks had stood, now was bareness; and from there you could look out over the trees to the colliery railway, and the new works at Stacks Gate. Connie had stood and looked, it was a breach in the pure seclusion of the wood. It let in the world. But she didn't tell Clifford.

This denuded place always made Clifford curiously angry. He had been through the war, had seen what it meant. But he didn't get really angry till he saw this bare hill. He was having it re-planted. But it made him hate Sir Geoffrey.

Clifford sat with a fixed face as the chair slowly mounted. When they came to the top of the rise he stopped; he would not risk the long and very jolty down-slope. He sat looking at the greenish sweep of the riding downwards, a clear way through the bracken and oaks. It swerved at the bottom of the hill and disappeared; but it had such a lovely easy curve, of knights riding and ladies on palfreys.

"I consider this is really the heart of England," said Clifford to Connie, as he sat there in the dim February sunshine.

"Do you?" she said, seating herself, in her blue knitted dress, on a stump by the path.

"I do! This is the old England, the heart of it; and I intend to keep it intact."

"Oh, yes!" said Connie. But, as she said it she heard the eleven-o'clock hooters at Stacks Gate colliery. Clifford was too used to the sound to notice.

"I want this wood perfect . . . untouched. I want nobody to trespass in it," said Clifford.

There was a certain pathos. The wood still had some of the mystery of wild, old England; but Sir Geoffrey's cuttings during the war had given it a blow. How still the trees were, with their crinkly, innumerable twigs against the sky, and their grey, obstinate trunks rising from the brown bracken! How safely the birds flitted among them! And once there had been deer, and archers, and monks paddling along on asses. The place remembered, still remembered.

Clifford sat in the pale sun, with the light on his smooth, rather blond hair, his reddish full face inscrutable.

"I mind more, not having a son, when I come here, than any other time," he said.

"But the wood is older than your family," said Connie gently.

"Quite!" said Clifford. "But we've preserved it. Except for us it would go . . .

it would be gone already, like the rest of the forest. One must preserve some of the Old England!"

"Must one?" said Connie. "If it has to be preserved, and preserved against the new England? It's sad, I know."

"If some of the old England isn't preserved, there'll be no England at all," said Clifford. "And we who have this kind of property, and the feeling for it, *must* preserve it."

There was a sad pause.

"Yes, for a little while," said Connie.

"For a little while! It's all we can do. We can only do our bit. I feel every man of my family has done his bit here, since we've had the place. One may go against convention, but one must keep up tradition." Again there was a pause.

"What tradition?" asked Connie.

"The tradition of England! of this!"

"Yes," she said slowly.

"That's why having a son helps; one is only a link in a chain," he said.

Connie was not keen on chains, but she said nothing. She was thinking of the curious impersonality of his desire for a son.

"I'm sorry we can't have a son," she said.

He looked at her steadily, with his full, pale-blue eyes.

"It would almost be a good thing if you had a child by another man," he said. "If we brought it up at Wragby, it would belong to us and to the place. I don't believe very intensely in fatherhood. If we had the child to rear, it would be our own, and it would carry on. Don't you think it's worth considering?"

Connie looked up at him at last. The child, her child, was just an "it" to him. It . . . it . . . it!

"But what about the other man?" she asked.

"Does it matter very much? Do these things really affect us very deeply? . . . You had that lover in Germany . . . what is it now? Nothing almost. It seems to me that it isn't these little acts and little connections we make in our lives that matter so very much. They pass away, and where are they? Where . . . Where are the snows of yesteryear? . . . It's what endures through one's life that matters; my own life matters to me, in its long continuance and development. But what do the occasional connections matter? And the occasional sexual connections specially. If people don't exaggerate them ridiculously, they pass like the mating of birds. And so they should. What does it matter? It's the life-long companionship that matters. It's the living together from day to day, not the sleeping together once or twice. You and I are married, no matter what happens to us. We have the habit of each other. And habit, to my thinking, is more vital than any occasional excitement. The long, slow, enduring thing . . . that's what we live by . . . not the occasional spasm of any sort. Little by little, living together, two people fall into a sort of unison, they vibrate so intricately to one another. That's the real secret of marriage, not sex; at least not the simple function of sex. You and I are interwoven in a marriage. If we stick to that we ought to be able to arrange this sex thing, as we arrange going to the dentist; since fate has given us a checkmate physically there."

Connie sat and listened in a sort of wonder, and a sort of fear. She did not know if he was right or not. There was Michaelis, whom she loved; so she said to herself. But her love was somehow only an excursion from her marriage with Clifford; the long, slow habit of intimacy, formed through years of suffering and patience. Perhaps the human soul needs excursions, and must not be denied them. But the point of an excursion is that you come home again.

"And wouldn't you mind *what* man's child I got?" she asked.

"Why, Connie, I should trust your natural instinct of decency and selection. You just wouldn't let the wrong sort of fellow touch you."

She thought of Michaelis! He was absolutely Clifford's idea of the wrong sort of fellow.

"But men and women may have different feelings about the wrong sort of fellow," she said.

"No," he replied. "You cared for me. I don't believe you would ever care for a man who was purely antipathetic to me. Your rhythm wouldn't let you."

She was silent. Logic might be unanswerable because it was so absolutely wrong.

"And should you expect me to tell you?" she asked, glancing up at him almost furtively.

"Not at all. I'd better not know. . . . But you do agree with me, don't you, that the casual sex thing is nothing, compared to the long life lived together? Don't you think one can just subordinate the sex thing to the necessities of a long life? Just use it, since that's what we're driven to? After all, *do* these temporary excitements matter? Isn't the whole problem of life the slow building up of an integral personality, through the years? living an integrated life? There's no point in a disintegrated life. If lack of sex is going to disintegrate you, then go out and have a love affair. If lack of a child is going to disintegrate you, then have a child if you possibly can. But only do these things so that you have an integrated life, that makes a long harmonious thing. And you and I can do that together. . . . don't you think? . . . if we adapt ourselves to the necessities, and at the same time weave the adaptation together into a piece with our steadily-lived life. Don't you agree?"

Connie was a little overwhelmed by his words. She knew he was right theoretically. But when she actually touched her steadily-lived life with him she hesitated. . . . Was it actually her destiny to go on weaving herself into his life all the rest of her life? Nothing else?

Was it just that? She was to be content to weave a steady life with him, all one fabric, but perhaps brocaded with the occasional flower of an adventure. But how could she know what she would feel next year? How could one ever know? How could one say Yes? for years and years? The little yes, gone on a breath! Why should one be pinned down by that butterfly word? Of course it had to flutter away and be gone, to be followed by other yes's and no's! Like the straying of butterflies.

"I think you're right, Clifford. And as far as I can see I agree with you. Only life may turn quite a new face on it all."

"But until life turns a new face on it all, you do agree?"

"Oh, yes! I think I do, really."

She was watching a brown spaniel that had run out of a side-path, and was looking toward them with lifted nose, making a soft, fluffy bark. A man with a gun strode swiftly, softly out after the dog, facing their way as if about to attack them; then stopped instead, saluted, and was turning down hill. It was only the new gamekeeper, but he had frightened Connie, he seemed to emerge with such a swift menace. That was how she had seen him, like a sudden rush of a threat out of nowhere.

He was a man in dark green velveteens and gaiters . . . the old style, with a red face and red moustache and distant eyes. He was going quickly down hill.

"Mellors!" called Clifford.

The man faced lightly round, and saluted with a quick little gesture, a soldier!

"Will you turn the chair round and get it started? That makes it easier," said Clifford.

The man at once slung his gun over his shoulder, and came forward with the same curious swift, yet soft movements, as if keeping invisible. He was moderately tall and lean, and was silent. He did not look at Connie at all, only at the chair.

"Connie, this is the new gamekeeper, Mellors. You haven't spoken to her ladyship yet, Mellors?"

"No, Sir!" came the ready, neutral words.

The man lifted his hat as he stood, showing his thick, almost fair hair. He stared straight into Connie's eyes, with a perfect, fearless, impersonal look, as if he wanted to see what she was like. He made her feel shy. She bent her head to him shyly, and he changed his hat to his left hand and made her a slight bow, like a gentleman; but he said nothing at all. He remained for a moment still, with his hat in his hand.

"But you've been here some time, haven't you?" Connie said to him.

"Eight months, Madam . . . your Ladyship!" he corrected himself calmly.

"And do you like it?"

She looked him in the eyes. His eyes narrowed a little, with irony, perhaps with impudence.

"Why, yes, thank you, your Ladyship! I was reared here. . . ." He gave another slight bow, turned, put his hat on, and strode to take hold of the chair. His voice on the last words had fallen into the heavy broad drag of the dialect . . . perhaps also in mockery, because there had been no trace of dialect before. He might almost be a gentleman. Anyhow, he was a curious, quick, separate fellow, alone, but sure of himself.

Clifford started the little engine, the man carefully turned the chair, and set it nose-forwards to the incline that curved gently to the dark hazel thicket.

"Is that all then, Sir Clifford?" asked the man.

"No, you'd better come along in case she sticks. The engine isn't really stong enough for the uphill work." The man glanced round for his dog . . . a thoughtful glance. The spaniel looked at him and faintly moved its tail. A little smile, mocking or teasing her, yet gentle, came into his eyes for a moment, then faded away, and his face was expressionless. They went fairly quickly down the slope, the man with his hand on the rail of the chair, steadying it. He looked like a free soldier rather than a servant. And something about him reminded Connie of Tommy Dukes.

When they came to the hazel grove, Connie suddenly ran forward and opened the gate into the park. As she stood holding it, the two men looked at her in passing. Clifford critically, the other man with a curious, cool wonder; impersonally wanting to see what she looked like. And she saw in his blue, impersonal eyes a look of suffering and detachment, yet a certain warmth. But why was he aloof, apart?

Clifford stopped the chair, once through the gate, and the man came quickly, courteously to close it.

"Why did you run to open?" asked Clifford in his quiet, calm voice, that showed he was displeased. "Mellors would have done it."

"I thought you would go straight ahead," said Connie.

"And leave you to run after us?" said Clifford.

"Oh, well, I like to run sometimes!"

Mellors took the chair again, looking perfectly unheeding, yet Connie felt he noted everything. As he pushed the chair up the steepish rise of the knoll in the park, he breathed rather quickly, through parted lips. He was rather frail, really. Curiously full of vitality, but a little frail and quenched. Her woman's instinct sensed it.

Connie fell back, let the chair go on. The day had greyed over: the small blue sky that had poised low on its circular rims of haze was closed in again, the lid was down, there was a raw coldness. It was going to snow. All grey, all grey! the world looked worn out.

The chair waited at the top of the pink path. Clifford looked around for Connie.

"Not tired, are you?" he asked.

"Oh, no!" she said.

But she was. A strange, weary yearning, a dissatisfaction had started in her. Clifford did not notice: those were not things he was aware of. But the stranger knew. To Connie, everything in her world and life seemed worn out, and her dissatisfaction was older than the hills.

They came to the house, and round to the back, where there were no steps. Clifford managed to swing himself over on to the low, wheeled house-chair; he was very strong and agile with his arms. Then Connie lifted the burden of his dead legs after him.

The keeper, waiting at attention to be dismissed, watched everything narrowly, missing nothing. He went pale, with a sort of fear, when he saw Connie lifting the inert legs of the man in her arms, into the other chair, Clifford pivoting round as she did so. He was frightened.

"Thanks, then, for the help, Mellors," said Clifford casually, as he began to wheel down the passage to the servants' quarters.

"Nothing else, Sir?" came the neutral voice, like one in a dream.

"Nothing. Good-morning!"

"Good-morning, Sir."

"Good-morning! It was kind of you to push the chair up that hill. . . . I hope it wasn't too heavy for you," said Connie, looking back at the keeper outside the door.

His eyes came to her in an instant, as if wakened up. He was aware of her.

"Oh, no, not heavy!" he said quickly. Then his voice dropped again into the broad sound of the vernacular: "Good-mornin' to your ladyship!"

"Who is your gamekeeper?" Connie asked at lunch.

"Mellors! You saw him," said Clifford.

"Yes, but where did he come from?"

"Nowhere! He was a Tevershall boy . . . son of a collier, I believe."

"And was he a collier himself?"

"Blacksmith on the pit-bank, I believe: overhead smith. But he was keeper here for two years before the war . . . before he joined up. My father always had a good opinion of him, so when he came back, and went to the pit for a blacksmith's job, I just took him back here as keeper. I was really very glad to get him . . . it's almost impossible to find a good man round here, for a gamekeeper . . . and it needs a man who knows the people."

"And isn't he married?"

"He was. But his wife went off with . . . with various men . . . but finally with a collier at Stacks Gate, and I believe she's living there still."

"So this man is alone?"

"More or less! He has a mother in the village . . . and a child, I believe."

Clifford looked at Connie, with his pale, slightly prominent blue eyes, in which a certain vagueness was coming. He seemed alert in the foreground, but the background was like the Midlands atmosphere, haze, smoky mist. And the haze seemed to be creeping forward. So when he stared at Connie in his peculiar way, giving her his peculiar, precise information, she felt all the background of his mind filling up with mist, with nothingness. And it frightened her. It made him seem impersonal, almost to idiocy.

And dimly she realized one of the great laws of the human soul: that when the emotional soul receives a wounding shock, which does not kill the body, the soul seems to recover as the body recovers. But this is only appearance. It is really only the mechanism of the reassumed habit. Slowly, slowly the wound to the soul begins to make itself felt, like a bruise, which only slowly deepens its terrible ache, till it fills all the psyche. And when we think we have recovered and forgotten, it is then that the terrible after-effects have to be encountered at their worst.

So it was with Clifford. Once he was "well," once he was back at Wragby, and writing his stories, and feeling sure of life, in spite of all, he seemed to forget, and to have recovered all his equanimity. But now, as the years went by, slowly, slowly, Connie felt the bruise of fear and horror coming up, and spreading in him. For a time it had been so deep as to be numb, as it were non-existent. Now slowly it began to assert itself in a spread of fear, almost paralysis. Mentally he still was alert. But the paralysis, the bruise of the too great shock was gradually spreading in his affective self.

And as it spread in him, Connie felt it spread in her. An inward dread, an emptiness, an indifference to everything gradually spread in her soul. When Clifford was aroused, he could still talk brilliantly, and, as it were, command the future: as when, in the wood, he talked about her having a child, and giving an heir to Wragby. But the day after, all the brilliant words seemed like dead leaves, crumpling up and turning to powder, meaning really nothing, blown away on any gust of wind. They were not the leafy words of an effective life, young with energy and belonging to the tree. They were the hosts of fallen leaves of a life that is ineffectual.

So it seemed to her everywhere. The colliers at Tevershall were talking again of a strike, and it seemed to Connie there again it was not a manifestation of energy, it was the bruise of the war that had been in abeyance, slowly rising to the surface and creating the great ache of unrest, and stupor of discontent. The bruise was deep, deep, deep . . . the bruise of the false inhuman war. It would take many years for the living blood of the generations to dissolve the vast black clot of bruised blood, deep inside their souls and bodies. And it would need a new hope.

Poor Connie! As the years drew on it was the fear of nothingness in her life that affected her. Clifford's mental life and hers gradually began to feel like nothingness. Their marriage, their integrated life based on a habit of intimacy, that he talked about: there were days when it all became utterly blank and nothing. It was words, just so many words. The only reality was nothingness, and over it a hypocrisy of words.

There was Clifford's success: the bitch-goddess! It was true he was almost famous, and his books brought him in a thousand pounds. His photograph appeared everywhere. There was a bust of him in one of the galleries, and a portrait of him in two galleries. He seemed the most modern of modern voices. With his uncanny lame instinct for publicity, he had become in four or five years one of the best known of the young "intellectuals." Where the intellect came in, Connie did not quite see. Clifford was really clever at that slightly humorous analysis of people and motives which leaves everything in bits at the end. But it was rather like puppies tearing the sofa cushions to bits; except that it was not young and playful, but curiously old, and rather obstinately conceited. It was weird and it was nothing. This was the feeling that echoed and re-echoed at the bottom of Connie's soul: it was all nothing, a wonderful display of nothingness. At the same time a display. A display! a display! a display!

Michaelis had seized upon Clifford as the central figure for a play; already he had sketched in the plot, and written the first act. For Michaelis was even better than Clifford at making a display of nothingness. It was the last bit of passion left in these men: the passion for making a display. Sexually they were passionless, even dead. And now it was not money that Michaelis was after. Clifford had never been primarily out for money, though he made it where he could, for money is the seal and stamp of success. And success was what they wanted. They wanted, both of them, to make a real display . . . a man's own very display of himself, that should capture for a time the vast populace.

It was strange . . . the prostitution to the bitch-goddess. To Connie, since she was really outside of it, and since she had grown numb to the thrill of it, it was again nothingness. Even the prostitution to the bitch-goddess was nothingness, though the men prostituted themselves innumerable times. Nothingness even that.

Michaelis wrote to Clifford about the play. Of course she knew about it long ago. And Clifford was again thrilled. He was going to be displayed again, this time somebody was going to display him, and to advantage. He invited Michaelis down to Wragby with Act I.

Michaelis came: in summer, in pale-colored suit and white suède gloves, with mauve orchids for Connie, very lovely, and Act I was a great success. Even Connie was thrilled . . . thrilled to what bit of marrow she had left. And Michaelis, thrilled by his power to thrill, was really wonderful . . . and quite beautiful, in Connie's eyes. She saw in him that ancient motionlessness of a race that can't be disillusioned any more, an extreme, perhaps, of impurity that is pure. On the far side of his supreme prostitution to the bitch-goddess he seemed pure, pure as an African ivory mask that dreams impurity into purity, in its ivory curves and planes.

His moment of sheer thrill with the two Chatterleys, when he simply carried Connie and Clifford away, was one of the supreme moments of Michaelis' life. He had succeeded: he had carried them away. Even Clifford was temporarily in love with him . . . if that is the way one can put it.

So next morning Mick was more uneasy than ever: restless, devoured, with his hands restless in his trouser pockets. Connie had not visited him the night . . . and he had not known where to find her. Coquetry! . . . at his moment of triumph.

He went up to her sitting-room in the morning. She knew he would come. And his restlessness was evident. He asked her about his play . . . did she think it good? He *had* to hear it praised. That affected him with the last thin thrill of passion beyond any sexual orgasm. And she praised it rapturously. Yet all the while, at the bottom of her soul, she knew it was nothing.

"Look here!" he said suddenly at last. "Why don't you and I make a clean thing of it? Why don't we marry?"

"But I am married," she said amazed, and yet feeling nothing.

"Oh, that! . . . he'll divorce you all right. . . . Why don't you and I marry? I want to marry. I know it would be the best thing for me . . . marry and lead a regular life. I lead the deuce of a life, simply tearing myself to pieces. Look here, you and I, we're made for one another . . . hand and glove. Why don't we marry? Do you see any reason why we shouldn't?"

Connie looked at him amazed: and yet she felt nothing. These men, they were all alike, they left everything out. They just went off from the top of their heads as if they were squibs, and expected you to be carried heavenwards along with their own thin sticks.

"But I am married already," she said. "I can't leave Clifford, you know."

"Why not? But why not?" he cried. "He'll hardly know you've gone, after six months. He doesn't know that anybody exists, except himself. Why, the man has no use for you at all, as far as I can see; he's entirely wrapped up in himself."

Connie felt there was truth in this. But she also felt that Mick was hardly making a display of selflessness.

"Aren't all men wrapped up in themselves?" she asked.

"Oh, more or less, I allow. A man's got to be, to get through. But that's not the point. The point is, what sort of a time can a man give a woman? Can he give her a damn good time, or can't he? If he can't he's no right to the woman. . . ." He paused and gazed at her with his full, hazel eyes, almost hypnotic. "Now, I consider," he added, "I can give a woman the darndest good time she can ask for. I think I can guarantee myself."

"And what sort of a good time?" asked Connie, gazing on him still with a sort of amazement, that looked like thrill; and underneath feeling nothing at all.

"Every sort of a good time, damn it, every sort! Dress, jewels up to a point, any night-club you like, know anybody you want to know, live the pace . . . travel and be somebody wherever you go. . . . Darn it, every sort of good time."

He spoke it almost in a brilliancy of triumph, and Connie looked at him as if dazzled, and really feeling nothing at all. Hardly even the surface of her mind was tickled at the glowing prospects he offered her. Hardly even her most outside self responded, that at any other time would have been thrilled. She just got no feeling from it all, she couldn't "go off." She just sat and stared and looked dazzled, and felt nothing, only somewhere she smelt the extraordinary unpleasant smell of the bitch-goddess.

Mick sat on tenterhooks, leaning forward in his chair, glaring at her almost hysterically: and whether he was more anxious out of vanity for her to say Yes! or whether he was more panic-stricken for fear she *should* say Yes—who can tell?

"I should have to think about it," she said. "I couldn't say now. It may seem to you Clifford doesn't count, but he does. When you think how disabled he is. . . ."

"Oh, damn it all! if a fellow's going to trade on his disabilities, I might begin to say how lonely I am, and always have been, and all the rest of the my-eye-Betty-Martin sob-stuff! Damn it all, if a fellow's got nothing but disabilities to recommend him. . . ."

He turned aside, working his hands furiously in his trouser pockets. That evening he said to her:

"You're coming round to my room tonight, aren't you? I don't darned know where your room is."

"All right!" she said.

He was a more excited lover that night, with his strange, small boy's frail nakedness. Connie found it impossible to come to her crisis before he had really finished his. And he roused a certain craving passion in her, with his little boy's nakedness and softness; she had to go on after he had finished, in the wild tumult and heaving of her loins, while he heroically kept himself up, and present in her, with all his will and self-offering, till she brought about her own crisis, with weird little cries.

When at last he drew away from her, he said, in a bitter, almost sneering little voice:

"You couldn't go off at the same time as a man, could you? You'd have to bring yourself off! You'd have to run the show!"

This little speech, at the moment, was one of the shocks of her life. Because that passive sort of giving himself was so obviously his only real mode of intercourse.

"What do you mean?" she said.

"You know what I mean. You keep on for hours after I've gone off . . . and I have to hang on with my teeth till you bring yourself off by your own exertions."

She was stunned by this unexpected piece of brutality, at the moment when she was glowing with a sort of pleasure beyond words, and a sort of love for him. Because after all, like so many modern men, he was finished almost before he had begun. And that forced the woman to be active.

"But you want me to go on, to get my own satisfaction?" she said.

He laughed grimly: "I want it!" he said. "That's good! I want to hang on with my teeth clenched, while you go for me!"

"But don't you?" she insisted.

He avoided the question. "All the darned women are like that," he said. "Either they don't go off at all, as if they were dead in there . . . or else they wait till a chap's really done, and then they start in to bring themselves off, and a chap's got to hang on. I never had a woman yet who went off just at the same moment as I did."

Connie only half heard this piece of novel, masculine information. She was only stunned by his feeling against her . . . his incomprehensible brutality. She felt so innocent.

"But you want me to have my satisfaction too, don't you?" she repeated.

"Oh, all right! I'm quite willing. But I'm darned if hanging on waiting for a woman to go off is much of a game for a man. . . ."

This speech was one of the crucial blows of Connie's life. It killed something in her. She had not been so very keen on Michaelis; till he started it, she did not want him. It was as if she never positively wanted him. But once he had started her, it seemed only natural for her to come to her own crisis with him. Almost she had loved him for it . . . almost that night she loved him, and wanted to marry him.

Perhaps instinctively he knew it, and that was why he had to bring down the whole show with a smash; the house of cards. Her whole sexual feeling for him, or for any man, collapsed that night. Her life fell apart from his as completely as if he had never existed.

And she went through the days drearily. There was nothing now but this empty treadmill of what Clifford called the integrated life, the long living together of two people, who are in the habit of being in the same house with one another.

Nothingness! To accept the great nothingness of life seemed to be the one end of living. All the many busy and important little things that make up the grand sum-total of nothingness!

Chapter Six

W hy don't men and women really like one another nowadays?" Connie asked Tommy Dukes, who was more or less her oracle.

"Oh, but they do! I don't think since the human species was invented, there has ever been a time when men and women have liked one another as much as they do today. Genuine liking! Take myself. . . . I really *like* women better than men; they are braver, one can be more frank with them."

Connie pondered this.

"Ah, yes, but you never have anything to do with them!" she said.

"I? What am I doing but talking perfectly sincerely to a woman at this moment?"

"Yes, talking. . . ."

"And what more could I do if you were a man, than talk perfectly sincerely to you?"

"Nothing perhaps. But a woman. . . ."

"A woman wants you to like her and talk to her, and at the same time love her and desire her; and it seems to me the two things are mutually exclusive."

"But they shouldn't be!"

"No doubt water ought not to be so wet as it is; it overdoes it in wetness. But there it is! I like women and talk to them, and therefore I don't love them and desire them. The two things don't happen at the same time in me."

"I think they ought to."

"All right. The fact that things ought to be something else than what they are is not my department."

Connie considered this. "It isn't true," she said. "Men can love women and talk to them. I don't see how they can love them *without* talking, and being friendly and intimate. How can they?"

"Well," he said, "I don't know. What's the use of my generalizing? I only know my own case. I like women, but I don't desire them. I like talking to them; but talking to them, though it makes me intimate in one direction, sets me poles apart from them as far as kissing is concerned. So there you are! But don't take me as a general example, probably I'm just a special case: one of the men who like women, but don't love women, and even hate them if they force me into a pretense of love, or an entangled appearance."

"But doesn't it make you sad?"

"Why should it? Not a bit! I look at Charlie May, and the rest of the men who have affairs. . . . No, I don't envy them a bit! If fate sent me a woman I wanted, well and good. Since I don't know any woman I want, and never see one . . . why, I presume I'm cold, and really *like* some women very much."

"Do you like me?"

"Very much! And you see there's no question of kissing between us, is there?"

"None at all!" said Connie. "But oughtn't there to be?"

"*Why*, in God's name? I like Clifford, but what would you say if I went and kissed him?"

"But isn't there a difference?"

"Where does it lie, as far as we're concerned? We're all intelligent human beings, and the male and female business is in abeyance. Just in abeyance. How would you like me to start acting up like a continental male at this moment, and parading the sex thing?"

"I should hate it."

"Well then! I tell you, if I'm really a male thing at all, I never run across the female of my species. And I don't miss her, I just *like* women. Who's going to force me into loving, or pretending to love them, working up the sex game?"

"No, I'm not. But isn't something wrong?"

"You may feel it, I don't."

"Yes, I feel something is wrong between men and women. A woman has no glamor for a man any more."

"Has a man for a woman?"

She pondered the other side of the question.

"Not much," she said truthfully.

"Then let's leave it alone, and just be decent and simple, like proper human beings with one another. Be damned to the artificial sex-compulsion! I refuse it!"

Connie knew he was right, really. Yet it left her feeling so forlorn, so forlorn and stray. Like a chip on a dreary pond, she felt. What was the point, of her or anything?

It was her youth which rebelled. These men seemed so old and cold. Everything seemed old and cold. And Michaelis let one down so; he was no good. The men didn't want one; they just didn't really want a woman, even Michaelis didn't.

And the bounders who pretended they did, and started working the sex game, they were worse than ever.

It was just dismal, and one had to put up with it. It was quite true, men had no real glamor for a woman: if you could fool yourself into thinking they had, even as she had fooled herself over Michaelis, that was the best you could do. Meanwhile you just lived on and there was nothing to it. She understood perfectly well why people had cocktail parties, and jazzed, and Charlestoned till they were ready to drop. You had to take it out some way or other, your youth, or it ate you up. But what a ghastly thing, this youth!

"What is your name?" she said playfully to the child. "Won't you tell me your name?"

Sniffs; then very affectedly in a piping voice: "Connie Mellors!"

"Connie Mellors! Well, that's a nice name! And did you come out with your Daddy, and he shot a pussy? But it was a bad pussy!"

The child looked at her, with bold, dark eyes of scrutiny, sizing her up, and her condolence.

"I wanted to stop with my Gran," said the little girl.

"Did you? But where is your Gran?"

The child lifted an arm, pointing down the drive. "At th' cottidge."

"At the cottage! And would you like to go back to her?"

Sudden, shuddering quivers of reminiscent sobs. "Yes!"

"Come then, shall I take you? Shall I take you to your Gran? Then your Daddy can do what he has to do." She turned to the man. "It is your little girl, isn't it?"

He saluted, and made a slight movement of the head in affirmation.

"I suppose I can take her to the cottage?"

"If your Ladyship wishes."

Again he looked into her eyes, with that calm, searching detached glance. A man very much alone, and on his own.

"Would you like to come with me to the cottage, to your Gran, dear?"

The child peeped up again. "Yes!" she simpered.

Connie disliked her; the spoilt, false little female. Nevertheless she wiped her face, and took her hand. The keeper saluted in silence.

"Good morning!" said Connie.

It was nearly a mile to the cottage, and Connie senior was well bored by Connie junior by the time the gamekeeper's picturesque little home was in sight. The child was already as full to the brim with tricks as a little monkey, and so self-assured.

At the cottage the door stood open, and there was a rattling heard inside. Connie lingered, the child slipped her hand, and ran indoors.

"Gran! Gran!"

"Why, are yer back a'ready!"

The grandmother had been blackleading the stove, it was Saturday morning. She came to the door in her sacking apron, a blacklead-brush in her hand, and a black smudge on her nose. She was a little, rather dry woman.

"Why, whatever?" she said, hastily wiping her arm across her face as she saw Connie standing outside.

"Good morning!" said Connie. "She was crying, so I just brought her home."

The grandmother looked round swiftly at the child:

"Why, wheer was yer Dad?"

The little girl clung to her grandmother's skirts and simpered.

"He was there," said Connie, "but he'd shot a poaching cat, and the child was upset."

"Oh, you'd no right t'ave bothered, Lady Chatterley, I'm sure! I'm sure it was very good of you, but you shouldn't 'ave bothered. Why, did ever you see!"—and the old woman turned to the child. "Fancy Lady Chatterley takin' all that trouble over yer! Why, she shouldn't 'ave bothered!"

"It was no bother, just a walk," said Connie, smiling.

"Why, I'm sure 'twas very kind of you, I must say! So she was crying! I knew there'd be something afore they got far. She's frightened of 'im, that's wheer it is. Seems 'e's almost a stranger to 'er, fair a stranger, and I don't think they're two as'd hit it off very easy. He's got funny ways."

Connie didn't know what to say.

"Look, Gran!" simpered the child.

The old woman looked down at the sixpence in the little girl's hand.

"An' sixpence an' all! Or, your Ladyship, you shouldn't, you shouldn't. Why, isn't Lady Chatterley good to yer! My word, you're a lucky girl this morning!"

She pronounced the name, as all the people did: Chat'ley. "Isn't Lady Chat'ley *good* to you!" Connie couldn't help looking at the old woman's nose, and the latter again vaguely wiped her face with the back of her wrist, but missed the smudge.

Connie was moving away. "Well, thank you ever so much, Lady Chat'ley, I'm sure. Say thank you to Lady Chat'ley!"—this last to the child.

"Thank you," piped the child.

"There's a dear!" laughed Connie, and she moved away, saying "Good morning," heartily relieved to get away from the contact. Curious, she thought, that that thin, proud man should have that little, sharp woman for a mother!

And the old woman, as soon as Connie was gone, rushed to the bit of mirror in the scullery, and looked at her face. Seeing it, she stamped her foot with impatience. "Of *course,* she had to catch me in my coarse apron, and a dirty face! Nice idea she'd get of me!"

Connie went slowly home to Wragby. "Home!" . . . it was a warm word to use for that great, weary warren. But then it was a word that had had its day. It was somehow cancelled. All the great words, it seemed to Connie, were cancelled for her generation: love, joy, happiness, home, mother, father, husband, all these great dynamic words were half dead now, and dying from day to day. Home was a place you lived in, love was a thing you didn't fool yourself about, joy was a word you applied to a good Charleston, happiness was a term of hypocrisy used to bluff other people, a father was an individual who enjoyed his own existence, a husband was a man you lived with and kept going in spirits. As for sex, the last of the great words, it was just a cocktail term for an excitement that bucked you up for a while, then left you more raggy than ever. Frayed! It was as if the very material you were made of was cheap stuff, and was fraying out to nothing.

All that really remained was a stubborn stoicism: and in that there was a certain pleasure. In the very experience of the nothingness of life, phase after phase, *étape* after *étape,* there was a certain grisly satisfaction. So that's *that!* Always this was the last utterance: home, love, marriage, Michaelis: So that's *that!*—And when one died, the last words to life would be: So that's *that!*—

Money? Perhaps one couldn't say the same there. Money one always wanted. Money, success, the bitch-goddess, as Tommy Dukes persisted in calling it, after Henry James, that was a permanent necessity. You couldn't spend your last sou, and say finally: So that's *that!*—No, if you lived even another ten minutes, you wanted a few more sous for something or other. Just to keep the business mechanically going, you needed money. You had to have it. Money you *have* to have. You needn't really have anything else. So that's *that!*—

Since, of course, it's not your own fault you are alive. Once you are alive, money is a necessity, and the only absolute necessity. All the rest you can get along without, at a pinch. But not money. Emphatically, that's *that!*—

She thought of Michaelis, and the money she might have had with him; and even that she didn't want. She preferred the lesser amount which she helped Clifford to make by his writing. That she actually helped to make.—"Clifford and I together, we make twelve hundred a year out of writing"; so she put it to herself. Make money! Make it! Out of nowhere! Wring it out of the thin air! The last feat to be humanly proud of! The rest all-my-eye-Betty-Martin.

So she plodded home to Clifford, to join forces with him again, to make another story out of nothingness: and a story meant money. Clifford seemed to care very much whether his stories were considered first-class literature or not. Strictly, she didn't care. Nothing in it! said her father. Twelve hundred pounds last year! was the retort simple and final.

If you were young, you just set your teeth, and bit on and held on, till the money began to flow from the invisible; it was a question of power. It was a question of will; a subtle, subtle, powerful emanation of will out of yourself brought back to you the mysterious nothingness of money: a word on a bit of paper. It was a sort of magic, certainly it was triumph. The bitch-goddess! Well, if one had to prostitute oneself, let it be to a bitch-goddess! One could always despise her even while one prostituted oneself to her, which was good.

Clifford, of course, had still many childish taboos and fetishes. He wanted to be thought "really good," which was all cock-a-hoopy nonsense. What was really good was what actually caught on. It was no good being really good and getting left with it. It seemed as if most of the "really good" men just missed the bus. After all you only lived one life, and if you missed the bus, you were just left on the pavement, along with the rest of the failures.

Connie was contemplating a winter in London with Clifford, next winter. He and she had caught the bus all right, so they might as well ride on top for a bit, and show it.

The worst of it was, Clifford tended to become vague, absent, and to fall into fits of vacant depression. It was the wound to his psyche coming out. But it made Connie want to scream. Oh, God, if the mechanism of the consciousness itself was going to go wrong, then what was one to do? Hang it all, one did one's bit! Was one to be let down *absolutely?*

Sometimes she wept bitterly, but even as she wept she was saying to herself:
Silly fool, wetting hankies! As if that would get you anywhere!

Since Michaelis, she had made up her mind she wanted nothing. That seemed
the simplest solution of the otherwise insoluble. She wanted nothing more than
what she'd got; only she wanted to get ahead with what she'd got: Clifford, the
stories, Wragby, the Lady Chatterley business, money and fame, such as it was
. . . she wanted to go ahead with it all. Love, sex, all that sort of stuff, just
water-ices! Lick it up and forget it. If you don't hang on to it in your mind, it's
nothing. Sex especially . . . nothing! Make up your mind to it, and you've solved
the problem. Sex and a cocktail: they both lasted about as long, had the same
effect, and amounted to about the same thing.

But a child, a baby! that was still one of the sensations. She would venture
very gingerly on that experiment. There was the man to consider, and it was
curious, there wasn't a man in the world whose children you wanted. Mick's
children! Repulsive thought! As lief have a child to a rabbit! Tommy Dukes?
. . . he was very nice, but somehow you couldn't associate him with a baby,
another generation. He ended in himself. And out of all the rest of Clifford's
pretty wide acquaintance, there was not a man who did not rouse her contempt,
when she thought of having a child by him. There were several who would have
been quite possible as lovers, even Mick. But as people to have children with!
Ugh! Humiliation and abomination.

So that was that!

Nevertheless, Connie had the child at the back of her mind. Wait! Wait! She
would sift the generations of men through her sieve, and see if she couldn't find
one who would do.—"Go ye into the streets and byways of Jerusalem, and see
if ye can find _a man._" It had been impossible to find a man in the Jerusalem
of the prophet, though there were thousands of male humans. But _a man!_ C'est
une autre chose!

She had an idea that he would have to be a foreigner: not an Englishman, still
less an Irishman. A real foreigner.

But wait! wait! Next winter she would get Clifford to London; the following
winter she would get him abroad to the South of France, Italy. Wait! She was
in no hurry about the child. That was her own private affair, and the one point
on which, in her own queer, female way, she was serious to the bottom of her
soul. She was not going to risk any chance comer, not she! One might take a
lover almost at any moment, but a man who should beget a child on one . . .
wait! wait! it's a very different matter.—"Go ye into the streets and byways of
Jerusalem. . . ." It was not a question of love; it was a question of _a man._ Why,
one might even rather hate him, personally. Yet if he was the man, what would
one's personal hate matter? This business concerned another part of oneself.

It had rained as usual, and the paths were too sodden for Clifford's chair, but
Connie would go out. She went out alone every day now, mostly in the wood,
where she was really alone. She saw nobody there.

This day, however, Clifford wanted to send a message to the keeper, and as the boy was laid up with influenza—somebody always seemed to have influenza at Wragby—Connie said she would call at the cottage.

The air was soft and dead, as if all the world were slowly dying. Grey and clammy and silent, even from the shuffling of the collieries, for the pits were working short time, and today they were stopped altogether. The end of all things!

In the wood all was utterly inert and motionless, only great drops fell from the bare boughs, with a hollow little crash. For the rest, among the old trees was depth within depth of grey, hopeless inertia, nothingness.

Connie walked dimly on. From the old wood came an ancient melancholy, somehow soothing to her, better than the harsh insentience of the outer world. She liked the *inwardness* of the remnant of forest, the unspeaking reticence of the old trees. They seemed a very power of silence, and yet a vital presence. They, too, were waiting: obstinately, stoically waiting, and giving off a potency of silence. Perhaps they were only waiting for the end; to be cut down, cleared away, the end of the forest, for them the end of all things. But perhaps their strong and aristocratic silence, the silence of strong trees, meant something else.

As she came out of the wood on the north side, the keeper's cottage, a rather dark, brown stone cottage, with gables and a handsome chimney, looked uninhabited, it was so silent and alone. But a thread of smoke rose from the chimney, and the little railed-in garden in the front of the house was dug and kept very tidy. The door was shut.

Now she was here she felt a little shy of the man, with his curious far-seeing eyes. She did not like bringing him orders, and felt like going away again. She knocked softly, no one came. She knocked again, but still not loudly. There was no answer. She peeped through the window, and saw the dark little room, with its almost sinister privacy, not wanting to be invaded.

She stood and listened, and it seemed to her she heard sounds from the back of the cottage. Having failed to make herself heard, her mettle was roused, she would not be defeated.

So she went around the side of the house. At the back of the cottage the land rose steeply, so the back yard was sunken, and enclosed by a low stone wall. She turned the corner of the house and stopped. In the little yard two paces beyond her, the man was washing himself, utterly unaware. He was naked to the hips, his velveteen breeches slipping down over his slender loins. And his white slim back was curved over a big bowl of soapy water, in which he ducked his head, shaking his head with a queer, quick little motion, lifting his slender white arms, and pressing the soapy water from his ears, quick, subtle as a weasel playing with water, and utterly alone. Connie backed away round the corner of the house, and hurried away to the wood. In spite of herself, she had had a shock. After all, merely a man washing himself; commonplace enough, Heaven knows!

Yet in some curious way it was a visionary experience: it had hit her in the middle of the body. She saw the clumsy breeches slipping down over the pure, delicate, white loins, the bones showing a little, and the sense of aloneness, of a creature purely alone, overwhelmed her. Perfect, white, solitary nudity of a creature that lives alone, and inwardly alone. And beyond that, a certain beauty of a pure creature. Not the stuff of beauty, not even the body of beauty, but a lambency, the warm, white flame of a single life, revealing itself in contours that one might touch: a body!

Connie had received the shock of vision in her womb, and she knew it; it lay inside her. But with her mind she was inclined to ridicule. A man washing himself in a backyard! No doubt with evil-smelling yellow soap!—She was rather annoyed; why should she be made to stumble on these vulgar privacies?

So she walked away from herself, but after a while she sat down on a stump. She was too confused to think. But in the coil of her confusion, she was determined to deliver her message to the fellow. She would not be balked. She must give him time to dress himself, but not time to go out. He was probably preparing to go out somewhere.

So she sauntered slowly back, listening. As she came near, the cottage looked just the same. A dog barked, and she knocked at the door, her heart beating in spite of herself.

She heard the man coming lightly downstairs. He opened the door quickly, and startled her. He looked uneasy himself, but instantly a laugh came on his face.

"Lady Chatterley!" he said. "Will you come in?"

His manner was so perfectly easy and good, she stepped over the threshold into the rather dreary little room.

"I only called with a message from Sir Clifford," she said in her soft, rather breathless voice.

The man was looking at her with those blue, all-seeing eyes of his, which made her turn her face aside a little. He thought her comely, almost beautiful, in her shyness, and he took command of the situation himself at once.

"Would you care to sit down?" he asked, presuming she would not. The door stood open.

"No thanks! Sir Clifford wondered if you would . . ." and she delivered her message, looking unconsciously into his eyes again. And now his eyes looked warm and kind, particularly to a woman, wonderfully warm, and kind, and at ease.

"Very good, your Ladyship. I will see to it at once."

Taking an order, his whole self had changed, glazed over with a sort of hardness and distance. Connie hesitated, she ought to go. But she looked round the clean, tidy, rather dreary little sitting-room with something like dismay.

"Do you live here quite alone?" she asked.

"Quite alone, your Ladyship."

"But your mother . . .?"

"She lives in her own cottage in the village."

"With the child?" asked Connie.

"With the child!"

And his plain, rather worn face took on an indefinable look of derision. It was a face that changed all the time, baffling.

"No," he said, seeing Connie stand at a loss, "my mother comes and cleans up for me on Saturdays; I do the rest myself."

Again Connie looked at him. His eyes were smiling again, a little mockingly, but warm and blue, and somehow kind. She wondered at him. He was in trousers and flannel shirt and a grey tie, his hair soft and damp, his face rather pale and worn-looking. When the eyes ceased to laugh they looked as if they had suffered a great deal, still without losing their warmth. But a pallor of isolation came over him, she was not really there for him.

She wanted to say so many things, and she said nothing. Only she looked up at him again, and remarked:

"I hope I didn't disturb you?"

The faint smile of mockery narrowed his eyes.

"Only combing my hair, if you don't mind. I'm sorry I hadn't a coat on, but then I had no idea who was knocking. Nobody knocks here, and the unexpected sounds ominous."

He went in front of her down the garden path to hold the gate. In his shirt, without the clumsy velveteen coat, she saw again how slender he was, thin, stooping a little. Yet, as she passed him, there was something young and bright in his fair hair, and his quick eyes. He would be a man about thirty-seven or eight.

She plodded on into the wood, knowing he was looking after her; he upset her so much, in spite of herself.

And he, as he went indoors, was thinking: "She's nice, she's real! she's nicer than she knows."

She wondered very much about him; he seemed so unlike a gamekeeper, so unlike a working-man anyhow; although he had something in common with the local people. But also something very uncommon.

"The gamekeeper, Mellors, is a curious kind of person," she said to Clifford: "he might almost be a gentleman."

"Might he?" said Clifford. "I hadn't noticed."

"But isn't there something special about him?" Connie insisted.

"I think he's quite a nice fellow, but I know very little about him. He only came out of the army last year, less than a year ago. From India, I rather think. He may have picked up certain tricks out there; perhaps he was an officer's servant, and improved on his position. Some of the men were like that. But it does them no good, they have to fall back into their old places when they get home again."

Connie gazed at Clifford contemplatively. She saw in him the peculiar tight rebuff against anyone of the lower classes who might be really climbing up, which she knew was characteristic of his breed.

"But don't you think there is something special about him?" she asked.

"Frankly, no! Nothing I had noticed."

He looked at her curiously, uneasily, half-suspiciously. And she felt he wasn't telling her the real truth; he wasn't telling himself the real truth, that was it. He disliked any suggestion of a really exceptional human being. People must be more or less at his level, or below it.

Connie felt again the tightness, niggardliness of the men of her generation. They were so tight, so scared of life!

Chapter Seven

When Connie went up to her bedroom she did what she had not done for a long time: took off all her clothes, and looked at herself naked in the huge mirror. She did not know what she was looking for, or at, very definitely, yet she moved the lamp till it shone full on her.

And she thought, as she had thought so often, . . . what a frail, easily hurt, rather pathetic thing a human body is, naked; somehow a little unfinished, incomplete!

She had been supposed to have a rather good figure, but now she was out of fashion: a little too female, not enough like an adolescent boy. She was not very tall, a bit Scottish and short; but she had a certain fluent, down-slipping grace that might have been beauty. Her skin was faintly tawny, her limbs had a certain stillness, her body should have had a full, down-slipping richness; but it lacked something.

Instead of ripening its firm, down-running curves, her body was flattening and going a little harsh. It was as if it had not had enough sun and warmth; it was a little greyish and sapless.

Disappointed of its real womanhood, it had not succeeded in becoming boyish, and unsubstantial, and transparent; instead it had gone opaque.

Her breasts were rather small, and dropping pear-shaped. But they were unripe, a little bitter, without meaning hanging there. And her belly had lost the fresh, round gleam it had had when she was young, in the days of her German boy, who had really loved her physically. Then it was young and expectant, with a real look of its own. Now it was going slack, and a little flat, thinner, but with a slack thinness. Her thighs, too, that used to look so quick and glimpsey in their female roundness, somehow they too were going flat, slack, meaningless.

Her body was going meaningless, going full and opaque, so much insignificant substance. It made her feel immensely depressed and hopeless. What hope was there? She was old, old at twenty-seven, with no gleam and sparkle in the flesh. Old through neglect and denial, yes denial. Fashionable women kept their bodies bright like delicate porcelain, by external attention. There was nothing inside the porcelain; but she was not even as bright as that. The mental life! Suddenly she hated it with a rushing fury, the swindle!

She looked in the other mirror's reflection at her back, her waist, her loins. She was getting thinner, but to her it was not becoming. The crumple of her waist at the back, as she bent back to look, was a little weary; and it used to be so gay-looking. And the longish slope of her haunches and her buttocks had lost its gleam and its sense of richness. Gone! Only the German boy had loved it, and he was ten years dead, very nearly. How time went by! Ten years dead, and she was only twenty-seven. That healthy boy with his fresh, clumsy sensuality that she had then been so scornful of! Where would she find it now? It was gone out of men. They had their pathetic, two-seconds spasms like Michaelis; but no healthy human sensuality, that warms the blood and freshens the whole being.

Still she thought the most beautiful part of her was the long-sloping fall of the haunches from the socket of the back, and the slumberous, round stillness of the buttocks. Like hillocks of sand the Arabs say, soft and downward-slipping with a long slope. Here the life still lingered hoping. But here too she was thinner, and going unripe, astringent.

But the front of her body made her miserable. It was already beginning to slacken, with a slack sort of thinness, almost withered, going old before it had ever really lived. She thought of the child she might somehow bear. Was she fit, anyhow?

She slipped into her nightdress, and went to bed, where she sobbed bitterly. And in her bitterness burned a cold indignation against Clifford, and his writings and his talk: against all the men of his sort who defrauded a woman even of her own body.

Unjust! Unjust! The sense of deep physical injustice burned to her very soul.

But in the morning, all the same, she was up at seven, and going downstairs to Clifford. She had to help him in all the intimate things, for he had no man, and refused a woman-servant. The housekeeper's husband, who had known him as a boy, helped him, and did any heavy lifting; but Connie did the personal things, and she did them willingly. It was a demand on her, but she had wanted to do what she could.

So she hardly ever went away from Wragby, and never for more than a day or two; when Mrs. Betts, the housekeeper, attended to Clifford. He, as was inevitable in the course of time, took all the service for granted. It was natural he should.

And yet, deep inside herself, a sense of injustice, of being defrauded, began to burn in Connie. The physical sense of injustice is a dangerous feeling, once it is awakened. It must have outlet, or it eats away the one in whom it is aroused. Poor Clifford, he was not to blame. His was the greater misfortune. It was all part of the general catastrophe.

And yet was he not in a way to blame? The lack of warmth, this lack of the simple, warm, physical contact, was he not to blame for that? He was never really warm, nor even kind, only thoughtful, considerate, in a well-bred, cold sort of way! But never warm as a man can be warm to a woman, as even Connie's father could be warm to her, with the warmth of a man who did himself well, and intended to, but who still could comfort a woman with a bit of his masculine glow.

But Clifford was not like that. His whole race was not like that. They were all inwardly hard and separate, and warmth to them was just bad taste. You had to get on without it, and hold your own; which was all very well if you were of the same class and race. Then you could keep yourself cold and be very estimable, and hold your own, and enjoy the satisfaction of holding it. But if you were of another class and another race it wouldn't do; there was no fun merely holding your own, and feeling you belonged to the ruling class. What was the point, when even the smartest aristocrats had really nothing positive of their own to hold, and their rule was really a farce, not rule at all? What was the point? It was all cold nonsense.

A sense of rebellion smoldered in Connie. What was the good of it all? What was the good of her sacrifice, her devoting her life to Clifford? What was she serving, after all? A cold spirit of vanity, that had no warm human contacts, and that was as corrupt as any low-born Jew, in craving for prostitution to the bitch-goddess, Success. Even Clifford's cool and contactless assurance that he belonged to the ruling class didn't prevent his tongue lolling out of his mouth, as he panted after the bitch-goddess. After all, Michaelis was really more dignified in the matter, and far, far more successful. Really, if you looked closely at Clifford, he was a buffoon, and a buffoon is more humiliating than a bounder.

As between the two men, Michaelis really had far more use for her than Clifford had. He had even more need of her. Any good nurse can attend to crippled legs! And as for the heroic effort, Michaelis was an heroic rat, and Clifford was very much of a poodle showing off.

There were people staying in the house, among them Clifford's Aunt Eva, Lady Bennerley. She was a thin woman of sixty, with a red nose, a widow, and still something of a "grande dame." She belonged to one of the best families, and had the character to carry it off. Connie liked her, she was so perfectly simple and frank, as far as she intended to be frank, and superficially kind. Inside herself she was a past-mistress in holding her own, and holding other people a little lower. She was not at all a snob: far too sure of herself. She was perfect at the social sport of coolly holding her own, and making other people defer to her.

She was kind to Connie, and tried to worm into her woman's soul with the sharp gimlet of her well-born observations.

"You're quite wonderful, in my opinion," she said to Connie. "You've done wonders for Clifford. I never saw any budding genius myself, and there he is all the rage."—Aunt Eva was quite complacently proud of Clifford's success. Another feather in the family cap. She didn't care a straw about his books, but why should she?

"Oh, I don't think it's my doing," said Connie.

"It must be! Can't be anybody else's. And it seems to me you don't get enough out of it."

"How?"

"Look at the way you are shut up here. I said to Clifford: 'If that child rebels one day, you'll have yourself to thank!'"

"But Clifford never denies me anything," said Connie.

"Look here, my dear child"—and Lady Bennerley laid her thin hand on Connie's arm. "A woman has to live her life, or live to repent not having lived it. Believe me!" And she took another sip of brandy, which maybe was her form of repentance.

"But I do live my life, don't I?"

"Not in my idea! Clifford should bring you to London and let you go about. His sort of friends are all right for him, but what are they for you? If I were you I should think it wasn't good enough. You'll let your youth slip by, and you'll spend your old age, and your middle age too, repenting it."

Her ladyship lapsed into contemplative silence, soothed by the brandy.

But Connie was not keen on going to London, and being steered into the smart world by Lady Bennerley. She didn't feel really smart, it wasn't interesting. And she did feel the peculiar, withering coldness under it all; like the soil of Labrador, which has gay little flowers on its surface, and a foot down is frozen.

Tommy Dukes was at Wragby, and another man, Harry Winterslow, and Jack Strangeways with his wife Olive. The talk was much more desultory than when only the cronies were there, and everybody was a bit bored, for the weather was bad and there was only billiards, and the pianola to dance to.

Olive was reading a book about the future, when babies would be bred in bottles, and women would be "immunized."

"Jolly good thing too!" she said. "Then a woman can live her own life." Strangeways wanted children, and she didn't.

"How'd you like to be immunized?" Winterslow asked her with an ugly smile.

"I hope I am; naturally," she said. "Anyhow the future's going to have more sense, and a woman needn't be dragged down by her *functions*."

"Perhaps she'll float off into space altogether," said Dukes.

"I do think sufficient civilization ought to eliminate a lot of the physical disabilities," said Clifford. "All the love business, for example; it might just as well go. I suppose it would if we could breed babies in bottles."

"No!" cried Olive. "That might leave all the more room for fun."

"I suppose," said Lady Bennerley, contemplatively, "if the love-business went, something else would take its place. Morphia, perhaps. A little morphine in all the air. It would be wonderfully refreshing for everybody."

"The government releasing ether into the air on Saturdays, for a cheerful week-end!" said Jack. "Sounds all right, but where should we be by Wednesday?"

"So long as you can forget your body you are happy," said Lady Bennerley. "And the moment you begin to be aware of your body, you are wretched. So, if civilization is any good, it has to help us forget our bodies, and then time passes happily without our knowing it."

"Help us to get rid of our bodies altogether," said Winterslow. "It's quite time man began to improve on his own nature, especially the physical side of it."

"Imagine if we floated like tobacco smoke," said Connie.

"It won't happen," said Dukes. "Our old show will come flop; our civilization is going to fall. It's going down the bottomless pit, down the chasm. And, believe me, the only bridge across the chasm will be the phallus!"

"Oh! do, *do* be impossible, General!" cried Olive.

"I believe our civilization is going to collapse," said Aunt Eva.

"And what will come after it?" asked Clifford.

"I haven't the faintest idea; but something, I suppose," said the elderly lady.

"Connie says people like wisps of smoke, and Olive says immunized women and babies in bottles, and Dukes says the phallus is the bridge to what comes next. I wonder what it will really be?" said Clifford.

"Oh, don't bother! Let's get on with today," said Olive. "Only hurry up with the breeding bottle, and let us poor women off."

"There might even be real men, in the next phase," said Tommy. "Real, intelligent, wholesome men, and wholesome nice women! Wouldn't that be a change, an enormous change from us? *We're* not men, and the women aren't women. We're only cerebrating makeshifts, mechanical and intellectual experiments. There may even come a civilization of genuine men and women, instead of our little lot of cleverjacks, all at the intelligence-age of seven. It would be even more amazing than men of smoke or babies in bottles."

"Oh, when people begin to talk about real women, I give up," said Olive.

"Certainly nothing but the spirit in us is worth having," said Winterslow.

"Spirits!" said Jack, drinking his whiskey-and-soda.

"Think so? Give me the resurrection of the body!" said Dukes. "But it'll come, in time, when we've shoved the cerebral stone away a bit, the money and the rest. Then we'll get a democracy of touch, instead of a democracy of pocket."

Something echoed inside Connie: "Give me the democracy of touch, the resurrection of the body!" She didn't at all know what it meant, but it comforted her, as meaningless things may do.

Anyhow everything was terribly silly, and she was exasperatedly bored by it all, by Clifford, by Aunt Eva, by Olive and Jack, and Winterslow, and even by Dukes. Talk, talk, talk! What hell it was, the continual rattle of it!

Then, when all the people went, it was no better. She continued plodding on, but exasperation and irritation had got hold of her body, she couldn't escape. The days seemed to grind by, with curious painfulness, yet nothing happened. Only she was getting thinner; even the housekeeper noticed it, and asked her about herself. Even Tommy Dukes insisted she was not well, though she said she was all right. Only she began to be afraid of the ghastly white tombstones, that peculiar loathsome whiteness of Carrara marble, detestable as false teeth, which stuck up on the hillside, under Tevershall Church, and which she saw with such grim plainness from the park. The bristling of the hideous false teeth of tombstones on the hill affected her with a grisly kind of horror. She felt the time not far off when she would be buried there, added to the ghastly host under the tombstones and the monuments, in these filthy Midlands.

She needed help, and she knew it; so she wrote a little *cri de coeur* to her sister, Hilda. "I'm not well lately, and I don't know what's the matter with me."

Down posted Hilda from Scotland, where she had taken up her abode. She came in March, alone, driving herself in a nimble two-seater. Up the drive she came, tooting up the incline, then sweeping round the oval of grass, where the two great wild beech-trees stood, on the flat in front of the house.

Connie had run out to the steps. Hilda pulled up her car, got out, and kissed her sister.

"But, Connie!" she cried. "Whatever is the matter?"

"Nothing!" said Connie, rather shame-facedly; but she knew how she had suffered in contrast to Hilda. Both sisters had the same rather golden, glowing skin, and soft brown hair, and naturally strong, warm physique. But now Connie was thin and earthy-looking, with a scraggy, yellowish neck, that stuck out of her jumper.

"But you're ill, child!" said Hilda, in the soft, rather breathless voice, that both sisters had alike. Hilda was nearly, but not quite, two years older than Connie.

"No, not ill. Perhaps I'm bored," said Connie a little pathetically.

The light of battle glowed in Hilda's face: she was a woman, soft and still as she seemed, of the old amazon sort, not made to fit with men.

"This wretched place!" she said softly, looking at poor old, lumbering Wragby with real hate. She looked soft and warm herself, as a ripe pear, and she was an amazon of the real old breed.

She went quietly in to Clifford. He thought how handsome she looked, but also he shrank from her. His wife's family did not have his sort of manners, or his sort of etiquette. He considered them rather outsiders, but once they got inside they made him jump through the hoop.

He sat square and well-groomed in his chair, his hair sleek and blond, and his face fresh, his blue eyes pale, and a little prominent, his expression inscrutable, but well-bred. Hilda thought it sulky and stupid, and he waited. He had an air of aplomb, but Hilda didn't care what he had an air of; she was up in arms, and if he'd been Pope or Emperor it would have been just the same.

"Connie's looking awfully unwell," she said in her soft voice, fixing him with her beautiful, glowering grey eyes. She looked so maidenly, so did Connie; but he well knew the stone of Scottish obstinacy underneath.

"She's a little thinner," he said.

"Haven't you done anything about it?"

"Do you think it necessary?" he asked, with his suavest English stiffness, for the two things often go together.

Hilda only glowered at him without replying; repartee was not her forte, nor Connie's; so she glowered, and he was much more uncomfortable than if she had said things.

"I'll take her to a doctor," said Hilda at length. "Can you suggest a good one round here?"

"I'm afraid I can't."

"Then I'll take her to London, where we have a doctor we trust."

Though boiling with rage, Clifford said nothing.

"I suppose I may as well stay the night," said Hilda, pulling off her gloves, "and I'll drive her to town tomorrow."

Clifford was yellow at the gills with anger, and at evening the whites of his eyes were a little yellow too. He ran to liver. But Hilda was consistently modest and maidenly.

"You must have a nurse or somebody to look after you personally. You should really have a man-servant," said Hilda as they sat, with apparent calmness, at coffee after dinner. She spoke in her soft, seemingly gentle way, but Clifford felt she was hitting him on the head with a bludgeon.

"You think so?" he said coldly.

"I'm sure! It's necessary. Either that, or father and I must take Connie away for some months. This can't go on."

"What can't go on?"

"Haven't you looked at the child?" asked Hilda, gazing at him full stare. He looked rather like a huge, boiled crayfish, at the moment; or so she thought.

"Connie and I will discuss it," he said.

"I've already discussed it with her," said Hilda.

Clifford had been long enough in the hands of nurses; he hated them, because they left him no real privacy. And a man-servant! . . . he couldn't stand a man hanging round him. Almost better any woman. But why not Connie?

The two sisters drove off in the morning, Connie looking rather like an Easter lamb, rather small beside Hilda, who held the wheel. Sir Malcolm was away, but the Kensington house was open.

The doctor examined Connie carefully, and asked her all about her life. "I see your photograph, and Sir Clifford's, in the illustrated papers sometimes. Almost notorieties, aren't you? That's how the quiet little girls grow up, though you're only a quiet little girl even now, in spite of the illustrated papers. No, no! There's nothing organically wrong, but it won't do! It won't do! Tell Sir Clifford he's got to bring you to town, to take you abroad, and amuse you. You've got to be amused, got to! Your vitality is much too low; no reserves, no reserves. The nerves of the heart a bit queer already: oh, yes. Nothing but nerves; I'd put you right in a month at Cannes or Biarritz. But it mustn't go on, *mustn't*, I tell you, or I won't be answerable for consequences. You're spending your life without renewing it. You've got to be amused, properly, healthily amused. You're spending your vitality without making any. Can't go on, you know. Depression! avoid depression!"

Hilda set her jaw, and that meant something.

Michaelis heard they were in town, and came running with roses. "Why, whatever's wrong?" he cried. "You're a shadow of yourself. Why, I never saw such a change! Why ever didn't you let me know? Come to Nice with me! Come down to Sicily! Go on, come to Sicily with me, it's lovely there just now. You want sun! You want life! Why, you're wasting away! Come away with me! Come to Africa! Oh, hang Sir Clifford! Chuck him, and come along with me. I'll marry you the minute he divorces you. Come along and try a life! God's love! That place Wragby would kill anybody. Beastly place! Foul place! Kill anybody! Come away with me into the sun! It's the sun you want, of course, and a bit of normal life."

But Connie's heart simply stood still at the thought of abandoning Clifford there and then. She couldn't do it. No . . . no! She just couldn't. She had to go back to Wragby.

Michaelis was disgusted. Hilda didn't like Michaelis, but she *almost* preferred him to Clifford. Back went the sisters to the Midlands.

Hilda talked to Clifford, who still had yellow eyeballs when they got back. He, too, in his way was overwrought; but he had to listen to all Hilda said, to all the doctor had said, not to what Michaelis had said, of course, and he sat mum through the ultimatum.

"Here is the address of a good man-servant, who was with an invalid patient of the doctor's till he died last month. He is really a good man, and fairly sure to come."

"But I'm *not* an invalid, and I will *not* have a man-servant," said Clifford, poor devil.

"And here are the addresses of two women; I saw one of them, she would do very well; a woman of about fifty, quiet, strong, kind, and in her way cultured. . . ."

Clifford only sulked, and would not answer.

"Very well, Clifford. If we don't settle something by tomorrow, I shall telegraph to father, and we shall take Connie away."

"Will Connie go?" asked Clifford.

"She doesn't want to, but she knows she must. Mother died of cancer, brought on by fretting. We're not running any risks."

So next day Clifford suggested Mrs. Bolton, the Tevershall parish nurse. Apparently Mrs. Betts had thought of her. Mrs. Bolton was just retiring from her parish duties to take up private nursing jobs. Clifford had a queer dread of delivering himself into the hands of a stranger, but this Mrs. Bolton had once nursed him through scarlet fever, and he knew her.

The two sisters at once called on Mrs. Bolton, in a newish house in a row, quite select for Tevershall. They found a rather good-looking woman of forty-odd, in a nurse's uniform, with a white collar and apron, just making herself tea, in a small, crowded sitting-room.

Mrs. Bolton was most attentive and polite, seemed quite nice, spoke with a bit of a broad slur, but in heavily correct English, and from having bossed the sick colliers for a good many years, had a very good opinion of herself, and a fair amount of assurance. In short, in her tiny way, one of the governing class in the village, very much respected.

"Yes, Lady Chatterley's not looking at all well! Why she used to be that bonny, didn't she now? But she's been failing all winter! Oh, it's hard, it is. Poor Sir Clifford! Eh, that war, it's a lot to answer for."

And Mrs. Bolton would come to Wragby at once, if Dr. Shardlow would let her off. She had another fortnight's parish nursing to do, by rights, but they might get a substitute, you know.

Hilda posted off to Dr. Shardlow, and on the following Sunday Mrs. Bolton drove up in Leiver's cab to Wragby, with two trunks. Hilda had talks with her;

Mrs. Bolton was ready at any moment to talk. And she seemed so young! the way the passion would flush in her rather pale cheek. She was forty-seven.

Her husband, Ted Bolton, had been killed in the pit, twenty-two years ago, twenty-two years last Christmas, just at Christmas time, leaving her with two children, one a baby in arms. Oh, the baby was married now—Edith—to a young man in Boots Cash Chemists in Sheffield. The other one was a school-teacher in Chesterfield, she came home week-ends, when she wasn't asked out anywhere. Young folks enjoyed themselves nowadays; not like when she, Ivy Bolton, was young.

Ted Bolton was twenty-eight when he was killed in an explosion down th' pit. The butty in front shouted to them all to lie down quick; there were four of them. And they all lay down in time, only Ted, and it killed him. Then at the enquiry, on the masters' side they said Ted had been frightened, and trying to run away, and not obeying orders, so it was like his fault really. So the compensation was only three hundred pounds, and they made out as if it was more of a gift than legal compensation, because it was really the man's own fault. And they wouldn't let her have the money down; she wanted to have a little shop. But they said she'd no doubt squander it, perhaps in drink! So she had to draw it thirty shillings a week. Yes, she had to go every Monday morning down to the offices, and stand there a couple of hours waiting her turn; yes, for almost four years she went every Monday. And what could she do with two little children on her hands? But Ted's mother was very good to her. When the baby could toddle she'd keep both the children for the day, while she, Ivy Bolton, went to Sheffield, and attended classes in ambulance, and then the fourth year she even took a nursing course and got qualified. She was determined to be independent and keep her children. So she was assistant at Uthwaite hospital, just a little place, for a while. But when the Company, the Tevershall Colliery Company, really Sir Geoffrey, saw that she could get on by herself, they were very good to her, gave her the parish nursing, and stood by her, she would say that for them. And she'd done it ever since, till now it was getting a bit too much for her, she needed something a bit lighter, there was such a lot of traipsing round if you were a district nurse.

"Yes, the Company's been very good to *me,* I always say it. But I should never forget what they said about Ted, for he was as steady and fearless a chap as ever set foot on the cage, and it was as good as branding him a coward. But there, he was dead, and could say nothing to none of 'em."

It was a queer mixture of feelings the woman showed as she talked. She liked the colliers, whom she had nursed for so long; but she felt very superior to them. She felt almost upper class; and at the same time a resentment against the ruling class smoldered in her. The masters! In a dispute between masters and men, she was always for the men. But when there was no question of contest, she was pining to be superior, to be one of the upper class. The upper classes fascinated her, appealing to her peculiar English passion for superiority. She was thrilled to come to Wragby, thrilled to talk to Lady Chatterley; my word, different from the common colliers' wives! She said so in so many words. Yet one could see a grudge against the Chatterleys peep out in her; the grudge against the masters.

"Why, yes, of course, it would wear Lady Chatterley out! It's a mercy she has a sister to come and help her. Men don't think; high and low alike, they take what a woman does for them for granted. Oh, I've told the colliers off about it many a time. But it's very hard for Sir Clifford, you know, crippled like that. They were always a haughty family, stand-offish in a way, as they've a right to be. But then, to be brought down like that! And it's very hard on Lady Chatterley, perhaps harder on her. What she misses! I only had Ted three years, but my word, while I had him I had a husband I could never forget. He was one in a thousand, and jolly as the day. Who'd ever have thought he'd get killed? I don't believe it to this day, somehow; I've never believed it, though I washed him with my own hands. But he was never dead for me, he never was. I never took it in."

This was a new voice in Wragby, very new for Connie to hear; it roused a new ear in her.

For the first week or so, Mrs. Bolton, however, was very quiet at Wragby; her assured, bossy manner left her, and she was nervous. With Clifford she was shy, almost frightened and silent. He liked that, and soon recovered his self-possession, letting her do things for him without even noticing her.

"She's a useful nonentity!" he said. Connie opened her eyes in wonder, but did not contradict him. So different are impressions on two different people!

And he soon became rather superb, somewhat lordly with the nurse. She had rather expected it, and he played up without knowing. So susceptible we are to what is expected of us! The colliers had been so like children, talking to her, and telling her what hurt them, while she bandaged them, or nursed them. They had always made her feel so grand, almost superhuman in her administrations. Now Clifford made her feel small, and like a servant, and she accepted it without a word, adjusting herself to the upper classes.

She came very mute, with her long, handsome face, and downcast eyes, to administer to him. And she said very humbly: "Shall I do this now, Sir Clifford? Shall I do that?"

"No, leave it for a time, I'll have it done later."

"Very well, Sir Clifford."

"Come in again in half-an-hour."

"Very well, Sir Clifford."

"And just take those old papers out, will you?"

"Very well, Sir Clifford."

She went softly, and in half-an-hour she came softly again. She was bullied, but she didn't mind. She was experiencing the upper classes. She neither resented nor disliked Clifford; he was just part of a phenomenon, the phenomenon of the high-class folks, so far unknown to her, but now to be known. She felt more at home with Lady Chatterley, and after all it's the mistress of the house matters most.

Mrs. Bolton helped Clifford to bed at night, and slept across the passage from his room, and came if he rang for her in the night. She also helped him in the morning, and soon valeted him completely, even shaving him, in her soft, tentative woman's way. She was very good and competent, and she soon knew how to have him in her power. He wasn't so very different from the colliers after all, when you lathered his chin, and softly rubbed the bristles. The standoffishness and the lack of frankness didn't bother her, she was having a new experience.

Clifford, however, inside himself, never quite forgave Connie for giving up her personal care of him to a strange hired woman. It killed, he said to himself, the real flower of the intimacy between him and her. But Connie didn't mind that. The fine flower of their intimacy was to her rather like an orchid, a bulb stuck parasitic on her tree of life, and producing, to her eyes, a rather shabby flower.

Now she had more time to herself she could softly play the piano, up in her room, and sing: "Touch not the nettle . . . for the bonds of love are ill to loose." She had not realized till lately how ill to loose they were, these bonds of love. But thank heaven she had loosened them! She was so glad to be alone, not always to have to talk to him. When he was alone he tapped-tapped-tapped on a typewriter, to infinity. But when he was not "working," and she was there, he talked, always talked; infinite small analysis of people and motives, and results, characters and personalities, till now she had had enough. For years she had loved it, until she had enough, and then suddenly it was too much. She was thankful to be alone.

It was as if thousands and thousands of little roots and threads of consciousness in him and her had grown together into a tangled mass, till they could crowd no more, and the plant was dying. Now quietly, subtly she was unravelling the tangle of his consciousness and hers, breaking the threads gently, one by one, with patience and impatience to get clear. But the bonds of such love are more ill to loose even than most bonds; though Mrs. Bolton's coming had been a great help.

But he still wanted the old intimate evenings of talk with Connie: talk or reading aloud. But now she could arrange that Mrs. Bolton should come at ten to disturb them. At ten o'clock Connie could go upstairs and be alone. Clifford was in good hands with Mrs. Bolton.

Mrs. Bolton ate with Mrs. Betts in the housekeeper's room, since they were all agreeable. And it was curious how much closer the servants' quarters seemed to have come; right up to the doors of Clifford's study, when before they were so remote. For Mrs. Betts would sometimes sit in Mrs. Bolton's room, and Connie heard their lowered voices, and felt somehow the strong, outer vibration of the working people almost invading the sitting-rooms, when she and Clifford were alone. So changed was Wragby merely by Mrs. Bolton's coming.

And Connie felt herself released, in another world; she felt she breathed differently. But still she was afraid of how many of her roots, perhaps mortal ones, were tangled with Clifford's. Yet still, she breathed freer, a new phase was going to begin in her life.

Chapter Eight

Mrs. Bolton also kept a cherishing eye on Connie, feeling she must extend to her her female and professional protection. She was always urging her ladyship to walk out, to drive to Uthwaite, to be in the air. For Connie had got into the habit of sitting still by the fire, pretending to read, or to sew feebly, and hardly going out at all.

It was a blowy day soon after Hilda had gone, that Mrs. Bolton said: "Now, why don't you go for a walk through the wood, and look at the daffs behind the keeper's cottage? They're the prettiest sight you'd see in a day's march. And you could put some in your room, wild daffs are always so cheerful-looking, aren't they?"

Connie took it in good part, even daffs for daffodils. Wild daffodils! After all, one should not stew in one's own juice. The spring came back. . . . "Seasons return, but not to me returns Day, or the sweet approach of Ev'n or Morn."

And the keeper, his thin, white body, like a lonely pistil of an invisible flower! She had forgotten him in her unspeakable depression. But now something roused . . . "Pale beyond porch and portal" . . . the thing to do was to pass the porches and the portals.

She was stronger, she could walk better, and in the wood the wind would not be so tiring as it was across the park, flattening against her. She wanted to forget, to forget the world, and all the dreadful carrion-bodied people. "Ye must be born again! I believe in the resurrection of the body! Except a grain of wheat fall into the earth and die, it shall by no means bring forth. When the crocus cometh forth I too will emerge and see the sun!" In the wind of March endless phrases swept through her consciousness.

Little gusts of sunshine blew, strangely bright, and lit up the celandines at the wood's edge, under the hazel-rods, they spangled out bright and yellow. And the wood was still, stiller, but yet gusty with crossing sun. The first windflowers were out, and all the wood seemed pale with the pallor of endless little anemones, sprinkling the shaken floor. "The world has grown pale with thy breath." But it was the breath of Persephone, this time; she was out of hell on a cold morning. Cold breaths of wind came, and overhead there was an anger of entangled wind caught among the twigs. It, too, was caught and trying to tear itself free, the wind, like Absalom. How cold the anemones looked, bobbing their naked white shoulders over crinoline skirts of green. But they stood it. A few first bleached little primroses, too, by the path, and yellow buds unfolding themselves.

The roaring and swaying was overhead, only cold currents came down below. Connie was strangely excited in the wood, and the color flew in her cheeks, and burned blue in her eyes. She walked ploddingly, picking a few primroses and the first violets, that smelled sweet and cold, sweet and cold. And she drifted on without knowing where she was.

Till she came to the clearing, at the far end of the wood, and saw the green-stained stone cottage, looking almost rosy, like the flesh underneath a mushroom, its stone warmed in a burst of sun. And there was a sparkle of yellow jasmine by the door; the closed door. But no sound; no smoke from the chimney; no dog barking.

She went quietly round to the back, where the bank rose up; she had an excuse, to see the daffodils.

And they were there, the short-stemmed flowers, rustling and fluttering and shivering, so bright and alive, but with nowhere to hide their faces, as they turned them away from the wind.

They shook their bright, sunny little rags in bouts of distress. But perhaps they liked it really; perhaps they really liked the tossing.

Constance sat down with her back to a young pine-tree, that swayed against her with curious life, elastic and powerful, rising up. The erect, alive thing, with its top in the sun! And she watched the daffodils turn golden, in a burst of sun that was warm on her hands and lap. Even she caught the faint, tarry scent of the flowers. And then, being so still and alone, she seemed to get into the current of her own proper destiny. She had been fastened by a rope, and jagging and snarring like a boat at its moorings; now she was loose and adrift.

The sunshine gave way to chill; the daffodils were in shadow, dipping silently. So they would dip through the day and the long cold night. So strong in their frailty!

She rose, a little stiff, took a few daffodils, and went down. She hated breaking the flowers, but she wanted just one or two to go with her. She would have to go back to Wragby and it walls, and now she hated it, especially its thick walls. Walls! Always walls! Yet one needed them in this wind.

When she got home Clifford asked her:

"Where did you go?"

"Right across the wood! Look, aren't the little daffodils adorable? To think they should come out of the earth!"

"Just as much out of the air and sunshine," he said.

"But modelled in the earth," she retorted, with a prompt contradiction, that surprised her a little.

The next afternoon she went to the wood again. She followed the broad riding that swerved round and up through the larches to a spring called John's Well. It was cold on this hillside, and not a flower in the darkness of larches. But the icy little spring softly pressed upwards from its tiny well-bed of pure, reddish-white pebbles. How icy and clear it was! brilliant! The new keeper had no doubt put in fresh pebbles. She heard the faint tinkle of water, as the tiny overflow trickled over and downhill. Even above the hissing boom of the larch-wood, that spread its bristling, leafless, wolfish darkness on the down-slope, she heard the tinkle as of tiny water-bells.

This place was a little sinister, cold, damp, Yet the well must have been a drinking-place for hundreds of years. Now no more. Its tiny cleared space was lush and cold and dismal.

She rose and went slowly towards home. As she went she heard a faint tapping away on the right, and stood still to listen. Was it hammering, or a woodpecker? It was surely hammering.

She walked on, listening. And then she noticed a narrow track between young fir-trees, a track that seemed to lead nowhere. But she felt it had been used. She turned down it adventurously, between the thick young firs, which gave way soon to the old oak wood. She followed the track, and the hammering drew nearer, in the silence of the windy wood, for trees make a silence even in their noise of wind.

She saw a secret little clearing, and a secret little hut made of rustic poles. And she had never been here before! She realized it was the quiet place where the growing pheasants were reared; the keeper in his shirt-sleeves was kneeling, hammering. The dog trotted forward with a short, sharp bark, and the keeper lifted his face suddenly and saw her. He had a startled look in his eyes.

He straightened himself and saluted, watching her in silence, as she came forward with weakening limbs. He resented the intrusion, he cherished his solitude as his only and last freedom in life.

"I wondered what the hammering was," she said, feeling weak and breathless, and a little afraid of him, as he looked so straight at her.

"Ah'm gettin' th' coops ready for th' young bods," he said, in broad vernacular.

She did not know what to say, and she felt weak.

"I should like to sit down a bit," she said.

"Come and sit 'ere i' th' 'ut," he said, going in front of her to the hut, pushing aside more timber and stuff, and drawing out a rustic chair, made of hazel sticks.

"Am Ah t'light yer a little fire?" he asked, with the curious naïveté of the dialect.

"Oh, don't bother," she replied.

But she looked at her hands: they were rather blue. So he quickly took some larch twigs to the little brick fireplace in the corner, and in a moment the yellow flame was running up the chimney. He made a place by the brick hearth.

"Sit 'ere then a bit, and warm yer," he said.

She obeyed him. He had that curious kind of protective authority she obeyed at once. So she sat and warmed her hands at the blaze, and dropped logs on the fire, whilst outside he was hammering again. She did not really want to sit, poked in a corner by the fire; she would rather have watched from the door, but she was being looked after, so she had to submit.

The hut was quite cozy, panelled with unvarnished deal, having a little rustic table and stool besides her chair, and a carpenter's bench, then a big box, tools, new boards, nails; and many things hung from pegs: axe, hatchet, traps, things in sacks, his coat. It had no window, the light came in through the open door. It was a jumble, but also it was a sort of little sanctuary.

She listened to the tapping of the man's hammer; it was not so happy. He was oppressed. Here was a trespass on his privacy, and a dangerous one! A woman! He had reached the point where all he wanted on earth was to be alone. And yet he was powerless to preserve his privacy; he was a hired man, and these people were his masters.

Especially he did not want to come into contact with a woman again. He feared it; for he had a big wound from old contacts. He felt if he could not be alone, and if he could not be left alone, he would die. His recoil away from the outer world was complete; his last refuge was this wood; to hide himself there!

Connie grew warm by the fire, which she had made too big: then she grew hot. She went and sat on the stool in the doorway, watching the man at work. He seemed not to notice her, but he knew. Yet he worked on, as if absorbedly, and his brown dog sat on her tail near him, and surveyed the untrustworthy world.

Slender, quiet and quick, the man finished the coop he was making, turned it over, tried the sliding door, then set it aside. Then he rose, went for an old coop, and took it to the chopping-log where he was working. Crouching, he tried the bars; some broke in his hands; he began to draw the nails. Then he turned the coop over and deliberated, and he gave absolutely no sign of awareness of the woman's presence.

So Connie watched him fixedly. And the same solitary aloneness she had seen in him naked, she now saw in him clothed: solitary, and intent, like an animal that works alone, but also brooding, like a soul that recoils away, away from all human contact. Silently, patiently, he was recoiling away from her even now. It was the stillness, and the timeless sort of patience, in a man impatient and passionate, that touched Connie's womb. She saw it in his bent head, the quick, quiet hands, the crouching of his slender, sensitive loins; something patient and withdrawn. She felt his experience had been deeper and wider than her own; much deeper and wider, and perhaps more deadly. And this relieved her of herself; she felt almost irresponsible.

So she sat in the doorway of the hut in a dream, utterly unaware of time and of particular circumstances. She was so drifted away that he glanced up at her quickly, and saw the utterly still, waiting look on her face. To him it was a look of waiting. And a little thin tongue of fire suddenly flickered in his loins, at the root of his back, and he groaned in spirit. He dreaded, with a repulsion almost of death, any further close human contact. He wished above all things she would go away, and leave him to his own privacy. He dreaded her will, her female will, and her modern female insistency. And above all he dreaded her cool, upper-class impudence of having her own way. For after all he was only a hired man. He hated her presence there.

Connie came to herself with sudden uneasiness. She rose. The afternoon was turning to evening, yet she could not go away. She went over to the man, who stood up at attention, his worn face stiff and blank, his eyes watching her.

"It is so nice here, so restful," she said. "I have never been here before."

"No?"

"I think I shall come and sit here sometimes."

"Yes!"

"Do you lock the hut when you're not here?"

"Yes, your Ladyship."

"Do you think I could have a key too, so that I could sit here sometimes? Are there two keys?"

"Not as Ah know on, ther' isna."

He had lapsed into the vernacular. Connie hesitated; he was putting up an opposition. Was it his hut, after all?

"Couldn't we get another key?" she asked in her soft voice, that underneath had the ring of a woman determined to get her way.

"Another!" he said, glancing at her with a flash of anger, touched with derision.

"Yes, a duplicate," she said, flushing.

" 'Appen Sir Clifford 'ud know," he said, putting her off.

"Yes!" she said, "he might have another. Otherwise we could have one made from the one you have. It would only take a day or so, I suppose. You could spare your key for so long."

"Ah canna tell yer, m'lady! Ah know nob'dy as ma'es keys round 'ere."

Connie suddenly flushed with anger.

"Very well!" she said. "I'll see to it."

"All right, your Ladyship."

Their eyes met. His had a cold, ugly look of dislike and contempt, and indifference to what would happen. Hers were hot with rebuff.

But her heart sank, she saw how utterly he disliked her, when she went against him. And she saw him in a sort of desperation.

"Good afternoon!"

"Afternoon, my Lady!" He saluted and turned abruptly away. She had wakened the sleeping dogs of old voracious anger in him, anger against the self-willed female. And he was powerless, powerless. He knew it!

And she was angry against the self-willed male. A servant too! She walked sullenly home.

She found Mrs. Bolton under the great beech tree on the knoll, looking for her.

"I just wondered if you'd be coming, my Lady," the woman said brightly.

"Am I late?" asked Connie.

"Oh . . . only Sir Clifford was waiting for his tea."

"Why didn't *you* make it then?"

"Oh, I don't think it's hardly my place. I don't think Sir Clifford would like it at all, my Lady."

"I don't see why not," said Connie.

She went indoors to Clifford's study, where the old brass kettle was simmering on the tray.

"Am I late, Clifford?" she said, putting down the few flowers and taking up the tea-caddy, as she stood before the tray in her hat and scarf. "I'm sorry! Why didn't you let Mrs. Bolton make the tea?"

'I didn't think of it," he said ironically. "I don't quite see her presiding at the tea-table."

"Oh, there's nothing sacrosanct about a silver tea-pot," said Connie.

He glanced up at her curiously.

"What did you do all afternoon?" he said.

"Walked and sat in a sheltered place. Do you know there are still berries on the big holly-tree?"

She took off her scarf, but not her hat, and sat down to make tea. The toast would certainly be leathery. She put the tea-cosy over the tea-pot, and rose to get a little glass for her violets. The poor flowers hung over, limp on their stalks.

"They'll revive again!" she said, putting them before him in their glass for him to smell.

"Sweeter than the lids of Juno's eyes," he quoted.

"I don't see a bit of connection with the actual violets," she said. "The Elizabethans are rather upholstered."

She poured him his tea.

"Do you think there is a second key to that little hut not far from John's Well, where the pheasants are reared?" she said.

"There may be. Why?"

"I happened to find it today—and I'd never seen it before. I think it's a darling place. I could sit there sometimes, couldn't I?"

"Was Mellors there?"

"Yes! That's how I found it; his hammering. He didn't seem to like my intruding at all. In fact he was almost rude when I asked about a second key."

"What did he say?"

"Oh, nothing: just his manner; and he said he knew nothing about keys."

"There may be one in father's study. Betts knows them all; they're all there. I'll get him to look."

"Oh, do!" she said.

"So Mellors was almost rude?"

"Oh, nothing, really! But I don't think he wanted me to have the freedom of the castle, quite."

"I don't suppose he did."

"Still, I don't see why he should mind. It's not his home, after all! It's not his private abode. I don't see why I shouldn't sit there if I want to."

"Quite!" said Clifford. "He thinks too much of himself, that man."

"Do you think he does?"

"Oh, decidedly! He thinks he's something exceptional. You know he had a wife he didn't get on with, so he joined up in 1915 and was sent out to India, I believe. Anyhow he was blacksmith to the cavalry in Egypt for a time; always was connected with horses, a clever fellow that way. Then some Indian colonel took a fancy to him, and he was made a lieutenant. Yes, they gave him a commission. I believe he went back to India with his colonel, and up to the northwest frontier. He was ill; he has a pension. He didn't come out of the army till last year, I believe, and then, naturally, it isn't easy for a man like that to get back to his own level. He's bound to flounder. But he does his duty all right, as far as I'm concerned. Only, I'm not having any of the Lieutenant Mellors touch."

"How could they make him an officer when he speaks broad Derbyshire?"

"He doesn't . . . . except by fits and starts. He can speak perfectly well, for him. I suppose he has an idea if he's come down to the ranks again, he'd better speak as the ranks speak."

"Why didn't you tell me about him before?"

"Oh, I've no patience with these romances. They're the ruin of all order. It's a thousand pities they ever happened."

Connie was inclined to agree. What was the good of discontented people who fitted in nowhere?

In the spell of fine weather Clifford, too, decided to go to the wood. The wind was cold, but not so tiresome, and the sunshine was like life itself, warm and full.

"It's amazing," said Connie, "how different one feels when there's a really fresh fine day. Usually one feels the very air is half dead. People are killing the very air."

"Do you think people are doing it?" he asked.

"I do. The steam of so much boredom, and discontent and anger out of all the people, just kills the vitality in the air. I'm sure of it."

"Perhaps some condition of the atmosphere lowers the vitality of the people?" he said.

"No, it's man that poisons the universe," she asserted.

"Fouls his own nest," remarked Clifford.

The chair puffed on. In the hazel copse catkins were hanging pale gold, and in sunny places the wood-anemones were wide open, as if exclaiming with the joy of life, just as good as in past days, when people could exclaim along with them. They had a faint scent of apple-blossom. Connie gathered a few for Clifford.

He took them and looked at them curiously.

"Thou still unravished bride of quietness," he quoted. "It seems to fit flowers so much better than Greek vases."

"Ravished is such a horrid word!" she said. "It's only people who ravish things."

"Oh, I don't know . . . snails and things," he said.

"Even snails only eat them, and bees don't ravish."

"She was angry with him, turning everything into words. Violets were Juno's eyelids, and windflowers were unravished brides. How she hated words, always coming between her and life: they did the ravishing, if anything did: ready-made words and phrases, sucking all the life-sap out of living things.

The walk with Clifford was not quite a success. Between him and Connie there was a tension that each pretended not to notice, but there it was. Suddenly, with all the force of her female instinct, she was shoving him off. She wanted to be clear of him, and especially of his consciousness, his words, his obsession with himself, his endless treadmill obsession with himself, and his own words.

The weather came rainy again. But after a day or two she went out in the rain, and she went to the wood. And once there, she went towards the hut. It was raining, but not so cold, and the wood felt so silent and remote, inaccessible in the dusk of rain.

She came to the clearing. No one there! The hut was locked. But she sat on the log doorstep, under the rustic porch, and snuggled into her own warmth. So she sat, looking at the rain, listening to the many noiseless noises of it, and to the strange soughings of wind in upper branches, when there seemed to be no wind. Old oak trees stood around, grey, powerful trunks, rain-blackened, round and vital, throwing off reckless limbs. The ground was fairly free of undergrowth, the anemones sprinkled, there was a bush or two, elder, or guelder-rose, and a purplish tangle of bramble; the old russet of bracken almost vanished under green anemone ruffs. Perhaps this was one of the unravished places. Unravished! The whole world was ravished.

Some things can't be ravished. You can't ravish a tin of sardines. And so many women are like that; and men. But the earth . . . !

The rain was abating. It was hardly making darkness among the oaks any more. Connie wanted to go; yet she sat on. But she was getting cold; yet the overwhelming inertia of her inner resentment kept her there as if paralyzed.

Ravished! How ravished one could be without ever being touched. Ravished by dead words become obscene, and dead ideas become obsessions.

A wet brown dog came running and did not bark, lifting a wet feather of a tail. The man followed in a wet black oilskin jacket, like a chauffeur, and face flushed a little. She felt him recoil in his quick walk, when he saw her. She stood up in the handbreath of dryness under the rustic porch. He saluted without speaking, coming slowly near. She began to withdraw.

"I'm just going," she said.

"Was yer waitin' to get in?" he asked, looking at the hut, not at her.

"No, I only sat a few minutes in the shelter," she said, with quiet dignity.

He looked at her. She looked cold.

"Sir Clifford 'adn't got no other key then?" he asked.

"No, but it doesn't matter. I can sit perfectly dry under this porch. Good afternoon!" She hated the excess of vernacular in his speech.

He watched her closely, as she was moving away. Then he hitched up his jacket, and put his hand in his breeches pocket, taking out the key of the hut.

" 'Appen yer'd better 'ave this key, an' mun fend for t'bods some other road."

"What do you mean?" she asked.

"I mean as 'appen Ah can find anuther pleece as'll du for rearin' th' pheasants. If yer want ter be 'ere, yo'll non want me messin' abaht a' th' time."

She looked at him, getting his meaning through the fog of the dialect.

"Why don't you speak ordinary English?" she said coldly.

"Me! Ah thowt it *wor*' ordinary."

She was silent for a few moments in anger.

"So if yer want t' key, yer'd better ta'e it. Or 'appen Ah'd better gi'e 't yer termorrer, an' clear all t' stuff aht fust. Would that du for yer?"

She became more angry.

"I didn't want your key," she said. "I don't want you to clear anything out at all. I don't in the least want to turn you out of your hut, thank you! I only wanted to be able to sit here sometimes, like today. But I can sit perfectly well under the porch, so please say no more about it."

He looked at her again with his wicked blue eyes.

"Why," he began, in the broad slow dialect, "your Ladyship's as welcome as Christmas ter th' hut an' th' key an' iverythink as it. On'y this time o' th' year ther's bods ter set, an' Ah've got ter be potterin' abaht a good bit, seein' after 'em, an' a'. Winter time Ah need 'ardly come nigh th' pleece. But what wi' spring, an' Sir Clifford wantin' ter start th' pheasants. . . . An' your Ladyship'd non want me tinkerin' around an' about when she was 'ere, all th' time."

She listened with a dim kind of amazement.

"Why should I mind your being here?" she asked.

He looked at her curiously.

"T' nuisance on me!" he said briefly, but significantly.

She flushed. "Very well!" she said finally. "I won't trouble you. But I don't think I should have minded at all sitting and seeing you look after the birds. I should have liked it. But since you think it interferes with you, I won't disturb you, don't be afraid. You are Sir Clifford's keeper, not mine."

The phrase sounded queer, she didn't know why. But she let it pass.

"Nay, your Ladyship. It's your Ladyship's own 'ut. It's as your Ladyship likes an' pleases, every time. Yer can turn me off at a wik's notice. It wor only . . ."

"Only what?" she asked, baffled.

He pushed back his hat in an odd comic way.

"On'y as 'appen yo'd like the place ter yersen, when yer did come, an' not me messin' abaht."

"But why?" she said, angry. "Aren't you a civilized human being? Do you think I ought to be afraid of you? Why should I take any notice of you and your being here or not? Why is it important?"

He looked at her, all his face glimmering with wicked laughter.

"It's not, your Ladyship. Not in the very least," he said.

"Well, why then?" she asked.

"Shall I get your Ladyship another key then?"

"No, thank you! I don't want it."

"Ah'll get it anyhow. We'd best 'ave two keys ter th' place."

"And I consider you are insolent," said Connie, with her color up, panting a little.

"Nay, nay!" he said quickly. "Dunna yer say that! Nay, nay! I niver meant nuthink. Ah on'y thought as if yo' come 'ere, Ah s'd 'ave ter clear out, an' it'd mean a lot o' work, settin' up somewheres else. But if your Ladyship isn't going ter take no notice o' me, then . . . it's Sir Clifford's 'ut, an' everythink is as your Ladyship likes, everythink is as your Ladyship likes an' pleases, barrin' yer take no notice o' me, doin' the bits of jobs as Ah've got ter do."

Connie went away completely bewildered. She was not sure whether she had been insulted and mortally offended, or not. Perhaps the man really only meant what he said; that he thought she would expect him to keep away. As if she would dream of it! And as if he could possibly be so important, he and his stupid presence.

She went home in confusion, not knowing what she thought or felt.

Chapter Nine

Connie was surprised at her own feeling of aversion for Clifford. What is more, she felt she had always really disliked him. Not hate: there was no passion in it. But a profound physical dislike. Almost it seemed to her, she had married him because she disliked him, in a secret, physical sort of way. But of course, she had married him really because in a mental way he attracted her and excited her. He had seemed, in some way, her master, beyond her.

Now the mental excitement had worn itself out and collapsed, and she was aware only of the physical aversion. It rose up in her from her depths: and she realized how it had been eating her life away.

She felt weak and utterly forlorn. She wished some help would come from outside. But in the whole world there was no help. Society was terrible because it was insane. Civilized society is insane. Money and so-called love are its two great manias; money a long way first. The individual asserts himself in his disconnected insanity in these two modes: money and love. Look at Michaelis! His life and activity were just insanity. His love was a sort of insanity.

And Clifford the same. All that talk! All that writing! All that wild struggling to push himself forward! It was just insanity. And it was getting worse, really maniacal.

Connie felt washed-out with fear. But at least, Clifford was shifting his grip from her on to Mrs. Bolton. He did not know it. Like many insane people, his insanity might be measured by the things he was *not* aware of; the great desert tracts in his consciousness.

Mrs. Bolton was admirable in many ways. But she had that queer sort of bossiness, endless assertion of her own will, which is one of the signs of insanity in modern woman. She *thought* she was utterly subservient and living for others.

Clifford fascinated her because he always, or so often, frustrated her will, as if by a finer instinct. He had a finer, subtler will of self-assertion than herself. This was his charm for her.

Perhaps that had been his charm, too, for Connie.

"It's a lovely day, today!" Mrs. Bolton would say in her caressive, persuasive voice. "I should think you'd enjoy a little run in your chair today, the sun's just lovely."

"Yes? Will you give me that book—there, that yellow one. And I think I'll have those hyacinths taken out."

"Why, they're so beautiful!" She pronounced it with the "y" sound: be-yutiful!— "And the scent is simply gorgeous."

"The scent is what I object to," he said. "It's a little funereal."

"Do you think so!" she exclaimed in surprise, just a little offended, but impressed. And she carried the hyacinths out of the room, impressed by his higher fastidiousness.

"Shall I shave you this morning, or would you rather do it yourself?" Always the same soft, caressive, subservient, yet managing voice.

"I don't know. Do you mind waiting a while. I'll ring when I'm ready."

"Very good, Sir Clifford!" she replied, so soft and submissive, withdrawing quietly. But every rebuff stored up new energy of will in her.

When he rang, after a time, she would appear at once. And then he would say:

"I think I'd rather you shaved me this morning."

Her heart gave a little thrill, and she replied with extra softness:

"Very good, Sir Clifford!"

She was very deft, with a soft, lingering touch, a little slow. At first he had resented the infinitely soft touch of her fingers on his face. But now he liked it, with a growing voluptuousness. He let her shave him nearly every day: her face near his, her eyes so very concentrated, watching that she did it right. And gradually her fingertips knew his cheeks and lips, his jaw and chin and throat perfectly. He was well-fed and well-groomed, his face and throat were handsome enough, and he was a gentleman.

She was handsome, too, pale, her face rather long and absolutely still, her eyes bright, but revealing nothing. Gradually, with infinite softness, almost with love, she was getting him by the throat, and he was yielding to her.

She now did almost everything for him, and he felt more at home with her, less ashamed of accepting her menial offices, than with Connie. She liked handling him. She loved having his body in her charge, absolutely, to the last menial offices. She said to Connie one day: "All men are babies, when you come to the bottom of them. Why, I've handled some of the toughest customers as ever went down Tevershall pit. But let anything ail them so that you have to do for them, and they're babies, just big babies. Oh, there's not much difference in men!"

At first Mrs. Bolton had thought there really was something different in a gentleman, a *real* gentleman, like Sir Clifford. So Clifford had got a good start of her. But gradually, as she came to the bottom of him, to use her own term, she found he was like the rest, a baby grown to man's proportions: but a baby with a queer temper and a fine manner and power in its control, and all sorts of odd knowledge that she had never dreamed of, with which he could still bully her.

Connie was sometimes tempted to say to him:

"For God's sake, don't sink so horribly into the hands of that woman!" But she found she didn't care for him enough to say it, in the long run.

It was still their habit to spend the evening together, till ten o'clock. Then they would talk, or read together, or go over his manuscript. But the thrill had gone out of it. She was bored by his manuscripts. But she still dutifully typed them out for him. But in time Mrs. Bolton would do even that.

For Connie had suggested to Mrs. Bolton that she should learn to use a typewriter. And Mrs. Bolton, always ready, had begun at once, and practiced assiduously. So now Clifford would sometimes dictate a letter to her, and she would take it down rather slowly, but correctly. And he was very patient, spelling for her the difficult words, or the occasional phrases in French. She was so thrilled, it was almost a pleasure to instruct her.

Now Connie would sometimes plead a headache as an excuse for going up to her room after dinner.

"Perhaps Mrs. Bolton will play piquet with you," she said to Clifford.

"Oh, I shall be perfectly all right. You go to your own room and rest, darling."

But no sooner had she gone, than he rang for Mrs. Bolton, and asked her to take a hand at piquet or bezique, or even chess. He had taught her all these games. And Connie found it curiously objectionable to see Mrs. Bolton, flushed and tremulous like a little girl, touching her queen or her knight with uncertain fingers, then drawing away again. And Clifford, faintly smiling with a half-teasing superiority, saying to her:

"You must say *j'adoube*!"

She looked up at him with bright, startled eyes, then murmured shyly, obediently: "*J'adoube*"!

Yes, he was educating her. And he enjoyed it, it gave him a sense of power. And she was thrilled. She was coming bit by bit into possession of all that the gentry knew, all that made them upper class: apart from the money. That thrilled her. And at the same time, she was making him want to have her there with him. It was a subtle deep flattery to him, her genuine thrill.

To Connie, Clifford seemed to be coming out in his true colors: a little vulgar, a little common, and uninspired; rather fat. Ivy Bolton's tricks and humble bossiness were also only too transparent. But Connie did wonder at the genuine thrill which the woman got out of Clifford. To say she was in love with him would be putting it wrongly. She was thrilled by her contact with a man of the upper class, this titled gentleman, this author who could write books and poems, and whose photograph appeared in the illustrated newspapers. She was thrilled to a weird passion. And his "educating" her roused in her a passion of excitement and response much deeper than any love affair could have done. In truth, the very fact that there could *be* no love affair left her free to thrill to her very marrow with this other passion, the peculiar passion of *knowing,* knowing as he knew.

There was no mistake that the woman was in some way in love with him: whatever force we give to the word love. She looked so handsome and so young, and her grey eyes were sometimes marvellous. At the same time, there was a lurking soft satisfaction about her, even of triumph, and private satisfaction. Ugh, that private satisfaction! How Connie loathed it!

But no wonder Clifford was caught by the woman! She absolutely adored him, in her persistent fashion, and put herself absolutely at his service, for him to use as he liked. No wonder he was flattered!

Connie heard long conversations going on between the two. Or rather, it was mostly Mrs. Bolton talking. She had unloosed to him the stream of gossip about Tevershall village. It was more than gossip. It was Mrs. Gaskell and George Eliot and Miss Mitford all rolled in one, with a great deal more, that these women left out. Once started, Mrs. Bolton was better than any book, about the lives of the people. She knew them all so intimately, and had such a peculiar, flamey zest in all their affairs, it was wonderful, if just a *trifle* humiliating to listen to her. At first she had not ventured to "talk Tevershall," as she called it, to Clifford. But once started, it went. Clifford was listening for "material," and he found it in plenty. Connie realized that his so-called genius was just this: a perspicuous talent for personal gossip, clever and apparently detached. Mrs. Bolton, of course, was very warm when she "talked Tevershall." Carried away, in fact. And it was marvellous, the things that happened and that she knew about. She would have run to dozens of volumes.

Connie was fascinated, listening to her. But afterwards always a little ashamed. She ought not to listen with this queer rabid curiosity. After all, one may hear the most private affairs of other people, but only in a spirit of respect for the struggling, battered thing which any human soul is, and in a spirit of fine, discriminative sympathy. For even satire is a form of sympathy. It is the way our sympathy flows and recoils that really determines our lives. And here lies the vast importance of the novel, properly handled. It can inform and lead into new places the flow of our sympathetic consciousness, and it can lead our sympathy away in recoil from things gone dead. Therefore, the novel, properly handled, can reveal the most secret places of life: for it is in the *passional* secret places of life, above all, that the tide of sensitive awareness needs to ebb and flow, cleansing and freshening.

But the novel, like gossip, can also excite spurious sympathies and recoils, mechanical and deadening to the psyche. The novel can glorify the most corrupt feelings, so long as they are *conventionally* "pure." Then the novel, like gossip, becomes at last vicious, and, like gossip, all the more vicious because it is always ostensibly on the side of the angels. Mrs. Bolton's gossip was always on the side of the angels. "And he was such a *bad* fellow, and she was such a *nice* woman." Whereas, as Connie could see even from Mrs. Bolton's gossip, the woman had been merely a mealy-mouthed sort, and the man angrily honest. But angry honesty

made a "bad man" of him, and mealy-mouthedness made a "nice woman" of
her, in the vicious, conventional channeling of sympathy by Mrs. Bolton.

For this reason, the gossip was humiliating. And for the same reason, most
novels, especially popular ones, are humiliating too. The public responds now
only to an appeal to its vices.

Nevertheless, one got a new vision of Tevershall village from Mrs. Bolton's
talk. A terrible, seething welter of ugly life it seemed: not at all the flat drabness
it looked from outside. Clifford of course knew by sight most of the people
mentioned; Connie knew only one or two. But it sounded really more like a
Central African jungle than an English village.

"I suppose you heard as Miss Allsopp was married last week! Would you ever!
Miss Allsopp, old James's daughter, the boot-and-shoe Allsopp. You know, they
built a house up at Pye Croft. The old man died last year from a fall: eighty-
three, he was, an' nimble as a lad. An' then he slipped on Bestwood Hill, on a
slide as the lad's 'ad made last winter, an' broke his thigh, and that finished him,
poor old man, it did seem a shame. Well, he left all his money to Tattie: didn't
leave the boys a penny. An' Tattie, I know, is five years . . . yes, she's fifty-
three last autumn. And you know they were such Chapel people, my word! She
taught Sunday School for thirty years, till her father died. And then she started
carrying on with a fellow from Kinbrook, I don't know if you know him, an
oldish fellow with a red nose, rather dandified, Willcock, as works in Harrison's
woodyard. Well, he's sixty-five if he's a day, yet you'd have thought they were
a pair of young turtledoves, to see them, arm-in-arm, and kissing at the gate:
yes, an' she sitting on his knee right in the bay window on Pye Croft Road, for
anybody to see. And he's got sons over forty: only lost his wife two years ago.
If old James Allsopp hasn't risen from his grave, it's because there is no rising:
for he kept her that strict! Now they're married and gone to live down at Kinbrook,
and they say she goes round in a dressing-gown from morning to night, a veritable
sight. I'm sure it's awful, the way the old ones go on! Why, they're a lot worse
than the young, and a sight more disgusting. I lay it down to the pictures, myself.
But you can't keep them away. I was always saying: go to a good instructive
film, but do for goodness sake keep away from these melodramas and love films.
Anyhow keep the children away! But there you are, the grown-ups are worse than
the children: and the old ones beat the band. Talk about morality; nobody cares
a thing. Folks does as they like, and much better off they are for it, I must say.
But they're having to draw their horns in nowadays, now th' pits are working
so bad, and they haven't got the money. And the grumbling they do, it's awful,
especially the women. The men are so good and patient! What can they do, poor
chaps! But the women, oh, they do carry on! They go and show off, giving
contributions for a wedding present for Princess Mary, and then when they see
all the grand things that's been given, they simply rave: who's she, any better
than anybody else! Why doesn't Swan & Edgar give me *one* fur coat, instead of
giving her six? I wish I'd kept my ten shillings! What's she going to give *me,* I
should like to know? Here I can't get a new spring coat, my dad's working that
bad, and she gets van-loads. It's time as poor folks had some money to spend,

rich ones 'as 'ad it long enough. I want a new spring coat, I do, an' wheer am I going to get it?—I say to them, be thankful you're well fed and well clothed, without all the new finery you want!—And they fly back at me: 'Why isn't Princess Mary thankful to go about in her old rags, then, an' have nothing? Folks like *her* get van-loads, an' I can't have a new spring coat. It's a damned shame. Princess! bloomin' rot about Princess! It's munney as matters, an' cos she's got lots, they give her more! Nobody's givin' me any, an' I've as much right as anybody else. Don't talk to me about education. It's munney as matters. I want a new spring coat, I do, an' I shan't get it, cos there's no munney.'—That's all they care about, clothes. They think nothing of giving seven or eight guineas for a winter coat—collier's daughters, mind you—and two guineas for a child's summer hat. And then they go to the Primitive Chapel in their two-guinea hat, girls as would have been proud of a three-and-sixpenny one in my day. I heard that at the Primitive Methodist anniversary this year, when they have a built-up platform for the Sunday School children, like a grandstand going almost up to th' ceiling, I heard Miss Thompson, who has the first class of girls in the Sunday School, say there'd be over a thousand pounds in new Sunday clothes sitting on that platform! And times are what they are! But you can't stop them. They're mad for clothes. And boys the same. The lads spend every penny on themselves, clothes, smoking, drinking in the Miner's Welfare, jaunting off to Sheffield two or three times a week. Why, it's another world. And they fear nothing, and they respect nothing, the young don't. The older men are that patient and good, really, they let the women take everything. And this is what it leads to. The women are positive demons. But the lads aren't like their dads. They're sacrificing nothing, they aren't: they're all for self. If you tell them they ought to be putting a bit by, for a home, they say: That'll keep, that will, I'm goin' t' enjoy mysen while I can. Owt else'll keep!—Oh, they're rough an' selfish, if you like. Everything falls on the older men, an' it's a bad lookout all round."

Clifford began to get a new idea of his own village. The place had always frightened him, but he had thought it more or less stable. Now—?

"Is there much socialism, bolshevism, among the people?" he asked.

"Oh!" said Mrs. Bolton, "You hear a few loud-mouthed ones. But they're mostly women who've got into debt. The men take no notice. I don't believe you'll ever turn our Tevershall men into reds. They're too decent for that. But the young ones blether sometimes. Not that they care for it really. They only want a bit of money in their pocket, to spend at the Welfare, or go gadding to Sheffield. That's all they care. When they've got no money, they'll listen to the reds spouting. But nobody believes in it, really."

"So you think there's no danger?"

"Oh, no! Not if trade was good, there wouldn't be. But if things were bad for a long spell, the young ones might go funny. I tell you, they're a selfish, spoilt lot. But I don't see how they'd ever do anything. They aren't ever serious about anything, except showing off on motorbikes and dancing at the Palais-de-danse in Sheffield. You can't *make* them serious. The serious ones dress up in evening clothes and go off to the Pally to show off before a lot of girls and dance these new Charlestons and what not. I'm sure sometimes the bus'll be full of young fellows in evening suits, collier lads, off to the Pally: let alone those that have gone with their girls in motors or on motor-bikes. They don't give a serious thought to a thing—save Doncaster races, and the Derby: for they all of them bet on every race. And football! But even football's not what it was, not by a long chalk. It's too much like hard work, they say. No, they'd rather be off on motor-bikes to Sheffield or Nottingham, Saturday afternoons."

"But what do they do when they get there?"

"Oh, hang round—and have tea in some fine tea-place like the Mikado—and go to the Pally or the Pictures or the Empire, with some girl. The girls are as free as the lads. They do just what they like."

"And what do they do when they haven't the money for these things?"

"They seem to get it, somehow. And they begin talking nasty then. But I don't see how you're going to get bolshevism, when all the lads want is just money to enjoy themselves, and the girls the same, with fine clothes: and they don't care about another thing. They haven't the brains to be socialists. They haven't enough seriousness to take anything really serious, and they never will have."

Connie thought, how extremely like all the rest of the classes the lower classes sounded. Just the same thing over again, Tevershall or Mayfair or Kensington. There was only one class nowadays: moneyboys. The moneyboy and the moneygirl, the only difference was how much you'd got, and how much you wanted.

Under Mrs. Bolton's influence, Clifford began to take a new interest in the mines. He began to feel he belonged. A new sort of self-assertion came into him. After all, he was the real boss in Tevershall, he was really the pits. It was a new sense of power, something he had till now shrunk from with dread.

Tevershall pits were running thin. There were only two collieries: Tevershall itself, and New London. Tevershall had once been a famous mine, and had made famous money. But its best days were over. New London was never very rich, and in ordinary times just got along decently. But now times were bad, and it was pits like New London that got left.

"There's a lot of Tevershall men left and gone to Stacks Gate and Whiteover," said Mrs. Bolton. "You've not seen the new works at Stacks Gate, opened after the war, have you, Sir Clifford? Oh, you must go one day, they're something quite new: great big chemical works at the pit-head, doesn't look a bit like a colliery. They say they get more money out of the chemical by-products than out of the coal—I forget what it is. And the grand new houses for the men, fair mansions! But a lot of Tevershall men got on there, and doin' well, a lot better than our own men. They say Tevershall's done, finished: only a question of a few more years, and it'll have to shut down. And New London'll go first. My word, won't it be funny, when there's no Tevershall pit working. It's bad enough during a strike, but my word, if it closes for good, it'll be like the end of the world. Even when I was a girl it was the best pit in the country, and a man counted himself lucky if he could work here. Oh, there's been some money made in Tevershall. And now the men say it's a sinking ship, and it's time they all got out. Doesn't it sound awful! But of course there's a lot as'll never go till they have to. They don't like these new fangled mines, such a depth, and all machinery to work them. Some of them simply dreads those iron men, as they call them, those machines for hewing the coal, where men always did it before. And they say it's wasteful as well. But what goes in waste is saved in wages, and a lot more. It seems soon there'll be no use for men on the face of the earth, it'll be all machines. But they say that's what folks said when they had to give up the old stocking frames. I can remember one or two. But my word, the more machines the more people, that's what it looks like. They say you can't get the same chemicals out of Tevershall coal as you can out of Stacks Gate, and that's funny, they're not three miles apart. But they say so. But everybody says it's a shame something can't be started, to keep the men going a bit better, and employ the girls. All the girls traipsing off to Sheffield every day! My word, it would be something to talk about if Tevershall Collieries took a new lease on life, after everybody saying they're finished, and a sinking ship, and the men ought to leave them like rats leave a sinking ship. But folks talk so much. Of course there was a boom during the war. When Sir Geoffrey made a trust of himself and got the money safe for ever, somehow. So they say! But they say even the masters and the owners don't get much out of it now. You can hardly believe it, can you! Why, I always thought the Pits would go on for ever and ever. Who'd have thought, when I was a girl! But New England's shut down, so is Colwick Wood: yes, it's fair haunting to go through that coppy and see Colwick Wood standing there deserted among the trees, and bushes growing up all over the pit-head, and the lines red rusty. It's like death itself, a dead colliery. Why, whatever we should do if Tevershall shut down—? it doesn't bear thinking of. Always that throng it's been, except at strikes, and even then the fan-wheels didn't stand, except when they fetched the ponies up. I'm sure it's a funny world, you don't know where you are from year to year, you really don't."

It was Mrs. Bolton's talk that really put a new fight into Clifford. His income, as she pointed out to him, was secure, from his father's trust, even though it was not large. The pits did not really concern him. It was the other world he wanted to capture, the world of literature and fame; the popular world, not the working world.

Now he realized the distinction between popular success and working success: the populace of pleasure and the populace of work. He, as a private individual, had been catering with his stories for the populace of pleasure. And he had caught on. But beneath the populace of pleasure lay the populace of work, grim, grimey, and rather terrible. They, too, had to have their providers. And it was a much grimmer business, providing for the populace of work, than for the populace of pleasure. While he was doing his stories, and "getting on" in the world, Tevershall was going to the wall.

He realized now that the bitch-goddess of success had two main appetites: one for flattery, adulation, stroking and tickling, such as writers and artists gave her; but the other a grimmer appetite for meat and bones. And the meat and bones for the bitch-goddess were provided by the men who made money in industry.

Yes, there were two great groups of dogs wrangling for the bitch-goddess: the

group of the flatterers, those who offered her amusement, stories, films, plays:
and the other, much less showy, much more savage breed, those who gave her
meat, the real substance of money. The well-groomed showy dogs of amusement
wrangled and snarled among themselves for the favors of the bitch-goddess. But
it was nothing to the silent fight-to-the-death that went on among the indis-
pensables, the bone-bringers.

But under Mrs. Bolton's influence, Clifford was tempted to enter this other
fight, to capture the bitch-goddess by brute means of industrial production.
Somehow he got his pecker up. In one way, Mrs. Bolton made a man of him,
as Connie never did. Connie kept him apart, and made him sensitive and conscious
of himself and his own states. Mrs. Bolton made him aware only of outside
things. Inwardly he began to go soft as pulp. But outwardly he began to be
effective.

He even roused himself to go to the mines once more: and when he was there,
he went down in a tub, and in a tub he was hauled out into the workings. Things
he had learned before the war, and seemed utterly to have forgotten, now came
back to him. He sat there, crippled, in a tub, with the underground manager
showing him the seam with a powerful torch. And he said little. But his mind
began to work.

He began to read again his technical works on the coal-mining industry, he
studied the Government reports, and he read with care the latest things on mining
and the chemistry of coal and of shale which were written in German. Of course
the most valuable discoveries were kept secret as far as possible. But once you
started a sort of research in the field of coal-mining, a study of methods and
means, a study of by-products and the chemical possibilities of coal, it was
astounding the ingenuity and the almost uncanny cleverness of the modern
technical mind, as if really the devil himself had lent fiend's wits to the technical
scientists of industry. It was far more interesting than art, than literature, poor
emotional half-witted stuff, was this technical science of industry. In this field,
men were like gods, or demons, inspired to discoveries, and fighting to carry
them out. In this activity, men were beyond any mental age calculable. But
Clifford knew that when it did come to the emotional and human life, these self-
made men were of a mental age of about thirteen, feeble boys. The discrepancy
was enormous and appalling.

But let that be. Let man slide down to general idiocy in the emotional and
"human" mind, Clifford did not care. Let all that go hang. He was interested in
the technicalities of modern coal-mining, and in pulling Tevershall out of the
hole.

He went down to the pit day after day, he studied, he put the general manager,
and the overhead manager, and the underground manager, and the engineers
through a mill they had never dreamed of. Power! He felt a new sense of power
flowing through him: power over all these men, over the hundreds and hundreds
of colliers. He was finding out: and he was getting things into his grip.

And he seemed verily to be re-born. *Now* life came into him! He had been
gradually dying, with Connie, in the isolated private life of the artist and the

conscious being. Now let all that go. Let it sleep. He simply felt life rush into
him out of the coal, out of the pit. The very stale air of the colliery was better
than oxygen to him. It gave him a sense of power, power. He was doing something:
and he was *going* to do something. He was going to win, to win: not as he had
won with his stories, mere publicity, amid a whole sapping of energy and malice.
But a man's victory.

At first he thought the solution lay in electricity: convert the coal into electric
power. Then a new idea came. The Germans invented a new locomotive engine
with a self-feeder, that did not need a fireman. And it was to be fed with a new
fuel, that burnt in small quantities at a great heat, under peculiar conditions.

The idea of a new concentrated fuel that burnt with a hard slowness at a fierce
heat was what first attracted Clifford. There must be some sort of external stimulus
to the burning of such fuel, not merely air supply. He began to experiment, and
got a clever young fellow who had proved brilliant in chemistry, to help him.

And he felt triumphant. He had at last got out of himself. He had fulfilled his
life-long secret yearning to get out of himself. Art had not done it for him. Art
had only made it worse. But now, now he had done it.

He was not aware how much Mrs. Bolton was behind him. He did not know
how much he depended on her. But for all that, it was evident that when he
was with her his voice dropped to an easy rhythm of intimacy, almost a trifle
vulgar.

With Connie, he was a little stiff. He felt he owed her everything, everything,
and he showed her the utmost respect and consideration, so long as she gave
him mere outward respect. But it was obvious he had a secred dread of her. The
new Achilles in him had a heel, and in this heel the woman, the woman like
Connie his wife, could lame him fatally. He went in a certain half-subservient
dread of her, and was extremely nice to her. But his voice was a little tense
when he spoke to her, and he began to be silent whenever she was present.

Only when he was alone with Mrs. Bolton did he really feel a lord and a
master, and his voice ran on with her almost as easily and garrulously as her
own could run. And he let her shave him or sponge all his body as if he were
a child, really as if he were a child.

Chapter Ten

Connie was a good deal alone now,
fewer people came to Wragby. Clifford no longer wanted them. He had turned
against even the cronies. He was queer. He preferred the radio, which he had

installed at some expense, with a good deal of success at last. He could sometimes get Madrid or Frankfort, even there in the uneasy Midlands.

And he would sit alone for hours listening to the loud-speaker bellowing forth. It amazed and stunned Connie. But there he would sit, with a blank entranced expression on his face, like a person losing his mind, and listen, or seem to listen, to the unspeakable thing.

Was he really listening? Or was it a sort of soporific he took, whilst something else worked on underneath in him? Connie did not know. She fled up to her room, or out of doors to the wood. A kind of terror filled her sometimes, a terror of the incipient insanity of the whole civilized species.

But now that Clifford was drifting off to his other weirdness of industrial activity, becoming almost a *creature,* with a hard, efficient shell of an exterior and a pulpy interior, one of the amazing crabs and lobsters of the modern, industrial and financial world, invertebrates of the crustacean order, with shells of steel, like machines, and inner bodies of soft pulp, Connie herself was really completely stranded.

She was not even free, for Clifford must have her there, he seemed to have a nervous terror that she should leave him. The curious pulpy part of him, the emotional and humanly-individual part, depended on her with terror, like a child, almost like an idiot. She must be there, there at Wragby, a Lady Chatterley, his wife. Otherwise he would be lost like an idiot on a moor.

This amazing dependence Connie realized with a sort of horror. She heard him with his pit managers, with the members of his Board, with young scientists, and she was amazed at his shrewd insight into things, his power, his uncanny material power over what is called practical men. He had become a practical man himself, and an amazingly astute and powerful one, a master. Connie attributed it to Mrs. Bolton's influence upon him, just at the crisis in his life.

But this astute and practical man was almost an idiot when left alone to his own emotional life. He worshipped Connie, she was his wife, a higher being, and he worshipped her with a queer, craven idolatry, like a savage, a worship based on enormous fear, and even hate of the power of the idol, the dread idol. All he wanted was for Connie to swear, to swear not to leave him, not to give him away.

"Clifford," she said to him—but this was after she had the key to the hut—"would you really like me to have a child one day?"

He looked at her with a furtive apprehension in his rather prominent pale eyes.

"I shouldn't mind, if it made no difference between us," he said.

"No difference to what?" she asked.

"To you and me; to our love for one another. If it's going to affect that, then I'm all against it. Why, I might even one day have a child of my own!"

She looked at him in amazement.

"I mean, it might come back to me one of these days."

She still stared in amazement, and he was uncomfortable.

"So you would not like it if I had a child?" she said.

"I tell you," he replied quickly, like a cornered dog. "I am quite willing, provided it doesn't touch your love for me. If it would touch that, I am dead against it."

Connie could only be silent in cold fear and contempt. Such talk was really the gabbling of an idiot. He no longer knew what he was talking about.

"Oh, it wouldn't make any difference to my feeling for you," she said, with a certain sarcasm.

"There!" he said. "That is the point. In that case I don't mind in the least. I mean it would be awfully nice to have a child running about the house, and feel one was building up a future for it. I should have something to strive for then, and I should know it was your child, shouldn't I, dear? And it would seem just the same as my own. Because it is you who count in these matters. You know that, don't you, dear? I don't enter, I am a cipher. You are the great I-am, as far as life goes. You know that, don't you? I mean, as far as I am concerned. I mean, but for you I am absolutely nothing. I live for your sake and your future. I am nothing to myself."

Connie heard it all with deepening dismay and repulsion. It was one of the ghastly half-truths that poison human existence. What man in his senses would say such things to a woman! But men aren't in their senses. What man with a spark of honor would put this ghastly burden of life-responsibility upon a woman, and leave her there, in the void?

Moreover, in half-an-hour's time, Connie heard Clifford talking to Mrs. Bolton, in a hot, impulsive voice, revealing himself in a sort of passionless passion to the woman, as if she were half mistress, half foster-mother to him. And Mrs. Bolton was carefully dressing him in evening clothes, for there were important business guests in the house.

Connie really sometimes felt she would die at this time. She felt she was being crushed to death by weird lies, and by the amazing cruelty of idiocy. Clifford's strange business efficiency in a way overawed her, and his declaration of private worship put her into a panic. There was nothing between them. She never even touched him nowadays, and he never touched her. He never even took her hand and held it kindly. No, and because they were so utterly out of touch, he tortured her with his declaration of idolatry. It was the cruelty of utter impotence. And she felt her reason would give way, or she would die.

She fled as much as possible to the wood. One afternoon, as she sat brooding, watching the water bubbling coldly in John's Well, the keeper had strode up to her.

"I got you a key made, my Lady!" he said, saluting, and he offered her the key.

"Thank you so much!" she said, startled.

"The hut's not very tidy, if you don't mind," he said. "I cleared it of what I could."

"But I didn't want you to trouble!" she said.

"Oh, it wasn't any trouble. I am setting the hens in about a week. But they won't be scared of you. I s'll have to see to them morning and night, but I shan't bother you any more than I can help."

"But you wouldn't bother me," she pleaded. "I'd rather not go to the hut at all, if I am going to be in the way."

He looked at her with his keen blue eyes. He seemed kindly, but distant. But at least he was sane, and wholesome, if even he looked thin and ill. A cough troubled him.

"You have a cough," she said.

"Nothing—a cold! The last pneumonia left me with a cough, but it's nothing."

He kept distant from her, and would not come any nearer.

She went fairly often to the hut, in the morning or in the afternoon, but he was never there. No doubt he avoided her on purpose. He wanted to keep his own privacy.

He had made the hut tidy, put the little table and chair near the fireplace, left a little pile of kindling and small logs, and put the tools and traps away as far as possible, effacing himself. Outside, by the clearing, he had built a low little roof of boughs and straw, a shelter for the birds, and under it stood the five coops. And, one day when she came, she found two brown hens sitting alert and fierce in the coops, sitting on pheasants' eggs, and fluffed out so proud and deep in all the heat of the pondering female blood. This almost broke Connie's heart. She, herself, was so forlorn and unused, not a female at all, just a mere thing of terrors.

Then all the five coops were occupied by hens, three brown and a grey and a black. All alike, they clustered themselves down on the eggs in the soft nestling ponderosity of the female urge, the female nature, fluffing out their feathers. And with brilliant eyes they watched Connie, as she crouched before them, and they gave short sharp clucks of anger and alarm, but chiefly of female anger at being approached.

Connie found corn in the corn-bin in the hut. She offered it to the hens in her hand. They would not eat it. Only one hen pecked at her hand with a fierce little jab, so Connie was frightened. But she was pining to give them something, the brooding mothers who neither fed themselves nor drank. She brought water in a little tin, and was delighted when one of the hens drank.

Now she came every day to the hens, they were the only things in the world that warmed her heart. Clifford's protestations made her go cold from head to foot. Mrs. Bolton's voice made her go cold, and the sound of the business men who came. An occasional letter from Michaelis affected her with the same sense of chill. She felt she would surely die if it lasted much longer.

Yet it was spring, and the bluebells were coming in the wood, and the leaf-buds on the hazels were opening like the spatter of green rain. How terrible it was that it should be spring, and everything cold-hearted, cold-hearted. Only the hens, fluffed so wonderfully on the eggs, were warm with their hot, brooding female bodies! Connie felt herself living on the brink of fainting all the time.

Then, one day, a lovely sunny day with great tufts of primroses under the hazels, and many violets dotting the paths, she came in the afternoon to the coops and there was one tiny, tiny perky chicken tinily prancing round in front of a coop, and the mother hen clucking in terror. The slim little chick was greyish-brown with dark markings, and it was the most alive little spark of a creature in seven kingdoms at that moment. Connie crouched to watch in a sort of ecstasy. Life, life! Pure, sparky, fearless new life! New life! So tiny and so utterly without fear! Even when it scampered a little scramblingly into the coop again, and disappeared under the hen's feathers in answer to the mother hen's wild alarm-cries, it was not really frightened; it took it as a game, the game of living. For in a moment a tiny sharp head was poking through the gold-brown feathers of the hen, and eyeing the Cosmos.

Connie was fascinated. And at the same time never had she felt so acutely the agony of her own female forlornness. It was becoming unbearable.

She had only one desire now, to go to the clearing in the wood. The rest was a kind of painful dream. But sometimes she was kept all day at Wragby, by her duties as hostess. And then she felt as if she, too, were going blank, just blank and insane.

One evening, guests or no guests, she escaped after tea. It was late, and she fled across the park like one who fears to be called back. The sun was setting rosy as she entered the wood, but she pressed on among the flowers. The light would last long overhead.

She arrived at the clearing, flushed and semi-conscious. The keeper was there, in his shirt-sleeves, just closing up the coops for the night, so the little occupants would be safe. But still one little trio was pattering about on tiny feet, alert drab mites, under the straw shelter, refusing to be called in by the anxious mother.

"I had to come and see the chickens!" she said, panting, glancing shyly at the keeper, almost unaware of him. "Are there any more?"

"Thirty-six so far!" he said. "Not bad!"

He, too, took a curious pleasure in watching the young things come out.

Connie crouched in front of the last coop. The three chicks had run in. But still their cheeky heads came poking sharply through the yellow feathers, then withdrawing, then only one beady little head eyeing forth from the vast mother-body.

"I'd love to touch them," she said, putting her fingers gingerly through the bars of the coop. But the mother-hen pecked at her hand fiercely, and Connie drew back startled and frightened.

"How she pecks at me! She hates me!" she said in a wondering voice. "But I wouldn't hurt them!"

The man standing above her laughed, and crouched down beside her, knees apart, and put his hand with quiet confidence slowly into the coop. The old hen pecked at him, but not so savagely. And slowly, softly, with sure gentle fingers, he felt among the old bird's feathers and drew out a faintly-peeping chick in his closed hand.

"There!" he said, holding out his hand to her. She took the little drab thing between her hands, and there it stood, on its impossible little stalks of legs, its atom of balancing life trembling through its almost weightless feet into Connie's hands. But it lifted its handsome, clean-shaped little head boldly, and looked sharply round, and gave a little "peep."

"So adorable! So cheeky!" she said softly.

The keeper, squatting beside her, was also watching with an amused face the bold little bird in her hands. Suddenly he saw a tear fall on to her wrist.

And he stood up, and stood away, moving to the other coop. For suddenly he was aware of the old flame shooting and leaping up in his loins, that he had hoped was quiescent for ever. He fought against it, turning his back to her. But it leapt, and leapt downward, circling in his knees.

He turned again to look at her. She was kneeling and holding her two hands slowly forward, blindly, so that the chicken should run in to the mother-hen again. And there was something so mute and forlorn in her, compassion flamed in his bowels for her.

Without knowing, he came quickly towards her and crouched beside her again, taking the chick from her hands, because she was afraid of the hen, and putting it back in the coop. At the back of his loins the fire suddenly darted stronger.

He glanced apprehensively at her. Her face was averted, and she was crying blindly, in all the anguish of her generation's forlornness. His heart melted suddenly, like a drop of fire, and he put out his hand and laid his fingers on her knee.

"You shouldn't cry," he said softly.

But then she put her hands over her face and felt that really her heart was broken and nothing mattered any more.

He laid his hand on her shoulder, and softly, gently, it began to travel down the curve of her back, blindly, with a blind stroking motion, to the curve of her crouching loins. And there his hand softly, softly, stroked the curve of her flank, in the blind instinctive caress.

She had found her scrap of handkerchief and was blindly trying to dry her face.

"Shall you come to the hut?" he said, in a quiet, neutral voice.

And closing his hand softly on her upper arm, he drew her up and led her slowly to the hut, not letting go of her till she was inside. Then he cleared aside the chair and table, and took a brown soldier's blanket from the tool-chest, spreading it slowly. She glanced at his face, as she stood motionless.

His face was pale and without expression, like that of a man submitting to fate.

"You lie there," he said softly, and he shut the door, so that it was dark, quite dark.

With a queer obedience, she lay down on the blanket. Then she felt the soft, groping, helplessly desirous hand touching her body, feeling for her face. The hand stroked her face softly, softly, with infinite soothing and assurance, and at last there was the soft touch of a kiss on her cheek.

She lay quite still, in a sort of sleep, in a sort of dream. Then she quivered as she felt his hand groping softly, yet with queer thwarted clumsiness among her clothing. Yet the hand knew, too, how to unclothe her where it wanted. He drew down the thin silk sheath, slowly, carefully, right down and over her feet. Then with a quiver of exquisite pleasure he touched the warm soft body, and touched her navel for a moment in a kiss. And he had to come into her at once, to enter the peace on earth of her soft, quiescent body. It was the moment of pure peace for him, the entry into the body of a woman.

She lay still, in a kind of sleep, always in a kind of sleep. The activity, the orgasm was his, all his; she could strive for herself no more. Even the tightness of his arms round her, even the intense movement of his body, and the springing seed in her, was a kind of sleep, from which she did not begin to rouse till he had finished and lay softly panting against her breast.

Then she wondered, just dimly wondered, why? Why was this necessary? Why had it lifted a great cloud from her and given her peace? Was it real? Was it real?

Her tormented modern-woman's brain still had no rest. Was it real? And she knew, if she gave herself to the man, it was real. But if she kept herself for herself, it was nothing. She was old; millions of years old, she felt. And at last, she could bear the burden of herself no more. She was to be had for the taking. To be had for the taking.

The man lay in a mysterious stillness. What was he feeling? What was he thinking? She did not know. He was a strange man to her, she did not know him. She must only wait, for she did not dare to break his mysterious stillness. He lay there with his arms round her, his body on hers, his wet body touching hers, so close. And completely unknown. Yet not unpeaceful. His very silence was peaceful.

She knew that, when at last he roused and drew away from her. It was like an abandonment. He drew her dress in the darkness down over her knees and stood for a few moments, apparently adjusting his own clothing. Then he quietly opened the door and went out.

She saw a very brilliant little moon shining above the afterglow over the oaks. Quickly she got up and arranged herself; she was tidy. Then she went to the door of the hut.

All the lower wood was in shadow, almost darkness. Yet the sky overhead was crystal. But it shed hardly any light. He came through the lower shadow towards her, his face lifted like a pale blotch.

"Shall we go, then?" he said.

"Where?"

"I'll go with you to the gate."

He arranged things his own way. He locked the door of the hut and came after her.

"You aren't sorry, are you?" he asked, as he went at her side.

"No! No! Are you?" she said.

"For that! No!" he said. Then after a while he added: "But there's the rest of things."

"What rest of things?" she said.

"Sir Clifford. Other folks. All the complications."

"Why complications?" she said, disappointed.

"It's always so. For you as well as for me. There's always complications." He walked on steadily in the dark.

"And are you sorry?" she said.

"In a way!" he replied, looking up at the sky. "I thought I'd done with it all. Now I've begun again."

"Begun what?"

"Life."

"Life!" she re-echoed, with a queer thrill.

"It's life," he said. "There's no keeping clear. And if you do keep clear you might almost as well die. So if I've got to be broken open again, I have."

She did not quite see it that way, but still . . .

"It's just love," she said cheerfully.

"Whatever that may be," he replied.

They went on through the darkening wood in silence, till they were almost at the gate.

"But you don't hate me, do you?" she said wistfully.

"Nay, nay," he replied. And suddenly he held her fast against his breast again, with the old connecting passion. "Nay, for me it was good, it was good. Was it for you?"

"Yes, for me too," she answered, a little untruthfully, for she had not been conscious of much.

He kissed her softly, softly, with the kisses of warmth.

"If only there weren't so many other people in the world," he said lugubriously.

She laughed. They were at the gate to the park. He opened it for her.

"I won't come any farther," he said.

"No!" And she held out her hand, as if to shake hands. But he took it in both his.

"Shall I come again?" she asked wistfully.

"Yes! Yes!"

She left him and went across the park.

He stood back and watched her going into the dark, against the pallor of the horizon. Almost with bitterness he watched her go. She had connected him up again, when he had wanted to be alone. She had cost him that bitter privacy of a man who at last wants only to be alone.

He turned into the dark of the wood. All was still, the moon had set. But he was aware of the noises of the night, the engines at Stacks Gate, the traffic on the main road. Slowly he climbed the denuded knoll. And from the top he could see the country, bright rows of lights at Stacks Gate, smaller lights at Tevershall pit, the yellow lights of Tevershall and lights everywhere, here and there, on the dark country, with the distant blush of furnaces, faint and rosy, since the night was clear, the rosiness of the outpouring of white-hot metal. Sharp, wicked electric lights at Stacks Gate! An undefinable quick of evil in them! And all the unease, the ever-shifting dread of the industrial night in the Midlands. He could hear the winding-engines at Stacks Gate turning down the seven-o'clock miners. The pit worked three shifts.

He went down again in to the darkness and seclusion of the wood. But he knew that the seclusion of the wood was illusory. The industrial noises broke the solitude, the sharp lights, though unseen, mocked it. A man could no longer be private and withdrawn. The world allows no hermits. And now he had taken the woman, and brought on himself a new cycle of pain and doom. For he knew by experience what it meant.

It was not woman's fault, nor even love's fault, nor the fault of sex. The fault lay there, out there, in those evil electric lights and diabolical rattlings of engines. There, in the world of the mechanical greedy, greedy mechanism and mechanized greed, sparkling with lights and gushing hot metal and roaring with traffic, there lay the vast evil thing, ready to destroy whatever did not conform. Soon it would destroy the wood, and the bluebells would spring no more. All vulnerable things must perish under the rolling and running of iron.

He thought with infinite tenderness of the woman. Poor forlorn thing, she was nicer than she knew, and oh! so much too nice for the tough lot she was in contact with. Poor thing, she too had some of the vulnerability of the wild hyacinths, she wasn't all tough rubber-goods and platinum, like the modern girl. And they would do her in! As sure as life, they would do her in, as they do in all naturally tender life. Tender! Somewhere she was tender, tender with a tenderness of the growing hyacinths, something that has gone out of the celluloid women of today. But he would protect her with his heart for a little while. For a little while, before the insentient iron world and the Mammon of mechanized greed did them both in, her as well as him.

He went home with his gun and his dog, to the dark cottage, lit the lamp, started the fire, and ate his supper of bread and cheese, young onions and beer. He was alone, in a silence he loved. His room was clean and tidy, but rather stark. Yet the fire was bright, the hearth white, the petroleum lamp hung right over the table, with its white, oil-cloth. He tried to read a book about India, but tonight he could not read. He sat by the fire in his shirt-sleeves, not smoking, but with a mug of beer in reach. And he thought about Connie.

To tell the truth, he was sorry for what had happened, perhaps most for her sake. He had a sense of foreboding. No sense of wrong or sin; he was troubled by no conscience in that respect. He knew that conscience was chiefly fear of society, or fear of oneself. He was not afraid of himself. But he was quite consciously afraid of society, which he knew by instinct to be a malevolent, partly-insane beast.

The woman! If she could be there with him, and there were nobody else in the world! The desire rose again, his penis began to stir like a live bird. At the same time an oppression, a dread of exposing himself and her to that outside Thing that sparkled viciously in the electric lights, weighed down his shoulders. She, poor thing, was just a young female creature to him; but a young female creature whom he had gone into and whom he desired again.

Stretching with the curious yawn of desire, for he had been alone and apart from man or woman for four years, he rose and took his coat again, and his gun, lowered the lamp and went out into the starry night, with the dog. Driven by desire and by dread of the malevolent Thing outside, he made his round in the wood, slowly, softly. He loved the darkness and folded himself into it. It fitted the turgidity of his desire which, in spite of all, was like a riches; the stirring restlessness of his penis, the stirring fire in his loins! Oh, if only there were other men to be with, to fight that sparkling electric Thing outside there, to preserve the tenderness of life, the tenderness of women, and the natural riches of desire. If only there were men to fight side by side with! But the men were all outside there, glorying in the Thing, triumphing or being trodden down in the rush of mechanized greed or of greedy mechanism.

Constance, for her part, had hurried across the park, home, almost without thinking. As yet she had no after-thought. She would be in time for dinner.

She was annoyed to find the doors fastened, however, so that she had to ring. Mrs. Bolton opened.

"Why, there you are, your Ladyship! I was beginning to wonder if you'd gone lost!" she said a little roguishly. "Sir Clifford hasn't asked for you, though; he's got Mr. Linley in with him, talking over something. It looks as if he'd stay to dinner, doesn't it, my Lady?"

"It does rather," said Connie.

"Shall I put dinner back a quarter of an hour? That would give you time to dress in comfort."

"Perhaps you'd better."

Mr. Linley was the general manager of the collieries, an elderly man from the north, with not quite enough punch to suit Clifford; not up to post-war conditions, nor post-war colliers either, with their "ca' canny" creed. But Connie liked Mr. Linley, though she was glad to be spared the toadying of his wife.

Linley stayed to dinner, and Connie was the hostess men liked so much, so modest, yet so attentive and aware, with big, wide blue eyes and a soft repose that sufficiently hid what she was really thinking. Connie had played this woman so much, it was almost second nature to her; but still, decidedly second. Yet it was curious how everything disappeared from her consciousness while she played it.

She waited patiently till she could go upstairs and think her own thoughts. She was always waiting, it seemed to be her *forte*.

Once in her room, however, she felt still vague and confused. She didn't know what to think. What sort of a man was he, really? Did he really like her? Not much, she felt. Yet he was kind. There was something, a sort of warm naïve kindness, curious and sudden, that almost opened her womb to him. But she felt he might be kind like that to any woman. Though even so, it was curiously soothing, comforting. And he was a passionate man, wholesome and passionate. But perhaps he wasn't quite individual enough; he might be the same with any woman as he had been with her. It really wasn't personal. She was only really a female to him.

But perhaps that was better. And after all, he was kind to the female in her, which no man had ever been. Men were very kind to the *person* she was, but rather cruel to the female, despising her or ignoring her altogether. Men were awfully kind to Constance Reid or to Lady Chatterley; but not to her womb they weren't kind. And he took no notice of Constance or of Lady Chatterley; he just softly stroked her loins or her breasts.

She went to the wood next day. It was a grey, still afternoon, with the dark-green dogs'-mercury spreading under the hazel copse, and all the trees making a silent effort to open their buds. Today she could almost feel it in her own body, the huge heave of the sap in the massive trees, upwards, up, up to the bud-tips, there to push into little flamey oak-leaves, bronze as blood. It was like a tide running turgid upward, and spreading on the sky.

She came to the clearing, but he was not there. She had only half expected him. The pheasant chicks were running lightly abroad, light as insects, from the coops where the yellow hens clucked anxiously. Connie sat and watched them, and waited. She only waited. Even the chicks she hardly saw. She waited.

The time passed with dream-like slowness, and he did not come. She had only half expected him. He never came in the afternoon. She must go home to tea. But she had to force herself to leave.

As she went home, a fine drizzle of rain fell.

"Is it raining again?" said Clifford, seeing her shake her hat.

"Just drizzle."

She poured tea in silence, absorbed in a sort of obstinacy. She did want to see the keeper today, to see if it were really real. If it were really real.

"Shall I read a little to you afterwards?" said Clifford.

She looked at him. Had he sensed something?

"The spring makes me feel queer—I thought I might rest a little," she said.

"Just as you like. Not feeling really unwell, are you?"

"No! Only rather tired—with the spring. Will you have Mrs. Bolton to play something with you?"

"No! I think I'll listen in."

She heard the curious satisfaction in his voice. She went upstairs to her bedroom. There she heard the loudspeaker begin to bellow, in an idiotically velveteen, genteel sort of voice, something about a series of street-cries, the very cream of genteel affectation imitating old criers. She pulled on her old violet-colored mackintosh, and slipped out of the house at the side door.

The drizzle of rain was like a veil over the world, mysterious, hushed, not cold. She got very warm as she hurried across the park. She had to open her light waterproof.

The wood was silent, still and secret in the evening drizzle of rain, full of the mystery of eggs and half-open buds, half-unsheathed flowers. In the dimness of it all trees glistened naked and dark as if they had unclothed themselves, and the green things on earth seemed to hum with greenness.

There was still no one at the clearing. The chicks had nearly all gone under the mother-hens, only one or two lost adventurous ones still dibbed about in the dryness under the straw roof-shelter. And they were doubtful of themselves.

So! He still had not been. He was staying away on purpose. Or perhaps something was wrong. Perhaps she should go to the cottage and see.

But she was born to wait. She opened the hut with her key. It was all tidy, the corn put in the bin, the blankets folded on the shelf, the straw neat in a corner; a new bundle of straw. The hurricane lamp hung on a nail. The table and chair had been put back where she had lain.

She sat down on a stool in the doorway. How still everything was! The fine rain blew very softly, filmily, but the wind made no noise. Nothing made any sound. The trees stood like powerful beings, dim, twilit, silent and alive. How alive everything was!

Night was drawing near again; she would have to go. He was avoiding her.

But suddenly he came striding into the clearing, in his black oilskin jacket like a chauffeur, shining with wet. He glanced quickly at the hut, half-saluted, then veered aside and went on to the coops. There he crouched in silence, looking carefully at everything, then carefully shutting the hens and chicks up safe against the night.

At last he came slowly towards her. She still sat on her stool. He stood before her under the porch.

"You came then," he said, using the intonation of the dialect.

"Yes," she replied, looking up at him. "You're late!"

"Ay!" he replied, looking away into the wood.

She rose slowly, drawing aside her stool.

"Did you want to come in?" she asked.

He looked down at her shrewdly.

"Won't folks be thinkin' somethink, you comin' here every night?" he said.

"Why?" She looked up at him, at a loss. "I said I'd come. Nobody knows."

"They soon will, though," he replied. "An' what then?"

She was at a loss for an answer.

"Why should they know?" she said.

"Folks always does," he said fatally.

Her lip quivered a little.

"Well, I can't help it," she faltered.

"Nay," he said. "You can help it by not comin'—if yer want to," he added, in a lower tone.

"But I don't want to," she murmured.

He looked away into the wood, and was silent.

"But what when folks finds out?" he asked at last. "Think about it! Think how lowered you'll feel, one of your husband's servants."

She looked up at his averted face.

"Is it," she stammered, "is it that you don't want me?"

"Think!" he said. "Think what if folks finds out—Sir Clifford an' a'—an' everybody talkin'—"

"Well, I can go away."

"Where to?"

"Anywhere! I've got money of my own. My mother left me twenty thousand pounds in trust, and I know Clifford can't touch it. I can go away."

"But 'appen you don't want to go away."

"Yes, yes! I don't care what happens to me."

"Ah, you think that! But you'll care! You'll have to care, everybody has. You've got to remember your ladyship is carrying on with a gamekeeper. It's not as if I was a gentleman. Yes, you'd care. You'd care."

"I shouldn't. What do I care about my ladyship! I hate it, really. I feel people are jeering every time they say it. And they are, they are! Even you jeer when you say it."

"Me!"

For the first time he looked straight at her, and into her eyes.

"I don't jeer at you," he said.

As he looked into her eyes she saw his own eyes go dark, quite dark, the pupils dilating.

'Don't you care about a' the risk?" he asked in a husky voice. "You should care. Don't care when it's too late!"

There was a curious warning pleading in his voice.

"But I've nothing to lose," she said fretfully. "If you knew what it is, you'd think I'd be glad to lose it. But are you afraid for yourself?"

"Ay!" he said briefly. "I am. I'm afraid. I'm afraid. I'm afraid o' things."

"What things?" she asked.

He gave a curious backward jerk of his head, indicating the outer world.

"Things! Everybody! The lot of 'em."

Then he bent down and suddenly kissed her unhappy face.

"Nay, I don't care," he said. "Let's have it, an' damn the rest. But if you was to feel sorry you'd ever done it—!"

"Don't put me off," she pleaded.

He put his fingers to her cheek and kissed her again suddenly.

"Let me come in then," he said softly. "An' take off your mackintosh."

He hung up his gun, slipped out of his wet leather jacket, and reached for the blankets.

"I brought another blanket," he said, "so we can put one over us if we like."

"I can't stay long," she said. "Dinner is half-past seven."

He looked at her swiftly, then at his watch.

"All right," he said.

He shut the door, and lit a tiny light in the hanging hurricane lamp.

"One time we'll have a long time," he said.

He put the blankets down carefully, one folded for her head. Then he sat down for a moment on the stool, and drew her to him, holding her close with one arm, feeling for her body with his free hand. She heard the catch of his intaken breath as he found her. Under her frail petticoat she was naked.

"Eh! what it is to touch thee!" he said, as his finger caressed the delicate, warm secret skin of her waist and hips. He put his face down and rubbed his cheek against her belly and against her thighs again and again. And again she wondered a little over the sort of rapture it was to him. She did not understand the beauty he found in her, through touch upon her living secret body, almost the ecstasy of beauty. For passion alone is awake to it. And when passion is dead, or absent, then the magnificent throb of beauty is incomprehensible and even a little despicable; warm, live beauty of contact, so much deeper than the beauty of vision. She felt the glide of his cheek on her thighs and belly and buttocks, and the close brushing of his moustache and his soft thick hair, and her knees began to quiver. Far down in her she felt a new stirring, a new nakedness emerging. And she was half afraid. Half she wished he would not caress her so. He was encompassing her somehow. Yet she was waiting, waiting.

And when he came into her, with an intensification of relief and consummation that was pure peace to him, still she was waiting. She felt herself a little left out. And she knew, partly it was her own fault. She willed herself into this separateness. Now perhaps she was condemned to it. She lay still, feeling his motion within her, his deep-sunk intentness, the sudden quiver of him at the springing of his seed, then slow-subsiding thrust. That thrust of the buttocks, surely it was a little ridiculous. If you were a woman, and apart in all the business, surely that thrusting of the man's buttocks was supremely ridiculous. Surely the man was intensely ridiculous in this posture and this act!

But she lay still, without recoil. Even, when he had finished, she did not rouse herself to get a grip on her own satisfaction, as she had done with Michaelis; she lay still, and the tears slowly filled and ran from her eyes.

He lay still, too. But he held her close and tried to cover her poor naked legs with his legs, to keep them warm. He lay on her with a close, undoubting warmth.

"Are ter cold?" he asked, in a soft, small voice, as if she were close, so close. Whereas she was left out, distant.

"No! But I must go," she said gently.

He sighed, held her closer, then relaxed to rest again.

He had not guessed her tears. He thought she was there with him.

"I must go," she repeated.

He lifted himself, kneeled beside her a moment, kissed the inner side of her thighs, then drew down her skirts, buttoning his own clothes unthinking, not even turning aside, in the faint, faint light from the lantern.

"Tha mun come ter th' cottage one time," he said, looking down at her with a warm, sure, easy face.

But she lay there inert, and was gazing up at him thinking. Stranger! Stranger! She even resented him a little.

He put on his coat and looked for his hat, which had fallen, then he slung on his gun.

"Come then!" he said, looking down at her with those warm, peaceful sort of eyes.

She rose slowly. She didn't want to go. She also rather resented staying. He helped her with her thin waterproof, and saw she was tidy.

Then he opened the door. The outside was quite dark. The faithful dog under the porch stood up with pleasure seeing him. The drizzle of rain drifted greyly past upon the darkness. It was quite dark.

"Ah mun ta'e th' lantern," he said. "The'll be nob'dy."

He walked just before her in the narrow path, swinging the hurricane lamp low, revealing the wet grass, the black shiny tree roots like snakes, wan flowers. For the rest, all was grey rain-mist and complete darkness.

"Tha mun come to the cottage one time," he said, "shall ta? We might as well be hung for a sheep as for a lamb."

It puzzled her, his queer, persistent wanting her, when there was nothing between them, when he never really spoke to her, and in spite of herself she resented the dialect. His "tha mun come" seemed not addressed to her, but some common woman. She recognized the foxglove leaves of the riding and knew, more or less, where they were.

"It's quarter past seven," he said, "you'll do it." He had changed his voice, seemed to feel her distance. As they turned the last bend in the riding towards the hazel wall and the gate, he blew out the light. "We'll see from here," he said, taking her gently by the arm.

But it was difficult, the earth under their feet was a mystery, but he felt his way by tread: he was used to it. At the gate he gave her his electric torch. "It's a bit lighter in the park," he said; "but take it for fear you get off th' path."

It was true, there seemed a ghost-glimmer of greyness in the open space of the park. He suddenly drew her to him and whipped his hand under her dress again, feeling her warm body with his wet, chill hand.

"I could die for the touch of a woman like thee," he said in his throat. "If tha would stop another minute."

She felt the sudden force of his wanting her again.

"No, I must run," she said, a little wildly.

"Ay," he replied, suddenly changed, letting her go.

She turned away, and on the instant she turned back to him saying: "Kiss me."

He bent over her indistinguishable and kissed her on the left eye. She held her mouth and he softly kissed it, but at once drew away. He hated mouth kisses.

"I'll come tomorrow," she said, drawing away; "if I can," she added.

"Ay! not so late," he replied out of the darkness. Already she could not see him at all. "Good night," she said.

"Good night, your Ladyship," his voice.

She stopped and looked back into the wet dark. She could just see the bulk of him. "Why did you say that?" she said.

"Nay," he replied. "Good night then, run!"

She plunged on in the dark-grey tangible night. She found the side door open, and slipped into her room unseen. As she closed the door the gong sounded, but she would take her bath all the same—she must take her bath. "But I won't be late any more," she said to herself; "it's too annoying."

The next day she did not go to the wood. She went instead with Clifford to Uthwaite. He could occasionally go out now in the car, and had got a strong young man as chauffeur, who could help him out of the car if need be. He particularly wanted to see his godfather, Leslie Winter, who lived at Shipley Hall, not far from Uthwaite. Winter was an elderly gentleman now, wealthy, one of the wealthy coal-owners who had had their hey-day in King Edward's time. King Edward had stayed more than once at Shipley, for the shooting. It was a handsome old stucco hall, very elegantly appointed, for Winter was a bachelor and prided himself on his style; but the place was beset by collieries. Leslie Winter was attached to Clifford, but personally did not entertain a great respect for him, because of the photographs in illustrated papers and the literature. The old man was a buck of the King Edward school, who thought life and the scribbling fellows were something else. Towards Connie the Squire was always rather gallant; he thought her an attractive demure maiden and rather wasted on Clifford, and it was a thousand pities she stood no chance of bringing forth an heir to Wragby. He himself had no heir.

Connie wondered what he would say if he knew that Clifford's gamekeeper had been having intercourse with her, and saying to her "tha mun come to th' cottage one time." He would detest and despise her, for he had come almost to hate the shoving forward of the working classes. A man of her own class he would not mind, for Connie was gifted from nature with this appearance of demure, submissive maidenliness, and perhaps it was part of her nature. Winter called her "dear child" and gave her a rather lovely miniature of an eighteenth-century lady, rather against her will.

But Connie was preoccupied with her affair with the keeper. After all Mr. Winter, who was really a gentleman and a man of the world, treated her as a person and a discriminating individual; he did not lump her together with all the rest of his female womanhood in his "thee" and "tha."

She did not go to the wood that day nor the next, nor the day following. She did not go so long as she felt, or imagined she felt, the man waiting for her, wanting her. But the fourth day she was terribly unsettled and uneasy. She still refused to go to the wood and open her thighs once more to the man. She thought of all the things she might do—drive to Sheffield, pay visits, and the thought of all these things was repellent. At last she decided to take a walk, not towards the wood, but in the opposite direction; she would go to Marehay, through the little iron gate in the other side of the park fence. It was a quiet grey day of spring, almost warm. She walked on unheeding, absorbed in thoughts she was not even conscious of. She was not really aware of anything outside her, till she was startled by the loud barking of the dog at Marehay Farm. Marehay Farm! Its pastures ran up to Wragby park fence, so they were neighbors, but it was some time since Connie had called.

"Bell!" she said to the big white bull-terrier. "Bell! have you forgotten me? Don't you know me?"—She was afraid of dogs, and Bell stood back and bellowed, and she wanted to pass through the farmyard on to the warren path.

Mrs. Flint appeared. She was a woman of Constance's own age, had been a school-teacher, but Connie suspected her of being rather a false little thing.

"Why, it's Lady Chatterley! Why!" And Mrs. Flint's eyes glowed again, and she flushed like a young girl. "Bell, Bell. Why! barking at Lady Chatterley! Bell! Be quiet!" She darted forward and slashed at the dog with a white cloth she held in her hand, then came forward to Connie.

"She used to know me," said Connie, shaking hands. The Flints were Chatterley tenants.

"Of course she knows your ladyship! She's just showing off," said Mrs. Flint, glowing and looking up with a sort of flushed confusion, "but it's so long since she's seen you. I do hope you are better."

"Yes, thanks, I'm all right."

"We've hardly seen you all winter. Will you come in and look at the baby?"

"Well!" Connie hesitated. "Just for a minute."

Mrs. Flint flew wildly in to tidy up, and Connie came slowly after her, hesitating in the rather dark kitchen where the kettle was boiling by the fire. Back came Mrs. Flint.

"I do hope you'll excuse me," she said. "Will you come in here."

They went into the living-room, where a baby was sitting on the rag hearthrug, and the table was roughly set for tea. A young servant-girl backed down the passage, shy and awkward.

The baby was a perky little thing of about a year, with red hair like its father, and cheeky pale-blue eyes. It was a girl, and not to be daunted. It sat among cushions and was surrounded with rag dolls and other toys in modern excess.

"Why, what a dear she is!" said Connie, "and how she's grown! A big girl! A big girl."

She had given it a shawl when it was born, and celluloid ducks for Christmas.

"There, Josephine! Who's that come to see you? Who's this, Josephine? Lady Chatterley—you know Lady Chatterley, don't you?"

The queer pert little mite gazed cheekily at Connie. Ladyships were still all the same to her.

"Come! Will you come to me?" said Connie to the baby.

The baby didn't care one way or another, so Connie picked her up and held her in her lap. How warm and lovely it was to hold a child in one's lap, and the soft little arms, the unconscious cheeky little legs.

"I was just having a rough cup of tea all by myself. Luke's gone to market, so I can have it when I like. Would you care for a cup, Lady Chatterley? I don't suppose it's what you're used to, but if you would . . ."

Connie would, though she didn't want to be reminded of what she was used to. There was a great relaying of the table, and the best cups brought and the best teapot.

"If only you wouldn't take any trouble," said Connie.

But if Mrs. Flint took no trouble, where was the fun! So Connie played with the child and was amused by its little female dauntlessness, and got a deep voluptuous pleasure out of its soft young warmth. Young life. And so fearless! So fearless, because so defenseless. All the older people, so narrow with fear.

She had a cup of tea, which was rather strong, and very good bread and butter, and bottled damsons. Mrs. Flint flushed and glowed and bridled with excitement, as if Connie were some gallant knight. And they had a real female chat, and both of them enjoyed it.

"It's a poor little tea, though," said Mrs. Flint.

"It's much nicer than at home," said Connie truthfully.

"Oh-h!" said Mrs. Flint, not believing, of course.

But at last Connie rose.

"I must go," she said. "My husband has no idea where I am. He'll be wondering all kinds of things."

"He'll never think you're here," laughed Mrs. Flint excitedly. "He'll be sending the crier round."

"Good-bye, Josephine," said Connie, kissing the baby and ruffling its red, wispy hair.

Mrs. Flint insisted on opening the locked and barred front door. Connie emerged in the farm's little front garden, shut in by a privet hedge. There were two rows of auriculas by the path, very velvety and rich.

"Lovely auriculas," said Connie.

"Recklesses, as Luke calls them," laughed Mrs. Flint. "Have some."

And eagerly she picked the velvet and primrose flowers.

"Enough! Enough!" said Connie.

They came to the little garden gate.

"Which way were you going?" asked Mrs. Flint.

"By the warren."

"Let me see! Oh, yes, the cows are in the gin close. But they're not up yet. But the gate's locked, you'll have to climb."

"I can climb," said Connie.

"Perhaps I can just go down the close with you."

They went down the poor, rabbit-bitten pasture. Birds were whistling in wild evening triumph in the wood. A man was calling up the last cows, which trailed slowly over the path-worn pasture.

"They're late, milking, tonight," said Mrs. Flint severely. "They know Luke won't be back till after dark."

They came to the fence, beyond which the young firwood bristled dense. There was a little gate, but it was locked. In the grass on the inside stood a bottle, empty.

"There's the keeper's empty bottle for his milk," explained Mrs. Flint. "We bring it as far as here for him, and then he fetches it himself."

"When?" said Connie.

"Oh, any time he's around. Often in the morning. Well, good-bye, Lady Chatterley! And do come again. It was so lovely having you."

Connie climbed the fence into the narrow path between the dense, bristling young firs. Mrs. Flint went running back across the pasture, in a sun-bonnet, because she was really a school teacher. Constance didn't like this dense new part of the wood; it seemed grotesque and choking. She hurried on with her head down, thinking of the Flint's baby. It was a dear little thing, but it would be a bit bow-legged like its father. It showed already, but perhaps it would grow out of it. How warm and fulfilling somehow to have a baby, and how Mrs. Flint showed it off! She had something anyhow that Connie hadn't got, and apparently couldn't have. Yes, Mrs. Flint had flaunted her motherhood. And Connie had been just a bit, just a little bit jealous. She couldn't help it.

She started out of her muse, and gave a little cry of fear. A man was there.

It was the keeper; he stood in the path like Balaam's ass, barring her way.

"How's this?" he said in surprise.

"How did you come?" she panted.

"How did you? Have you been to the hut?"

"No! No! I went to Marehay."

He looked at her curiously, searchingly, and she hung her head a little guiltily.

"And were you going to the hut now?" he asked rather sternly.

"No! I mustn't. I stayed at Marehay. No one knows where I am. I'm late. I've got to run."

"Giving me the slip, like?" he said, with a faint ironic smile.

"No! No, not that. Only—"

"Why, what else?" he said. And he stepped up to her, and put his arm around her. She felt the front of his body terribly near to her, and alive.

"Oh, not now, not now," she cried, trying to push him away.

"Why not? It's only six o'clock. You've got half-an-hour. Nay! Nay! I want you."

He held her fast and she felt his urgency. Her old instinct was to fight for her freedom. But something else in her was strange and inert and heavy. His body was urgent against her, and she hadn't the heart any more to fight.

He looked around.

"Come—come here! Through here," he said, looking penetratingly into the dense fir-trees, that were young and not more than half-grown.

He looked back at her. She saw his eyes, tense and brilliant, fierce, not loving. But her will had left her. A strange weight was on her limbs. She was giving way. She was giving up.

He led her through the wall of prickly trees, that were difficult to come through, to a place where was a little space and a pile of dead boughs. He threw one or two dry ones down, put his coat and waistcoat over them, and she had to lie down there under the boughs of the tree, like an animal, while he waited, standing there in his shirt and breeches, watching her with haunted eyes. But still he was provident—he made her lie properly, properly. Yet he broke the band of her underclothes, for she did not help him, only lay inert.

He too had bared the front part of his body and she felt his naked flesh against her as he came into her. For a moment he was still inside her, turgid there and quivering. Then as he began to move, in the sudden helpless orgasm, there awoke in her new strange thrills rippling inside her. Rippling, rippling, rippling, like a flapping overlapping of soft flames, soft as feathers, running to points of brilliance, exquisite, exquisite and melting her all molten inside. It was like bells rippling up and up to a culmination. She lay unconscious of the wild little cries she uttered at the last. But it was over too soon, too soon, and she could no longer force her own conclusion with her own activity. This was different, different. She could do nothing. She could no longer harden and grip for her own satisfaction upon him. She could only wait, wait and moan in spirit as she felt him withdrawing, withdrawing and contracting, coming to the terrible moment when he would slip out of her and be gone. Whilst all her womb was open and soft, and softly clamoring, like a sea-anemone under the tide, clamoring for him to come in again and make a fulfillment for her. She clung to him unconscious in passion, and he never quite slipped from her, and she felt the soft bud of him within her stirring, and strange rhythms flushing up into her with a strange rhythmic growing motion, swelling and swelling till it filled all her cleaving consciousness, and then began again the unspeakable motion that was not really motion, but pure deepening whirlpools of sensation swirling deeper and deeper through all her tissue and consciousness, till she was one perfect concentric fluid of feeling, and she lay there crying in unconscious inarticulate cries. The voice out of the uttermost night, the life! The man heard it beneath him with a kind of awe, as his life sprang out into her. And as it subsided, he subsided too and lay utterly still, unknowing, while her grip on him slowly relaxed, and she lay inert. And they lay and knew nothing, not even of each other, both lost. Till at last he began to rouse and become aware of his defenseless nakedness, and she was aware that his body was loosening its clasp on her. He was coming apart; but in her breast she felt she could not bear him to leave her uncovered. He must cover her now for ever.

But he drew away at last, and kissed her and covered her over, and began to cover himself. She lay looking up to the boughs of the tree, unable as yet to move. He stood and fastened up his breeches, looking round. All was dense and silent, save for the awed dog that lay with its paws against its nose. He sat down again on the brushwood and took Connie's hand in silence.

She turned and looked at him. "We came off together that time," he said.

She did not answer.

"It's good when it's like that. Most folks live their lives through and they never know it," he said, speaking rather dreamily.

She looked into his brooding face.

"Do they?" she said. "Are you glad?"

He looked back into her eyes. "Glad," he said. "Ay, but never mind." He did not want her to talk. And he bent over her and kissed her, and she felt, so he must kiss her for ever.

At last she sat up.

"Don't people often come off together?" she asked with naïve curiosity.

"A good many of them never. You can see by the raw look of them." He spoke unwittingly, regretting he had begun.

"Have you come off like that with other women?"

He looked at her amused.

"I don't know," he said, "I don't know."

And she knew he would never tell her anything he didn't want to tell her. She watched his face, and the passion for him moved in her bowels. She resisted it as far as she could, for it was the loss of herself to herself.

He put on his waistcoat and his coat, and pushed a way through to the path again.

The last level rays of the sun touched the wood. "I won't come with you," he said; "better not."

She looked at him wistfully before she turned. His dog was waiting so anxiously for him to go, and he seemed to have nothing whatever to say. Nothing left.

Connie went slowly home, realizing the depth of the other thing in her. Another self was alive in her, burning molten and soft in her womb and bowels, and with this self she adored him. She adored him till her knees were weak as she walked. In her womb and bowels she was flowing and alive now and vulnerable, and helpless in adoration of him as the most naïve woman.—It feels like a child, she said to herself; it feels like a child in me.—And so it did, as if her womb, that had always been shut, had opened and filled with new life, almost a burden, yet lovely.

"If I had a child!" she thought to herself; "if I had him inside me as a child!"— and her limbs turned molten at the thought, and she realized the immense difference between having a child to oneself, and having a child to a man whom one's bowels yearned towards. The former seemed in a sense ordinary: but to have a child to a man whom one adored in one's bowels and one's womb, it made her feel she was very different from her old self, and as if she was sinking deep, deep to the center of all womanhood and the sleep of creation.

It was not the passion that was new to her, it was the yearning adoration. She knew she had always feared it, for it left her helpless; she feared it still, lest if she adored him too much, then she would lose herself, become effaced, and she did not want to be effaced, a slave, like a savage woman. She must not become a slave. She feared her adoration, yet she would not at once fight against it. She knew she could fight it. She had a devil of self-will in her breast that could have fought the full soft heaving adoration of her womb and crushed it. She could even now do it, or she thought so, and she could then take up her passion with her own will.

Ah! yes, to be passionate like a Bacchante, like a Bacchanal fleeing through the woods, to call on Iacchos, the bright phallus that had no independent personality behind it, but was pure god-servant to the woman! The man, the individual, let him not dare intrude. He was but a temple-servant, the bearer and keeper of the bright phallus, her own.

So, in the flux of a new awakening, the old hard passion flamed in her for a time, and the man dwindled to a contemptible object, the mere phallus-bearer, to be torn to pieces when his service was performed. She felt the force of the Bacchae in her limbs and her body, the woman gleaming and rapid, beating down the male; but while she felt this, her heart was heavy. She did not want it, it was known and barren, birthless; the adoration was her treasure. It was so fathomless, so soft, so deep and so unknown. No, no, she would give up her hard bright female power; she was weary of it, stiffened with it; she would sink in the new bath of life, in the depths of her womb and her bowels that sang the voiceless song of adoration. It was early yet to begin to fear the man.

"I walked over by Marehay, and I had tea with Mrs. Flint," she said to Clifford. "I wanted to see the baby. It's so adorable, with hair like red cobwebs. Such a dear! Mr. Flint had gone to market, so she and I and the baby had tea together. Did you wonder where I was?"

"Well, I wondered, but I guessed you had dropped in somewhere to tea," said Clifford jealously. With a sort of second sight he sensed something new in her, something to him quite incomprehensible, but he ascribed it to the baby. He thought that all that ailed Connie was that she did not have a baby; automatically bring one forth, so to speak.

"I saw you go across the park to the iron gate, my Lady," said Mrs. Bolton; "so I thought perhaps you'd called at the Rectory."

"I nearly did, then I turned towards Marehay instead."

The eyes of the two women met: Mrs. Bolton's grey and bright and searching; Connie's blue and veiled and strangely beautiful. Mrs. Bolton was almost sure she had a lover, yet how could it be, and who could it be? Where was there a man?

"Oh, it's so good for you, if you go out and see a bit of company sometimes," said Mrs. Bolton. "I was saying to Sir Clifford, it would do her ladyship a world of good if she'd go out among people more."

"Yes, I'm glad I went, and such a quaint dear cheeky baby, Clifford," said Connie. "It's got hair just like spiderwebs, and bright orange, and the oddest, cheekiest, pale-blue china eyes. Of course, it's a girl, or it wouldn't be so bold, bolder than any little Sir Francis Drake."

"You're right, my Lady—a regular little Flint. They were always a forward, sandy-headed family," said Mrs. Bolton.

"Wouldn't you like to see it, Clifford? I've asked them to tea for you to see it."

"Who?" he asked, looking at Connie in great uneasiness.

"Mrs. Flint and the baby, next Monday."

"You can have them to tea in your room," he said.

"Why, don't you want to see the baby?" she cried.

"Oh, I'll see it, but I don't want to sit through a tea-time with them."

"Oh," said Connie, looking at him with wide veiled eyes.

She did not really see him, he was somebody else.

"You can have a nice cozy tea up in your room, my Lady, and Mrs. Flint will be more comfortable than if Sir Clifford was there," said Mrs. Bolton.

She was sure Connie had a lover, and something in her soul exulted. But who was he? Who was he? Perhaps Mrs. Flint would provide a clue.

Clifford was very uneasy. He would not let her go after dinner, and she had wanted so much to be alone. She looked at him, but was curiously submissive.

"Shall we play a game, or shall I read to you, or what shall it be?" he asked uneasily.

"You read to me," said Connie.

"What shall I read—verse or prose? Or drama?"

"Read Racine," she said.

It had been one of his stunts in the past, to read Racine in the real French grand manner, but he was rusty now, and a little self-conscious; he really preferred the loudspeaker. But Connie was sewing, sewing a little silk frock of primrose silk, cut out of one of her dresses, for Mrs. Flint's baby. Between coming home and dinner she had cut it out, and she sat in the soft quiescent rapture of herself, sewing, while the noise of the reading went on.

Inside herself she could feel the humming of passion, like the after-humming of deep bells.

Clifford said something to her about the Racine. She caught the sense after the words had gone.

"Yes! Yes!" she said, looking up at him. "It is splendid."

Again he was frightened at the deep blue haze of her eyes, and of her soft stillness, sitting there. She had never been so utterly soft and still. She fascinated him helplessly, as if some perfume about her intoxicated him. So he went on helplessly with his reading, and the throaty sound of the French was like the wind in the chimneys to her. Of the Racine she heard not one syllable.

She was gone in her own soft rapture, like a forest soughing with the dim, glad moan of spring, moving into bud. She could feel in the same world with her the man, the nameless man, moving on beautiful feet, beautiful in the phallic mystery. And in herself, in all her veins, she felt him and his child. His child was in all her veins, like a twilight.

"For hands she hath none, nor eyes, nor feet, nor golden Treasure of hair . . ."

She was like a forest, like the dark interlacing of the oak-wood, humming inaudibly with myriad unfolding buds. Meanwhile the birds of desire were asleep in the vast interlaced intricacy of her body.

But Clifford's voice went on, clapping and gurgling with unusual sounds. How extraordinary it was! How extraordinary he was, bent there over the book, queer and rapacious and civilized, with broad shoulders and no real legs! What a strange creature, with the sharp, cold, inflexible will of some bird, and no warmth, no warmth at all! One of those creatures of the afterwards, that have no soul, but an extra-alert will, cold will. She shuddered a little, afraid of him. But then, the soft warm flame of life was stronger than he, and the real things were hidden from him.

The reading finished. She was startled. She looked up, and was more startled still to see Clifford watching her with pale, uncanny eyes, like hate.

"Thank you *so* much! You do read Racine beautifully!" she said softly.

"Almost as beautifully as you listen to him," he said cruelly.

"What are you making?" he asked.

"I'm making a child's dress, for Mrs. Flint's baby."

He turned away. A child! A child! That was all her obsession.

"After all," he said, in a declamatory voice, "one gets all one wants out of Racine. Emotions that are ordered and given shape are more important than disorderly emotions."

She watched him with wide, vague, veiled eyes.

"Yes, I'm sure they are," she said.

"The modern world has only vulgarized emotion by letting it loose. What we need is classic control."

"Yes," she said slowly, thinking of him listening with vacant face to the emotional idiocy of the radio. "People pretend to have emotions, and they really feel nothing. I suppose that is being romantic."

"Exactly!" he said.

As a matter of fact, he was tired. This evening had tired him. He would rather have been with his technical books, or his pit-manager, or listening-in to the radio.

Mrs. Bolton came in with two glasses of malted milk: for Clifford, to make him sleep, and for Connie to fatten her again. It was a regular night-cap she had introduced.

Connie was glad to go, when she had drunk her glass, and thankful she needn't help Clifford to bed. She took his glass and put it on the tray, then took the tray, to leave it outside.

"Good night, Clifford! *Do* sleep well! The Racine gets into one like a dream. Good night!"

She had drifted to the door. She was going without kissing him good night. He watched her with sharp, cold eyes. So! She did not even kiss him good night, after he had spent an evening reading to her. Such depths of callousness in her! Even if the kiss was but a formality, it was on such formalities that life depends. She was a bolshevik, really. Her instincts were bolshevistic. He gazed coldly and angrily at the door whence she had gone. Anger!

And again the dread of the night came on him. He was a networks of nerves, and when he was not braced up to work, and so full of energy: or when he was not listening-in, and so utterly neuter: then he was haunted by anxiety and a sense of dangerous impending void. He was afraid. And Connie could keep the fear off him, if she would. But it was obvious she wouldn't, she wouldn't. She was callous, cold and callous to all that he did for her. He gave up his life for her, and she was callous to him. She only wanted her own way. "The lady loves her will."

Now it was a baby she was obsessed by. Just so that it should be her own, all her own, and not his!

Clifford was so healthy, considering. He looked so well and ruddy, in the face, his shoulders were broad and strong, his chest deep, he had put on flesh. And yet, at the same time, he was afraid of death. A terrible hollow seemed to menace him somewhere, somehow, a void, and into this void his energy would collapse. Energyless, he felt at times he was dead, really dead.

So his rather prominent pale eyes had a queer look, furtive, and yet a little cruel, so cold: and at the same time, almost impudent. It was a very odd look, this look of impudence: as if he were triumphing over life in spite of life. "Who knoweth the mysteries of the will—for it can triumph even against the angels—"

But his dread was the nights when he could not sleep. Then it was awful indeed, when annihilation pressed in on him on every side. Then it was ghastly, to exist without having any life: lifeless, in the night, to exist.

But now he could ring for Mrs. Bolton. And she would always come. That was a great comfort. She would come in her dressing-gown, with her hair in a plait down her back, curiously girlish and dim, though the brown plait was streaked with grey. And she would make him coffee or camomile tea, and she would play chess or piquet with him. She had a woman's queer faculty of playing even chess well enough, when she was three parts asleep, well enough to make her worth beating. So, in the silent intimacy of the night, they sat, or she sat and he lay on the bed, with the reading-lamp shedding its solitary light on them, she almost gone in sleep, he almost gone in a sort of fear, and they played, played together—then they had a cup of coffee and a biscuit together, hardly speaking, in the silence of night, but being a reassurance to one another.

And this night she was wondering who Lady Chatterley's lover was. And she was thinking of her own Ted, so long dead, yet for her never quite dead. And when she thought of him, the old, old grudge against the world rose up, but especially against the masters, that they had killed him. They had not really killed him. Yet, to her, emotionally, they had. And somewhere deep in herself, because of it, she was a nihilist, and really anarchic.

In her half-sleep, thoughts of her Ted and thoughts of Lady Chatterley's unknown lover commingled, and then she felt she shared with the other woman a great grudge against Sir Clifford and all he stood for. At the same time she was playing piquet with him, and they were gambling sixpences. And it was a source of satisfaction to be playing piquet with a baronet, and even losing sixpences to him.

When they played cards, they always gambled. It made him forget himself. And he usually won. Tonight, too, he was winning. So he would not go to sleep till the first dawn appeared. Luckily it began to appear at half-past four or thereabouts.

Connie was in bed, and fast asleep all this time. But the keeper, too, could not rest. He had closed the coops and made his round of the wood, then gone home and eaten supper. But he did not go to bed. Instead he sat by the fire and thought.

He thought of his boyhood in Tevershall, and of his five or six years of married life. He thought of his wife, and always bitterly. She had seemed so brutal. But he had not seen her now since 1915, in the spring when he joined up. Yet there she was, not three miles away, and more brutal than ever. He hoped never to see her again while he lived.

He thought of his life abroad, as a soldier. India, Egypt, then India again: the blind, thoughtless life with the horses: the colonel who had loved him and whom he had loved: the several years that he had been an officer, a lieutenant with a very fair chance of being a captain. Then the death of the colonel from pneumonia, and his own narrow escape from death: his damaged health: his deep restlessness: his leaving the army and coming back to England to be a working man again.

He was temporizing with life. He had thought he would be safe, at least for a time, in this wood. There was no shooting as yet: he had to rear the pheasants. He would have no guns to serve. He would be alone, and apart from life, which was all he wanted. He had to have some sort of a background. And this was his native place. There was even his mother, though she had never meant very much to him. And he could go on in life, existing from day to day, without connection and without hope. For he did not know what to do with himself.

He did not know what to do with himself. Since he had been an officer for some years, and had mixed among the other officers and civil servants, with their wives and families, he had lost all ambition to "get on." There was a toughness, a curious rubber-necked toughness and unlivingness about the middle and upper classes, as he had known them, which just left him feeling cold and different from them.

So, he had come back to his own class. To find there, what he had forgotten during his absence of years, a pettiness and a vulgarity of manner extremely distasteful. He admitted now at last, how important manner was. He admitted, also, how important it was even *to pretend* not to care about the halfpence and the small things of life. But among the common people there was no pretense. A penny more or less on the bacon was worse than a change in the Gospel. He could not stand it.

And again, there was the wage-squabble. Having lived among the owning classes, he knew the utter futility of expecting any solution of the wage-squabble. There was no solution, short of death. The only thing was not to care, not to care about the wages.

Yet, if you were poor and wretched you *had* to care. Anyhow, it was becoming the only thing they did care about. The *care* about money was like a great cancer, eating away individuals of all classes. He refused to care about money.

And what then? What did life offer apart from the care of money. Nothing.

Yet he could live alone, in the wan satisfaction of being alone, and raise pheasants to be shot ultimately by fat men after breakfast. It was futility, futility to the *n*th power.

But why care, why bother? And he had not cared nor bothered till now, when this woman had come into his life. He was nearly ten years older than she. And he was a thousand years older in experience, starting from the bottom. The connection between them was growing closer. He could see the day when it would clinch up and they would have to make a life together. "For the bonds of love are ill to loose!"

And what then? What then? Must he start again, with nothing to start on? Must he entangle this woman? Must he have the horrible broil with her lame husband? And also some sort of horrible broil with his own brutal wife, who hated him? Misery! lots of misery! And he was no longer young and merely buoyant. Neither was he the insouciant sort. Every bitterness and every ugliness would hurt him: and the woman!

But even if they got clear of Sir Clifford and of his own wife, even if they got clear, what were they going to do? What was he, himself, going to do? What was he going to do with his life? For he must do something. He couldn't be a mere hanger-on, on her money and his own very small pension.

It was insoluble. He could only think of going to America, to try a new air. He disbelieved in the dollar utterly. But perhaps, perhaps there was something else.

He could not rest nor even go to bed. After sitting in a stupor of bitter thoughts until midnight, he got suddenly from his chair and reached for his coat and gun.

"Come on, lass," he said to the dog. "We're best outside."

It was a starry night, but moonless. He went on a slow, scrupulous, soft-stepping and stealthy round. The only thing he had to contend with was the colliers setting snares for rabbits, particularly the Stacks Gate colliers, on the Marehay side. But it was breeding season, and even colliers respected it a little. Nevertheless the stealthy beating of the round in search of poachers soothed his nerves and took his mind off his thoughts.

But when he had done his slow, cautious beating of his bounds—it was nearly a five-mile walk—he was tired. He went to the top of the knoll and looked out. There was no sound save the noise, the faint shuffling noise from Stacks Gate colliery, that never ceased working: and there were hardly any lights, save the brilliant electric rows at the works. The world lay darkly and fumily sleeping. It was half-past two. But even in its sleep it was an uneasy, cruel world, stirring with the noise of a train or some great lorry on the road, and flashing with some rosy lightning-flash from the furnaces. It was a world of iron and coal, the cruelty of iron and the smoke of coal, and the endless, endless greed that drove it all. Only greed, greed stirring in its sleep.

It was cold, and he was coughing. A fine cold draught blew over the knoll. He thought of the woman. Now he would have given all he had or even might have to hold her warm in his arms, both of them wrapped in one blanket, and sleep. All hopes of eternity and all gain from the past he would have given to have her there, to be wrapped warm with him in one blanket, and sleep, only sleep. It seemed the sleep with the woman in his arms was the only necessity.

He went to the hut, and wrapped himself in the blanket and lay on the floor to sleep. But he could not, he was cold. And besides, he felt cruelly his own unfinished nature. He felt his own unfinished condition of aloneness cruelly. He wanted her, to touch her, to hold her fast against him in one moment of completeness and rest.

He got up again and went out, towards the park gates this time: then slowly along the path towards the house. It was nearly four o'clock, still clear and cold, but no sign of dawn. He was so used to the dark, he could see well.

Slowly, slowly the great house drew him, as a magnet. He wanted to be near her. It was not desire, not that. It was the cruel sense of unfinished aloneness, that needed a silent woman folded in his arms. Perhaps he could find her. Perhaps he could even call her out to him: or find some way in to her. For the need was imperious.

He slowly, silently climbed the incline to the hall. Then he came round the great trees at the top of the knoll, on to the drive, which made a grand sweep round a lozenge of grass in front of the entrance. He could already see the two magnificent beeches which stood in this big level lozenge in front of the house, detaching themselves darkly in the dark air.

There was the house, low and long and obscure, with one light burning downstairs, in Sir Clifford's room. But which room she was in, the woman who held the other end of the frail thread which drew him so mercilessly, that he did not know.

He went a little nearer, gun in hand, and stood motionless on the drive, watching the house. Perhaps even now he could find her, come at her in some way. The house was not impregnable: he was as clever as burglars are. Why not come to her?

He stood motionless, waiting, while the dawn faintly and imperceptibly paled behind him. He saw the light in the house go out. But he did not see Mrs. Bolton come to the window and draw back the old curtain of dark-blue silk, and stand herself in the dark room, looking out on the half-dark of the approaching day, looking for the longed-for dawn, waiting for Clifford to be really reassured that it was daybreak. For when he was sure of daybreak, he would sleep almost at once.

She stood blind with sleep at the window, waiting. And as she stood, she started, and almost cried out. For there was a man out there on the drive, a black figure in the twilight. She woke up greyly, and watched, but without making a sound to disturb Sir Clifford.

The daylight began to rustle into the world, and the dark figure seemed to go smaller and more defined. She made out the gun and gaiters and baggy jacket— it would be Oliver Mellors, the keeper. Yes, there was the dog nosing around like a shadow, and waiting for him!

And what did the man want? Did he want to rouse the house? What was he standing there for, transfixed, looking up at the house like a love-sick male dog outside the house where the bitch is!

Goodness! The knowledge went through Mrs. Bolton like a shot. He was Lady Chatterley's lover! He! He!

To think of it! Why, she, Ivy Bolton, had once been a tiny bit in love with him herself! When he was a lad of sixteen and she a woman of twenty-six. It was when she was studying, and he had helped her a lot with the anatomy and things she had had to learn. He'd been a clever boy, had a scholarship for Sheffield Grammar School, and learned French and things: and then after all had become an overhead blacksmith shoeing horses, because he was fond of horses, he said: but really because he was frightened to go out and face the world, only he'd never admit it.

But he'd been a nice lad, a nice lad, had helped her a lot, so clever at making things clear to you. He was quite as clever as Sir Clifford: and always one for the women. More with women than men, they said.

Till he'd gone and married that Bertha Coutts, as if to spite himself. Some people do marry to spite themselves, because they're disappointed or something. And no wonder it had been a failure.—For years he was gone, all the time of

the war: and a lieutenant and all: quite the gentleman, really quite the gentleman!—
Then to come back to Tevershall and go as a gamekeeper! Really, some people
can't take their chances when they've got them! And talking broad Derbyshire
again like the worst, when she, Ivy Bolton, knew he spoke like any gentleman,
really.

Well, well! So her ladyship had fallen for him! Well, her ladyship wasn't the
first: there was something about him. But fancy! A Tevershall lad born and bred,
and she her ladyship in Wragby Hall! My word, that was a slap back at the high-
and-mighty Chatterleys!

But he, the keeper, as the day grew, had realized: it's no good! It's no good
trying to get rid of your own aloneness. You've got to stick to it all your life.
Only at times, at times, the gap will be filled in. At times! But you have to wait
for the times. Accept your own aloneness and stick to it, all your life. And then
accept the times when the gap is filled in, when they come. But they've got to
come. You can't force them.

With a sudden snap the bleeding desire that had drawn him after her broke.
He had broken it, because it must be so. There must be a coming together on
both sides. And if she wasn't coming to him, he wouldn't track her down. He
mustn't. He must go away, till she came.

He turned slowly, ponderingly, accepting again the isolation. He knew it was
better so. She must come to him: it was no use trailing after her. No use!

Mrs. Bolton saw him disappear, saw his dog run after him.

"Well, well!" she said. "He's the one man I never thought of; and the one
man I might have thought of. He was nice to me when he was a lad, after I lost
Ted. Well, well! Whatever would *he* say if he knew!"

And she glanced triumphantly at the already sleeping Clifford, as she stepped
softly from the room.

Chapter Eleven

Connie was sorting out one of the
Wragby lumber rooms. There were several: the house was a warren, and the
family never sold anything. Sir Geoffrey's father had liked pictures and Sir
Geoffrey's mother had liked cinquecento furniture. Sir Geoffrey himself had liked
old carved oak chests, vestry chests. So it went on through the generations. Clifford
collected very modern pictures, at very moderate prices.

So in the lumber room there were bad Sir Edwin Landseers and pathetic
William Henry Hunt birds' nests: and other Academy stuff, enough to frighten

the daughter of an R.A. She determined to look through it one day, and clear it all. And the grotesque furniture interested her.

Wrapped up carefully to preserve it from damage and dry-rot was the old family cradle, of rosewood. She had to unwrap it, to look at it. It had a certain charm: she looked at it a long time.

"It's a thousand pities it won't be called for," sighed Mrs. Bolton, who was helping. "Though cradles like that are out-of-date nowadays."

"It might be called for. I might have a child," said Connie casually, as if saying she might have a new hat.

"You mean, if anything happened to Sir Clifford!" stammered Mrs. Bolton.

"No! I mean as things are. It's only muscular paralysis with Sir Clifford—it doesn't affect *him*," said Connie, lying as naturally as breathing.

Clifford had put the idea into her head. He had said: "Of course, *I* may have a child yet. I'm not really mutilated at all. The potency may easily come back even if the muscles of the hips and legs are paralyzed. And then the seed may be transferred."

He really felt, when he had his periods of energy and worked so hard at the question of the mines, as if his sexual potency were returning. Connie had looked at him in terror. But she was quite quick-witted enough to use his suggestion for her own preservation. For she would have a child if she could: but not his.

Mrs. Bolton was for a moment breathless, flabbergasted. Then she didn't believe it: she saw in it a ruse. Yet doctors could do such things nowadays. They might sort of graft seed.

"Well, my Lady, I only hope and pray you may. It would be lovely for you: and for everybody. My word, a child in Wragby, what a difference it would make!"

"Wouldn't it!" said Connie.

And she chose three R.A. pictures of sixty years ago, to send to the Duchess of Shortlands for that lady's next charitable bazaar. She was called "the bazaar duchess," and she would be delighted with the three framed R.A.'s. She might even call, on the strength of them. How furious Clifford was when she called!

But oh, my dear! Mrs. Bolton was thinking to herself. Is it Oliver Mellors' child you're preparing us for? Oh, my dear, that *would* be a Tevershall baby in the Wragby cradle, my word! Wouldn't shame it, neither!

Among other monstrosities in this lumber room was a largish black japanned box, excellently and ingeniously made some sixty or seventy years ago, and fitted with every imaginable object. On top was a concentrated toilet set: brushes, bottles, mirrors, combs, boxes, even three beautiful little razors in safety sheaths, shaving-bowl and all. Underneath came a sort of escritoire outfit: blotters, pens, ink-bottles, paper, envelopes, memorandum books: and then a perfect sewing outfit, with three different-sized scissors, thimbles, needles, silks, and cottons, darning egg, all of the very best quality and perfectly finished. Then there was a little medicine store, with bottles labelled Laudanum, Tincture of Myrrh, Ess. Cloves, and so on: but empty. Everything was perfectly new, and the whole thing, when shut up, was as big as a small, but fat week-end bag. And inside, it fitted together like a puzzle. The bottles could not possibly have spilled: there wasn't room.

The thing was wonderfully made and contrived, excellent craftsmanship of the Victorian order. But somehow it was monstrous. Some Chatterley must even have felt it, for the thing had never been used. It had a peculiar soullessness.

Yet Mrs. Bolton was thrilled.

"Look what beautiful brushes, so expensive, even the shaving brushes, three perfect ones! No! and those scissors! They're the best that money could buy. Oh, I call it lovely!"

"Do you?" said Connie. "Then you have it."

"Oh, no, my Lady!"

"Of course! It will only lie here till Doomsday. If you won't have it, I'll send it to the Duchess as well as the pictures, and she doesn't deserve so much. Do have it!"

"Oh, your Ladyship! Why, I shall never be able to thank you."

"You needn't try," laughed Connie.

And Mrs. Bolton sailed down with the huge and very black box in her arms, flushing bright pink in her excitement.

Mr. Betts drove her in the trap to her house in the village, with the box. And she *had* to have a few friends in, to show it: the school-mistress, the chemist's wife, Mrs. Weedon the under-cashier's wife. They thought it marvellous. And then started the whisper of Lady Chatterley's child.

"Wonders'll never cease!" said Mrs. Weedon.

But Mrs. Bolton was *convinced,* if it did come, it would be Sir Clifford's child. So there!

Not long after, the rector said gently to Clifford:

"And may we really hope for an heir to Wragby? Ah, that would be the hand of God in mercy, indeed!"

"Well! We may *hope,* "said Clifford, with a faint irony, and, at the same time, a certain conviction. He had begun to believe it really possible it might even be *his* child.

Then one afternoon came Leslie Winter, Squire Winter, as everybody called him: lean, immaculate, and seventy: and every inch a gentleman, as Mrs. Bolton said to Mrs. Betts. Every millimeter, indeed! And with his old-fashioned, rather haw-haw! manner of speaking, he seemed more out-of-date than bag-wigs. Time, in her flight, drops these fine old feathers.

They discussed the collieries. Clifford's idea was, that his coal, even the poor sort, could be made into hard concentrated fuel that would burn at great heat if fed with certain damp, acidulated air at a fairly strong pressure. It had long been observed that in a particularly strong, wet wind the pit-bank burned very vivid, gave off hardly any fumes, and left a fine powder of ash, instead of the slow pink gravel.

"But where will you find the proper engines for burning your fuel?" asked Winter.

"I'll make them myself. And I'll use my fuel myself. And I'll sell electric power. I'm certain I could do it."

"If you can do it, then splendid, splendid, my dear boy. Haw! Splendid! If I can be of any help, I shall be delighted. I'm afraid I am a little out-of-date, and my collieries are like me. But who knows, when I'm gone, there may be men like you. Splendid! It will employ all the men again, and you won't have to sell your coal, or fail to sell it. A splendid idea, and I hope it will be a success. If I had sons of my own, no doubt they would have up-to-date ideas for Shipley: no doubt! By the way, dear boy, is there any foundation to the rumor that we may entertain hopes of an heir to Wragby?"

"Is there a rumor?" asked Clifford.

"Well, my dear boy, Marshall from Fillingwood asked *me,* that's all I can say about a rumor. Of course, I wouldn't repeat it for the world, if there were no foundation."

"Well, Sir," said Clifford uneasily, but with strange bright eyes. "There is a hope. There is a hope."

Winter came across the room and wrung Clifford's hand.

"My dear boy, my dear lad, can you believe what it means to me, to hear that! And to hear you are working in the hopes of a son: and that you may again employ every man at Tevershall. Ah my boy! to keep up the level of the race, and to have work waiting for any man who cares to work!—"

The old man was really moved.

Next day Connie was arranging tall yellow tulips in a glass vase.

"Connie," said Clifford, "did you know there was a rumor that you are going to supply Wragby with a son and heir?"

Connie felt dim with terror, yet she stood quite still, touching the flowers.

"No!" she said. "Is it a joke? Or malice?"

He paused before he answered:

"Neither, I hope. I hope it may be a prophecy."

Connie went on with her flowers.

"I had a letter from father this morning," she said. "He wants to know if I am aware he has accepted Sir Alexander Cooper's invitation for me for July and August, to the Villa Esmeralda in Venice."

"July *and* August?" said Clifford.

"Oh, I wouldn't stay all that time. Are you sure you wouldn't come?"

"I won't travel abroad," said Clifford, promptly.

She took her flowers to the window.

"Do you mind if I go?" she said. "You know it was promised, for this summer."

"For how long would you go?"

"Perhaps three weeks."

There was a silence for a time.

"Well," said Clifford slowly, and a little gloomily: "I suppose I could stand it for three weeks: if I were absolutely sure you'd want to come back."

"I should want to come back," she said, with a quiet simplicity, heavy with conviction. She was thinking of the other man.

Clifford felt her conviction, and somehow he believed her, he believed it was for him. He felt immensely relieved, joyful at once.

"In that case," he said, "I think it would be all right. Don't you?"

"I think so," she said.

"You'd enjoy the change?"

She looked up at him with strange blue eyes.

"I should like to see Venice again," she said, "and to bathe from one of the shingle islands across the lagoon. But you know I loathe Lido! And I don't fancy I shall like Sir Alexander Cooper and Lady Cooper. But if Hilda is there, and we have a gondola of our own: yes, it will be rather lovely. I *do* wish you'd come."

She said it sincerely. She would so love to make him happy, in these ways.

"Ah, but think of me, though, at the Gare du Nord: at Calais quay!"

"But why not? I see other men carried in litter-chairs, who have been wounded in the war. Besides, we'd motor all the way."

"We should need to take two men."

"Oh, no! We'd manage with Field. There would always be another man there."

But Clifford shook his head.

"Not this year, dear! Not this year! Next year, probably, I'll try."

She went away gloomily. Next year! What would next year bring? She herself did not really want to go to Venice: not now, now there was the other man. But she was going as a sort of discipline: and also because, if she had a child, Clifford would think she had a lover in Venice.

It was already May, and in June they were supposed to start. Always these arrangements! Always one's life arranged for one! Wheels that worked one and drove one, and over which one had no real control!

It was May, but cold and wet again. A cold wet May, good for corn and hay! Much the corn and hay matter nowadays! Connie had to go into Uthwaite, which was their little town, where the Chatterleys were still *the* Chatterleys. She went alone, Field driving her.

In spite of May and a new greenness, the country was dismal. It was rather chilly, and there was smoke in the rain, and a certain sense of exhaust vapor in the air. One just had to live from one's resistance. No wonder these people were ugly and tough.

The car ploughed uphill through the long squalid straggle of Tevershall, the blackened brick dwellings, the black slate roofs glistening their sharp edges, the mud black with coal-dust, the pavements wet and black. It was as if dismalness had soaked through and through everything. The utter negation of natural beauty, the utter negation of the gladness of life, the utter absence of the instinct for shapely beauty which every bird and beast has, the utter death of the human intuitive faculty was appalling. The stacks of soap in the grocers' shops, the rhubarb and lemons in the green-grocers'! the awful hats in the milliners'! all went by ugly, ugly, ugly, followed by the plaster-and-gilt horror of the cinema with its wet picture announcements, "A Woman's Love!", and the new big Primitive chapel, primitive enough in its stark brick and big panes of greenish and raspberry glass in the windows. The Wesleyan chapel, higher up, was of blackened brick and stood behind iron railings and blackened shrubs. The Congregational chapel, which thought itself superior, was built of rusticated sandstone and had a steeple, but not a very high one. Just beyond were the new school buildings, expensive pink brick, and gravelled playground inside iron railings, all very imposing, and mixing the suggestion of a chapel and a prison. Standard Five girls were having a singing lesson, just finishing the la-me-do-la exercises and beginning a "sweet children's song." Anything more unlike song, spontaneous song, would be impossible to imagine: a strange bawling yell that followed the outlines of a tune. It was not like savages: savages have subtle rhythms. It was not like animals: animals *mean* something when they yell. It was like nothing on earth, and it was called singing. Connie sat and listened with her heart in her boots, as Field was filling petrol. What could possibly become of such a people, a people in whom the living intuitive faculty was dead as nails, and only queer mechanical yells and uncanny will power remained?

A coal-cart was coming down-hill, clanking in the rain. Field started upwards, past the big but weary-looking drapers' and clothing shops, the post-office, into the little marketplace of forlorn space, where Sam Black was peering out of the door of the "Sun," that called itself an inn, not a pub, and where the commercial travellers stayed, and was bowing to Lady Chatterley's car.

The church was away to the left among black trees. The car slid on down-hill, past the Miners Arms. It had already passed the Wellington, the Nelson, the Three Tunns and the Sun, now it passed the Miners Arms, then the Mechanics Hall, then the new and almost gaudy Miners Welfare and so, past a few new "villas," out into the blackened road between dark hedges and dark green fields, towards Stacks Gate.

Tevershall! That was Tevershall! Merrie England! Shakespeare's England! No, but the England of today, as Connie had realized since she had come to live in it. It was producing a new race of mankind, over-conscious in the money and social and political side, on the spontaneous, intuitive side dead,—but dead! Half-corpses, all of them: but with a terrible insistent consciousness in the other half. There was something uncanny and underground about it all. It was an underworld. And quite incalcuable. How shall we understand the reactions in half-corpses? When Connie saw the great lorries full of steel-workers from Sheffield, weird, distorted, smallish beings like men, off for an excursion to Matlock, her bowels fainted and she thought: Ah, God, what has man done to man? What have the leaders of men been doing to their fellow-men? They have reduced them to less than humanness; and now there can be no fellowship any more! It is just a nightmare.

She felt again in a wave of terror the grey, gritty hopelessness of it all. With such creatures for the industrial masses, and the upper classes as she knew them, there was no hope, no hope any more. Yet she was wanting a baby, and an heir to Wragby! An heir to Wragby! She shuddered with dread.

Yet Mellors had come out of all this!—Yes, but he was as apart from it all as she was. Even in him there was no fellowship left. It was dead. The fellowship was dead. There was only apartness and hopelessness, as far as all this was concerned. And this was England, the vast bulk of England: as Connie knew, since she had motored from the center of it.

The car was rising towards Stacks Gate. The rain was holding off, and in the air came a queer pellucid gleam of May. The country rolled away in long undulations, south towards the Peak, east towards Mansfield and Nottingham. Connie was travelling south.

As she rose on to the high country, she could see on her left, on a height above the rolling land the shadowy, powerful bulk of Warsop Castle, dark grey, with below it the reddish plastering of miners' dwellings, newish, and below those the plumes of dark smoke and white steam from the great colliery which put so many thousand pounds per annum into the pockets of the Duke and the other shareholders. The powerful old castle was a ruin, yet still it hung its bulk on the low skyline, over the black plumes and the white that waved on the damp air below.

A turn, and they ran on the high level to Stacks Gate. Stacks Gate, as seen from the highroad, was just a huge and gorgeous new hotel, the Coningsby Arms, standing red and white and gilt in barbarous isolation off the road. But if you looked, you saw on the left rows of handsome "modern" dwellings, set down like a game of dominoes, with spaces and gardens: a queer game of dominoes that some weird "masters" were playing on the surprised earth. And beyond these blocks of dwellings, at the back, rose all the astonishing and frightening overhead erections of a really modern mine, chemical works and long galleries, enormous, and of shapes not before known to man. The head-stocks and pit-bank of the mine itself were insignificant among the huge new installations. And in front of this, the game of dominoes stood forever in a sort of surprise, waiting to be played.

This was Stacks Gate, new on the face of the earth, since the war. But as a matter of fact, though even Connie did not know it, down-hill half a mile below the "hotel" was old Stacks Gate, with a little old colliery and blackish old brick dwellings, and a chapel or two and a shop or two and a little pub or two.

But that didn't count any more. The vast plumes of smoke and vapor rose from the new works up above, and this was now Stacks Gate: no chapel, no pubs, even no shops. Only the great "works," which are the modern Olympia with temples to all the gods: then the model dwellings: then the hotel. The hotel in actuality was nothing but a miners' pub, though it looked first-classy.

Even since Connie's arrival at Wragby this new place had arisen on the face of the earth, and the model dwellings had filled with riff-raff drifting in from anywhere, to poach Clifford's rabbits among other occupations.

The car ran on along the uplands, seeing the rolling county spread out. The county; it had once been a proud and lordly county. In front, looming again and hanging on the brow of the sky-line, was the huge and splendid bulk of Chadwick Hall, more window than wall, one of the most famous Elizabethan houses. Noble it stood alone above a great park, but out of date, passed over. It was still kept up, but as a show place. "Look how our ancestors lorded it!"

That was the past. The present lay below. God alone knows where the future lies. The car was already turning, between little old blackened miners' cottages, to descend to Uthwaite. And Uthwaite, on a damp day, was sending up a whole array of smoke plumes and steam, to whatever gods there be. Uthwaite down in the valley, with all the steel threads of the railways to Sheffield drawn through it, and the coal-mines and the steel-works sending up smoke and glare from long tubes, and the pathetic little corkscrew spire of the church, that is going to tumble down, still pricking the fumes, always affected Connie strangely. It was an old market-town, center of the dales. One of the chief inns was the Chatterley Arms. There, in Uthwaite, Wragby was known as Wragby, as if it were a whole place, not just a house, as it was to outsiders: Wragby Hall, near Tevershall: Wragby, a "seat."

The miners' cottages, blackened, stood flush on the pavement, with that intimacy and smallness of colliers' dwellings over a hundred years old. They lined all the way. The road had become a street, and as you sank, you forgot instantly the open, rolling country where the castles and big houses still dominated, but like ghosts. Now you were just above the tangle of naked railway-lines, and foundries and other "works" rose about you, so big you were only aware of walls. And iron clanked with a huge reverberating clank, and huge lorries shook the earth, and whistles screamed.

Yet again, once you had got right down and into the twisted and crooked heart of the town, behind the church, you were in the world of two centuries ago, in the crooked streets where the Chatterley Arms stood, and the old pharmacy, streets which used to lead out to the wild open world of the castles and stately couchant houses.

But at the corner a policeman held up his hand as three lorries loaded with iron rolled past, shaking the poor old church. And not till the lorries were past could he salute her ladyship.

So it was. Upon the old crooked burgess streets hordes of oldish, blackened miners' dwellings crowded, lining the roads out. And immediately after these came the newer, pinker rows of rather larger houses, plastering the valley: the homes of more modern workmen. And beyond that again, in the wide rolling regions of the castles, smoke waved against steam, and patch after patch of raw reddish brick showed the newer mining settlements, sometimes in the hollows, sometimes gruesomely ugly along the sky-line of the slopes. And between, in between, were the tattered remnants of the old coaching and cottage England, even the England of Robin Hood, where the miners prowled with the dismalness of suppressed sporting instincts, when they were not at work.

England, my England! But which is *my* England? The stately homes of England make good photographs, and create the illusion of a connection with the Elizabethans. The handsome old halls are here, from the days of Good Queen Anne and Tom Jones. But smuts fall and blacken on the drab stucco, that has long ceased to be golden. And one by one, like the stately homes, they are abandoned. Now they are being pulled down. As for the cottages of England—there they are—great plasterings of brick dwellings on the hopeless countryside.

Now they are pulling down the stately homes, the Georgian halls are going. Fritchley, a perfect old Georgian mansion, was even now, as Connie passed in the car, being demolished. It was in perfect repair: till the war the Weatherleys had lived in style there. But now it was too big, too expensive, and the country had become too uncongenial. The gentry were departing to pleasanter places, where they could spend their money without having to see how it was made.

This is history. One England blots out another. The mines had made the halls wealthy. Now they were blotting them out, as they had already blotted out the cottages. The industrial England blots out the agricultural England. One meaning blots out another. The new England blots out the old England. And the continuity is not organic, but mechanical.

Connie, belonging to the leisured classes, had clung to the remnants of the old England. It had taken her years to realize that it was really blotted out by this terrifying new and gruesome England, and that the blotting out would go on till it was complete. Fritchley was gone, Eastwood was gone, Shipley was going: Squire Winter's beloved Shipley.

Connie called for a moment at Shipley. The park gates, at the back, opened just near the level crossing of the colliery railway; the Shipley colliery itself stood just beyond the trees. The gates stood open, because through the park was a right-of-way that the colliers used. They hung around the park.

The car passed the ornamental ponds, in which the colliers threw their newspapers, and took the private drive to the house. It stood above, aside, a very pleasant stucco building from the middle of the eighteenth century. It had a beautiful alley of yew trees, that had approached an older house, and the hall stood serenely spread out, winking its Georgian panes as if cheerfully. Behind, there were really beautiful gardens.

Connie liked the interior much better than Wragby. It was much lighter, more alive, shapen and elegant. The rooms were panelled with creamy-painted panelling, the ceilings were touched with gilt, and everything was kept in exquisite order, all the appointments were perfect, regardless of expense. Even the corridors managed to be ample and lovely, softly curved and full of life.

Leslie Winter was alone. He had adored his house. But his park was bordered by three of his own collieries. He had been a generous man in his ideas. He had almost welcomed the colliers in his park. Had the miners not made him rich! So, when he saw the gangs of unshapely men lounging by his ornamental waters— not on the *private* part of the park; no, he drew the line there—he would say: "The miners are perhaps not so ornamental as deer, but they are far more profitable."

But that was in the golden—monetarily—latter half of Queen Victoria's reign. Miners were then "good working men."

Winter had made this speech, half apologetic, to his guest, the then Prince of Wales. And the Prince had replied, in his rather guttural English:

"You are quite right. If there were coal under Sandringham, I would open a mine on the lawns, and think it first-rate landscape gardening. Oh, I am quite willing to exchange roe-deer for colliers, at the price. Your men are good men, too, I hear."

But then, the Prince had perhaps an exaggerated idea of the beauty of money, and the blessings of industrialism.

However, the Prince had been a King, and the King had died, and now there was another King, whose chief function seemed to be to open soup-kitchens.

And the good working men were somehow hemming Shipley in. New mining villages crowded on the park, and the squire felt somehow that the population was alien. He used to feel, in a good-natured but quite grand way, lord of his own domain and of his own colliers. Now, by a subtle pervasion of the new spirit, he had somehow been pushed out. It was he who did not belong any more. There was no mistaking it. The mines, the industry had a will of its own, and this will was against the gentleman-owner. All the colliers took part in the will, and it was hard to live up against it. It either shoved you out of the place, or out of life altogether.

Squire Winter, a soldier, had stood it out. But he no longer cared to walk in the park after dinner. He almost hid, indoors. Once he had walked, bare-headed, and in his patent-leather shoes and purple silk socks, with Connie down to the gate, talking to her in his well-bred rather haw-haw fashion. But when it came to passing the little gangs of colliers who stood and stared without either salute or anything else, Connie felt how the lean, well-bred old man winced, winced as an elegant antelope stag in a cage winces from the vulgar stare. The colliers were not *personally* hostile: not at all. But their spirit was cold, and shoving him out. And deep down, there was a profound grudge. They "worked for him." And in their ugliness, they resented his elegant, well-groomed, well-bred existence. "Who's he!" It was the *difference* they resented.

And somewhere, in his secret English heart, being a good deal of a soldier, he believed they were right to resent the difference. He felt himself a little in the wrong, for having all the advantages. Nevertheless he represented a system, and he would not be shoved out.

Except by death. Which came on him soon after Connie's call, suddenly. And he remembered Clifford handsomely in his will.

The heirs at once gave out the order for the demolishing of Shipley. It cost too much to keep up. No one would live there. So it was broken up. The avenue of yews was cut down. The park was denuded of its timber, and divided into lots. It was near enough to Uthwaite. In the strange, bald desert of this still-one-more no-man's-land, new little streets of semi-detacheds were run up, very desirable! The Shipley Hall Estate!

Within a year of Connie's last call, it had happened. There stood Shipley Hall Estate, an array of red-brick semi-detached "villas" in new streets. No one would have dreamed that the stucco hall had stood there twelve months before.

But this is a later stage of King Edward's landscape gardening, the sort that has an ornamental coal-mine on the lawn.

One England blots out another. The England of the Squire Winters and the Wragby Halls was gone, dead. The blotting out was only not yet complete.

What would come after? Connie could not imagine. She could only see the new brick streets spreading into the fields, the new erections rising at the collieries, the new girls in their silk stockings, the new collier lads lounging into the Pally or the Welfare. The younger generation were utterly unconscious of the Old England. There was a gap in the continuity of consciousness, almost American: but industrial really. What next?

Connie always felt there was no next. She wanted to hide her head in the sand: or at least, in the bosom of a living man.

The world was so complicated and weird and gruesome! The common people were so many, and really, so terrible. So she thought as she was going home, and saw the colliers trailing from the pits, grey-black, distorted, one shoulder higher than the other, slurring their heavy iron-shod boots. Underground grey faces, whites of eyes rolling, necks cringing from the pit roof, shoulders out of shape. Men! Men! Alas, in some way patient and good men. In other ways, non-existent. Something that men *should* have was bred and killed out of them. Yet they were men. They begot children. One might bear a child to them. Terrible, terrible thought! They were good and kindly. But they were only half, only the grey half of a human being. As yet, they were "good." But even that was the goodness of their halfness. Supposing the dead in them ever rose up! But no, it was too terrible to think of. Connie was absolutely afraid of the industrial masses. They seemed so *weird* to her. A life with utterly no beauty in it, no intuition, always "in the pit."

Children from such men. Oh, God! Oh, God!

Yet Mellors had come from such a father. Not quite. Forty years had made a difference, an appalling difference in manhood. The iron and the coal had eaten deep into the bodies and souls of the men.

Incarnate ugliness, and alive! What would become of them all? Perhaps with the passing of the coal they would disappear again, off the face of the earth. They had appeared out of nowhere in their thousands, when the coal had called for them. Perhaps they were only weird fauna of the coal-seams. Creatures of another reality, they were elementals, serving the elements of coal, as the metal-workers were elementals, serving the element of iron. Men not men, but animas of coal and iron and clay. Fauna of the elements, carbon, iron, silicon: elementals. They had perhaps some of the weird, inhuman beauty of minerals, the luster of coal, the weight and blueness and resistance of iron, the transparency of glass. Elemental creatures, weird and distorted, of the mineral world! They belonged to the coal, the iron, the clay, as fish belong to the sea and worms to dead wood. The anima of mineral disintegration!

Connie was glad to be home, to bury her head in the sand. She was glad even to babble to Clifford. For her fear of the mining and iron Midlands affected her with a queer feeling that went all over her, like influenza.

"Of course, I had to have tea in Miss Bentley's shop," she said.

"Really! Winter would have given you tea."

"Oh, yes, but I daren't disappoint Miss Bentley."

Miss Bentley was a sallow old maid with a rather large nose and romantic disposition, who served tea with a careful intensity worthy of a sacrament.

"Did she ask after me?" said Clifford.

"Of course!—*May* I ask your Ladyship how Sir Clifford is?—I believe she ranks you even higher than Nurse Cavell!"

"And I suppose you said I was blooming."

"Yes! And she looked as rapt as if I had said the heavens had opened to you. I said if she ever came to Tevershall she was to come to see you."

"Me! Whatever for! See me!"

"Why, yes, Clifford. You can't be so adored without making some slight return. Saint George of Cappadocia was nothing to you, in her eyes."

"And do you think she'll come?"

"Oh, she blushed! and looked quite beautiful for a moment, poor thing! Why don't men marry the women who would really adore them?"

"The women start adoring too late. But did she say she'd come?"

"Oh!" Connie imitated the breathless Miss Bentley, "your Ladyship, if ever I should dare to presume!"

"Dare to presume! how absurd! But I hope to God she won't turn up. And how was her tea?"

"Oh, Lipton's and *very* strong! But, Clifford, do you realize you are the *Roman de la rose* of Miss Bentley and lots like her?"

"I'm not flattered, even then."

"They treasure up every one of your pictures in the illustrated papers, and probably pray for you every night. It's rather wonderful."

She went upstairs to change.

That evening he said to her:

"You do think, don't you, that there is something eternal in marriage?"

She looked at him.

"But Clifford, you make eternity sound like a lid or a long, long chain that trailed after one, no matter how far one went."

He looked at her, annoyed.

"What I mean," he said, "is that if you go to Venice, you won't go in the hopes of some love affair that you can take *au grand sérieux*, will you?"

"A love affair in Venice *au grand sérieux*? No, I assure you! No, I'd never take a love affair in Venice more than *au très petit sérieux*.'"

She spoke with a queer kind of contempt. He knitted his brows, looking at her.

Coming downstairs in the morning, she found the keeper's dog Flossie sitting in the corridor outside Clifford's room, and whimpering very faintly.

"Why, Flossie!" she said softly. "What are you doing here?"

And she quietly opened Clifford's door. Clifford was sitting up in bed, with the bed-table and typewriter pushed aside, and the keeper was standing attention at the foot of the bed. Flossie ran in. With a faint gesture of head and eyes, Mellors ordered her to the door again, and she slunk out.

"Oh, good morning, Clifford!" Connie said. "I didn't know you were so busy."

Then she looked at the keeper, saying good morning to him. He murmured his reply, looking at her as if vaguely. But she felt a whiff of passion touch her, from his mere presence.

"Did I interrupt you, Clifford? I'm sorry."

"No, it's nothing of any importance."

She slipped out of the room again, and up to the blue boudoir on the first floor. She sat in the window, and saw him go down the drive, with his curious, silent motion, effaced. He had a natural sort of quiet distinction, an aloof pride, and also a certain look of frailty. A hireling! One of Clifford's hirelings! "The fault, dear Brutus, is not in our stars, but in ourselves, that we are underlings."

Was he an underling? Was he? What did he think of *her?*

It was a sunny day, and Connie was working in the garden, and Mrs. Bolton was helping her. For some reason, the two women had drawn together, in one of the unaccountable flows and ebbs of sympathy that exist between people. They were pegging down carnations, and putting in small plants for the summer. It was work they both liked. Connie especially felt a delight in putting the soft roots of young plants into a soft black puddle, and cradling them down. On this spring morning she felt a quiver in her womb, too, as if the sunshine had touched it and made it happy.

"It is many years since you lost your husband?" she said to Mrs. Bolton, as she took up another little plant and laid it in its hole.

"Twenty-three!" said Mrs. Bolton, as she carefully separated the young columbines into single plants. "Twenty-three years since they brought him home."

Connie's heart gave a lurch, at the terrible finality of it. "Brought him home!"

"Why did he get killed, do you think?" she asked. "He was happy with you?"

It was a woman's question to a woman. Mrs. Bolton put aside a strand of hair from her face, with the back of her hand.

"I don't know, my Lady! He sort of wouldn't give in to things: he wouldn't really go with the rest. And then he hated ducking his head for anything on earth. A sort of obstinacy, that *gets* itself killed. You see, he didn't really care. I lay it down to the pit. He ought never to have been down the pit. But his dad made him go down, as a lad; and then, when you're over twenty, it's not very easy to come out."

"Did he say he hated it?"

"Oh, no! Never! He never said he hated anything. He just made a funny face. He was one of those who wouldn't take care: like some of the first lads as went off so blithe to the war and got killed right away. He wasn't really wezzle-brained. But he wouldn't care. I used to say to him: 'You care for nought nor nobody!' But he did! The way he sat when my first baby was born, motionless, and the sort of fatal eyes he looked at me with, when it was over! I had a bad time, but I had to comfort *him*. 'It's all right, lad, it's all right!' I said to him. And he gave me a look, and that funny sort of smile. He never said anything. But I don't believe he had any right pleasure with me at nights after; he'd never really let himself go. I used to say to him: 'Oh, let thysen go, lad!'—I'd talk broad to him sometimes. And he said nothing. But he wouldn't let himself go, or he couldn't. He didn't want me to have any more children. I always blamed his mother, for letting him in th' room. He'd no right t'ave been there. Men makes so much more of things than they should, once they start brooding."

"Did he mind so much?" said Connie in wonder.

"Yes, he sort of couldn't take it for natural, all that pain. And it spoilt his pleasure in his bit of married love. I said to him: If I don't care, why should you? It's my look-out!—But all he'd ever say was: It's not right!"

"Perhaps he was too sensitive," said Connie.

"That's it! When you come to know men, that's how they are: too sensitive in the wrong place. And I believe, unbeknown to himself, he hated the pit, just hated it. He looked so quiet when he was dead, as if he'd got free. He was such a nice-looking lad. It just broke my heart to see him, so still and pure looking, as if he'd *wanted* to die. Oh, it broke my heart, that did. But it was the pit."

She wept a few bitter tears, and Connie wept more. It was a warm spring day, with a perfume of earth and of yellow flowers, many things rising to bud, and the garden still with the very sap of sunshine.

"It must have been terrible for you!" said Connie.

"Oh, my Lady! I never realized at first. I could only say: Oh, my lad, what did you want to leave me for!—That was all my cry. But somehow I felt he'd come back."

"But he *didn't* want to leave you," said Connie.

"Oh, no, my Lady! That was only my silly cry. And I kept expecting him back. Especially at nights. I kept waking up, thinking: Why, he's not here with me!— It was as if my *feelings* wouldn't believe he'd gone. I just felt he'd *have* to come back and talk to me, so I could feel him with me. That was all I wanted, to feel him there with me, warm. And it took me a thousand shocks before I knew he wouldn't come back, it took me years."

"The touch of him," said Connie.

"That's it, my Lady, the touch of him! I've never got over it to this day, and never shall. And if there's a heaven above, he'll be there, and warm up against me so I can sleep."

Connie glanced at the handsome, brooding face in fear. Another passionate one out of Tevershall! The touch of him! For the bonds of love are ill to loose!

"It's terrible, once you've got a man into your blood." she said.

"Oh, my Lady! And that's what makes you feel so bitter. You feel folks *wanted* him killed. You feel the pit fair *wanted* to kill him. Oh, I felt, if it hadn't been for the pit, an' them as runs the pit, there'd have been no leaving me. But they all *want* to separate a woman and a man, if they're together."

"If they're physically together," said Connie.

"That's right, my Lady! There's a lot of hard-hearted folks in the world. And every morning when he got up and went to th' pit, I felt it was wrong, wrong. But what else could he do? What can a man do?"

A queer hate flared in the woman.

"But can a touch last so long?" Connie asked suddenly. "That you could feel him so long?"

"Oh, my Lady, what else is there to last? Children grows away from you. But the man, well—! But even *that* they'd like to kill in you, the very thought of the touch of him. Even your own children! Ah, well! We might have drifted apart, who knows. But the feeling's something different. It's 'appen better never to care. But there, when I look at women who's never really been warmed through by a man, well, they seem to me poor dool-owls after all, no matter how they may dress up and gad. No, I'll abide by my own. I've not much respect for people."

Chapter Twelve

Connie went to the wood directly after lunch. It was really a lovely day, the first dandelions making suns, the first daisies so white. The hazel thicket was a lacework of half-open leaves, and the last dusty perpendicular of the catkins. Yellow celandines now were in crowds, flat open, pressed back in urgency, and the yellow glitter of themselves. It was the yellow, the powerful yellow of early summer. And primroses were broad, and full of pale abandon, thick-clustered primroses no longer shy. The lush, dark green of hyacinths was a sea, with buds rising like pale corn, while in the riding the forget-me-nots were fluffing up, and columbines were unfolding their ink-purple riches, and there were bits of blue bird's eggshell under a bush. Everywhere the bud-knots and the leap of life!

The keeper was not at the hut. Everything was serene, brown chickens running lustily. Connie walked on towards the cottage, because she wanted to find him.

The cottage stood in the sun, off the wood's edge. In the little garden the double daffodils rose in tufts, near the wide-open door, and red double daisies made a border to the path. There was the bark of a dog, and Flossie came running.

The wide-open door! so he was at home. And the sunlight falling on the red-brick floor! As she went up the path, she saw him through the window, sitting at the table in his shirt-sleeves, eating. The dog wuffed softly, slowly wagging her tail.

He rose, and came to the door, wiping his mouth with a red handkerchief, still chewing.

"May I come in?" she said.

"Come in!"

The sun shone into the bare room, which still smelled of a mutton chop, done in a dutch oven before the fire, because the dutch oven still stood on the fender, with the black potato-saucepan on a piece of paper beside it on the white hearth. The fire was red, rather low, the bar dropped, the kettle singing.

On the table was his plate, with potatoes and the remains of the chop; also bread in a basket, salt, and a blue mug with beer. The tablecloth was white oil-cloth. He stood in the shade.

"You are very late," she said. "Do go on eating!"

She sat down on a wooden chair, in the sunlight by the door.

"I had to go to Uthwaite," he said, sitting down at the table but not eating.

"Do eat," she said.

But he did not touch the food.

"Shall y'ave something?" he asked her. "Shall y'ave a cup of tea? t'kettle's on t' boil." He half rose again from his chair.

"If you'll let me make it myself," she said, rising. He seemed sad, and she felt she was bothering him.

"Well, teapot's in there,"—he pointed to a little, drab corner cupboard; "an' cups. An' tea's on th' mantel over yer 'ead."

She got the black teapot, and the tin of tea from the mantelshelf. She rinsed the teapot with hot water, and stood a moment wondering where to empty it.

"Throw it out," he said, aware of her. "It's clean."

She went to the door and threw the drop of water down the path. How lovely it was here, so still, so really woodland. The oaks were putting out ochre yellow leaves; in the garden the red daisies were like red plush buttons. She glanced at the big, hollow sandstone slab of the threshold, now crossed by so few feet.

"But it's lovely here," she said. "Such a beautiful stillness, everything alive and still."

He was eating again, rather slowly and unwillingly, and she could feel he was discouraged. She made the tea in silence, and set the teapot on the hob, as she knew the people did. He pushed his plate aside and went to the back place; she heard a latch click, then he came back with cheese on a plate, and butter.

She set the two cups on the table: there were only two.

"Will you have a cup of tea?" she said.

"If you like. Sugar's in th' cupboard, and there's a little cream-jug. Milk's in a jug in th' pantry."

"Shall I take your plate away?" she asked him. He looked up at her with a faint ironical smile.

"Why . . . if you like," he said, slowly eating bread and cheese. She went to the back, into the penthouse scullery, where the pump was. On the left was a door, no doubt the pantry door. She unlatched it, and almost smiled at the place he called a pantry; a long narrow whitewashed slip of a cupboard. But it managed to contain a little barrel of beer, as well as a few dishes and bits of food. She took a little milk from the yellow jug.

"How do you get your milk?" she asked him, when she came back to the table.

"Flints! They leave me a bottle at the warren end. You know, where I met you!"

But he was discouraged.

She poured out the tea, poising the cream-jug.

"No milk," he said; then he seemed to hear a noise, and looked keenly through the doorway.

" 'Appen we'd better shut," he said.

"It seems a pity," she replied. "Nobody will come, will they?"

"Not unless it's one time in a thousand, but you never know."

"And even then it's no matter," she said. "It's only a cup of tea. Where are the spoons?"

He reached over, and pulled open the table drawer. Connie sat at table in the sunshine of the doorway.

"Flossie!" he said to the dog, who was lying on a little mat at the stair foot. "Go an' hark, hark!"

He lifted his finger, and his "hark!" was very vivid. The dog trotted out to reconnoitre.

"Are you sad today?" she asked him.

He turned his blue eyes quickly and gazed direct on her.

"Sad! No, bored! I had to go getting summonses for two poachers I caught, and oh, well I don't like people."

He spoke cold, good English, and there was anger in his voice.

"Do you hate being a gamekeeper?" she asked.

"Being a gamekeeper, no! So long as I'm left alone. But when I have to go messing around at the police station, and various other places, and waiting for a lot of fools to attend to me . . . oh, well, I get mad . . ." and he smiled, with a certain faint humor.

"Couldn't you be really independent?" she asked.

"Me? I suppose I could, if you mean manage to exist on my pension. I could! But I've got to work, or I should die. That is, I've got to have something that keeps me occupied. And I'm not in a good enough temper to work for myself. It's got to be a sort of job for somebody else, or I should throw it up in a month, out of bad temper. So altogether I'm very well off here, especially lately. . . ."

He laughed at her again, with mocking humor.

"But why are you in a bad temper?" she asked. "Do you mean you are *always* in a bad temper?"

"Pretty well," he said, laughing. "I don't quite digest my bile."

"But what bile?" she said.

"Bile!" he said. "Don't you know what that is?" She was silent, and disappointed. He was taking no notice of her.

"I'm going away for a while next month," she said.

"You are! Where to?"

"Venice."

"Venice! With Sir Clifford? For how long?"

"For a month or so," she replied. "Clifford won't go."

"He'll stay here?" he asked.

"Yes! He hates to travel as he is."

"Ay, poor devil!" he said, with sympathy.

There was a pause.

"You won't forget me when I'm gone, will you?" she asked. Again he lifted his eyes and looked full at her.

"Forget?" he said. "You know nobody forgets. It's not a question of memory."

She wanted to say: "What, then?" but she didn't. Instead, she said in a mute kind of voice: "I told Clifford I might have a child."

Now he really looked at her, intense and searching.

"You did?" he said at last. "And what did he say?"

"Oh, he wouldn't mind. He'd be glad, really, so long as it seemed to be his." She dared not look up at him.

He was silent a long time, then he gazed again on her face.

"No mention of *me,* of course?" he said.

"No. No mention of you," she said.

"No, he'd hardly swallow me as a substitute breeder.—Then where are you supposed to be getting the child?"

"I might have a love affair in Venice," she said.

"You might," he replied slowly. "So that's why you're going?"

"Not to have the love affair," she said, looking up at him, pleading.

"Just the appearance of one," he said.

There was silence. He was staring out of the window, with a faint grin, half mockery, half bitterness, on his face. She hated his grin.

"You've not taken any precautions against having a child then?" he asked her suddenly. "Because I haven't."

"No," she said faintly. "I should hate that."

He looked at her, then again with the peculiar subtle grin out of the window. There was a tense silence.

At last he turned to her and said satirically:

"That was why you wanted me, then, to get a child?"

She hung her head.

"No. Not really," she said.

"What then, *really?*" he asked, rather bitingly.

She looked up at him reproachfully, saying: "I don't know." He broke into a laugh.

"Then I'm damned if I do," he said.

There was a long pause of silence, a cold silence.

"Well," he said at last. "It's as your Ladyship likes. If you get the baby, Sir Clifford's welcome to it. I shan't have lost anything. On the contrary, I've had a very nice experience; very nice, indeed!" And he stretched in a half suppressed sort of yawn. "If you've made use of me," he said, "it's not the first time I've been made use of; and I don't suppose it's ever been as pleasant as this time; though, of course, one can't feel tremendously dignified about it." He stretched again, curiously, his muscles quivering and his jaw oddly set.

"But I didn't make use of you," she said, pleading.

"At your Ladyship's service," he replied.

"No," she said. "I liked your body."

"Did you?" he replied, and he laughed. "Well then, we're quits, because I liked yours."

He looked at her with queer darkened eyes.

"Would you like to go upstairs now?" he asked her, in a strangled sort of voice.

"No, not here. Not now!" she said heavily, though if he had used any power over her, she would have gone, for she had no strength against him.

He turned his face away again, and seemed to forget her.

"I want to touch you like you touch me," she said. "I've never really touched you."

He looked at her, and smiled again. "Now?" he said.

"No! No! Not here! At the hut. Would you mind?"

"How do I touch you?" he asked.

"When you feel me."

He looked at her, and met her heavy, anxious eyes.

"And do you like it when I touch you?" he asked, laughing at her still.

"Yes, do you?" she said.

"Oh, me!" Then he changed his tone. "Yes," he said. "You know without asking." Which was true.

She rose and picked up her hat. "I must go," she said.

"Will you go?" he replied politely.

She wanted him to touch her, to say something to her, but he said nothing, only waited politely.

"Thank you for the tea," she said.

"I haven't thanked your Ladyship for doing me the honors of my teapot," he said.

She went down the path; and he stood in the doorway, faintly grinning. Flossie came running with her tail lifted. And Connie had to plod dumbly across into the wood, knowing he was standing there watching her, with that incomprehensible grin on his face.

She walked home very much downcast and annoyed. She didn't at all like his saying he had been made use of; because, in a sense, it was true. But he oughtn't to have said it. Therefore, again, she was divided between two feelings; resentment against him, and a desire to make it up with him.

She passed a very uneasy and irritated tea-time, and at once went to her room. But when she was there it was no good; she could neither sit nor stand. She would have to do something about it. She would have to go back to the hut; if he was not there, well and good.

She slipped out of the side door, and took her way direct and a little sullen. When she came to the clearing she was terribly uneasy. But there he was again, in his shirt-sleeves, stooping, letting the hens out of the coops, among the chicks that were now growing a little gawky, but were much more trim than hen-chickens.

She went straight across to him.

"You see, I've come!" she said.

"Ay, I see it!" he said, straightening his back, and looking at her with a faint amusement.

"Do you let the hens out now?" she asked.

"Yes, they've sat themselves to skin and bone," he said. "An' now they're not all that anxious to come out an' feed. There's no self in a sitting hen; she's all in the eggs or the chicks."

The poor mother-hens; such blind devotion; even to eggs not their own! Connie looked at them in compassion. A helpless silence fell between the man and the woman.

"Shall us go i' th' 'ut?" he asked.

"Do you want me?" she asked, in a sort of mistrust.

"Ay, if you want to come."

She was silent.

"Come then!" he said.

And she went with him to the hut. It was quite dark when he had shut the door, so he made a small light in the lantern, as before.

"Have you left your underthings off?" he asked her.

"Yes!"

"Ay, well, then I'll take my things off too."

He spread the blankets, putting one at the side for a coverlet. She took off her hat, and shook her hair. He sat down, taking off his shoes and gaiters, and undoing his cord breeches.

"Lie down then!" he said, when he stood in his shirt. She obeyed in silence, and he lay beside her, and pulled the blanket over them both.

"There!" he said.

And he lifted her dress right back, till he came even to her breasts. He kissed them softly, taking the nipples in his lips in tiny caresses.

"Eh, but tha'rt nice, tha'rt nice!" he said, suddenly rubbing his face with a snuggling movement against her warm belly.

And she put her arms round him under his shirt, but she was afraid, afraid of his thin, smooth, naked body, that seemed so powerful, afraid of the violent muscles. She shrank, afraid.

And when he said, with a sort of little sigh: "Eh, tha'rt nice!" something in her quivered, and something in her spirit stiffened in resistance: stiffened from the terribly physical intimacy, and from the peculiar haste of his possession. And this time the sharp ecstasy of her own passion did not overcome her; she lay with her hands inert on his striving body, and do what she might, her spirit seemed to look on from the top of her head, and the butting of his haunches seemed ridiculous to her, and the sort of anxiety of his penis to come to its little evacuating crisis seemed farcical. Yes, this was love, this ridiculous bouncing of the buttocks, and the wilting of the poor insignificant, moist little penis. This was the divine love! After all, the moderns were right when they felt contempt for the performance; for it was a performance. It was quite true, as some poets said, that the God who created man must have had a sinister sense of humor, creating him a reasonable being, yet forcing him to take this ridiculous posture, and driving him with blind craving for this ridiculous performance. Even a Maupassant found it a humiliating anti-climax. Men despised the intercourse act, and yet did it.

Cold and derisive her queer female mind stood apart, and though she lay perfectly still, her impulse was to heave her loins, and throw the man out, escape his ugly grip, and the butting overriding of his absurd haunches. His body was a foolish, impudent, imperfect thing, a little disgusting in its unfinished clumsiness. For surely a complete evolution would eliminate this performance, this "function."

And yet when he had finished, soon over, and lay very still, receding into silence, and a strange, motionless distance, far, farther than the horizon of her awareness, her heart began to weep. She could feel him ebbing away, ebbing away, leaving her there like a stone on the shore. He was withdrawing, his spirit was leaving her. He knew.

And in real grief, tormented by her own double consciousness and reaction, she began to weep. He took no notice, or did not even know. The storm of weeping swelled and shook her, and shook him.

"Ay!" he said. "It was no good that time. You wasn't there."—So he knew! Her sobs became violent.

"But what's amiss?" he said. "It's once in a while that way."

"I . . . I can't love you," she sobbed, suddenly feeling her heart breaking.

"Canna ter? Well, dunna fret! There's no law says tha's got to. Ta'e it for what it is."

He still lay with his hand on her breast. But she had drawn both her hands from him.

His words were small comfort. She sobbed aloud.

"Nay, nay!" he said. "Ta'e the thick wi' th' thin. This wor' a bit o' thin for once."

She wept bitterly, sobbing: "But I want to love you, and I can't. It only seems horrid."

He laughed a little, half bitter, half amused.

"It isna horrid," he said, "even if tha thinks it is. An' tha canna ma'e it horrid. Dunna fret thysen about lovin' me. Tha'lt niver force thysen to 't. There's sure to be a bad nut in a basketful. Tha mun ta'e th' rough wi' th' smooth."

He took his hand away from her breast, not touching her. And now she was untouched she took an almost perverse satisfaction in it. She hated the dialect: the *thee* and the *tha* and the *thysen*. He could get up if he liked, and stand there above her buttoning down those absurd corduroy breeches, straight in front of her. After all, Michaelis had had the decency to turn away. This man was so assured in himself he didn't know what a clown other people found him, a half-bred fellow.

Yet, as he was drawing away, to rise silently and leave her, she clung to him in terror.

"Don't! Don't go! Don't leave me! Don't be cross with me! Hold me! Hold me fast!" she whispered in blind frenzy, not even knowing what she said, and clinging to him with uncanny force. It was from herself she wanted to be saved, from her own inward anger and resistance. Yet how powerful was that inward resistance that possessed her!

He took her in his arms again and drew her to him, and suddenly she became small in his arms, small and nestling. It was gone, and she began to melt in marvellous peace. And as she melted small and wonderful in his arms, she became inifinitely desirable to him, all his blood vessels seemed to scald with intense yet tender desire, for her, for her softness, for the penetrating beauty of her in his arms, passing into his blood. And softly, with that marvellous swoon-like caress of his hand in pure soft desire, softly he stroked the silky slope of her loins, down, down between her soft warm buttocks, coming nearer and nearer to the very quick of her. And she felt him like a flame of desire, yet tender, and she felt herself melting in the flame. She let herself go. She felt his penis risen against her with silent amazing force and assertion, and she let herself go to him. She yielded with a quiver that was like death, she went all open to him. And oh, if he were not tender to her now, how cruel, for she was all open to him and helpless!

She quivered again at the potent inexorable entry inside her, so strange and terrible. It might come with the thrust of a sword in her softly-opened body, and that would be death. She clung in a sudden anguish of terror. But it came with a strange slow thrust of peace, the dark thrust of peace and a ponderous, primordial tenderness, such as made the world in the beginning. And her terror subsided in her breast, her breast dared to be gone in peace, she held nothing. She dared to let go everything, all herself, and be gone in the flood.

And it seemed she was like the sea, nothing but dark waves rising and heaving, heaving with a great swell, so that slowly her whole darkness was in motion, and she was ocean rolling its dark, dumb mass. Oh, and far down inside her the deeps parted and rolled asunder, in long, far-travelling billows, and ever, at the quick of her, the depths parted and rolled asunder, from the center of soft plunging, as the plunger went deeper and deeper, touching lower, and she was deeper and deeper and deeper disclosed, and heavier the billows of her rolled away to some shore, uncovering her, and closer and closer plunged the palpable unknown, and further and further rolled the waves of herself away from herself, leaving her, till suddenly, in a soft, shuddering convulsion, the quick of all her plasm was touched, she knew herself touched, the consummation was upon her, and she was gone. She was gone, she was not, and she was born: a woman.

Ah, too lovely, too lovely! In the ebbing she realized all the loveliness. Now all her body clung with tender love to the unknown man, and blindly to the wilting penis, as it so tenderly, frailly, unknowingly withdrew, after the fierce thrust of its potency. As it drew out and left her body, the secret, sensitive thing, she gave an unconscious cry of pure loss, and she tried to put it back. It had been so perfect! And she loved it so!

And only now she became aware of the small, bud-like reticence and tenderness of the penis, and a little cry of wonder and poignancy escaped her again, her woman's heart crying out over the tender frailty of that which had been the power.

"It was so lovely!" she moaned. "It was so lovely!" But he said nothing, only softly kissed her, lying still above her. And she moaned with a sort of bliss, as a sacrifice, and a new-born thing.

And now in her heart the queer wonder of him was awakened. A man! the strange potency of manhood upon her! Her hands strayed over him, still a little afraid. Afraid of that strange, hostile, slightly repulsive thing that he had been to her, a man. And now she touched him, and it was the sons of god with the daughters of men. How beautiful he felt, how pure in tissue! How lovely, how lovely, strong, and yet pure and delicate, such stillness of the sensitive body! Such utter stillness of potency and delicate flesh! How beautiful! How beautiful! Her hands came timorously down his back to the soft, smallish globes of the buttocks. Beauty! What beauty! a sudden little flame of new awareness went through her. How was it possible this beauty here, where she had previously been repelled? The unspeakable beauty to the touch, of the warm, living buttocks! The life within life, the sheer warm, potent loveliness. And the strange weight of the balls between his legs! What a mystery! What a strange heavy weight of mystery, that could lie soft and heavy in one's hand! The roots, root of all that is lovely, the primeval root of all full beauty.

She clung to him, with a hiss of wonder that was almost awe, terror. He held her close, but he said nothing. He would never say anything. She crept nearer to him, nearer, only to be near the sensual wonder of him. And out of his utter, incomprehensible stillness, she felt again the slow, momentous, surging rise of the phallus again, the other power. And her heart melted out with a kind of awe.

And this time his being within her was all soft and iridescent, purely soft and iridescent, such as no consciousness could seize. Her whole self quivered unconscious and alive, like plasm. She could not know what it was. She could not remember what it had been. Only that it had been more lovely than anything ever could be. Only that. And afterwards she was utterly still, utterly unknowing, she was not aware for how long. And he was still with her, in an unfathomable silence along with her. And of this, they would never speak.

When awareness of the outside began to come back, she clung to his breast, murmuring: "My love! my love!" And he held her silently. And she curled on his breast, perfect.

But his silence was fathomless. His hands held her like flowers, so still and strange. "Where are you?" she whispered to him. "Where are you? Speak to me! Say something to me!"

He kissed her softly, murmuring: "Ay, my lass!"

But she did not know what he meant, she did not know where he was. In his silence he seemed lost to her.

"You love me, don't you?" she murmured.

"Ay, tha knows!" he said.

"But tell me!" she pleaded.

"Ay! Ay! 'asn't ter felt it?" he said dimly, but softly and surely. And she clung close to him, closer. He was so much more peaceful in love than she was, and she wanted him to reassure her.

"You do love me!" she whispered, assertive. And his hands stroked her softly, as if she were a flower, without the quiver of desire, but with delicate nearness. And still there haunted her a restless necessity to get a grip on love.

"Say you'll always love me!" she pleaded.

"Ay!" he said, abstractedly. And she felt her questions driving him away from her.

"Mustn't we get up?" he said at last.

"No!" she said.

But she could feel his consciousness straying, listening to the noises outside.

"It'll be nearly dark," he said. And she heard the pressure of circumstance in his voice. She kissed him, with a woman's grief at yielding up her hour.

He rose, and turned up the lantern, then began to pull on his clothes, quickly disappearing inside them. Then he stood there, above her, fastening his breeches and looking down at her with dark, wide eyes, his face a little flushed and his hair ruffled, curiously warm and still and beautiful in the dim light of the lantern, so beautiful, she would never tell him how beautiful. It made her want to cling fast to him, to hold him, for there was a warm, half-sleepy remoteness in his beauty that made her want to cry out and clutch him, to have him. She would never have him. So she lay on the blanket with curved, soft naked haunches, and he had no idea what she was thinking, but to him she too was beautiful, the soft, marvellous thing he could go into, beyond everything.

"I love thee that I can go into thee," he said.

"Do you like me?" she said, her heart beating.

"It heals it all up, that I can go into thee. I love thee that tha opened to me. I love thee that I came into thee like that."

He bent down and kissed her soft flank, rubbed his cheek against it, then covered it up.

"And will you never leave me?" she said.

"Dunna ask them things," he said.

"But you do believe I love you?" she said.

"Tha loved me just now, wider than iver tha thout tha would. But who knows what'll 'appen, once tha starts thinkin' about it!"

"No, don't say those things!—And you don't really think that I wanted to make use of you, do you?"

"How?"

"To have a child—?"

"Now anybody can 'ave any childt i' th' world," he said, as he sat down fastening on his leggings.

"Ah no!" she cried. "You don't mean it?"

"Eh well!" he said, looking at her under his brows. "This wor t' best."

She lay still. He softly opened the door. The sky was dark blue, with crystalline, turquoise rim. He went out, to shut up the hens, speaking softly to his dog. And she lay and wondered at the wonder of life, and of being.

When he came back she was still lying there, glowing like a gipsy. He sat on the stool by her.

"Tha mun come one naight ter th' cottage, afore tha goos; sholl ter?" he asked, lifting his eyebrows as he looked at her, his hands dangling between his knees.

"Sholl ter?" she echoed, teasing.

He smiled.

"Ay, sholl ter?" he repeated.

"Ay!" she said, imitating the dialect sound.

"Yi!" he said.

"Yi!" she repeated.

"An' slaip wi' me," he said. "It needs that. When sholt come?"

"When sholl I?" she said.

"Nay," he said, "tha canna do't. When sholt come then?"

" 'Appen Sunday," she said.

" 'Appen a' Sunday! Ay!"

He laughed at her quickly.

"Nay, tha canna," he protested.

"Why canna I?" she said.

He laughed. Her attempts at the dialect were so ludicrous, somehow.

"Coom then, tha mun goo!" he said.

"Mun I?" she said.

"Maun Ah!" he corrected.

"Why should I say *maun* when you say *mun*," she protested. "You're not playing fair."

"Arena Ah!" he said, leaning forward and softly stroking her face.

"Th'art good cunt, though, are'nt ter? Best bit o' cunt left on earth. When ter likes! When tha'rt willin'!"

"What is cunt?" she said.

"An' doesn't ter know? Cunt! It's thee down theer; an' what I get when I'm i'side thee; it's a' as it is, all on't."

"All on't," she teased. "Cunt! It's like fuck then."

"Nay, nay! Fuck's only what you do. Animals fuck. But cunt's a lot more than that. It's thee, dost see: an' tha'rt a lot besides an animal, aren't ter? even ter fuck! Cunt! Eh, that's the beauty o' thee, lass."

She got up and kissed him between the eyes that looked at her so dark and soft and unspeakably warm, so unbearably beautiful.

"Is it?" she said. "And do you care for me?"

He kissed her without answering.

"Tha mun goo, let me dust thee," he said.

His hand passed over the curves of her body, firmly, without desire, but with soft, intimate knowledge.

As she ran home in the twilight the world seemed a dream; the trees in the park seemed bulging and surging at anchor on a tide, and the heave of the slope to the house was alive.

Chapter Thirteen

On Sunday Clifford wanted to go into the wood. It was a lovely morning, the pear blossom and plum had suddenly appeared in the world in a wonder of white here and there.

It was cruel for Clifford, while the world bloomed, to have to be helped from chair to bath-chair. But he had forgotten, and even seemed to have a certain conceit of himself in his lameness. Connie still suffered, having to lift his inert legs into place. Mrs. Bolton did it now, or Field.

She waited for him at the top of the drive, at the edge of the screen of beeches. His chair came puffing along with a sort of valetudinarian slow importance. As he joined his wife he said:

"Sir Clifford on his foaming steed!"

"Snorting, at least!" she laughed.

He stopped and looked around at the facade of the long, low old brown house.

"Wragby doesn't wink an eyelid!" he said. "But then why should it? I ride upon the achievements of the mind of man, and that beats a horse."

"I suppose it does. And the souls in Plato riding up to heaven in a two-horse chariot would go in a Ford car now," she said.

"Or a Rolls-Royce: Plato was an aristocrat!"

"Quite! No more black horse to thrash and maltreat. Plato never thought we'd go one better than his black steed and his white steed, and have no steeds at all, only an engine!"

"Only an engine and gas!" said Clifford.

"I hope I can have some repairs done to the old place next year. I think I shall have about a thousand to spare for that: but work costs so much!" he added.

"Oh, good!" said Connie. "If only there aren't more strikes!"

"What would be the use of their striking again! Merely ruin the industry, what's left of it: and surely the owls are beginning to see it!"

"Perhaps they don't mind ruining the industry," said Connie.

"Ah, don't talk like a woman! The industry fills their bellies, even if it can't keep their pockets quite so flush," he said, using terms of speech that oddly had a twang of Mrs. Bolton.

"But didn't you say the other day that you were a conservative-anarchist?" she asked innocently.

"And did you understand what I meant?" he retorted. "All I meant is, people can be what they like and feel what they like and do what they like, strictly privately, so long as they keep the *form* of life intact, and the apparatus."

Connie walked on in silence a few paces. Then she said, obstinately:

"It sounds like saying an egg may go as addled as it likes, so long as it keeps its shell on whole. But addled eggs do break of themselves."

"I don't think people are eggs," he said. "Not even angels' eggs, my dear little evangelist."

He was in rather high feather this bright morning. The larks were trilling away over the park, the distant pit in the hollow was fuming silent steam. It was almost like old days, before the war. Connie didn't really want to argue. But then she did not really want to go to the wood with Clifford either. So she walked beside his chair in a certain obstinacy of spirit.

"No," he said. "There will be no more strikes, if the thing is properly managed."

"Why not?"

"Because strikes will be made as good as impossible."

"But will the men let you?" she asked.

"We shan't ask them. We shall do it while they aren't looking: for their own good, to save the industry."

"For your own good, too," she said.

"Naturally! For the good of everybody. But for their good even more than mine. I can live without the pits. They can't. They'll starve if there are no pits. I've got other provision."

They looked up the shallow valley at the mine, and beyond it, at the black-lidded houses of Tevershall crawling like some serpent up the hill. From the old brown church the bells were ringing: Sunday, Sunday, Sunday!

"But will the men let you dictate terms?" she said.

"My dear, they will have to: if one does it gently."

"But mightn't there be a mutual understanding?"

"Absolutely: when they realize that the industry comes before the individual."

"But must you own the industry?" she said.

"I don't. But to the extent I do own it, yes, most decidedly. The ownership of property has now become a religious question: as it has been since Jesus and St. Francis. The point is *not:* take all thou hast and give to the poor, but use all thou hast to encourage the industry and give work to the poor. It's the only way to feed all the mouths and clothe all the bodies. Giving away all we have to the poor spells starvation for the poor just as much as for us. And universal starvation is no high aim. Even general poverty is no lovely thing. Poverty is ugly."

"But the disparity?"

"That is fate. Why is the star Jupiter bigger than the star Neptune? You can't start altering the make-up of things!"

"But when this envy and jealousy and discontent has once started," she began.

"Do your best to stop it. Somebody's *got* to be boss of the show."

"But who is the boss of the show?" she asked.

"The men who own and run the industries."

There was a long silence.

"It seems to me they're a bad boss," she said.

"Then you suggest what they should do."

"They don't take their boss-ship seriously enough," she said.

"They take it far more seriously than you take your ladyship," he said.

"That's thrust upon me. I don't really want it," she blurted out. He stopped the chair and looked at her.

"Who's shirking their responsibility now!" he said. "Who is trying to get away *now* from the responsibility of their own boss-ship, as you call it?"

"But I don't want any boss-ship," she protested.

"Ah! But that is funk. You've got it: fated to it. And you should live up to it. Who has given the colliers all they have that's worth having; all their political liberty, and their education, such as it is; their sanitation, their health-conditions, their books, their music, everything? Who has given it to them? Have colliers given it to the colliers? No! All the Wragbys and Shipleys in England have given their part, and must go on giving. There's your responsibility."

Connie listened, and flushed very red.

"I'd like to give something," she said. "But I'm not allowed. Everything is to be sold and paid for now; and all the things you mention now, Wragby and Shipley *sell* them to the people, at a good profit. Everything is sold. You don't give one heart-beat of real sympathy. And besides, who has taken away from the people their natural life and manhood, and given them this industrial horror? Who has done that?"

"And what must I do?" he asked, green. "Ask them to come and pillage me?"

"Why is Tevershall so ugly, so hideous? Why are their lives so hopeless?"

"They built their own Tevershall. That's part of their display of freedom. They built themselves their pretty Tevershall, and they live their own pretty lives. I can't live their lives for them. Every beetle must live its own life."

"But you make them work for you. They live the life of your coal mine."

"Not at all. Every beetle finds its own food. Not one man is forced to work for me."

"Their lives are industrialized and hopeless, and so are ours," she cried.

"I don't think they are. That's just a romantic figure of speech, a relic of the swooning and die-away romanticism. You don't look at all a hopeless figure standing there, Connie, my dear."

Which was true. For her dark blue eyes were flashing, color was hot in her cheeks, she looked full of a rebellious passion far from the dejection of hopelessness. She noticed, in the tussocky places of the grass, cottony young cowslips standing up still bleared in their down. And she wondered with rage, why it was she felt Clifford was so *wrong,* yet she couldn't say it to him, she could not say exactly *where* he was wrong.

"No wonder the men hate you," she said.

"They don't!" he replied. "And don't fall into errors: in your sense of the word, they are *not* men. They are animals you don't understand and never could. Don't thrust your illusions on other people. The masses were always the same, and will always be the same. Nero's slaves were extremely little different from our colliers or the Ford motor-car workmen. I mean Nero's mine slaves and his field slaves. It is the masses: they are the unchangeable. An individual may emerge from the masses. But the emergence doesn't alter the mass. The masses are unalterable. It is one of the most momentous facts of social science. *Panem et circenses!* Only today education is one of the bad substitutes for a circus. What is wrong today is that we've made a profound hash of the circuses part of the program, and poisoned our masses with a little education."

When Clifford became really aroused in his feelings about the common people, Connie was frightened. There was something devastatingly true in what he said. But it was a truth that killed.

Seeing her pale and silent, Clifford started the chair again, and no more was said till he halted again at the wood gate, which she opened.

"And what we need to take up now," he said, "is whips, not swords. The masses have been ruled since time began, and, till time ends, ruled they will have to be. It is sheer hypocrisy and farce to say they can rule themselves."

"But can you rule them?" she asked.

"I? Oh, yes! Neither my mind nor my will is crippled, and I don't rule with my legs. I can do my share of ruling: absolutely, my share; and give me a son, and he will be able to rule his portion after me."

"But he wouldn't be your own son, of your own ruling class; or, perhaps not," she stammered.

"I don't care who his father may be, so long as he is a healthy man not below normal intelligence. Give me the child of any healthy, normally intelligent man, and I will make a perfectly competent Chatterley of him. It is not who begets us that matters, but where fate places us. Place any child among the ruling classes, and he will grow up, to his own extent, a ruler. Put kings' and dukes' children among the masses, and they'll be little plebians, mass products. It is the overwhelming pressure of environment."

"Then the common people aren't a race, and the aristocrats aren't blood," she said.

"No, my child! All that is romantic illusion. Aristocracy is a function, a part of fate. And the masses are a functioning of another part of fate. The individual hardly matters. It is a question of which function you are brought up to and adapted to. It is not the individuals that make an aristocracy: it is the functioning of the aristocratic whole. And it is the functioning of the whole mass that makes the common man what he is."

"Then there is no common humanity between us all!"

"Just as you like. We all need to fill our bellies. But when it comes to expressive or executive functioning, I believe there is a gulf and an absolute one, between the ruling and the serving classes. The two functions are opposed. And the function determines the individual."

Connie looked at him with dazed eyes.

"Won't you come on?" she said.

And he started his chair. He had said his say. Now he lapsed into his peculiar and rather vacant apathy, that Connie found so trying. In the wood, anyhow, she was determined not to argue.

In front of them ran the open cleft of the riding, between the hazel walls and the grey trees. The chair puffed slowly on, slowly surging into the forget-me-nots that rose up in the drive like milk froth, beyond the hazel shadows. Clifford steered the middle course, where feet passing had kept a channel through the flowers. But Connie, walking behind, had watched the wheels jolt over the woodruff and the bugle, and squash the little yellow cups of the creeping-jenny. Now they made a wake through the forget-me-nots.

All the flowers were there, the first bluebells in blue pools, like standing water.

"You are quite right about its being beautiful," said Clifford. "It is so amazingly. What is *quite* so lovely as an English spring!"

Connie thought it sounded as if even the spring bloomed by Act of Parliament. An English spring! Why not an Irish one? or Jewish? The chair moved slowly ahead, past tufts of sturdy bluebells that stood up like wheat and over grey burdock leaves. Then they came to the open place where the trees had been felled, the light flooded in rather stark. And the bluebells made sheets of bright blue color, here and there, sheering off into lilac and purple. And between, the bracken was lifting its brown curled heads, like legions of young snakes with a new secret to whisper to Eve.

Clifford kept the chair going till he came to the brow of the hill; Connie followed slowly behind. The oak buds were opening soft and brown. Everything came tenderly out of the old hardness. Even the snaggy craggy oak trees put out the softest leaves, spreading thin, brown little wings like young bat wings in the light. Why had men never any newness in them, any freshness to come forth with? Stale men!

Clifford stopped the chair at the top of the rise and looked down. The bluebells washed blue like flood-water over the broad riding, and lit up the down-hill with a warm blueness.

"It's a very fine color in itself," said Clifford, "but useless for making a painting."

"Quite!" said Connie, completely uninterested.

"Shall I venture as far as the spring?" said Clifford.

"Will the chair get up again?" she said.

"We'll try; nothing venture, nothing win!"

And the chair began to advance slowly, joltingly down the beautiful broad riding washed over with blue encroaching hyacinths. Oh last of all ships, through the hyacinthian shallows! Oh pinnace on the last wild waters, sailing on the last voyage of our civilization! Whither, Oh weird wheeled ship, your slow course steering! Quiet and complacent, Clifford sat at the wheel of adventure: in his old black hat and tweed jacket, motionless and cautious. Oh captain, my Captain, our splendid trip is done! Not yet though! Downhill in the wake, came Constance in her grey dress, watching the chair jolt downwards.

They passed the narrow track to the hut. Thank heaven it was not wide enough for the chair: hardly wide enough for one person. The chair reached the bottom of the slope, and swerved round, to disappear. And Connie heard a low whistle behind her. She glanced sharply round: the keeper was striding down-hill towards her, his dog keeping behind him.

"Is Sir Clifford going to the cottage?" he asked, looking into her eyes.

"No, only to the well."

"Ah! Good! Then I can keep out of sight. But I shall see you tonight. I shall wait for you at the park gate about ten."

He looked again direct into her eyes.

"Yes," she faltered.

They heard the Papp! Papp! of Clifford's horn, tooting for Connie. She "Coo-eed!" in reply. The keeper's face flickered with a little grimace, and with his hand he softly brushed her breast upwards, from underneath. She looked at him, frightened, and started running down the hill, calling Coo-ee! again to Clifford. The man above watched her, then turned, grinning faintly, back into his path.

She found Clifford slowly mounting to the spring, which was half-way up the slope of the dark larch-wood. He was there by the time she caught him up.

"She did that all right," he said, referring to the chair.

Connie looked at the great grey leaves of burdock that grew out ghostly from the edge of the larch-wood. The people call it Robin Hood's Rhubarb. How silent and gloomy it seemed by the well! Yet the water bubbled so bright, wonderful! And there were bits of eye-bright and strong blue bugle. And there, under the bank, the yellow earth was moving. A mole! It emerged, rowing its pink hands, and waving its blind gimlet of a face, with the tiny nose-tip uplifted.

"It seems to see with the end of its nose," said Connie.

"Better than with its eyes!" he said. "Will you drink?"

"Will you?"

She took an enamel mug from a twig on a tree, and stooped to fill it for him. He drank in sips. Then she stooped again, and drank a little herself.

"So icy!" she said, gasping.

"Good, isn't it! Did you wish?"

"Did you?"

"Yes, I wished. But I won't tell."

She was aware of the rapping of a woodpecker, then of the wind, soft and eerie through the larches. She looked up. White clouds were crossing the blue.

"Clouds!" she said.

"White lambs only," he replied.

A shadow crossed the little clearing. The mole had swum out on to the soft yellow earth.

"Unpleasant little beast, we ought to kill him," said Clifford.

"Look! he's like a parson in a pulpit," said she.

She gathered some sprigs of woodruff and brought them to him.

"New-mown hay!" he said. "Doesn't it smell like the romantic ladies of the last century, who had their heads screwed on the right way after all!"

She was looking at the white clouds.

"I wonder if it will rain," she said.

"Rain! Why! Do you want it to?"

They started on the return journey, Clifford jolting cautiously down-hill. They came to the dark bottom of the hollow, turned to the right, and after a hundred yards swerved up the foot of the long slope, where bluebells stood in the light.

"Now, old girl!" said Clifford, putting the chair to it.

It was a steep and jolty climb. The chair plugged slowly, in a struggling unwilling fashion. Still, she nosed her way up unevenly, till she came to where the hyacinths were all around her, then she balked, struggled, jerked a little way out of the flowers, then stopped.

"We'd better sound the horn and see if the keeper will come," said Connie. "He could push her a bit. For that matter, I will push. It helps."

"We'll let her breathe," said Clifford. "Do you mind putting a scotch under the wheel?"

Connie found a stone, and they waited. After a while Clifford started his motor again, then set the chair in motion. It struggled and faltered like a sick thing, with curious noises.

"Let me push!" said Connie, coming up behind.

"No! Don't push!" he said angrily. "What's the good of the damned thing, if it has to be pushed! Put the stone under!"

There was another pause, then another start; but more ineffectual than before.

"You *must* let me push," she said. "Or sound the horn for the keeper."

"Wait!"

She waited; and he had another try, doing more harm than good.

"Sound the horn, then, if you won't let me push," she said.

"Hell! Be quiet a moment!"

She was quiet a moment: he made shattering efforts with the little motor.

"You'll only break the thing down altogether, Clifford," she remonstrated: "besides wasting your nervous energy."

"If I could only get out and look at the damned thing!" he said, exasperated. And he sounded the horn stridently. "Perhaps Mellors can see what's wrong."

They waited, among the mashed flowers under a sky softly curdling with clouds. In the silence a wood-pigeon began to coo, roo-hoo hoo! roo-hoo hoo! Clifford shut her up with a blast on the horn.

The keeper appeared directly, striding inquiringly round the corner. He saluted.

"Do you know anything about motors?" asked Clifford sharply.

"I'm afraid I don't. Has she gone wrong?"

"Apparently!" snapped Clifford.

The man crouched solicitously by the wheel, and peered at the little engine.

"I'm afraid I know nothing at all about these mechanical things, Sir Clifford," he said calmly. "If she has enough petrol and oil—"

"Just look carefully and see if you can see anything broken," snapped Clifford.

The man laid his gun against a tree, took off his coat and threw it beside it. The brown dog sat guard. Then he sat down on his heels and peered under the chair, poking with his finger at the greasy little engine, and resenting the grease-marks on his clean Sunday shirt.

"Doesn't seem anything broken," he said. And he stood up, pushing back his hat from his forehead, rubbing his brow and apparently studying.

"Have you looked at the rods underneath?" asked Clifford. "See if they are all right!"

The man lay flat on his stomach on the floor, his neck pressed back, wriggling under the engine and poking with his finger. Connie thought what a pathetic sort of thing a man was, feeble and small looking, when he was lying on his belly on the big earth.

"Seems all right as far as I can see," came his muffled voice.

"I don't suppose you can do anything," said Clifford.

"Seems as if I can't!" And he scrambled up and sat on his heels, collier fashion. "There's certainly nothing obviously broken."

Clifford started his engine, then put her in gear. She would not move.

"Run her a bit hard, like," suggested the keeper.

Clifford resented the interference: but he made his engine buzz like a bluebottle. Then she coughed and snarled and seemed to go better.

"Sounds as if she'd come clear," said Mellors.

But Clifford had already jerked her into gear. She gave a sick lurch and ebbed weakly forwards.

"If I give her a push, she'll do it," said the keeper, going behind.

"Keep off!" snapped Clifford. "She'll do it by herself."

"But Clifford!" put in Connie from the bank, "you know it's too much for her. Why are you so obstinate!"

Clifford was pale with anger. He jabbed at his levers. The chair gave a sort of scurry, reeled on a few more yards, and came to her end amid a particularly promising patch of bluebells.

"She's done!" said the keeper. "Not power enough."

"She's been up here before," said Clifford coldly.

"She won't do it this time," said the keeper.

Clifford did not reply. He began doing things with his engine, running her fast and slow as if to get some sort of tune out of her. The wood re-echoed with weird noises. Then he put her in gear with a jerk, having jerked off his brake.

"You'll rip her inside out," murmured the keeper.

The chair charged in a sick lurch sideways at the ditch.

"Clifford!" cried Connie, rushing forward.

But the keeper had got the chair by the rail. Clifford, however, putting on all his pressure, managed to steer into the riding, and with a strange noise the chair was fighting the hill. Mellors pushed steadily behind, and up she went, as if to retrieve herself.

"You see, she's doing it!" said Clifford victorious, glancing over his shoulder. There he saw the keeper's face.

"Are you pushing her?"

"She won't do it without."

"Leave her alone. I asked you not."

"She won't do it."

"Let her try!" snarled Clifford, with all his emphasis.

The keeper stood back: then turned to fetch his coat and gun. The chair seemed to strangle immediately. She stood inert. Clifford, seated a prisoner, was white with vexation. He jerked at the levers with his hand, his feet were no good. He got queer noises out of her. In savage impatience he moved little handles and got more noises out of her. But she would not budge. No, she would not budge. He stopped the engine and sat rigid with anger.

Constance sat on the bank and looked at the wretched and trampled bluebells. "Nothing quite so lovely as an English spring." "I can do my share of ruling." "What we need to take up now is whips, not swords." "The ruling classes!"

The keeper strode up with his coat and gun, Flossie cautiously at his heels. Clifford asked the man to do something or other to the engine. Connie, who understood nothing at all of the technicalities of motors, and who had had experience of breakdowns, sat patiently on the bank as if she were a cipher. The keeper lay on his stomach again. The ruling classes and the serving classes!

He got to his feet and said patiently:

"Try her again, then."

He spoke in a quiet voice, almost as if to a child.

Clifford tried her, and Mellors stepped quickly behind and began to push. She was going, the engine doing about half the work, the man the rest.

Clifford glanced round yellow with anger.

"Will you get off there!"

The keeper dropped his hold at once, and Clifford added: "How shall I know what she is doing!"

The man put his gun down and began to pull on his coat. He'd done.

The chair began slowly to run backwards.

"Clifford, your brake!" cried Connie.

She, Mellors, and Clifford moved at once, Connie and the keeper jostling lightly. The chair stood. There was a moment of dead silence.

"It's obvious I'm at everybody's mercy!" said Clifford. He was yellow with anger.

No one answered. Mellors was slinging his gun over his shoulder, his face queer and expressionless, save for an abstracted look of patience. The dog Flossie, standing on guard almost between her master's legs, moved uneasily, eyeing the chair with great suspicion and dislike, and very much perplexed between the three human beings. The *tableau vivant* remained set among the squashed bluebells, nobody proffering a word.

"I expect she'll have to be pushed," said Clifford at last, with an affectation of *sang froid*.

No answer. Mellors' abstracted face looked as if he had heard nothing. Connie glanced anxiously at him. Clifford, too, glanced round.

"Do you mind pushing her home, Mellors!" he said in a cold, superior tone. "I hope I have said nothing to offend you," he added, in a tone of dislike.

"Nothing at all, Sir Clifford! Do you want me to push that chair?"

"If you please."

The man stepped up to it: but this time it was without effect. The brake was jammed. They poked and pulled, and the keeper took off his gun and his coat once more. And now Clifford said never a word. At last the keeper heaved the back of the chair off the ground, and with an instantaneous push of his foot, tried to loosen the wheels. He failed, the chair sank. Clifford was clutching the sides. The man gasped with the weight.

"Don't do it!" cried Connie to him.

"If you'll pull the wheel that way, so!" he said to her, showing her how.

"No! You mustn't lift it! You'll strain yourself," she said, flushed now with anger.

But he looked into her eyes and nodded. And she had to go and take hold of the wheel, ready. He heaved and she tugged, and the chair reeled.

"For God's sake!" cried Clifford in terror.

But it was all right, and the brake was off. The keeper put a stone under the wheel, and went to sit on the bank, his heart beating and his face white with the effort, semiconscious. Connie looked at him, and almost cried with anger. There was a pause and a dead silence. She saw his hands trembling on his thighs.

"Have you hurt yourself?" she asked, going to him.

"No. No!" he turned away almost angrily.

There was dead silence. The back of Clifford's fair head did not move. Even the dog stood motionless. The sky had clouded over.

At last he sighed, and blew his nose on his red handkerchief.

"That pneumonia took a lot out of me," he said.

No one answered. Connie calculated the amount of strength it must have taken to heave up that chair and the bulky Clifford: too much, far too much! If it hadn't killed him!

He rose, and again picked up his coat, slinging it through the handle of the chair.

"Are you ready, then, Sir Clifford?"

"When you are!"

He stooped and took out the scotch, then put his weight against the chair. He was paler than Connie had ever seen him: and more absent. Clifford was a heavy man: and the hill was steep. Connie stepped to the keeper's side.

"I'm going to push too!" she said.

And she began to shove with a woman's turbulent energy of anger. The chair went faster. Clifford looked round.

"Is that necessary?" he said.

"Very! Do you want to kill the man! If you'd let the motor work while it would—"

But she did not finish. She was already panting. She slackened off a little, for it was surprisingly hard work.

"Ay! slower!" said the man at her side, with a faint smile of the eyes.

"Are you sure you've not hurt yourself?" she said fiercely.

He shook his head. She looked at his smallish, short, alive hand, browned by the weather. It was the hand that caressed her. She had never even looked at it before. It seemed so still, like him, with a curious inward stillness that made her want to clutch it, as if she could not reach it. All her soul suddenly swept towards him: he was so silent, and out of reach! And he felt his limbs revive. Shoving with his left hand, he laid his right on her round white wrist, softly enfolding her wrist, with caress. And the flame of strength went down his back and his loins, reviving him. And she bent suddenly and kissed his hand. Meanwhile the back of Clifford's head was held sleek and motionless, just in front of them.

At the top of the hill they rested, and Connie was glad to let go. She had had fugitive dreams of friendship between these two men: one her husband, the other the father of her child. Now she saw the screaming absurdity of her dreams. The two males were as hostile as fire and water. They mutually exterminated one another. And she realized for the first time, what a queer subtle thing hate is. For the first time, she had consciously and definitely hated Clifford, with vivid hate: as if he ought to be obliterated from the face of the earth. And it was strange, how free and full of life it made her feel, to hate him and to admit it fully to herself.—"Now, I've hated him, I shall never be able to go on living with him," came the thought into her mind.

On the level the keeper could push the chair alone. Clifford made a little conversation with her, to show his complete composure: about Aunt Eva, who was at Dieppe, and about Sir Malcolm, who had written to ask would Connie drive with him in his small car, to Venice, or would she and Hilda go by train.

"I'd much rather go by train," said Connie. "I don't like long motor drives, especially when there's dust. But I shall see what Hilda wants."

"She will want to drive her own car, and take you with her," he said.

"Probably!—I must help up here. You've no idea how heavy this chair is."

She went to the back of his chair, and plodded side by side with the keeper, shoving up the pink path. She did not care who saw.

"Why not let me wait, and fetch Field. He is strong enough for the job," said Clifford.

"It's so near," she panted.

But both she and Mellors wiped the sweat from their faces when they came to the top. It was curious, but this bit of work together had brought them much closer than they had been before.

"Thanks so much, Mellors," said Clifford, when they were at the house door. "I must get a different sort of motor, that's all. Won't you go to the kitchen and have a meal? it must be about time."

"Thank you, Sir Clifford. I was going to my mother for dinner today, Sunday."

"As you like."

Mellors slung into his coat, looked at Connie, saluted, and was gone. Connie, furious, went upstairs.

At lunch she could not contain her feelings.

"Why are you so abominably inconsiderate, Clifford?" she said to him.

"Of whom?"

"Of the keeper! If that is what you call the ruling classes, I'm sorry for you."

"Why?"

"A man who's been ill, and isn't strong! My word, if I were the serving classes, I'd let you wait for service. I'd let you whistle."

"I quite believe it."

"If he'd been sitting in a chair with paralyzed legs, and behaved as you behaved, what would you have done for *him?*"

"My dear evangelist, this confusing of persons and personalities is in bad taste."

"And your nasty, sterile want of common sympathy is in the worst taste imaginable. *Noblesse oblige!* You and your ruling class!"

"And to what should it oblige me? To have a lot of unnecessary emotions about my gamekeeper? I refuse. I leave it all to my evangelist."

"As if he weren't a man as much as you are, my word!"

"My gamekeeper to boot, and I pay him two pounds a week and give him a house."

"Pay him! What do you think you pay him for, with two pounds a week and a house?"

"His services."

"Bah! I would tell you to keep your two pounds a week and your house."

"Probably he would like to; but can't afford the luxury!"

"You and *rule!*" she said. "You don't rule, don't flatter yourself. You have only got more than your share of the money, and make people work for you for two pounds a week, or threaten them with starvation. Rule! What do you give forth of rule? Why, you're dried up! You only bully with your money, like any Jew or any Schieber!"

"You are very elegant in your speech, Lady Chatterley!"

"I assure you, you were very elegant altogether out there in the wood. I was utterly ashamed of you. Why, my father is ten times the human being you are: you *gentleman!*"

He reached and rang the bell for Mrs. Bolton. But he was yellow at the gills.

She went up to her room, furious, saying to herself: "Him and buying people! Well, he doesn't buy me, and therefore there's no need for me to stay with him. Dead fish of a gentleman, with his celluloid soul! And how they take one in, with their manners and their mock wistfulness and gentleness. They've got about as much feeling as celluloid has."

She made her plans for the night, and determined to get Clifford off her mind. She didn't want to hate him. She didn't want to be mixed up very intimately with him in any sort of feeling. She wanted him not to know anything at all about herself: and especially, not to know anything about her feeling for the keeper. This squabble of her attitude to the servants was an old one. He found her too familiar, she found him stupidly insentient, tough and india rubbery where other people were concerned.

She went downstairs calmly, with her old demure bearing, at dinner time. He was still yellow at the gills: in for one of his liver bouts, when he was really very queer.—He was reading a French book.

"Have you ever read Proust?" he asked her.

"I've tried, but he bores me."

"He's really very extraordinary."

"Possibly! But he bores me: all that sophistication! He doesn't have feelings, he only has streams of words about feelings. I'm tired of self-important mentalities."

"Would you prefer self-important animalities?"

"Perhaps! But one might possibly get something that wasn't self-important."

"Well, I like Proust's subtlety and his well-bred anarchy."

"It makes you very dead, really."

"There speaks my evangelical little wife."

They were at it again, at it again! But she couldn't help fighting him. He seemed to sit there like a skeleton, sending out a skeleton's cold grizzly *will* against her. Almost she could feel the skeleton clutching her and pressing her to its cage of ribs. He, too, was really up in arms: and she was a little afraid of him.

She went upstairs as soon as possible, and went to bed quite early. But at half-past nine she got up, and went outside to listen. There was no sound. She slipped on a dressing-gown and went downstairs. Clifford and Mrs. Bolton were playing cards, gambling. They would probably go on until midnight.

Connie returned to her room, threw her pajamas on the tossed bed, put on a thin tennis-dress and over that a woolen day-dress, put on rubber tennis-shoes, and then a light coat. And she was ready. If she met anybody, she was just going out for a few minutes. And in the morning, when she came in again, she would just have been for a little walk in the dew, as she fairly often did before breakfast. For the rest, the only danger was that someone should go into her room during the night. But that was most unlikely: not one chance in a hundred.

Betts had not yet locked up. He fastened up the house at ten o'clock, and unfastened it again at seven in the morning. She slipped out silently and unseen. There was a half-moon shining, enough to make a little light in the world, not enough to show her up in her dark-grey coat. She walked quickly across the park, not really in the thrill of the assignation, but with a certain anger and rebellion burning in her heart. It was not the right sort of heart to take to a love-meeting. But *à la guerre comme à la guerre!*

Chapter Fourteen

When she got near the park gate, she heard the click of the latch. He was there, then, in the darkness of the wood, and had seen her!

"You are good and early," he said out of the dark. "Was everything all right?"

"Perfectly easy."

He shut the gate quietly after her, and made a spot of light on the dark ground, showing the pallid flowers still standing there open in the night. They went on apart, in silence.

"Are you sure you didn't hurt yourself this morning with that chair?" she asked.

"No, no!"

"When you had that pneumonia, what did it do to you?"

"Oh nothing! It left my heart not so strong and the lungs not so elastic. But it always does that."

"And you ought not to make violent physical efforts?"

"Not often."

She plodded on in an angry silence.

"Did you hate Clifford?" she said at last.

"Hate him, no! I've met too many like him to upset myself hating him. I know beforehand I don't care for his sort, and I let it go at that."

"What is his sort?"

"Nay, you know better than I do. The sort of youngish gentleman, a bit like a lady, and no balls."

"What balls?"

"Balls! A man's balls!"

She pondered this.

"But is it a question of that?" she said, a little annoyed.

"You say a man's got no brain, when he's a fool: and no heart, when he's mean; and no stomach when he's a funker. And when he's got none of that spunky wild bit of a man in him, you say he's got no balls. When he's sort of tame."

She pondered this.

"And is Clifford tame?" she asked.

"Tame, and nasty with it: like most such fellows, when you come up against 'em."

"And do you think you're not tame?"

"Maybe not quite!"

At length she saw in the distance a yellow light.

She stood still.

"There is a light!" she said.

"I always leave a light in the house," he said.

She went on again at his side, but not touching him, wondering why she was going with him at all.

He unlocked, and they went in, he bolting the door behind them. As if it were a prison, she thought! The kettle was singing by the red fire, there were cups on the table.

She sat in the wooden armchair by the fire. It was warm after the chill outside.

"I'll take off my shoes, they are wet," she said.

She sat with her stockinged feet on the bright steel fender. He went to the pantry, bringing food: bread and butter and pressed tongue. She was warm: she took off her coat. He hung it on the door.

"Shall you have cocoa or tea or coffee to drink?" he asked.

"I don't think I want anything," she said, looking at the table. "But you eat."

"Nay, I don't care about it. I'll just feed the dog."

He tramped with a quiet inevitability over the brick floor, putting food for the dog in a brown bowl. The spaniel looked up at him anxiously.

"Ay, this thy supper, tha nedna look as if tha wouldna get it!" he said.

He set the bowl on the stairfoot mat, and sat himself on a chair by the wall, to take off his leggings and boots. The dog, instead of eating, came to him again, and sat looking up at him, troubled.

He slowly unbuckled his leggings. The dog edged a little nearer.

"What's amiss wi' thee then? Art upset because there's somebody else here? Tha'rt a female, tha art! Go an' eat thy supper."

He put his hand on her head, and the bitch leaned her head sideways against him. He slowly, softly pulled the long silky ear.

"There!" he said. "There! Go an' eat thy supper! Go!"

He tilted his chair towards the pot on the mat, and the dog meekly went, and fell to eating.

"Do you like dogs?" Connie asked him.

"No, not really. They're too tame and clinging."

He had taken off his leggings and was unlacing his heavy boots. Connie had turned from the fire. How bare the little room was! Yet over his head on the wall hung a hideous enlarged photograph of a young married couple, apparently him and a bold-faced young woman, no doubt his wife.

"Is that you?" Connie asked him.

He twisted and looked at the enlargement above his head.

"Ay! Taken just afore we was married, when I was twenty-one." He looked at it impassively.

"Do you like it?" Connie asked him.

"Like it? No! I never liked the thing. But she fixed it all up to have it done, like."

He returned to pulling off his boots.

"If you don't like it, why do you keep it hanging there? Perhaps your wife would like to have it," she said.

He looked up at her with a sudden grin.

"She carted off iverything as was worth taking from th'ouse," he said. "But she left *that*!"

"Then why do you keep it? For sentimental reasons?"

"Nay, I niver look at it. I hardly knowed it wor theer. It's been theer sin' we come to this place."

"Why don't you burn it?" she said.

He twisted round again and looked at the enlarged photograph. It was framed in a brown-and-gilt frame, hideous. It showed a clean shaven, alert, very young looking man in a rather high collar, and a somewhat plump, bold young woman with hair fluffed out and crimped, and wearing a dark satin blouse.

"It wouldn't be a bad idea, would it?" he said.

He pulled off his boots, and put on a pair of slippers. He stood up on the chair, and lifted down the photograph. It left a big pale place on the greenish wallpaper.

"No use dusting it now," he said, setting the thing against the wall.

He went to the scullery, and returned with hammer and pincers. Sitting where he had sat before, he started to tear off the back-paper from the big frame and to pull out the sprigs that held the backboard in position, working with the immediate quiet absorption that was characteristic of him.

He soon had the nails out: then he pulled out the backboards, then the enlargement itself, in its solid white mount. He looked at the photograph with amusement.

"Shows me for what I was, a young curate, and her for what she was, a bully," he said. "The prig and the bully!"

"Let me look!" said Connie.

He did look indeed very clean shaven and very clean altogether, one of the clean young men of twenty years ago. But even in the photograph his eyes were alert, and dauntless. And the woman was not altogether a bully, though her jowl was heavy. There was a touch of appeal in her.

"One never should keep these things," said Connie.

"That one shouldn't! One should never have them made!"

He broke the cardboard photograph and mount over his knee, and when it was small enough, put it on the fire.

"It'll spoil the fire, though," he said.

The glass and the backboards he carefully took upstairs.

The frame he knocked asunder with a few blows of the hammer, making the stucco fly. Then he took the pieces into the scullery.

"We'll burn that tomorrow," he said. "There's too much plaster-molding on it."

Having cleared away, he sat down.

"Did you love your wife?" she asked him.

"Love?" he said. "Did you love Sir Clifford?"

But she was not going to be put off.

"But you cared for her?" she insisted.

"Cared?" he grinned.

"Perhaps you care for her now," she said.

"Me!" His eyes widened. "Ah, no, I can't think of her," he said quietly.

"Why?"

But he shook his head.

"They why don't you get a divorce? She'll come back to you one day," said Connie.

He looked up at her sharply.

"She wouldn't come within a mile of me. She hates me a lot worse than I hate her."

"You'll see, she'll come back to you."

"That she never shall. That's done. It would make me sick to see her."

"You will see her. And you're not even legally separated, are you?"

"No."

"Ah, well, then she'll come back, and you'll have to take her in."

He gazed at Connie fixedly. Then he gave the queer toss of his head.

"You may be right. I was a fool ever to come back here. But I felt stranded and had to go somewhere. A man's a poor bit of a wastrel, blown about. But you're right. I'll get a divorce and get clear. I hate those things like death, officials and courts and judges. But I've got to get through with it. I'll get a divorce.

And she saw his jaw set. Inwardly she exulted.

"I think I will have a cup of tea now," she said.

He rose to make it. But his face was set.

As they sat at the table she asked him:

"Why did you marry her? She was commoner than yourself. Mrs. Bolton told me about her. She could never understand why you married her."

He looked at her fixedly.

"I'll tell you," he said. "The first girl I had, I began with when I was sixteen. She was a schoolmaster's daughter over at Ollerton, pretty, beautiful really. I was supposed to be a clever sort of young fellow from Sheffield Grammar School, with a bit of French and German, very much up aloft. She was the romantic sort that hated commonness. She egged me on to poetry and reading: in a way, she made a man of me. I read and I thought like a house on fire, for her. And I was a clerk in Butterley Offices, a thin, white-faced fellow fuming with all the things I read. And about *everything* I talked to her: but everything. We talked ourselves into Persepolis and Timbuctoo. We were the most literary-cultured couple in ten counties. I held forth with rapture to her, positively with rapture. I simply went up in smoke. And she adored me. The serpent in the grass was sex. She somehow didn't have any; at least where it's supposed to be. I got thinner and crazier. Then I said we'd got to be lovers. I talked her into it, as usual. So she let me. I was excited, and she never wanted it. She just didn't want it. She adored me, she loved me to talk to her and kiss her: in that way she had a passion for me. But the other, she just didn't want it. And there are lots of women like her. And it was just the other that I *did* want. So there we split. I was cruel, and left her. Then I took on with another girl, a teacher, who had made a scandal by carrying on with a married man and driving him nearly out of his mind. She was a soft, white-skinned, soft sort of a woman, older than me, and played the fiddle. And she was a demon. She loved everything about love, except the sex. Clinging, caressing, creeping into you in every way: but if you forced her to sex itself, she just ground her teeth and sent out hate. I forced her to it, and she could simply numb me with hate because of it. So I was balked again. I loathed all that. I wanted a woman who wanted me, and wanted *it*.

"Then came Bertha Coutts. They'd lived next door to us when I was a little lad, so I knew 'em all right. And they were common. Well, Bertha went away to some place or other in Birmingham; she said, as a lady's companion; everybody else said, as a waitress or something in an hotel. Anyhow, just when I was more than fed up with that other girl, when I was twenty-one, back comes Bertha, with airs and grace and smart clothes and a sort of bloom on her: a sort of sensual bloom that you'd see sometimes on a woman, or on a trolly. Well I was in a state of murder. I chucked up my job at Butterley because I thought I was a weed, clerking there: and I got on as overhead blacksmith at Tevershall: shoeing horses mostly. It had been my dad's job, and I'd always been with him. It was a job I liked: handling horses: and it came natural to me. So I stopped talking 'fine,' as they call it, talking proper English, and went back to talking broad. I still read books, at home, but I blacksmithed and had a pony-trap of my own, and was My Lord Duckfoot. My dad left me three hundred pounds when he died. So I took on with Bertha, and I was glad she was common. I wanted her to be common. I wanted to be common myself. Well, I married her, and she wasn't bad. Those other 'pure' women had nearly taken all the balls out of me, but she was all right that way. She wanted me, and made no bones about it. And I was as pleased as punch. That was what I wanted: a woman who *wanted* me to fuck her. So I fucked her like a good un. And I think she despised me a bit, for being so pleased about it, and bringin' her her breakfast in bed sometimes. She sort of let things go, didn't get me a proper dinner when I came home from work, and if I said anything, flew out at me. And I flew back, hammer and tongs. She flung a cup at me, and I took her by the scruff of the neck and squeezed the life out of her. That sort of thing! But she treated me with insolence. And she got so's she'd never see me when I wanted her; never. Always put me off, brutal as you like. And then when she'd put me right off, and I didn't want her, she'd come all lovey-dovey, and get me. And I always went. But when I had her, she'd never come off when I did. Never! She'd just wait. If I kept back for half an hour, she'd keep back longer. And when I'd come and really finished then she'd start on her own account, and I had to stop inside her till she brought herself off, wriggling and shouting, she'd clutch clutch with herself down there, an' then she'd come off, fair in ecstasy. And then she'd say: That was lovely! Gradually, I got sick of it: and she got worse. She sort of got harder and harder to bring off, and she'd sort of tear at me down there, as if it was a beak tearing me. By God, you think a woman's soft down there, like a fig. But I tell you the old rampers have beaks between their legs, and they tear at you with it till you're sick. Self! Self! Self! all self! tearing and shouting! They talk about men's selfishness, but I doubt if it can ever touch a woman's blind beakishness, once she's gone that way. Like an old trull! And she couldn't help it. I told her about it, I told her how I hated it. And she'd even try. She'd try to lie still and let *me* work the business. She'd try. But it was no good. She got no feeling off it, from my working. She had to work the thing herself, grind her own coffee. And it came back on her like a raving necessity; she had to let herself go, and tear, tear, tear, as if she had no sensation in her except in the top of her beak, the very outside top tip, that rubbed and tore. That's how old whores used to be, so men used to say. It was a low kind of self-will in her, a raving sort of self-will: like in a woman who drinks. Well, in the end I couldn't stand it. We slept apart. She herself had started it, in her bouts, when she wanted to be clear of me, when she said I bossed her. She had started having a room for herself. But the time came when I wouldn't have her coming to my room. I wouldn't.

"I hated her. And she hated me. My God, how she hated me before that child was born! I often think that she conceived it out of hate. Anyhow, after the child was born I left her alone. And then came the war, and I joined up. And I didn't come back till I knew she was with that fellow at Stacks Gate."

He broke off, pale in the face.

"And what is the man at Stacks Gate like?" asked Connie.

"A big baby sort of fellow, very low-mouthed. She bullies him, and they both drink."

"My word, if she came back!"

"My God, yes! I should just go, disappear again."

There was a silence. The pasteboard in the fire had turned to grey ash.

"So when you did get a woman who wanted you," said Connie, "you got a bit too much of a good thing."

"Ay! Seems so! Yet even then I'd rather have her than the never-never ones: the white love of my youth, and that other poison-smelling lily, and the rest."

"What about the rest?" said Connie.

"The rest? There is no rest. Only to my experience the mass of women are like this: most of them want a man, but don't want the sex, but they put up with it, as part of the bargain. The more old-fashioned sort just lie there like nothing and let you go ahead. They don't mind afterwards: then they like you. But the actual thing itself is nothing to them, a bit distasteful. And most men like it that way. I hate it. But the sly sort of women who are like that pretend they're not. They pretend they're passionate and have thrills. But it's all cockaloopy.

They make it up.—Then there's the ones that love everything, every kind of feeling and cuddling and going off, every kind except the natural one. They always make you go off when you're *not* in the only place you should be, when you go off.—Then there's the hard sort, that are the devil to bring off at all, and bring themselves off, like my wife. They want to be the active party.—Then there's the sort that's just dead inside: but dead: and they know it. Then there's the sort that puts you out before you really 'come,' and go on writhing their loins till they bring themselves off against your thighs. But they're mostly the Lesbian sort. It's astonishing how Lesbian women are, consciously or unconsciously. Seems to me they're nearly all Lesbian."

"And do you mind?" asked Connie.

"I could kill them. When I'm with a woman who's really Lesbian, I fairly howl in my soul, wanting to kill her."

"And what do you do?"

"Just get away as fast as I can."

"But do you think Lesbian women any worse than homosexual men?"

"*I* do! Because I've suffered more from them. In the abstract, I've no idea. When I get with a Lesbian woman, whether she knows she's one or not, I see red. No, no! But I wanted to have nothing to do with any woman any more. I wanted to keep to myself: keep my privacy and my decency."

He looked pale, and his brows were somber.

"And were you sorry when I came along?" she said.

"I was sorry and I was glad."

"And what are you now?"

"I'm sorry, from the outside: all the complications and the ugliness and recrimination that's bound to come, sooner or later. That's when my blood sinks, and I'm low. But when my blood comes up, I'm glad. I'm even triumphant. I was really getting bitter. I thought there was no real sex left: never a woman who'd really 'come' naturally with a man: except black women, and somehow, well, we're white men: and they're a bit like mud."

"And now, are you glad of me?" she asked.

"Yes. When I can forget the rest. When I can't forget the rest, I want to get under the table and die."

"Why under the table?"

"Why?" he laughed. "Hide, I suppose. Baby!"

"You do seem to have had awful experiences of women," she said.

"You see, I couldn't fool myself. That's where most men manage. They take an attitude, and accept a lie. I could never fool myself. I knew what I wanted with a woman, and I could never say I'd got it when I hadn't."

"But have you got it now?"

"Looks as if I might have."

"Then why are you so pale and gloomy?"

"Bellyfull of remembering: and perhaps afraid of myself."

She sat in silence. It was growing late.

"And you do think it's important, a man and a woman?" she asked him.

"For me it is. For me it's the core of my life: if I have a right relation with a woman."

"And if you didn't get it?"

"Then I'd have to do without."

Again she pondered, before she asked:

"And do you think you've always been right with women?"

"God, no! I let my wife get to what she was: my fault a good deal. I spoilt her. And I'm very mistrustful. You'll have to expect it. It takes a lot to make me trust anybody, inwardly. So perhaps I'm a fraud too. I mistrust. And tenderness is not to be mistaken."

She looked at him.

"You don't mistrust with your body, when your blood comes up," she said. "You don't mistrust then, do you?"

"No, alas! That's how I've got into all the trouble. And that's why my mind mistrusts so thoroughly."

"Let your mind mistrust. What does it matter!"

The dog sighed with discomfort on the mat. The ash-clogged fire sank.

"We *are* a couple of battered warriors," said Connie.

"Are you battered too?" he laughed. "And here we are returning to the fray!"

"Yes! I feel really frightened."

"Ay!"

He got up, and put her shoes to dry, and wiped his own and set them near the fire. In the morning he would grease them. He poked the ash of pasteboard as much as possible out of the fire. "Even burnt, it's filthy," he said. Then he brought sticks and put them on the hob for the morning. Then he went out awhile with the dog.

When he came back Connie said: "I want to go out, too, for a minute."

She went alone into the darkness. There were stars overhead. She could smell flowers on the night air. And she could feel her shoes getting wetter again. But she felt like going away, right away from him and everybody.

It was chilly. She shuddered, and returned to the house. He was sitting in front of the low fire.

"Ugh! Cold!" she shuddered.

He put the sticks on the fire, and fetched more, till they had a good crackling chimneyful of blaze. The rippling running yellow flame made them both happy, warmed their faces and their souls.

"Never mind!" she said, taking his hand as he sat silent and remote. "One does one's best."

"Ay"—He sighed, with a twist of a smile.

She slipped over to him, and into his arms, as he sat there before the fire.

"Forget then!" she whispered. "Forget!"

He held her close, in the running warmth of the fire. The flame itself was like a forgetting. And her soft, warm, ripe weight! Slowly his blood turned, and began to ebb back into strength and reckless vigor again.

"And perhaps the women *really* wanted to be there and love you properly, only perhaps they couldn't. Perhaps it wasn't all their fault," she said.

"I know it. Do you think I don't know what a broken-backed snake that's been trodden on I was myself!"

She clung to him suddenly. She had not wanted to start all this again. Yet some perversity had made her.

"But you're not now," she said. "You're not that now: a broken-backed snake that's been trodden on."

"I don't know what I am. There's black days ahead," he repeated with a prophetic gloom.

"No! You're not to say it!"

He was silent. But she could feel the black void of despair inside him. That was the death of all desire, the death of all love: this despair that was like the dark cave inside the men, in which their spirit was lost.

"And you talk so coldly about sex," she said. "You talk as if you had only wanted your own pleasure and satisfaction."

She was protesting nervously against him.

"Nay!" he said. "I wanted to have my pleasure and satisfaction of a woman, and I never got it: because I could never get my pleasure and satisfaction of *her* unless she got hers of me at the same time. And it never happened. It takes two."

"But you never believed in your women. You don't even believe really in me," she said.

"I don't know what believing in a woman means."

"That's it, you see!"

She still was curled on his lap. But his spirit was grey and absent, he was not there for her. And everything she said drove him further.

"But what *do* you believe in?" she insisted.

"I don't know."

"Nothing, like all the men I've ever known," she said.

They were both silent. Then he roused himself and said:

"Yes, I do believe in something. I believe in being warm-hearted. I believe especially in being warm-hearted in love, in fucking with a warm heart. I believe if men could fuck with warm hearts, and the women take it warm-heartedly, everything would come all right. It's all this cold-hearted fucking that is death and idiocy."

"But you don't fuck me cold-heartedly," she protested.

"I don't want to fuck you at all. My heart's as cold as cold potatoes just now."

"Oh!" she said, kissing him mockingly. "Let's have them *sautées*." He laughed, and sat erect.

"It's a fact!" he said. "Anything for a bit of warm-heartedness. But the women don't like it. Even you don't really like it. You like good, sharp, piercing cold-hearted fucking, and then pretending it's all sugar. Where's your tenderness for me? You're as suspicious of me as a cat is of a dog. I tell you it takes two even to be tender and warm-hearted. You love fucking all right: but you want it to be called something grand and mysterious, just to flatter your own self-importance. Your own self-importance is more to you, fifty times more, than any man, or being together with a man."

"But that's what I'd say of you. Your own self-importance is everything to you."

"Ay! Very well then!" he said, moving as if he wanted to rise. "Let's keep apart then. I'd rather die than do any more cold-hearted fucking."

She slid away from him, and he stood up.

"And do you think *I* want it?" she said.

"I hope you don't," he replied. "But anyhow, you go to bed an' I'll sleep down here."

She looked at him. He was pale, his brows were sullen, he was as distant in recoil as the cold pole. Men were all alike.

"I can't go home till morning," she said.

"No! Go to bed. It's a quarter to one."

"I certainly won't," she said.

He went across and picked up his boots.

"Then I'll go out!" he said.

He began to put on his boots. She stared at him.

"Wait!" she faltered. "Wait! What's come between us?"

He was bent over, lacing his boot, and did not reply. The moments passed. A dimness came over her, like a swoon. All her consciousness died, and she stood there wide-eyed, looking at him from the unknown, knowing nothing any more.

He looked up, because of the silence, and saw her wide-eyed and lost. And as if a wind tossed him he got up and hobbled over to her, one shoe off and one shoe on, and took her in his arms, pressing her against his body, which somehow felt hurt right through. And there he held her, and there she remained.

Till his hands reached blindly down and felt for her, and felt under the clothing to where she was smooth and warm.

"Ma lass!" he murmured. "Ma little lass! Dunna let's fight! Dunna let's niver fight! I love thee an' th' touch on thee. Dunna argue wi' me! Dunna! Dunna! Dunna! Let's be together."

She lifted her face and looked at him.

"Don't be upset," she said steadily. "It's no good being upset. Do you really want to be together with me?"

She looked with wide, steady eyes into his face. He stopped, and went suddenly still, turning his face aside. All his body went perfectly still, but did not withdraw.

Then he lifted his head and looked into her eyes, with his odd, faintly mocking grin, saying: "Ay-ay! Let's be together on oath."

"But really?" she said, her eyes filling with tears.

"Ay really! Heart an' belly an' cock."

He still smiled faintly down at her, with the flicker of irony in his eyes, and a touch of bitterness.

She was silently weeping, and he lay with her and went into her there on the hearthrug, and so they gained a measure of equanimity. And then they went quickly to bed, for it was growing chill, and they had tired each other out. And she nestled up to him, feeling small and enfolded, and they both went to sleep at once, fast in one sleep. And so they lay and never moved, till the sun rose over the wood and day was beginning.

Then he woke up and looked at the light. The curtains were drawn. He listened to the loud wild calling of blackbirds and thrushes in the wood. It would be a brilliant morning, about half-past five, his hour for rising. He had slept so fast! It was such a new day! The woman was still curled asleep and tender. His hand moved on her, and she opened her blue wondering eyes, smiling unconsciously into his face.

"Are you awake?" she said to him.

He was looking into her eyes. He smiled, and kissed her. And suddenly she roused and sat up.

"Fancy that I am here!" she said.

She looked round the whitewashed little bedroom with its sloping ceiling and gable window where the white curtains were closed. The room was bare save for a little yellow-painted chest of drawers, and a chair: and the smallish white bed in which she lay.

"Fancy that we are here!" she said, looking down at him. He was lying watching her, stroking her breasts with his fingers, under the thin night-dress. When he was warm and smoothed out, he looked young and handsome. His eyes could look so warm. And she was fresh and young like a flower.

"I want to take this off!" he said, gathering the thin batiste night-dress and pulling it over her head. She sat there with bare shoulders and longish breasts faintly golden. He loved to make her breasts swing softly, like bells.

"You must take off your pyjamas too," she said.

"Eh nay!"

"Yes! Yes!" she commanded.

And he took off his old cotton pyjama-jacket and pushed down the trousers. Save for his hands and wrists and face and neck he was white as milk, with fine slender muscular flesh. To Connie he was suddenly piercingly beautiful again, as when she had seen him that afternoon washing himself.

Gold of sunshine touched the closed white curtains. She felt it wanted to come in.

"Oh! do let's draw the curtains! The birds are singing so! Do let the sun in," she said.

He slipped out of bed with his back to her, naked and white and thin, and went to the window, stooping a little, drawing the curtains and looking out for a moment. The back was white and fine, the small buttocks beautiful with exquisite, delicate manliness, the back of the neck ruddy and delicate and yet strong.

There was an inward, not an outward strength in the delicate and yet strong body.

"But you are beautiful!" she said. "So pure and fine! Come!" She held her arms out.

He was ashamed to turn to her, because of his aroused nakedness.

He caught his shirt off the floor, and held it to him, coming to her.

"No!" she said, still holding out her beautiful slim arms from her drooping breasts. "Let me see you!"

He dropped the shirt and stood still, looking towards her. The sun through the low window sent a beam that lit up his thighs and slim belly, and the erect phallus rising darkish and hot-looking from the little cloud of vivid gold-red hair. She was startled and afraid.

"How strange!" she said slowly. "How strange he stands there! So big! and so dark and cocksure! Is he like that?"

The man looked down the front of his slender white body, and laughed. Between the slim breasts the hair was dark, almost black. But at the root of the belly, where the phallus rose thick and arching, it was gold-red, vivid in a little cloud.

"So proud!" she murmured, uneasy. "And so lordly! Now I know why men are so overbearing. But he's lovely, *really*. Like another being! A bit terrifying! But lovely really! And he comes to *me*!—" She caught her lower lip between her teeth, in fear and excitement.

The man looked down in silence at his tense phallus, that did not change.— "Ay!" he said at last, in a little voice. "Ay ma lad! Tha'rt theer right enough. Yi, tha mun rear thy head! Theer on thy own, eh? an ta'es no count o' nob'dy! Tha ma'es nowt o' me, John Thomas. Art boss? of me? Eh well, tha'rt more cocky than me, an' tha says less. John Thomas! Dost want *her*? Dost want my lady Jane? Tha's dipped me in again, tha hast. Ay, an' tha comes up smilin'.— Ax 'er than! Ax lady Jane! Say: Lift up you heads o' ye gates, that the king of glory may come in. Ay, th' cheek on thee! Cunt, that's what tha'rt after. Tell lady Jane tha wants cunt. John Thomas, an' th' cunt o'lady Jane!—"

"Oh, don't tease him" said Connie, crawling on her knees on the bed towards him and putting her arms round his white slender loins, and drawing him to her so that her hanging, swinging breasts touched the tip of the stirring, erect phallus, and caught the drop of moisture. She held the man fast.

"Lie down!" he said. "Lie down! Let me come!"

He was in a hurry now.

And afterwards, when they had been quite still, the woman had to uncover the man again, to look at the mystery of the phallus.

"And now he's tiny, and soft like a little bud of life!" she said, taking the soft small penis in her hand. "Isn't he somehow lovely! so on his own, so strange! And *so* innocent! And he comes so far into me! You must *never* insult him, you know. He's mine too. He's not only yours. He's mine! And so lovely and innocent!" An she held the penis soft in her hand.

He laughed.

"Blest be the tie that binds our hearts in kindred love," he said.

"Of course!" she said. "Even when he's soft and little I feel my heart simply tied to him. And how lovely your hair is here! quite quite different!"

"That's John Thomas' hair, not mine!" he said.

"John Thomas! John Thomas!" and she quickly kissed the soft penis, that was beginning to stir again.

"Ay!" said the man, stretching his body almost painfully. "He's got his root in my soul, has that gentleman! An' sometimes I don't know what ter do wi' him. Ay, he's got a will of his own, an' it's hard to suit him. Yet I wouldn't have him killed."

"No wonder men have always been afraid of him!" she said. "He's rather terrible."

The quiver was going through the man's body, as the stream of consciousness again changed its direction, turning downwards. And he was helpless, as the penis in slow soft undulations filled and surged and rose up, and grew hard, standing there hard and overweening, in its curious towering fashion. The woman too trembled a little as she watched.

"There! Take him then! He's thine," said the man.

And she quivered, and her own mind melted out. Sharp soft waves of unspeakable pleasure washed over her as he entered her, and started the curious molten thrilling that spread and spread till she was carried away with the last, blind flush of extremity.

He heard the distant hooters of Stacks Gate for seven o'clock. It was Monday morning. He shivered a little, and with his face between her breasts pressed her soft breasts up over his ears, to deafen him.

She had not even heard the hooters. She lay perfectly still, her soul washed transparent.

"You must get up, mustn't you?" he muttered.

"What time?" came her colorless voice.

"Seven o'clock blowers a bit sin'."

"I suppose I must."

She was resenting, as she always did, the compulsion from outside.

He sat up and looked blankly out of the window.

"You do love me, don't you?" she asked calmly.

He looked down at her.

"Tha knows what tha knows. What dost ax for!" he said, a little fretfully.

"I want you to keep me, not to let me go," she said.

His eyes seemed full of a warm, soft darkness that could not think.

"When? Now?"

"Now, in your heart. Then I want to come and live with you always, soon."

He sat on the bed, with his head dropped, unable to think.

"Don't you want it?" she asked.

"Ay!" he said.

Then with the same eyes darkened with another flame of consciousness, almost like sleep, he looked at her.

"Dunna ax me nowt now," he said. "Let me be. I like thee. I luv thee when tha lies theer. A woman's a lovely thing when 'er's deep ter fuck, and cunt's good. Ah luv thee, thy legs, an' th' shape on thee, an' th' womanness on thee. Ah luv th' womanness on thee. Ah luv thee wi' my ba's an' wi' my heart. But dunna ax me nowt. Dunna ma'e me say nowt. Let me stop as I am while I can. Tha can ax me ivrything after. Now let me be, let me be!"

And softly, he laid his hand over her mound of Venus, on the soft brown maiden-hair, and himself sat still and naked on the bed, his face motionless in physical abstraction, almost like the face of Buddha. Motionless, and in the invisible flame of another consciousness, he sat with his hand on her, and waited for the turn.

After a while, he reached for his shirt and put it on, dressed himself swiftly in silence, looked at her once as she still lay naked and faintly golden like a Gloire de Dijon rose on the bed, and was gone. She heard him downstairs opening the door.

And she still lay musing, musing. It was very hard to go: to go out of his house. He called from the foot of the stairs: "Half-past seven!" She sighed, and got out of bed. The bare little room! Nothing in it at all but the small chest of drawers and the smallish bed. But the board floor was scrubbed clean. And in the corner by the window gable was a shelf with some books, and some from a circulating library. She looked. There were books about bolshevist Russia, books of travel, a volume about the atom and the electron, another about the composition of the earth's core, and the causes of earthquakes: then a few novels: then three books on India. So! He was a reader after all.

The sun fell on her naked limbs through the gable window. Outside she saw the dog Flossie roaming round. The hazel-brake was misted with green, and dark-green dogs'-mercury under. It was a clear clean morning with birds flying and triumphantly singing. If only she could stay! If only there weren't the other ghastly world of smoke and iron! If only *he* would make her a world.

She came downstairs, down the steep, narrow wooden stairs. Still, she would be content with this little house, if only it were in a world of its own.

He was washed and fresh, and the fire was burning.

"Will you eat anything?" he said.

"No! Only lend me a comb."

She followed him into the scullery, and combed her hair before the handbreath of mirror by the back door. Then she was ready to go.

She stood in the little front garden, looking at the dewy flowers, the grey bed of pinks in bud already.

"I would like to have all the rest of the world disappear," she said, "and live with you here."

"It won't disappear," he said.

They went almost in silence through the lovely dewy wood. But they were together in a world of their own.

It was bitter to her to go on to Wragby.

"I want soon to come and live with you altogether," she said as she left him.

He smiled unanswering.

She got home quietly and unremarked, and went up to her room.

Chapter Fifteen

There was a letter from Hilda on the breakfast tray. "Father is going to London this week, and I shall call for you on Thursday week, June 17th. You must be ready so that we can go at once. I don't want to waste time at Wragby, it's an awful place. I shall probably stay the night at Retford with the Colemans, so I should be with you for lunch Thursday. Then we could start at tea-time, and sleep perhaps in Grantham. It is no use our spending an evening with Clifford. If he hates your going, it would be no pleasure to him."

So! She was being pushed around on the chessboard again.

Clifford hated her going, but it was only because he didn't feel *safe* in her absence. Her presence, for some reason, made him feel safe, and free to do the things he was occupied with. He was a great deal at the pits, and wrestling in spirit with the almost hopeless problems of getting out his coal in the most economical fashion, and then selling it when he'd got it out. He knew he ought to find some way of *using* it, or converting it, so that he needn't sell it, or needn't have the chagrin of failing to sell it. But if he made electric power, could he sell that or use it? And to convert into oil was as yet too costly and elaborate. To keep industry alive there must be more industry, like a madness.

It was a madness, and it required a madman to succeed in it. Well, he was a little mad. Connie thought so. His very intensity and acumen in the affairs of the pits seemed like a manifestation of madness to her, his very inspirations were the inspirations of insanity.

He talked to her of all his serious schemes, and she listened in a kind of wonder, and let him talk. Then his flow ceased, and he turned on the loudspeaker, and became a blank, while apparently his schemes coiled on inside him like a kind of dream.

And every night now he played pontoon, that game of the Tommies, with Mrs. Bolton, gambling with sixpences. And again, in the gambling he was gone in a kind of unconscious, or blank intoxication, or intoxication of blankness, whatever it was. Connie could not bear to see him. But when she had gone to bed, he and Mrs. Bolton would gamble on till two and three in the morning, safely, and with strange lust. Mrs. Bolton was caught in the lust as much as Clifford: the more so, as she nearly always lost.

She told Connie one day: "I lost twenty-three shillings to Sir Clifford last night."

"And did he take the money from you?" asked Connie aghast.

"Why, of course, my Lady! Debt of honor!"

Connie expostulated roundly and was angry with both of them. The upshot was, Sir Clifford raised Mrs. Bolton's wages a hundred a year, and she could gamble on that. Meanwhile it seemed to Connie, Clifford was really going deader.

She told him at length she was leaving on the seventeenth.

"Seventeenth!" he said. "And when will you be back?"

"By the twentieth of July at the latest."

"Yes! the twentieth of July."

Strangely and blankly he looked at her, with the vagueness of a child, but with the queer blank cunning of an old man.

"You won't let me down, will you?" he said.

"How?"

"While you're away. I mean, you're sure to come back?"

"I'm as sure as I can be of anything, that I shall come back."

"Yes! Well! Twentieth of July."

Yet he really wanted her to go. That was so curious. He wanted her to go, positively, to have her little adventures and perhaps become pregnant, and all that. At the same time, he was afraid of her going.

She was quivering, watching her real opportunity for leaving him altogether, waiting till the time, herself, himself, should be ripe.

She sat and talked to the keeper of her going abroad.

"And then when I come back," she said, "I can tell Clifford I must leave him. And you and I can go away. They never need even know it is you. We can go to another country. Shall we? To Africa or Australia. Shall we?"

She was quite thrilled by her plan.

"You've never been to the Colonies, have you?" he asked her.

"No! Have you?"

"I've been in India, and South Africa, and Egypt."

"Why shouldn't we go to South Africa?"

"We might!" he said slowly.

"Or don't you want to?" she asked.

"I don't care. I don't much care what I do."

"Doesn't it make you happy? Why not? We shan't be poor. I have about six hundred a year. I wrote and asked. It's not much, but it's enough, isn't it?"

"It's riches to me."

"Oh, how lovely it will be!"

"But I ought to get divorced, and so ought you, unless we're going to have complications."

There was plenty to think about.

Another day she asked him about himself. They were in the hut, and there was a thunderstorm.

"And weren't you happy, when you were a lieutenant and an officer and a gentleman?"

"Happy? All right. I liked my Colonel."

"Did you love him?"

"Yes! I loved him."

"And did he love you?"

"Yes! In a way, he loved me.

"Tell me about him."

"What is there to tell? He had risen from the ranks. He loved the army. And he had never married. He was twenty years older than me. He was a very intelligent man: and alone in the army, as such a man is: a passionate man in his way: and a very clever officer. I lived under his spell while I was with him. I sort of let him run my life. And I never regret it."

"And did you mind very much when he died?"

"I was as near death myself. But when I came to, I knew another part of me was finished. But then I had always known it would finish in death. All things do, as far as that goes."

She sat and ruminated. The thunder crashed outside. It was like being in a little ark in the Flood.

"You seem to have such a lot *behind* you," she said.

"Do I? It seems to me I've died once or twice already. Yet here I am, pegging on, and in for more trouble."

She was thinking hard, yet listening to the storm.

"And weren't you happy as an officer and a gentleman, when your Colonel was dead?"

"No! They were a mingy lot." He laughed suddenly. "The Colonel used to say: Lad, the English middle classes have to chew every mouthful thirty times because their guts are so narrow, a bit as big as a pea would give them a stoppage. They're the mingiest set of ladylike snipe ever invented: full of conceit of themselves, frightened even if their boot-laces aren't correct, rotten as high game, and always in the right. That's what finishes me up. Kow-tow, kow-tow, arse-licking till their tongues are tough: yet they're always in the right. Prigs on top of everything. Prigs! A generation of ladylike prigs with half a ball each.—"

Connie laughed. The rain was rushing down.

"He hated them!"

"No," said he. "He didn't bother. He just disliked them. There's a difference. Because, as he said, the Tommies are getting just as priggish and half-balled and narrow-gutted. It's the fate of mankind, to go that way."

"The common people, too, the working people?"

"All the lot. Their spunk is gone dead. Motor cars and cinemas and aeroplanes suck that last bit out of them. I tell you, every generation breeds a more rabbity generation, with india rubber tubing for guts and tin legs and tin faces. Tin people! It's all a steady sort of bolshevism just killing off the human thing, and worshipping the mechanical thing. Money, money, money! All the modern lot get their real kick out of killing the old human feeling out of man, making mincemeat of the old Adam and the old Eve. They're all alike. The world is all alike: kill off the human reality, a quid for every foreskin, two quid for each pair of balls. What is cunt but machine-fucking!—It's all alike. Pay 'em money to cut off the world's cock. Pay money, money, money to them that will take spunk out of mankind, and leave 'em all little twiddling machines."

He sat there in the hut, his face pulled to mocking irony. Yet even then, he had one ear set backwards, listening to the storm over the wood. It made him feel so alone.

"But won't it ever come to an end?" she said.

"Ay, it will. It'll achieve its own salvation. When the last real man is killed, and they're *all* tame: white, black, yellow, all colors of tame ones: then they'll *all* be insane. Because the root of sanity is in the balls. Then they'll all be *insane,* and they'll make their grand *auto de fê.* You know *auto da fê* means act of faith? Ay, well, they'll make their own grand little act of faith. They'll offer one another up."

"You mean kill one another?"

"I do, duckie! If we go on at our present rate then in a hundred years' time there won't be ten thousand people in this island: there may not be ten. They'll have lovingly wiped each other out." The thunder was rolling further away.

"How nice!" she said.

"Quite nice! To contemplate the extermination of the human species and the long pause that follows before some other species crops up, it calms you more than anything else. And if we go on in that way, with everybody, intellectuals, artists, government, industrialists and workers all frantically killing off the last human feeling, the last bit of their intuition, the last healthy instinct; if it goes on in algebraical progression, as it is going on: then ta-tah! to the human species! Good-bye! darling! the serpent swallows itself and leaves a void, considerably messed up, but not hopeless. Very nice! When savage wild dogs bark in Wragby, and savage wild pit-ponies stamp on Tevershall pit-bank! *te deum laudamus!*"

Connie laughed, but not very happily.

"Then you ought to be pleased that they are all bolshevists," she said. "You ought to be pleased that they hurry on towards the end."

"So I am. I don't stop 'em. Because I couldn't if I would."

"Then why are you so bitter?"

"I'm not! If my cock gives its last crow, I don't mind."

"But if you have a child?" she said.

He dropped his head.

"Why," he said at last. "It seems to me a wrong and bitter thing to do, to bring a child into this world."

"No! Don't say it! Don't say it!" she pleaded. "I think I'm going to have one. Say you'll be pleased." She laid her hand on his.

"I'm pleased for you to be pleased," he said. "But for me it seems a ghastly treachery to the unborn creature."

"Ah, no!" she said, shocked. "Then you can't ever really want me! You *can't* want me, if you feel that!"

Again he was silent, his face sullen. Outside there was only the threshing of the rain.

"It's not quite true!" she whispered. "It's not quite true! There's another truth." She felt he was bitter now partly because she was leaving him, deliberately going away to Venice. And this half pleased her.

She pulled open his clothing and uncovered his belly, and kissed his navel. Then she laid her cheek on his belly, and pressed her arm around his warm, silent, loins. They were alone in the flood.

"Tell me you want a child, in hope!" she murmured, pressing her face against his belly. "Tell me you do!"

"Why!" he said at last: and she felt the curious quiver of changing consciousness and relaxation going through his body. "Why, I've thought sometimes if one but tried, here among th' colliers even! They workin' bad now, an' not earnin' much. If a man could say to 'em: Dunna think o' nowt but th' money. When it comes ter *wants,* we want but little. Let's not live for money—"

She softly rubbed her cheek on his belly, and gathered his balls in her hand. The penis stirred softly, with strange life, but did not rise up. The rain beat bruisingly outside.

"Let's live for summat else. Let's not live ter make money, neither for us-selves nor for anybody else. Now we're forced to. We're forced to make a bit for us-selves, an' a fair lot for th' bosses. Let's stop it! Bit by bit, let's stop it. We needn't rant an' rave. Bit by bit, let's drop the whole industrial life, an' go back. The least little bit o' money'll do. For everybody, me an' you, bosses an' masters, even th' king. The least little bit o' money'll really do. Just make up your mind to it, an' you've got out o' th' mess." He paused, then went on:

"An' I'd tell 'em: Look! Look at Joe! He moves lovely! Look how he moves, alive and aware. He's beautiful! An' look at Jonah! He's clumsy, he's ugly, because he's niver willin' to rouse himself. I'd tell 'em: Look! look at yourselves! one shoulder higher than t'other, legs twisted, feet all lumps! What have yer done ter yerselves, wi' the blasted work? Spoilt yerselves. No need to work that much. Take yer clothes off an' look at yourselves. Yer ought ter be alive an' beautiful, an' yer ugly an' half dead. So I'd tell 'em. An' I'd get my men to wear different clothes: 'appen close red trousers, bright red, an' little short white jackets. Why, if men had red, fine legs, that alone would change them in a month. They'd begin to be men again, to be men! An' the women could dress as they liked. Because if once the men walked with legs close bright scarlet, and buttocks nice and showing scarlet under a little white jacket: then the women 'ud begin to be women. It's because th' men *aren't* men, that th' women have to be.—An' in time pull down Tevershall and build a few beautiful buildings, that would hold us all. An' clean the country up again. An' not have many children, because the world is overcrowded.

"But I wouldn't preach to the men: only strip 'em an' say: Look at yourselves! That's workin' for money!—Hark at yourselves! That's working for money. You've been working for money! Look at Tevershall! It's horrible. That's because it was built while you was working for money. Look at your girls! They don't care about you, you don't care about them. It's because you've spent your time working an' caring for money. You can't talk nor move nor live, you can't properly be with a woman. You're not alive. Look at yourselves!"

There fell a complete silence. Connie was half listening, and threading in the hair at the root of his belly a few forget-me-nots that she had gathered on the way to the hut. Outside the world had gone still, and a little icy.

"You've got four kinds of hair," she said to him. "On your chest it's nearly black, and your hair isn't dark on your head: but your moustache is hard and dark red, and your hair here, your love-hair, is like a little bush of bright red-gold mistletoe. It's the loveliest of all!"

He looked down and saw the milky bits of forget-me-nots in the hair on his groin.

"Ay! That's where to put forget-me-nots, in the man-hair, or the maiden-hair. But don't you care about the future?"

She looked up at him.

"Oh, I do, terribly!" she said.

"Because when I feel the human world is doomed, has doomed itself by its own mingy beastliness, then I feel the Colonies aren't far enough. The moon wouldn't be far enough, because even there you could look back and see the earth, dirty, beastly, unsavory among all the stars: made foul by men. Then I feel I've swallowed gall, and it's eating my inside out, and nowhere's far enough away to get away. But when I get a turn, I forget it all again. Though it's a shame, what's been done to people these last hundred years: men turned into nothing but labor-insects, and all their manhood taken away, and all their real life. I'd wipe the machines off the face of the earth again, and end the industrial epoch absolutely, like a black mistake. But since I can't, an' nobody can, I'd better hold my peace, an' try an' live my own life: if I've got one to live, which I rather doubt."

The thunder had ceased outside, but the rain which had abated, suddenly came striking down, with a last blench of lightning and mutter of departing storm. Connie was uneasy. He had talked so long now, and he was really talking to himself, not to her. Despair seemed to come down on him completely, and she was feeling happy, she hated despair. She knew her leaving him, which he had only just realized inside himself, had plunged him back into this mood. And she triumphed a little.

She opened the door and looked at the straight, heavy rain, like a steel curtain, and had a sudden desire to rush out into it, to rush away. She got up, and began swiftly pulling off her stockings, then her dress and underclothing, and he held his breath. Her pointed keen animal breasts tipped and stirred as she moved. She was ivory-colored in the greenish light. She slipped on her rubber shoes again and ran out with a wild little laugh, holding up her breasts to the heavy rain and spreading her arms, and running blurred in the rain with the eurythmic dance-movements she had learned so long ago in Dresden. It was a strange pallid figure lifting and falling, bending so the rain beat and glistened on the full haunches, swaying up again and coming belly-forward through the rain, then stooping again so that only the full loins and buttocks were offered in a kind of homage towards him, repeating a wild obeisance.

He laughed wryly, and threw off his clothes. It was too much. He jumped out, naked and white, with a little shiver, into the hard slanting rain. Flossie sprang before him with a frantic little bark. Connie, her hair all wet and sticking to her head, turned her hot face and saw him. Her blue eyes blazed with excitement as she turned and ran fast, with a strange charging movement, out of the clearing and down the path, the wet boughs whipping her. She ran, and he saw nothing but the round wet head, the wet back leaning forward in flight, the round buttocks twinkling: a wonderful cowering female nakedness in flight.

She was nearly at the wide riding when he came up and flung his naked arm round her soft naked-wet middle. She gave a shriek and straightened herself, and the heap of her soft, chill flesh came up against his body. He pressed it all up against him, madly, the heap of soft, chilled female flesh that became quickly warm as flame, in contact. The rain streamed on them till they smoked. He gathered her lovely, heavy posteriors one in each hand and pressed them in towards him in a frenzy, quivering motionless in the rain. Then suddenly he tipped her up and fell with her on the path, in the roaring silence of the rain, and short and sharp, he took her, short and sharp and finished, like an animal.

He got up in an instant, wiping the rain from his eyes.

"Come in," he said, and they started running back to the hut. He ran straight and swift: he didn't like the rain. But she came slower, gathering forget-me-nots and campion and bluebells, running a few steps and watching him fleeting away from her.

When she came with her flowers, panting to the hut, he had already started a fire, and the twigs were crackling. Her sharp breasts rose and fell, her hair was plastered down with rain, her face was flushed ruddy and her body glistened and trickled. Wide-eyed and breathless, with a small wet head and full, trickling, naïve haunches, she looked another creature.

He took the old sheet and rubbed her down, she standing like a child. Then he rubbed himself, having shut the door of the hut. The fire was blazing up. She ducked her head in the other end of the sheet, and rubbed her wet hair.

"We're drying ourselves together on the same towel, we shall quarrel!" he said.

She looked up for a moment, her hair all odds and ends.

"No!" she said, her eyes wide. "It's not a towel, it's a sheet."

And she went on busily rubbing her head, while he busily rubbed his.

Still panting with their exertions, each wrapped in an army blanket, but the front of the body open to the fire, they sat on a log side by side before the blaze, to get quiet. Connie hated the feel of the blanket against her skin. But now the sheet was all wet.

She dropped her blanket and kneeled on the clay hearth, holding her head to the fire, and shaking her hair to dry it. He watched the beautiful curving drop of her haunches. That fascinated him today. How it sloped with a rich down-slope to the heavy roundness of her buttocks! And in between, folded in the secret warmth, the secret entrances!

He stroked her tail with his hand, long and subtly taking in the curves and the globefulness.

"Tha's got such a nice tail on thee," he said, in the throaty caressive dialect. "Tha's got the nicest arse of anybody. It's the nicest, nicest woman's arse as is! An' ivry bit of it is woman, woman sure as nuts. Tha'rt not one o' them button-arsed lasses as should be lads, are ter! Tha's got a real soft sloping bottom on thee, as a man loves in 'is guts. It's a bottom as could hold the world up, it is."

All the while he spoke he exquisitely stroked the rounded tail, till it seemed as if a slippery sort of fire came from it into his hands. And his finger-tips touched the two secret openings to her body, time after time, with a soft little brush of fire.

"An' if tha shits an' if tha pisses, I'm glad. I don't want a woman as couldna shit nor piss."

Connie couldn't help a sudden snort of astonished laughter, but he went on unmoved.

"Tha'rt real, tha art! Tha'rt real, even a bit of a bitch. Here tha shits an' here tha pisses: an' I lay my hand on 'em both an' like thee for it. I like thee for it. Tha's got a proper, woman's arse, proud of itself. It's none ashamed of itself, this isna."

He laid his hand close and firm over her secret places, in a kind of close greeting.

"I like it," he said. "I like it! An' if I only lived ten minutes, an' stroked thy arse an' got to know it, I should reckon I'd lived *one* life, sees ter! Industrial system or not! Here's one o' my lifetimes."

She turned round and climbed into his lap, clinging to him. "Kiss me!" she whispered.

And she knew the thought of their separation was latent in both their minds, and at last she was sad.

She sat on his thighs, her head against his breast, and her ivory-gleaming legs loosely apart, the fire glowing unequally upon them. Sitting with his head dropped, he looked at the folds of her body in the fire-glow, and at the fleece of soft brown hair that hung down to a point between her open thighs. He reached to the table behind, and took up a bunch of flowers, still so wet that drops of rain fell on the floor.

"Flowers stops out of doors all weathers," he said. "They have no houses."

"Not even a hut!" she murmured.

With quiet fingers he threaded a few forget-me-not flowers in the fine brown fleece of the mount of Venus.

"There!" he said. "There's forget-me-nots in the right place!"

She looked down at the milky odd little flowers among the brown maiden-hair at the lower tip of her body.

"Doesn't it look pretty!" she said.

"Pretty as life," he replied.

And he stuck a pink campion-bud among the hair.

"There! That's me where you won't forget me! That's Moses in the bulrushes."

"You don't mind, do you, that I'm going away?" she asked wistfully, looking up into his face.

But his face was inscrutable, under the heavy brows. He kept it quite blank.

"You do as you wish," he said.

And he spoke in good English.

"But I won't go if you don't wish it," she said, clinging to him.

There was silence. He leaned and put another piece of wood on the fire. The flame glowed on his silent, abstracted face. She waited, but he said nothing.

"Only I thought it would be a good way to begin a break with Clifford. I do want a child. And it would give me a chance to, to—" she resumed.

"To let them think a few lies," he said.

"Yes, that among other things. Do you want them to think the truth?"

"I don't care what they think."

"I do! I don't want them handling me with their unpleasant cold minds, not while I'm still at Wragby. They can think what they like when I'm finally gone."

He was silent.

"But Sir Clifford expects you to come back to him?"

"Oh, I must come back," she said: and there was silence.

"And would you have a child in Wragby?" he asked.

She closed her arm round his neck.

"If you wouldn't take me away, I should have to," she said.

"Take you where to?"

"Anywhere! away! But right away from Wragby."

"When?"

"Why, when I come back."

"But what's the good of coming back, doing the thing twice, if you're once gone?" he said.

"Oh, I must come back. I've promised! I've promised so faithfully. Besides, I come back to you, really."

"To your husband's gamekeeper?"

"I don't see that that matters," she said.

"No?" He mused a while. "And when would you think of going away again, then; finally? When exactly?"

"Oh, I don't know. I'd come back from Venice. And then we'd prepare everything."

"How prepare?"

"Oh, I'd tell Clifford. I'd have to tell him."

"Would you!"

He remained silent. She put her arms fast round his neck.

"Don't make it difficult for me," she pleaded.

"Make what difficult?"

"For me to go to Venice and arrange things."

A little smile, half a grin, flickered on his face.

"I don't make it difficult," he said. "I only want to find out just what you are after. But you don't really know yourself. You want to take time: get away and look at it. I don't blame you. I think you're wise. You may prefer to stay mistress of Wragby. I don't blame you. I've no Wragbys to offer. In fact, you know what you'll get out of me. No, no, I think you're right! I really do! And I'm not keen on coming to live on you, being kept by you. There's that too."

She felt, somehow, as if he were giving her tit for tat.

"But you want me, don't you?" she asked.

"Do you want me?"

"You know I do. *That's* evident."

"Quite! And *when* do you want me?"

"You know we can arrange it all when I come back. Now I'm out of breath with you. I must get calm and clear."

"Quite! Get calm and clear!"

She was a little offended.

"But you trust me, don't you?" she said.

"Oh, absolutely!"

She heard the mockery in his tone.

"Tell me, then," she said flatly, "do you think it would be better if I *don't* go to Venice?"

"I'm sure it's better if you *do* go to Venice," he replied in the cool, slightly mocking voice.

"You know it's next Thursday?" she said.

"Yes!"

She now began to muse. At last she said:

"And we *shall* know better where we are when I come back, shan't we?"

"Oh, surely!"

The curious gulf of silence between them!

"I've been to the lawyer about my divorce," he said, a little constrainedly.

She gave a slight shudder.

"Have you!" she said. "And what did he say?"

"He said I ought to have done it before; that may be a difficulty. But since I was in the army, he thinks it will go through all right. If only it doesn't bring *her* down on my head!"

"Will she have to know?"

"Yes! she is served with a notice: so is the man she lives with, the co-respondent."

"Isn't it hateful, all the performances! I suppose I'd have to go through it with Clifford."

There was a silence.

"And of course," he said, "I have to live an exemplary life for the next six or eight months. So if you go to Venice, there's temptation removed for a week or two, at least."

"Am I temptation!" she said, stroking his face. "I'm so glad I'm temptation to you! Don't let's think about it! You frighten me when you start thinking: you roll me out flat. Don't let's think about it. We can think so much when we are apart. That's the whole point! I've been thinking, I *must* come to you for another night before I go. I must come once more to the cottage. Shall I come on Thursday night?"

"Isn't that when your sister will be there?"

"Yes! But she said we would start at tea-time. So we could start at tea-time. But she could sleep somewhere else and I could sleep with you."

"But then she'd have to know."

"Oh, I shall tell her. I've more or less told her already. I must talk it all over with Hilda. She's a great help, so sensible."

He was thinking of her plan.

"So you'd start off from Wragby at tea-time, as if you were going to London? Which way were you going?"

"By Nottingham and Grantham."

"And then your sister would drop you somewhere and you'd walk or drive back here? Sounds very risky, to me."

"Does it? Well then, Hilda could bring me back. She could sleep at Mansfield, and bring me back here in the evening, and fetch me again in the morning. It's quite easy."

"And the people who see you?"

"I'll wear goggles and a veil."

He pondered for some time.

"Well," he said. "You please yourself, as usual."

"But wouldn't it please you?"

"Oh, yes! It'd please me all right," he said a little grimly. "I might as well smite while the iron's hot."

"Do you know what I thought?" she said suddenly. "It suddenly came to me. You are the 'Knight of the Burning Pestle!' "

"Ay! And you? Are you the Lady of the Red-Hot Mortar?"

"Yes!" she said. "Yes! You're Sir Pestle and I'm Lady Mortar."

"All right, then I'm knighted. John Thomas is Sir John, to your Lady Jane."

"Yes! John Thomas is knighted! I'm my-lady-maiden-hair, and you must have flowers too. Yes!"

She threaded two pink campions in the bush of red-gold hair above his penis.

"There!" she said. "Charming! Charming! Sir John!"

And she pushed a bit of forget-me-not in the dark hair of his breast.

"And you won't forget me *there,* will you?" she kissed him on the breast, and made two bits of forget-me-not lodge one over each nipple, kissing him again.

"Make a calendar of me!" he said. He laughed and the flowers shook from his breast.

"Wait a bit!" he said.

He rose, and opened the door of the hut. Flossie, lying in the porch, got up and looked at him.

"Ay, it's me!" he said.

The rain had ceased. There was a wet, heavy perfumed stillness. Evening was approaching.

He went out and down the little path in the opposite direction from the riding. Connie watched his thin, white figure, and it looked to her like a ghost, an apparition moving away from her.

When she could see it no more, her heart sank. She stood in the door of the hut, with a blanket round her, looking into the drenched motionless silence.

But he was coming back, trotting strangely, and carrying flowers. She was a little afraid of him, as if he were not quite human. And when he came near, his eyes looked into hers, but she could not understand the meaning.

He had brought columbines and campions, and new-mown-hay, and oak-tufts and honeysuckle in small bud. He fastened fluffy young oak-sprays round her breasts, sticking in tufts of bluebells and campion: and in her navel he poised a pink campion flower, and in her maiden-hair were forget-me-nots and woodruff.

"That's you in all your glory!" he said. "Lady Jane, at her wedding with John Thomas."

And he stuck flowers in the hair of his own body, and wound a bit of creeping-jenny round his penis, and stuck a single bell of a hyacinth in his navel. She watched him with amusement, his odd intentness. And she pushed a campion flower in his moustache, where it stuck dangling under his nose.

"This is John Thomas marryin' Lady Jane," he said. "An' we mun let Constance an' Oliver go their ways. Maybe—"

He spread out his hand with a gesture, and then he sneezed, sneezing away the flowers from his nose and his navel. He sneezed again.

"Maybe what?" she said, waiting for him to go on.

"Eh?" he said.

"Maybe what? Go on with what you were going to say," she insisted.

"Ay, what *was* I going to say?"

He had forgotten. And it was one of the disappointments of her life, that he never finished.

A yellow ray of sun shone over the trees.

"Sun!" he said. "And time you went. Time, my lady, time! What's that as flies without wings, your ladyship? Time! Time!"

He reached for his shirt.

"Say good night! to John Thomas," he said, looking down at his penis. "He's safe in the arms of creeping-jenny! Not much burning pestle about him just now."

And he put his flannel shirt over his head.

"A man's most dangerous moment," he said, when his head emerged, "is when he's getting into his shirt. Then he puts his head in a bag. That's why I prefer those American shirts, that you put on like a jacket." She still stood watching him. He stepped into his short drawers, and buttoned them round his waist.

"Look at Jane!" he said. "In all her blossoms! Who'll put blossoms on you next year, Jinny? Me, or somebody else? 'Good-bye my bluebell, farewell to you!' I hate that song, it's early war days." He had sat down, and was pulling on his stockings. She still stood unmoving. He laid his hand on the slope of her buttocks. "Pretty little lady Jane!" he said. "Perhaps in Venice you'll find a man who'll put jasmine in your maiden-hair, and a pomegranate flower in your navel. Poor little lady Jane!"

"Don't say those things!" she said. "You only say them to hurt me."

He dropped his head. Then he said, in dialect:

"Ay, maybe I do, maybe I do! Well then, I'll say nowt, an' ha' done wi't. But tha mun dress thysen, an' go back to thy stately homes of England, how beautiful they stand. Time's up. Time's up for Sir John, an' for little lady Jane! Put thy shimmy on, Lady Chatterley! Tha might be anybody, standin' there be-out even a shimmy, an' a few rags o' flowers. There then, there then, I'll undress thee, tha bob-tailed young throstle." And he took the leaves from her hair, kissing her damp hair, and the flowers from her breasts, and kissed her breasts, and kissed her navel, and kissed her maiden-hair, where he left the flowers threaded. "They mun stop while they will," he said. "So! There th'art bare again, nowt but a bare-arsed lass an' a bit of a lady Jane! Now put thy shimmy on, for tha mun go, or else Lady Chatterley's goin' to be late for dinner, an' where 'ave yer been to my pretty maid!"

She never knew how to answer him when he was in this condition of the vernacular. So she dressed herself and prepared to go a little ignominiously home to Wragby. Or so she felt it: a little ignominiously home.

He would accompany her to the broad riding. His young pheasants were all right under the shelter.

When he and she came out on to the riding, there was Mrs. Bolton faltering palely towards them.

"Oh, my Lady, we wondered if anything had happened!"

"No! Nothing has happened."

Mrs. Bolton looked into the man's face, that was smooth and new-looking with love. She met his half-laughing, half-mocking eyes. He always laughed at mischance. But he looked at her kindly.

"Evening, Mrs. Bolton! Your Ladyship will be all right now, so I can leave you. Good night to your Ladyship! Good night, Mrs. Bolton!"

He saluted and turned away.

Chapter Sixteen

Connie arrived home to an ordeal of cross-questioning. Clifford had been out at tea-time, had come in just before the storm, and where was her ladyship? Nobody knew, only Mrs. Bolton suggested she had gone for a walk into the wood. Into the wood, in such a storm!—Clifford for once let himself get into a state of nervous frenzy. He started at every flash of lightning, and blenched at every roll of thunder. He looked at the icy thunder-rain as if it were the end of the world. He got more and more worked up.

Mrs. Bolton tried to soothe him.

"She'll be sheltering in the hut, till it's over. Don't worry, her ladyship is all right."

"I don't like her being in the wood in a storm like this! I don't like her being in the wood at all! She's been gone now more than two hours. When did she go out?"

"A little while before you came in."

"I didn't see her in the park. God knows where she is and what has happened to her."

"Oh, nothing's happened to her. You'll see, she'll be home directly after the rain stops. It's just the rain that's keeping her."

But her ladyship did not come home directly the rain stopped. In fact time went by, the sun came out for his last yellow glimpse, and there was still no sign of her. The sun was set, it was growing dark, and the first dinner-gong had rung.

"It's no good!" said Clifford in a frenzy. "I'm going to send out Field and Betts to find her."

"Oh, don't do that!" cried Mrs. Bolton. "They'll think there's a suicide or something. Oh, don't start a lot of talk going—Let me slip over to the hut and see if she's not there. I'll find her all right."

So, after some persuasion, Clifford allowed her to go.

And so Connie had come upon her in the drive, alone and palely loitering.

"You mustn't mind me coming to look for you, my Lady! But Sir Clifford worked himself up into such a state. He made sure you were struck by lightning, or killed by a falling tree. And he was determined to send Field and Betts to the wood to find the body. So I thought I'd better come, rather than set all the servants agog."

She spoke nervously. She could still see on Connie's face the smoothness and the half-dream of passion, and she could feel the irritation against herself.

"Quite!" said Connie. And she could say no more.

The two women plodded on through the wet world, in silence, while great drops splashed like explosions in the wood. When they came to the park, Connie strode ahead, and Mrs. Bolton panted a little. She was getting plumper.

"How foolish of Clifford to make a fuss!" said Connie at length, angrily, really speaking to herself.

"Oh, you know what men are! They like working themselves up. But he'll be all right as soon as he sees your ladyship."

Connie was very angry that Mrs. Bolton knew her secret: for certainly she knew it.

Suddenly Constance stood still on the path.

"It's monstrous that I should have to be followed!" she said, her eyes flashing.

"Oh, your Ladyship, don't say that! He'd certainly have sent the two men, and they'd have come straight to the hut. I didn't know where it was, really."

Connie flushed darker with rage, at the suggestion. Yet, while her passion was on her, she could not lie. She could not even pretend there was nothing between herself and the keeper. She looked at the other woman, who stood so sly, with her head dropped: yet somehow, in her femaleness, an ally.

"Oh well!" she said. "If it is so, it is so. I don't mind!"

"Why, you're all right, my Lady! You've only been sheltering in the hut. It's absolutely nothing."

They went on to the house. Connie marched into Clifford's room, furious with him, furious with his pale, overwrought face and prominent eyes.

"I must say, I don't think you need send the servants after me!" she burst out.

"My God!" he exploded. "Where have you been, woman? You've been gone hours, hours, and in a storm like this! What the hell do you go to that bloody wood for? What have you been up to? It's hours even since the rain stopped, hours! Do you know what time it is? You're enough to drive anybody mad. Where have you been? What in the name of hell have you been doing?"

"And what if I don't choose to tell you?" She pulled her hat from her head and shook her hair.

He looked at her with his eyes bulging, and yellow coming into the whites. It was very bad for him to get into these rages: Mrs. Bolton had a weary time with him, for days after. Connie felt a sudden qualm.

"But, really!" she said, milder. "Anyone would think I'd been I don't know where! I just sat in the hut during all the storm, and made myself a little fire, and was happy."

She spoke now easily. After all, why work him up any more! He looked at her suspiciously.

"And look at your hair!" he said; "look at yourself!"

"Yes!" she replied calmly. "I ran out into the rain with no clothes on."

He stared at her speechless.

"You must be mad!" he said.

"Why? To like a shower bath from the rain?"

"And how did you dry yourself?"

"On an old towel and at the fire."

He still stared at her in a dumbfounded way.

"And supposing anybody came," he said.

"Who would come?"

"Who? Why, anybody! And Mellors. Does he come? He must come in the evenings."

"Yes, he came later, when it had cleared up, to feed the pheasants with corn."

She spoke with amazing nonchalance. Mrs. Bolton, who was listening in the next room, heard in sheer admiration. To think a woman would carry it off so naturally!

"And suppose he'd come while you were running about in the rain with nothing on, like a maniac?"

"I suppose he'd have had the fright of his life, and cleared out as fast as he could."

Clifford still stared at her transfixed. What he thought in his under-consciousness he would never know. And he was too much taken aback to form one clear thought in his upper consciousness. He just simply accepted what she said, in a sort of blank. And he admired her. He could not help admiring her. She looked flushed and handsome and smooth: love-smooth.

"At least," he said, subsiding, "you'll be lucky if you've got off without a severe cold."

"Oh, I haven't got a cold," she replied. She was thinking to herself of the other man's words: Tha's got the nicest woman's arse of anybody! She wished, she dearly wished she could tell Clifford that this had been said to her, during the famous thunderstorm. However! She bore herself rather like an offended queen and went upstairs to change.

That evening, Clifford wanted to be nice to her. He was reading one of the latest scientific-religious books: he had a streak of a spurious sort of religion in him, and was egocentrically concerned with the future of his own ego. It was like his habit to make conversation to Connie about some book, since the conversation between them had to be made, almost chemically. They had almost chemically to concoct it in their heads.

"What do you think of this, by the way?" he said, reaching for his book. "You'd have no need to cool your ardent body by running out in the rain, if only we had a few more aeons of evolution behind us. Ah, here it is!—'The universe shows us two aspects: on one side it is physically wasting, on the other it is spiritually ascending.' "

Connie listened, expecting more. But Clifford was waiting. She looked at him in surprise.

"And if it spiritually ascends," she said, "what does it leave down below, in the place where its tail used to be?"

"Ah!" he said. "Take the man for what he means. *Ascending* is the opposite of his *wasting,* I presume."

"Spiritually blown out, so to speak!"

"No. But seriously, without joking: do you think there is anything in it?"

She looked at him again.

"Physically wasting?" she said. "I see you getting fatter, and I'm not wasting myself. Do you think the sun is smaller than he used to be? He's not, to me. And I suppose the apple Adam offered Eve wasn't really much bigger, if any, than one of our orange pippins. Do you think it was?"

"Well, hear how he goes on: 'It is thus slowly passing, with a slowness inconceivable in our measures of time, to new creative conditions, amid which the physical world, as we at present know it, will be represented by a ripple barely to be distinguished from nonentity.' "

She listened with a glisten of amusement. All sorts of improper things suggested themselves. But she only said:

"What silly hocus-pocus! As if his little conceited consciousness could know what was happening as slowly as all that! It only means *he's* a physical failure on earth, so he wants to make the whole universe a physical failure. Priggish little impertinence!"

"Oh, but listen! Don't interrupt the great man's solemn words!—The present type of order in the world has risen from an unimaginable past, and will find its grave in an unimaginable future. There remains the inexhaustive realm of abstract forms, and creativity with its shifting character ever determined afresh by its own creatures, and God, upon whose wisdom all forms of order depend.— There, that's how he winds up!"

Connie sat listening contemptuously.

"He's spiritually blown out," she said. "What a lot of stuff! Unimaginables, and types of order in graves, and realms of abstract forms, and creativity with a shifty character, and God mixed up with forms of order! Why, it's idiotic!"

"I must say, it is a little vaguely conglomerate, a mixture of gases, so to speak," said Clifford. "Still, I think there is something in the idea that the universe is physically wasting and spiritually ascending."

"Do you? Then let it ascend, so long as it leaves me safely and solidly physically here below."

"Do you like your physique?" he asked.

"I love it!" And through her mind went the words: It's the nicest, nicest woman's arse as is!

"But that is really rather extraordinary, because there's no denying it's an encumbrance. But then, I suppose a woman doesn't take a supreme pleasure in the life of the mind."

"Supreme pleasure?" she said, looking up at him. "Is that sort of idiocy the supreme pleasure of the life of the mind? No, thank you! Give me the body. I believe the life of the body is a greater reality than the life of the mind: when the body is really awakened to life. But so many people, like your famous wind-machine, have only got minds tacked on to their physical corpses."

He looked at her in wonder.

"The life of the body," he said, "is just the life of the animals."

"And that's better than the life of professional corpses. But it's not true! The human body is only just coming to real life. With the Greeks it gave a lovely flicker, then Plato and Aristotle killed it, and Jesus finished it off. But now the body is coming really to life, it is really rising from the tomb. And it will be a lovely, lovely life in the lovely universe, the life of the human body."

"My dear, you speak as if you were ushering it all in! True, you are going away on a holiday: but don't please be quite so indecently elated about it. Believe me, whatever God there is is slowly eliminating the guts and alimentary system from the human being, to evolve a higher, more spiritual being."

"Why should I believe you, Clifford, when I feel that whatever God there is has at last wakened up in my guts, as you call them, and is rippling so happily there, like dawn? Why should I believe you, when I feel so very much the contrary?"

"Oh, exactly! And what has caused this extraordinary change in you? running out stark naked in the rain, and playing Bacchante? Desire for sensation, or the anticipation of going to Venice?"

"Both! Do you think it is horrid of me to be so thrilled at going off?" she said.

"Rather horrid to show it so plainly."

"Then I'll hide it."

"Oh, don't trouble! You almost communicate a thrill to me. I almost feel that it is *I* who am going off."

"Well, why don't you come?"

"We've gone over all that. And, as a matter of fact, I suppose your greatest thrill comes from being able to say a temporary farewell to all this. Nothing so thrilling, for the moment, as Good-bye-to-it-all!—But every parting means a meeting elsewhere. And every meeting is a new bondage."

"I am not going to enter any new bondages."

"Don't boast, while the gods are listening," he said.

She pulled up short.

"No! I won't boast!" she said.

But she was thrilled, none the less, to be going off; to feel bonds snap. She couldn't help it.

Clifford, who couldn't sleep, gambled all night with Mrs. Bolton, till she was too sleepy almost to live.

And the day came around for Hilda to arrive. Connie had arranged with Mellors that if everything promised well for their night together, she would hang a green shawl out of the window. If there were frustration, a red one.

Mrs. Bolton helped Connie to pack.

"It will be so good for your ladyship to have a change."

"I think it will. You don't mind having Sir Clifford on your hands alone for a time, do you?"

"Oh, no! I can manage him quite all right. I mean, I can do all he needs me to do. Don't you think he's better than he used to be?"

"Oh, much! You do wonders with him."

"Do I though! But men are all alike: just babies and you have to flatter them and wheedle them and let them think they're having their own way. Don't you find it so, my Lady?"

"I'm afraid I haven't much experience."

Connie paused in her occupation.

"Even your husband, did you have to manage him, and wheedle him like a baby?" she asked, looking at the other woman.

Mrs. Bolton paused too.

"Well!" she said. "I had to do a good bit of coaxing with him too. But he always knew what I was after, I must say that. But he generally gave in to me."

"He was never the lord and master thing?"

"No! At least, there'd be a look in his eyes sometimes, and then I knew *I'd* got to give in. But usually he gave in to me. No, he was never lord and master.

But neither was I. I knew when I could go no further with him, and then I gave in: though it cost me a good bit, sometimes."

"And what if you had held out against him?"

"Oh, I don't know. I never did. Even when he was in the wrong, if he was fixed, I gave in. You see, I never wanted to break what was between us. And if you really set your will against a man, that finishes it. If you care for a man, you have to give in to him once he's really determined; whether you're in the right or not, you have to give in. Else you break something. But I must say, Ted 'ud give in to me sometimes, when I was set on a thing, and in the wrong. So I suppose it cuts both ways."

"And that's how you are with all your patients?" asked Connie.

"Oh, that's different. I don't care at all, in the same way. I know what's good for them, or I try to, and then I just contrive to manage them for their own good. It's not like anybody as you're really fond of. It's quite different. Once you've been really fond of a man, you can be affectionate to almost any man, if he needs you at all. But it's not the same thing. You don't really *care*. I doubt, once you've *really* cared, if you can ever really care again."

These words frightened Connie.

"Do you think one can only care once?" she asked.

"Or never. Most women never care, never begin to. They don't know what it means. Nor men either. But when I see a woman as cares, my heart stands still for her."

"And do you think men easily take offense?"

"Yes! If you wound them on their pride. But aren't women the same? Only, our two prides are a bit different."

Connie pondered this. She began again to have some misgiving about her going away. After all, was she not giving her man the go-by, if only for a short time? And he knew it. That's why he was so queer and sarcastic.

Still! the human existence is a good deal controlled by the machine of external circumstance. She was in the power of this machine. She couldn't extricate herself all in five minutes. She didn't even want to.

Hilda arrived in good time on Thursday morning, in a nimble two-seater car, with her suitcase strapped firmly behind. She looked as demure and maidenly as ever, but she had the same will of her own. She had the very hell of a will of her own, as her husband had found out. But her husband was now divorcing her. Yes, she even made it easy for him to do that, though she had no lover. For the time being, she was "off" men. She was very well content to be quite her own mistress: and mistress of her two children, whom she was going to bring up "properly," whatever that may mean.

Connie was only allowed a suitcase, also. But she had sent on a trunk to her father, who was going by train. No use taking a car to Venice. And Italy was much too hot to motor in, in July. He was going comfortably by train. He had just come down from Scotland.

So, like a demure arcadian field-marshal, Hilda arranged the material part of the journey. She and Connie sat in the upstairs room, chatting.

"But, Hilda!" said Connie, a little frightened. "I want to stay near here tonight. Not here: near here!"

Hilda fixed her sister with grey, inscrutable eyes. She seemed so calm: and she was so often furious.

"Where, near here?" she asked softly.

"Well, you know I love somebody, don't you?"

"I gathered there was something."

"Well, he lives near here, and I want to spend this last night with him. I must! I've promised."

Connie became insistent.

Hilda bent her Minerva-like head in silence. Then she looked up.

"Do you want to tell me who he is," she said.

"He's our gamekeeper," faltered Connie, and she flushed vividly, like a shamed child.

"Connie!" said Hilda, lifting her nose slightly with disgust: a motion she had from her mother.

"I know: but he's lovely, really. He really understands tenderness," said Connie, trying to apologize for him.

Hilda, like a ruddy, rich-colored Athena, bowed her head and pondered. She was really violently angry. But she dared not show it, because Connie, taking after her father, would straightway become obstreperous and unmanageable.

It was true, Hilda did not like Clifford: his cool assurance that he was somebody! She thought he made use of Connie shamefully and impudently. She had hoped her sister *would* leave him. But, being solid Scotch middle class, she loathed any "lowering" of oneself, or the family. She looked up at last.

"You'll regret it," she said.

"I shan't," cried Connie, flushing red. "He's quite the exception. I *really* love him. He's lovely as a lover."

Hilda still pondered.

"You'll get over him quite soon," she said, "and live to be ashamed of yourself because of him."

"I shan't! I hope I'm going to have a child of his."

"*Connie!*" said Hilda, hard as a hammer-stroke, and pale with anger.

"I shall, if I possibly can. I should be fearfully proud if I had a child by him."

It was no use talking to her. Hilda pondered.

"And doesn't Clifford suspect?" she said.

"Oh, no! Why should he?"

"I've no doubt you've given him plenty of occasion for suspicion," said Hilda.

"Not at all."

"And tonight's business seems quite gratuitous folly. Where does the man live?"

"In the cottage at the other end of the wood."

"Is he a bachelor?"

"No! His wife left him."

"How old?"

"I don't know. Older than me."

Hilda became more angry at every reply, angry as her mother used to be, in a kind of paroxysm. But she still hid it.

"I would give up tonight's escapade if I were you," she advised calmly.

"I can't! I *must* stay with him tonight, or I can't go to Venice at all. I just can't."

Hilda heard her father over again, and she gave way, out of mere diplomacy. And she consented to drive to Mansfield, both of them, to dinner, to bring Connie back to the lane-end after dark, and to fetch her from the lane-end the next morning, herself sleeping in Mansfield, only half-an-hour away, good going. But she was furious. She stored it up against her sister, this balk in her plans.

Connie flung an emerald-green shawl over her windowsill.

On the strength of her anger, Hilda warmed towards Clifford. After all, he had a mind. And if he had no sex, functionally, all the better; so much the less to quarrel about. Hilda wanted no more of that sex business, where men became nasty, selfish little horrors. Connie really had less to put up with than many women, if she did but know it.

And Clifford decided that Hilda, after all, was a decidedly intelligent woman, and would make a man a first-rate help-meet, if he were going in for politics, for example. Yes, she had none of Connie's silliness, Connie was more a child: you had to make excuses for her, because she was not altogether dependable.

There was an early cup of tea in the hall, where doors were open to let in the sun. Everybody seemed to be panting a little.

"Goodbye, Connie girl! Come back to me safely."

"Goodbye, Clifford! Yes, I shan't be long." Connie was almost tender.

"Goodbye, Hilda! You will keep an eye on her, won't you?"

"I'll even keep two!" said Hilda. "She shan't go very far astray."

"It's a promise!"

"Goodbye, Mrs. Bolton. I know you'll look after Sir Clifford nobly."

"I'll do what I can, your Ladyship."

"And write to me if there is any news, and tell me about Sir Clifford, how he is."

"Very good, your Ladyship, I will. And have a good time, and come back and cheer us up."

Everybody waved. The car went off. Connie looked back and saw Clifford sitting at the top of the steps in his house-chair. After all, he was her husband: Wragby was her home: circumstance had done it.

Mrs. Chambers held the gate and wished her ladyship a happy holiday. The car slipped out of the dark spinney that masked the park, on to the highroad where the colliers were trailing home. Hilda turned to the Crosshill Road, that was not a main road, but ran to Mansfield. Connie put on goggles. They ran beside the railway, which was in a cutting below them. Then they crossed the cutting on a bridge.

"That's the lane to the cottage!" said Connie.

Hilda glanced at it impatiently.

"It's a frightful pity we can't go straight off!" she said. "We could have been in Pall Mall by nine o'clock."

"I'm sorry for your sake," said Connie, from behind her goggles.

They were soon at Mansfield, that once-romantic, now utterly disheartening colliery town. Hilda stopped at the hotel named in the motor-car book, and took a room. The whole thing was utterly uninteresting, and she was almost too angry to talk. However, Connie *had* to tell her something of the man's history.

"*He*! *He*! What name do you call him by? You only say *he*," said Hilda.

"I've never called him by any name: nor he me: which is curious, when you come to think of it. Unless we say Lady Jane and John Thomas. But his name is Oliver Mellors."

"And how would you like to be Mrs. Oliver Mellors, instead of Lady Chatterley?"

"I'd love it."

There was nothing to be done with Connie. And anyhow, if the man had been a lieutenant in the army in India for four or five years, he must be more or less presentable. Apparently he had character. Hilda began to relent a little.

"But you'll be through with him in a while," she said, "and then you'll be ashamed of having been connected with him. One *can't* mix up with the working people."

"But you are such a socialist! you're always on the side of the working classes."

"I may be on their side in a political crisis, but being on their side makes me know how impossible it is to mix one's life with theirs. Not out of snobbery, but just because the whole rhythm is different."

Hilda had lived among the real political intellectuals, so she was disastrously unanswerable.

The nondescript evening in the hotel dragged out, and at last they had a nondescript dinner. Then Connie slipped a few things into a little silk bag, and combed her hair once more.

"After all, Hilda," she said, "love can be wonderful; when you feel you *live,* and are in the very middle of creation." It was almost like bragging on her part.

"I suppose every mosquito feels the same," said Hilda.

"Do you think it does? How nice for it!"

The evening was wonderfully clear and long-lingering even in the small town. It would be half-light all night. With a face like a mask, from resentment, Hilda started her car again, and the two sped back on their tracks, taking the other road, through Bolsover.

Connie wore her goggles and disguising cap, and she sat in silence. Because of Hilda's opposition, she was fiercely on the side of the man, she would stand by him through thick and thin.

They had their headlights on, by the time they passed Crosshill, and the small lit-up train that chuffed past in the cutting made it seem like real night. Hilda had calculated the turn into the lane at the bridge-end. She slowed up rather suddenly and swerved off the road, the lights glaring white into the grassy, overgrown lane. Connie looked out. She saw a shadowy figure, and she opened the door.

"Here we are!" she said softly.

But Hilda had switched off the lights, and was absorbed backing, making the turn.

"Nothing on the bridge?" she asked shortly.

"You're all right," said the man's voice.

She backed on to the bridge, reversed, let the car run forward a few yards along the road, then backed into the lane, under a wych-elm tree, crushing the grass and bracken. Then all the lights went out. Connie stepped down. The man stood under the trees.

"Did you wait long?" Connie asked.

"Not so very," he replied.

They both waited for Hilda to get out. But Hilda shut the door of the car and sat tight.

"This is my sister Hilda. Won't you come and speak to her? Hilda! This is Mr. Mellors."

The keeper lifted his hat, but went no nearer.

"Do walk down to the cottage with us, Hilda," Connie pleaded. "It's not far."

"What about the car?"

"People do leave them in the lanes. You have the key."

Hilda was silent, deliberating. Then she looked backwards down the lane.

"Can I back round that bush?" she said.

"Oh, yes!" said the keeper.

She backed slowly round the curve, out of sight of the road, locked the car, and got down. It was night, but luminous dark. The hedges rose high and wild, by the unused lane, and very dark seeming. There was a fresh sweet scent on the air. The keeper went ahead, then came Connie, then Hilda, and in silence. He lit up the difficult places with a flashlight torch, and they went on again, while an owl softly hooted over the oaks, and Flossie padded silently around. Nobody could speak. There was nothing to say.

At length Connie saw the yellow light of the house, and her heart beat fast. She was a little frightened. They trailed on, still in Indian file.

He unlocked the door and preceded them into the warm but bare little room. The fire burned low and red in the grate. The table was set with two plates and two glasses, on a proper white tablecloth for once. Hilda shook her hair and looked round the bare, cheerless room. Then she summoned her courage and looked at the man.

He was moderately tall, and thin, and she thought him good-looking. He kept a quiet distance of his own, and seemed absolutely unwilling to speak.

"Do sit down, Hilda," said Connie.

"Do!" he said. "Can I make you tea or anything, or will you drink a glass of beer? It's moderately cool."

"Beer!" said Connie.

"Beer for me, please!" said Hilda, with a mock sort of shyness. He looked at her and blinked.

He took a blue jug and tramped to the scullery. When he came back with the beer, his face had changed again.

Connie sat down by the door, and Hilda sat in his seat, with the back to the wall, against the window corner.

"That is his chair," said Connie softly. And Hilda rose as if it had burnt her.

"Sit yer still, sit yer still! Ta'e ony cheer as yo'n a mind to, none of us is th' big bear," he said, with complete equanimity.

And he brought Hilda a glass, and poured her beer first from the blue jug.

"As for cigarettes," he said, "I've got none, but 'appen you've got your own. I dunna smoke, mysen. Shall y' eat summat?"—He turned direct to Connie: "Shall t'eat a smite o' summat, if I bring it thee? Tha can usually do wi' a bite." He spoke the vernacular with a curious calm assurance, as if he were the landlord of the inn.

"What is there?" asked Connie, flushing.

"Boiled ham, cheese, pickled wa'nuts, if yer like.—Nowt much."

"Yes," said Connie. "Won't you, Hilda?"

Hilda looked up at him.

"Why do you speak Yorkshire?" she said softly.

"That! That's non Yorkshire, that's Derby."

He looked back at her with that faint, distant grin.

"Derby, then! Why do you speak Derby? You spoke natural English at first."

"Did Ah though? An' canna Ah change if Ah'n a mind to it? Nay, nay, let me talk Derby if it suits me. If yo'n nowt against it."

"It sounds a little affected," said Hilda.

"Ay, 'appen so! An' up i' Tevershall yo'd sound affected." He looked again at her, with a queer calculating distance, along his cheekbones, as if to say: Yi, an' who are you?

He tramped away to the pantry for the food.

The sisters sat in silence. He brought another plate, and knife and fork. Then he said:

"An' if it's the same to you, I s'll ta'e my coat off, like I allers do."

And he took off his coat, and hung it on the peg, then sat down to the table, in his shirtsleeves: a shirt of thin, cream-colored flannel.

" 'Elp yerselves!" he said. " 'Elp yerselves! Dunna wait f'r axin'!"

He cut the bread, then sat motionless. Hilda felt, as Connie once used to, his power of silence and distance. She saw his smallish, sensitive, loose hand on the table. He was no simple working man, not he: he was acting! Acting!

"Still!" she said, as she took a little cheese. "It would be more natural if you spoke to us in normal English, not in vernacular."

He looked at her, feeling her devil of a will.

"Would it?" he said in the normal English. "Would it? Would anything that was said between you and me be quite natural, unless you said you wished me to hell before your sister ever saw me again: and unless I said something almost as unpleasant back again? Would anything else be natural?"

"Oh, yes!" said Hilda. "Just good manners would be quite natural."

"Second nature, so to speak!" he said: then he began to laugh. "Nay," he said. "I'm weary o' manners. Let me be!"

Hilda was frankly baffled and furiously annoyed. After all, he might show that he realized he was being honored. Instead of which, with his play-acting and lordly airs, he seemed to think it was he who was conferring the honor. Just impudence! Poor misguided Connie, in the man's clutches!

The three ate in silence. Hilda looked to see what his table manners were like. She could not help realizing that he was instinctively much more delicate and well-bred than herself. She had a certain Scottish clumsiness. And moreover, he had all the quiet self-contained assurance of the English, no loose edges. It would be very difficult to get the better of him.

"And do you really think," she said, a little more humanly, "it's worth the risk?"

"Is what worth what risk?"

"This escapade with my sister."

He flickered his irritating grin.

"Yo' maun ax 'er!"

Then he looked at Connie.

"Tha comes o' thine own accord, lass, doesn't yer? It's non me as forces thee?"

Connie looked at Hilda.

"I wish you wouldn't cavil, Hilda."

"Naturally, I don't want to. But someone has to think about things. You've got to have some continuity in your life. You can't just go making a mess."

There was a moment's pause.

"Eh, continuity!" he said. "An' what by that? What continuity 'ave yer got i' *your* life? I thought you was gettin' divorced. What continuity's that? Continuity o' yer own stubbornness. I can see that much. An' what good's it goin' to do yer? Yo'll be sick o' yer continuity afore yer a fat sight older. A stubborn woman an' 'er own self-will: ay, they make a fast continuity, they do. Thank heaven, it isn't me as 'as got th' 'andlin' of yer!"

"What right have you to speak like that to me?" said Hilda.

"Right! What right ha' yo' ter start harnessin' other folks i' your Continuity? Leave folks to their own continuities."

"My dear man, do you think I am concerned with you?" said Hilda softly.

"Ay," he said. "Yo' are. For it's a force-put. Yo' more or less my sister-in-law."

"Still far from it, I assure you."

"Not a' that far, I assure *you*. I've got my own sort o' continuity, back your life! Good as yours, any day. An' if your sister there comes ter me for a bit o' cunt an' tenderness, she knows what she's after. She's been in my bed afore: which you 'aven't, thank the Lord, with your continuity." There was a dead pause, before he added: "—Eh, I don't wear me breeches arse-forrards. An' if I get a windfall, I thank my stars. A man gets a lot of enjoyment out o' that lass theer, which is more than anybody gets out o' th' likes o' you. Which is a pity, for you might 'appen a' bin a good apple, 'stead of a handsome crab. Women like you needs proper graftin'."

He was looking at her with an odd, flickering smile, faintly sensual and appreciative.

"And men like you," she said, "ought to be segregated: justifying their own vulgarity and selfish lust."

"Ay, ma'am. It's a mercy there's a few men left like me. But you deserve what you get: to be left severely alone."

Hilda had risen and gone to the door. He rose and took his coat from the peg.

"I can find my way quite well alone," she said.

"I doubt you can't," he replied easily.

They tramped in ridiculous file down the lane again, in silence. An owl still hooted. He knew he ought to shoot it.

The car stood untouched, a little dewy. Hilda got in and started the engine. The other two waited.

"All I mean," she said from her entrenchment, "is that I doubt if you'll find it's been worth it, either of you!"

"One man's meat is another man's poison," he said, out of the darkness. "But it's meat an' drink to me."

The lights flared out.

"Don't make me wait in the morning, Connie."

"No, I won't. Good night!"

The car rose slowly on to the highroad, then slid swiftly away, leaving the night silent.

Connie timidly took his arm, and they went down the lane. He did not speak. At length she drew him to a standstill.

"Kiss me!" she murmured.

"Nay, wait a bit! Let me simmer down," he said.

That amused her. She still kept hold of his arm, and they went quickly down the lane, in silence. She was so glad to be with him, just now. She shivered, knowing that Hilda might have snatched her away. He was inscrutably silent.

When they were in the cottage again, she almost jumped with pleasure, that she should be free of her sister.

"But you were horrid to Hilda," she said to him.

"She should ha' been slapped in time."

"But why? and she's *so* nice."

He didn't answer, went round doing the evening chores, with a quiet, inevitable sort of motion. He was outwardly angry, but not with her. So Connie felt. And his anger gave him a peculiar handsomeness, an inwardness and glisten that thrilled her and made her limbs go molten.

Still he took no notice of her.

Till he sat down and began to unlace his boots. Then he looked up at her from under his brows, on which the anger still sat firm.

"Shan't you go up?" he said. "There's a candle!"

He jerked his head swiftly to indicate the candle burning on the table. She took it obediently, and he watched the full curve of her hips as she went up the first stairs.

It was a night of sensual passion, in which she was a little startled and almost unwilling: yet pierced again with piercing thrills of sensuality, different, sharper, more terrible than the thrills of tenderness, but, at the moment, more desirable. Though a little frightened, she let him have his way, and the reckless, shameless sensuality shook her to her foundations, stripped her to the very last, and made a different woman of her. It was not really love. It was not voluptuousness. It was sensuality sharp and searing as fire, burning the soul to tinder.

Burning out the shames, the deepest, oldest shames, in the most secret places. It cost her an effort to let him have his way and his will of her. She had to be a passive, consenting thing, like a slave, a physical slave. Yet the passion licked round her, consuming, and when the sensual flame of it pressed through her bowels and breast, she really thought she was dying: yet a poignant, marvellous death.

She had often wondered what Abélard meant, when he said that in their year of love he and Heloïse had passed through all the stages and refinements of passion. The same thing, a thousand years ago: ten thousand years ago! The same on the Greek vases, everywhere! The refinements of passion, the extravagances of sensuality! And necessary, forever necessary, to burn out false shames and smelt out the heaviest ore of the body into purity. With the fire of sheer sensuality.

In the short summer night she learnt so much. She would have thought a woman would have died of shame. Instead of which, the shame died. Shame, which is fear: the deep organic shame, the old, old physical fear which crouches in the bodily roots of us, and can only be chased away by the sensual fire, at last it was roused up and routed by the phallic hunt of the man, and she came to the very heart of the jungle of herself. She felt, now, she had come to the real bedrock of her nature, and was essentially shameless. She was her sensual self, naked and unashamed. She felt a triumph, almost a vainglory. So! That was how it was! That was life! That was how oneself really was! There was nothing left to disguise or be ashamed of. She shared her ultimate nakedness with a man, another being.

And what a reckless devil the man was! really like a devil! One had to be strong to bear him. But it took some getting at, the core of the physical jungle, the last and deepest recess of organic shame. The phallus alone could explore it. And how he had pressed in on her!

And how, in fear, she had hated it. But how she had really wanted it! She knew now. At the bottom of her soul, fundamentally, she had needed this phallic hunting out, she had secretly wanted it, and she had believed that she would never get it. Now suddenly there it was, and a man was sharing her last and final nakedness, she was shameless.

What liars poets and everybody were! They made one think one wanted sentiment. When what one supremely wanted was this piercing, consuming, rather awful sensuality. To find a man who dared do it, without shame or sin or final misgiving! If he had been ashamed afterwards, and made one feel ashamed, how awful! What a pity most men are so doggy, a bit shameful, like Clifford! Like Michaelis even! Both sensually a bit doggy and humiliating. The supreme pleasure of the mind! And what is that to a woman? What is it, really, to the man either? He becomes merely messy and doggy, even in his mind. It needs sheer sensuality even to purify and quicken the mind. Sheer fiery sensuality, not messiness.

Ah God, how rare a thing a man is! They are all dogs that trot and sniff and copulate. To have found a man who was not afraid and not ashamed! She looked at him now, sleeping so like a wild animal asleep, gone, gone in the remoteness of it. She nestled down, not to be away from him.

Till his rousing waked her completely. He was sitting up in bed, looking down at her. She saw her own nakedness in his eyes, immediate knowledge of her. And the fluid, male knowledge of herself seemed to flow to her from his eyes and wrap her voluptuously. Oh, how voluptuous and lovely it was to have limbs and body half-asleep, heavy and suffused with passion!

"Is it time to wake up?" she said.

"Half-past six."

She had to be at the lane-end at eight. Always, always, always this compulsion on one!

"I might make the breakfast and bring it up here: should I?" he said.

"Oh, yes!"

Flossie whimpered gently below. He got up and threw off his pyjamas, and rubbed himself with a towel. When the human being is full of courage and full of life, how beautiful it is! So she thought, as she watched him in silence.

"Draw the curtain, will you?"

The sun was shining already on the tender green leaves of morning, and the wood stood bluey-fresh, in the nearness. She sat up in bed, looking dreamily out through the dormer window, her naked arms pushing her naked breasts together. He was dressing himself. She was half-dreaming of life, a life together with him: just a life.

He was going, fleeing from her dangerous, crouching nakedness.

"Have I lost my nightie altogether?" she said.

He pushed his hand down in the bed, and pulled out the bit of flimsy silk.

"I knowed I felt silk at my ankles," he said.

But the night-dress was slit almost in two.

"Never mind!" she said. "It belongs here, really. I'll leave it."

"Ay, leave it, I can put it between my legs at night, for company. There's no name or mark on it, is there?"

She slipped on the torn thing, and sat dreamily looking out of the window. The window was open, the air of morning drifted in, and the sound of birds. Birds flew continuously past. Then she saw Flossie roaming out. It was morning.

Downstairs she heard him making the fire, pumping water, going out at the back door. By and by came the smell of bacon, and at length he came upstairs with a huge black tray that would only just go through the door. He set the tray on the bed, and poured out the tea. Connie squatted in her night-dress, and fell on her food hungrily. He sat on the one chair, with his plate on his knees.

"How good it is!" she said. "How nice to have breakfast together."

He ate in silence, his mind on the time that was quickly passing. That made her remember.

"Oh, how I wish I could stay here with you, and Wragby were a million miles away! It's Wragby I'm going away from really. You know that, don't you?"

"Ay!"

"And you promise we will live together and have a life together, you and me! You promise me, don't you?"

"Ay! When we can."

"Yes! And we *will*! We *will*, won't we?" She leaned over, making the tea spill, catching his wrist.

"Ay!" he said, tidying up the tea.

"We can't possibly *not* live together now, can we?" she said appealingly.

He looked up at her with his flickering grin.

"No!" he said. "Only, you've got to start in twenty-five minutes."

"Have I?" she cried. Suddenly he held up a warning finger, and rose to his feet.

Flossie had given a short bark, then three loud sharp yaps of warning.

Silent, he put his plate on the tray and went downstairs. Constance heard him go down the garden path. A bicycle bell tinkled outside there.

"Morning, Mr. Mellors! Registered letter!"

"Oh, ay! Got a pencil?"

"Here y'are!"

There was a pause.

"Canada!" said the stranger's voice.

"Ay! That's a mate o' mine out there in British Columbia. Dunno what he's got to register."

" 'Appen sent y'a fortune, like."

"More like wants summat."

Pause.

"Well! Lovely day again!"

"Ay!"

"Morning!"

"Morning!"

After a time he came upstairs again, looking a little angry.

"Postman," he said.

"Very early!" she replied.

"Rural round; he's mostly here by seven, when he does come."

"Did your mate send you a fortune?"

"No! Only some photographs and papers about a place out there in British Columbia."

"Would you go there?"

"I thought perhaps we might."

"Oh, yes! I believe it's lovely!"

But he was put out by the postman's coming.

"Them damned bikes, they're on you afore you know where you are. I hope he twigged nothing."

"After all, what could he twig?"

"You must get up now, and get ready. I'm just goin' ter look round outside."

She saw him go reconnoitering into the lane, with dog and gun. She went downstairs and washed, and was ready by the time he came back, with the few things in the little silk bag.

He locked up, and they set off, but through the wood, not down the lane. He was being wary.

"Don't you think one lives for times like last night?" she said to him.

"Ay! But there's the rest o' times to think on," he replied, rather short.

They plodded on down the overgrown path, he in front, in silence.

"And we *will* live together and make a life together, won't we?" she pleaded.

"Ay!" he replied, striding on without looking round. "When t' time comes! Just now you're off to Venice or somewhere."

She followed him dumbly, with sinking heart. Oh, now she *was* to go!

At last he stopped.

"I'll just strike across here," he said, pointing to the right.

But she flung her arms round his neck, and clung to him.

"But you'll keep the tenderness for me, won't you?" she whispered. "I loved last night. But you'll keep the tenderness for me, won't you?"

He kissed her and held her close for a moment. Then he sighed, and kissed her again.

"I must go an' look if th' car's there."

He strode over the low brambles and bracken, leaving a trail through the fern. For a minute or two he was gone. Then he came striding back.

"Car's not there yet," he said. "But there's the baker's cart on t' road."

He seemed anxious and troubled.

"Hark!"

They heard a car softly hoot as it came nearer. It slowed up on the bridge.

She plunged with utter mournfulness in his track through the fern, and came to a huge holly hedge. He was just behind her.

"Here! Go through there!" he said, pointing to a gap. "I shan't come out."

She looked at him in despair. But he kissed her and made her go. She crept in sheer misery through the holly and through the wooden fence, stumbled down the little ditch and up into the lane, where Hilda was just getting out of the car in vexation.

"Why, you're there!" said Hilda. "Where's *he?*"

"He's not coming."

Connie's face was running with tears as she got into the car with her little bag. Hilda snatched up the motoring helmet with the disfiguring goggles.

"Put it on!" she said. And Connie pulled on the disguise, then the long motoring coat, and she sat down, a goggling, inhuman, unrecognizable creature. Hilda started the car with a business-like motion. They heaved out of the lane, and were away down the road. Connie had looked round, but there was no sight of him. Away! Away! She sat in bitter tears. The parting had come so suddenly, so unexpectedly. It was like death.

"Thank goodness you'll be away from him for some time!" said Hilda, turning to avoid Crosshill village.

Chapter Seventeen

You see, Hilda," said Connie after lunch, when they were nearing London, "you have never known either real tenderness or real sensuality: and if you do know them, with the same person, it makes a great difference."

"For mercy's sake, don't brag about your experiences!" said Hilda. "I've never met the man yet who was capable of intimacy with a woman, giving himself up to her. That was what I wanted. I'm not keen on their self-satisfied tenderness, and their sensuality. I'm not content to be any man's little petsywetsy, nor his *chair à plaisir* either. I wanted a complete intimacy, and I didn't get it. That's enough for me."

Connie pondered this. Complete intimacy! She supposed that meant revealing everything concerning yourself to the other person, and his revealing everything concerning himself. But that was a bore. And all that weary self-consciousness between a man and a woman! a disease!

"I think you're too conscious of yourself all the time, with everybody," she said to her sister.

"I hope at least I haven't a slave nature," said Hilda.

"But perhaps you have! Perhaps you are a slave to your own idea of yourself."

Hilda drove in silence for some time after this piece of unheard-of insolence from that chit Connie.

"At least I'm not a slave to somebody else's idea of me: and the somebody else a servant of my husband's," she retorted at last, in crude anger.

"You see, it's not so," said Connie calmly.

She had always let herself be dominated by her elder sister. Now, though somewhere inside herself she was weeping, she was free of the dominion of *other women*. Ah! that in itself was a relief, like being given another life: to be free of the strange dominion and obsession of *other women*. How awful they were, women!

She was glad to be with her father, whose favorite she had always been. She and Hilda stayed in a little hotel off Pall Mall, and Sir Malcolm was in his club. But he took his daughters out in the evening, and they liked going with him.

He was still handsome and robust, though just a little afraid of the new world that had sprung up around him. He had got a second wife in Scotland, younger than himself, and richer. But he had as many holidays away from her as possible: just as with his first wife.

Connie sat next to him at the opera. He was moderately stout, and had stout thighs, but they were still strong and well-knit, the thighs of a healthy man who had taken his pleasure in life. His good-humored selfishness, his dogged sort of independence, his unrepenting sensuality, it seemed to Connie she could see them all in his well-knit, straight thighs. Just a man! And now becoming an old man, which is sad. Because in his strong, thick male legs there was none of the alert sensitiveness and power of tenderness which is the very essence of youth, that which never dies, once it is there.

Connie woke up to the existence of legs. They became more important to her than faces, which are no longer very real. How few people had live, alert legs. She looked at the men in the stalls. Great puddingy thighs in black pudding-cloth, or lean wooden sticks in black funeral stuff, or well-shaped young legs without any meaning whatever, either sensuality or tenderness or sensitiveness, just mere leggy ordinariness that pranced around. Not even any sensuality like her father's. They were all daunted, daunted out of existence.

But the women were not daunted. The awful mill-posts of most females! really shocking, really enough to justify murder! Or the poor thin legs! or the trim neat things in silk stockings, without the slightest look of life! Awful, the millions of meaningless legs prancing meaninglessly around!

But she was not happy in London. The people seemed so spectral and blank. They had no alive happiness, no matter how brisk and good-looking they were. It was all barren. And Connie had a woman's blind craving for happiness, to be assured of happiness.

In Paris at any rate she felt a bit of sensuality still. But what a weary, tired worn-out sensuality. Worn-out for lack of tenderness. Oh! Paris was sad. One of the saddest towns: weary of its now-mechanical sensuality, weary of the tension of money, money, money, weary even of resentment and conceit, just weary to death, and still not sufficiently Americanized or Londonized to hide the weariness under a mechanical jig-jig-jig! Ah, these manly he-men, these flaneurs, these oglers, these eaters of good dinners! How weary they were! Weary, worn-out for lack of a little tenderness given and taken. The efficient, sometimes charming women knew a thing or two about the sensual realities: they had that pull over their jigging English sisters. But they knew even less of tenderness. Dry, with the endless dry tension of will, they too were wearing out. The human world was just getting worn out. Perhaps it would turn fiercely destructive. A sort of anarchy! Clifford and his conservative anarchy! Perhaps it wouldn't be conservative much longer. Perhaps it would develop into a very radical anarchy.

Connie found herself shrinking and afraid of the world. Sometimes she was happy for a little while in the Boulevards or in the Bois or the Luxembourg

Gardens. But already Paris was full of Americans and English, strange Americans in the oddest uniforms, and the usual dreary English that are so hopeless abroad.

She was glad to drive on. It was suddenly hot weather, so Hilda was going through Switzerland and over the Brenner, then through the Dolomites down to Venice. Hilda loved all the managing and the driving and being mistress of the show. Connie was quite content to keep quiet.

And the trip was really quite nice. Only, Connie kept saying to herself: Why don't I really care? Why am I never really thrilled? How awful, that I don't really care about the landscape any more! But I don't. It's rather awful. I'm like Saint Bernard, who could sail down the lake of Lucerne without ever noticing that there were even mountains and green water. I just don't care for landscape any more. Why should one stare at it? Why should one? I refuse to.

No, she found nothing vital in France or Switzerland or the Tyrol or Italy. She just was carted through it all. And it was all less real than Wragby. Less real than the awful Wragby! She felt she didn't care if she never saw France or Switzerland or Italy again. They'd keep. Wragby was more real.

As for people! people were all alike, with very little differences. They all wanted to get money out of you: or, if they were travellers, they wanted to get enjoyment, perforce, like squeezing blood out of a stone. Poor mountains! poor landscape! it all had to be squeezed and squeezed and squeezed again, to provide a thrill, to provide enjoyment. What did people mean, with their simply *determined* enjoying of themselves?

No! said Connie to herself. I'd rather be at Wragby, where I can go about and be still, and not stare at anything or do any performing of any sort. This tourist performance of enjoying oneself is too hopelessly humiliating: it's such a failure.

She wanted to go back to Wragby, even to Clifford, even to poor crippled Clifford. He wasn't such a fool as this swarming holiday lot, anyhow.

But in her inner consciousness she was keeping touch with the other man. She mustn't let her connection with him go: oh, she mustn't let it go, or she was lost, lost utterly in this world of riff-raffy expensive people and joy-hogs. Oh, the joy-hogs! Oh, "enjoying oneself!" Another modern form of sickness.

They left the car in Mestre, in a garage, and took the regular steamer over to Venice. It was a lovely summer afternoon, the shallow lagoon rippled, the full sunshine made Venice, turning its back to them across the water, look dim.

At the station quay they changed to a gondola, giving the man the address. He was a regular gondolier in white-and-blue blouse, not very good-looking, not at all impressive.

"Yes! The Villa Esmeralda! Yes! I know it! I have been the gondolier for a gentleman there. But a fair distance out!"

He seemed a rather childish, impetuous fellow. He rowed with a certain exaggerated impetuosity, through the dark side-canals with the horrible, slimy green walls, the canals that go through the poorer quarters, where the washing hangs high up on ropes, and there is a slight, or strong odor of sewage.

But at last he came to one of the open canals with pavement on either side, and looping bridges, that run straight, at right angles to the Grand Canal. The two women stayed under a little awning, the man was perched above, behind them.

"Are the signorine staying long at the Villa Esmeralda?" he asked, rowing easy, and wiping his perspiring face with a white-and-blue handkerchief.

"Some twenty days: we are both married ladies," said Hilda, in her curious hushed voice, that made her Italian sound so foreign.

"Ah! Twenty days!" said the man. There was a pause. After which he asked: "Do the signore want a gondolier for the twenty days or so that they will stay at the Villa Esmeralda? Or by the day, or by the week?"

Connie and Hilda considered. In Venice, it is always preferable to have one's own gondola, as it is preferable to have one's own car on land.

"What is there at the Villa? what boats?"

"There is a motor-launch, also a gondola. But—" The *but* meant: they won't be your property.

"How much do you charge?"

It was about thirty shillings a day, or ten pounds a week.

"Is that the regular price?" asked Hilda.

"Less, Signora, less. The regular price—"

The sisters considered.

"Well," said Hilda, "come tomorrow morning, and we will arrange it. What is your name?"

His name was Giovanni, and he wanted to know at what time he should come, and then for whom should he say he was waiting. Hilda had no card. Connie gave him one of hers. He glanced at it swiftly, with his hot, southern blue eyes, then glanced again.

"Ah!" he said, lighting up, "Milady! Milady! isn't it?"

"Milady Constanza!" said Connie.

He nodded, repeating: "Milady Constanza!'" and putting the card carefully away in his blouse.

The Villa Esmeralda was quite a long way out, on the edge of the lagoon looking towards Chioggia. It was not a very old house, and pleasant, with the terraces looking seawards, and below, quite a big garden with dark trees, walled in from the lagoon.

Their host was a heavy, rather coarse Scotchman who had made a good fortune in Italy before the war, and had been knighted for his ultrapatriotism during the war. His wife was a thin, pale, sharp kind of person with no fortune of her own, and the misfortune of having to regulate her husband's rather sordid amorous exploits. He was terribly tiresome with the servants. But having had a slight stroke during the winter, he was now more manageable.

The house was pretty full. Besides Sir Malcolm and his two daughters, there were seven more people, a Scotch couple, again with two daughters; a young Italian Contessa, a widow; a young Georgian prince, and a youngish English clergyman who had had pneumonia and was being chaplain to Sir Alexander for his health's sake. The prince was penniless, good looking, would make an excellent chauffeur, with the necessary impudence, and basta! The contessa was a quiet little puss with a game on somewhere. The clergyman was a raw simple fellow from a Bucks vicarage: luckily he had left his wife and two children at home. And the Guthries, the family of four, were good solid Edinburgh middle-class, enjoying everything in a solid fashion, and daring everything while risking nothing.

Connie and Hilda ruled out the prince at once. The Guthries were more or less their own sort, substantial, but boring: and the girls wanted husbands. The chaplain was not a bad fellow, but too deferential. Sir Alexander, after his slight stroke, had a terrible heaviness in his joviality, but he was still thrilled at the presence of so many handsome young women. Lady Cooper was a quiet, catty person who had a thin time of it, poor thing, and who watched every other woman with a cold watchfulness that had become her second nature, and who said cold, nasty little things which showed what an utterly low opinion she had of all human nature. She was also quite venomously overbearing with the servants, Connie found: but in a quiet way. And she skilfully behaved so that Sir Alexander should think that *he* was lord and monarch of the whole caboosh, with his stout, would-be-genial paunch, and his utterly boring jokes, his humorosity, as Hilda called it.

Sir Malcolm was painting. Yes, he still would do a Venetian lagoonscape, now and then, in contrast to his Scottish landscapes. So in the morning he was rowed off with a huge canvas, to his "site." A little later, Lady Cooper would be rowed off into the heart of the city, with sketching-block and colors. She was an inveterate water-color painter, and the house was full of rose-colored palaces, dark canals, swaying bridges, medieval façades, and so on. A little later the Guthries, the prince, the countess, Sir Alexander and sometimes Mr. Lind, the chaplain, would go off to the Lido where they would bathe; coming home to a late lunch at half-past one.

The house-party, as a house-party, was distinctly boring. But this did not trouble the sisters. They were out all the time. Their father took them to the exhibition, miles and miles of weary paintings. He took them to all the cronies of his in the Villa Lucchese, he sat with them on warm evenings in Piazza, having got a table at Florian's: he took them to the theater, to the Goldoni plays. There were illuminated water-fêtes, there were dances. This was a holiday-place of all holiday-places. The Lido with its acres of sun-pinked or pyjamaed bodies, was like a strand with an endless heap of seals come up for mating. Too many people in Piazza, too many limbs and trunks of humanity on the Lido, too many gondolas, too many motor launches, too many steamers, too many pigeons, too many ices, too many cocktails, too many men servants wanting tips, too many languages rattling, too much, too much sun, too much smell of Venice, too many cargoes of strawberries, too many silk shawls, too many huge, raw-beef slices of watermelon on stalls: too much enjoyment, altogether far too much enjoyment!

Connie and Hilda went around in their sunny frocks. There were dozens of people they knew, dozens of people knew them. Michaelis turned up like a bad penny. "Hullo! Where you staying? Come and have an ice cream or something! Come with me somewhere in my gondola." Even Michaelis *almost* sunburned: though sun-cooked is more appropriate to the look of the mass of human flesh.

It was pleasant in a way. It was *almost* enjoyment. But anyhow, with all the cocktails, all the lying in warmish water and sunbathing on hot sand in hot sun, jazzing with your stomach up against some fellow in the warm nights, cooling off with ices, it was a complete narcotic. And that was what they all wanted, a drug: the slow water, a drug; the sun, a drug; jazz, a drug; cigarettes, cocktails, ices, vermouth. To be drugged! Enjoyment! Enjoyment!

Hilda half liked being drugged. She liked looking at all the women, speculating about them. The women were absorbingly interested in the women. How does she look? What man has she captured? what fun is she getting out of it?—The men were like great dogs in white flannel trousers, waiting to be patted, waiting to wallow, waiting to plaster some woman's stomach against their own, in jazz.

Hilda liked jazz, because she could plaster her stomach against the stomach of some so-called man, and let him control her movements from the visceral center, here and there across the floor, and then she could break loose and ignore "the creature." He had been merely made use of. Poor Connie was rather unhappy. She wouldn't jazz, because she simply couldn't plaster her stomach against some "creature's" stomach. She hated the conglomerate mass of nearly nude flesh on the Lido: there was hardly enough water to wet them all. She disliked Sir Alexander and Lady Cooper. She did not want Michaelis or anybody else trailing her.

The happiest times were when she got Hilda to go with her away across the Lagoon, far across to some lonely shingle-bank, where they could bathe quite alone, the gondola remaining on the inner side of the reef.

Then Giovanni got another gondolier to help him, because it was a long way and he sweated terrifically in the sun. Giovanni was very nice: affectionate, as the Italians are, and quite passionless. The Italians are not passionate: passion has deep reserves. They are easily moved, and often affectionate, but they rarely have any abiding passion of any sort.

So Giovanni was already devoted to his ladies, as he had been devoted to cargoes of ladies in the past. He was perfectly ready to prostitute himself to them, if they wanted him: he secretly hoped they would want him. They would give him a handsome present, and it would come in very handy, as he was just going to be married. He told them about his marriage, and they were suitably interested.

He thought this trip to some lonely bank across the lagoon probably meant business: business being *l'amore,* love. So he got a mate to help him, for it *was* a long way; and after all, they were two ladies. Two ladies, two mackerels! Good arithmetic! Beautiful ladies too! He was justly proud of them. And though it was the Signora who paid him and gave him orders, he rather hoped it would be the young milady who would select him for *l'amore.* She would give more money too.

The mate he brought was called Daniele. He was not a regular gondolier, so he had none of the cadger and prostitute about him. He was a sandola man, a sandola being a big boat that brings in fruit and produce from the islands.

Daniele was beautiful, tall and well-shapen, with a light round head of little, close, pale-blond curls, and a good-looking man's face, a little like a lion, and long-distance blue eyes. He was not effusive, loquacious, and bibulous like Gio-

vanni. He was silent and he rowed with a strength and ease as if he were alone
on the water. The ladies were ladies, remote from him. He did not even look at
them. He looked ahead.

He was a real man, a little angry when Giovanni drank too much wine and
rowed awkwardly, with effusive shoves of the great oar. He was a man as Mellors
was a man, unprostituted. Connie pitied the wife of the easily-overflowing Giovanni. But Daniele's wife could be one of those sweet Venetian women of the
people whom one still sees, modest and flower-like, in the back of that labyrinth
of a town.

Ah, how sad that man first prostitutes woman, then woman prostitutes man.
Giovanni was pining to prostitute himself, dribbling like a dog, wanting to give
himself to a woman. And for money!

Connie looked at Venice far off, low and rose-colored upon the water. Built
of money, blossomed of money, and dead with money. The money-deadness!
Money, money, money, prostitution and deadness.

Yet Daniele was still a man capable of a man's free allegiance. He did not
wear the gondolier's blouse: only the knitted blue jersey. He was a little wild,
uncouth and proud. So he was hireling to the rather doggy Giovanni, who was
hireling again of two women. So it is! When Jesus refused the devil's money, he
left the devil like a Jewish banker, master of the whole situation.

Connie would come home from the blazing light of the lagoon in a kind of
stupor, to find letters from home. Clifford wrote regularly. He wrote very good
letters: they might all have been printed in a book. And for this reason Connie
found them not very interesting.

She lived in the stupor of the light of the lagoon, the lapping saltiness of the
water, the space, the emptiness, the nothingness: but health, health, complete
stupor of health. It was gratifying, and she was lulled away in it, not caring for
anything. Besides, she was pregnant. She knew now. So the stupor of sunlight
and the lagoon salt and sea-bathing and lying on shingle and finding shells and
drifting away, away in a gondola was completed by the pregnancy inside her,
another fulness of health, satisfying and stupefying.

She had been at Venice a fortnight, and she was to stay another ten days or
a fortnight. The sunshine blazed over any count of time, and the fulness of
physical health made forgetfulness complete. She was in a sort of stupor of well-
being.

From which a letter of Clifford roused her.

"We, too, have had our mild local excitement. It appears the truant wife of
Mellors, the keeper, turned up at the cottage, and found herself unwelcome. He
packed her off and locked the door. Report has it, however, that when he returned
from the wood he found the no longer fair lady firmly established in his bed, in
puris naturalibus; or one should say, in *impuris naturalibus.* She had broken a
window and got in that way. Unable to evict the somewhat manhandled Venus
from his couch, he beat a retreat and retired, it is said, to his mother's house
in Tevershall. Meanwhile, the Venus of Stacks Gate is established in the cottage,
which she claims is her home, and Apollo, apparently, is domiciled in Tevershall.

"I repeat this from hearsay, as Mellors has not come to me personally. I had the particular bit of local garbage from our garbage bird, our ibis, our scavenging turkey-buzzard, Mrs. Bolton. I would not have repeated it had she not exclaimed: her Ladyship will go no more to the wood if *that* woman's going to be about!

"I like your picture of Sir Malcolm striding into the sea with white hair blowing and pink flesh glowing. I envy you that sun. Here it rains. But I don't envy Sir Malcolm his inveterate mortal carnality. However, it suits his age. Apparently one grows more carnal and more mortal as one grows older. Only youth has a taste of immortality—"

This news affected Connie in her state of semi-stupified well-being with vexation amounting to exasperation. Now she had got to be bothered by that beast of a woman! Now she must start and fret! She had no letter from Mellors. They had agreed not to write at all, but now she wanted to hear from him personally. After all, he was the father of the child that was coming. Let him write!

But how hateful! How everything was messed up. How foul those low people were! How nice it was here, in the sunshine and the indolence, compared to that dismal mess of that English midlands! After all, a clear sky was almost the most important thing in life.

She did not mention the fact of her pregnancy, even to Hilda. She wrote to Mrs. Bolton for exact information.

Duncan Forbes, an artist, friend of theirs, had arrived at the Villa Esmeralda, coming north from Rome. Now he made a third in the gondola, and he bathed with them across the lagoon, and was their escort: a quiet, almost taciturn young man, very advanced in his art.

She had a letter from Mrs. Bolton: "You will be pleased, I am sure, my Lady, when you see Sir Clifford. He's looking quite blooming and working very hard, and very hopeful. Of course, he is looking forward to seeing you among us again. It is a dull house without my Lady, and we shall all welcome her presence among us once more.

"About Mr. Mellors, I don't know how much Sir Clifford told you. It seems his wife came back all of a sudden one afternoon, and he found her sitting on the doorstep when he came in from the wood. She said she was come back to him and wanted to live with him again, as she was his legal wife, and he wasn't going to divorce her. Because it seems Mr. Mellors was trying for a divorce. But he wouldn't have anything to do with her, and wouldn't let her in the house, and did not go in himself; he went back into the wood without even opening the door.

"But when he came back after dark, he found the house broken into, so he went upstairs to see what she'd done, and he found her in bed without a rag on her. He offered her money, but she said she was his wife and he must take her back. I don't know what sort of a scene they had. His mother told me about it, she's terribly upset. Well, he told her he'd rot rather than ever live with her again, so he took his things and went straight to his mother's on Tevershall hill. He stopped the night and went to the wood next day through the park, never going near the cottage. It seems he never saw his wife that day. But the day after she was at her brother Dan's at Beggarlee, swearing and carrying on, saying she was his legal wife, and that he'd been having women at the cottage, because she'd found a scent-bottle in his drawer, and gold-tipped cigarette-ends on the ashheap, and I don't know what all. Then it seems the postman, Fred Kirk, says he heard somebody talking in Mr. Mellors' bedroom early one morning, and a motor car had been in the lane.

"Mr. Mellors stayed on with his mother, and went to the wood through the park, and it seems she stayed on at the cottage. Well, there was no end of talk. So at last Mr. Mellors and Tom Phillips went to the cottage and fetched away most of the furniture and bedding, and unscrewed the handle of the pump, so she was forced to go. But instead of going back to Stacks Gate she went and lodged with that Mrs. Swain at Beggarlee, because her brother Dan's wife wouldn't have her. And she kept going to old Mrs. Mellors' house, to catch him, and she began swearing he'd got in bed with her in the cottage, and she went to a lawyer to make him pay her an allowance. She's grown heavy, and more common than ever, and as strong as a bull. And she goes about saying the most awful things about him, how he has women at the cottage, and how he behaved to her when they were married, the low, beastly things he did to her, and I don't know what all. I'm sure it's awful, the mischief a woman can do, once she starts talking. And no matter how low she may be, there'll be some as will believe her, and some of the dirt will stick. I'm sure the way she makes out that Mr. Mellors was one of those low, beastly men with women, is simply shocking. And people are only too ready to believe things against anybody, especially things like that. She declares she'll never leave him alone while he lives. Though what I say is, if he was so beastly to her, why is she so anxious to go back to him? But, of course, she's coming near her change of life, for she's years older than he is. And these common, violent women always go partly insane when the change of life comes upon them."—

This was a nasty blow to Connie. Here she was, sure as life, coming in for her share of the lowness and dirt. She felt angry with him for not having got clear of a Bertha Coutts: nay, for ever having married her. Perhaps he had a certain hankering after lowness. Connie remembered the last night she had spent with him, and shivered. He had known all that sensuality, even with a Bertha Coutts! It was really rather disgusting. It would be well to be rid of him, clear of him altogether. He was perhaps really common, really low.

She had a revulsion against the whole affair, and almost envied the Guthrie girls their gawky inexperience and crude maidenliness. And she now dreaded the thought that anybody would know about herself and the keeper. How unspeakably humiliating! She was weary, afraid, and felt a craving for utter respectability, even for the vulgar and deadening respectability of the Guthrie girls. If Clifford knew about her affair, how unspeakably humiliating! She was afraid, terrified of society and its unclean bite. She almost wished she could get rid of the child again, and be quite clear. In short, she fell into a state of funk.

As for the scent-bottle, that was her own folly. She had not been able to refrain from perfuming his one or two handkerchiefs and his shirts in the drawer, just out of childishness, and she had left a little bottle of Coty's Wood-violet perfume, half empty, among his things. She wanted him to remember her in the perfume. As for the cigarette-ends, they were Hilda's.

She could not help confiding a little in Duncan Forbes. She didn't say she had been the keeper's lover, she only said she liked him, and told Forbes the history of the man.

"Oh," said Forbes, "you'll see, they'll never rest till they've pulled the man down and done him in. If he has refused to creep up into the middle classes, when he had a chance; and if he's a man who stands up for his own sex, then they'll do him in. It's the one thing they won't let you be, straight and open in your sex. You can be as dirty as you like. In fact the more dirt you do on sex, the better they like it. But if you believe in your own sex, and won't have it done dirt to: they'll down you. It's the one insane taboo left: sex as a natural and vital thing. They won't have it, and they'll kill you before they'll let you have it. You'll see, they'll hound that man down. And what's he done, after all? If he's made love to his wife all ends on, hasn't he a right to? She ought to be proud of it. But you see, even a low bitch like that turns on him, and uses the hyena instinct of the mob against sex, to pull him down. You have to snivel and feel sinful or awful about your sex, before you're allowed to have any. Oh, they'll hound the poor devil down."

Connie had a revulsion in the opposite direction now. What had he done, after all? What had he done to herself, Connie, but give her an exquisite pleasure, and a sense of freedom and life? He had released her warm, natural sexual flow. And for that they would hound him down.

No, no, it should not be. She saw the image of him, naked white with tanned face and hands, looking down and addressing his erect penis as if it were another being, the odd grin flickering on his face. And she heard his voice again: Tha's got the nicest woman's arse of anybody! And she felt his hand warmly and softly closing over her tail again, over her secret places, like a benediction. And the warmth ran through her womb, and the little flames flickered in her knees, and she said: Oh no! I mustn't go back on it! I must not go back on him. I must stick to him and to what I had of him, through everything. I had no warm, flamy life till he gave it me. And I won't go back on it.

She did a rash thing. She sent a letter to Ivy Bolton, enclosing a note to the keeper, and asking Mrs. Bolton to give it to him. And she wrote to him: "I am very much distressed to hear of all the trouble your wife is making for you, but don't mind it, it is only a sort of hysteria. It will all blow over as suddenly as it came. But I'm awfully sorry about it, and I do hope you are not minding very much. After all, it isn't worth it. She is only a hysterical woman who wants to hurt you. I shall be home in ten days' time, and I hope everything will be all right."

A few days later came a letter from Clifford. He was evidently upset.

"I am delighted to hear you are prepared to leave Venice on the sixteenth. But if you are enjoying it, don't hurry home. We miss you, Wragby misses you. But it is essential that you should get your full amount of sunshine, sunshine and pyjamas, as the advertisements of the Lido say. So please do stay on a little longer, if it is cheering you up and preparing you for our sufficiently awful winter. Even today, it rains.

"I am assiduously, admirably looked after by Mrs. Bolton. She is a queer specimen. The more I live, the more I realize what strange creatures human beings are. Some of them might just as well have a hundred legs, like a centipede, or six, like a lobster. The human consistency and dignity one has been led to expect from one's fellowmen seem actually non-existent. One doubts if they exist to any startling degree even in oneself.

"The scandal of the keeper continues and gets bigger like a snowball. Mrs. Bolton keeps me informed. She reminds me of a fish which, though dumb, seems to be breathing silent gossip through its gills, while ever it lives. All goes through the sieve of her gills, and nothing surprises her. It is as if the events of other people's lives were the necessary oxygen of her own.

"She is preoccupied with the Mellors scandal, and if I will let her begin, she takes me down to the depths. Her great indignation, which even then is like the indignation of an actress playing a role, is against the wife of Mellors, whom she persists in calling Bertha Coutts. I have been to the depths of the muddy lives of the Bertha Couttses of this world, and when, released from the current of gossip, I slowly rise to the surface again, I look at the daylight in wonder that it ever should be.

"It seems to me absolutely true, that our world, which appears to us the surface of all things, is really the *bottom* of a deep ocean: all our trees are submarine growths, and we are weird, scaly-clad submarine fauna, feeding ourselves on offal like shrimps. Only occasionally the soul rises gasping through the fathomless fathoms under which we live, far up to the surface of the ether, where there is true air. I am convinced that the air we normally breathe is a kind of water, and men and women are a species of fish.

"But sometimes the soul does come up, shoots like a kittiwake into the light, with ecstasy, after having preyed on the submarine depths. It is our mortal destiny, I suppose, to prey upon the ghastly subaqueous life of our fellow men, in the submarine jungle of mankind. But our immortal destiny is to escape, once we have swallowed our swimmy catch, up again into the bright ether, bursting out from the surface of Old Ocean into real light. Then one realizes one's eternal nature.

"When I hear Mrs. Bolton talk, I feel myself plunging down, down, to the depths where the fish of human secrets wriggle and swim. Carnal appetite makes one seize a beakful of prey: then up, up again, out of the dense into the ethereal, from the wet into the dry. To you I can tell the whole process. But with Mrs. Bolton I only feel the downward plunge, down, horribly, among the seaweeds and the pallid monsters of the very bottom.

"I am afraid we are going to lose our gamekeeper. The scandal of the truant wife, instead of dying down, has reverberated to greater and greater dimensions. He is accused of all unspeakable things, and curiously enough, the woman has managed to get the bulk of the colliers' wives behind her, gruesome fish, and the village is putrescent with talk.

"I hear this Bertha Coutts besieges Mellors in his mother's house, having ransacked the cottage and the hut. She seized one day upon her own daughter, as that chip of the female block was returning from school; but the little one, instead of kissing the loving mother's hand, bit it firmly, and so received from the other hand a smack in the face which sent her reeling into the gutter: whence she was rescued by an indignant and harassed grandmother.

"The woman has blown off an amazing quantity of poison-gas. She has aired in detail all those incidents of her conjugal life which are usually buried down in the deepest grave of matrimonial silence, between married couples. Having chosen to exhume them, after ten years of burial, she has a weird array. I hear these details from Linley and the doctor: the latter being amused. Of course, there is really nothing in it. Humanity has always had a strange avidity for unusual sexual postures, and if a man likes to use his wife, as Benvenuto Cellini says, 'in the Italian way,' well that is a matter of taste. But I had hardly expected our gamekeeper to be up to so many tricks. No doubt Bertha Coutts herself first put him up to them. In any case, it is a matter of their own personal squalor, and nothing to do with anybody else.

"However, everybody listens: as I do myself. A dozen years ago, common decency would have hushed the thing. But common decency no longer exists, and the colliers' wives are all up in arms and unabashed in voice. One would think every child in Teic, for the past fifty years, had been an immaculate conception, and every one of our nonconformist females was a shining Joan of Arc. That our estimable gamekeeper should have about him a touch of Rabelais seems to make him more monstrous and shocking than a murderer like Crippen. Yet these people in Tevershall are a loose lot, if one is to believe all accounts.

"The trouble is, however, the execrable Bertha Coutts has not confined herself to her own experiences and sufferings. She has discovered, at the top of her voice, that her husband has been 'keeping' women down at the cottage, and has made a few random shots at naming the women. This has brought a few decent names trailing through the mud, and the thing has gone quite considerably too far. An injunction has been taken out against the woman.

"I have had to interview Mellors about the business, as it was impossible to keep the woman away from the wood. He goes about as usual, with his Miller-of-the-Dee air, I care for nobody, no, not I, if nobody care for me! Nevertheless, I shrewdly suspect he feels like a dog with a tin can tied to its tail: though he makes a very good show of pretending the tin can isn't there. But I hear that in the village the women call away their children if he is passing, as if he were the Marquis de Sade in person. He goes on with a certain impudence, but I am afraid the tin can is firmly tied to his tail, and that inwardly he repeats, like Don Rodrigo in the Spanish ballad: 'Ah, now it bites me where I most have sinned!"

"I asked him if he thought he would be able to attend to his duty in the wood, and he said he did not think he had neglected it. I told him it was a nuisance to have the woman trespassing: to which he replied that he had no power to arrest her. Then I hinted at the scandal and its unpleasant course. 'Ay,' he said. 'Folks should do their own fuckin', then they wouldn't want to listen to a lot of clatfart about another man's.'

"He said it with some bitterness, and no doubt it contains the real germ of truth. The mode of putting it, however, is neither delicate nor respectful. I hinted as much, and then I heard the tin can rattle again. 'It's not for a man i' the shape you're in, Sir Clifford, to twit me for havin' a cod atween my legs.'

"These things, said indiscriminately to all and sundry, of course do not help him at all, and the rector, and Linley, and Burroughs all think it would be as well if the man left the place.

"I asked him if it was true that he entertained ladies down at the cottage, and all he said was: 'Why what's that to you, Sir Clifford?' I told him I intended to have decency observed on my estate, to which he replied: 'Then you mun button the mouths o' a' th' women.'—When I pressed him about his manner of life at the cottage, he said: 'Surely you might ma'e a scandal out o' me an' my bitch Flossie. You've missed summat there.' As a matter of fact, for an example of impertinence he'd be hard to beat.

"I asked him if it would be easy for him to find another job. He said: 'If you're hintin' that you'd like to shunt me out of this job, it'd be as easy as wink.' So he made no trouble at all about leaving at the end of next week, and apparently is willing to initiate a young fellow, Joe Chambers, into as many mysteries of the craft as possible. I told him I would give him a month's wages extra, when he left. He said he'd rather I kept my money, as I'd no occasion to ease my conscience. I asked him what he meant, and he said: 'You don't owe me nothing extra, Sir Clifford, so don't pay me nothing extra. If you think you see my shirt hanging out, just tell me.'

"Well, there is the end of it for the time being. The woman has gone away: we don't know where to: but she is liable to arrest if she shows her face in Tevershall. And I hear she is mortally afraid of gaol, because she merits it so well. Mellors will depart on Saturday week, and the place will soon become normal again.

"Meanwhile, my dear Connie, if you would enjoy the stay in Venice or in Switzerland till the beginning of August, I should be glad to think you were out of all this buzz of nastiness, which will have died quite away by the end of the month.

"So you see, we are deep-sea monsters, and when the lobster walks on mud, he stirs it up for everybody. We must perforce take it philosophically."—The irritation, and the lack of any sympathy in any direction, of Clifford's letter, had a bad effect on Connie. But she understood it better when she received the following from Mellors: "The cat is out of the bag, along with various other pussies. You have heard that my wife Bertha came back to my unloving arms, and took up her abode in the cottage: where, to speak disrespectfully, she smelled a rat in the shape of a little bottle of Coty. Other evidence she did not find, at least for some days, when she began to howl about the burnt photograph. She noticed the glass and the backboard in the spare bedroom. Unfortunately, on the backboard somebody had scribbled little sketches, and the initials, several times repeated: C. S. R. This, however, afforded no clue until she broke into the hut, and found one of your books, an autobiography of the actress Judith, with your name, Constance Stewart Reid, on the front page. After this, for some days she went round loudly saying that my paramour was no less a person than Lady Chatterley herself. The news came at last to the rector, Mr. Burroughs, and to Sir Clifford. They then proceeded to take legal steps against my liege lady, who for her part disappeared, having always had a mortal fear of the police.

"Sir Clifford asked to see me, so I went to him. He talked around things and seemed annoyed with me. Then he asked if I knew that even her ladyship's name had been mentioned. I said I never listened to scandal, and was surprised to hear this bit from Sir Clifford himself. He said, of course, it was a great insult, and I told him there was Queen Mary on a calendar in the scullery, no doubt because Her Majesty formed part of my harem. But he didn't appreciate the sarcasm. He as good as told me I was a disreputable character who walked about with all of my breeches' buttons undone, and I as good as told him he'd nothing to unbutton anyhow, so he gave me the sack, and I leave on Saturday week, and the place thereof shall know me no more.

"I shall go to London, and my old landlady, Mrs. Inger, 17 Coburg Square, will either give me a room or will find one for me.

"Be sure your sins will find you out, especially if you're married and her name's Bertha.—"

There was not a word about herself, or to her. Connie resented this. He might have said some few words of consolation or reassurance. But she knew he was leaving her free, free to go back to Wragby and to Clifford. She resented that too. He need not be so falsely chivalrous. She wished he had said to Clifford: "Yes, she is my lover and mistress and I am proud of it!" But his courage wouldn't carry him so far.

So her name was coupled with his in Tevershall! It was a mess. But that would soon die down.

She was angry, with the complicated and confused anger that made her inert. She did not know what to do nor what to say, so she said and did nothing. She went on at Venice just the same, rowing out in the gondola with Duncan Forbes, bathing, letting the days slip by. Duncan, who had been rather depressingly in love with her ten years ago, was in love with her again. But she said to him: "I only want one thing of men, and that is, that they should leave me alone."

So Duncan left her alone: really quite pleased to be able to. All the same, he offered her a soft stream of a queer, inverted sort of love. He wanted to be *with* her.

"Have you ever thought," he said to her one day, "how very little people are connected with one another. Look at Daniele! He is handsome as a son of the sun. But see how alone he looks in his handsomeness. Yet I bet he has a wife and family, and couldn't possibly go away from them."

"Ask him," said Connie.

Duncan did so. Daniele said he was married, and had two children, both male, aged seven and nine. But he betrayed no emotion over the fact.

"Perhaps only people who are capable of real togetherness have that look of being alone in the universe," said Connie. "The others have a certain stickiness, they stick to the mass, like Giovanni."—"And," she thought to herself, "like you, Duncan."

Chapter Eighteen

S he had to make up her mind what to do. She would leave Venice on the Saturday that he was leaving Wragby: in six days' time. This would bring her to London on the Monday following, and she would then see him. She wrote to him to the London address, asking him to send her a letter to Hartland's hotel, and to call for her on the Monday evening at seven.

Inside herself, she was curiously and complicatedly angry, and all her responses were numb. She refused to confide even in Hilda, and Hilda, offended by her steady silence, had become rather intimate with a Dutch woman. Connie hated those rather stifling intimacies between women, intimacies into which Hilda always entered ponderously.

Sir Malcolm decided to travel with Connie, and Duncan could come on with Hilda. The old artist always did himself well: he took berths on the Orient Express, in spite of Connie's dislike of *trains de luxe,* the atmosphere of vulgar depravity there is aboard them nowadays. However, it would make the journey to Paris shorter.

Sir Malcolm was always uneasy going back to his wife. It was a habit carried over from the first wife. But there would be a house-party for the grouse, and he wanted to be well ahead. Connie, sunburnt and handsome, sat in silence, forgetting all about the landscape.

"A little dull for you, going back to Wragby," said her father, noticing her glumness.

"I'm not sure I shall go back to Wragby," she said, with startling abruptness, looking into his eyes with her big blue eyes. His big blue eyes took on the frightened look of a man whose social conscience is not quite clear.   .

"You mean you'll stay on in Paris a while?"

"No! I mean never go back to Wragby."

He was bothered by his own little problems, and sincerely hoped he was getting none of hers to shoulder.

"How's that, all at once?" he asked.

"I'm going to have a child."

It was the first time she had uttered the words to any living soul, and it seemed to mark a cleavage in her life.

"How do you know?" said her father.

She smiled.

"How *should* I know?"

"But not Clifford's child, of course?"

"No! Another man's."

She rather enjoyed tormenting him.

"Do I know the man?" asked Sir Malcolm.

"No! You've never seen him."

There was a long pause.

"And what are your plans?"

"I don't know. That's the point."

"No patching it up with Clifford?"

"I suppose Clifford would take it," said Connie. "He told me, after last time you talked to him, he wouldn't mind if I had a child, so long as I went about it discreetly."

"Only sensible thing he could say, under the circumstances. Then I suppose it'll be all right."

"In what way?" said Connie, looking into her father's eyes. They were big blue eyes rather like her own, but with a certain uneasiness in them, a look sometimes of an uneasy little boy, sometimes a look of sullen selfishness, usually goodhumored and wary.

"You can present Clifford with an heir to all the Chatterleys, and put another baronet in Wragby."

Sir Malcolm's face smiled with a half-sensual smile.

"But I don't think I want to," she said.

"Why not? Feeling entangled with the other man? Well! If you want the truth from me, my child, it's this. The world goes on. Wragby stands and will go on standing. The world is more or less a fixed thing, and, externally, we have to adapt ourselves to it. Privately, in my private opinion, we can please ourselves. Emotions change. You may like one man this year and another next. But Wragby still stands. Stick to Wragby as far as Wragby sticks to you. Then please yourself. But you'll get very little out of making a break. You can make a break if you wish. You have an independent income, the only thing that never lets you down. But you won't get much out of it. Put a little baronet in Wragby. It's an amusing thing to do."

And Sir Malcolm sat back and smiled again. Connie did not answer.

"I hope you had a real man at last," he said to her after a while, sensually alert.

"I did. That's the trouble. There aren't many of them about," she said.

"No, by God!" he mused. "There aren't! Well, my dear, to look at you, he was a lucky man. Surely he wouldn't make trouble for you?"

"Oh, no! He leaves me my own mistress entirely."

"Quite! Quite! A genuine man would."

Sir Malcolm was pleased. Connie was his favorite daughter, he had always liked the female in her. Not so much of her mother in her as in Hilda. And he had always disliked Clifford. So he was pleased, and very tender with his daughter, as if the unborn child were his child.

He drove with her to Hartland's hotel, and saw her installed: then went round to his club. She had refused his company for the evening.

She found a letter from Mellors. "I won't come round to your hotel, but I'll wait for you outside the Golden Cock in Adam Street at seven."

There he stood, tall and slender, and so different, in a formal suit of thin dark cloth. He had a natural distinction, but he had not the cut-to-pattern look of her class. Yet, she saw at once, he could go anywhere. He had a native breeding which was really much nicer than the cut-to-pattern class thing.

"Ah, there you are! How well you look!"

"Yes! But not you."

She looked in his face anxiously. It was thin, and the cheekbones showed. But his eyes smiled at her, and she felt at home with him. There it was: suddenly, the tension of keeping up her appearances fell from her. Something flowed out of him physically, that made her feel inwardly at ease and happy, at home. With a woman's now alert instinct for happiness, she registered it at once. "I'm happy when he's there!" Not all the sunshine of Venice had given her this inward expansion and warmth.

"Was it horrid for you?" she asked as she sat opposite him at table. He was too thin; she saw it now. His hand lay as she knew it, with that curious loose forgottenness of a sleeping animal. She wanted so much to take it and kiss it. But she did not quite dare.

"People are always horrid," he said.

"And did you mind very much?"

"I minded, as I always shall mind. And I knew I was a fool to mind."

"Did you feel like a dog with a tin can tied to its tail? Clifford said you felt like that."

He looked at her. It was cruel of her at that moment: for his pride had suffered bitterly.

"I suppose I did," he said.

She never knew the fierce bitterness with which he resented insult.

There was a long pause.

"And did you miss me?" she asked.

"I was glad you were out of it."

Again there was a pause.

"But did people *believe* about you and me?" she asked.

"No! I don't think so for a moment."

"Did Clifford?"

"I should say not. He put it off without thinking about it. But naturally it made him want to see the last of me."

"I'm going to have a child."

The expression died utterly out of his face, out of his whole body. He looked at her with darkened eyes, whose look she could not understand at all: like some dark-flamed spirit looking at her.

"Say you're glad!" she pleaded, groping for his hand. And she saw a certain exultance spring up in him. But it was netted down by things she could not understand.

"It's the future," he said.

"But aren't you glad?" she persisted.

"I have such a terrible mistrust of the future."

"But you needn't be troubled by any responsibility. Clifford would have it as his own, he'd be glad."

She saw him go pale, and recoil under this. He did not answer.

"Shall I go back to Clifford and put a little baronet into Wragby?" she asked.

He looked at her, pale and very remote. The ugly little grin flickered on his face.

"You wouldn't have to tell him who the father was."

"Oh!" she said; "he'd take it even then, if I wanted him to."

He thought for a time.

"Ay!" he said at last, to himself. "I suppose he would."

There was silence. A big gulf was between them.

"But you don't want me to go back to Clifford, do you?" she asked him.

"What do you want yourself?" he replied.

"I want to live with you," she said simply.

In spite of himself, little flames ran over his belly as he heard her say it, and he dropped his head. Then he looked up at her again, with those haunted eyes.

"If it's worth it to you," he said. "I've got nothing."

"You've got more than most men. Come, you know it," she said.

"In one way, I know it." He was silent for a time, thinking. Then he resumed: "They used to say I had too much of the woman in me. But it's not that. I'm not a woman because I don't want to shoot birds, neither because I don't want to make money, or get on. I could have got on in the army, easily, but I didn't like the army. Though I could manage the men all right: they liked me and they had a bit of a holy fear of me when I got mad. No, it was stupid, dead-handed higher authority that made the army dead: absolutely fool-dead. I like men, and men like me. But I can't stand the twaddling bossy impudence of the people who run this world. That's why I can't get on. I hate the impudence of money, and I hate the impudence of class. So in the world as it is, what have I to offer a woman?"

"But why offer anything? It's not a bargain. It's just that we love one another," she said.

"Nay, nay! It's more than that. Living is moving and moving on. My life won't get down the proper gutters, it just won't. So I'm a bit of a waste ticket by myself. And I've no business to take a woman into my life, unless my life does something and gets somewhere, inwardly at least, to keep us both fresh. A man must offer a woman *some* meaning in his life, if it's going to be an isolated life, and if she's a genuine woman. I can't be just your male concubine."

"Why not?" she said.

"Why, because I can't. And you would soon hate it."

"As if you couldn't trust me," she said.

The grin flickered on his face.

"The money is yours, the position is yours, the decisions will lie with you. I'm not just my lady's fucker, after all."

"What else are you?"

"You may well ask. It no doubt is invisible. Yet I'm something to myself at least. I can see the point of my own existence, though I can quite understand nobody else's seeing it."

"And will your existence have less point, if you live with me?"

He paused a long time before replying:

"It might."

She, too, stayed to think about it.

"And what is the point of your existence?"

"I tell you, it's invisible. I don't believe in the world, not in money, nor in advancement, nor in the future of our civilization. If there's got to be a future for humanity, there'll have to be a very big change from what now is."

"And what will the real future have to be like?"

"God knows! I can feel something inside me, all mixed up with a lot of rage. But what it really amounts to, I don't know."

"Shall I tell you?" she said, looking into his face. "Shall I tell you what you have that other men don't have, and that will make the future? Shall I tell you?"

"Tell me, then," he replied.

"It's the courage of your own tenderness, that's what it is, like when you put your hand on my tail and say I've got a pretty tail."

The grin came flickering on his face.

"That!" he said.

Then he sat thinking.

"Ay!" he said. "You're right. It's that really. It's that all the way through. I knew it with the men. I had to be in touch with them, physically, and not go back on it. I had to be bodily aware of them and a bit tender to them, even if I put 'em through hell. It's a question of awareness, as Buddha said. But even he fought shy of the bodily awareness, and that natural physical tenderness which is the best, even between men; in a proper manly way. Makes 'em really manly, not so monkeyish. Ay! it's tenderness, really; it's cunt-awareness. Sex is really only touch, the closest of all touch. And it's touch we're afraid of. We're only half-conscious, and half alive. We've got to come alive and aware. Especially the English have got to get into touch with one another, a bit delicate and a bit tender. It's our crying need."

She looked at him.

"Then why are you afraid of me?" she said.

He looked at her a long time before he answered.

"It's the money, really, and the position. It's the world in you."

"But isn't there tenderness in me?" she said wistfully.

He looked down at her, with darkened, abstract eyes.

"Ay! It come an' goes, like in me."

"But can't you trust it between you and me?" she asked, gazing anxiously at him.

She saw his face all softening down, losing its armor.

"Maybe!" he said.

They were both silent.

"I want you to hold me in your arms," she said. "I want you to tell me you are glad we are having a child."

She looked so lovely and warm and wistful, his bowels stirred towards her.

"I suppose we can go to my room," he said. "Though it's scandalous again."

But she saw the forgetfulness of the world coming over him again, his face taking the soft, pure look of tender passion.

They walked by the remoter streets to Coburg Square, where he had a room at the top of the house, an attic room where he cooked for himself on a gas range. It was small, but decent and tidy.

She took off her things, and made him do the same. She was lovely in the soft first flush of her pregnancy.

"I ought to leave you alone," he said.

"No!" she said. "Love me! Love me, and say you'll keep me. Say you'll keep me! Say you'll never let me go, to the world nor to anybody!"

She crept close against him, clinging fast to his thin, strong naked body, the only home she had ever known.

"Then I'll keep thee," he said. "If tha wants it, then I'll keep thee."

He held her round and fast.

"And say you're glad about the child," she repeated. "Kiss it! Kiss my womb and say you're glad it's there."

But that was more difficult for him.

"I've a dread of puttin' children i' th' world," he said. "I've such a dread o' th' future for 'em."

"But you've put it into me. Be tender to it, and that will be its future already. Kiss it!"

He quivered, because it was true. "Be tender to it, and that will be its future."— At that moment he felt a sheer love for the woman. He kissed her belly and her mount of Venus, to kiss close to the womb and the fetus within the womb.

"Oh, you love me! You love me!" she said, in a little cry like one of her blind, inarticulate love cries. And he went in to her softly, feeling the stream of tenderness flowing in release from his bowels to hers, the bowels of compassion kindled between them.

And he realized as he went in to her that this was the thing he had to do, to come into tender touch, without losing his pride or his dignity or his integrity as a man. After all, if she had money and means, and he had none, he should be too proud and honorable to hold back his tenderness from her on that account.

"I stand for the touch of bodily awareness between human beings," he said to himself, "and the touch of tenderness. And she is my mate. And it is a battle against the money, and the machine, and the insentient ideal monkeyishness of the world. And she will stand behind me there. Thank God I've got a woman! Thank God I've got a woman who is with me, and tender and aware of me. Thank God she's not a bully, nor a fool. Thank God she's a tender, aware woman." And as his seed sprang in her, his soul sprang towards her too, in the creative act that is far more than procreative.

She was quite determined now that there should be no parting between him and her. But the ways and means were still to settle.

"Did you hate Bertha Coutts?" she asked him.

"Don't talk to me about her."

"Yes! You must let me. Because once you liked her. And once you were as intimate with her as you are with me. So you have to tell me. Isn't it rather terrible, when you've been intimate with her, to hate her so? Why is it?"

"I don't know. She sort of kept her will ready against me, always, always: her ghastly female will: her freedom! A woman's ghastly freedom that ends in the most beastly bullying! Oh, she always kept her freedom against me, like vitriol in my face."

"But she's not free of you even now. Does she still love you?"

"No, no! If she's not free of me, it's because she's got that mad rage, she must try to bully me."

"But she must have loved you."

"No! Well, in specks, she did. She was drawn to me. And I think even that she hated. She loved me in moments. But she always took it back, and started bullying. Her deepest desire was to bully me, and there was no altering her. Her *will* was wrong, from the first."

"But perhaps she felt you didn't really love her, and she wanted to make you."

"My God, it was bloody making."

"But you didn't really love her, did you? You did her that wrong."

"How could I? I began to. I began to love her. But somehow, she always ripped me up. No, don't let's talk of it. It was a doom, that was. And she was a doomed woman. This last time, I'd have shot her like I shoot a stoat, if I'd but been allowed: a raving, doomed thing in the shape of a woman! If only I could have shot her, and ended the whole misery! It ought to be allowed. When a woman gets absolutely possessed by her own will, her own will set against everything, then it's fearful, and she should be shot at last."

"And shouldn't men be shot at last, if they get possessed by their own will."

"Ay!—the same! But I must get free of her, or she'll be at me again. I wanted to tell you. I must get a divorce if I possibly can. So we must be careful. We mustn't really be seen together, you and I. I never, *never* could stand it if she came down on me and you."

Connie pondered this.

"Then we can't be together?" she said.

"Not for six months or so. But I think my divorce will go through in September, then till March."

"But the baby will probably be born at the end of February," she said.

He was silent.

"I could wish the Cliffords and Berthas all dead," she said.

"It's not being very tender to them," she said.

"Tender to them? Yea, even then the tenderest thing you could do for them, perhaps, would be to give them death. They can't live. They only frustrate life. Their souls are awful inside them. Death ought to be sweet to them. And I ought to be allowed to shoot them."

"But you wouldn't do it," she said.

"I would though! and with less qualms than I shoot a weasel. It anyhow has a prettiness and a loneliness. But they are legion. Oh, I'd shoot them."

"Then perhaps it is just as well you daren't."

"Well."

Connie had now plenty to think of. It was evident he wanted absolutely to be free of Bertha Coutts. And she felt he was right. The last attack had been too grim.—This meant her living alone, till spring. Perhaps she could get divorced from Clifford. But how? If Mellors were named, then there was an end to *his* divorce. How loathsome! Couldn't one go right away, to the far ends of the earth, and be free from it all?

One could not. The far ends of the world are not five minutes from Charing Cross, nowadays. While the wireless is active, there are no far ends of the earth. Kings of Dahomey and Lamas of Tibet listen in to London and New York.

Patience! Patience! The world is a vast and ghastly intricacy of mechanism, and one has to be very wary, not to get mangled by it.

Connie confided in her father.

"You see, father, he was Clifford's gamekeeper: but he was an officer in the army in India. Only he is like Colonel C. E. Florence, who preferred to become a private soldier again."

Sir Malcolm, however, had no sympathy with the unsatisfactory mysticism of the famous C. E. Florence. He saw too much advertisement behind all the humility. It looked just the sort of conceit the knight most loathed, the conceit of self-abasement.

"Where did your gamekeeper spring from?" asked Sir Malcolm irritably.

"He was a collier's son in Tevershall. But he's absolutely presentable."

The knight artist became more angry.

"Looks to me like a gold-digger," he said. "And you're a pretty easy gold-mine, apparently."

"No, father, it's not like that. You'd know if you saw him. He's a man. Clifford always detested him for not being humble."

"Apparently he had a good instinct, for once."

What Sir Malcolm could not bear, was the scandal of his daughter's having an intrigue with a gamekeeper. He did not mind the intrigue: he minded the scandal.

"I care nothing about the fellow. He's evidently been able to get around you all right. But by God, think of all the talk. Think of your stepmother, how she'll take it!"

"I know," said Connie. "Talk is beastly: especially if you live in society. And he wants so much to get his own divorce. I thought we might perhaps say it was another man's child, and not mention Mellors' name at all."

"Another man's! What other man's?"

"Perhaps Duncan Forbes. He has been our friend all his life. And he's a fairly well-known artist. And he's fond of me."

"Well I'm damned! Poor Duncan. And what's he going to get out of it?"

"I don't know. But he might rather like it, even."

"He might, might he? Well, he's a funny man, if he does. Why, you've never had an affair with him, have you?"

"No! But he doesn't really want it. He only loves me to be near him, but not to touch him."

"My God, what a generation!"

"He would like me most of all to be a model for him to paint from. Only I never wanted to."

"God help him! But he looks down-trodden enough for anything."

"Still, you wouldn't mind so much the talk about him?"

"My God, Connie, all the bloody contriving!"

"I know! It's sickening! But what can I do?"

"Contriving, conniving; conniving, contriving! Makes a man think he's lived too long."

"Come, father, if you haven't done a good deal of contriving and conniving in your time, you may talk."

"But it was different, I assure you."

"It's *always* different."

Hilda arrived, also furious when she heard of the new developments. And she also simply could not stand the thought of a public scandal about her sister and a gamekeeper. Too, too humiliating!

"Why should we not just disappear, separately, to British Columbia, and have no scandal?" said Connie.

But that was no good. The scandal would come out just the same. And if Connie was going with the man, she'd better be able to marry him. This was Hilda's opinion. Sir Malcolm wasn't sure. The affair might still blow over.

"But will you see him, father?"

Poor Sir Malcolm! he was by no means keen on it. And poor Mellors, he was still less keen. Yet the meeting took place: lunch in a private room at the club, the two men alone, looking one another up and down.

Sir Malcolm drank a fair amount of whiskey, Mellors also drank. And they talked all the while about India, on which the younger man was well informed.

This lasted during the meal. Only when coffee was served, and the waiter had gone, Sir Malcolm lit a cigar and said, heartily:

"Well, young man, and what about my daughter?"

The grin flickered on Mellors' face.

"Well, Sir, and what about her?"

"She's to have a child of yours, I understand."

"I have that honor!" grinned Mellors.

"Honor by God!" Sir Malcolm gave a little squirting laugh, and became Scotch and lewd. "Honor! How was the going, eh? Good, my boy, what?"

"Good!"

"I'll bet it was! Ha-ha! My daughter, chip of the old block, what! I never went back on a good bit of fucking, myself. Though her mother, oh, holy saints!" he rolled his eyes to heaven. "But you warmed her up, oh, you warmed her up, I can see that. Ha-ha! My blood in her! You set fire to her haystack all right. Ha-ha-ha! I was jolly glad of it, I can tell you. She needed it. Oh, she's a nice girl, she's a nice girl, and I knew she'd be good going, if only some damned man would set her stack on fire! Ha-ha-ha! A gamekeeper, oh, my boy! Bloody good poacher, if you ask me. Ha-ha! But now, look here, speaking seriously, what are we going to do about it? Speaking seriously, you know!"

Speaking seriously, they didn't get very far. Mellors, though a little tipsy, was much the soberer of the two. He kept the conversation as intelligent as possible: which isn't saying much.

"So you're a gamekeeper! Oh, you're quite right! That sort of game is worth a man's while, eh, what? The test of a woman is when you pinch her bottom. You can tell just by the feel of her bottom if she's going to come up all right. Ha-ha! I envy you, my boy. How old are you?"

"Thirty-nine."

The knight lifted his eyebrows.

"As much as that! Well, you've another good twenty years, by the look of you. Oh, gamekeeper or not, you're a good cock. I can see that with one eye shut. Not like that blasted Clifford! A lily-livered hound with never a fuck in him, never had. I like you, my boy. I'll bet you've a good cod on you: oh, you're a bantam, I can see that. You're a fighter. Gamekeeper! ha-ha, by crickey, I wouldn't trust my game to you! But look here, seriously, what are we going to do about it? The world's full of blasted old women."

Seriously, they didn't do anything about it, except establish the old freemasonry of male sensuality between them.

"And look here, my boy, if ever I can do anything for you, you can rely on me. Gamekeeper? Christ, but it's rich! I like it! Oh, I like it! Shows the girl's got spunk. What? After all, you know, she has her own income: moderate, moderate, but above starvation. And I'll leave her what I've got. By God, I will. She deserves it, for showing spunk, in a world of old women. I've been struggling to get myself clear of the skirts of old women for seventy years, and haven't managed it yet. But you're the man, I can see that."

"I'm glad you think so. They usually tell me, in a sideways fashion, that I'm the monkey."

"Oh, they would! My dear fellow, what could you be but a monkey, to all the old women."

They parted most genially, and Mellors laughed inwardly all the time for the rest of the day.

The following day he had lunch with Connie and Hilda at some discreet place.

"It's a very great pity it's such an ugly situation all round," said Hilda.

"I had a lot o' fun out of it," said he.

"I think you might have avoided putting children into the world until you were both free to marry and have children."

"The Lord blew a bit too soon on the spark," said he.

"I think the Lord had nothing to do with it. Of course, Connie has enough money to keep you both, but the situation is unbearable."

"But then, you don't have to bear more than a small corner of it, do you?" said he.

"If you'd been in her own class."

"Or if I'd been in a cage at the Zoo."

There was silence.

"I think," said Hilda, "it will be best if she names quite another man as co-respondent, and you stay out of it altogether."

"But I thought I'd put my foot right in."

"I mean, in the divorce proceedings."

He gazed at her in wonder. Connie had not dared mention the Duncan scheme to him.

"I don't follow," he said.

"We have a friend who would probably agree to be named as co-respondent, so that your name need not appear," said Hilda.

"You mean a man?"

"Of course!"

"But she's got no other?"

He looked in wonder at Connie.

"No, no!" she said hastily. "Only that old friendship, quite simple, no love."

"Then why should the fellow take the blame? If he's had nothing out of you?"

"Some men are chivalrous and don't only count what they get out of a woman," said Hilda.

"One for me, eh? But who's the johnny?"

"A friend whom we've known since we were children in Scotland, an artist."

"Duncan Forbes!" he said at once, for Connie had talked of him. "And how would you shift the blame on to him?"

"They could stay together in some hotel, or she could even stay in his apartment."

"Seems to me like a lot of fuss for nothing," he said.

"What else do you suggest?" said Hilda. "If your name appears, you will get no divorce from your wife, who is apparently quite an impossible person to be mixed up with."

"All that!" he said grimly.

There was a long silence.

"We could go right away," he said.

"There is no right away for Connie," said Hilda. "Clifford is too well known."

Again the silence of pure frustration.

"The world is what it is. If you want to live together without being persecuted, you will have to marry. To marry, you both have to be divorced. So how are you both going about it?"

He was silent for a long time.

"How are *you* going about it for us?" he said.

"We will see if Duncan will consent to figure as co-respondent: then we must get Clifford to divorce Connie: and you must go on with your divorce, and you must both keep apart till you are free."

"Sounds like a lunatic asylum."

"Possibly! And the world would look on you as lunatics: or worse."

"What is worse?"

"Criminals, I suppose."

"Hope I can plunge in the dagger a few more times yet," he said grinning. Then he was silent, and angry.

"Well!" he said at last. "I agree to anything. The world is a raving idiot, and no man can kill it: though I'll do my best. But you're right. We must rescue ourselves as best we can."

He looked in humiliation, anger, wariness and misery at Connie.

"Ma lass!" he said. "The world's goin' to put salt on thy tail."

"Not if we don't let it," she said.

She minded this conniving against the world less than he did.

Duncan, when approached, also insisted on seeing the delinquent gamekeeper, so there was a dinner, this time in his flat: the four of them. Duncan was a rather short, broad, dark-skinned, taciturn Hamlet of a fellow with straight black hair and a weird Celtic conceit of himself. His art was all tubes and valves and spirals and strange colors, ultra modern, yet with a certain power, even a certain purity of form and tone: only Mellors thought it cruel and repellent. He did not venture to say so, for Duncan was almost insane on the point of his art; it was a personal cult, a personal religion with him.

They were looking at the pictures in the studio, and Duncan kept his smallish brown eyes on the other man. He wanted to hear what the gamekeeper would say. He knew already Connie's and Hilda's opinions.

"It is like a pure bit of murder," said Mellors at last; a speech Duncan by no means expected from a gamekeeper.

"And who is murdered?" asked Hilda, rather coldly and sneeringly.

"Me! It murders all the bowels of compassion in a man."

A wave of pure hate came out of the artist. He heard the note of dislike in the other man's voice, and the note of contempt. And he himself loathed the mention of bowels of compassion. Sickly sentiment!

Mellors stood rather tall and thin, worn-looking, gazing with flickering detachment that was something like the dancing of a moth on the wing, at the pictures.

"Perhaps stupidity is murdered; sentimental stupidity," sneered the artist.

"Do you think so? I think all these tubes and corrugated vibrations are stupid enough for anything and pretty sentimental. They show a lot of self-pity and an awful lot of nervous self-opinion, seems to me."

In another wave of hate, the artist's face looked yellow. But with a sort of silent hauteur he turned the pictures to the wall.

"I think we may go to the dining-room," he said.

And they trailed off, dismally.

After coffee, Duncan said:

"I don't at all mind posing as the father of Connie's child. But only on the condition that she'll come and pose as a model for me. I've wanted her for years, and she's always refused." He uttered it with the dark finality of an inquisitor announcing an *auto da fé*.

"Ah!" said Mellors. "You only do it on condition, then?"

"Quite! I only do it on that condition." The artist tried to put the utmost contempt of the other person into his speech. He put a little too much.

"Better have me as a model at the same time," said Mellors. "Better do us in a group, Vulcan and Venus under the net of art. I used to be a blacksmith, before I was a gamekeeper."

"Thank you," said the artist. "I don't think Vulcan has a figure that interests me."

"Not even if it was tubified and tittivated up?"

There was no answer. The artist was too haughty for further words.

It was a dismal party, in which the artist henceforth steadily ignored the presence of the other man, and talked only briefly, as if the words were wrung out of the depths of his gloomy portentousness, to the women.

"You didn't like him, but he's better than that, really. He's really kind," Connie explained as they left.

"He's a little black pup with a corrugated distemper," said Mellors.

"No, he wasn't nice today."

"And will you go and be a model to him?"

"Oh, I don't really mind any more. He won't touch me. And I don't mind anything, if it paves the way to a life together for you and me."

"But he'll only shit on you on canvas."

"I don't care. He'll only be painting his own feelings for me, and I don't mind if he does that. I wouldn't have him touch me, not for anything. But if he thinks he can do anything with his owlish arty staring, let him stare. He can make as many empty tubes and corrugations out of me as he likes. It's his funeral. He hated you for what you said: that his tubified art is sentimental and self-important. But of course it's true."

Chapter Nineteen

*D*ear Clifford, I am afraid what you foresaw has happened. I am really in love with another man, and I do hope you will divorce me. I am staying at present with Duncan in his flat. I told you he was at Venice with us. I'm awfully unhappy for your sake: but do try to take it quietly. You don't really need me any more, and I can't bear to come back to Wragby. I'm most awfully sorry. But do try to forgive me, and divorce me and find someone better. I'm not really the right person for you, I am too impatient and selfish, I suppose. But I can't ever come back to live with you again. And I feel so frightfully sorry about it all, for your sake. But if you don't let yourself get worked up, you'll see you won't mind so frightfully. You didn't really care about me personally. So do forgive me and get rid of me."

Clifford was not *inwardly* surprised to get this letter. Inwardly, he had known for a long time she was leaving him. But he had absolutely refused any outward admission of it. Therefore, outwardly, it came as the most terrible blow and shock to him. He had kept the surface of his confidence in her quite serene.

And that is how we are. By strength of will we cut off our inner intuitive knowledge from admitted consciousness. This causes a state of dread, or apprehension, which makes the blow ten times worse when it does fall.

Clifford was like a hysterical child. He gave Mrs. Bolton a terrible shock, sitting up in bed ghastly and blank.

"Why, Sir Clifford, whatever's the matter?"

No answer! She was terrified lest he had had a stroke. She hurried and felt his face, took his pulse.

"Is there a pain? Do try and tell me where it hurts you. Do tell me!"

No answer!

"Oh, dear! Oh, dear! Then I'll telephone to Sheffield for Dr. Carrington, and Dr. Lecky may as well run round straight away."

She was moving to the door, when he said in a hollow tone:

"No!"

She stopped and gazed at him. His face was yellow, blank, and like the face of an idiot.

"Do you mean you'd rather I didn't fetch the doctor?"

"Yes! I don't want him," came the sepulchral voice.

"Oh, but, Sir Clifford, you're ill, and I daren't take the responsibility. I *must* send for the doctor, or *I* shall be blamed."

A pause; then the hollow voice said:

"I'm not ill. My wife isn't coming back."—It was as if an image spoke.

"Not coming back? You mean her ladyship?" Mrs. Bolton moved a little nearer to the bed. "Oh, don't you believe it. You can trust her ladyship to come back."

The image in the bed did not change, but it pushed a letter over the counterpane.

"Read it!" said the sepulchral voice.

"Why, if it's a letter from her ladyship, I'm sure her ladyship wouldn't want me to read her letter to you, Sir Clifford. You can tell me what she says, if you wish."

But the face with the fixed blue eyes sticking out did not change.

"Read it!" repeated the voice.

"Why, if I must, I do it to obey you, Sir Clifford," she said.

And she read the letter.

"Well I *am* surprised at her ladyship," she said. "She promised so faithfully she'd come back!"

The face in the bed seemed to deepen its expression of wild, but motionless distraction. Mrs. Bolton looked at it and was worried. She knew what she was up against: male hysteria. She had not nursed soldiers without learning something about that very unpleasant disease.

She was a little impatient of Sir Clifford. Any man in his senses must have *known* his wife was in love with somebody else, and was going to leave him. Even, she was sure, Sir Clifford was inwardly absolutely aware of it, only he wouldn't admit it to himself. If he would have admitted it, and prepared himself for it! or if he would have admitted it, and actively struggled with his wife against it: that would have been acting like a man. But no! he knew it, and all the time tried to kid himself it wasn't so. He felt the devil twisting his tail, and pretended it was the angels smiling on him. This state of falsity had now brought on that crisis of falsity and dislocation, hysteria, which is a form of insanity. "It comes," she thought to herself, hating him a little, "because he always thinks of himself. He's so wrapped up in his own immortal self, that when he does get a shock he's like a mummy tangled in its own bandages. Look at him!"

But hysteria is dangerous: and she was a nurse, it was her duty to pull him out. Any attempt to rouse his manhood and his pride would only make him worse: for his manhood was dead, temporarily if not finally. He would only squirm softer and softer, like a worm, and become more dislocated.

The only thing was to release his self-pity. Like the lady in Tennyson, he must weep or he must die.

So Mrs. Bolton began to weep first. She covered her face with her hands and burst into little wild sobs. "I would never have believed it of her ladyship, I wouldn't!" She wept, suddenly summoning up all her old grief and sense of woe, and weeping the tears of her own bitter chagrin. Once she started her weeping was genuine enough, for she had had something to weep for.

Clifford thought of the way he had been betrayed by the woman Connie, and in a contagion of grief, tears filled his eyes and began to run down his cheeks. He was weeping for himself. Mrs. Bolton, as soon as she saw the tears running over his blank face, hastily wiped her own wet cheeks on her little handkerchief, and leaned towards him.

"Now don't you fret, Sir Clifford!" she said, in a luxury of emotion. "Now, don't you fret; don't, you'll only do yourself an injury!"

His body shivered suddenly in an indrawn breath of silent sobbing, and the tears ran quicker down his face. She laid her hand on his arm, and her own tears fell again. Again the shiver went through him, like a convulsion, and she laid her arm round his shoulder. "There, there! There, there! Don't you fret, then, don't you! Don't you fret!" she moaned to him, while her own tears fell. And she drew him to her, and held her arms round his great shoulders, while he laid his face on her bosom and sobbed, shaking and hulking his huge shoulders, whilst she softly stroked his dusky-blond hair and said: "There! There! There! There, then! There, then! Never you mind! Never you mind, then!"

And he put his arms round her and clung to her like a child, wetting the bib of her starched white apron, and the bosom of her pale-blue cotton dress, with his tears. He had let himself go altogether, at last.

So at length she kissed him, and rocked him on her bosom, and in her heart she said to herself: "Oh, Sir Clifford! Oh, high and mighty Chatterleys! Is this what you've come down to!" And finally he even went to sleep, like a child. And she felt worn out, and went to her own room, where she laughed and cried at once with a hysteria of her own. It was so ridiculous! It was so awful! such a come-down! so shameful! And it *was* so upsetting as well.

After this, Clifford became like a child with Mrs. Bolton. He would hold her hand, and rest his head on her breast, and when she once lightly kissed him, he said: "Yes! Do kiss me! Do kiss me!" And when she sponged his great blond body, he would say the same: "Do kiss me!" and she would lightly kiss his body, anywhere, half in mockery.

And he lay with a queer, blank face like a child, with a bit of the wonderment of a child. And he would gaze on her with wide, childish eyes, in a relaxation of madonna-worship. It was sheer relaxation on his part, letting go all his manhood, and sinking back to a childish position that was really perverse. And then he would put his hand into her bosom and feel her breasts, and kiss them in exaltation, the exaltation of perversity, of being a child when he was a man.

Mrs. Bolton was both thrilled and ashamed, she both loved and hated it. Yet she never rebuffed nor rebuked him. And they drew into a closer physical intimacy, an intimacy of perversity, when he was a child stricken with an apparent candor and an apparent wonderment, that looked almost like a religious exaltation: the perverse and literal rendering of "except ye become again as a little child."— While she was the Magna Mater, full of power and potency, having the great blond child-man under her will and her stroke entirely.

The curious thing was that when this child-man, which Clifford was now and which he had been becoming for years, emerged into the world, he was much sharper and keener than the real man he used to be. This perverted child-man was now a *real* business man; when it was a question of affairs, he was an absolute he-man, sharp as a needle, and impervious as a bit of steel. When he was out among men, seeking his own ends, and "making good" his colliery workings, he had an almost uncanny shrewdness, hardness, and a straight sharp punch. It was as if his very passivity and prostitution to the Magna Mater gave him insight into material business affairs, and lent him a certain remarkable inhuman force. The wallowing in private emotion, the utter abasement of his manly self, seemed to lend him a second nature, cold, almost visionary, business-clever. In business he was quite inhuman.

And in this Mrs. Bolton triumphed. "How he's getting on!" she would say to herself in pride. "And that's my doing! My word, he'd never have got on like this with Lady Chatterley. She was not the one to put a man forward. She wanted too much for herself."

At the same time, in some corner of her weird female soul, how she despised him and hated him! He was to her the fallen beast, the squirming monster. And while she aided and abetted him all she could, away in the remotest corner of her ancient healthy womanhood she despised him with a savage contempt that knew no bounds. The merest tramp was better than he.

His behavior with regard to Connie was curious. He insisted on seeing her again. He insisted, moreover, on her coming to Wragby. On this point he was finally and absolutely fixed. Connie had promised to come back to Wragby, faithfully.

"But is it any use?" said Mrs. Bolton. "Can't you let her go, and be rid of her?"

"No! She said she was coming back, and she's got to come."

Mrs. Bolton opposed him no more. She knew what she was dealing with.

"I needn't tell you what effect your letter has had on me," he wrote to Connie to London. "Perhaps you can imagine it if you try, though no doubt you won't trouble to use your imagination on my behalf.

"I can only say one thing in answer: I must see you personally, here at Wragby, before I can do anything. You promised faithfully to come back to Wragby, and I hold you to the promise. I don't believe anything nor understand anything until I see you personally, here under normal circumstances. I needn't tell you that nobody here suspects anything, so your return would be quite normal. Then if you feel, after we have talked things over, that you still remain in the same mind, no doubt we can come to terms."

Connie showed this letter to Mellors.

"He wants to begin his revenge on you," said he, handing the letter back.

Connie was silent. She was somewhat surprised to find that she was afraid of Clifford. She was afraid to go near him. She was afraid of him as if he were evil and dangerous.

"What shall I do?" she said.

"Nothing, if you don't want to do anything."

She replied, trying to put Clifford off. He answered: "If you don't come back to Wragby now, I shall consider that you are coming back one day, and act accordingly. I shall just go on the same, and wait for you here, if I wait for fifty years."

She was frightened. This was bullying of an insidious sort. She had no doubt he meant what he said. He would not divorce her, and the child would be his, unless she could find some means of establishing its illegitimacy.

After a time of worry and harassment, she decided to go to Wragby. Hilda would go with her. She wrote this to Clifford. He replied: "I shall not welcome your sister, but I shall not deny her the door. I have no doubt she has connived at your desertion of your duties and responsibilities, so do not expect me to show pleasure in seeing her."

They went to Wragby. Clifford was away when they arrived. Mrs. Bolton received them.

"Oh, your Ladyship, it isn't the happy home-coming we hoped for, is it?" she said.

"Isn't it!" said Connie.

So this woman knew! How much did the rest of the servants know or suspect?

She entered the house which now she hated with every fiber in her body. The great, rambling mass of a place seemed evil to her, just a menace over her. She was no longer its mistress, she was its victim.

"I can't stay long here," she whispered to Hilda, terrified.

And she suffered going into her own bedroom, re-entering into possession as if nothing had happened. She hated every minute inside the Wragby walls.

They did not meet Clifford till they went down to dinner. He was dressed, and with a black tie: rather reserved, and very much the superior gentleman. He behaved perfectly politely during the meal, and kept a polite sort of conversation going: but it seemed all touched with insanity.

"How much do the servants know?" asked Connie when the woman was out of the room.

"Of your intentions? Nothing whatsoever."

"Mrs. Bolton knows."

He changed color.

"Mrs. Bolton is not exactly one of the servants," he said.

"Oh, I don't mind."

There was tension till after coffee, when Hilda said she would go up to her room.

Clifford and Connie sat in silence when she had gone. Neither would begin to speak. Connie was so glad that he wasn't taking the pathetic line, she kept him up to as much haughtiness as possible. She just sat silent and looked down at her hands.

"I suppose you don't at all mind having gone back on your word?" he said at last.

"I can't help it," she murmured.

"But if you can't, who can?"

"I suppose nobody."

He looked at her with curious cold rage. He was used to her. She was as it were embedded in his will. How dared she now go back on him, and destroy the fabric of his daily existence? How dared she try to cause this derangement of his personality!

"And for *what* do you want to go back on everything?" he insisted.

"Love!" she said. It was best to be hackneyed.

"Love of Duncan Forbes? But you didn't think that worth having, when you met me. Do you mean to say you now love him better than anything else in life?"

"One changes," she said.

"Possibly! Possibly you may have whims. But you still have to convince me of the importance of the change. I merely don't believe in your love of Duncan Forbes."

"But why *should* you believe in it? You have only to divorce me, not to believe in my feelings."

"And why should I divorce you?"

"Because I don't want to live here any more. And you really don't want me."

"Pardon me! I don't change. For my part, since you are my wife, I should prefer that you should stay under my roof in dignity and quiet. Leaving aside personal feelings, and I assure you, on my part it is leaving aside a great deal, it is bitter as death to me to have this order of life broken up, here in Wragby, and the decent round of daily life smashed, just for some whim of yours."

After a time of silence she said:

"I can't help it. I've got to go. I expect I shall have a child." He, too, was silent for a time.

"And is it for the child's sake you must go?" he asked at length.

She nodded.

"And why? Is Duncan Forbes so keen on his spawn?"

"Surely keener than you would be," she said.

"But really? I want my wife, and I see no reason for letting her go. If she likes to bear a child under my roof, she is welcome, and the child is welcome, provided that the decency and order of life is preserved. Do you mean to tell me that Duncan Forbes has a greater hold over you? I don't believe it."

There was a pause.

"But don't you see," said Connie. "I *must* go away from you, and I *must* live with the man I love."

"No, I don't see it! I don't give tuppence for your love, nor for the man you love. I don't believe in that sort of cant."

"But, you see, I do."

"Do you? My dear Madam, you are too intelligent, I assure you, to believe in your own love for Duncan Forbes. Believe me, even now you really care more for me. So why should I give in to such nonsense!"

She felt he was right there. And she felt she could keep silent no longer.

"Because it isn't Duncan that I *do* love," she said, looking up at him. "We only said it was Duncan, to spare your feelings."

"To spare my feelings?"

"Yes! Because who I really love, and it'll make you hate me, is Mr. Mellors, who was our gamekeeper here."

If he could have sprung out of his chair, he would have done so. His face went yellow, and his eyes bulged with disaster as he glared at her.

Then he dropped back in the chair, gasping and looking up at the ceiling.

At length he sat up.

"Do you mean to say you're telling me the truth?" he asked, looking gruesome.

"Yes! You know I am."

"And when did you begin with him?"

"In the spring."

He was silent like some beast in a trap.

"And it *was* you, then, in the bedroom at the cottage?"

So he had really inwardly known all the time.

"Yes!"

He still leaned forward in his chair, gazing at her like a cornered beast.

"My God, you ought to be wiped off the face of the earth!"

"Why?" she ejaculated faintly.

But he seemed not to hear her.

"That scum! That bumptious lout! That miserable cad! And carrying on with him all the time, while you were here and he was one of my servants! My God, my God, is there any limit to the beastly lowness of women!"

He was beside himself with rage, as she knew he would be.

"And you mean to say you want to have a child to a cad like that?"

"Yes! I'm going to."

"You're going to! You mean you're sure! How long have you been sure?"

"Since June."

He was speechless, and the queer blank look of a child came over him again.

"You'd wonder," he said at last, "that such beings were ever allowed to be born."

"What beings?" she asked.

He looked at her weirdly, without an answer. It was obvious he couldn't even accept the fact of the existence of Mellors, in any connection with his own life. It was sheer, unspeakable, impotent hate.

"And do you mean to say you'd marry him?—and bear his foul name?" he asked at length.

"Yes, that's what I want."

He was again as if dumbfounded.

"Yes!" he said at last. "That proves what I've always thought about you is correct: you're not normal, you're not in your right senses. You're one of those half-insane, perverted women who must run after depravity, the *nostalgie de la boue.*"

Suddenly he had become almost wistfully moral, seeing himself the incarnation of good, and people like Mellors and Connie the incarnation of mud, of evil. He seemed to be growing vague, inside a nimbus.

"So don't you think you'd better divorce me and have done with it?" she said.

"No! You can go where you like, but I shan't divorce you," he said idiotically.

"Why not?"

He was silent, in the silence of imbecile obstinacy.

"Would you even let the child be legally yours, and your heir?" she said.

"I care nothing about the child."

"But if it's a boy it will be legally your son, and it will inherit your title, and have Wragby."

"I care nothing about that," he said.

"But you *must*! I shall prevent the child from being legally yours, if I can. I'd so much rather it were illegitimate and mine: if it can't be Mellors'."

"Do as you like about that."

He was immovable.

"And won't you divorce me?" she said. "You can use Duncan as a pretext! There'd be no need to bring in the real name. Duncan doesn't mind."

"*I* shall never divorce you," he said, as if a nail had been driven in.

"But why? Because I want you to?"

"Because I follow my own inclination, and I'm not inclined to."

It was useless. She went upstairs, and told Hilda the upshot.

"Better get away tomorrow," said Hilda, "and let him come to his senses."

So Connie spent half the night packing her really private and personal effects. In the morning she had her trunks sent to the station, without telling Clifford. She decided to see him only to say good-bye, before lunch.

But she spoke to Mrs. Bolton.

"I must say good-bye to you, Mrs. Bolton. You know why, but I can trust you not to talk."

"Oh, you can trust me, your Ladyship, though it's a sad blow for us here, indeed. But I hope you'll be happy with the other gentleman."

"The other gentleman! It's Mr. Mellors, and I care for him. Sir Clifford knows. But don't say anything to anybody. And if one day you think Sir Clifford may be willing to divorce me, let me know, will you? I should like to be properly married to the man I care for."

"I'm sure you would, my Lady. Oh, you can trust me. I'll be faithful to Sir Clifford, and I'll be faithful to you, for I can see you're both right in your own ways."

"Thank you! And look! I want to give you this—may I?—" So Connie left Wragby once more, and went on with Hilda to Scotland. Mellors went into the country and got work on a farm. The idea was, he should get his divorce, if possible, whether Connie got hers or not. And for six months he should work at farming, so that eventually he and Connie could have some small farm of their own, into which he could put his energy. For he would have to have some work, even hard work, to do, and he would have to make his own living, even if her capital started him.

So they would have to wait till spring was in, till the baby was born, till the early summer came round again.

The Grange Farm,
Old Heanor, 29 September.

"I got on here with a bit of contriving, because I knew Richards, the company engineer, in the army. It is a farm belonging to Butler & Smitham Colliery Company, they use it for raising hay and oats for the pit-ponies; not a private concern. But they've got cows and pigs and all the rest of it, and I get thirty shillings a week as laborer. Rowley, the farmer, puts me on to as many jobs as he can, so that I can learn as much as possible between now and next Easter. I've not heard a thing about Bertha. I've no idea why she didn't show up at the divorce, nor where she is nor what she's up to. But if I keep quiet till March I suppose I shall be free. And don't you bother about Sir Clifford. He'll want to get rid of you one of these days. If he leaves you alone, it's a lot.

"I've got lodgings in a bit of an old cottage in Engine Row, very decent. The man is engine-driver at High Park, tall, with a beard, and very chapel. The woman is a birdy bit of a thing who loves anything superior, King's English and allow-me! all the time. But they lost their only son in the war, and it's sort of knocked a hole in them. There's a long gawky lass of a daughter training for a school teacher, and I help her with her lessons sometimes, so we're quite the family. But they're very decent people, and only too kind to me. I expect I'm more coddled than you are.

"I like farming all right. It's not inspiring, but then I don't ask to be inspired. I'm used to horses, and cows, though they are very female, have a soothing effect on me. When I sit with my head in her side, milking, I feel very solaced. They have six rather fine Herefords. Oat-harvest is just over and I enjoyed it, in spite of sore hands and a lot of rain. I don't take much notice of people, but get on with them all right. Most things one just ignores.

"The pits are working badly; this is a colliery district like Tevershall, only prettier. I sometimes sit in the Wellington and talk to the men. They grumble a lot, but they're not going to alter anything. As everybody says, the Notts-Derby miners have got their hearts in the right place. But the rest of their anatomy must be in the wrong place, in a world that has no use for them. I like them, but they don't cheer me much: not enough of the old fighting-cock in them. They talk a lot about nationalism, nationalization of royalties, nationalization of the whole industry. But you can't nationalize coal and leave all the other industries as they are. They talk about putting coal to new uses, like Sir Clifford is trying to do. It may work here and there, but not as a general thing, I doubt. Whatever you make you've got to sell it. The men are very apathetic. They feel the whole damned thing is doomed, and I believe it is. And they are doomed along with it. Some of the young ones spout about a Soviet, but there's not much conviction in them. There's no sort of conviction about anything, except that it's all a muddle and a hole. Even under a Soviet you've still got to sell coal: and that's the difficulty.

"We've got this great industrial population, and they've got to be fed, so the damn show has to be kept going somehow. The women talk a lot more than the men nowadays, and they are a sight more cocksure. The men are limp, they feel a doom somewhere, and they go about as if there was nothing to be done. Anyhow nobody knows what should be done, in spite of all the talk. The young ones get mad because they've no money to spend. Their whole life depends on spending money, and now they've got none to spend. That's our civilization and our education: bring up the masses to depend entirely on spending money, and then the money gives out. The pits are working two days, two-and-a-half days a week, and there's no sign of betterment even for the winter. It means a man bringing up a family on twenty-five and thirty shillings. The women are the maddest of all. But then they're the maddest for spending, nowadays.

"If you could only tell them that living and spending isn't the same thing! But it's no good. If only they were educated to *live* instead of earn and spend, they could manage very happily on twenty-five shillings. If the men wore scarlet trousers, as I said, they wouldn't think so much of money: if they could dance and hop and skip, and sing and swagger and be handsome, they could do with very little cash. And amuse the women themselves, and be amused by the women. They ought to learn to be naked and handsome, and to sing in a mass and dance the old group dances, and carve the stools they sit on, and embroider their own emblems. Then they wouldn't need money. And that's the only way to solve the industrial problem: train the people to be able to live, and live in handsomeness, without needing to spend. But you can't do it. They're all one-track minds nowadays. Whereas the mass of people oughtn't even to try to think, because they *can't*! They should be alive and frisky, and acknowledge the great god Pan. He's the only god for the masses, forever. The few can go in for higher cults if they like. But let the mass be forever pagan.

"But the colliers aren't pagan, far from it. They're a sad lot, a deadened lot of men: dead to their women, dead to life. The young ones scoot about on motorbikes with girls, and jazz when they get a chance. But they're very dead. And it needs money. Money poisons you when you've got it, and starves you when you haven't.

"I'm sure you're sick of all this. But I don't want to harp on myself, and I've nothing happening to me. I don't like to think too much about you, in my head, that only makes a mess of us both. But of course what I live for now is for you and me to live together. I'm frightened, really. I feel the devil in the air, and he'll try to get us. Or not the devil, Mammon: which I think, after all, is only the mass-will of people, wanting money and hating life. Anyhow I feel great grasping white hands in the air, wanting to get hold of the throat of anybody who tries to live, to live beyond money, and squeeze the life out. There's a bad time coming. There's a bad time coming, boys, there's a bad time coming! If things go on as they are, there's nothing lies in the future but death and destruction, for these industrial masses. I feel my inside turn to water sometimes, and there you are, going to have a child by me. But never mind. All the bad times that ever have been, haven't been able to blow the crocus out: not even the love of women. So they won't be able to blow out my wanting you, nor the little glow there is between you and me. We'll be together next year. And though I'm frightened, I believe in your being with me. A man has to fend and fettle for the best, and then trust in something beyond himself. You can't insure against the future, except by really believing in the best bit of you, and in the power beyond it. So I believe in the little flame between us. For me now, it's the only thing in the world. I've got no friends, not inward friends. Only you. And now the little flame is all I care about in my life. There's the baby, but that is a side issue. It's my Pentecost, the forked flame between me and you. The old Pentecost isn't quite right. Me and God is a bit uppish, somehow. But the little forked flame between me and you: there you are! That's what I abide by, and will abide by, Cliffords and Berthas, colliery companies and governments and the money-mass of people all notwithstanding.

"That's why I don't like to start thinking about you actually. It only tortures me, and does you no good. I don't want you to be away from me. But if I start fretting it wastes something. Patience, always patience. This is my fortieth winter. And I can't help all the winters that have been. But this winter I'll stick to my little pentecost flame, and have some peace. And I won't let the breath of people blow it out. I believe in a higher mystery, that doesn't let even the crocus be blown out. And if you're in Scotland and I'm in the Midlands, and I can't put my arms round you, and wrap my legs round you, yet I've got something of you. My soul softly flaps in the little pentecost flame with you, like the peace of fucking. We fucked a flame into being. Even the flowers are fucked into being between the sun and the earth. But it's a delicate thing, and takes patience and the long pause.

"So I love chastity now, because it is the peace that comes of fucking. I love being chaste now. I love it as snowdrops love the snow. I love this chastity, which is the pause of peace of our fucking, between us now like a snowdrop of forked white fire. And when the real spring comes, when the drawing together comes, then we can fuck the little flame brilliant and yellow, brilliant. But not now, not yet! Now is the time to be chaste, it is so good to be chaste, like a river of cool water in my soul. I love the chastity now that it flows between us. It is like fresh water and rain. How can men want wearisomely to philander! What a misery to be like Don Juan, and impotent ever to fuck oneself into peace, and the little flame alight, impotent and unable to be chaste in the cool between-whiles, as by a river.

"Well, so many words, because I can't touch you. If I could sleep with my arms round you, the ink could stay in the bottle. We could be chaste together just as we can fuck together. But we have to be separate for a while, and I suppose it is really the wiser way. If only one were sure.

"Never mind, never mind, we won't get worked up. We really trust in the little flame, in the unnamed god that shields it from being blown out. There's so much of you here with me, really, that it's a pity you aren't all here.

"Never mind about Sir Clifford. If you don't hear anything from him, never mind. He can't really do anything to you. Wait, he will want to get rid of you at last, to cast you out. And if he doesn't, we'll manage to keep clear of him. But he will. In the end he will want to spew you out as the abominable thing.

"Now I can't even leave off writing to you.

"But a great deal of us is together, and we can but abide by it, and steer our courses to meet soon. John Thomas says good night to lady Jane, a little droopingly, but with a hopeful heart."

*O*wing to the existence of various pir-
ated editions of *Lady Chatterley's Lover,* I brought out in 1929 a cheap popular
edition, produced in France and offered to the public at Sixty Francs, hoping at
least to meet the European demand. The pirates, in the United States certainly,
were prompt and busy. The first stolen edition was being sold in New York
almost within a month of the arrival in America of the first genuine copies from
Florence. It was a facsimile of the original, produced by the photographic method,
and was sold, even by reliable booksellers, to the unsuspecting public as if it
were the original first edition. The price was usually fifteen dollars, whereas the
price of the original was ten dollars: and the purchaser was left in fond ignorance
of the fraud.

This gallant attempt was followed by others. I am told there was still another
facsimile edition produced in New York or Philadelphia: and I myself possess a
filthy-looking book bound in a dull orange cloth, with green label, smearily
produced by photography, and containing my signature forged by the little boy
of the piratical family. It was when this edition appeared in London, from New
York, towards the end of 1928, and was offered to the public at thirty shillings,
that I put out from Florence my little second edition of two hundred copies,
which I offered at a guinea. I had wanted to save it for a year or more, but had
to launch it against the dirty orange pirate. But the number was too small. The
orange pirate persisted.

Then I have had in my hand a very funereal volume, bound in black and
elongated to look like a bible or long hymn-book, gloomy. This time the pirate
was not only sober, but earnest. He has not one, but two title-pages, and on each
is a vignette representing the American Eagle, with six stars round his head and
lightning splashing from his paw, all surrounded by a laurel wreath in honour
of his latest exploit in literary robbery. Altogether it is a sinister volume,—like
Captain Kidd with his face blackened, reading a sermon to those about to walk
the plank. Why the pirate should have elongated the page, by adding a false page-
heading, I don't know. The effect is peculiarly depressing, sinisterly high-brow.
For of course this book also was produced by the photographic process. The

signature anyhow is omitted. And I am told this lugubrious tome sells for ten, twenty, thirty, and fifty dollars, according to the whim of the bookseller and the gullibility of the purchaser.

That makes three pirated editions in the United States for certain. I have heard mentioned the report of a fourth, another facsimile of the original. But since I haven't seen it, I want not to believe in it.

There is, however, the European pirated edition of fifteen hundred, produced by a Paris firm of booksellers, and stamped *Imprimé en Allemagne:* Printed in Germany. Whether printed in Germany or not, it was certainly printed, not photographed, for some of the spelling errors of the original are corrected. And it is a very respectable volume, a very close replica of the original, but lacking the signature and it gives itself away also by the green-and-yellow silk edge of the back-binding. This edition is sold to the trade at one hundred francs, and offered to the public at three hundred, four hundred, five hundred francs. Very unscrupulous booksellers are said to have forged the signature and offered the book as the original signed edition. Let us hope it is not true. But it all sounds very black against the "trade". Still there is some relief. Certain booksellers will not handle the pirated edition at all. Both sentimental and business scruples prevent them. Others handle it, but not very warmly. And apparently they would all rather handle the authorized edition. So that sentiment does genuinely enter in, against the pirates, even if not strong enough to keep them out altogether.

None of these pirated editions has received any sort of authorization from me, and from none of them have I received a penny. A semi-repentant bookseller of New York did, however, send me some dollars which were, he said my 10% royalty on all copies sold in his shop. "I know", he wrote, "it is but a drop in the bucket". He meant of course, a drop out of the bucket. And since, for a drop, it was quite a nice little sum, what a beautiful bucketful there must have been for the pirates!

I received a belated offer from the European Pirates, who found the booksellers stiff-necked, offering me a royalty on all copies sold in the past as well as the future, if I would authorize their edition. Well, I thought to myself, in a world of: Do him or you will be done by him,—why not?—When it came to the point, however, pride rebelled. It is understood that Judas is always ready with a kiss. But that I should have to kiss him back—!

So I managed to get published the little cheap French edition, photographed down from the original, and offered at sixty francs. English publishers urge me to make an expurgated edition, promising large returns, perhaps even a little bucket, one of those children's sea-side pails!—and insisting that I should show the public that here is a fine novel, apart from all "purple" and all "words". So I begin to be tempted and start in to expurgate. But impossible! I might as well try to clip my own nose into shape with scissors. The book bleeds.

And in spite of all antagonism, I put forth this novel as an honest, healthy book, necessary for us to-day. The words that shock so much at first don't shock at all after a while. Is this because the mind is depraved by habit? Not a bit. It is that the words merely shocked the eye, they never shocked the mind at all.

People without minds may go on being shocked, but they don't matter. People with minds realize that they aren't shocked, and never really were: and they experience a sense of relief.

And that is the whole point. We are today, as human beings, evolved and cultured far beyond the taboos which are inherent in our culture. This is a very important fact to realize. Probably, to the Crusaders, mere words were potent and evocative to a degree we can't realize. The evocative power of the so-called obscene words must have been very dangerous to the dim-minded, obscure, violent natures of the Middle Ages, and perhaps are still too strong for slow-minded, half-evoked lower natures to-day. But real culture makes us give to a word only those mental and imaginative reactions which belong to the mind, and saves us from violent and indiscriminate physical reactions which may wreck social decency. In the past, man was too weak-minded, or crude-minded, to contemplate his own physical body and physical functions, without getting all messed up with physical reactions that overpowered him. It is no longer so. Culture and civilization have taught us to separate the reactions. We now know the act does not necessarily follow on the thought. In fact, thought and action, word and deed, are two separate forms of consciousness, two separate lives which we lead. We need, very sincerely, to keep a connection. But while we think, we do not act, and while we act we do not think. The great necessity is that we should act according to our thoughts, and think according to our acts. But while we are in thought we cannot really act, and while we are in action we cannot really think. The two conditions, of thought and action, are mutually exclusive. Yet they should be related in harmony.

And this is the real point of this book. I want men and women to be able to think sex, fully, completely, honestly and cleanly.

Even if we can't act sexually to our complete satisfaction, let us at least think sexually, complete and clear. All this talk of young girls and virginity, like a blank white sheet on which nothing is written, is pure nonsense. A young girl and a young boy is a tormented tangle, a seething confusion of sexual feelings and sexual thoughts which only the years will disentangle. Years of honest thoughts of sex, and years of struggling action in sex will bring us at last where we want to get, to our real and accomplished chastity, our completeness, when our sexual act and our sexual thought are in harmony, and the one does not interfere with the other.

Far be it from me to suggest that all women should go running after gamekeepers for lovers. Far be it from me to suggest that they should be running after anybody. A great many men and women to-day are happiest when they abstain and stay sexually apart, quite clean: and at the same time, when they understand and realize sex more fully. Ours is the day of realization rather than action. There has been so much action in the past, especially sexual action, a wearying repetition over and over, without a corresponding thought, a corresponding realization. Now our business is to realize sex. To-day the full conscious realization of sex is even more important than the act itself. After centuries of obfuscation, the mind demands to know and know fully. The body is a good deal in abeyance, really.

When people act in sex, nowadays, they are half the time acting up. They do it because they think it is expected of them. Whereas as a matter of fact it is the mind which is interested, and the body has to be provoked. The reason being that our ancestors have so assiduously acted sex without ever thinking it or realizing it, that now the act tends to be mechanical, dull and disappointing, and only fresh mental realization will freshen up the experience.

The mind has to catch up, in sex: indeed, in all the physical acts. Mentally, we lag behind in our sexual thought, in a dimness, a lurking, grovelling fear which belongs to our raw, somewhat bestial ancestors. In this one respect, sexual and physical, we have left the mind unevolved. Now we have to catch up, and make a balance between the consciousness of the body's sensations and experiences, and these sensations and experiences themselves. Balance up the consciousness of the act, and the act itself. Get the two in harmony. It means having a proper reverence for sex, and a proper awe of the body's strange experience. It means being able to use the so-called obscene words, because these are a natural part of the mind's consciousness of the body. Obscenity only comes in when the mind despises and fears the body, and the body hates and resists the mind.

When we read of the case of Colonel Barker, we see what is the matter. Colonel Barker was a woman who masqueraded as a man. The "Colonel" married a wife, and lived five years with her in "conjugal happiness". And the poor wife thought all the time she was married normally and happily to a real husband. The revelation at the end is beyond all thought cruel for the poor woman. The situation is monstrous. Yet there are thousands of women to-day who might be so deceived, and go on being deceived. Why? Because they know nothing, they can't think sexually at all; they are morons in this respect. It is better to give all girls this book, at the age of seventeen.

The same with the case of the venerable schoolmaster and clergyman, for years utterly "holy and good": and at the age of sixty-five, tried in the police courts for assaulting little girls. This happens at the moment when the Home Secretary, himself growing elderly, is most loudly demanding and enforcing a mealy-mouthed silence about sexual matters. Doesn't the experience of that other elderly, most righteous and "pure" gentleman, make him pause at all?

But so it is. The mind has an old grovelling fear of the body and the body's potencies. It is the mind we have to liberate, to civilize on these points. The mind's terror of the body has probably driven more men mad than ever could be counted. The insanity of a great mind like Swift's is at least partly traceable to this cause. In the poem to his mistress Celia, which has the maddened refrain "But—Celia, Celia, Celia s***s," (the word rhymes with spits), we see what can happen to a great mind when it falls into panic. A great wit like Swift could not see how ridiculous he made himself. Of course Celia s***s! Who doesn't? And how much worse if she didn't. It is hopeless. And then think of poor Celia, made to feel iniquitous about her proper natural function, by her "lover". It is monstrous. And it comes from having taboo words, and from not keeping the mind sufficiently developed in physical and sexual consciousness.

In contrast to the puritan hush! hush!, which produces the sexual moron, we have the modern young jazzy and high-brow person who has gone one better, and won't be hushed in any respect, and just "does as she likes". From fearing the body, and denying its existence, the advanced young go to the other extreme and treat it as a sort of toy to be played with, a slightly nasty toy, but still you can get some fun out of it, before it lets you down. These young people scoff at the importance of sex, take it like a cocktail, and flout their elders with it. These young ones are advanced and superior. They despise a book like *Lady Chatterley's Lover*. It is much too simple and ordinary for them. The naughty words they care nothing about, and the attitude to love they find old-fashioned. Why make a fuss about it. Take it like a cocktail! The book, they say, shows the mentality of a boy of fourteen. But perhaps the mentality of a boy of fourteen, who still has a little natural awe and proper fear in fact of sex, is more wholesome than the mentality of the young cocktaily person who has no respect for anything and whose mind has nothing to do but play with the toys of life, sex being one of the chief toys, and who loses his mind in the process. Heliogabulus, indeed!

So, between the stale grey puritan who is likely to fall into sexual indecency in advanced age, and the smart jazzy person of the young world, who says: "We can do anything. If we can think a thing we can do it", and then the low uncultured person with a dirty mind, who looks for dirt—this book has hardly a space to turn in. But to them all I say the same: Keep your perversions if you like them—your perversion of puritanism, your perversion of smart licentiousness, your perversion of a dirty mind. But I stick to my book and my position: Life is only bearable when the mind and the body are in harmony, and there is a natural balance between them, and each has a natural respect for the other.

And it is obvious, there is no balance and no harmony now. The body is at the best the tool of the mind, at the worst, the toy. The business man keeps himself "fit", that is, keeps his body in good working order, for the sake of his business, and the usual young person who spends much time on keeping fit does so as a rule out of self-conscious self-absorption, narcissism. The mind has a stereotyped set of ideas and "feelings", and the body is made to act up, like a trained dog: to beg for sugar, whether it wants sugar or whether it doesn't, to shake hands when it would dearly like to snap the hand it has to shake. The body of men and women to-day is just a trained dog. And of no one is this more true than of the free and emancipated young. Above all, their bodies are the bodies of trained dogs. And because the dog is trained to do things the old-fashioned dog never did, they call themselves free, full of real life, the real thing.

But they know perfectly well it is false. Just as the business man knows, somewhere, that he's all wrong. Men and women aren't really dogs: they only look like it and behave like it. Somewhere inside there is a great chagrin and a gnawing discontent. The body is, in its spontaneous natural self, dead or paralysed. It has only the secondary life of a circus dog, acting up and showing off: and then collapsing.

What life could it have, of itself? The body's life is the life of sensations and emotions. The body feels real hunger, real thirst, real joy in the sun or the snow, real pleasure in the smell of roses or the look of a lilac bush; real anger, real sorrow, real love, real tenderness, real warmth, real passion, real hate, real grief. All the emotions belong to the body, and are only recognised by the mind. We may hear the most sorrowful piece of news, and only feel a mental excitement. Then, hours after, perhaps in sleep, the awareness may reach the bodily centres, and true grief wrings the heart.

How different they are, mental feelings and real feelings. To-day, many people live and die without having had any real feelings—though they have had a "rich emotional life" apparently, having showed strong mental feeling. But it is all counterfeit. In magic, one of the so-called "occult" pictures represents a man standing, apparently, before a flat table mirror, which reflects him from the waist to the head, so that you have the man from head to waist, then his reflection downwards from waist to head again. And whatever it may mean in magic, it means what we are to-day, creatures whose active emotional self has no real existence, but is all reflected downwards from the mind. Our education from the start has *taught* us a certain range of emotions, what to feel and what not to feel, and how to feel the feelings we allow ourselves to feel. All the rest is just non-existent. The vulgar criticism of any new good book is: Of course nobody ever felt like that!—People allow themselves to feel a certain number of finished feelings. So it was in the last century. This feeling only what you allow yourselves to feel at last kills all capacity for feeling, and in the higher emotional range you feel nothing at all: This has come to pass in our present century. The higher emotions are strictly dead. They have to be faked.

And by higher emotions we mean love in all its manifestations, from genuine desire to tender love, love of our fellowmen, and love of God: we mean love, joy, delight, hope, true indignant anger, passionate sense of justice and injustice, truth and untruth, honour and dishonour, and real belief in *anything*: for belief is a profound emotion that has the mind's connivance. All these things, to-day, are more or less dead. We have in their place the loud and sentimental counterfeit of all such emotion.

Never was an age more sentimental, more devoid of real feeling, more exaggerated in false feeling, than our own. Sentimentality and counterfeit feeling have become a sort of game, everybody trying to outdo his neighbour. The radio and the film are mere counterfeit emotion all the time, the current press and literature the same. People wallow in emotion: counterfeit emotion. They lap it up: they live in it and on it. They ooze with it.

And at times, they seem to get on very well with it all. And then, more and more, they break down. They go to pieces. You can fool yourself for a long time about your own feelings. But not forever. The body itself hits back at you, and hits back remorselessy in the end.

As for other people—you can fool most people all the time, and all people most of the time, but not all people all the time, with false feelings. A young couple fall in counterfeit love, and fool themselves and each other completely. But, alas, counterfeit love is good cake but bad bread. It produces a fearful emotional indigestion. Then you get a modern marriage, and a still more modern separation.

The trouble with counterfeit emotion is that nobody is really happy, nobody is really contented, nobody has any peace. Everybody keeps on rushing to get away from the counterfeit emotion which is in themselves worst of all. They rush from the false feelings of Peter to the false feelings of Adrian, from the counterfeit emotions of Margaret to those of Virginia, from film to radio, from Eastbourne to Brighton, and the more it changes the more it is the same thing.

Above all things love is a counterfeit feeling to-day. Here, above all things, the young will tell you, is the greatest swindle. That is, if you take it seriously. Love is all right if you take it lightly, as an amusement. But if you begin taking it seriously you are let down with a crash.

There are, the young women say, no *real* men to love. And there are, the young men say, no *real* girls to fall in love with. So they go on falling in love with unreal ones, on either side; which means, if you can't have real feelings, you've got to have counterfeit ones: since some feelings you've *got* to have: like falling in love. There are still some young people who would *like* to have real feelings, and they are bewildered to death to know why they can't. Especially in love.

But especially in love, only counterfeit emotions exist nowadays. We have all been taught to mistrust everybody emotionally, from parents downwards, or upwards. Don't trust *anybody* with your real emotions: if you've got any: that is the slogan of to-day. Trust them with your money, even, but *never* with your feelings. They are bound to trample on them.

I believe there has never been an age of greater mistrust between persons than ours to-day: under a superficial but quite genuine social trust. Very few of my friends would pick my pocket, or let me sit on a chair where I might hurt myself. But practically all my friends would turn my real emotions to ridicule. They can't help it; it's the spirit of the day. So there goes love, and there goes friendship: for each implies a fundamental emotional sympathy. And hence, counterfeit love, which there is no escaping.

And with counterfeit emotions there is no real sex at all. Sex is the one thing you cannot really swindle; and it is the centre of the worst swindling of all, emotional swindling. Once come down to sex, and the emotional swindle must collapse. But in all the approaches to sex, the emotional swindle intensifies more and more. Till you get there. Then collapse.

Sex lashes out against counterfeit emotion, and is ruthless, devastating against false love. The peculiar hatred of people who have not loved one another, but who have pretended to, even perhaps have imagined they really did love, is one of the phenomena of our time. The phenomenon, of course, belongs to all time. But to-day it is almost universal. People who thought they loved one another dearly, dearly, and went on for years, ideal: lo! suddenly the most profound and vivid hatred appears. If it doesn't come out fairly young, it saves itself till the happy couple are nearing fifty, the time of the great sexual change—and then—cataclysm!

Nothing is more startling. Nothing is more staggering, in our age, than the intensity of the hatred people, men and women, feel for one another when they have once "loved" one another. It breaks out in the most extraordinary ways. And when you know people intimately, it is almost universal. It is the charwoman as much as the mistress, and the duchess as much as the policeman's wife.

And it would be too horrible, if one did not remember that in all of them, men and women alike, it is the organic reaction against counterfeit love. All love to-day is counterfeit. It is a stereotyped thing. All the young know just how they ought to feel and how they ought to behave, in love. And they feel and they behave like that. And it is counterfeit love. So that revenge will come back at them, ten-fold. The sex, the very sexual organism in man and woman alike accumulates a deadly and desperate rage, after a certain amount of counterfeit love has been palmed off on it, even if itself has given nothing but counterfeit love. The element of counterfeit in love at last maddens, or else kills, sex, the deepest sex in the individual. But perhaps it would be safe to say that it *always* enrages the inner sex, even if at last it kills it. There is always the period of rage. And the strange thing is, the worst offenders in the counterfeit-love game fall into the greatest rage. Those whose love has been a bit sincere are always gentler, even though they have been most swindled.

Now the real tragedy is here: that we are none of us all of a piece, none of us *all* counterfeit, or *all* true love. And in many a marriage, in among the counterfeit there flickers a little flame of the true thing, on both sides. The tragedy is, that in an age peculiarly conscious of counterfeit, peculiarly suspicious of substitute and swindle in emotion, particularly sexual emotion, the rage and mistrust against the counterfeit element is likely to overwhelm and extinguish the small, true flame of real loving communion, which might have made two lives happy. Herein lies the danger of harping only on the counterfeit and the swindle of emotion, as most "advanced" writers do. Though they do it, of course, to counterbalance the hugely greater swindle of the sentimental "sweet" writers.

Perhaps I shall have given some notion of my feeling about sex, for which I have been so monotonously abused. When a "serious" young man said to me the other day: "I can't believe in the regeneration of England by sex, you know," I could only say, "I'm sure you can't." He had no sex, anyhow: poor, self-conscious, uneasy, narcissus-monk as he was. And he didn't know what it meant, to have any. To him, people only had minds, or no minds, mostly no minds, so they were only there to be gibed at, and he wandered round ineffectively seeking for gibes or for truth, tight shut in inside his own ego.

Now when brilliant young people like this talk to me about sex: or scorn to: I say nothing. There is nothing to say. But I feel a terrible weariness. To them, sex means just plainly and simply, a lady's underclothing, and the fumbling therewith. They have read all the love literature, *Anna Karenina,* all the rest, and looked at statues and pictures of Aphrodite, all very laudable. Yet when it comes to actuality, to to-day, sex means to them meaningless young women and expensive underthings. Whether they are young men from Oxford, or working-men, it is the same. The story from the modish summer-resort, where city ladies take up with young mountaineer "dancing partners" for a season—or less—is typical. It was end of September, the summer visitors had almost all gone. Young

John, the young mountain farmer, had said goodbye to his "lady" from the capital, and was lounging about alone. "Ho, John! you'll be missing your lady!" "Nay!" he said. "Only she had such nice underclothes."

That is all sex means to them: just the trimmings. The regeneration of England with that? Good God! Poor England, she will have to regenerate the sex in her young people, before they do any regenerating of her. It isn't England that needs regeneration, it is her young.

They accuse me of barbarism. I want to drag England down to the level of savages. But it is this crude stupidity, deadness, about sex which I find barbaric and savage. The man who finds a woman's underclothing the most exciting part about her is a savage. Savages are like that. We read of the woman-savage who wore three overcoats on top of one another to excite her man: and did it. That ghastly crudity of seeing in sex nothing but a functional act and a certain fumbling with clothes is, in my opinion, a low degree of barbarism, savagery. And as far as sex goes, our white civilisation is crude, barbaric, and uglily savage: especially England and America.

Witness Bernard Shaw, one of the greatest exponents of our civilisation. He says clothes arouse sex and lack of clothes tends to kill sex—speaking of muffled-up women or our present bare-armed and bare-legged sisters: and scoffs at the Pope for wanting to cover women up; saying that the last person in the world to know anything about sex is the Chief Priest of Europe: and that the one person to ask about it would be the chief Prostitute of Europe, if there were such a person.

Here we see the flippancy and vulgarity of our chief thinkers, at least. The half-naked women of to-day certainly do not rouse much sexual feeling in the muffled-up men of to-day—who don't rouse much sexual feeling in the women, either.—But why? Why does the bare woman of to-day rouse so much less sexual feeling than the muffled-up woman of Mr. Shaw's muffled-up eighties? It would be silly to make it a question of mere muffling.

When a woman's sex is in itself dynamic and alive, then it is a power in itself, beyond her reason. And of itself it emits its peculiar spell, drawing men in the first delight of desire. And the woman has to protect herself, hide herself as much as possible. She veils herself in timidity and modesty, because her sex is a power in itself, exposing her to the desire of men. If a woman in whom sex was alive and positive were to expose her naked flesh as women do to-day, then men would go mad for her. As David was mad for Bathsheba.

But when a woman's sex has lost its dynamic call, and is in a sense dead or static, then the woman *wants* to attract men, for the simple reason that she finds she no longer does attract them. So all the activity that used to be unconscious and delightful becomes conscious and repellant. The woman exposes her flesh more and more, and the more she exposes, the more men are sexually repelled by her. But let us not forget that the men are *socially* thrilled, while sexually repelled. The two things are opposites, to-day. Socially, men like the gesture of the half-naked woman, half-naked in the street. It is *chic,* it is a declaration of defiance and independence, it is modern, it is free, it is popular because it is strictly a-sexual, or anti-sexual. Neither men nor women *want* to feel real desire, to-day. They want the counterfeit, mental substitute.

But we are very mixed, all of us, and creatures of many diverse and often opposing desires. The very men who encourage women to be most daring and sexless complain most bitterly of the sexlessness of women. The same with women. The women who adore men so tremendously for their social smartness and sexlessness as males, hate them most bitterly for not being "men". In public, *en masse,* and socially, everybody to-day wants counterfeit sex. But at certain hours in their lives, all individuals hate counterfeit sex with deadly and maddened hate, and those who have dealt it out most perhaps have the wildest hate of it, in the other person—or persons.

The girls of to-day could muffle themselves up to the eyes, wear crinolines and chignons and all the rest, and though they would not, perhaps, have the peculiar hardening effect on the hearts of men that our half-naked women truly have, neither would they exert any more real sexual attraction. If there is no sex to muffle up, it's no good muffling. Or not much good. Man is often willing to be deceived—for a time—even by muffled-up nothingness.

The point is, when women are sexually alive and quivering and helplessly attractive, beyond their will, then they always cover themselves, and drape themselves with clothes, gracefully. The extravagance of 1880 bustles and such things was only a forewarning of approaching sexlessness.

While sex is a power in itself, women try all kinds of fascinating disguise, and men flaunt. When the Pope insists that women shall cover their naked flesh in church, it is not sex he is opposing, but the sexless tricks of female immodesty. The Pope, and the priests, conclude that the flaunting of naked women's flesh in street and church produces a bad, "unholy" state of mind both in men and women. And they are right. But not because the exposure arouses sexual desire: it doesn't, or very rarely: even Mr. Shaw knows that. But when women's flesh arouses no sort of desire, something is specially wrong! Something is sadly wrong. For the naked arms of women to-day arouse a feeling of flippancy, cynicism and vulgarity which is indeed the very last feeling to go to church with, if you have any respect for the Church. The bare arms of women in an Italian church are really a mark of disrespect, given the tradition.

The Catholic Church, especially in the south, is neither anti-sexual, like the northern Churches, nor a-sexual, like Mr. Shaw and such social thinkers. The Catholic Church recognises sex, and makes of marriage a sacrament based on the sexual communion, for the purpose of procreation. But procreation in the south, is not the bare and scientific fact, and act, that it is in the north. The act of procreation is still charged with all the sensual mystery and importance of the old past. The man is potential creator, and in this has his splendour. All of which has been stripped away by the northern Churches and the Shavian logical triviality.

But all this which has gone in the north, the Church has tried to keep in the south, knowing that it is of basic importance in life. The sense of being a potential creator and lawgiver, as father and husband, is perhaps essential to the day-by-day life of a man, if he is to live full and satisfied. The sense of the eternality of marriage is perhaps necessary to the inward peace, both of men and women. Even if it carry a sense of doom, it is necessary. The Catholic Church does not spend its time reminding the people that in heaven there is no marrying nor giving in marriage. It insists: if you marry, you marry for ever! And the people accept the decree, the doom, and the dignity of it. To the priest, sex is the clue to marriage and marriage is the clue to the daily life of the people and the Church is the clue to the greater life.

So that sexual lure in itself is not deadly to the Church. Much more deadly is the anti-sexual defiance of bare arms and flippancy, "freedom", cynicism, irreverence. Sex may be obscene in church, or blasphemous, but never cynical and atheist. Potentially, the bare arms of women to-day are cynical, atheist, in the dangerous, vulgar form of atheism. Naturally the Church is against it. The Chief Priest of Europe knows more about sex than Mr. Shaw does, anyhow, because he knows more about the essential nature of the human being. Traditionally, he has a thousand years' experience. Mr. Shaw jumped up in a day. And Mr. Shaw, as a dramatist, has jumped up to play tricks with the counterfeit sex of the modern public. No doubt he can do it. So can the cheapest film. But it is equally obvious that he *cannot* touch the deeper sex of the real individual, whose existence he hardly seems to suspect.

And, as a parallel to himself, Mr. Shaw suggests that the Chief Prostitute of Europe would be the one to consult about sex, not the Chief Priest. The parallel is just. The Chief Prostitute of Europe would know truly as much about sex as Mr. Shaw himself does. Which is, not much. Just like Mr. Shaw, the Chief Prostitute of Europe would know an immense amount about the counterfeit sex of men, the shoddy thing that is worked by tricks. And just like him, she would know nothing at all about the real sex in a man, that has the rhythm of the seasons and the years, the crisis of the winter solstice and the passion of Easter. This the Chief Prostitute would know nothing about, positively, because to be a prostitute she would have to have lost it. But even then, she would know more than Mr. Shaw. She would know that the profound, rhythmic sex of a man's inward life *existed*. She would know, because time and again she would have been up against it. All the literature of the world shows the prostitute's ultimate impotence in sex, her inability to keep a man, her rage against the profound instinct of fidelity in a man, which is, as shown by world-history, just a little deeper and more powerful than his instinct of faithless sexual promiscuity. All the literature of the world shows how profound is the instinct of fidelity in both man and woman, how men and women both hanker restlessly after the satisfaction of this instinct, and fret at their own inability to find the real mode of fidelity. The instinct of fidelity is perhaps the deepest instinct in the great complex we call sex. Where there is real sex there is the underlying passion for fidelity. And the prostitute knows this, because she is up against it. She can only keep men who have no real sex, the counterfeits: and these she despises. The men with real sex leave her inevitably, as unable to satisfy their real desire.

The Chief Prostitute knows so much. So does the Pope, if he troubles to think of it, for it is all in the traditional consciousness of the Church. But the Chief

Dramatist knows nothing of it. He has a curious blank in his make-up. To him, all sex is infidelity and only infidelity is sex. Marriage is sexless, null. Sex is only manifested in infidelity, and the queen of sex is the chief prostitute. If sex crops up in marriage, it is because one party falls in love with somebody else, and wants to be unfaithful. Infidelity is sex, and prostitutes know all about it. Wives know nothing and are nothing in that respect.

This is the teaching of the Chief Dramatists and Chief Thinkers of our generation. And the vulgar public agrees with them entirely. Sex is a thing you don't have except to be naughty with. Apart from naughtiness, that is, apart from infidelity and fornication, sex doesn't exist. Our chief thinkers, ending in the flippantly cock-sure Mr. Shaw, have taught this trash so thoroughly, that it has almost become a fact. Sex is almost non-existent, apart from the counterfeit forms of prostitution and shallow fornication. And marriage is empty, hollow.

Now this question of sex and marriage is of paramount importance. Our social life is established on marriage, and marriage, the sociologists say, is established upon property. Marriage has been found the best method of conserving property and stimulating production. Which is all there is to it.

But is it? We are just in the throes of a great revolt against marriage, a passionate revolt against its ties and restrictions. In fact, at least three-quarters of the unhappiness of modern life could be laid at the door of marriage. There are few married people to-day, and few unmarried, who have not felt an intense and vivid hatred against marriage itself, marriage as an institution and an imposition upon human life. Far greater than the revolt against governments is this revolt against marriage.

And everybody, pretty well, takes it for granted that as soon as we can find a possible way out of it, marriage will be abolished. The Soviet abolishes marriage: or did. If new "modern" states spring up, they will almost certainly follow suit. They will try to find some social substitute for marriage, and abolish the hated yoke of conjugality. State support of motherhood, state support of children, and independence of women. It is on the programme of every great scheme of reform. And it means, of course, the abolition of marriage.

The only question to ask ourselves is, do we really want it? Do we want the absolute independence of women, State support of motherhood and of children, and consequent doing away with the necessity of marriage? Do we want it? Because all that matters is that men and women shall do what they *really* want to do. Though here, as everywhere, we must remember that man has a double set of desires, the shallow and the profound, the personal, superficial, temporary desires, and the inner, impersonal, great desires that are fulfilled in long periods of time. The desires of the moment are easy to recognise, but the others, the deeper ones, are difficult. It is the business of our Chief Thinkers to tell us of our deeper desires, not to keep shrilling our little desires in our ears.

Now the Church is established upon a recognition of some, at least, of the greatest and deepest desires in man, desires that take years, or a life-time, or even centuries to fulfil. And the Church, celibate as its priesthood may be, built as it may be upon the lonely rock of Peter, or of Paul, really rests upon the indissolubility of marriage. Make marriage in any serious degree unstable, dissoluble, destroy the permanency of marriage, and the Church falls. Witness the enormous decline of the Church of England.

The reason being that the Church is established upon the element of *union* in mankind. And the first element of union in the Christian world is the marriage-tie. The marriage-tie, the marriage bond, take it which way you like, is the fundamental connecting link in Christian society. Break it, and you will have to go back to the overwhelming dominance of the State, which existed before the Christian era. The Roman State was all-powerful, the Roman Fathers represented the State, the Roman family was the father's estate, held more or less in fee for the State itself. It was the same in Greece, with not so much feeling for the *permanence* of property, but rather a dazzling splash of the moment's possessions. The family was much more insecure in Greece than in Rome.

But, in either case, the family was the man, as representing the State. There are States where the family is the woman: or there have been. There are States where the family hardly exists, priest States where the priestly control is everything, even functioning as family control. Then there is the Soviet State, where again family is not supposed to exist, and the State controls every individual direct, mechanically, as the great religious States, such as early Egypt, may have controlled every individual direct, through priestly surveillance and ritual.

Now the question is, do we want to go back, or forward, to any of these forms of State control? Do we want to be like the Romans under the Empire, or even under the Republic? Do we want to be, as far as our family and our freedom is concerned, like the Greek citizens of a City State in Hellas? Do we want to imagine ourselves in the strange priest-controlled, ritual-fulfilled condition of the earlier Egyptians? Do we want to be bullied by a Soviet?

For my part, I have to say NO! every time. And having said it, we have to come back and consider the famous saying, that perhaps the greatest contribution to the social life of man made by Christianity is—marriage. Christianity brought marriage into the world: marriage as we know it. Christianity established the little autonomy of the family within the greater rule of the State. Christianity made marriage in some respects inviolate, not to be violated by the State. It is marriage, perhaps, which had given man the best of his freedom, given him his little kingdom of his own within the big kingdom of the State, given him his foothold of independence on which to stand and resist an unjust State. Man and wife, a king and queen with one or two subjects, and a few square yards of territory of their own: this, really, is marriage. It is a true freedom because it is a true fulfilment, for man, woman, and children.

Do we, then, want to break marriage? If we do break it, it means we all fall to a far greater extent under the direct sway of the State. Do we want to fall under the direct sway of the State, any State? For my part, I don't.

And the Church created marriage by making it a sacrament, a sacrament of man and woman united in the sex communion, and never to be separated, except by death. And even when separated by death, still not freed from the marriage. Marriage, as far as the individual went, eternal. Marriage, making one complete body out of two incomplete ones, and providing for the complex development of the man's soul and the woman's soul in unison, throughout a life-time. Marriage sacred and inviolable, the great way of earthly fulfilment for man and woman, in unison, under the spiritual rule of the Church.

This is Christianity's great contribution to the life of man, and it is only too easily overlooked. Is it, or is it not, a great step in the direction of life-fulfilment, for men and women? Is it, or is it not? Is marriage a great help to the fulfilment of man and woman, or is it a frustration? It is a very important question indeed, and every man and woman must answer it.

If we are to take the Nonconformist, protestant idea of ourselves: that we are all isolated individual souls, and our supreme business is to save our own souls; then marriage surely is a hindrance. If I am only out to save my own soul, I'd better leave marriage alone. As the monks and hermits knew. But also, if I am only out to save other people's souls, I had also best leave marriage alone, as the apostles knew, and the preaching saints.

But supposing I am neither bent on saving my own soul nor other people's souls? Supposing Salvation seems incomprehensible to me, as I confess it does. "Being saved" seems to me just jargon, the jargon of self-conceit. Supposing, then, that I cannot see this Saviour and Salvation stuff, supposing that I see the soul as something which must be developed and fulfilled throughout a life-time, sustained and nourished, developed and further fulfilled, to the very end; what then?

Then I realise that marriage, or something like it, is essential, and that the old Church knew best the enduring needs of man, beyond the spasmodic needs of to-day and yesterday. The Church established marriage for life, for the fulfilment of the soul's living life, not postponing it till the after-death.

The old Church knew that life is here our portion, to be lived, to be lived in fulfilment. The stern rule of Benedict, the wild flights of Francis of Assisi, these were coruscations in the steady heaven of the Church. The rhythm of life itself was preserved by the Church hour by hour, day by day, season by season, year by year, epoch by epoch, down among the people, and the wild coruscations were accommodated to this permanent rhythm. We feel it, in the south, in the country, when we hear the jangle of the bells at dawn, at noon, at sunset, marking the hours with the sound of mass or prayers. It is the rhythm of the daily sun. We feel it in the festivals, the processions, Christmas, the Three Kings, Easter, Pentecost, St. John's Day, All Saints, All Souls. This is the wheeling of the year, the movement of the sun through solstice and equinox, the coming of the seasons, the going of the seasons. And it is the inward rhythm of man and woman, too, the sadness of Lent, the delight of Easter, the wonder of Pentecost, the fires of St. John, the candles on the graves of All Souls, the lit-up tree of Christmas, all representing kindled rhythmic emotions in the souls of men and women. And men experience the great rhythm of emotion man-wise, women experience it woman-wise, and in the unison of men and women it is complete.

Augustine said that God created the universe new every day: and to the living, emotional soul, this is true. Every dawn dawns upon an entirely new universe, every Easter lights up an entirely new glory of a new world opening in utterly new flower. And the soul of man and the soul of woman is new in the same way, with the infinite delight of life and the evernewness of life. So a man and a woman are new to one another throughout a life-time, in the rhythm of marriage that matches the rhythm of the year.

Sex is the balance of male and female in the universe, the attraction, the repulsion, the transit of neutrality, the new attraction, the new repulsion, always different, always new. The long neuter spell of Lent, when the blood is low, and the delight of the Easter kiss, the sexual revel of spring, the passion of mid-summer, the slow recoil, revolt, and grief of autumn, greyness again, then the sharp stimulus of winter of the long nights. Sex goes through the rhythm of the year, in man and woman, ceaselessly changing: the rhythm of the sun in his relation to the earth. Oh, what a catastrophe for man when he cut himself off from the rhythm of the year, from his unison with the sun and the earth. Oh, what a catastrophe, what a maiming of love when it was made a personal, merely personal feeling, taken away from the rising and the setting of the sun, and cut off from the magic connection of the solstice and the equinox! This is what is the matter with us. We are bleeding at the roots, because we are cut off from the earth and sun and stars, and love is a grinning mockery, because, poor blossom, we plucked it from its stem on the tree of Life, and expected it to keep on blooming in our civilised vase on the table.

Marriage is the clue to human life, but there is no marriage apart from the wheeling sun and the nodding earth, from the straying of the planets and the magnificance of the fixed stars. Is not a man different, utterly different, at dawn from what he is at sunset? and a woman too? And does not the changing harmony and discord of their variation make the secret music of life?

And is it not so throughout life? A man is different at thirty, at forty, at fifty, at sixty, at seventy: and the woman at his side is different. But is there not some strange conjunction in their differences? Is there not some peculiar harmony, through youth, the period of child-birth, the period of florescence and young children, the period of the woman's change of life, painful yet also a renewal, the period of waning passion but mellowing delight of affection, the dim, unequal period of the approach of death, when the man and woman look at one another with the dim apprehension of separation that is not really a separation: is there not, throughout it all, some unseen, unknown interplay of balance, harmony, completion, like some soundless symphony which moves with a rhythm from phase to phase, so different, so very different in the various movements, and yet one symphony, made out of the soundless singing of two strange and incompatible lives, a man's and a woman's?

This is marriage, the mystery of marriage, marriage which fulfils itself here, in this life. We may well believe that in heaven there is no marrying or giving in marriage. All this has to be fulfilled here, and if it is not fulfilled here, it will never be fulfilled. The great saints only live, even Jesus only lives to add a new fulfilment and a new beauty to the permanent sacrament of marriage.

But—and this *but* crashes through our heart like a bullet—marriage is no marriage that is not basically and permanently phallic, and that is not linked up with the sun and the earth, the moon and the fixed stars and the planets, in the rhythm of days, in the rhythm of months, in the rhythm of quarters, of years, of decades and of centuries. Marriage is no marriage that is not a correspondence of blood. For the blood is the substance of the soul, and of the deepest consciousness. It is by blood that we are: and it is by the heart and the liver that we live and move and have our being. In the blood, knowing and being, or feeling, are one and undivided: no serpent and no apple has caused a split. So that only when the conjunction is of the blood, is marriage truly marriage. The blood of man and the blood of woman are two eternally different streams, that can never be mingled. Even scientifically we know it. But therefore they are the two rivers that encircle the whole of life, and in marriage the circle is complete, and in sex the two rivers touch and renew one another, without ever commingling or confusing. We know it. The phallus is a column of blood that fills the valley of blood of a woman. The great river of male blood touches to its depths the great river of female blood—yet neither breaks its bounds. It is the deepest of all communions, as all the religions, in practice, know. And it is one of the greatest mysteries, in fact, the greatest, as almost every initiation shows, showing the supreme achievement of the mystic marriage.

And this is the meaning of the sexual act: this Communion, this touching on one another of the two rivers, Euphrates and Tigris,—to use old jargon—and the enclosing of the land of Mesopotamia, where Paradise was, or the Park of Eden, where man had his beginning. This is marriage, this circuit of the two rivers, this communion of the two blood-streams, this, and nothing else: as all the religions know.

Two rivers of blood, are man and wife, two distinct eternal streams, that have the power of touching and communing and so renewing, making new one another, without any breaking of the subtle confines, any confusing or commingling. And the phallus is the connecting-link between the two rivers, that establishes the two streams in a oneness, and gives out of their duality a single circuit, forever. And this, this oneness gradually accomplished throughout a life-time in twoness, is the highest achievement of time or eternity. From it all things human spring, children and beauty and well-made things; all the true creations of humanity. And all we know of the will of God is that He wishes this, this oneness, to take place, fulfilled over a lifetime, this oneness within the great dual blood-stream of humanity.

Man dies, and woman dies, and perhaps separate the souls go back to the Creator. Who knows? But we know that the oneness of the blood-stream of man and woman in marriage completes the universe, as far as humanity is concerned, completes the streaming of the sun and the flowing of the stars.

There is, of course, the counterpart to all this, the counterfeit. There is counterfeit marriage, like nearly all marriage to-day. Modern people are just personalities, and modern marriage takes place when two people are "thrilled" by each other's personality: when they have the same tastes in furniture or books or sport or amusement, when they love "talking" to one another, when they admire one another's "minds". Now this, this affinity of mind and personality is an excellent basis of friendship between the sexes, but a disastrous basis for marriage. Because marriage inevitably starts the sex-activity, and the sex-activity is, and always was and will be, in some way hostile to the mental, *personal* relationship between man and woman. It is almost an axiom that the marriage of two *personalities* will end in a startling physical hatred. People who are personally devoted to one another at first end by hating one another with a hate which they cannot account for, which they try to hide, for it makes them ashamed, and which is none the less only too painfully obvious, especially to one another. In people of strong individual feeling the irritation that accumulates in marriage increases only too often to a point of rage that is close akin to madness. And, apparently, all without reason.

But the real reason is, that the exclusive sympathy of nerves and mind and personal interest is, alas, hostile to blood-sympathy, in the sexes. The modern cult of personality is excellent for friendship between the sexes, and fatal for marriage. On the whole, it would be better if modern people didn't marry. They could remain so much more true to what they are, to their own personality.

But marriage or no marriage, the fatal thing happens. If you have only known personal sympathy and personal love, then rage and hatred will sooner or later take possession of the soul, because of the frustration and denial of blood-sympathy, blood-contact. In celibacy, the denial is withering and souring, but in marriage, the denial produces a sort of rage. And we can no more avoid this, nowadays, than we can avoid thunder-storms. It is part of the phenomenon of the psyche. The important point is that sex itself comes to subserve the personality and the personal "love" entirely, without ever giving sexual satisfaction or fulfilment. In fact, there is probably far more sexual activity in a "personal" marriage than in a blood-marriage. Woman sighs for a perpetual lover: and in the personal marriage, relatively, she gets him. And how she comes to hate him, with his never-ending desire, which never gets anywhere or fulfils anything!

It is a mistake I have made, talking of sex I have always inferred that sex meant blood-sympathy and blood-contact. Technically this is so. But as a matter of fact, nearly all modern sex is a pure matter of nerves, cold and bloodless. This is personal sex. And this white, cold, nervous, "poetic" personal sex, which is practically all the sex that moderns know, has a very peculiar physiological effect, as well as psychological. The two blood-streams are brought into contact, in man and woman, just the same as in the urge of blood-passion and blood-desire. But whereas the contact in the urge of blood-desire is positive, making a newness in the blood, in the insistence of this nervous, personal desire the blood-contact becomes frictional and destructive, there is a resultant whitening and impoverishment of the blood. Personal or nervous or spiritual sex is destructive to the blood, has a katabolistic activity, whereas coition in warm blood-desire is an activity of metabolism. The katabolism of "nervous" sex-activity may produce for a time a sort of ecstasy and a heightening of consciousness. But this, like the effect of alcohol or drugs, is the result of the decomposition of certain corpuscles in the blood, and is a process of impoverishment. This is one of the many reasons for the failure of energy in modern people; sexual activity, which ought to be refreshing and renewing, becomes exhaustive and debilitating. So that when the young man fails to believe in the regeneration of England by sex, I am constrained to agree with him. Since modern sex is practically all personal and nervous, and, in effect, exhaustive, disintegrative. The disintegrative effect of modern sex-activity is undeniable. It is only less fatal than the disentegrative effect of masturbation, which is more deadly still.

So that at last I begin to see the point of my critics' abuse of my exalting of sex. They only know one form of sex: in fact, to them there *is* only one form of sex: the nervous, personal, disintegrative sort, the "white" sex. And this, of course, is something to be flowery and false about, but nothing to be very hopeful about. I quite agree. And I quite agree, we can have no hope of the regeneration of England from such sort of sex.

At the same time, I cannot see any hope of regeneration for a sexless England. An England that has lost its sex seems to me nothing to feel very hopeful about. And nobody feels very hopeful about it. Though I may have been a fool for insisting on sex where the current sort of sex is just what I *don't* mean and *don't* want, still I can't go back on it all and believe in the regeneration of England by pure sexlessness. A sexless England!—it doesn't ring very hopeful, to me.

And the other, the warm blood-sex that establishes the living and re-vitalising connection between man and woman, how are we to get that back? I don't know. Yet get it back we must: or the younger ones must, or we are all lost. For the bridge to the future is the phallus, and there's the end of it. But not the poor, nervous counterfeit phallus of modern "nervous" love. Not that.

For the new impulse to life will never come without blood-contact; the true, positive blood-contact, not the nervous negative reaction. And the essential blood-contact is between man and woman, always has been so, always will be. The contact of positive sex. The homosexual contacts are secondary, even if not merely substitutes of exasperated reaction from the utterly unsatisfactory nervous sex between men and women.

If England is to be regenerated—to use the phrase of the young man who seemed to think there was need of *regeneration*—the very word is his—then it will be by the arising of a new blood-contact, a new touch, and a new marriage. It will be a phallic rather than a sexual regeneration. For the phallus is only the great old symbol of godly vitality in a man, and of immediate contact.

It will also be a renewal of marriage: the true phallic marriage. And, still further, it will be marriage set again in relationship to the rhythmic cosmos. The rhythm of the cosmos is something we cannot get away from, without bitterly impoverishing our lives. The Early Christians tried to kill the old pagan rhythm of cosmic ritual, and to some extent succeeded. They killed the planets and the zodiac, perhaps because astrology had already become debased to fortune-telling. They wanted to kill the festivals of the year. But the Church, which knows that man doth not live by man alone, but by the sun and moon and earth in their revolutions, restored the sacred days and feasts almost as the pagans had them, and the Christian peasants went on very much as the pagan peasants had gone, with the sunrise pause for worship, and the sunset, and noon, the three great daily moments of the sun: then the new holy-day, one in the ancient seven-cycle: then Easter and the dying and rising of God, Pentecost, Midsummer Fire, the November dead and the spirits of the grave, then Christmas, then Three Kings. For centuries the mass of people lived in this rhythm, under the Church. And it is down in the mass that the roots of religion are eternal. When the mass of a people loses the religious rhythm, that people is dead, without hope. But Protestantism came and gave a great blow to the religious and ritualistic rhythm of the year, in human life. Nonconformity *almost* finished the deed. Now you have a poor, blind, disconnected people with nothing but politics and bank-holidays to satisfy the eternal human need of living in ritual adjustment to the cosmos in its revolutions, in eternal submission to the greater laws. And marriage, being one of the greater necessities, has suffered the same from the loss of the sway of the greater laws, the cosmic rhythms which should sway life always. Mankind has got to get back to the rhythm of the cosmos, and the permanence of marriage.

All this is post-script, or afterthought, to my novel, *Lady Chatterley's Lover*. Man has little needs and deeper needs. We have fallen into the mistake of living from our little needs till we have almost lost our deeper needs in a sort of madness. There is a little morality, which concerns persons and the little needs of man: and this, alas, is the morality we live by. But there is a deeper morality, which concerns all womanhood, all manhood, and nations, and races, and classes of men. This greater morality affects the destiny of mankind over long stretches of time, applies to man's greater needs, and is often in conflict with the little morality of the little needs. The tragic consciousness has taught us, even, that one of the greater needs of man is a knowledge and experience of death; every man needs to know death in his own body. But the greater consciousness of the pre-tragic and post-tragic epochs teaches us—though we have not yet reached the post-tragic epoch—that the greatest need of man is the renewal forever of the complete rhythm of life and death, the rhythm of the sun's year, the body's year of a lifetime, and the greater year of the stars, the soul's year of immortality. This is our need, our imperative need. It is a need of the mind and soul, body, spirit and sex: all. It is no use asking for a Word to fulfil such a need. No Word, no Logos, no Utterance will ever do it. The Word is uttered, most of it: we need only pay true attention. But who will call us to the Deed, the great Deed of the Seasons and the year, the Deed of the soul's cycle, the Deed of a woman's life at one with a man's, the little Deed of the moon's wandering, the bigger Deed of the sun's, and the biggest, of the great still stars? It is the *Deed* of life we have now to learn: we are supposed to have learnt the Word, but, alas, look at us. Word-perfect we may be, but Deed-demented. Let us prepare now for the death of our present "little" life, and the re-emergence in a bigger life, in touch with the moving cosmos.

It is a question, practically, of relationship. We *must* get back into relation, vivid and nourishing relation to the cosmos and the universe. The way is through daily ritual, and the re-awakening. We *must* once more practise the ritual of dawn and noon and sunset, the ritual of the kindling fire and pouring water, the ritual of the first breath, and the last. This is an affair of the individual and the household, a ritual of day. The ritual of the moon in her phases, of the morning star and the evening star is for men and women separate. Then the ritual of the seasons, with the Drama and the Passion of the soul embodied in procession and dance, this is for the community, an act of men and women, a whole community, in togetherness. And the ritual of the great events in the year of stars is for nations and whole peoples. To these rituals we must return: or we must evolve them to suit our needs. For the truth is, we are perishing for lack of fulfilment of our greater needs, we are cut off from the great sources of our inward nourishment and renewal, sources which flow eternally in the universe. Vitally, the human race is dying. It is like a great uprooted tree, with its roots in the air. We must plant ourselves again in the universe.

It means a return to ancient forms. But we shall have to create these forms again, and it is more difficult than the preaching of an evangel. The Gospel came to tell us we were all saved. We look at the world to-day and realise that humanity, alas, instead of being saved from sin, whatever that may be, is almost completely lost, lost to life, and near to nullity and extermination. We have to go back, a long way, before the idealist conceptions began, before Plato, before the tragic idea of life arose, to get on to our feet again. For the gospel of salvation through the Ideals and escape from the body coincided with the tragic conception of human life. Salvation and tragedy are the same thing, and they are now both beside the point.

Back, before the idealist religions and philosophies arose and started man on the great excursion of tragedy. The last three thousand years of mankind have been an excursion into ideals, bodilessness, and tragedy, and now the excursion is over. And it is like the end of a tragedy in the theatre. The stage is strewn with dead bodies, worse still, with meaningless bodies, and the curtain comes down.

But in life, the curtain never comes down on the scene. There the dead bodies lie, and the inert ones, and somebody has to clear them away, somebody has to carry on. It is the day after. To-day is already the day after the end of the tragic and idealist epoch. Utmost inertia falls on the remaining protagonists. Yet we have to carry on.

Now we have to re-establish the great relationships which the grand idealists, with their underlying pessimism, their belief that life is nothing but futile conflict, to be avoided even unto death, destroyed for us. Buddha, Plato, Jesus, they were all three utter pessimists as regards life, teaching that the only happiness lay in abstracting oneself from life, the daily, yearly, seasonal life of birth and death and fruition, and in living in the "immutable" or eternal spirit. But now, after almost three thousand years, now that we are almost abstracted entirely from the rhythmic life of the seasons, birth and death and fruition, now we realise that such abstraction is neither bliss nor liberation, but nullity. It brings null inertia. And the great saviours and teachers only cut us off from life. It was the tragic *excursus*.

The universe is dead for us, and how is it to come to life again? "Knowledge" has killed the sun, making it a ball of gas, with spots; "knowledge" has killed the moon, it is a dead little earth fretted with extinct craters as with smallpox; the machine has killed the earth for us, making it a surface, more or less bumpy, that you travel over. How, out of all this, are we to get back the grand orbs of the soul's heavens, that fill us with unspeakable joy? How are we to get back Apollo, and Attis, Demeter, Persephone, and the halls of Dis? How even see the star Hesperus, or Betelguese?

We've got to get them back, for they are the world our soul, our greater consciousness, lives in. The world of reason and science, the moon, a dead lump of earth, the sun, so much gas with spots: this is the dry and sterile little world the abstracted mind inhabits. The world of our little consciousness, which we know in our pettifogging *apartness*. This is how we know the world when we know it apart from ourselves, in the mean separateness of everything. When we know the world in togetherness with ourselves, we know the earth hyacinthine or Plutonic, we know the moon gives us our body as delight upon us, or steals it away, we know the purring of the great gold lion of the sun, who licks us like a lioness her cubs, making us bold, or else, like the red, angry lion, dashes at us with open claws. There are many ways of knowing, there are many sorts of knowledge. But the two ways of knowing, for man, are knowing in terms of apartness, which is mental, rational, scientific, and knowing in terms of togetherness, which is religious and poetic. The Christian religion lost, in Protestantism finally, the togetherness with the universe, the togetherness of the body, the sex, the emotions, the passions, with the earth and sun and stars.

But relationship is threefold. First, there is the relation to the living universe. Then comes the relation of man to woman. Then comes the relation of man to man. And each is a blood-relationship, not mere spirit or mind. We have abstracted the universe into Matter and Force, we have abstracted men and women into separate personalities—personalities being isolated units, incapable of togetherness—so that all three great relationships are bodiless, dead.

None, however, is quite so dead as the man-to-man relationship. I think, if we came to analyse to the last what men feel about one another to-day, we should find that every man feels every other man as a menace. It is a curious thing, but the more mental and ideal men are, the more they seem to feel the bodily presence of any other man a menace, a menace, as it were, to their very being. Every man that comes near me threatens my very existence: nay, more, my very being.

This is the ugly fact which underlies our civilisation. As the advertisement of one of the war novels said, it is an epic of "friendship and hope, mud and blood", which means, of course, that the friendship and hope must end in mud and blood.

When the great crusade against sex and the body started in full blast with Plato, it was a crusade for "ideals", and for this "spiritual" knowledge in apartness. Sex is the great unifier. In its big, slower vibration it is the warmth of heart which makes people happy together, in togetherness. The idealist philosophies and religions set out deliberately to kill this. And they did it. Now they have done it. The last great ebullition of friendship and hope was squashed out in mud and blood. Now men are all separate little entities. While "kindness" is the glib order of the day—everybody *must* be "kind"—underneath this "kindness" we find a coldness of heart, a lack of heart, a callousness, that is very dreary. Every man *is* a menace to every other man.

Men only know one another in menace. Individualism has triumphed. If I am a sheer individual, then every other being, every other man especially, is over against me as a menace to me. This is the peculiarity of our society to-day. We are all extremely sweet and "nice" to one another, because we merely fear one another.

The sense of isolation, followed by the sense of menace and of fear, is bound to arise as the feeling of oneness and community with our fellow-men declines, and the feeling of individualism and personality, which is existence in isolation, increases. The so-called "cultured" classes are the first to develop "personality" and individualism, and the first to fall into this state of unconscious menace and fear. The working-classes retain the old blood-warmth of oneness and togetherness some decades longer. Then they lose it too. And then class-consciousness becomes rampant, and class-hate. Class-hate and class-consciousness are only a sign that the old togetherness, the old blood-warmth has collapsed, and every man is really aware of himself in apartness. Then we have these hostile groupings of men for the sake of opposition, strife. Civil strife becomes a necessary condition of self-assertion.

This, again, is the tragedy of social life today. In the old England, the curious blood-connection held the classes together. The squires might be arrogant, violent, bullying and unjust, yet in some ways they were *at one* with the people, part of the same blood-stream. We feel it in Defoe or Fielding. And then, in the mean Jane Austen, it is gone. Already this old maid typifies "personality" instead of character, the sharp knowing in apartness instead of knowing in togetherness, and she is, to my feeling, thoroughly unpleasant, English in the bad, mean, snobbish sense of the word, just as Fielding is English in the good, generous sense.

So, in *Lady Chatterley's Lover* we have a man, Sir Clifford, who is purely a personality, having lost entirely all connection with his fellow-men and women, except those of usage. All warmth is gone entirely, the hearth is cold, the heart does not humanly exist. He is a pure product of our civilisation, but he is the death of the great humanity of the world. He is kind by rule, but he does not know what warm sympathy means. He is what he is. And he loses the woman of his choice.

The other man still has the warmth of a man, but he is being hunted down, destroyed. Even it is a question if the woman who turns to him will really stand by him and his vital meaning.

I have been asked many times if I intentionally made Clifford paralysed, if it is symbolic. And literary friends say, it would have been better to have left him whole and potent, and to have made the woman leave him nevertheless.

As to whether the "symbolism" is intentional—I don't know. Certainly not in the beginning, when Clifford was created. When I created Clifford and Connie, I had no idea what they were or why they were. They just came, pretty much as they are. But the novel was written, from start to finish, three times. And when I read the first version, I recognised that the lameness of Clifford was symbolic of the paralysis, the deeper emotional or passional paralysis, of most men of his sort and class today. I realised that it was perhaps taking an unfair advantage of Connie, to paralyse him technically. It made it so much more vulgar of her to leave him. Yet the story came as it did, by itself, so I left it alone. Whether we call it symbolism or not, it is, in the sense of its happening, inevitable.

And these notes, which I write now almost two years after the novel was finished, are not intended to explain or expound anything: only to give the emotional beliefs which perhaps are necessary as a background to the book. It is so obviously a book written in defiance of convention that perhaps some reason should be offered for the attitude of defiance: since the silly desire to *épater le bourgeois,* to bewilder the commonplace person, is not worth entertaining. If I use the taboo words, there is a reason. We shall never free the phallic reality from the "uplift" taint till we give it its own phallic language, and use the obscene words. The greatest blasphemy of all against the phallic reality is this "lifting it to a higher plane". Likewise, if the lady marries the gamekeeper—she hasn't done it yet—it is not class-spite, but in spite of class.

Finally, there are the correspondents who complain that I describe the pirated editions—some of them—but not the original. The original first edition, issued in Florence, is bound in hard covers, dullish mulberry-red paper with my phœnix (symbol of immortality, the bird rising new from the nest of flames) printed in black on the cover, and a white paper label on the back. The paper is good, creamy hand-rolled Italian paper, but the print, though nice, is ordinary, and the binding is just the usual binding of a little Florentine shop. There is no expert bookmaking in it: yet it is a pleasant volume, much more so than many far "superior" books.

And if there are many spelling errors—there are—it is because the book was set up in a little Italian printing shop, such a family affair, in which nobody knew one word of English. They none of them knew any English at all, so they were spared all blushes: and the proofs were terrible. The printer would do fairly well for a few pages, then he would go drunk, or something. And then the words danced weird and *macabre,* but not English. So that if still some of the hosts of errors exist, it is a mercy they are not more.

Then one paper wrote pitying the poor printer who was deceived into printing the book. Not deceived at all. A white-moustached little man who has just married a second wife, he was told: Now the book contains such-and-such words, in English, and it describes certain things. Don't you print it if you think it will get you into trouble!—What does it describe?" he asked. And when told, he said, with the short indifference of a Florentine: "O! *ma*! but we do it every day!"—And it seemed, to him, to settle the matter entirely. Since it was nothing political or out of the way, there was nothing to think about. Everyday concerns, commonplace.

But it was a struggle, and the wonder is the book came out as well as it did. There was just enough type to set up a half of it: so the half was set up, the thousand copies were printed and, as a measure of caution, the two hundred on ordinary paper, the little second edition, as well: then the type was distributed, and the second half set up.

Then came the struggle of delivery. The book was stopped by the American customs almost at once. Fortunately in England there was a delay. So that practically the whole edition—at least eight hundred copies, surely—must have gone to England.

Then came the storms of vulgar vituperation. But they were inevitable. "But we do it every day," says a little Italian printer. "Monstrous and horrible!" shrieks a section of the British press. "Thank you for a really sexual book about sex, at last. I am so tired of a-sexual books," says one of the most distinguished citizens of Florence to me—an Italian. "I don't know—I don't know—if it's not a bit too strong," says a timid Florentine critic—an Italian. "Listen, Signor Lawrence, you find it really necessary to *say* it?" I told him I did, and he pondered.— "Well, one of them was a brainy vamp, and the other was a sexual moron," said an American woman, referring to the two men in the book—"so I'm afraid Connie had a poor choice—*as usual*!"

Pornography
and
Obscenity

What they are depends, as usual, entirely on the individual. What is pornography to one man is the laughter of genius to another.

The word itself, we are told, means 'pertaining to harlots'—the graph of the harlot. But nowadays, what is a harlot? If she was a woman who took money from a man in return for going to bed with him—really, most wives sold themselves, in the past, and plenty of harlots gave themselves, when they felt like it, for nothing. If a woman hasn't got a tiny streak of a harlot in her, she's a dry stick as a rule. And probably most harlots had somewhere a streak of womanly generosity. Why be so cut and dried? The law is a dreary thing, and its judgments have nothing to do with life.

The same with the word *obscene:* nobody knows what it means. Suppose it were derived from *obscena:* that which might not be represented on the stage; how much further are you? None! What is obscene to Tom is not obscene to Lucy or Joe, and really, the meaning of a word has to wait for majorities to decide it. If a play shocks ten people in an audience, and doesn't shock the remaining five hundred, then it is obscene to ten and innocuous to five hundred; hence the play is not obscene, by majority. But *Hamlet* shocked all the Cromwellian Puritans, and shocks nobody to-day, and some of Aristophanes shocks everybody to-day, and didn't galvanize the later Greeks at all, apparently. Man is a changeable beast, and words change their meanings with him, and things are not what they seemed, and what's what becomes what isn't, and if we think we know where we are it's only because we are so rapidly being translated to somewhere else. We have to leave everything to the majority, everything to the majority, everything to the mob, the mob, the mob. They know what is obscene and what isn't, they do. If the lower ten million doesn't know better than the upper ten men, then there's something wrong with mathematics. Take a vote on it! Show hands, and prove it by count! Vox populi, vox Dei. Odi profanum vulgus! Profanum vulgus.

So it comes down to this: if you are talking to the mob, the meaning of your words is the mob-meaning, decided by majority. As somebody wrote to me: the American law on obscenity is very plain, and America is going to enforce the law. Quite, my dear, quite, quite, quite! The mob knows all about obscenity. Mild little words that rhyme with spit or farce are the height of obscenity. Supposing a printer put 'h' in the place of 'p', by mistake, in that mere word spit? Then the great American public knows that this man has committed an obscenity, an indecency, that his act was lewd, and as a compositor he was pornographical. You can't tamper with the great public, British or American. Vox populi, vox Dei, don't you know. If you don't we'll let you know it. At the same time, this vox Dei shouts with praise over moving-pictures and books and newspaper accounts that seem, to a sinful nature like mine, completely disgusting and obscene. Like a real prude and Puritan, I have to look the other way. When obscenity becomes mawkish, which is its palatable form for the public, and when the Vox populi, vox Dei, is hoarse with sentimental indecency, then I have to steer away, like a Pharisee, afraid of being contaminated. There is a certain kind of sticky universal pitch that I refuse to touch.

So again, it comes down to this: you accept the majority, the mob, and its decisions, or you don't. You bow down before the Vox populi, vox Dei, or you plug your ears not to hear its obscene howl. You perform your antics to please the vast public, Deus ex machina, or you refuse to perform for the public at all, unless now and then to pull its elephantine and ignominious leg.

When it comes to the meaning of anything, even the simplest word, then you must pause. Because there are two great categories of meaning, forever separate. There is mob-meaning, and there is individual meaning. Take even the word *bread*. The mob-meaning is merely: stuff made with white flour into loaves that you eat. But take the individual meaning of the word bread: the white, the brown, the corn-pone, the homemade, the smell of bread just out of the oven, the crust, the crumb, the unleavened bread, the shew-bread, the staff of life, sour-dough bread, cottage loaves, French bread, Viennese bread, black bread, a yesterday's loaf, rye, Graham, barley, rolls, Bretzeln, Kringeln, scones, damper, matsen— there is no end to it all, and the word bread will take you to the ends of time and space, and far-off down avenues of memory. But this is individual. The word bread will take the individual off on his own journey, and its meaning will be his own meaning, based on his own genuine imaginative reactions. And when a word comes to us in its individual character, and starts in us the individual responses, it is a great pleasure to us. The American advertisers have discovered this, and some of the cunningest American literature is to be found in advertisements of soap-suds, for example. These advertisements are *almost* prose-poems. They give the word soap-suds a bubbly, shiny individual meaning, which is very skilfully poetic, would, perhaps, be quite poetic to the mind which could forget that the poetry was bait on a hook.

Business is discovering the individual, dynamic meaning of words, and poetry is losing it. Poetry more and more tends to far-fetch its word-meanings, and this results once again in mob-meanings, which arouse only a mob-reaction in the individual. For every man has a mob self and an individual self, in varying proportions. Some men are almost all mob-self, incapable of imaginative individual responses. The worst specimens of mob-self are usually to be found in the professions, lawyers, professors, clergymen and so on. The business man, much maligned, has a tough outside mob-self, and a scared, floundering, yet still alive individual self. The public, which is feeble-minded like an idiot, will never be able to preserve its individual reactions from the tricks of the exploiter. The public is always exploited and always will be exploited. The methods of exploitation merely vary. To-day the public is tickled into laying the golden egg. With imaginative words and individual meanings it is tricked into giving the great goose-cackle of mob-acquiescence. Vox populi, vox Dei. It has always been so, and will always be so. Why? Because the public has not enough wit to distinguish between mob-meanings and individual meanings. The mass is forever vulgar, because it can't distinguish between its own original feelings and feelings which are diddled into existence by the exploiter. The public is always profane, because it is controlled from the outside, by the trickster, and never from the inside, by its own sincerity. The mob is always obscene, because it is always second-hand.

Which brings us back to our subject of pornography and obscenity. The reaction to any word may be, in any individual, either a mob-reaction or an individual reaction. It is up to the individual to ask himself: Is my reaction individual, or am I merely reacting from my mob-self?

When it comes to the so-called obscene words, I should say that hardly one person in a million escapes mob-reaction. The first reaction is almost sure to be mob-reaction, mob-indignation, mob-condemnation. And the mob gets no further. But the real individual has second thoughts and says: am I really shocked? Do I *really* feel outraged and indignant? And the answer of any individual is bound to be: No, I am not shocked, not outraged, nor indignant. I know the word, and take it for what it is, and I am not going to be jockeyed into making a mountain out of a mole-hill, not for all the law in the world.

Now if the use of a few so-called obscene words will startle man or woman out of a mob-habit into an individual state, well and good. And word prudery is so universal a mob-habit that it is time we were startled out of it.

But still we have only tackled obscenity, and the problem of pornography goes even deeper. When a man is startled into his individual self, he still may not be able to know, inside himself, whether Rabelais is or is not pornographic: and over Aretino or even Boccaccio he may perhaps puzzle in vain, torn between different emotions.

One essay on pornography, I remember, comes to the conclusion that pornography in art is that which is calculated to arouse sexual desire, or sexual excitement. And stress is laid on the fact, whether the author or artist *intended* to arouse sexual feelings. It is the old vexed question of intention, become so dull to-day, when we know how strong and influential our unconscious intentions are. And why a man should be held guilty of his conscious intentions, and innocent of his unconscious intentions, I don't know, since every man is more made up of unconscious intentions than of conscious ones. I am what I am, not merely what I think I am.

However! We take it, I assume, that *pornography* is something base, something unpleasant. In short, we don't like it. And why don't we like it? Because it arouses sexual feelings?

I think not. No matter how hard we may pretend otherwise, most of us rather like a moderate rousing of our sex. It warms us, stimulates us like sunshine on a grey day. After a century or two of Puritanism, this is still true of most people. Only the mob-habit of condemning any form of sex is too strong to let us admit it naturally. And there are, of course, many people who are genuinely repelled by the simplest and most natural stirrings of sexual feeling. But these people are perverts who have fallen into hatred of their fellow men: thwarted, disappointed, unfulfilled people, of whom, alas, our civilization contains so many. And they nearly always enjoy some unsimple and unnatural form of sex excitement, secretly.

Even quite advanced art critics would try to make us believe that any picture or book which had 'sex appeal' was *ipso facto* a bad book or picture. This is just canting hypocrisy. Half the great poems, pictures, music, stories of the whole world are great by virtue of the beauty of their sex appeal. Titian or Renoir, the *Song of Solomon* or *Jane Eyre,* Mozart or *Annie Laurie,* the loveliness is all interwoven with sex appeal, sex stimulus, call it what you will. Even Michael Angelo, who rather hated sex, can't help filling the Cornucopia with phallic acorns. Sex is a very powerful, beneficial and necessary stimulus in human life, and we are all grateful when we feel its warm, natural flow through us, like a form of sunshine.

So we can dismiss the idea that sex appeal in art is pornography. It may be so to the grey Puritan, but the grey Puritan is a sick man, soul and body sick, so why should we bother about his hallucinations? Sex appeal, of course, varies enormously. There are endless different kinds, and endless degrees of each kind. Perhaps it may be argued that a mild degree of sex appeal is not pornographical, whereas a high degree is. But this is a fallacy. Boccaccio at his hottest seems to me less pornographical than *Pamela* or *Clarissa Harlowe* or even *Jane Eyre,* or a host of modern books or films which pass uncensored. At the same time Wagner's *Tristan and Isolde* seems to me very near to pornography, and so, even, do some quite popular Christian hymns.

What is it, then? It isn't a question of sex appeal, merely: nor even a question of deliberate intention on the part of the author or artist to arouse sexual excitement. Rabelais sometimes had a deliberate intention, so in a different way, did Boccaccio. And I'm sure poor Charlotte Bronte, or the authoress of *The Sheik* did *not* have any deliberate intention to stimulate sex feelings in the reader. Yet I find *Jane Eyre* verging towards pornography and Boccaccio seems to me always fresh and wholesome.

The late British Home Secretary, who prides himself on being a very sincere Puritan, grey, grey in every fibre, said with indignant sorrow in one of his outbursts on improper books: '—and these two young people, who had been perfectly pure up till that time, after reading this book went and had sexual intercourse together!!!' *One up to them!* is all we can answer. But the grey Guardian of British Morals seemed to think that if they had murdered one another, or worn each other to rags of nervous prostration, it would have been much better. The grey disease!

Then what is pornography, after all this? It isn't sex appeal or sex stimulus in art. It isn't even a deliberate intention on the part of the artist to arouse or to excite sexual feelings. There's nothing wrong with sexual feelings in themselves, so long as they are straight-forward and not sneaking or sly. The right sort of sex stimulus is invaluable to human daily life. Without it the world grows grey. I would give everybody the gay Renaissance stories to read, they would help to shake off a lot of grey self-importance, which is our modern civilized disease.

But even I would censor genuine pornography, rigorously. It would not be very difficult. In the first place, genuine pornography is almost always underworld, it doesn't come into the open. In the second, you can recognize it by the insult it offers, invariably, to sex, and to the human spirit.

Pornography is the attempt to insult sex, to do dirt on it. This is unpardonable. Take the very lowest instance, the picture post-card sold underhand, by the underworld, in most cities. What I have seen of them have been of an ugliness to make you cry. The insult to the human body, the insult to a vital human relationship! Ugly and cheap they make the human nudity, ugly and degraded they make the sexual act, trivial and cheap and nasty.

It is the same with the books they sell in the underworld. They are either so ugly they make you ill, or so fatuous you can't imagine anybody but a cretin or a moron reading them, or writing them.

It is the same with the dirty limericks that people tell after dinner, or the dirty stories one hears commercial travellers telling each other in a smoke-room. Occasionally there is a really funny one, that redeems a great deal. But usually they are just ugly and repellant, and the so-called 'humour' is just a trick of doing dirt on sex.

Now the human nudity of a great many modern people is just ugly and degraded, and the sexual act between modern people is just the same, merely ugly and degrading. But this is nothing to be proud of. It is the catastrophe of our civilization. I am sure no other civilization, not even the Roman, has showed such a vast proportion of ignominious and degraded nudity, and ugly, squalid dirty sex. Because no other civilization has driven sex into the underworld, and nudity to the W.C.

The intelligent young, thank Heaven, seem determined to alter in these two respects. They are rescuing their young nudity from the stuffy, pornographical hole-and-corner underworld of their elders, and they refuse to sneak about the sexual relation. This is a change the elderly grey ones of course deplore, but it is in fact a very great change for the better, and a real revolution.

But it is amazing how strong is the will in ordinary, vulgar people, to do dirt on sex. It was one of my fond illusions, when I was young, that the ordinary healthy-seeming sort of men, in railway carriages, or the smoke-room of an hotel or a pullman, were healthy in their feelings and had a wholesome rough devil-may-care attitude toward sex. All wrong! All wrong! Experience teaches that common individuals of this sort have a disgusting attitude toward sex, a disgusting contempt of it, a disgusting desire to insult it. If such fellows have intercourse with a woman, they triumphantly feel that they have done her dirt, and now she is lower, cheaper, more contemptible than she was before.

It is individuals of this sort that tell dirty stories, carry indecent picture post-cards, and know the indecent books. This is the great pornographical class—the really common men-in-the-street and women-in-the-street. They have as great a hate and contempt of sex as the greyest Puritan, and when an appeal is made to them, they are always on the side of the angels. They insist that a film-heroine shall be a neuter, a sexless thing of washed-out purity. They insist that real sex-feeling shall only be shown by the villain or villainess, low lust. They find a Titian or a Renoir really indecent, and they don't want their wives and daughters to see it.

Why? Because they have the grey disease of sex-hatred, coupled with the yellow disease of dirt lust. The sex functions and the excrementory functions in the human body work so close together, yet they are, so to speak, utterly different in direction. Sex is a creative flow, the excrementory flow is towards dissolution, decreation, if we may use such a word. In the really healthy human being the distinction between the two is instant, our profoundest instincts are perhaps our instincts of opposition between the two flows.

But in the degraded human being the deep instincts have gone dead, and then the two flows become identical. *This* is the secret of really vulgar and of por-nographical people: the sex flow and the excrement flow is the same thing to them. It happens when the psyche deteriorates, and the profound controlling instincts collapse. Then sex is dirt and dirt is sex, and sexual excitement becomes a playing with dirt, and any sign of sex in a woman becomes a show of her dirt. This is the condition of the common, vulgar human being whose name is legion, and who lifts his voice and it is the Vox populi, vox Dei. And this is the source of all pornography.

And for this reason we must admit that *Jane Eyre* or Wagner's *Tristan* are much nearer to pornography than is Boccaccio. Wagner and Charlotte Bronte were both in the state where the strongest instincts have collapsed, and sex has become something slightly obscene, to be wallowed in, but despised. Mr. Roch-ester's sex passion is not 'respectable' till Mr. Rochester is burned, blinded, disfigured and reduced to helpless dependence. Then, thoroughly humbled and humiliated, it may be merely admitted. All the previous titillations are slightly indecent, as in *Pamela* or *The Mill on the Floss* or *Anna Karenina*. As soon as there is sex excitement with a desire to spite the sexual feeling, to humiliate it and degrade it, the element of pornography enters.

For this reason, there is an element of pornography in nearly all nineteenth-century literature and very many so-called pure people have a nasty pornographical side to them, and never was the pornographical appetite stronger than it is to-day. It is a sign of a diseased condition of the body politic. But the way to treat the disease is to come out into the open with sex and sex stimulus. The real pornographer truly dislikes Boccaccio, because the fresh healthy naturalness of the Italian story-teller makes the modern pornographical shrimp feel the dirty worm he is. To-day Boccaccio should be given to everybody young or old, to read if they like. Only a natural fresh openness about sex will do any good, now we are being swamped by secret or semi-secret pornography. And perhaps the Renaissance story-tellers, Boccaccio, Lasca and the rest, are the best antidote we can find now, just as more plasters of Puritanism are the most harmful remedy we can resort to.

The whole question of pornography seems to me a question of secrecy. Without secrecy there would be no pornography. But secrecy and modesty are two utterly different things. Secrecy has always an element of fear in it, amounting very often to hate. Modesty is gentle and reserved. To-day, modesty is thrown to the winds, even in the presence of the grey guardians. But secrecy is hugged, being a vice in itself. And the attitude of the grey ones is: Dear young ladies, you may abandon all modesty, so long as you hug your dirty little secret.

This 'dirty little secret' has become infinitely precious to the mob of people to-day. It is a kind of hidden sore or inflammation which, when rubbed or scratched, gives off sharp thrills that seem delicious. So the dirty little secret is rubbed and scratched more and more, till it becomes more and more secretly inflamed, and the nervous and psychic health of the individual is more and more impaired. One might easily say that half the love novels and half the love-films to-day depend entirely for their success on the secret rubbing of the dirty little secret. You can call this sex-excitement if you like, but it is sex-excitement of a secretive, furtive sort, quite special. The plain and simple excitement, quite open and wholesome, which you find in some Boccaccio stories is not for a minute to be confused with the furtive excitement aroused by rubbing the dirty little secret in all secrecy in modern bestsellers. This furtive, sneaking, cunning rubbing of an inflamed spot in the imagination is the very quick of modern pornography, and it is a beastly and very dangerous thing. You can't so easily expose it, because of its very furtiveness and its sneaking cunning. So the cheap and popular modern love-novel and love-film flourishes and is even praised by moral guardians, because you get the sneaking thrill fumbling under all the purity of dainty underclothes, without one single gross word to let you know what is happening.

Without secrecy there would be no pornography. But if pornography is the result of sneaking secrecy, what is the result of pornography? What is the effect on the individual?

The effect on the individual is manifold, and always pernicious. But one effect is perhaps inevitable. The pornography of to-day, whether it be the pornography of the rubber-goods shop or the pornography of the popular novel, film and play, is an invariable stimulant to the vice of self abuse, onanism, masturbation, call it what you will. In young or old, man or woman, boy or girl, modern pornography is a direct provocative of masturbation. It cannot be otherwise. When the grey ones wail that the young man and the young woman went and had sexual intercourse, they are bewailing the fact that the young man and the young woman didn't go separately and masturbate. Sex must go somewhere, especially in young people. So, in our glorious civilization, it goes in masturbation. And the mass of our popular literature, the bulk of our popular amusements just exists to provoke masturbation. Masturbation is the one thoroughly secret act of the human being, more secret even than excrementation. It is the one functional result of sex-secrecy, and it is stimulated and provoked by our glorious popular literature of pretty pornography, which rubs on the dirty secret without letting you know what is happening.

Now I have heard men, teachers and clergymen, commend masturbation as the solution of an otherwise insoluble sex problem. This at least is honest. The sex problem is there, and you can't just will it away. There it is, and under the ban of secrecy and taboo in mother and father, teacher, friend and foe, it has found its own solution, the solution of masturbation.

But what about the solution? Do we accept it? Do all the grey ones of this world accept it? If so, they must now accept it openly. We can none of us pretend any longer to be blind to the fact of masturbation, in young and old, man and woman. The moral guardians who are prepared to censor all open and plain portrayal of sex must now be made to give their only justification: We prefer that the people shall masturbate. If this preference is open and declared, then the existing forms of censorship are justified. If the moral guardians prefer that the people shall masturbate, then their present behaviour is correct, and popular amusements are as they should be. If sexual intercourse is deadly sin, and masturbation is comparatively pure and harmless, then all is well. Let things continue as they now are.

Is masturbation so harmless, though? Is it even comparatively pure and harmless? Not to my thinking. In the young, a certain amount of masturbation is inevitable, but not therefore natural. I think, there is no boy or girl who masturbates without feeling a sense of shame, anger and futility. Following the excitement comes the shame, anger, humiliation and the sense of futility. This sense of futility and humiliation deepens as the years go on, into a suppressed rage, because of the impossibility of escape. The one thing that it seems impossible to escape from, once the habit is formed, is masturbation. It goes on and on, on into old age, in spite of marriage or love affairs or anything else. And it always carries this secret feeling of futility and humiliation, futility and humiliation. And this is, perhaps, the deepest and most dangerous cancer of our civilization. Instead of being a comparatively pure and harmless vice, masturbation is certainly the most dangerous sexual vice that a society can be afflicted with, in the long run. Comparatively pure it may be—purity being what it is. But harmless!!!

The great danger of masturbation lies in its merely exhaustive nature. In sexual intercourse, there is a give and take. A new stimulus enters as the native stimulus departs. Something quite new is added as the old surcharge is removed. And this is so in all sexual intercourse where two creatures are concerned, even in the homosexual intercourse. But in masturbation there is nothing but loss. There is no reciprocity. There is merely the spending away of a certain force, and no return. The body remains, in a sense, a corpse, after the act of self-abuse. There is no change, only deadening. There is what we call dead loss. And this is not the case in any act of sexual intercourse between two people. Two people may destroy one another in sex. But they cannot just produce the null effect of masturbation.

The only positive effect of masturbation is that it seems to release a certain mental energy, in some people. But it is mental energy which manifests itself always in the same way, in a vicious circle of analysis and impotent criticism, or else a vicious circle of false and easy sympathy, sentimentalities. The sentimentalism and the niggling analysis, often self-analysis, of most of our modern literature, is a sign of self-abuse. It is the manifestation of masturbation, the sort of conscious activity stimulated by masturbation, whether male or female. The outstanding feature of such consciousness is that there is no real object, there is only subject. This is just the same whether it be a novel or a work of science. The author never escapes from himself, he pads along within the vicious circle of himself. There is hardly a writer living who gets out of the vicious circle of himself—or a painter either. Hence the lack of creation, and the stupendous amount of production. It is a masturbation result, within the vicious circle of the self. It is self-absorption made public.

And of course the process is exhaustive. The real masturbation of Englishmen began only in the nineteenth century. It has continued with an increasing emptying of the real vitality and the real *being* of men, till now people are little more than shells of people. Most of the responses are dead, most of the awareness is dead, nearly all the constructive activity is dead, and all that remains is a sort of shell, a half-empty creature fatally self-preoccupied and incapable of either giving or taking. Incapable either of giving or taking, in the vital self. And this is masturbation result. Enclosed within the vicious circle of the self, with no vital contacts outside, the self becomes emptier and emptier, till it is almost a nullus, a nothingness.

But null or nothing as it may be, it still hangs on to the dirty little secret, which it must still secretly rub and inflame. Forever the vicious circle. And it has a weird, blind will of its own.

One of my most sympathetic critics wrote: 'If Mr. Lawrence's attitude to sex were adopted, then two things would disappear, the love lyric and the smoking-room story.' And this, I think, is true. But it depends on which love-lyric he means. If it is the: *Who is Sylvia, what is she?*—then it may just as well disappear. All that pure and noble and heaven-blessed stuff is only the counterpart to the smoking-room story. *Du bist wie eine Blume!* Jawohl! One can see the elderly gentleman laying his hands on the head of the pure maiden and praying God to keep her forever so pure, so clean and beautiful. Very nice for him! Just pornography! tickling the dirty little secret and rolling his eyes to heaven! He knows perfectly well that if God keeps the maiden so clean and pure and beautiful—in his vulgar sense of clean and pure—for a few more years, then she'll be an unhappy old maid, and not pure nor beautiful at all, only stale and pathetic. Sentimentality is a sure sign of pornography. Why should 'sadness strike through the heart' of the old gentleman, because the maid was pure and beautiful? Anybody but a masturbator would have been glad and would have thought: What a lovely bride for some lucky man!—But no, not the self-enclosed, pornographic masturbator. Sadness has to strike into his beastly heart!—Away with such love-lyrics, we've had too much of their pornographic poison, tickling the dirty little secret and rolling the eyes to heaven.

But if it is a question of the sound love-lyric, *'My love is like a red, red rose——!'* then we are on other ground. My love is like a red, red rose only when she's *not* like a pure, pure lily. And nowadays the pure, pure lilies are mostly festering, anyhow. Away with them and their lyrics. Away with the pure, pure lily lyric, along with the smoking-room story. They are counterparts, and the one is as pornographic as the other. *Du bist wie eine Blume*—is really as pornographic as a dirty story: tickling the dirty little secret and rolling the eyes to heaven. But oh, if only Robert Burns had been accepted for what he is, then love might still have been like a red, red rose.

The vicious circle, the vicious circle! The vicious circle of masturbation! The vicious circle of self-consciousness that is never *fully* self-conscious, never fully and openly conscious, but always harping on the dirty little secret. The vicious circle of secrecy, in parents, teachers, friends—everybody. The specially vicious circle of family. The vast conspiracy of secrecy in the press, and at the same time, the endless tickling of the dirty little secret. The endless masturbation! and the endless purity! The vicious circle!

How to get out of it? There is only one way: Away with the secret! No more secrecy! The only way to stop the terrible mental itch about sex is to come out quite simply and naturally into the open with it. It is terribly difficult, for the secret is cunning as a crab. Yet the thing to do is to make a beginning. The man who said to his exasperating daughter: 'My child, the only pleasure I ever had out of you was the pleasure I had in begetting you'—has already done a great deal to release both himself and her from the dirty little secret.

How to get out of the dirty little secret! It is, as a matter of fact, extremely difficult for us secretive moderns. You can't do it by being wise and scientific about it, like Dr. Marie Stopes: though to be wise and scientific like Dr. Marie Stopes is better than to be utterly hypocritical, like the grey ones. But by being wise and scientific in the serious and earnest manner you only tend to disinfect the dirty little secret, and either kill sex altogether with too much seriousness and intellect, or else leave it a miserable disinfected secret. The unhappy 'free and pure' love of so many people who have taken out the dirty little secret and thoroughly disinfected it with scientific words is apt to be more pathetic even than the common run of dirty-little-secret love. The danger is, that in killing the dirty little secret, you kill dynamic sex altogether, and leave only the scientific and deliberate mechanism.

This is what happens to many of those who become seriously 'free' in their sex, free and pure. They have mentalized sex till it is nothing at all, nothing at all but a mental quantity. And the final result is disaster, every time.

The same is true, in an even greater proportion, of the emancipated bohemians: and very many of the young are bohemian to-day, whether they ever set foot in Bohemia or not. But the bohemian is 'sex free'. The dirty little secret is no secret either to him or her. It is, indeed, a most blatantly open question. There is nothing they don't say: everything that can be revealed is revealed. And they do as they wish.

And then what? They have apparently killed the dirty little secret, but somehow, they have killed everything else too. Some of the dirt still sticks, perhaps; sex remains still dirty. But the thrill of secrecy is gone. Hence the terrible dreariness and depression of modern Bohemia, and the inward dreariness and emptiness of so many young people of to-day. They have killed, they imagine, the dirty little secret. The thrill of secrecy is gone. Some of the dirt remains. And for the rest, depression, inertia, lack of life. For sex is the fountain-head of our energetic life, and now the fountain ceases to flow.

Why? For two reasons. The idealists along the Marie Stopes line, and the young bohemians of to-day have killed the dirty little secret as far as their personal self goes. But they are still under its dominion socially. In the social world, in the press, in literature, film, theatre, wireless, everywhere purity and the dirty little secret reigns supreme. At home, at the dinner table, it is just the same. It is the same wherever you go. The young girl, and the young woman is by tacit assumption pure, virgin, sexless. *Du bist wie eine Blume.* She, poor thing, knows quite well that flowers, even lilies, have tippling yellow anthers and a sticky stigma, sex, rolling sex. But to the popular mind flowers are sexless things, and when a girl is told she is like a flower, it means she is sexless and ought to be sexless. She herself knows quite well she isn't sexless and she isn't merely like a flower. But how bear up against the great social lie forced on her? She can't! She succumbs, and the dirty little secret triumphs. She loses her interest in sex, as far as men are concerned, but the vicious circle of masturbation and self-consciousness encloses her even still faster.

This is one of the disasters of young life to-day. Personally, and among themselves, a great many, perhaps a majority of the young people of to-day have come out into the open with sex and laid salt on the tail of the dirty little secret. And this is a very good thing. But in public, in the social world, the young are still entirely under the shadow of the grey elderly ones. The grey elderly ones belong to the last century, the eunuch century, the century of the mealy-mouthed lie, the century that has tried to destroy humanity, the nineteenth century. All our grey ones are left over from this century. And they rule us. They rule us with the grey, mealy-mouthed, canting lie of that great century of lies which, thank God, we are drifting away from. But they rule us still with the lie, for the lie, in the name of the lie. And they are too heavy and too numerous, the grey ones. It doesn't matter what government it is. They are all grey ones, left over from the last century, the century of mealy-mouthed liars, the century of purity and the dirty little secret.

So there is one cause for the depression of the young: the public reign of the mealy-mouthed lie, purity and the dirty little secret, which they themselves have privately overthrown. Having killed a good deal of the lie in their own private lives, the young are still enclosed and imprisoned within the great public lie of the grey ones. Hence the excess, the extravagance, the hysteria, and then the weakness, the feebleness, the pathetic silliness of the modern youth. They are all in a sort of prison, the prison of a great lie and a society of elderly liars. And this is one of the reasons, perhaps the main reason why the sex-flow is dying out of the young, the real energy is dying away. They are enclosed within a lie, and the sex won't flow. For the length of a complete lie is never more than three generations, and the young are the fourth generation of the nineteenth century lie.

The second reason why the sex-flow is dying is of course, that the young, in spite of their emancipation, are still enclosed within the vicious circle of self-conscious masturbation. They are thrown back into it, when they try to escape, by the enclosure of the vast public lie of purity and the dirty little secret. The most emancipated bohemians, who swank most about sex, are still utterly self-conscious and enclosed within the narcissus-masturbation circle. They have perhaps less sex even than the grey ones. The whole thing has been driven up into their heads. There isn't even the lurking hole of a dirty little secret. Their sex is more mental than their arithmetic; and as vital physical creatures they are more non-existent than ghosts. The modern bohemian is indeed a kind of ghost, not even narcissus, only the image of narcissus reflected on the face of the audience. The dirty little secret is most difficult to kill. You may put it to death publicly a thousand times, and still it reappears, like a crab, stealthily from under the submerged rocks of the personality. The French, who are supposed to be so open about sex, will perhaps be the last to kill the dirty little secret. Perhaps they don't want to. Anyhow mere publicity won't do it.

You may parade sex abroad, but you will not kill the dirty little secret. You may read all the novels of Marcel Proust, with everything there in all detail. Yet you will not kill the dirty little secret. You will perhaps only make it more cunning. You may even bring about a state of utter indifference and sex-inertia, still without killing the dirty little secret. Or you may be the most wispy and enamoured little Don Juan of modern days, and still the core of your spirit merely be the dirty little secret. That is to say, you will still be in the narcissus-masturbation circle, the vicious circle of self-enclosure. For whenever the dirty little secret exists, it exists as the centre of the vicious circle of masturbation self-enclosure. And whenever you have the vicious circle of masturbation self-enclosure, you have at the core the dirty little secret. And the most high-flown sex-emancipated young people to-day are perhaps the most fatally and nervously enclosed within the masturbation self-enclosure. Nor do they want to get out of it, for there would be nothing left to come out.

But some people surely do want to come out of the awful self-enclosure. To-day, practically everybody is self-conscious and imprisoned in self-consciousness. It is the joyful result of the dirty little secret. Vast numbers of people don't want to come out of the prison of their self-consciousness: they have so little left to come out with. But some people, surely, want to escape this doom of self-enclosure which is the doom of our civilization. There is surely a proud minority that wants once and for all to be free of the dirty little secret.

And the way to do it is, first, to fight the sentimental lie of purity and the dirty little secret wherever you meet it, inside yourself or in the world outside.

Fight the great lie of the nineteenth century, which has soaked through our sex and our bones. It means fighting with almost every breath, for the lie is ubiquitous.

Then secondly, in his adventure of self-consciousness a man must come to the limits of himself and become aware of something beyond him. A man must be self-conscious enough to know his own limits, and to be aware of that which surpasses him. What surpasses me is the very urge of life that is within me, and this life urges me to forget myself and to yield to the stirring half-born impulse to smash up the vast lie of the world, and make a new world. If my life is merely to go on in a vicious circle of self-enclosure, masturbating self-consciousness, it is worth nothing to me. If my individual life is to be enclosed within the huge corrupt lie of society to-day, purity and the dirty little secret, then it is worth not much to me. Freedom is a very great reality. But it means, above all things, freedom from lies. It is first, freedom from myself, from the lie of myself, from the lie of my all-importance, even to myself; it is freedom from the self-conscious masturbating thing I am, self-enclosed. And second, freedom from the vast lie of the social world, the lie of purity and the dirty little secret. All the other monstrous lies lurk under the cloak of this one primary lie. The monstrous lie of money lurks under the cloak of purity. Kill the purity-lie, and the money-lie will be defenceless.

We have to be sufficiently conscious, and self-conscious, to know our own limits and to be aware of the greater urge within us and beyond us. Then we cease to be primarily interested in ourselves. Then we learn to leave ourselves alone, in all the affective centres: not to force our feelings in any way, and never to force our sex. Then we make the great onslaught on to the outside lie, the inside lie being settled. And that is freedom and the fight for freedom.

The greatest of all lies in the modern world is the lie of purity and the dirty little secret. The grey ones left over from the nineteenth century are the embodiment of this lie. They dominate in society, in the press, in literature, everywhere. And, naturally, they lead the vast mob of the general public along with them.

Which means, of course, perpetual censorship of anything that would militate against the lie of purity and the dirty little secret, and perpetual encouragement of what may be called permissible pornography, pure, but tickling the dirty little secret under the delicate underclothing. The grey ones will pass and will commend floods of evasive pornography, and will suppress every outspoken word.

The law is a mere figment. In his article on the 'Censorship of Books', in the *Nineteenth Century,* Viscount Brentford, the late Home Secretary, says: 'Let it be remembered that the publishing of an obscene book, the issue of an obscene post-card or pornographic photograph—are all offences against the law of the land, and the Secretary of State who is the general authority for the maintenance of law and order most clearly and definitely cannot discriminate between one offence and another in discharge of his duty.'

So he winds up, *ex cathedra* and infallible. But only ten lines above he has written: 'I agree, that if the law were pushed to its logical conclusion, the printing and publication of such books as *The Decameron,* Benvenuto Cellini's *Life,* and Burton's *Arabian Nights* might form the subject of proceedings. But the ultimate sanction of all law is public opinion, and I do not believe for one moment that prosecution in respect of books that have been in circulation for many centuries would command public support.'

Ooray then for public opinion! It only needs that a few more years shall roll. But now we see that the Secretary of State most clearly and definitely *does* discriminate between one offence and another in discharge of his duty. Simple and admitted discrimination on his part! Yet what is this public opinion? Just more lies on the part of the grey ones. They would suppress Benvenuto to-morrow, if they dared. But they would make laughing-stocks of themselves, because *tradition* backs up Benvenuto. It isn't public opinion at all. It is the grey ones afraid of making still bigger fools of themselves. But the case is simple. If the grey ones are going to be backed by a general public, then every new book that would smash the mealy-mouthed lie of the nineteenth century will be suppressed as it appears. Yet let the grey ones beware. The general public is nowadays a very unstable affair, and no longer loves its grey ones so dearly, with their old lie. And there is another public, the small public of the minority, which hates the lie and the grey ones that perpetuate the lie, and which has its own dynamic ideas about pornography and obscenity. You can't fool all the people all the time, even with purity and a dirty little secret.

And this minority public knows well that the books of many contemporary writers, both big and lesser fry, are far more pornographical than the liveliest story in *The Decameron:* because they tickle the dirty little secret and excite to private masturbation, which the wholesome Boccaccio never does. And the minority public knows full well that the most obscene painting on a Greek vase—*Thou still unravished bride of quietness*—is not as pornographical as the close-up kisses on the film, which excite men and women to secret and separate masturbation.

And perhaps one day even the general public will desire to look the thing in the face, and see for itself the difference between the sneaking masturbation pornography of the press, the film, and present-day popular literature, and then the creative portrayals of the sexual impulse that we have in Boccaccio or the Greek vase-paintings or some Pompeian art, and which are necessary for the fulfilment of our consciousness.

As it is, the public mind is to-day bewildered on this point, bewildered almost to idiocy. When the police raided my picture show, they did not in the least know what to take. So they took every picture where the smallest bit of the sex organ of either man or woman showed. Quite regardless of subject or meaning or anything else: they would allow anything, these dainty policemen in a picture show, except the actual sight of a fragment of the human *pudenda*. This was the police test. The dabbing on of a postage stamp—especially a green one that could be called a leaf—would in most cases have been quite sufficient to satisfy this 'public opinion'.

It is, we can only repeat, a condition of idiocy. And if the purity-with-a-dirty-little-secret lie is kept up much longer, the mass of society will really be an idiot, and a dangerous idiot at that. For the public is made up of individuals. And each individual has sex, and is pivoted on sex. And if, with purity and dirty little secrets you drive every individual into the masturbation self-enclosure, and keep him there, then you will produce a state of general idiocy. For the masturbation self-enclosure produces idiots. Perhaps if we are all idiots, we shan't know it. But God preserve us.

The Virgin
and
the Gipsy

One

When the vicar's wife went off with a young and penniless man the scandal knew no bounds. Her two little girls were only seven and nine years old respectively. And the vicar was such a good husband. True, his hair was grey. But his moustache was dark, he was handsome, and still full of furtive passion for his unrestrained and beautiful wife.

Why did she go? Why did she burst away with such an *éclat* of revulsion, like a touch of madness?

Nobody gave any answer. Only the pious said she was a bad woman. While some of the good women kept silent. They knew.

The two little girls never knew. Wounded, they decided that it was because their mother found them negligible.

The ill wind that blows nobody any good swept away the vicarage family on its blast. Then lo and behold! the vicar, who was somewhat distinguished as an essayist and a controversialist, and whose case had aroused sympathy among the bookish men, received the living of Papplewick. The Lord had tempered the wind of misfortune with a rectorate in the north country.

The rectory was a rather ugly stone house down by the river Papple, before you come into the village. Further on, beyond where the road crosses the stream, were the big old stone cottonmills, once driven by water. The road curved uphill, into the bleak stone streets of the village.

The vicarage family received decided modification, upon its transference into the rectory. The vicar, now the rector, fetched up his old mother and his sister, and a brother from the city. The two little girls had a very different milieu from the old home.

The rector was now forty-seven years old; he had displayed an intense and not very dignified grief after the flight of his wife. Sympathetic ladies had stayed him from suicide. His hair was almost white, and he had a wild-eyed, tragic look. You had only to look at him, to know how dreadful it all was, and how he had been wronged.

Yet somewhere there was a false note. And some of the ladies, who had sympathised most profoundly with the vicar, secretly rather disliked the rector.

There was a certain furtive self-righteousness about him, when all was said and done.

The little girls, of course, in the vague way of children, accepted the family verdict. Granny, who was over seventy and whose sight was failing, became the central figure in the house. Aunt Cissie, who was over forty, pale, pious, and gnawed by an inward worm, kept house. Uncle Fred, a stingy and grey-faced man of forty, who just lived dingily for himself, went into town every day. And the rector, of course, was the most important person, after Granny.

They called her The Mater. She was one of those physically vulgar, clever old bodies who had got her own way all her life by buttering the weaknesses of her men-folk. Very quickly she took her cue. The rector still "loved" his delinquent wife, and would "love her" till he died. Therefore hush! The rector's feeling was sacred. In his heart was enshrined the pure girl he had wedded and worshipped.

Out in the evil world, at the same time, there wandered a disreputable woman who had betrayed the rector and abandoned his little children. She was now yoked to a young and despicable man, who no doubt would bring her the degradation she deserved. Let this be clearly understood, and then hush! For in the pure loftiness of the rector's heart still bloomed the pure white snowflower of his young bride. This white snow-flower did not wither. That other creature, who had gone off with that despicable young man, was none of his affair.

The Mater, who had been somewhat diminished and insignificant as a widow in a small house, now climbed into the chief arm-chair in the rectory, and planted her old bulk firmly again. She was not going to be dethroned. Astutely she gave a sigh of homage to the rector's fidelity to the pure white snowflower, while she pretended to disapprove. In sly reverence for her son's great love, she spoke no word against that nettle which flourished in the evil world, and which had once been called Mrs Arthur Saywell. Now, thank heaven, having married again, she was no more Mrs Arthur Saywell. No woman bore the rector's name. The pure white snowflower bloomed *in perpetuum,* without nomenclature. The family even thought of her as She-who-was-Cynthia.

All this was water on the Mater's mill. It secured her against Arthur's ever marrying again. She had him by his feeblest weakness, his skulking self-love. He had married an imperishable white snowflower. Lucky man! He had been injured! Unhappy man! He had suffered. Ah, what a heart of love! And he had—forgiven! Yes, the white snowflower was forgiven. He even had made provision in his will for her, when that other scoundrel—But hush! Don't even *think* too near to that horrid nettle in the rank outer world! She-who-was-Cynthia. Let the white snow-flower bloom inaccessible on the heights of the past. The present is another story.

The children were brought up in this atmosphere of cunning self-sanctification and of unmentionability. They too, saw the snowflower on inaccessible heights. They too knew that it was throned in lone splendour aloft their lives, never to be touched.

At the same time, out of the squalid world sometimes would come a rank, evil smell of selfishness and degraded lust, the smell of that awful nettle, She-who-was-Cynthia. This nettle actually contrived, at intervals, to get a little note through to her girls, her children. And at this the silver-haired Mater shook inwardly with hate. For if She-who-was-Cynthia ever came back, there wouldn't be much left of the Mater. A secret gust of hate went from the old granny to the girls, children of that foul nettle of lust, that Cynthia who had had such an affectionate contempt for the Mater.

Mingled with all this, was the children's perfectly distinct recollection of their real home, the Vicarage in the south, and their glamorous but not very dependable mother, Cynthia. She had made a great glow, a flow of life, like a swift and dangerous sun in the home, forever coming and going. They always associated her presence with brightness, but also with danger; with glamour, but with fearful selfishness.

Now the glamour was gone, and the white snowflower, like a porcelain wreath, froze on its grave. The danger of instability, the peculiarly *dangerous* sort of selfishness, like lions and tigers, was also gone. There was now a complete stability, in which one could perish safely.

But they were growing up. And as they grew, they became more definitely confused, more actively puzzled. The Mater, as she grew older, grew blinder. Somebody had to lead her about. She did not get up till towards midday. Yet blind or bed-ridden, she held the house.

Besides, she wasn't bed-ridden. Whenever the *men* were present, the Mater was in her throne. She was too cunning to court neglect. Especially as she had rivals.

Her great rival was the younger girl, Yvette. Yvette had some of the vague, careless blitheness of She-who-was-Cynthia. But this one was more docile. Granny perhaps had caught her in time. Perhaps!

The rector adored Yvette, and spoiled her with a doting fondness; as much as to say: am I not a soft-hearted, indulgent old boy! He liked to have weaknesses to a hair's-breadth. She knew them, this opinion of himself, and the Mater knew his and she traded on them by turning them into decorations for him, for his character. He wanted, in his own eyes, to have a fascinating character, as women want to have fascinating dresses. And the Mater cunningly put beauty-spots over his defects and deficiencies. Her mother-love gave her the clue to his weaknesses, and she hid them for him with decorations. Whereas She-who-was-Cynthia—! But don't mention *her,* in this connection. In her eyes, the rector was almost hump-backed and an idiot.

The funny thing was, Granny secretly hated Lucille, the elder girl, more than the pampered Yvette. Lucille, the uneasy and irritable, was more conscious of being under Granny's power, than was the spoilt and vague Yvette.

On the other hand, Aunt Cissie hated Yvette. She hated her very name. Aunt Cissie's life had been sacrificed to the Mater, and Aunt Cissie knew it, and the Mater knew she knew it. Yet as the years went on, it became a convention. The convention of Aunt Cissie's sacrifice was accepted by everybody, including the self-same Cissie. She prayed a good deal about it. Which also showed that she had her own private feelings somewhere, poor thing. She had ceased to be Cissie, she had lost her life and her sex. And now, she was creeping towards fifty, strange green flares of rage would come up in her, and at such times, she was insane.

But Granny held her in her power. And Aunt Cissie's one object in life was to look after The Mater.

Aunt Cissie's green flares of hellish hate would go up against all young things, sometimes. Poor thing, she prayed and tried to obtain forgiveness from heaven. But what had been done to her, *she* could not forgive, and the vitriol would spurt in her veins sometimes.

It was not as if the Mater were a warm, kindly soul. She wasn't. She only seemed it, cunningly. And the fact dawned gradually on the girls. Under her old-fashioned lace cap, under her silver hair, under the black silk of her stout, forward-bulging body, this old woman had a cunning heart, seeking forever her own female power. And through the weakness of the unfresh, stagnant men she had bred, she kept her power, as her years rolled on, from seventy to eighty, and from eighty on the new lap, towards ninety.

For in the family there was a whole tradition of "loyalty"; loyalty to one another, and especially to the Mater. The Mater, of course, was the pivot of the family. The family was her own extended ego. Naturally she covered it with her power. And her sons and daughters, being weak and disintegrated, naturally were loyal. Outside the family, what was there for them but danger and insult and ignominy? Had not the rector experienced it, in his marriage. So now, caution! Caution and loyalty, fronting the world! Let there be as much hate and friction *inside* the family, as you like. To the outer world, a stubborn fence of unison.

Two

But it was not until the girls finally came home from school, that they felt the full weight of Granny's dear old hand on their lives. Lucille was now nearly twenty-one, and Yvette nineteen. They had been to a good girls' school, and had had a finishing year in Lausanne, and were quite the usual thing, tall young creatures with fresh, sensitive faces and bobbed hair and young-manly, deuce-take-it manners.

"What's so awfully *boring* about Papplewick," said Yvette, as they stood on the Channel boat watching the grey, grey cliffs of Dover draw near, "is that there are no *men* about. Why doesn't Daddy have some good old sports for friends? As for Uncle Fred, he's the limit!"

"Oh, you never know what will turn up," said Lucille, more philosophic.

"You jolly well know what to expect," said Yvette. "Choir on Sundays, and I hate mixed choirs. Boys' voices are *lovely*, when there are no women. And Sunday School and Girls' Friendly, and socials, all the dear old souls that enquire after Granny! Not a decent young fellow for miles."

"Oh I don't know!" said Lucille. "There's always the Framleys. And you know Gerry Somercotes *adores* you."

"Oh but I *hate* fellows who adore me!" cried Yvette, turning up her sensitive nose. "They *bore* me. They hang on like lead."

"Well what *do* you want, if you can't stand being adored? *I* think it's perfectly all right to be adored. You know you'll never marry them, so why not let them go on adoring, if it amuses them."

"Oh but I *want* to get married," cried Yvette.

"Well in that case, let them go on adoring you till you find one that you can *possibly* marry."

"I never should, that way. Nothing puts me off like an adoring fellow. They *bore* me so! They make me feel beastly."

"Oh, so they do me, if they get pressing. But at a distance, I think they're rather nice."

"I should like to fall *violently* in love."

"Oh, very likely! I shouldn't! I should hate it. Probably so would you, if it actually happened. After all, we've got to settle down a bit, before we know what we want."

"But don't you *hate* going back to Pepplewick?" cried Yvette, turning up her young sensitive nose.

"No, not particularly. I suppose we shall be rather bored. I wish Daddy would get a car. I suppose we shall have to drag the old bikes out. Wouldn't you like to get up to Tansy Moor?"

"Oh, *love* it! Though it's an awful *strain,* shoving an old push-bike up those hills."

The ship was nearing the grey cliffs. It was summer, but a grey day. The two girls wore their coats with fur collars turned up, and little *chic* hats pulled down over their ears. Tall, slender, fresh-faced, naive, yet confident, too confident, in their school-girlish arrogance, they were so terribly English. They seemed so free, and were as a matter of fact so tangled and tied up, inside themselves. They seemed so dashing and unconventional, and were really so conventional, so, as it were, shut up indoors inside themselves. They looked like bold, tall young sloops, just slipping from the harbour, into the wide seas of life. And they were, as a matter of fact, two poor young rudderless lives, moving from one chain anchorage to another.

The rectory struck a chill into their hearts as they entered. It seemed ugly, and almost sordid, with the dank air of that middle-class, degenerated comfort which has ceased to be comfortable and has turned stuffy, unclean. The hard, stone house struck the girls as being unclean, they could not have said why. The shabby furniture seemed somehow sordid, nothing was fresh. Even the food at meals had that awful dreary sordidness which is so repulsive to a young thing coming from abroad. Roast beef and wet cabbage, cold mutton and mashed potatoes, sour pickles, inexcusable puddings.

Granny, who "loved a bit of pork," also had special dishes, beef-tea and rusks, or a small savoury custard. The grey-faced Aunt Cissie ate nothing at all. She would sit at table, and take a single lonely and naked boiled potato on to her plate. She never ate meat. So she sat in sordid durance, while the meal went on, and Granny quickly slobbered her portion—lucky if she spilled nothing on her protuberant stomach. The food was not appetising in itself: how could it be, when Aunt Cissie hated food herself, hated the fact of eating, and never could keep a maidservant for three months. The girls ate with repulsion, Lucille bravely bearing up, Yvette's tender nose showing her disgust. Only the rector, white-haired, wiped his long grey moustache with his serviette, and cracked jokes. He too was getting heavy and inert, sitting in his study all day, never taking exercise. But he cracked sarcastic little jokes all the time, sitting there under the shelter of the Mater.

The country, with its steep hills and its deep, narrow valleys, was dark and gloomy, yet had a certain powerful strength of its own. Twenty miles away was the black industrialism of the north. Yet the village of Papplewick was comparatively lonely, almost lost, the life in it stony and dour. Everything was stone, with a hardness that was almost poetic, it was so unrelenting.

It was as the girls had known: they went back into the choir, they helped in the parish. But Yvette struck absolutely against Sunday School, the Band of Hope, the Girls Friendlies—indeed against all those functions that were conducted by determined old maids and obstinate, stupid elderly men. She avoided church duties as much as possible, and got away from the rectory whenever she could. The Framleys, a big, untidy, jolly family up at the Grange, were an enormous standby. And if anybody asked her out to a meal, even if a woman in one of the workmen's houses asked her to stay to tea, she accepted at once. In fact, she was rather thrilled. She liked talking to the working men, they had often such fine, hard heads. But of course they were in another world.

So the months went by. Gerry Somercotes was still an adorer. There were others, too, sons of farmers or mill-owners. Yvette really ought to have had a good time. She was always out to parties and dances, friends came for her in their motor-cars, and off she went to the city, to the afternoon dance in the chief hotel, or in the gorgeous new Palais de Danse, called the Pally.

Yet she always seemed like a creature mesmerised. She was never free to be quite jolly. Deep inside her worked an intolerable irritation, which she thought she *ought* not to feel, and which she hated feeling, thereby making it worse. She never understood at all whence it arose.

At home, she truly was irritable, and outrageously rude to Aunt Cissie. In fact Yvette's awful temper became one of the family by-words.

Lucille, always more practical, got a job in the city as private secretary to a man who needed somebody with fluent French and shorthand. She went back and forth every day, by the same train as Uncle Fred. But she never travelled with him, and wet or fine, bicycled to the station, while he went on foot.

The two girls were both determined that what they wanted was a really jolly social life. And they resented with fury that the rectory was, for their friends, impossible. There were only four rooms downstairs: the kitchen, where lived the two discontented maid-servants: the dark dining-room: the rector's study: and the big, "homely," dreary living-room or drawing-room. In the dining-room there was a gas fire. Only in the living-room was a good hot fire kept going. Because of course, here Granny reigned.

In this room the family was assembled. At evening, after dinner, Uncle Fred and the rector invariably played cross-word puzzles with Granny.

"Now, Mater, are you ready? N blank blank blank blank W: a Siamese functionary."

"Eh? Eh? M blank blank blank blank W?"

Granny was hard of hearing.

"No Mater. Not M! N blank blank blank blank W: a Siamese functionary."

"N blank blank blank blank W: a Chinese functionary."

"SIAMESE."

"Eh?"

"SIAMESE! SIAM!"

"A Siamese functionary! Now what can that be?" said the old lady profoundly, folding her hands on her round stomach. Her two sons proceeded to make suggestions, at which she said Ah! Ah! The rector was amazingly clever at cross-word puzzles. But Fred had a certain technical vocabulary.

"This certainly is a hard nut to crack," said the old lady, when they were all stuck.

Meanwhile Lucille sat in a corner with her hands over her ears, pretending to read, and Yvette irritably made drawings, or hummed loud and exasperating tunes, to add to the family concert. Aunt Cissie continually reached for a chocolate, and her jaws worked ceaselessly. She literally lived on chocolates. Sitting in the distance, she put another into her mouth, then looked again at the parish magazine. Then she lifted her head, and saw it was time to fetch Granny's cup of Horlicks.

While she was gone, in nervous exasperation Yvette would open the window. The room was never fresh, she imagined it smelt: smelt of Granny. And Granny, who was hard of hearing, heard like a weasel when she wasn't wanted to.

"Did you open the window, Yvette? I think you might remember there are older people than yourself in the room," she said.

"It's stifling! It's unbearable! No wonder we've all of us always got colds."

"I'm sure the room is large enough, and a good fire burning." The old lady gave a little shudder. "A draught to give us all our death."

"Not a draught at all," roared Yvette. "A breath of fresh air."

The old lady shuddered again, and said:

"Indeed!"

The rector, in silence, marched to the window and firmly closed it. He did not look at his daughter meanwhile. He hated thwarting her. But she must know what's what!

The cross-word puzzles, invented by Satan himself, continued till Granny had had her Horlicks, and was to go to bed. Then came the ceremony of Goodnight! Everybody stood up. The girls went to be kissed by the blind old woman. The rector gave his arm, and Aunt Cissie followed with a candle.

But this was already nine o'clock, although Granny was really getting old, and should have been in bed sooner. But when she was in bed, she could not sleep, till Aunt Cissie came.

"You see," said Granny, "I have *never* kept alone. For fifty-four years I never slept a night without the Pater's arm round me. And when he was gone, I tried to sleep alone. But as sure as my eyes closed to sleep, my heart nearly jumped out of my body, and I lay in a palpitation. Oh, you may think what you will, but it was a fearful experience, after fifty-four years of perfect married life! I would have prayed to be taken first, but the Pater, well, no I don't think he would have been able to bear up."

So Aunt Cissie slept with Granny. And she hated it. She said *she* could never sleep. And she grew greyer and greyer, and the food in the house got worse, and Aunt Cissie had to have an operation.

But The Mater rose as ever, towards noon, and at the mid-day meal, she presided from her arm-chair, with her stomach protruding, her reddish, pendulous face, that had a sort of horrible majesty, dropping soft under the wall of her high brow, and her blue eyes peering unseeing. Her white hair was getting scanty, it was altogether a little indecent. But the rector jovially cracked his jokes to her, and she pretended to disapprove. But she was perfectly complacent, sitting in her ancient obesity, and after meals, getting the wind from her stomach, pressing her bosom with her hand as she "rifted" in gross physical complacency.

What the girls minded most was that, when they brought their young friends to the house, Granny always was there, like some awful idol of old flesh, consuming all the attention. There was only the one room for everybody. And there sat the old lady, with Aunt Cissie keeping an acrid guard over her. Everybody must be presented first to Granny: she was ready to be genial, she liked company. She had to know who everybody was, where they came from, every circumstance of their lives. And then, when she was *au fait,* she could get hold of the conversation.

Nothing could be more exasperating to the girls. "Isn't old Mrs. Saywell wonderful! She takes *such* an interest in life, at nearly ninety!"

"She does take an interest in people's affairs, if that's life," said Yvette.

Then she would immediately feel guilty. After all, it *was* wonderful to be nearly ninety, and have such a clear mind! And Granny never *actually* did anybody any harm. It was more that she was in the way. And perhaps it was rather awful to hate somebody because they were old and in the way.

Yvette immediately repented, and was nice. Granny blossomed forth into reminiscences of when she was a girl, in the little town in Buckinghamshire. She talked and talked away, and was *so* entertaining. She really *was* rather wonderful.

Then in the afternoon Lottie and Ella and Bob Framley came, with Leo Wetherell.

"Oh, come in!"—and in they all trooped to the sitting-room, where Granny, in her white cap, sat by the fire.

"Granny, this is Mr. Wetherell."

"Mr. What-did-you-say? You must excuse me, I'm a little deaf!"

Granny gave her hand to the uncomfortable young man, and gazed silently at him, sightlessly.

"You are not from our parish?" she asked him.

"Dinnington!" he shouted.

"We want to go to a picnic tomorrow, to Bonsall Head, in Leo's car. We can all squeeze in," said Ella, in a low voice.

"Did you say Bonsall Head?" asked Granny.

"Yes!"

There was a blank silence.

"Did you say you were going in a car?"

"Yes! In Mr. Wetherell's."

"I hope he's a good driver. It's a very dangerous road."

"He's a *very* good driver."

"Not a very good driver?"

"Yes! He *is* a very good driver."

"If you go to Bonsall Head, I think I must send a message to Lady Louth."

Granny always dragged in this miserable Lady Louth, when there was company.

"Oh, we shan't go that way," cried Yvette.

"Which way?" said Granny. "You must go by Heanor."

The whole party sat, as Bob expressed it, like stuffed ducks, fidgeting on their chairs.

Aunt Cissie came in—and then the maid with the tea. There was the eternal and everlasting piece of bought cake. Then appeared a plate of little fresh cakes. Aunt Cissie had actually sent to the baker's.

"Tea, Mater!"

The old lady gripped the arms of her chair. Everybody rose and stood, while she waded slowly across, on Aunt Cissie's arm, to her place at table.

During tea Lucille came in from town, from her job. She was simply worn out, with black marks under her eyes. She gave a cry, seeing all the company.

As soon as the noise had subsided, and the awkwardness was resumed, Granny said:

"You have never mentioned Mr. Wetherell to me, have you, Lucille?"

"I don't remember," said Lucille.

"You can't have done. The name is strange to me."

Yvette absently grabbed another cake, from the now almost empty plate. Aunt Cissie, who was driven almost crazy by Yvette's vague and inconsiderate ways, felt the green rage fuse in her heart. She picked up her own plate, on which was the one cake she allowed herself, and said with vitriolic politeness, offering it to Yvette:

"Won't you have mine?"

"Oh thanks!" said Yvette, starting in her angry vagueness. And with an appearance of the same insouciance, she helped herself to Aunt Cissie's cake also, adding as an afterthought: "If you're sure you don't want it."

She now had two cakes on her plate. Lucille had gone white as a ghost, bending to her tea. Aunt Cissie sat with a green look of poisonous resignation. The awkwardness was an agony.

But Granny, bulkily enthroned and unaware, only said, in the centre of the cyclone:

"If you are motoring to Bonsall Head tomorrow, Lucille, I wish you would take a message from me to Lady Louth."

"Oh!" said Lucille, giving a queer look across the table at the sightless old woman. Lady Louth was the King Charles' Head of the family, invariably produced by Granny for the benefit of visitors. "Very well!"

"She was so very kind last week. She sent her chauffeur over with a Cross-word Puzzle book for me."

"But you thanked her then," cried Yvette.

"I should like to send her a note."

"We can post it," cried Lucille.

"Oh, no! I should like you to take it. When Lady Louth called last time. . . ."

The young ones sat like a shoal of young fishes dumbly mouthing at the surface of the water, while Granny went on about Lady Louth. Aunt Cissie, the two girls knew, was still helpless, almost unconscious in a paroxysm of rage about the cake. Perhaps, poor thing, she was praying.

It was a mercy when the friends departed. But by that time the two girls were both haggard-eyed. And it was then that Yvette, looking round, suddenly saw the stony, implacable will-to-power in the old and motherly-seeming Granny. She sat there bulging backwards in her chair, impassive, her reddish, pendulous old face rather mottled, almost unconscious, but implacable, her face like a mask that hid something stony, relentless. It was the static inertia of her unsavoury power. Yet in a minute she would open her ancient mouth to find out every detail about Leo Wetherell. For the moment she was hibernating in her oldness, her agedness. But in a minute her mouth would open, her mind would flicker awake, and with her insatiable greed for life, other people's life, she would start on her quest for every detail. She was like the old toad which Yvette had watched, fascinated, as it sat on the ledge of the beehive, immediately in front of the little entrance by which the bees emerged, and which, with a demonish lightning-like snap of its pursed jaws, caught every bee as it came out to launch into the air, swallowed them one after the other, as if it could consume the whole hive-full, into its aged, bulging, purse-like wrinkledness. It had been swallowing bees as they launched into the air of spring, year after year, year after year, for generations:

But the gardener, called by Yvette, was in a rage, and killed the creature with a stone.

" 'Appen tha *art* good for th' snails," he said, as he came down with the stone. "But tha 'rt none goin' ter emp'y th' bee-'ive into thy guts."

Three

The next day was dull and low, and the roads were awful, for it had been raining for weeks, yet the young ones set off on their trip, without taking Granny's message either. They just slipped out while she was making her slow trip upstairs after lunch. Not for anything would they have called at Lady Louth's house. That widow of a knighted doctor, a harmless person indeed, had become an obnoxity in their lives.

Six young rebels, they sat very perkily in the car as they swished through the mud. Yet they had a peaked look too. After all, they had nothing really to rebel against, any of them. They were left so very free in their movements. Their parents let them do almost entirely as they liked. There wasn't really a fetter to break, nor a prison-bar to file through, nor a bolt to shatter. The keys of their lives were in their own hands. And there they dangled inert.

It is very much easier to shatter prison bars than to open undiscovered doors to life. As the younger generation finds out, somewhat to its chagrin. True, there was Granny. But poor old Granny, you couldn't actually say to her: "Lie down and die, you old woman!" She might be an old nuisance, but she never really *did* anything. It wasn't fair to hate her.

So the young people set off on their jaunt, trying to be very full of beans. They could really do as they liked. And so, of course, there was nothing to do but sit in the car and talk a lot of criticism of other people, and silly flirty gallantry that was really rather a bore. If there had only been a few "strict orders" to be disobeyed! But nothing: beyond the refusal to carry the message to Lady Louth, of which the rector would approve, because he didn't encourage King Charles' Head either.

They sang, rather scrappily, the latest would-be comic songs, as they went through the grim villages. In the great park the deer were in groups near the road, roe deer and fallow, nestling in the gloom of the afternoon under the oaks by the road, as if for the stimulus of human company.

Yvette insisted on stopping and getting out to talk to them. The girls, in their Russian boots, tramped through the damp grass, while the deer watched them with big, unfrightened eyes. The hart trotted away mildly, holding back his head, because of the weight of the horns. But the doe, balancing her big ears, did not rise from under the tree, with her half-grown young ones, till the girls were almost in touch. Then she walked lightfoot away, lifting her tail from her spotted flanks, while the young ones nimbly trotted.

"Aren't they awfully dainty and nice!" cried Yvette. "You'd wonder they could lie so cosily in this horrid wet grass."

—"Well I suppose they've got to lie down *sometime*," said Lucille. "And it's *fairly* dry under the tree." She looked at the crushed grass, where the deer had lain.

Yvette went and put her hand down, to feel how it felt.

"Yes!" she said, doubtfully, "I believe it's a bit warm."

The deer had bunched again a few yards away, and were standing motionless in the gloom of the afternoon. Away below the slopes of grass and trees, beyond the swift river with its balustraded bridge, sat the huge ducal house, one or two chimneys smoking bluely. Behind it rose purplish woods.

The girls, pushing their fur collars up to their ears, dangling one long arm, stood watching in silence, their wide Russian boots protecting them from the wet grass. The great house squatted square and creamy-grey below. The deer, in little groups, were scattered under the old trees close by. It all seemed so still, so unpretentious, and so sad.

"I wonder where the Duke is now," said Ella.

"Not here, wherever he is," said Lucille. "I expect he's abroad where the sun shines."

The motor horn called from the road, and they heard Leo's voice:

"Come on boys! If we're going to get to the Head and down to Amberdale for tea, we'd better move."

They crowded into the car again, with chilled feet, and set off through the park, past the silent spire of the church, out through the great gates and over the bridge, on into the wide, damp, stony village of Woodlinkin, where the river ran. And thence, for a long time, they stayed in the mud and dark and dampness of the valley, often with sheer rock above them; the water brawling on one hand, the steep rock or dark trees on the other.

Till, through the darkness of overhanging trees, they began to climb, and Leo changed the gear. Slowly the car toiled up through the whitey-grey mud, into the stony village of Bolehill, that hung on the slope, round the old cross, with its steps, that stood where the road branched, on past the cottages whence came a wonderful smell of hot tea-cakes, and beyond, still upwards, under dripping trees and past broken slopes of bracken, always climbing. Until the cleft became shallower, and the trees finished, and the slopes on either side were bare, gloomy grass, with low dry-stone walls. They were emerging on to the Head.

The party had been silent for some time. On either side the road was grass, then a low stone fence, and the swelling curve of the hill-summit, traced with the low, dry-stone walls. Above this, the low sky.

The car ran out, under the low, grey sky, on the naked tops.

"Shall we stay a moment?" called Leo.

"Oh yes!" cried the girls.

And they scrambled out once more, to look around. They knew the place quite well. But still, if one came to the Head, one got out to look.

The hills were like the knuckles of a hand, the dales were below, between the fingers, narrow, steep, and dark. In the deeps a train was steaming, slowly pulling north: a small thing of the underworld. The noise of the engine re-echoed curiously upwards. Then came the dull, familiar sound of blasting in a quarry.

Leo, always on the go, moved quickly.

"Shall we be going?" he said. "Do we *want* to get down to Amberdale for tea? Or shall we try somewhere nearer?"

They all voted for Amberdale, for the Marquis of Grantham.

"Well, which way shall we go back? Shall we go by Codnor and over Crosshill, or shall we go by Ashbourne?"

There was the usual dilemma. Then they finally decided on the Codnor top road. Off went the car, gallantly.

They were on the top of the world, now, on the back of the fist. It was naked, too, as the back of your fist, high under heaven, and dull, heavy green. Only it was veined with a network of old stone walls, dividing the fields, and broken here and there with ruins of old lead-mines and works. A sparse stone farm bristled with six naked sharp trees. In the distance was a patch of smokey grey stone, a hamlet. In some fields grey, dark sheep fed silently, somberly. But there was not a sound nor a movement. It was the roof of England, stony and arid as any roof. Beyond, below, were the shires.

" 'And see the coloured counties,' " said Yvette to herself. Here anyhow they were not coloured. A stream of rooks trailed out from nowhere. They had been walking, pecking, on a naked field that had been manured. The car ran on between the grass and the stone walls of the upland lane, and the young people were silent, looking out over the far network of stone fences, under the sky, looking for the curves downward that indicated a drop to one of the underneath, hidden dales.

Ahead was a light cart, driven by a man, and trudging along at the side was a woman, sturdy and elderly, with a pack on her back. The man in the cart had caught her up, and now was keeping pace.

The road was narrow. Leo sounded the horn sharply. The man on the cart looked round, but the woman on foot only trudged steadily, rapidly forward, without turning her head.

Yvette's heart gave a jump. The man on the cart was a gipsy, one of the black, loose-bodied, handsome sort. He remained seated on his cart, turning round and gazing at the occupants of the motor-car, from under the brim of his cap. And his pose was loose, his gaze insolent in its indifference. He had a thin black moustache under his thin, straight nose, and a big silk handkerchief of red and yellow tied round his neck. He spoke a word to the woman. She stood a second, solid, to turn round and look at the occupants of the car, which had now drawn quite close. Leo honked the horn again, imperiously. The woman, who had a grey-and-white kerchief tied round her head, turned sharply, to keep pace with the cart, whose driver also had settled back, and was lifting the reins, moving his loose, light shoulders. But still he did not pull aside.

Leo made the horn scream, as he put the brakes on and the car slowed up near the back of the cart. The gipsy turned round at the din, laughing in his dark face under his dark-green cap, and said something which they did not hear, showing white teeth under the line of black moustache, and making a gesture with his dark, loose hand.

"Get out o' the way then!" yelled Leo.

For answer, the man delicately pulled the horse to a standstill, as it curved to the side of the road. It was a good roan horse, and a good, natty, dark-green cart.

Leo, in a rage, had to jam on the brake and pull up too.

"Don't the pretty young ladies want to hear their fortunes?" said the gipsy on the cart, laughing except for his dark, watchful eyes, which went from face to face, and lingered on Yvette's young, tender face.

She met his dark eyes for a second, their level search, their insolence, their complete indifference to people like Bob and Leo, and something took fire in her breast. She thought: "He is stronger than I am! He doesn't care!"

"Oh yes! let's!" cried Lucille at once.

"Oh yes!" chorused the girls.

"I say! What about the time?" cried Leo.

"Oh bother the old time! Somebody's always dragging in time by the forelock," cried Lucille.

"Well, if you don't mind *when* we get back, *I* don't!" said Leo heroically.

The gipsy man had been sitting loosely on the side of his cart, watching the faces. He now jumped softly down from the shaft, his knees a bit stiff. He was apparently a man something over thirty, and a beau in his way. He wore a sort of shooting-jacket, double-breasted, coming only to the hips, of dark green-and-black frieze; rather tight black trousers, black boots, and a dark-green cap; with the big yellow-and-red bandanna handkerchief round his neck. His appearance was curiously elegant, and quite expensive in its gipsy style. He was handsome, too, pressing in his chin with the old, gipsy conceit, and now apparently not heeding the strangers any more, as he led his good roan horse off the road, preparing to back his cart.

The girls saw for the first time a deep recess in the side of the road, and two caravans smoking. Yvette got quickly down. They had suddenly come upon a disused quarry, cut into the slope of the road-side, and in this sudden lair, almost like a cave, were three caravans, dismantled for the winter. There was also deep at the back, a shelter built of boughs, as a stable for the horse. The grey, crude rock rose high above the caravans, and curved round towards the road. The floor was heaped chips of stone, with grasses growing among. It was a hidden, snug winter camp.

The elderly woman with the pack had gone in to one of the caravans, leaving the door open. Two children were peeping out, shewing black heads. The gipsy man gave a little call, as he backed his cart into the quarry, and an elderly man came out to help him untackle.

The gipsy himself went up the steps into the newest caravan, that had its door closed. Underneath, a tied-up dog ranged forth. It was a white hound spotted liver-coloured. It gave a low growl as Leo and Bob approached.

At the same moment, a dark-faced gipsy-woman with a pink shawl or kerchief round her head and big gold ear-rings in her ears, came down the steps of the newest caravan, swinging her flounced, voluminous green skirt. She was handsome in a bold, dark, long-faced way, just a bit wolfish. She looked like one of the bold, loping Spanish gipsies.

"Good-morning, my ladies and gentlemen," she said, eyeing the girls from her bold, predative eyes. She spoke with a certain foreign stiffness.

"Good afternoon!" said the girls.

"Which beautiful little lady like to hear her fortune? Give me her little hand?"

She was a tall woman, with a frightening way of reaching forward her neck like a menace. Her eyes went from face to face, very active, heartlessly searching out what she wanted. Meanwhile the man, apparently her husband, appeared at the top of the caravan steps smoking a pipe, and with a small, black-haired child in his arms. He stood on his limber legs, casually looking down on the group, as if from a distance, his long black lashes lifted from his full, conceited, impudent black eyes. There was something peculiarly transfusing in his stare. Yvette felt it, felt it in her knees. She pretended to be interested in the white-and-liver-coloured hound.

"How much do you want, if we all have our fortunes told?" asked Lottie Framley, as the six fresh-faced young Christians hung back rather reluctantly from this pagan pariah woman.

"All of you? ladies and gentlemen, all?" said the woman shrewdly.

"I don't want mine told! You go ahead!" cried Leo.

"Neither do I," said Bob. "You four girls."

"The four ladies?" said the gipsy woman, eyeing them shrewdly, after having looked at the boys. And she fixed her price. "Each one give me a sheeling, and a little bit more for luck? a little bit!" She smiled in a way that was more wolfish than cajoling, and the force of her will was felt, heavy as iron beneath the velvet of her words.

"All right," said Leo. "Make it a shilling a head. Don't spin it out too long."

"Oh, *you!*" cried Lucille at him. "We want to hear it *all.*"

The woman took two wooden stools, from under a caravan, and placed them near the wheel. Then she took the tall, dark Lottie Framley by the hand, and bade her sit down.

"You don't care if everybody hear?" she said, looking up curiously into Lottie's face.

Lottie blushed dark with nervousness, as the gipsy woman held her hand, and stroked her palm with hard, cruel-seeming fingers.

"Oh, I don't mind," she said.

The gipsy woman peered into the palm, tracing the lines of the hand with a hard, dark forefinger. But she seemed clean.

And slowly she told the fortune, while the others, standing listening, kept on crying out: "Oh, that's Jim Baggaley! Oh, I don't believe it! Oh, that's not true! A fair woman who lives beneath a tree! why whoever's that?" until Leo stopped them with a manly warning:

"Oh, hold on, girls! You give everything away."

Lottie retired blushing and confused, and it was Ella's turn. She was much more calm and shrewd, trying to read the oracular words. Lucille kept breaking out with: Oh, I say! the gipsy man at the top of the steps stood imperturbable, without any expression at all. But his bold eyes kept staring at Yvette, she could feel them on her cheek, on her neck, and she dared not look up. But Framley would sometimes look up at him, and got a level stare back, from the handsome face of the male gipsy, from the dark conceited proud eyes. It was a peculiar look, in the eyes that belonged to the tribe of the humble: the pride of the pariah, the half-sneering challenge of the outcast, who sneered at law-abiding men, and went his own way. All the time, the gipsy man stood there, holding his child in his arms, looking on without being concerned.

Lucille was having her hand read,—"You have been across the sea, and there you met a man—a brown-haired man—but he was too old—."

"Oh, I *say!*" cried Lucille, looking round at Yvette.

But Yvette was abstracted, agitated, hardly heeding: in one of her mesmerised states.

"You will marry in a few years—not now, but a few years—perhaps four—and you will not be rich, but you will have plenty—enough—and you will go away, a long journey."

"With my husband, or without?" cried Lucille.

"With him—."

When it came to Yvette's turn, and the woman looked up boldly, cruelly, searching for a long time in her face, Yvette said nervously:

"I don't think I want mine told. No, I won't have mine told! No I won't, really!"

"You are afraid of some thing?" said the gipsy woman cruelly.

"No, it's not that—" Yvette fidgetted.

"You have some secret? You are afraid I shall say it. Come, would you like to go in the caravan, where nobody' hears?"

The woman was curiously insinuating; while Yvette was always wayward, perverse. The look of perversity was on her soft, frail young face now, giving her a queer hardness.

"Yes!" she said suddenly. "Yes! I might do that!"

"Oh, I say!" cried the others. "Be a sport!"

"I don't think you'd *better!*" cried Lucille.

"Yes!" said Yvette, with that hard little way of hers. "I'll do that. I'll go in the caravan."

The gipsy woman called something to the man on the steps. He went into the caravan for a moment or two, then re-appeared, and came down the steps, setting the small child on its uncertain feet, and holding it by the hand. A dandy, in his polished black boots, tight black trousers and tight dark-green jersey, he walked slowly across, with the toddling child, to where the elderly gipsy was giving the roan horse a feed of oats, in the bough shelter between pits of grey rock, with dry bracken upon the stone-chip floor. He looked at Yvette as he passed, staring her full in the eyes, with his pariah's bold yet dishonest stare. Something hard inside her met his stare. But the surface of her body seemed to turn to water. Nevertheless, something hard in her registered the peculiar pure lines of his face, of his straight, pure nose, of his cheeks and temples. The curious dark, suave purity of all his body, outlined in the green jersey: a purity like a living sneer.

And as he loped slowly past her, on his flexible hips, it seemed to her still that he was stronger than she was. Of all the men she had ever seen, this one was the only one who was stronger than she was, in her own kind of strength, her own kind of understanding.

So, with curiosity, she followed the woman up the steps of the caravan, the skirts of her well-cut tan coat swinging and almost showing her knees, under the pale-green cloth dress. She had long, long-striding, fine legs, too slim rather than too thick, and she wore curiously-patterned pale-and-fawn stockings of fine wool, suggesting the legs of some delicate animal.

At the top of the steps she paused and turned, debonair, to the others, saying in her naive, lordly way, so off-hand:

"I won't let her be long."

Her grey fur collar was open, showing her soft throat and pale green dress, her little, plaited tan-coloured hat came down to her ears, round her soft, fresh face. There was something soft and yet overbearing, unscrupulous, about her. She knew the gipsy man had turned to look at her. She was aware of the pure dark nape of his neck, the black hair groomed away. He watched as she entered his house.

What the gipsy told her, no one ever knew. It was a long time to wait, the others felt. Twilight was deepening on the gloom, and it was turning raw and cold. From the chimney of the second caravan came smoke and a smell of rich food. The horse was fed, a yellow blanket strapped round him, the two gipsy men talked together in the distance, in low tones. There was a peculiar feeling of silence and secrecy in that lonely, hidden quarry.

At last the caravan door opened, and Yvette emerged, bending forward and stepping with long, witch-like slim legs down the steps. There was a stooping, witch-like silence about her as she emerged on the twilight.

"Did it seem long?" she said vaguely, not looking at anybody and keeping her own counsel hard within her soft, vague waywardness. "I hope you weren't bored! Wouldn't tea be nice! Shall we go?"

"You get in!" said Bob. "I'll pay."

The gipsy-woman's full, metallic skirts of jade-green alpaca came swinging down the steps. She rose to her height, a big, triumphant-looking woman with a dark-wolf face. The pink cashmere kerchief, stamped with red roses, was slipping to one side over her black and crimped hair. She gazed at the young people in the twilight with bold arrogance.

Bob put two half-crowns in her hand.

"A little bit more, for luck, for your young lady's luck," she wheedled, like a wheedling wolf. "Another bit of silver, to bring you luck."

"You've got a shilling for luck, that's enough," said Bob calmly and quietly, as they moved away to the car.

"A little bit of silver! Just a little bit, for your luck in love!"

Yvette, with the sudden long, startling gestures of her long limbs, swung round as she was entering the car, and with long arm outstretched, strode and put something into the gipsy's hand, then stepped, bending her height, into the car.

"Prosperity to the beautiful young lady, and the gipsy's blessing on her," came the suggestive, half-sneering voice of the woman.

The engine *birred!* then *birred!* again more fiercely, and started. Leo switched on the lights, and immediately the quarry with the gipsies fell back into the blackness of night.

"Goodnight!" called Yvette's voice, as the car started. But hers was the only voice that piped up, chirpy and impudent in its nonchalance. The headlights glared down the stone lane.

"Yvette, you've got to tell us what she said to you," cried Lucille, in the teeth of Yvette's silent will *not* to be asked.

"Oh, nothing at *all* thrilling," said Yvette, with false warmth. "Just the usual old thing: a dark man who means good luck, and a fair one who means bad: and a death in the family, which if it means Granny, won't be so *very* awful: and I shall marry when I'm twenty-three, and have heaps of money and heaps of love, and two children. All sounds very nice, but it's a bit too much of a good thing, you know."

"Oh, but why did you give her more money?"

"Oh well, I wanted to! You *have* to be a bit lordly with people like that—."

Four

There was a terrific rumpus down at the rectory, on account of Yvette and the Window Fund. After the war, Aunt Cissie had set her heart on a stained glass window in the church, as a memorial for the men of the parish who had fallen. But the bulk of the fallen had been nonconformists, so the memorial took the form of an ugly little monument in front of the Wesleyan chapel.

This did not vanquish Aunt Cissie. She canvassed, she had bazaars, she made the girls get up amateur theatrical shows, for her precious window. Yvette, who quite liked the acting and showing-off part of it, took charge of the farce called *Mary in the Mirror,* and gathered in the proceeds, which were to be paid to the Window Fund when accounts were settled. Each of the girls was supposed to have a money-box for the Fund.

Aunt Cissie, feeling that the united sums must now almost suffice, suddenly called in Yvette's box. It contained fifteen shillings. There was a moment of green horror.

"Where is all the rest?"

"Oh!" said Yvette, casually. "I just borrowed it. It wasn't so awfully much."

"What about the three pounds thirteen for *Mary in the Mirror?*" asked Aunt Cissie, as if the jaws of Hell were yawning.

"Oh quite! I just borrowed it. I can pay it back."

Poor Aunt Cissie! The green tumour of hate burst inside her, and there was a ghastly, abnormal scene, which left Yvette shivering with fear and nervous loathing.

Even the rector was rather severe.

"If you needed money, why didn't you tell me?" he said coldly. "Have you ever been refused anything in reason?"

"I—I thought it didn't matter," stammered Yvette.

"And what have you done with the money?"

"I suppose I've spent it," said Yvette, with wide, distraught eyes and a peaked face.

"Spent it, on what?"

"I can't remember everything: stockings and things, and I gave some of it away."

Poor Yvette! Her lordly airs and ways were already hitting back at her, on the reflex. The rector was angry: his face had a snarling, doggish look, a sort of sneer. He was afraid his daughter was developing some of the rank, tainted qualities of She-who-was-Cynthia.

"You *would* do the large with somebody else's money, wouldn't you?" he said, with a cold, mongrel sort of sneer, which showed what an utter unbeliever he was, at the heart. The inferiority of a heart which has no core of warm belief in it, no pride in life. He had utterly no belief in her.

Yvette went pale, and very distant. Her pride, that frail, precious flame which everybody tried to quench, recoiled like a flame blown far away, on a cold wind, as if blown out, and her face, white now and still like a snowdrop, the white snowflower of his conceit, seemed to have no life in it, only this pure, strange abstraction.

"He has no belief in me!" she thought in her soul. "I am really nothing to him. I am nothing, only a shameful thing. Everything is shameful, everything is shameful!"

A flame of passion or rage, while it might have overwhelmed or infuriated her, would not have degraded her as did her father's unbelief, his final attitude of a sneer against her.

He became a little afraid, in the silence of sterile thought. After all, he needed the *appearance* of love and belief and bright life, he would never dare to face the fat worm of his own unbelief, that stirred in his heart.

"What have you to say for yourself?" he asked.

She only looked at him from that senseless snowdrop face which haunted him with fear, and gave him a helpless sense of guilt. That other one, She-who-was-Cynthia, she had looked back at him with the same numb, white fear, the fear of his degrading unbelief, the worm which was his heart's core. He *knew* his heart's core was a fat, awful worm. His dread was lest anyone else should know. His anguish of hate was against anyone who knew, and recoiled.

He saw Yvette recoiling, and immediately his manner changed to the worldly old good-humoured cynic which he affected.

"Ah well!" he said. "You have to pay it back, my girl, that's all. I will advance you the money out of your allowance. But I shall charge you four per-cent a month interest. Even the devil himself must pay a percentage on his debts. Another time, if you can't trust yourself, don't handle money which isn't your own. Dishonesty isn't pretty."

Yvette remained crushed, and deflowered and humiliated. She crept about, trailing the rays of her pride. She had a revulsion even from herself. Oh, why had she ever touched the leprous money! Her whole flesh shrank as if it were defiled. Why was that? Why, why was that?

She admitted herself wrong in having spent the money. "Of course I shouldn't have done it. They are quite right to be angry," she said to herself.

But where did the horrible wincing of her flesh come from? Why did she feel she had caught some physical contagion?

"Where you're so *silly,* Yvette," Lucille lectured her: poor Lucille was in great distress—"is that you give yourself away to them all. You might *know* they'd find out. I could have raised the money for you, and saved all this bother. It's perfectly awful! But you never will think beforehand where your actions are going to land you! Fancy Aunt Cissie saying all those things to you! How *awful!* Whatever would Mamma have said, if she'd heard it?"

When things went very wrong, they thought of their mother, and despised their father and all the low brood of the Saywells. Their mother, of course, had belonged to a higher, if more dangerous and "immoral" world. More selfish, decidedly. But with a showier gesture. More unscrupulous and more easily moved to contempt: but not so humiliating.

Yvette always considered that she got her fine, delicate flesh from her mother. The Saywells were all a bit leathery, and grubby somewhere inside. But then the Saywells never let you down. Whereas the fine She-who-was-Cynthia had let the rector down with a bang, and his little children along with him. Her little children! They could not quite forgive her.

Only dimly, after the row, Yvette began to realise the other sanctity of herself, the sanctity of her sensitive, clean flesh and blood, which the Saywells with their so-called morality, succeeded in defiling. They always wanted to defile it. They were the life unbelievers. Whereas, perhaps She-who-was-Cynthia had only been a moral unbeliever.

Yvette went about dazed and peaked and confused. The rector paid in the money to Aunt Cissie, much to that lady's rage. The helpless tumour of her rage was still running. She would have liked to announce her niece's delinquency in the parish magazine. It was anguish to the destroyed woman that she could not publish the news to all the world. The selfishness! The selfishness! The selfishness!

Then the rector handed his daughter a little account with himself: her debt to him, interest thereon, the amount deducted from her small allowance. But to her credit he had placed a guinea, which was the fee he had to pay for complicity.

"As father of the culprit," he said humorously, "I am fined one guinea. And with that I wash the ashes out of my hair."

He was always generous about money. But somehow, he seemed to think that by being free about money he could absolutely call himself a generous man. Whereas he used money, even generosity, as a hold over her.

But he let the affair drop entirely. He was by this time more amused than anything, to judge from appearances. He thought still he was safe.

Aunt Cissie, however, could not get over her convulsion. One night when Yvette had gone rather early miserably, to bed, when Lucille was away at a party, and she was lying with soft, peaked limbs aching with a sort of numbness and defilement, the door softly opened, and there stood Aunt Cissie, pushing her grey-green face through the opening of the door. Yvette started up in terror.

"Liar! Thief! Selfish little beast!" hissed the maniacal face of Aunt Cissie. "You little hypocrite! You liar! You selfish beast! You greedy little beast!"

There was such extraordinary impersonal hatred in that grey-green mask, and those frantic words, that Yvette opened her mouth to scream with hysterics. But Aunt Cissie shut the door as suddenly as she had opened it, and disappeared. Yvette leaped from her bed and turned the key. Then she crept back, half demented with fear of the squalid abnormal, half numbed with paralysis of damaged pride. And amid it all, up came a bubble of distracted laughter. It *was* so filthily ridiculous!

Aunt Cissie's behaviour did not hurt the girl so very much. It was after all somewhat fantastic. Yet hurt she was: in her limbs, in her body, in her sex, hurt. Hurt, numbed, and half destroyed, with only her nerves vibrating and jangled. And still so young, she could not conceive what was happening.

Only she lay and wished she were a gipsy. To live in a camp, in a caravan, and never set foot in a house, not know the existence of a parish, never look at a church. Her heart was hard with repugnance, against the rectory. She loathed these houses with their indoor sanitation and their bathrooms, and their extraordinary repulsiveness. She hated the rectory, and everything it implied. The whole stagnant, sewerage sort of life, where sewerage is never mentioned, but where it seems to smell from the centre of every two-legged inmate, from Granny to the servants, was foul. If gipsies had no bathrooms, at least they had no sewerage. There was fresh air. In the rectory there was *never* fresh air. And in the souls of the people, the air was stale till it stank.

Hate kindled her heart, as she lay with numbed limbs. And she thought of the words of the gipsy woman: "There is a dark man who never lived in a house.

He loves you. The other people are treading on your heart. They will tread on your heart till you think it is dead. But the dark man will blow the one spark up into fire again, good fire. You will see what good fire."

Even as the woman was saying it, Yvette felt there was some duplicity somewhere. But she didn't mind. She hated with the cold, acrid hatred of a child the rectory interior, the sort of putridity in the life. She liked that big, swarthy, wolf-like gipsy-woman, with the big gold rings in her ears, the pink scarf over her wavy black hair, the tight bodice of brown velvet, the green, fan-like skirt. She liked her dusky, strong, relentless hands, that had pressed so firm, like wolf's paws, in Yvette's own soft palm. She liked her. She liked the danger and the covert fearlessness of her. She liked her covert, unyielding sex, that was immoral, but with a hard, defiant pride of its own. Nothing would ever get that woman under. She would despise the rectory and the rectory morality, utterly! She would strangle Granny with one hand. And she would have the same contempt for Daddy and for Uncle Fred, as men, as she would have for fat old slobbery Rover, the Newfoundland dog. A great, sardonic female contempt, for such domesticated dogs, calling themselves men.

And the gipsy man himself! Yvette quivered suddenly, as if she had seen his big, bold eyes upon her, with the naked insinuation of desire in them. The absolutely naked insinuation of desire made her lie prone and powerless in the bed, as if a drug had cast her in a new, molten mould.

She never confessed to anybody that two of the ill-starred Window Fund pounds had gone to the gipsy woman. What if Daddy and Aunt Cissie knew *that!* Yvette stirred luxuriously in the bed. The thought of the gipsy had released the life of her limbs, and crystallised in her heart the hate of the rectory: so that now she felt potent, instead of impotent.

When, later, Yvette told Lucille about Aunt Cissie's dramatic interlude in the bedroom doorway, Lucille was indignant.

"Oh, hang it all!" cried she. "She might let it drop now. I should think we've heard enough about it by now! Good heavens, you'd think Aunt Cissie was a perfect bird of paradise! Daddy's dropped it, and after all, it's his business if it's anybody's. Let Aunt Cissie shut up!"

It was the very fact that the rector had dropped it, and that he again treated the vague and inconsiderate Yvette as if she were some specially-licensed being, that kept Aunt Cissie's bile flowing. The fact that Yvette really was most of the time unaware of other people's feelings, and being unaware, couldn't care about them, nearly sent Aunt Cissie mad. Why should that young creature, with a delinquent mother, go through life as a privileged being, even unaware of other people's existence, though they were under her nose.

Lucille at this time was very irritable. She seemed as if she simply went a little unbalanced, when she entered the rectory. Poor Lucille, she was so thoughtful and responsible. She did all the extra troubling, thought about doctors, medicines, servants, and all that sort of thing. She slaved conscientiously at her job all day in town, working in a room with artificial light from ten till five. And she came home to have her nerves rubbed almost to frenzy by Granny's horrible and persistent inquisitiveness and parasitic agedness.

The affair of the Window Fund had apparently blown over, but there remained a stuffy tension in the atmosphere. The weather continued bad. Lucille stayed at home on the afternoon of her half holiday, and did herself no good by it. The rector was in his study, she and Yvette were making a dress for the latter young woman, Granny was resting on the couch.

The dress was of blue silk velours, French material, and was going to be very becoming. Lucille made Yvette try it on again: she was nervously uneasy about the hang, under the arms.

"Oh bother!" cried Yvette, stretching her long, tender, childish arms, that tended to go bluish with the cold. "Don't be so frightfully *fussy,* Lucille! It's quite all right."

"If that's all the thanks I get, slaving my half day away making dresses for you, I might as well do something for myself!"

"Well, Lucille! You know I never *asked* you! You know you can't bear it unless you *do* supervise," said Yvette, with that irritating blandness of hers, as she raised her naked elbows and peered over her shoulder into the long mirror.

"Oh yes! you never *asked* me!" cried Lucille. "As if I didn't know what you meant, when you started sighing and flouncing about."

"I!" said Yvette, with vague surprise. "Why, when did I start sighing and flouncing about?"

"Of course you know you did."

"Did I? No, I didn't know! When was it?" Yvette could put a peculiar annoyance into her mild, straying questions.

"I shan't do another thing to this frock, if you don't stand still and *stop* it," said Lucille, in her rather sonorous, burning voice.

"You know you are most awfully nagging and irritable, Lucille," said Yvette, standing as if on hot bricks.

"Now Yvette!" cried Lucille, her eyes suddenly flashing in her sister's face, with wild flashes. "Stop it at once! Why should everybody put up with your abominable and overbearing temper!"

"Well, I don't know about *my* temper," said Yvette, writhing slowly out of the half-made frock, and slipping into her dress again.

Then, with an obstinate little look on her face, she sat down again at the table, in the gloomy afternoon, and began to sew at the blue stuff. The room was littered with blue clippings, the scissors were lying on the floor, the work-basket was spilled in chaos all over the table, and a second mirror was perched perilously on the piano.

Granny, who had been in a semi-coma, called a doze, roused herself on the big, soft couch and put her cap straight.

"I don't get much peace for my nap," she said, slowly feeling her thin white hair, to see that it was in order. She had heard vague noises.

Aunt Cissie came in, fumbling in a bag for a chocolate.

"I never saw such a mess!" she said. "You'd better clear some of that litter away, Yvette."

"All right," said Yvette. "I will in a minute."

"Which means never!" sneered Aunt Cissie, suddenly darting and picking up the scissors.

There was silence for a few moments, and Lucille slowly pushed her hands in her hair, as she read a book.

"You'd better clear away, Yvette," persisted Aunt Cissie.

"I will, before tea," replied Yvette, rising once more and pulling the blue dress over her head, flourishing her long, naked arms through the sleeveless armholes. Then she went between the mirrors, to look at herself once more.

As she did so, she sent the second mirror, that she had perched carelessly on the piano, sliding with a rattle to the floor. Luckily it did not break. But everybody started badly.

"She's smashed the mirror!" cried Aunt Cissie.

"Smashed a mirror! Which mirror! Who's smashed it?" came Granny's sharp voice.

"I haven't smashed anything," came the calm voice of Yvette. "It's quite all right."

"You'd better not perch it up there again," said Lucille.

Yvette, with a little impatient shrug at all the fuss, tried making the mirror stand in another place. She was not successful.

"If one had a fire in one's own room," she said crossly, "one needn't have a lot of people fussing when one wants to sew."

"Which mirror are you moving about?" asked Granny.

"One of our own, that came from the Vicarage," said Yvette rudely.

"Don't break it in *this* house, wherever it came from," said Granny.

There was a sort of family dislike for the furniture that had belonged to She-who-was-Cynthia. It was most of it shoved into the kitchen, and the servants' bedrooms.

"Oh, *I'm* not superstitious," said Yvette, "about mirrors or any of that sort of thing."

"Perhaps you're not," said Granny. "People who never take the responsibility for their own actions usually don't care what happens."

"After all," said Yvette, "I may say it's my own looking-glass, even if I did break it."

"And I say," said Granny, "that there shall be no mirrors broken in *this* house, if we can help it; no matter who they belong to, or did belong to. Cissie, have I got my cap straight?"

Aunt Cissie went over and straightened the old lady. Yvette loudly and irritatingly trilled a tuneless tune.

"And now, Yvette, will you please clear away," said Aunt Cissie.

"Oh bother!" cried Yvette angrily. "It's simply *awful* to live with a lot of people who are always nagging and fussing over trifles."

"What people, may I ask?" said Aunt Cissie ominously.

Another row was imminent. Lucille looked up with a queer cast in her eyes. In the two girls, the blood of She-who-was-Cynthia was roused.

"Of course you may ask! You know quite well I mean the people in this beastly house," said the outrageous Yvette.

"At least," said Granny, "we don't come of half-depraved stock."

There was a second's electric pause. Then Lucille sprang from her low seat, with sparks flying from her.

"You shut up!" she shouted, in a blast full upon the mottled majesty of the old lady.

The old woman's breast began to heave with heaven knows what emotions. The pause this time, as after the thunderbolt, was icy.

Then Aunt Cissie, livid, sprang upon Lucille, pushing her like a fury.

"Go to your room!" she cried hoarsely. "Go to your room!"

And she proceeded to push the white but fiery-eyed Lucille from the room. Lucille let herself be pushed, while Aunt Cissie vociferated:

"Stay in your room till you've apologised for this!—till you've apologised to the Mater for this!"

"I shan't apologise!" came the clear voice of Lucille, from the passage, while Aunt Cissie shoved her.

Aunt Cissie drove her more wildly upstairs.

Yvette stood tall and bemused in the sitting-room, with the air of offended dignity, at the same time bemused, which was so odd on her. She still was bare-armed, in the half-made blue dress. And even *she* was half-aghast at Lucille's attack on the majesty of age. But also, she was coldly indignant against Granny's aspersion of the maternal blood in their veins.

"Of course I meant no offence," said Granny.

"Didn't you!" said Yvette coolly.

"Of course not. I only said we're not depraved, just because we happen to be superstitious about breaking mirrors."

Yvette could hardly believe her ears. Had she heard right? Was it possible! Or was Granny, at her age, just telling a barefaced lie?

Yvette knew that the old woman was telling a cool, barefaced lie. But already, so quickly, Granny believed her own statement.

The rector appeared, having left time for a lull.

"What's wrong?" he asked cautiously, genially.

"Oh, nothing!" drawled Yvette. "Lucille told Granny to shut up, when she was saying something. And Aunt Cissie drove her up to her room. *Tant de bruit pour une omelette!* Though Lucille *was* a bit over the mark, that time."

The old lady couldn't quite catch what Yvette said.

"Lucille really will have to learn to control her nerves," said the old woman. "The mirror fell down, and it worried me. I said so to Yvette, and she said something about superstitions and the people in the beastly house. I told her the people in the house were not depraved, if they happened to mind when a mirror was broken. And at that Lucille flew at me and told me to shut up. It really is disgraceful how these children give way to their nerves. I know it's nothing but nerves."

Aunt Cissie had come in during this speech. At first even she was dumb. Then it seemed to her, it was as Granny had said.

"I have forbidden her to come down until she comes to apologise to the Mater," she said.

"I doubt if she'll apologise," said the calm, queenly Yvette, holding her bare arms.

"And I don't want any apology," said the old lady. "It is merely nerves. I don't know what they'll come to, if they have nerves like that, at their age! She must take Vibrofat.—I am sure Arthur would like his tea, Cissie!"

Yvette swept her sewing together, to go upstairs. And again she trilled her tune, rather shrill and tuneless. She was trembling inwardly.

"More glad rags!" said her father to her, genially.

"More glad rags!" she re-iterated sagely, as she sauntered upstairs, with her day dress over one arm. She wanted to console Lucille, and ask her how the blue stuff hung now.

At the first landing, she stood as she nearly always did, to gaze through the window that looked to the road and the bridge. Like the Lady of Shalott, she seemed always to imagine that someone would come along singing *Tirra-lirra!* or something equally intelligent, by the river.

Five

It was nearly tea-time. The snow-drops were out by the short drive going to the gate from the side of the house, and the gardener was pottering at the round, damp flower-beds, on the wet grass that sloped to the stream. Past the gate went the whitish muddy road, crossing the stone bridge almost immediately, and winding in a curve up to the steep, clustering, stony, smoking northern village, that perched over the grim stone mills which Yvette could see ahead down the narrow valley, their tall chimney long and erect.

The rectory was on one side the Papple, in the rather steep valley, the village was beyond and above, further down, on the other side the swift stream. At the back of the rectory the hill went up steep, with a grove of dark, bare larches, through which the road disappeared. And immediately across stream from the rectory, facing the house, the river-bank rose steep and bushy, up to the sloping, dreary meadows, that sloped up again to dark hillsides of trees, with grey rock cropping out.

But from the end of the house, Yvette could only see the road curving round past the wall with its laurel hedge, down to the bridge, then up again round the shoulder to that first hard cluster of houses in Papplewick village, beyond the dry-stone walls of the steep fields.

She always expected *something* to come down the slant of the road from Papplewick, and she always lingered at the landing window. Often a cart came, or a motor-car, or a lorry with stone, or a laborer, or one of the servants. But never anybody who sang *Tirra-lirra!* by the river. The tirralirraing days seemed to have gone by.

This day, however, round the corner on the white-grey road, between the grass and the low stone walls, a roan horse came stepping bravely and briskly down-hill, driven by a man in a cap, perched on the front of his light cart. The man swayed loosely to the swing of the cart, as the horse stepped down-hill, in the silent sombreness of the afternoon. At the back of the cart, long duster-brooms of reed and feather stuck out, nodding on their stalks of cane.

Yvette stood close to the window, and put the casement-cloth curtains behind her, clutching her bare upper arms with the hands.

At the foot of the slope the horse started into a brisk trot to the bridge. The cart rattled on the stone bridge, the brooms bobbed and flustered, the driver sat as if in a kind of dream, swinging along. It was like something seen in a sleep.

But as he crossed the end of the bridge, and was passing along the rectory wall, he looked up at the grim stone house that seemed to have backed away from the gate, under the hill. Yvette moved her hands quickly on her arms. And as quickly, from under the peak of his cap, he had seen her, his swarthy predative face was alert.

He pulled up suddenly at the white gate, still gazing upwards at the landing window; while Yvette, always clasping her cold and mottled arms, still gazed abstractedly down at him, from the window.

His head gave a little, quick jerk of signal, and he led his horse well aside, on to the grass. Then, limber and alert, he turned back the tarpaulin of the cart, fetched out various articles, pulled forth two or three of the long brooms of reed or turkey-feathers, covered the cart, and turned towards the house, looking up at Yvette as he opened the white gate.

She nodded to him, and flew to the bathroom to put on her dress, hoping she had disguised her nod so that he wouldn't be sure she had nodded. Meanwhile she heard the hoarse deep roaring of that old fool, Rover, punctuated by the yapping of that young idiot, Trixie.

She and the housemaid arrived at the same moment at the sitting-room door.

"Was it the man selling brooms?" said Yvette to the maid. "All right!" and she opened the door. "Aunt Cissie, there's a man selling brooms, Shall I go?"

"What sort of a man?" said Aunt Cissie, who was sitting at tea with the rector and the Mater: the girls having been excluded for once from the meal.

"A man with a cart," said Yvette.

"A gipsy," said the maid.

Of course Aunt Cissie rose at once. She had to look at him.

The gipsy stood at the back door, under the steep dark bank where the larches grew. The long brooms flourished from one hand, and from the other hung various objects of shining copper and brass: a saucepan, a candlestick, plates of beaten copper. The man himself was neat and dapper, almost rakish, in his dark green cap and double-breasted green check coat. But his manner was subdued, very quiet: and at the same time proud, with a touch of condescension and aloofness.

"Anything today, lady?" he said, looking at Aunt Cissie with dark, shrewd, searching eyes, but putting a very quiet tenderness into his voice.

Aunt Cissie saw how handsome he was, saw the flexible curve of his lips under the line of black moustache, and she was fluttered. The merest hint of roughness or aggression on the man's part would have made her shut the door contemptuously in his face. But he managed to insinuate such a subtle suggestion of submission into his male bearing, that she began to hesitate.

"The candlestick is lovely!" said Yvette. "Did you make it?"

And she looked up at the man with her naïve, childlike eyes, that were as capable of double meanings as his own.

"Yes lady!" He looked back into her eyes for a second, with that naked suggestion of desire which acted on her like a spell, and robbed her of her will. Her tender face seemed to go into a sleep.

"It's awfully nice!" she murmured vaguely.

Aunt Cissie began to bargain for the candlestick: which was a low, thick stem of copper, rising from a double bowl. With patient aloofness the man attended to her, without ever looking at Yvette, who leaned against the doorway and watched in a muse.

"How is your wife?" she asked him suddenly, when Aunt Cissie had gone indoors to show the candlestick to the rector, and ask him if he thought it was worth it.

The man looked fully at Yvette, and a scarcely discernible smile curled his lips. His eyes did not smile: the insinuation in them only hardened to a glare.

"She's all right. When are you coming that way again?" he murmured, in a low, caressive, intimate voice.

"Oh, I don't know," said Yvette vaguely.

"You come Fridays, when I'm there," he said. Yvette gazed over his shoulder as if she had not heard him. Aunt Cissie returned, with the candlestick and the money to pay for it. Yvette turned nonchalant away, trilling one of her broken tunes, abandoning the whole affair with a certain rudeness.

Nevertheless, hiding this time at the landing window, she stood to watch the man go. What she wanted to know, was whether he really had any power over her. She did not intend him to see her this time.

She saw him go down to the gate, with his brooms and pans, and out to the cart. He carefully stowed away his pans and his brooms, and fixed down the tarpaulin over the cart. Then with a slow, effortless spring of his flexible loins, he was on the cart again, and touching the horse with the reins. The roan horse was away at once, the cart-wheels grinding uphill, and soon the man was gone, without looking round. Gone like a dream which was only a dream, yet which she could not shake off.

"No, he hasn't any power over me!" she said to herself: rather disappointed really, because she wanted somebody, or something to have power over her.

She went up to reason with the pale and overwrought Lucille, scolding her for getting into a state over nothing.

"What does it *matter,*" she expostulated, "if you told Granny to shut up! Why, everybody ought to be told to shut up, when they're being beastly. But she didn't mean it, you know. No, she didn't mean it. And she's quite sorry she said it. There's absolutely no reason to make a fuss. Come on, let's dress ourselves up and sail down to dinner like duchesses. Let's have our own back that way. Come on, Lucille!"

There was something strange and mazy, like having cobwebs over one's face, about Yvette's vague blitheness; her queer, misty side-stepping from an unpleasantness. It was cheering too. But it was like walking in one of those autumn mists, when gossamer strands blow over your face. You don't quite know where you are.

She succeeded, however, in persuading Lucille, and the girls got out their best party frocks: Lucille in green and silver, Yvette in a pale lilac colour with turquoise chenille threading. A little rouge and powder, and their best slippers, and the gardens of paradise began to blossom. Yvette hummed and looked at herself, and put on her most *dégagé* airs of one of the young marchionesses. She had an odd way of slanting her eyebrows and pursing her lips, and to all appearances detaching herself from every earthly consideration, and floating through the cloud of her own pearl-coloured reserves. It was amusing, and not quite convincing.

"Of course I am beautiful, Lucille," she said blandly. "And you're perfectly lovely, now you look a bit reproachful. Of course you're the most aristocratic of the two of us, with your nose! And now your eyes look reproachful, that adds an appealing look, and you're perfect, perfectly lovely. But I'm more *winning,* in a way.—Don't you agree?" She turned with arch, complicated simplicity to Lucille.

She was truly simple in what she said. It was just what she thought. But it gave no hint of the very different *feeling* that also preoccupied her: the feeling that she had been looked upon, not from the outside, but from the inside, from her secret female self. She was dressing herself up and looking her most dazzling, just to counteract the effect that the gipsy had had on her, when he had looked at her, and seen none of her pretty face and her pretty ways, but just the dark, tremulous, potent secret of her virginity.

The two girls started downstairs in state when the dinner-gong rang: but they waited till they heard the voice of the men. Then they sailed down and into the sitting-room, Yvette preening herself in her vague, debonair way, always a little bit absent; and Lucille shy, ready to burst into tears.

"My goodness gracious!" exclaimed Aunt Cissie, who was still wearing her dark-brown knitted sports coat. "What an apparition! Wherever do you think you're going?"

"We're dining with the family," said Yvette naively, "and we've put on our best gewgaws in honour of the occasion."

The rector laughed aloud, and Uncle Fred said:

"The family feels itself highly honoured."

Both the elderly men were quite gallant, which was what Yvette wanted.

"Come and let me feel your dresses, do!" said Granny. "Are they your best? It *is* a shame I can't see them."

"Tonight, Mater," said Uncle Fred, "we shall have to take the young ladies in to dinner, and live up to the honour. Will you go with Cissie?"

"I certainly will," said Granny. "Youth and beauty must come first."

"Well, tonight Mater!" said the rector, pleased.

And he offered his arm to Lucille, while Uncle Fred escorted Yvette.

But it was a draggled, dull meal, all the same. Lucille tried to be bright and sociable, and Yvette really was most amiable, in her vague, cobwebby way. Dimly, at the back of her mind, she was thinking: Why are we all only like mortal pieces of furniture? Why is nothing *important?*

That was her constant refrain, to herself: Why is nothing important? Whether she was in church, or at a party of young people, or dancing in the hotel in the city, the same little bubble of a question rose repeatedly on her consciousness: Why is nothing important?

There were plenty of young men to make love to her: even devotedly. But with impatience she had to shake them off. Why were they so unimportant?— so irritating!

She never even thought of the gipsy. He was a perfectly negligible incident. Yet the approach of Friday loomed strangely significant. "What are we doing on Friday?" she said to Lucille. To which Lucille replied that they were doing nothing. And Yvette was vexed.

Friday came, and in spite of herself she thought all day of the quarry off the road up high Bonsall Head. She wanted to be there. That was all she was conscious of. She wanted to be there. She had not even a dawning idea of going there. Besides, it was raining again. But as she sewed the blue dress, finishing it for the party up at Lambley Close, tomorrow, she just felt that her soul was up there, at the quarry, among the caravans, with the gipsies. Like one lost, or whose soul was stolen, she was not present in her body, the shell of her body. Her intrinsic body was away, at the quarry, among the caravans.

The next day, at the party, she had no idea that she was being sweet to Leo. She had no idea that she was snatching him away from the tortured Ella Framley. Not until, when she was eating her pistachio ice, he said to her:

"Why don't you and me get engaged, Yvette? I'm absolutely sure it's the right thing for us both."

Leo was a bit common, but good-natured, and well-off. Yvette quite liked him. But engaged! How perfectly silly! She felt like offering him a set of her silk underwear, to get engaged to.

"But I thought it was Ella!" she said, in wonder.

"Well! It might ha' been, but for you. It's your doings, you know! Ever since those gipsies told your fortune, I felt it was me or nobody, for you, and you or nobody, for me."

"Really!" said Yvette, simply lost in amazement. "Really!"

"Didn't you feel a bit the same?" he asked.

"Really!" Yvette kept on gasping softly, like a fish.

"You felt a bit the same, didn't you?" he said.

"What? About what?" she asked, coming to.

"About me, as I feel about you."

"Why? What? Getting engaged, you mean? I? no! Why how *could* I? I could never have dreamed of such an impossible thing."

She spoke with her usual heedless candour, utterly unoccupied with his feelings.

"What was to prevent you?" he said, a bit nettled. "I thought you did."

"Did you *really now?*" she breathed in amazement, with that soft, virgin, heedless candour which made her her admirers and her enemies.

She was so completely amazed, there was nothing for him to do but twiddle his thumbs in annoyance.

The music began, and he looked at her.

"No! I won't dance any more," she said, drawing herself up and gazing away rather loftily over the assembly, as if he did not exist. There was a touch of puzzled wonder on her brow, and her soft, dim virgin face did indeed suggest the snow-drop of her father's pathetic imagery.

"But of course *you* will dance," she said, turning to him with young condescension. "Do ask somebody to have this with you."

He rose, angry, and went down the room.

She remained soft and remote in her amazement. Expect Leo to propose to her! She might as well have expected old Rover the Newfoundland dog to propose to her. Get engaged, to any man on earth? No, good heavens, nothing more ridiculous could be imagined!

It was then, in a fleeting side-thought, that she realised that the gipsy existed. Instantly, she was indignant. Him, of all things! Him! Never!

"Now why?" she asked herself, again in hushed amazement. "Why? It's *absolutely* impossible: absolutely! So why is it?"

This was a nut to crack. She looked at the young men dancing, elbows out, hips prominent, waists elegantly in. They gave her no clue to her problem. Yet she did particularly dislike the forced elegance of the waists and the prominent hips, over which the well-tailored coats hung with such effeminate discretion.

"There is something about me which they don't see and never would see," she said angrily to herself. And at the same time, she was relieved that they didn't and couldn't. It made life so very much simpler.

And again, since she was one of the people who are conscious in visual images, she saw the dark-green jersey rolled on the black trousers of the gipsy, his fine, quick hips, alert as eyes. They were elegant. The elegance of these dancers seemed so stuffed, hips merely wadded with flesh. Leo the same, thinking himself such a fine dancer! and a fine figure of a fellow!

Then she saw the gipsy's face; the straight nose, the slender mobile lips, and the level, significant stare of the black eyes, which seemed to shoot her in some vital, undiscovered place, unerring.

She drew herself up angrily. How dared he look at her like that! So she gazed glaringly at the insipid beaux on the dancing floor. And she despised them. Just as the raggle-taggle gipsy women despise men who are not gipsies, despise their dog-like walk down the streets, she found herself despising this crowd. Where among them was the subtle, lonely, insinuating challenge that could reach her?

She did not want to mate with a house-dog.

Her sensitive nose turned up, her soft brown hair fell like a soft sheath round her tender, flower-like face, as she sat musing. She seemed so virginal. At the same time, there was a touch of the tall young virgin *witch* about her, that made the house-dog men shy off. She might metamorphose into something uncanny before you knew where you were.

This made her lonely, in spite of all the courting. Perhaps the courting only made her lonelier.

Leo, who was a sort of mastiff among the house-dogs, returned after his dance, with fresh cheery-O! courage.

"You've had a little think about it, haven't you?" he said, sitting down beside her: a comfortable, well-nourished, determined sort of fellow. She did not know why it irritated her so unreasonably, when he hitched up his trousers at the knee, over his good-sized but not very distinguished legs, and lowered himself assuredly on to a chair.

"Have I?" she said vaguely. "About what?"

"You know what about," he said. "Did you make up your mind?"

"Make up my mind about what?" she asked, innocently.

In her upper consciousness, she truly had forgotten.

"Oh!" said Leo, settling his trousers again. "About me and you getting engaged, you know." He was almost as off-hand as she.

"Oh that's *absolutely* impossible," she said, with mild amiability, as if it were some stray question among the rest. "Why, I never even thought of it again. Oh, don't talk about that sort of nonsense! That sort of thing is *absolutely* impossible," she re-iterated like a child.

"That sort of thing is, is it?" he said, with an odd smile at her calm, distant assertion. "Well what sort of thing *is* possible, then? You don't want to die an old maid, do you?"

"Oh I don't mind," she said absently.

"I do," he said.

She turned round and looked at him in wonder.

"Why?" she said. "Why should you mind if I was an old maid?"

"Every reason in the world," he said, looking up at her with a bold, meaningful smile, that wanted to make its meaning blatant, if not patent.

But instead of penetrating into some deep, secret place, and shooting her there, Leo's bold and patent smile only hit her on the outside of the body, like a tennis ball, and caused the same kind of sudden irritated reaction.

"I think this sort of thing is awfully silly," she said, with minx-like spite. "Why, you're practically engaged to—to—" she pulled herself up in time—"probably half a dozen other girls. I'm not flattered by what you've said. I should hate it if anybody knew!—Hate it!—I shan't breathe a word of it, and I hope you'll have the sense not to.—There's Ella!"

And keeping her face averted from him, she sailed away like a tall, soft flower, to join poor Ella Framley.

Leo flapped his white gloves.

"Catty little bitch!" he said to himself. But he was of the mastiff type, he rather liked the kitten to fly in his face. He began definitely to single her out.

Six

The next week it poured again with rain. And this irritated Yvette with strange anger. She had intended it should be fine. Especially she insisted it should be fine towards the week-end. Why, she did not ask herself.

Thursday, the half-holiday, came with a hard frost, and sun. Leo arrived with his car, the usual bunch. Yvette disagreeably and unaccountably refused to go.

"No thanks, I don't feel like it," she said.

She rather enjoyed being Mary-Mary-quite-contrary.

Then she went for a walk by herself, up the frozen hills, to the Black Rocks.

The next day also came sunny and frosty. It was February, but in the north country the ground did not thaw in the sun. Yvette announced that she was going for a ride on her bicycle, and taking her lunch, as she might not be back till afternoon.

She set off, not hurrying. In spite of the frost, the sun had a touch of spring. In the park, the deer were standing in the distance, in the sunlight, to be warm. One doe, white spotted, walked slowly across the motionless landscape.

Cycling, Yvette found it difficult to keep her hands warm, even when bodily she was quite hot. Only when she had to walk up the long hill, to the top, and there was no wind.

The upland was very bare and clear, like another world. She had climbed on to another level. She cycled slowly, a little afraid of taking the wrong lane, in the vast maze of stone fences. As she passed along the lane she thought was the right one, she heard a faint tapping noise, with a slight metallic resonance.

The gipsy man was seated on the ground with his back to the cart-shaft, hammering a copper bowl. He was in the sun, bare-headed, but wearing his green jersey. Three small children were moving quietly round, playing in the horse's shelter: the horse and cart were gone. An old woman, bent, with a kerchief round her head, was cooking over a fire of sticks. The only sound was the rapid, ringing tap-tap-tap; of the small hammer on the dull copper.

The man looked up at once, as Yvette stepped from her bicycle, but he did not move, though he ceased hammering. A delicate, barely discernible smile of triumph was on his face. The old woman looked round, keenly, from under her dirty grey hair. The man spoke a half-audible word to her, and she turned again to her fire. He looked up at Yvette.

"How are you all getting on?" she asked politely.

"All right, eh! You sit down a minute?" He turned as he sat, and pulled a stool from under the caravan for Yvette. Then, as she wheeled her bicycle to the side of the quarry, he started hammering again, with that bird-like, rapid light stroke.

Yvette went to the fire to warm her hands.

"Is this the dinner cooking?" she asked childishly, of the old gipsy, as she spread her long, tender hands, mottled red with the cold, to the embers.

"Dinner, yes!" said the old woman. "For him! And for the children."

She pointed with the long fork at the three black-eyed, staring children, who were staring at her from under their black fringes. But they were clean. Only the old woman was not clean. The quarry itself they had kept perfectly clean.

Yvette crouched in silence, warming her hands. The man rapidly hammered away with intervals of silence. The old hag slowly climbed the steps to the third, oldest caravan. The children began to play again, like little wild animals, quiet and busy.

"Are they your children?" asked Yvette, rising from the fire and turning to the man.

He looked her in the eyes, and nodded.

"But where's your wife?"

"She's gone out with the basket. They're all gone out, cart and all, selling things. I don't go selling things. I make them, but I don't go selling them. Not often. I don't often."

"You make all the copper and brass things?" she said.

He nodded, and again offered her the stool. She sat down.

"You said you'd be here on Fridays," she said. "So I came this way, as it was so fine."

"Very fine day!" said the gipsy, looking at her cheek, that was still a bit blanched by the cold, and the soft hair over her reddened ear, and the long, still mottled bands on her knee.

"You get cold, riding a bicycle?" he asked.

"My hands!" she said, clasping them nervously.

"You didn't wear gloves?"

"I did, but they weren't much good."

"Cold comes through," he said.

"Yes!" she replied.

The old woman came slowly, grotesquely down the steps of the caravan, with some enamel plates.

"The dinner cooked, eh?" he called softly.

The old woman muttered something, as she spread the plates near the fire. Two pots hung from a long iron horizontal-bar, over the embers of the fire. A little pan seethed on a small iron tripod. In the sunshine, heat and vapour wavered together.

He put down his tools and the pot, and rose from the ground.

"You eat something along of us?" he asked Yvette, not looking at her.

"Oh, I brought my lunch," said Yvette.

"You eat some stew?" he said. And again he called quietly, secretly to the old woman, who muttered in answer, as she slid the iron pot towards the end of the bar.

"Some beans, and some mutton in it," he said.

"Oh thanks awfully!" said Yvette. Then suddenly taking courage, added: "Well yes, just a very little, if I may."

She went across to untie her lunch from her bicycle, and he went up the steps to his own caravan. After a minute, he emerged, wiping his hands on a towel.

"You want to come up and wash your hands?" he said.

"No, I think not," she said. "They are clean."

He threw away his wash-water, and set off down the road with a high brass jug, to fetch clean water from the spring that trickled into a small pool, taking a cup to dip it with.

When he returned, he set the jug and the cup by the fire, and fetched himself a short log, to sit on. The children sat on the floor, by the fire, in a cluster, eating beans and bits of meat with spoon or fingers. The man on the log ate in silence, absorbedly. The woman made coffee in the black pot on the tripod, hobbling upstairs for the cups. There was silence in the camp. Yvette sat on her stool, having taken off her hat and shaken her hair in the sun.

"How many children have you?" Yvette asked suddenly.

"Say five," he replied slowly, as he looked up into her eyes.

And again the bird of her heart sank down and seemed to die. Vaguely, as in a dream, she received from him the cup of coffee. She was aware only of his silent figure, sitting like a shadow there on the log, with an enamel cup in his hand, drinking his coffee in silence. Her will had departed from her limbs, he had power over her: his shadow was on her.

And he, as he blew his hot coffee, was aware of one thing only, the mysterious fruit of her virginity, her perfect tenderness in the body.

At length he put down his coffee-cup by the fire, then looked round at her. Her hair fell across her face, as she tried to sip from the hot cup. On her face was that tender look of sleep, which a nodding flower has when it is full out, like a mysterious early flower, she was full out, like a snowdrop which spreads its three white wings in a flight into the waking sleep of its brief blossoming. The waking sleep of her full-opened virginity, entranced like a snowdrop in the sunshine, was upon her.

The gipsy, supremely aware of her, waited for her like the substance of shadow, as shadow waits and is there.

At length his voice said, without breaking the spell:

"You want to go in my caravan, now, and wash your hands?"

The childlike, sleep-waking eyes of her moment of perfect virginity looked into his, unseeing. She was only aware of the dark, strange effluence of him bathing her limbs, washing her at last purely will-less. She was aware of *him,* as a dark, complete power.

"I think I might," she said.

He rose silently, then turned to speak, in a low command, to the old woman. And then again he looked at Yvette, and putting his power over her, so that she had no burden of herself, or of action.

"Come!" he said.

She followed simply, followed the silent, secret, overpowering motion of his body in front of her. It cost her nothing. She was gone in his will.

He was at the top of the steps, and she at the foot, when she became aware of an intruding sound. She stood still, at the foot of the steps. A motor-car was coming. He stood at the top of the steps, looking round strangely. The old woman harshly called something, as with rapidly increasing sound, a car rushed near. It was passing.

Then they heard the cry of a woman's voice, and the brakes on the car. It had pulled up, just beyond the quarry.

The gipsy came down the steps, having closed the door of the caravan.

"You want to put your hat on," he said to her.

Obediently she went to the stool by the fire, and took up her hat. He sat down by the cart-wheel, darkly, and took up his tools. The rapid tap-tap-tap of his hammer, rapid and angry now like the sound of a tiny machine-gun, broke out just as the voice of the woman was heard crying:

"May we warm our hands at the camp fire?"

She advanced, dressed in a sleek but bulky coat of sable fur. A man followed, in a blue great-coat; pulling off his fur gloves and pulling out a pipe.

"It looked so tempting," said the woman in the coat of many dead little animals, smiling a broad, half-condescending, half-hesitant simper, around the company.

No one said a word.

She advanced to the fire, shuddering a little inside her coat, with the cold. They had been driving in an open car.

She was a very small woman, with a rather large nose: probably a Jewess. Tiny almost as a child, in that sable coat she looked much more bulky than she should, and her wide, rather resentful brown eyes of a spoilt Jewess gazed oddly out of her expensive get-up.

She crouched over the low fire, spreading her little hands, on which diamonds and emeralds glittered.

"Ugh!" she shuddered. "Of course we ought not to have come in an open car! But my husband won't even let me say I'm cold!" She looked round at him with her large, childish, reproachful eyes, that had still the canny shrewdness of a bourgeois Jewess: a rich one, probably.

Apparently she was in love, in a Jewess's curious way, with the big, blond man. He looked back at her with his abstracted blue eyes, that seemed to have no lashes, and a small smile creased his smooth, curiously naked cheeks. The smile didn't mean anything at all.

He was a man one connects instantly with winter sports, Ski-ing and skating. Athletic, unconnected with life, he slowly filled his pipe, pressing in the tobacco with long, powerful reddened finger.

The Jewess looked at him to see if she got any response from him. Nothing at all, but that odd, blank smile. She turned again to the fire, tilting her eyebrows and looking at her small, white, spread hands.

He slipped off his heavily lined coat, and appeared in one of the handsome, sharp-patterned knitted jerseys, in yellow and grey and black, over well-cut trousers, rather wide. Yes, they were both expensive! And he had a magnificent figure, an athletic, prominent chest. Like an experienced camper, he began building the fire together, quietly: like a soldier on campaign.

"D'you think they'd mind if we put some fircones on, to make a blaze?" he asked of Yvette, with a silent glance at the hammering gipsy.

"Love it, I should think," said Yvette, in a daze, as the spell of the gipsy slowly left her, feeling stranded and blank.

The man went to the car, and returned with a little sack of cones, from which he drew a handful.

"Mind if we make a blaze?" he called to the gipsy.

"Eh?"

"Mind if we make a blaze with a few cones?"

"You go ahead!" said the gipsy.

The man began placing the cones lightly, carefully on the red embers. And soon, one by one, they caught fire, and burned like roses of flame, with a sweet scent.

"Ah lovely! lovely!" cried the little Jewess, looking up at her man again. He looked down at her quite kindly, like the sun on ice. "Don't you love fire! Oh, I love it!" the little Jewess cried to Yvette, across the hammering.

The hammering annoyed her. She looked round with a slight frown on her fine little brows, as if she would bid the man stop. Yvette looked round too. The gipsy was bent over his copper bowl, legs apart, head down, lithe arm lifted. Already he seemed so far from her.

The man who accompanied the little Jewess strolled over to the gipsy, and stood in silence looking down on him, holding his pipe to his mouth. Now they were two men, like two strange male dogs, having to sniff one another.

"We're on our honeymoon," said the little Jewess, with an arch, resentful look at Yvette. She spoke in a rather high, defiant voice, like some bird, a jay, or a crook, calling.

"Are you really?" said Yvette.

"Yes! Before we're married! Have you heard of Simon Fawcett?"—she named a wealthy and well-known engineer of the north country. "Well, I'm Mrs. Fawcett, and he's just divorcing me!" She looked at Yvette with curious defiance and wistfulness.

"Are you really!" said Yvette.

She understood now the look of resentment and defiance in the little Jewess' big, childlike brown eyes. She was an honest little thing, but perhaps her honesty was *too* rational. Perhaps it partly explained the notorious unscrupulousness of the well-known Simon Fawcett.

"Yes! As soon as we get the divorce, I'm going to marry Major Eastwood."

Her cards were now all on the table. She was not going to deceive anybody.

Behind her, the two men were talking briefly. She glanced round, and fixed the gipsy with her big brown eyes.

He was looking up, as if shyly, at the big fellow in the sparkling jersey, who was standing pipe in mouth, man to man, looking down.

"With the horses back of Arras," said the gipsy, in a low voice.

They were talking war. The gipsy had served with the artillery teams, in the Major's own regiment.

"Ein schöner Mensch!" said the Jewess. "A handsome man, eh?"

For her, too, the gipsy was one of the common men, the Tommies.

"Quite handsome!" said Yvette.

"You are cycling?" asked the Jewess in a tone of surprise.

"Yes! Down to Papplewick. My father is rector of Papplewick: Mr. Saywell!"

"Oh!" said the Jewess. "I know! A clever writer! Very clever! I have read him."

The fir-cones were all consumed already, the fire was a tall pile now of crumbling, shattering fire-roses. The sky was clouding over for afternoon. Perhaps towards evening it would snow.

The Major came back, and slung himself into his coat.

"I thought I remembered his face" he said. "One of our grooms, A. I. man with horses."

"Look!" cried the Jewess to Yvette. Why don't you let us motor you down to Normanton. We live in Scoresby. We can tie the bicycle on behind."

"I think I will," said Yvette.

"Come!" called the Jewess to the peeping children, as the blond man wheeled away the bicycle. "Come! Come here!" and taking out her little purse, she held out a shilling.

"Come!" she cried. "Come and take it!"

The gipsy had laid down his work, and gone into his caravan. The old woman called hoarsely to the children, from the enclosure. The two elder children came stealing forward. The Jewess gave them the two bits of silver, a shilling and a florin, which she had in her purse, and again the hoarse voice of the unseen old woman was heard.

The gipsy descended from his caravan and strolled to the fire. The Jewess searched his face with the peculiar bourgeois boldness of her race.

"You were in the war, in Major's Eastwood's regiment!" she said.

"Yes, lady!"

"Imagine you both being here now!—It's going to snow—" she looked up at the sky.

"Later on," said the man, looking at the sky.

He too had gone inaccessible. His race was very old, in its peculiar battle with established society, and had no conception of winning. Only now and then it could score.

But since the war, even the old sporting chance of scoring now and then, was pretty well quenched. There was no question of yielding. The gipsy's eyes still had their bold look: but it was hardened and directed far away, the touch of insolent intimacy was gone. He had been through the war.

He looked at Yvette.

"You're going back in the motor-car?" he said.

"Yes!" she replied, with a rather mincing mannerism. "The weather is so treacherous!"

"Treacherous weather!" he repeated, looking at the sky.

She could not tell in the least what his feelings were. In truth, she wasn't very much interested. She was rather fascinated, now, by the little Jewess, mother of two children, who was taking her wealth away from the well-known engineer and transferring it to the penniless, sporting young Major Eastwood, who must be five or six years younger than she. Rather intriguing!

The blond man returned.

"A cigarette, Charles!" cried the little Jewess, plaintively.

He took out his case, slowly, with his slow, athletic movement. Something sensitive in him made him slow, cautious, as if he had hurt himself against people. He gave a cigarette to his wife, then one to Yvette, then offered the case, quite simply, to the gipsy. The gipsy took one.

"Thank you sir!"

And he went quietly to the fire, and stooping, lit it at the red embers. Both women watched him.

"Well goodbye!" said the Jewess, with her odd bourgeois free-masonry. "Thank you for the warm fire."

"Fire is everybody's," said the gipsy.

The young child came toddling to him.

"Goodbye! said Yvette. "I hope it won't snow for you."

"We don't mind a bit of snow," said the gipsy.

"Don't you?" said Yvette. "I should have thought you would!"

"No!" said the gipsy.

She flung her scarf royally over her shoulder, and followed the fur coat of the Jewess, which seemed to walk on little legs of its own.

Seven

Yvette was rather thrilled by the East-woods, as she called them. The little Jewess had only to wait three months now, for the final decree. She had boldly rented a small summer cottage, by the moors up at Scoresby, not far from the hills. Now it was dead winter, and she and the Major lived in comparative isolation, without any maid-servant. He had already resigned his commission in the regular army, and called himself Mr. Eastwood. In fact, they were already Mr. and Mrs. Eastwood, to the common world.

The little Jewess was thirty-six, and her two children were both over twelve years of age. The husband had agreed that she should have the custody, as soon as she was married to Eastwood.

So there they were, this queer couple, the tiny, finely-formed little Jewess with her big, resentful reproachful eyes, and her mop of carefully-barbered black, curly hair, an elegant little thing in her way; and the big, pale-eyed young man, powerful and wintry, the remnant surely of some old uncanny Danish stock: living together in a small modern house near the moors and the hills, and doing their own housework.

It was a funny household. The cottage was hired furnished, but the little Jewess had brought along her dearest pieces of furniture. She had an odd little taste for the rococco, strange curving cupboards inlaid with mother of pearl, tortoiseshell, ebony, heaven knows what; strange tall flamboyant chairs, from Italy, with sea-green brocade: astonishing saints with wind-blown, richly-coloured carven garments and pink faces: shelves of weird old Saxe and Capo di Monte figurines: and finally, a strange assortment of astonishing pictures painted on the back of glass, done, probably in the early years of the nineteenth century, or in the late eighteenth.

In this crowded and extraordinary interior she received Yvette, when the latter made a stolen visit. A whole system of stoves had been installed into the cottage, every corner was warm, almost hot. And there was the tiny rococco figurine of the Jewess herself, in a perfect little frock, and an apron, putting slices of ham on the dish, while the great snow-bird of a major, in a white sweater and grey trousers, cut bread, mixed mustard, prepared coffee, and did all the rest. He had even made the dish of jugged hare which followed the cold meats and caviare.

The silver and the china were really valuable, part of the bride's trousseau. The Major drank beer from a silver mug, the little Jewess and Yvette had champagne in lovely glasses, the Major brought in coffee. They talked away. The little Jewess had a burning indignation against her first husband. She was intensely moral, so moral, that she was a divorcée. The Major too, strange wintry bird, so powerful, handsome, too, in his way, but pale round the eyes as if he had no eyelashes, like a bird, he too had a curious indignation against life, because of the false morality. That powerful, athletic chest hid a strange, snowy sort of anger. And his tenderness for the little Jewess was based on his sense of outraged justice, the abstract morality of the north blowing him, like a strange wind, into isolation.

As the afternoon drew on, they went to the kitchen, the Major pushed back his sleeves, showing his powerful athletic white arms, and carefully, deftly washed the dishes, while the women wiped. It was not for nothing his muscles were trained. Then he went round attending to the stoves of the small house, which only needed a moment or two of care each day. And after this, he brought out the small, closed car and drove Yvette home, in the rain, depositing her at the back gate, a little wicket among the larches, through which the earthen steps sloped downwards to the house.

She was really amazed by this couple.

"Really, Lucille!" she said. "I do meet the most extraordinary people!" And she gave a detailed description.

"I think they sound rather nice!" said Lucille. "I like the Major doing the housework, and looking so frightfully Bond-streety with it all. I should think, *when they're married,* it would be rather fun knowing them."

"Yes!" said Yvette vaguely. "Yes! Yes, it would!"

The very strangeness of the connection between the tiny Jewess and that pale-eyed, athletic young officer made her think again of her gipsy, who had been utterly absent from her consciousness, but who now returned with sudden painful force.

"What is it, Lucille," she asked, "that brings people together? People like the Eastwoods, for instance? and Daddy and Mamma, so frightfully unsuitable?— and that gipsy woman who told my fortune, like a great horse, and the gipsy man, so fine and delicately cut? What is it?"

"I suppose it's sex, whatever that is," said Lucille.

"Yes, what is it? It's not really anything *common,* like common sensuality, you know, Lucille. It really isn't!"

"No, I suppose not," said Lucille. "Anyhow I suppose it needn't be."

"Because you see, the *common* fellows, you know, who make a girl feel *low:* nobody cares much about them. Nobody feels any connection with them. Yet they're supposed to be the sexual sort."

"I suppose," said Lucille, "there's the low sort of sex, and there's the other sort, that isn't low. It's frightfully complicated, really! I *loathe* common fellows.

And I never feel anything *sexual*—" she laid a rather disgusted stress on the word—"for fellows who aren't common. Perhaps I haven't got any sex."

"That's just it!" said Yvette. "Perhaps neither of us has. Perhaps we haven't really *got* any sex, to connect us with men."

"How horrible it sounds: *connect us with men!*" cried Lucille, with revulsion. "Wouldn't you hate to be connected with men that way? Oh I think it's an awful pity there has to *be* sex! It would be so much better if we could still be men and women, without that sort of thing."

Yvette pondered. Far in the background was the image of the gipsy as he had looked round at her, when she had said: The weather is so treacherous. She felt rather like Peter when the cock crew, as she denied him. Or rather, she did not deny the gipsy; she didn't care about his part in the show, anyhow. It was some hidden part of herself which she denied: that part which mysteriously and unconfessedly responded to him. And it was a strange, lustrous black cock which crew in mockery of her.

"Yes!" she said vaguely. "Yes! Sex is an awful bore, you know Lucille. When you haven't got it, you feel you *ought* to have it, somehow. And when you've got it—or *if* you have it—" she lifted her head and wrinkled her nose disdainfully— "you hate it.'"

"Oh I don't know!" cried Lucille. "I think I should *like* to be awfully in love with a man."

"You think so!" said Yvette, again wrinkling her nose. "But if you were you wouldn't."

"How do you know?" asked Lucille.

"Well, I don't really," said Yvette. "But I think so! Yes, I think so!"

"Oh, it's very likely!" said Lucille disgustedly. "And anyhow one would be sure to get out of love again, and it would be merely disgusting."

"Yes," said Yvette. "It's a problem." She hummed a little tune.

"Oh hang it all, it's not a problem for us two, yet. We're neither of us really in love, and we probably never shall be, so the problem is settled that way."

"I'm not so sure!" said Yvette sagely. "I'm not so sure. I believe, one day, I shall fall *awfully* in love."

"Probably you never will," said Lucille brutally. "That's what most old maids are thinking all the time."

Yvette looked at her sister from pensive but apparently insouciant eyes.

"Is it?" she said. "Do you really think so, Lucille? How perfectly awful for them, poor things! Why ever do they *care?*"

"Why do they?" said Lucille. "Perhaps they don't, really.—Probably it's all because people say: *Poor old girl, she couldn't catch a man.*"

"I suppose it is!" said Yvette. "They get to mind the beastly things people always do say about old maids. What a shame!"

"Anyhow we have a good time, and we do have lots of boys who make a fuss of us," said Lucille.

"Yes!" said Yvette. "Yes! But I couldn't possibly marry any of them."

"Neither could I," said Lucille. "But why shouldn't we! Why should we bother about marrying, when we have a perfectly good time with the boys who are awfully good sorts, and you must say, Yvette, awfully sporting and *decent* to us."

"Oh, they are!" said Yvette absently.

"I think it's time to think of marrying somebody," said Lucille, when, you feel you're *not* having a good time any more. Then marry, and just settle down."

"Quite!" said Yvette.

But now, under all her bland, soft amiability, she was annoyed with Lucille. Suddenly she wanted to turn her back on Lucille.

Besides, look at the shadows under poor Lucille's eyes, and the wistfulness in the beautiful eyes themselves. Oh, if some awfully nice, kind, protective sort of man would but marry her! And if the sporting Lucille would let him!

Yvette did not tell the rector, nor Granny, about the Eastwoods. It would only have started a lot of talk which she detested. The rector wouldn't have minded, for himself, privately. But he too knew the necessity of keeping as clear as possible from that poisonous, many-headed serpent, the tongue of the people.

"But I don't *want* you to come if your father doesn't know," cried the little Jewess.

"I suppose I'll have to tell him," said Yvette. "I'm sure he doesn't mind, really. But if he knew, he'd have to, I suppose."

The young officer looked at her with an odd amusement, bird-like and unemotional, in his keen eyes. He too was by way of falling in love with Yvette. It was her peculiar virgin tenderness, and her straying, absent-minded detachment from things, which attracted him.

She was aware of what was happening, and she rather preened herself. Eastwood piqued her fancy. Such a smart young officer, awfully good class, so calm and amazing with a motor-car, and quite a champion swimmer, it was intriguing to see him quietly, calmly washing dishes, smoking his pipe, doing his job so alert and skilful. Or, with the same interested care with which he made his investigation into the mysterious inside of an automobile, concocting jugged hare in the cottage kitchen. Then going out in the icy weather and cleaning his car till it looked like a live thing, like a cat when she has licked herself. Then coming in to talk so unassumingly and responsively, if briefly, with the little Jewess. And apparently, never bored. Sitting at the window with his pipe, in bad weather, silent for hours, abstracted, musing, yet with his athletic body alert in its stillness.

Yvette did not flirt with him. But she *did* like him.

"But what about your future?" she asked him.

"What about it?" he said, taking his pipe from his mouth, the unemotional point of a smile in his bird's eyes.

"A career! Doesn't every man have to carve out a career?—like some huge goose with gravy?" She gazed with odd naïveté into his eyes.

"I'm perfectly all right today, and I shall be all right tomorrow," he said, with a cold, decided look. "Why shouldn't my future be continuous todays and tomorrows?"

He looked at her with unmoved searching.

"Quite!" she said. "I hate jobs, and all that side of life." But she was thinking of the Jewess's money.

To which he did not answer. His anger was of the soft, snowy sort, which comfortably muffles the soul.

They had come to the point of talking philosophically together. The little Jewess looked a bit wan. She was curiously naïve and not possessive, in her attitude to the man. Nor was she at all catty with Yvette. Only rather wan, and dumb.

Yvette, on a sudden impulse, thought she had better clear herself.

"I think life's *awfully* difficult," she said.

"Life is!" cried the Jewess.

"What's so beastly, is that one is supposed to *fall in love,* and get married!" said Yvette, curling up her nose.

"Don't you *want* to fall in love and get married?" cried the Jewess, with great glaring eyes of astounded reproach.

"No, not particularly!" said Yvette. "Especially as one feels there's nothing else to do. It's an awful chickencoop one has to run into."

"But you don't know what love is?" cried the Jewess.

"No!" said Yvette. "Do you?"

"I!" bawled the tiny Jewess. "I! My goodness, don't I!" She looked with reflective gloom at Eastwood, who was smoking his pipe, the dimples of his disconnected amusement showing on his smooth, scrupulous face. He had a very fine, smooth skin, which yet did not suffer from the weather, so that his face looked naked as a baby's. But it was not a round face: it was characteristic enough, and took queer ironical dimples, like a mask which is comic but frozen.

"Do you mean to say you don't know what love is?" insisted the Jewess.

"No!" said Yvette, with insouciant candour. "I don't believe I do! Is it awful of me, at my age?"

"Is there never any man that makes you feel quite, quite different?" said the Jewess, with another big-eyed look at Eastwood. He smoked, utterly unimplicated.

"I don't think there is," said Yvette. "Unless—yes!—unless it is that gipsy"— she had put her head pensively sideways.

"Which gipsy?" bawled the little Jewess.

"The one who was a Tommy and looked after horses in Major Eastwood's regiment in the war," said Yvette coolly.

The little Jewess gazed at Yvette with great eyes of stupor.

"You're not in love with that *gipsy!*" she said.

"Well!" said Yvette. "I don't know. He's the only one that makes me feel— different! He really is!"

"But how? How? Has he ever *said* anything to you?"

"No! No!"

"Then how? What has he done?"

"Oh, just looked at me!"

"How?"

"Well you see, I don't know. But different! Yes, different! Different, quite different from the way any man ever looked at me."

"But *how* did he look at you?" insisted the Jewess.

"Why—as if he really, but *really, desired* me," said Yvette, her meditative face looking like the bud of a flower.

"What a vile fellow! What *right* had he to look at you like that?" cried the indignant Jewess.

"A cat may look at a king," calmly interposed the Major, and now his face had the smiles of a cat's face.

"You think he oughtn't to?" asked Yvette, turning to him.

"Certainly not! A gipsy fellow, with half a dozen dirty women trailing after him! Certainly not!" cried the tiny Jewess.

"I wondered!" said Yvette. "Because it *was* rather wonderful, really! And it *was* something quite different in my life."

"I think," said the Major, taking his pipe from his mouth, "that desire is the most wonderful thing in life. Anybody who can really feel it, is a king, and I envy nobody else!" He put back his pipe.

The Jewess looked at him stupefied.

"But Charles!" she cried. "Every common low man in Halifax feels nothing else!"

He again took his pipe from his mouth.

"That's merely appetite," he said.

And he put back his pipe.

"You think the gipsy is a real thing?" Yvette asked him. He lifted his shoulders.

"It's not for me to say," he replied. "If I were you, I should know, I shouldn't be asking other people."

"Yes—but—" Yvette trailed out.

"Charles! You're wrong! How *could* it be a real thing! As if she could possibly marry him and go round in a caravan!"

"I didn't say marry him," said Charles.

"Or a love affair! Why it's monstrous! What would she think of herself!—That's not love! That's—that's prostitution!"

Charles smoked for some moments.

"That gipsy was the best man we had, with horses. Nearly died of pneumonia. I thought he *was* dead. He's a resurrected man to me. I'm a resurrected man myself, as far as that goes." He looked at Yvette. "I was buried for twenty hours under snow," he said. "And not much the worse for it, when they dug me out."

There was a frozen pause in the conversation.

"Life's awful!" said Yvette.

"They dug me out by accident," he said.

"Oh!—" Yvette trailed slowly. "It might be destiny, you know."

To which he did not answer.

Eight

The rector heard about Yvette's intimacy with the Eastwoods, and she was somewhat startled by the result. She had thought he wouldn't care. Verbally, in his would-be humorous fashion, he was so entirely unconventional, such a frightfully good sport. As he said himself, he was a conservative anarchist; which meant, he was like a great many more people, a mere unbeliever. The anarchy extended to his humorous talk, and his secret thinking. The conservatism based on a mongrel fear of the anarchy, controlled every action. His thoughts, secretly, were something to be scared of. Therefore, in his life, he was fanatically afraid of the unconventional.

When his conservatism and his abject sort of fear were uppermost, he always lifted his lip and bared his teeth a little, in a dog-like sneer.

"I hear your latest friends are the half-divorced Mrs. Fawcett and the *maquereau* Eastwood," he said to Yvette.

She didn't know what a *maquereau* was, but she felt the poison in the rector's fangs.

"I just know them," she said. "They're awfully nice, really. And they'll be married in about a month's time."

The rector looked at her insouciant face with hatred. Somewhere inside him, he was cowed, he had been born cowed. And those who are born cowed are natural slaves, and deep instinct makes them fear with prisonous fear those who might suddenly snap the slave's collar round their necks.

It was for this reason the rector had so abjectly curled up, who still so abject curled up before She-who-was-Cynthia: because of his slave's fear of her contempt, the contempt of a born-free nature for a base-born nature.

Yvette too had a free-born quality. She too, one day, would know him, and clap the slave's collar of her contempt round his neck.

But should she? He would fight to the death, this time, first. The slave in him was cornered this time, like a cornered rat, and with the courage of a cornered rat.

"I suppose they're your sort!" he sneered.

504

"Well they are, really," she said, with that blithe vagueness. "I do like them awfully. They seem so solid, you know, so honest."

"You've got a peculiar notion of honesty!" he sneered. "A young sponge going off with a woman older than himself, so that he can live on her money! The woman leaving her home and her children! I don't know where you get your idea of honesty. Not from me, I hope.—And you seem to be very well acquainted with them, considering you say you just know them. Where did you meet them?"

"When I was out bicycling. They came along in their car, and we happened to talk. She told me at once who she was, so that I shouldn't make a mistake. She *is* honest."

Poor Yvette was struggling to bear up.

"And how often have you seen them since?"

"Oh, I've just been over twice."

"Over where?"

"To their cottage in Scoresby."

He looked at her in hate, as if he could kill her. And he backed away from her, against the window-curtains of his study, like a rat at bay. Somewhere in his mind he was thinking unspeakable depravities about his daughter, as he had thought them of She-who-was-Cynthia. He was powerless against the lowest insinuations of his own mind. And these depravities which he attributed to the still-uncowed, but frightened girl in front of him, made him recoil, showing all his fangs in his handsome face.

"So you just know them, do you?" he said. "Lying is in your blood, I see. I don't believe you get it from me."

Yvette half averted her mute face, and thought of Granny's bare-faced prevarication. She did not answer.

"What takes you creeping round such couples?" he sneered. "Aren't there enough decent people in the world, for you to know? Anyone would think you were a stray dog, having to run round indecent couples, because the decent ones wouldn't have you. Have you got something worse than lying, in your blood?"

"What have I got, worse than lying in my blood?" she asked. A cold deadness was coming over her. Was she abnormal, one of the semi-criminal abnormals? It made her feel cold and dead.

In his eyes, she was just brazening out the depravity that underlay her virgin, tender, bird-like face. She-who-was-Cynthia had been like this: a snow-flower. And he had convulsions of sadistic horror, thinking what might be the *actual* depravity of She-who-was-Cynthia. Even his *own* love for her, which had been the lust love of the born cowed, had been a depravity, in secret, to him. So what must an illegal love be?

"You know best yourself, what you have got," he sneered. "But it is something you had best curb, and quickly, if you don't intend to finish in a criminal-lunacy asylum."

"Why?" she said, pale and muted, numbed with frozen fear. "Why criminal lunacy? What have I done?"

"That is between you and your Maker," he jeered. "I shall never ask. But certain tendencies end in criminal lunacy, unless they are curbed in time."

"Do you mean like knowing the Eastwoods?" asked Yvette, after a pause of numb fear.

"Do I mean like nosing round such people as Mrs. Fawcett, a Jewess, and ex-Major Eastwood, a man who goes off with an older woman for the sake of her money? Why yes, I do!"

"But you *can't* say that," cried Yvette. "He's an awfully simple, straightforward man."

"He is apparently one of your sort."

"Well.—In a way, I thought he was. I thought you'd like him too," she said, simply, hardly knowing what she said.

The rector backed into the curtains, as if the girl menaced him with something fearful.

"Don't say any more," he snarled, abject. "Don't say any more. You've said too much, to implicate you. I don't want to learn any more horrors."

"But what horrors?" she persisted.

The very naïveté of her unscrupulous innocence repelled him, cowed him still more.

"Say no more!" he said, in a low, hissing voice. "But I will kill you before you shall go the way of your mother."

She looked at him, as he stood there backed against the velvet curtains of his study, his face yellow, his eyes distraught like a rat's with fear and rage and hate, and a numb, frozen loneliness came over her. For her too, the meaning had gone out of everything.

It was hard to break the frozen, sterile silence that ensued. At last, however, she looked at him. And in spite of herself, beyond her own knowledge, the contempt for him was in her young, clear, baffled eyes. It fell like the slave's collar over his neck, finally. .

"Do you mean I mustn't know the Eastwoods?" she said.

"You can know them if you wish," he sneered. "But you must not expect to associate with your Granny, and your Aunt Cissie, and Lucille, if you do. I cannot have *them* contaminated. Your Granny was a faithful wife and a faithful mother, if ever one existed. She has already had one shock of shame and abomination to endure. She shall never be exposed to another."

Yvette heard it all dimly, half hearing."

"I can send a note and say you disapprove," she said dimly.

"You follow your own course of action. But remember, you have to choose between clean people, and reverence for your Granny's blameless old age, and people who are unclean in their minds and their bodies."

Again there was a silence. Then she looked at him, and her face was more puzzled than anything. But somewhere at the back of her perplexity was that peculiar calm, virgin contempt of the free-born for the base-born. He, and all the Saywells, were base-born.

"All right," she said. "I'll write and say you disapprove."

He did not answer. He was partly flattered, secretly triumphant, but abjectedly.

"I have tried to keep this from your Granny and Aunt Cissie," he said. "It need not be public property, since you choose to make your friendship clandestine."

There was a dreary silence.

"All right," she said. "I'll go and write."

And she crept out of the room.

She addressed her little note to Mrs. Eastwood.

"Dear Mrs. Eastwood, Daddy doesn't approve of my coming to see you. So you will understand if we have to break if off. I'm awfully sorry—." That was all.

Yet she felt a dreary blank when she had posted her letter. She was now even afraid of her own thoughts. She wanted, now, to be held against the slender, fine-shaped breast of the gipsy. She wanted him to hold her in his arms, if only for once, for once, and comfort and confirm her. She wanted to be confirmed by him, against her father, who had only a repulsive fear of her.

And at the same time she cringed and winced, so that she could hardly walk, for fear the thought was obscene, a criminal lunacy. It seemed to wound her heels as she walked, the fear. The fear, the great cold fear of the base-born, her father, everything human and swarming. Like a great bog humanity swamped her, and she sank in, weak at the knees, filled with repulsion and fear of every person she met.

She adjusted herself, however, quite rapidly to her new conception of people. She had to live. It is useless to quarrel with one's bread and butter. And to expect a great deal out of life is puerile. So, with the rapid adaptability of the post-war generation, she adjusted herself to the new facts. Her father was what he was. He would always play up to appearances. She would do the same. She too would play up to appearances.

So, underneath the blithe, gossamer-straying insouciance, a certain hardness formed, like rock crystallising in her heart. She lost her illusions in the collapse of her sympathies. Outwardly, she seemed the same. Inwardly she was hard and detached, and, unknown to herself, revengeful.

Outwardly she remained the same. It was part of her game. While circumstances remained as they were, she must remain, at least in appearance, true to what was expected of her.

But the revengefulness came out in her new vision of people. Under the rector's apparently gallant handsomeness, she saw the weak, feeble nullity. And she despised him. Yet still, in a way, she liked him too. Feelings are so complicated.

It was Granny whom she came to detest with all her soul. That obese old woman, sitting there in her blindness like some great red-blotched fungus, her neck swallowed between her heaped-up shoulders and her rolling, ancient chins, so that she was neckless as a double potato, her Yvette really hated, with that pure, sheer hatred which is almost a joy. Her hate was so clear, that while she was feeling strong, she enjoyed it.

The old woman sat with her big, reddened face pressed a little back, her lace cap perched on her thin white hair, her stub nose still assertive, and her old mouth shut like a trap. This motherly old soul, her mouth gave her away. It always had been one of the compressed sort. But in her great age, it had gone like a toad's lipless, the jaw pressing up like the lower jaw of a trap. The look Yvette most hated, was the look of that lower jaw pressing relentlessly up, with an ancient prognathous thrust, so that the snub nose in turn was forced to press upwards, and the whole face was pressed a little back, beneath the big, wall like forehead. The will, the ancient, toad-like obscene *will* in the old woman, was fearful, once you saw it: a toad-like self-will that was godless, and less than human! It belonged to the old, enduring race of toads, or tortoises. And it made one feel that Granny would never die. She would live on like these higher reptiles, in a state of semi-coma, forever.

Yvette dared not even suggest to her father that Granny was not perfect. He would have threatened his daughter with the lunatic asylum. That was the threat he always seemed to have up his sleeve: the lunatic asylum. Exactly as if a distaste for Granny and for that horrible house of relatives was in itself a proof of lunacy, dangerous lunacy.

Yet in one of her moods of irritable depression, she did once fling out:

"How perfectly beastly, this house is! Aunt Lucy comes, and Aunt Nell, and Aunt Alice, and they make a ring like a ring of crows, with Granny and Aunt Cissie, all lifting their skirts up and warming their legs at the fire, and shutting Lucille and me out. We're nothing but outsiders in this beastly house!"

Her father glanced at her curiously. But she managed to put a petulance into her speech, and a mere cross rudeness into her look, so that he could laugh, as at a childish tantrum. Somewhere, though, he knew that she coldly, venomously meant what she said, and he was wary of her.

Her life seemed now nothing but an irritable friction against the unsavoury household of the Saywells, in which she was immersed. She loathed the rectory with a loathing that consumed her life, a loathing so strong, that she could not really go away from the place. While it endured, she was spell-bound to it, in revulsion.

She forgot the Eastwoods again. After all! what was the revolt of the little Jewess, compared to Granny and the Saywell bunch! A husband was never more than a semicasual thing! But a family!—an awful, smelly family that would never disperse, stuck half dead round the base of a fungoid old woman! How was one to cope with that?"

She did not forget the gipsy entirely. But she had no time for him. She, who was bored almost to agony, and who had nothing at all to do, she had not time to think even, seriously, of anything. Time being, after all, only the current of the soul in its flow.

She saw the gipsy twice. Once he came to the house, with things to sell. And she, watching him from the landing window, refused to go down. He saw her too, as he was putting his things back into his cart. But he too gave no sign. Being of a race that exists only to be harrying the outskirts of our society, forever hostile and living only by spoil, he was too much master to himself, and too wary, to expose himself openly to the vast and gruesome clutch of our law. He had been through the war. He had been enslaved against his will, that time.

So now, he showed himself at the rectory, and slowly, quietly busied himself at his cart outside the white gate, with that air of silent and forever-unyielding outsideness which gave him his lonely, predative grace. He knew she saw him. And she should see him unyielding, quietly hawking his copper vessels, on an old, old war-path against such as herself.

Such as herself? Perhaps he was mistaken. Her heart, in its stroke, now rang hard as his hammer upon his copper, beating against circumstances. But he struck stealthily on the outside, and she still more secretly on the inside of the establishment. She liked him. She liked the quiet, noiseless clean-cut presence of him. She liked that mysterious endurance in him, which endures in opposition, without any idea of victory. And she liked that peculiar added relentlessness, the disillusion in hostility, which belongs to after the war. Yes, if she belonged to any side, and to any clan, it was to his. Almost she could have found in her heart to go with him, and be a pariah gipsy-woman.

But she was born inside the pale. And she liked comfort, and a certain prestige. Even as a mere rector's daughter, one did have a certain prestige. And she liked that. Also she liked to chip against the pillars of the temple, from the inside. She wanted to be safe under the temple roof. Yet she enjoyed chipping fragments off the supporting pillars. Doubtless many fragments had been whittled away from the pillars of the Philistine, before Samson pulled the temple down.

"I'm not sure one shouldn't have one's fling till one is twenty-six, and then give in, and marry!"

This was Lucille's philosophy, learned from older women. Yvette was twenty-one. It meant she had five more years in which to have this precious fling. And the fling meant, at the moment, the gipsy. The marriage, at the age of twenty-six, meant Leo or Gerry.

So, a woman could eat her cake and have her bread and butter.

Yvette, pitched in gruesome, deadlocked hostility to the Saywell household, was very old and very wise: with the agedness and the wisdom of the young, which always overleaps the agedness and the wisdom of the old, or the elderly.

The second time, she met the gipsy by accident. It was March, and sunny weather, after unheard-of rains. Celandines were yellow in the hedges, and primroses among the rocks. But still there came a smell of sulphur from far-away steel-works, out of the steel-blue sky.

And yet it was spring.

Yvette was cycling slowly along by Codnor Gate, past the lime quarries, when she saw the gipsy coming away from the door of a stone cottage. His cart stood there in the road. He was returning with his brooms and copper things, to the cart.

She got down from her bicycle. As she saw him, she loved with curious tenderness, the slim lines of his body in the green jersey, the turn of his silent face. She felt she knew him better than she knew anybody on earth, even Lucille, and belonged to him, in some way, for ever.

"Have you made anything new and nice?" she asked innocently, looking at his copper things.

"I don't think," he said, glancing back at her.

The desire was still there, still curious and naked, in his eyes. But it was more remote, the boldness was diminished. There was a tiny glint, as if he might dislike her. But this dissolved again, as he saw her looking among his bits of copper and brasswork. She searched them diligently.

There was a little oval brass plate, with a queer figure like a palm-tree beaten upon it.

"I like that," she said. "How much is it?"

"What you like," he said.

This made her nervous: he seemed off-hand, almost mocking.

"I'd rather you said," she told him, looking up at him.

"You give me what you like," he said.

"No!" she said, suddenly. "If you won't tell me I won't have it."

"All right," he said. "Two shilling."

She found half-a-crown, and he drew from his pocket a handful of silver, from which he gave her her sixpence.

"The old gipsy dreamed something about you," he said, looking at her with curious, searching eyes.

"Did she!" cried Yvette, at once interested. "What was it?"

"She said: Be braver in your heart, or you lose your game. She said it this way: Be braver in your body, or your luck will leave you. And she said as well: Listen for the voice of water."

Yvette was very much impressed.

"And what does it mean?" she asked.

"I asked her," he said. "She says she don't know."

"Tell me again what it was," said Yvette.

" 'Be braver in your body, or your luck will go.' And: 'Listen for the voice of water.' "

He looked in silence at her soft, pondering face. Something almost like a perfume seemed to flow from her young bosom direct to him, in a grateful connection.

"I'm to be braver in my body, and I'm to listen for the voice of water! All right!" she said. "I don't understand, but perhaps I shall."

She looked at him with clear eyes. Man or woman is made up of many selves. With one self, she loved this gipsy man. With many selves, she ignored him or had a distaste for him.

"You're not coming up to the Head no more?" he asked.

Again she looked at him absently.

"Perhaps I will," she said, "some time. Some time!"

"Spring weather!" he said, smiling faintly and glancing round at the sun. "We're going to break camp soon, and go away."

"When?" she said.

"Perhaps next week."

"Where to?"

Again he made a move with his head.

"Perhaps up north," he said.

She looked at him.

"All right!" she said. "Perhaps I *will* come up before you go, and say goodbye! to your wife and to the old woman who sent me the message."

Nine

Yvette did not keep her promise. The few March days were lovely, and she let them slip. She had a curious reluctance always, towards taking action, or making any real move of her own. She always wanted someone else to make a move for her, as if she did not want to play her own game of life.

She lived as usual, went out to her friends, to parties, and danced with the undiminished Leo. She wanted to go up and say goodbye to the gipsies. She wanted to. And nothing prevented her.

On the Friday afternoon especially she wanted to go. It was sunny, and the last yellow crocuses down the drive were in full blaze, wide open, the first bees rolling in them. The Papple rushed under the stone bridge, uncannily full, nearly filling the arches. There was the scent of a mezereon tree.

And she felt too lazy, too lazy, too lazy. She strayed in the garden by the river, half dreamy, expecting something. While the gleam of spring sun lasted, she would be out of doors. Indoors Granny, sitting back like some awful old prelate, in her bulk of black silk and her white lace cap, was warming her feet by the fire, and hearing everything that Aunt Nell had to say. Friday was Aunt Nell's day. She usually came for lunch, and left after an early tea. So the mother and the large, rather common daughter, who was a widow at the age of forty, sat gossiping by the fire, while Aunt Cissie prowled in and out. Friday was the rector's day for going to town: it was also the housemaid's half day.

Yvette sat on a wooden seat in the garden, only a few feet above the bank of the swollen river, which rolled a strange, uncanny mass of water. The crocuses were passing in the ornamental beds, the grass was dark green where it was mown, the laurels looked a little brighter. Aunt Cissie appeared at the top of the porch steps, and called to ask if Yvette wanted that early cup of tea. Because of the river just below, Yvette could not hear what Aunt Cissie said, but she guessed, and shook her head. An early cup of tea, indoors, when the sun actually shone? No thanks!

She was conscious of her gipsy, as she sat there musing in the sun. Her soul had the half painful, half easing knack of leaving her, and straying away to some place, to somebody that had caught her imagination. Some days she would be all the Framleys, even though she did not go near them. Some days, she was all the time in spirit with the Eastwoods. And today it was the gipsies. She was up at their encampment in the quarry. She saw the man hammering his copper, lifting his head to look at the road; and the children playing in the horseshelter: and the women, the gipsy's wife and the strong, elderly woman, coming home with their packs, along with the elderly man. For this afternoon, she felt intensely that *that* was home for her: the gipsy camp, the fire, the stool, the man with the hammer, the old crone.

It was part of her nature, to get these fits of yearning for some place she knew; to be in a certain place; with somebody who meant home to her. This afternoon it was the gipsy camp. And the man in the green jersey made it home to her. Just to be where he was, that was to be at home. The caravans, the brats, the other women: everything was natural to her, her home, as if she had been born there. She wondered if the gipsy was aware of her: if he could see her sitting on the stool by the fire; if he would lift his head and see her as she rose, looking at him slowly and significantly, turning towards the steps of his caravan. Did he know? Did he know?

Vaguely she looked up the steep of dark larch trees north of the house, where unseen the road climbed, going towards the Head. There was nothing, and her glance strayed down again. At the foot of the slope the river turned, thrown back harshly, ominously, against the low rocks across stream, then pouring past the garden to the bridge. It was unnaturally full, and whitey-muddy, and ponderous, "Listen for the voice of water," she said to herself. "No need to listen for it, if the voice means the noise!"

And again she looked at the swollen river breaking angrily as it came round the bend. Above it the black-looking kitchen garden hung, and the hard-natured fruit trees. Everything was on the tilt, facing south and south-west, for the sun. Behind, above the house and the kitchen garden hung the steep little wood of withered-seeming larches. The gardener was working in the kitchen garden, high up there, by the edge of the larch-wood.

She heard a call. It was Aunt Cissie and Aunt Nell. They were on the drive, waving Goodbye! Yvette waved back. Then Aunt Cissie, pitching her voice against the waters, called:

"I shan't be long. Don't forget Granny is alone!"

"All right!" screamed Yvette rather ineffectually.

And she sat on her bench and watched the two undignified, long-coated women walk slowly over the bridge and begin the curving climb on the opposite slope, Aunt Nell carrying a sort of suit-case in which she brought a few goods for Granny and took back vegetables or whatever the rectory garden or cupboard was yielding. Slowly the two figures diminished, on the whitish, up-curving road, laboring slowly up towards Papplewick village. Aunt Cissie was going as far as the village for something.

The sun was yellowing to decline. What a pity! Oh what a pity the sunny day was going, and she would have to turn indoors, to those hateful rooms, and Granny! Aunt Cissie would be back directly: it was past five. And all the others would be arriving from town, rather irritable and tired, soon after six.

As she looked uneasily round, she heard, across the running of water, the sharp noise of a horse and cart rattling on the road hidden in the larch trees. The gardener was looking up too. Yvette turned away again, lingering, strolling by the full river a few paces, unwilling to go in; glancing up the road to see if Aunt Cissie were coming. If she saw her, she would go indoors.

She heard somebody shouting, and looked round. Down the path through the larch-trees the gipsy was bounding. The gardener, away beyond, was also running. Simultaneously she became aware of a great roar, which, before she could move, accumulated to a vast deafening snarl. The gipsy was gesticulating. She looked round, behind her.

And to her horror and amazement, round the bend of the river she saw a shaggy, tawny wavefront of water advancing like a wall of lions. The roaring sound wiped out everything. She was powerless, too amazed and wonder-struck, she wanted to see it.

Before she could think twice, it was near, a roaring cliff of water. She almost fainted with horror. She heard the scream of the gipsy, and looked up to see him bounding upon her, his black eyes starting out of his head.

"Run!" he screamed, seizing her arm.

And in the instant the first wave was washing her feet from under her, swirling, in the insane noise, which suddenly for some reason seemed like stillness, with a devouring flood over the garden. The horrible mowing of water!

The gipsy dragged her heavily, lurching, plunging, but still keeping foot-hold both of them, towards the house. She was barely conscious: as if the flood was in her soul.

There was one grass-banked terrace of the garden, near the path round the house. The gipsy clawed his way up this terrace to the dry level of the path, dragging her after him, and sprang with her past the windows to the porch steps. Before they got there, a new great surge of water came mowing, mowing trees down even, and mowed them down too.

Yvette felt herself gone in an agonising millrace of icy water, whirled, with only the fearful grip of the gipsy's hand on her wrist. They were both down and gone. She felt a dull but stunning bruise somewhere.

Then he pulled her up. He was up, streaming forth water, clinging to the stem of the great wisteria that grew against the wall, crushed against the wall by the water. Her head was above water, he held her arm till it seemed dislocated: but she could not get her footing. With a ghastly sickness like a dream, she struggled and struggled, and could not get her feet. Only his hand was locked on her wrist.

He dragged her nearer till her one hand caught his leg. He nearly went down again. But the wisteria held him, and he pulled her up to him. She clawed at him, horribly, and got to her feet, he hanging on like a man torn in two, to the wisteria trunk.

The water was above her knees. The man and she looked into each other's ghastly streaming faces.

"Get to the steps!" he screamed.

It was only just round the corner: four strides! She looked at him: she could not go. His eyes glared on her like a tiger's, and he pushed her from him. She clung to the wall, and the water seemed to abate a little. Round the corner she staggered, but staggering, reeled and was pitched up against the cornice of the balustrade of the porch steps, the man after her.

They got on to the steps, when another roar was heard amid the roar, and the wall of the house shook. Up heaved the water round their legs again, but the gipsy had opened the hall door. In they poured with the water, reeling to the stairs. And as they did so, they saw the short but strange bulk of Granny emerge in the hall, away down from the dining-room door. She had her hands lifted and clawing, as the first water swirled round her legs, and her coffin-like mouth was opened in a hoarse scream.

Yvette was blind to everything but the stairs. Blind, unconscious of everything save the steps rising beyond the water, she clambered up like a wet, shuddering cat, in a state of unconsciousness. It was not till she was on the landing, dripping and shuddering till she could not stand erect, clinging to the banisters, while the house shook and the water raved below, that she was aware of the sodden gipsy, in paroxysms of coughing at the head of the stairs, his cap gone, his black hair over his eyes, peering between his washed-down hair at the sickening heave of water below, in the hall. Yvette, fainting, looked too, and saw Granny bob up, like a strange float, her face purple, her blind blue eyes bolting, spume hissing from her mouth. One old purple hand clawed at a banister rail, and held for a moment, showing the glint of a wedding ring.

The gipsy, who had coughed himself free and pushed back his hair, said to that awful float-like face below:

"Not good enough! Not good enough!"

With a low thud like thunder, the house was struck again, and shuttered, and a strange cracking, rattling, spitting noise began. Up heaved the water like a sea. The hand was gone, all sign of anything was gone, but upheaving water.

Yvette turned in blind unconscious frenzy, staggering like a wet cat to the upper stair-case, and climbing swiftly. It was not till she was at the door of her room that she stopped, paralysed by the sound of a sickening, tearing crash' while the house swayed.

"The house is coming down!" yelled the green-white face of the gipsy, in her face.

He glared into her crazed face.

"Where is the chimney? the back chimney?—which room? The chimney will stand—."

He glared with strange ferocity into her face, forcing her to understand. And she nodded with a strange, crazed poise, nodded quite serenely, saying:

"In here! In here! It's all right."

They entered her room, which had a narrow fire-place. It was a back room with two windows, one on each side the great chimney-flue. The gipsy, coughing bitterly and trembling in every limb, went to the window to look out.

Below, between the house and the steep rise of the hill, was a wild mill-race, of water rushing with refuse, including Rover's green dog-kennel. The gipsy coughed and coughed, and gazed down blankly. Tree after tree went down, mown by the water, which must have been ten feet deep.

Shuddering and pressing his sodden arms on his sodden breast, a look of resignation on his livid face, he turned to Yvette. A fearful tearing noise tore the house, then there was a deep, watery explosion. Something had gone down, some part of the house, the floor heaved and wavered beneath them. For some moments both were suspended, stupefied. Then he roused.

"Not good enough! Not good enough! This will stand. This here will stand. See that chimney! like a tower. Yes! All right! All right. You take your clothes off and go to bed. You'll die of the cold."

"It's all right! It's quite all right!" she said to him, sitting on a chair and looking up into his face with her white, insane little face, round which the hair was plastered.

"No!" he cried. "No! Take your things off and I rub you with this towel. I rub myself. If the house falls then die warm. If it don't fall, then live, not die of pneumonia."

Coughing, shuddering violently, he pulled up his jersey hem and wrestled with all his shuddering, cold-cracked might, to get off his wet, tight jersey.

"Help me!" he cried, his face muffled.

She seized the edge of the jersey, obediently, and pulled with all her might. The garment came over his head, and he stood in his braces.

"Take your things off! Rub with this towel!" he commanded ferociously, the savageness of the war on him. And like a thing obsessed, he pushed himself out of his trousers, and got out of his wet, clinging shirt, emerging slim and livid, shuddering in every fibre with cold and shock.

He seized a towel, and began quickly to rub his body, his teeth chattering like plates rattling together. Yvette dimly saw it was wise. She tried to get out of her dress. He pulled the horrible wet death-gripping thing off her, then, resuming his rubbing, went to the door, tip-toeing on the wet floor.

There he stood, naked, towel in hand, petrified. He looked west, towards where the upper landing window had been, and was looking into the sunset, over an insane sea of waters, bristling with uptorn trees and refuse. The end corner of the house, where porch had been, and the stairs, had gone. The wall had fallen, leaving the floors sticking out. The stairs had gone.

Motionless, he watched the water. A cold wind blew in upon him. He clenched his rattling teeth with a great effort of will, and turned into the room again, closing the door.

Yvette, naked, shuddering so much that she was sick, was trying to wipe herself dry.

"All right!" he cried. "All right! The water don't rise no more! All right!"

With his towel he began to rub her, himself shaking all over, but holding her

gripped by the shoulder, and slowly, numbedly rubbing her tender body, even
trying to rub up into some dryness the pitiful hair of her small head.

Suddenly he left off.

"Better lie in the bed," he commanded, "I want to rub myself."

His teeth went snap-snap-snap-snap, in great snaps, cutting off his words. Yvette
crept shaking and semi-conscious into her bed. He, making strained efforts to
hold himself still and rub himself warm, went again to the north window, to
look out.

The water had risen a little. The sun had gone down, and there was a reddish
glow. He rubbed his hair into a black, wet tangle, then paused for breath, in a
sudden access of shuddering, then looked out again, then rubbed again on his
breast, and began to cough afresh, because of the water he had swallowed. His
towel was red: he had hurt himself somewhere: but he felt nothing.

There was still the strange huge noise of water, and the horrible bump of
things bumping against the walls. The wind was rising with sundown, cold and
hard. The house shook with explosive thuds, and weird, weird frightening noises
came up.

A terror creeping over his soul, he went again to the door. The wind, roaring
with the waters, blew in as he opened it. Through the awesome gap in the house
he saw the world, the waters, the chaos of horrible waters, the twilight, the perfect
new moon high above the sunset, a faint thing, and clouds pushing dark into
the sky, on the cold, blustery wind.

Clenching his teeth again, fear mingling with resignation, or fatalism, in his
soul, he went into the room and closed the door, picking up her towel to see if
it were drier than his own, and less blood-stained, again rubbing his head, and
going to the window.

He turned away, unable to control his spasms of shivering. Yvette had disappeared right under the bedclothes, and nothing of her was visible but a shivering
mound under the white quilt. He laid his hand on this shivering mound, as if
for company. It did not stop shivering.

"All right!" he said. "All right! Water's going down."

She suddenly uncovered her head and peered out at him from a white face.
She peered into his greenish, curiously calm face, semi-conscious. His teeth were
chattering unheeded, as he gazed down at her, his black eyes still full of the fire
of life and a certain vagabond calm of fatalistic resignation.

"Warm me!" she moaned, with chattering teeth. "Warm me! I shall die of
shivering."

A terrible convulsion went through her curled-up white body, enough indeed
to rupture her and cause her to die.

The gipsy nodded, and took her in his arms, and held her in a clasp like a
vice, to still his own shuddering. He himself was shuddering fearfully, and only
semi-conscious. It was the shock.

The vice-like grip of his arms round her seemed to her the only stable point
in her consciousness. It was a fearful relief to her heart, which was strained to
bursting. And though his body, wrapped round her strange and lithe and powerful,

like tentacles, rippled with shuddering as an electric current, still the rigid tension of the muscles that held her clenched steadied them both, and gradually the sickening violence of the shuddering, caused by shock, abated, in his body first, then in hers, and the warmth revived between them. And as it roused, their tortured, semiconscious minds became unconscious, they passed away into sleep.

Ten

The sun was shining in heaven before men were able to get across the Papple with ladders. The bridge was gone. But the flood had abated, and the house, that leaned forwards as if it were making a stiff bow to the stream, stood now in mud and wreckage, with a great heap of fallen masonry and debris at the south-west corner. Awful were the gaping mouths of rooms!

Inside, there was no sign of life. But across-stream the gardener had come to reconnoitre, and the cook appeared, thrilled with curiosity. She had escaped from the back door and up through the larches to the high-road, when she saw the gipsy bound past the house: thinking he was coming to murder somebody. At the little top gate she had found his cart standing. The gardener had led the horse away to the Red Lion up at Darley, when night had fallen.

This the men from Papplewick learned when at last they got across the stream with ladders, and to the back of the house. They were nervous, fearing a collapse of the building, whose front was all undermined and whose back was choked up. They gazed with horror at the silent shelves of the rector's rows of books, in his torn-open study; at the big brass bed-stead of Granny's room, the bed so deep and comfortably made, but one brass leg of the bed-stead perched tentatively over the torn void; at the wreckage of the maid's room upstairs. The housemaid and the cook wept. Then a man climbed in cautiously through a smashed kitchen window, into the jungle and morass of the ground floor. He found the body of the old woman: or at least he saw her foot, in its flat black slipper, muddily protruding from a mudheap of debris. And he fled.

The gardener said he was sure that Miss Yvette was not in the house. He had seen her and the gipsy swept away. But the policeman insisted on a search, and the Framley boys rushing up at last, the ladders were roped together. Then the whole party set up a loud yell. But without result. No answer from within.

A ladder was up, Bob Framley climbed, smashed a window, and clambered into Aunt Cissie's room. The perfect homely familiarity of everything terrified him like ghosts. The house might go down any minute.

They had just got the ladder up to the top floor, when men came running from Darley, saying the old gipsy had been to the Red Lion for the horse and cart, leaving word that his son had seen Yvette at the top of the house. But by that time the policeman was smashing the window of Yvette's room.

Yvette, fast asleep, started from under the bed-clothes with a scream, as the glass flew. She clutched the sheets round her nakedness. The policeman uttered a startled yell, which he converted into a cry of: Miss Yvette! Miss Yvette! He turned round on the ladder, and shouted to the faces below.

"Miss Yvette's in bed!—in bed!"

And he perched there on the ladder, an unmarried man, clutching the window in peril, not knowing what to do.

Yvette sat up in bed, her hair in a matted tangle, and stared with wild eyes, clutching up the sheets at her naked breast. She had been so very fast asleep, that she was still not there.

The policeman, terrified at the flabby ladder, climbed into the room, saying:

"Don't be frightened, Miss! Don't you worry any more about it. You're safe now."

And Yvette, so dazed, thought he meant the gipsy. Where was the gipsy? This was the first thing in her mind. Where was her gipsy of this world's-end night?

He was gone! He was gone! And a policeman was in the room! A policeman! She rubbed her hand over her dazed brow.

"If you'll get dressed, Miss, we can get you down to safe ground. The house is likely to fall. I suppose there's nobody in the other rooms?"

He stepped gingerly into the passage, and gazed in terror through the torn-out end of the house, and far-off saw the rector coming down in a motor-car, on the sunlit hill.

Yvette, her face gone numb and disappointed, got up quickly, closing the bed-clothes, and looked at herself a moment, then opened her drawers for clothing. She dressed herself, then looked in a mirror, and saw her matted hair with horror. Yet she did not care. The gipsy was gone, anyhow.

Her own clothes lay in a sodden heap. There was a great sodden place on the carpet where his had been, and two blood-stained filthy towels. Otherwise there was no sign of him.

She was tugging at her hair when the policeman tapped at her door. She called him to come in. He saw with relief that she was dressed and in her right senses.

"We'd better get out of the house as soon as possible, Miss," he reiterated. "It might fall any minute."

"Really!" said Yvette calmly. "Is it as bad as that?"

There were great shouts. She had to go to the window. There, below, was the rector, his arms wide open, tears streaming down his face.

" 'I'm perfectly all right, Daddy!" she said, with the calmness of her contradictory feelings. She would keep the gipsy a secret from him. At the same time, tears ran down her face.

"Don't you cry, Miss, don't you cry! The rector's lost his mother, but he's thanking his stars to have his daughter. We all thought you were gone as well, we did that!"

"Is Granny drowned?" said Yvette.

"I'm afraid she is, poor lady!" said the policeman, with a grave face.

Yvette wept away into her hanky, which she had had to fetch from a drawer.

"Dare you go down that ladder, Miss?" said the policeman.

Yvette looked at the sagging depth of it, and said promptly to herself: No! Not for anything!—But then she remembered the gipsy's saying: "Be braver in the body."

"Have you been in all the other rooms?" she said, in her keeping, turning to the policeman.

"Yes, Miss! But you was the only person in the house, you know, save the old lady. Cook got away in time, and Lizzie was up at her mother's. It was only you and the poor old lady we was fretting about. Do you think you dare go down that ladder?"

"Oh, yes!" said Yvette with indifference. The gipsy was gone anyway.

And now the rector in torment watched his tall, slender daughter slowly stepping backwards down the sagging ladder, the policeman, peering heroically from the smashed window, holding the ladder's top ends.

At the foot of the ladder Yvette appropriately fainted in her father's arms, and was borne away with him, in the car, by Bob, to the Framely home. There the poor Lucille, a ghost of ghosts, wept with relief till she had hysterics, and even Aunt Cissie cried out among her tears: "Let the old be taken and the young spared! Oh I *can't* cry for the Mater, now Yvette is spared!"

And she wept gallons.

The flood was caused by the sudden bursting of the great reservoir, up in Papple Highdale, five miles from the rectory. It was found out later that an ancient, perhaps even a Roman mine tunnel, unsuspected, undreamed of, beneath the reservoir dam, had collapsed, undermining the whole dam. That was why the Papple had been, for the last day, so uncannily full. And then the dam had burst.

The rector and the two girls stayed on at the Framley's, till a new home could be found. Yvette did not attend Granny's funeral. She stayed in bed.

Telling her tale, she only told how the gipsy had got her inside the porch, and she had crawled to the stairs out of the water. It was known that he had escaped: the old gipsy had said so, when he fetched the horse and cart from the Red Lion. Yvette could tell little. She was vague, confused, she seemed hardly to remember anything. But that was just like her.

It was Bob Framley who said:

"You know, I think that gipsy deserves a medal."

The whole family was suddenly struck.

"Oh, we *ought* to thank him!" cried Lucille.

The rector himself went with Bob in the car. But the quarry was deserted. The gipsies had lifted camp and gone, no one knew whither.

And Yvette, lying in bed, moaned in her heart: Oh, I love him! I love him! I love him!—The grief over him kept her prostrate. Yet practically, she too was acquiescent in the fact of his disappearance. Her young soul knew the wisdom of it.

But after Granny's funeral, she received a little letter, dated from some unknown place.

"Dear Miss, I see in the paper you are all right after your ducking, as is the same with me. I hope I see you again one day, maybe at Tideswell cattle fair, or maybe we come that way again. I come that day to say goodbye! and I never said it, well, the water give no time, but I live in hopes. Your obdt. servant Joe Boswell."

And only then she realised that he had a name.

Love Among the Haystacks

I

The two large fields lay on a hillside facing south. Being newly cleared of hay, they were golden green, and they shone almost blindingly in the sunlight. Across the hill, half-way up, ran a high hedge, that flung its black shadow finely across the molten glow of the sward. The stack was being built just above the hedge. It was of great size, massive, but so silvery and delicately bright in tone that it seemed not to have weight. It rose dishevelled and radiant among the steady, golden-green glare of the field. A little farther back was another, finished stack.

The empty wagon was just passing through the gap in the hedge. From the far-off corner of the bottom field, where the sward was still striped grey with winrows, the loaded wagon launched forward, to climb the hill to the stack. The white dots of the hay-makers showed distinctly among the hay.

The two brothers were having a moment's rest, waiting for the load to come up. They stood wiping their brows with their arms, sighing from the heat and the labour of placing the last load. The stack they rode was high, lifting them up above the hedge-tops, and very broad, a great slightly-hollowed vessel into which the sunlight poured, in which the hot, sweet scent of hay was suffocating. Small and inefficacious the brothers looked, half-submerged in the loose, great trough, lifted high up as if on an altar reared to the sun.

Maurice, the younger brother, was a handsome young fellow of twenty-one, careless and debonair, and full of vigour. His grey eyes, as he taunted his brother, were bright and baffled with a strong emotion. His swarthy face had the same peculiar smile, expectant and glad and nervous, of a young man roused for the first time in passion.

'Tha sees,' he said, as he leaned on the pommel of his fork, 'tha thowt as tha'd done me one, didna ter?' He smiled as he spoke, then fell again into his pleasant torment of musing.

'I thought nowt—tha knows so much,' retorted Geoffrey, with the touch of a sneer. His brother had the better of him. Geoffrey was a very heavy, hulking fellow, a year older than Maurice. His blue eyes were unsteady, they glanced away quickly; his mouth was morbidly sensitive. One felt him wince away, through the whole of his great body. His inflamed self-consciousness was a disease in him.

'Ah but though, I know tha did,' mocked Maurice. 'Tha went slinkin' off'— Geoffrey winced convulsively—'thinking as that wor the last night as any of us'ud ha'e ter stop here, an' so tha'd leave me to sleep out, though it wor thy turn——'

He smiled to himself, thinking of the result of Geoffrey's ruse.

'I didna go slinkin' off neither,' retorted Geoffrey, in his heavy, clumsy manner, wincing at the phrase. 'Didna my feyther send me to fetch some coal——'

'Oh yes, oh yes—we know all about it. But tha sees what tha missed, my lad.'

Maurice, chuckling, threw himself on his back in the bed of hay. There was absolutely nothing in his world, then, except the shallow ramparts of the stack, and the blazing sky. He clenched his fists tight, threw his arms across his face, and braced his muscles again. He was evidently very much moved, so acutely that it was hardly pleasant, though he still smiled. Geoffrey, standing behind him, could just see his red mouth, with the young moustache like black fur, curling back and showing the teeth in a smile. The elder brother leaned his chin on the pommel of his fork, looking out across the country.

Far away was the faint blue heap of Nottingham. Between, the country lay under a haze of heat, with here and there a flag of colliery smoke waving. But near at hand, at the foot of the hill, across the deep-hedged high road, was only the silence of the old church and the castle farm, among their trees. The large view only made Geoffrey more sick. He looked away, to the wagons crossing the field below him, the empty cart like a big insect moving down hill, the load coming up, rocking like a ship, the brown head of the horse ducking, the brown knees lifted and planted strenuously. Geoffrey wished it would be quick.

'Tha didna think——'

Geoffrey started, coiled within himself, and looked down at the handsome lips moving in speech below the brown arms of his brother.

'Tha didna think 'er'd be thur wi' me—or tha wouldna ha' left me to it,' Maurice said, ending with a little laugh of excited memory. Geoffrey flushed with hate, and had an impulse to set his foot on that moving, taunting mouth, which was there below him. There was silence for a time, then, in a peculiar tone of delight, Maurice's voice came again, spelling out the words, as it were:

> 'Ich bin klein, mein Herz ist rein,
> Ist niemand d'rin als Christ allein.'

Maurice chuckled, then, convulsed at a twinge of recollection, keen as pain, he twisted over, pressed himself into the hay.

'Can thee say thy prayers in German?' came his muffled voice.

'I non want,' growled Geoffrey.

Maurice chuckled. His face was quite hidden, and in the dark he was going over again his last night's experiences.

'What about kissing 'er under th' ear, Sonny,' he said, in a curious, uneasy tone. He writhed, still startled and inflamed by his first contact with love.

Geoffrey's heart swelled within him, and things went dark. He could not see the landscape.

'An' there's just a nice two-handful of her bosom,' came the low, provocative tones of Maurice, who seemed to be talking to himself.

The two brothers were both fiercely shy of women, and until this hay harvest, the whole feminine sex had been represented by their mother and in presence of any other women they were dumb louts. Moreover, brought up by a proud mother, a stranger in the country, they held the common girls as beneath them, because beneath their mother, who spoke pure English, and was very quiet. Loud-mouthed and broad-tongued the common girls were. So these two young men had grown up virgin but tormented.

Now again Maurice had the start of Geoffrey, and the elder brother was deeply mortified. There was a danger of his sinking into a morbid state, from sheer lack of living, lack of interest. The foreign governess at the Vicarage, whose garden lay beside the top field, had talked to the lads through the hedge, and had fascinated them. There was a great elder bush, with its broad creamy flowers crumbling on to the garden path, and into the field. Geoffrey never smelled elder-flower without starting and wincing, thinking of the strange foreign voice that had so startled him as he mowed out with the scythe in the hedge bottom. A baby had run through the gap, and the Fräulein, calling in German, had come brushing down the flowers in pursuit. She had started so on seeing a man standing there in the shade, that for a moment she could not move: and then she had blundered into the rake which was lying by his side. Geoffrey, forgetting she was a woman when he saw her pitch forward, had picked her up carefully, asking: 'Have you hurt you?'

Then she had broken into a laugh, and answered in German, showing him her arms, and knitting her brows. She was nettled rather badly.

'You want a dock leaf,' he said. She frowned in a puzzled fashion.

'A dock leaf?' she repeated. He had rubbed her arms with the green leaf.

And now, she had taken to Maurice. She had seemed to prefer himself at first. Now she had sat with Maurice in the moonlight, and had let him kiss her. Geoffrey sullenly suffered, making no fight.

Unconsciously, he was looking at the Vicarage garden. There she was, in a golden-brown dress. He took off his hat, and held up his right hand in greeting to her. She, a small, golden figure, waved her hand negligently from among the potato rows. He remained, arrested, in the same posture, his hat in his left hand, his right arm upraised, thinking. He could tell by the negligence of her greeting that she was waiting for Maurice. What did she think of himself? Why wouldn't she have him?

Hearing the voice of the wagoner leading the load, Maurice rose. Geoffrey still stood in the same way, but his face was sullen, and his upraised hand was slack with brooding. Maurice faced up-hill. His eyes lit up and he laughed. Geoffrey dropped his own arm, watching.

'Lad!' chuckled Maurice. 'I non knowed 'er wor there.' He waved his hand clumsily. In these matters Geoffrey did better. The elder brother watched the girl. She ran to the end of the path, behind the bushes, so that she was screened from the house. Then she waved her handkerchief wildly. Maurice did not notice the manœuvre. There was the cry of a child. The girl's figure vanished, reappeared holding up a white childish bundle, and came down the path. There she put down her charge, sped up-hill to a great ash-tree, climbed quickly to a large horizontal bar that formed the fence there, and, standing poised, blew kisses with both her hands, in a foreign fashion that excited the brothers. Maurice laughed aloud, as he waved his red handkerchief.

'Well, what's the danger?' shouted a mocking voice from below. Maurice collapsed, blushing furiously.

'Nowt!' he called.

There was a hearty laugh from below.

The load rode up, sheered with a hiss against the stack, then sank back again upon the scotches. The brothers ploughed across the mass of hay, taking the forks. Presently a big, burly man, red and glistening, climbed to the top of the load. Then he turned round, scrutinized the hillside from under his shaggy brows. He caught sight of the girl under the ash-tree.

'Oh, that's who it is,' he laughed. 'I thought it was some such bird, but I couldn't see her.'

The father laughed in a hearty, chaffing way, then began to teem the load. Geoffrey, on the stack above, received his great forkfuls, and swung them over to Maurice, who took them, placed them, building the stack. In the intense sunlight, the three worked in silence, knit together in a brief passion of work. The father stirred slowly for a moment, getting the hay from under his feet. Geoffrey waited, the blue tines of his fork glittering in expectation: the mass rose, his fork swung beneath it, there was a light clash of blades, then the hay was swept on to the stack, caught by Maurice, who placed it judiciously. One after another, the shoulders of the three men bowed and braced themselves. All wore light blue, bleached shirts, that stuck close to their backs. The father moved mechanically, his thick, rounded shoulders bending and lifting dully: he worked monotonously. Geoffrey flung away his strength. His massive shoulders swept and flung the hay extravagantly.

'Dost want to knock me ower?' asked Maurice angrily. He had to brace himself against the impact. The three men worked intensely, as if some will urged them. Maurice was light and swift at the work, but he had to use his judgement. Also, when he had to place the hay along the far ends, he had some distance to carry it. So he was too slow for Geoffrey. Ordinarily, the elder would have placed the hay as far as possible where his brother wanted it. Now, however, he pitched his forkfuls into the middle of the stack. Maurice strode swiftly and handsomely across the bed, but the work was too much for him. The other two men, clenched in their receive and deliver, kept up a high pitch of labour. Geoffrey still flung the hay at random. Maurice was perspiring heavily with heat and exertion, and was getting worried. Now and again, Geoffrey wiped his arm across his brow, mechanically, like an animal. Then he glanced with satisfaction at Maurice's moiled condition, and caught the next forkful.

'Wheer dost think thou'rt hollin' it, fool!' panted Maurice, as his brother flung a forkful out of reach.

'Wheer I've a mind,' answered Geoffrey.

Maurice toiled on, now very angry. He felt the sweat trickling down his body: drops fell into his long black lashes, blinding him, so that he had to stop and angrily dash his eyes clear. The veins stood out in his swarthy neck. He felt he would burst, or drop, if the work did not soon slacken off. He heard his father's fork dully scrape the cart bottom.

'There, the last,' the father panted. Geoffrey tossed the last light lot at random, took off his hat, and, steaming in the sunshine as he wiped himself, stood complacently watching Maurice struggle with clearing the bed.

'Don't you think you've got your bottom corner a bit far out?' came the father's voice from below. 'You'd better be drawing in now, hadn't you?'

'I thought you said next load,' Maurice called, sulkily.

'Aye! All right. But isn't this bottom corner——?'

Maurice, impatient, took no notice.

Geoffrey strode over the stack, and stuck his fork in the offending corner. 'What—here?' he bawled in his great voice.

'Aye—isn't it a bit loose?' came the irritating voice.

Geoffrey pushed his fork in the jutting corner, and, leaning his weight on the handle, shoved. He thought it shook. He thrust again with all his power. The mass swayed.

'What art up to, tha fool!' cried Maurice, in a high voice.

'Mind who tha'rt callin' a fool,' said Geoffrey, and he prepared to push again. Maurice sprang across, and elbowed his brother aside. On the yielding, swaying bed of hay, Geoffrey lost his foothold, and fell grovelling. Maurice tried the corner.

'It's solid enough,' he shouted angrily.

'Aye—all right,' came the conciliatory voice of the father; 'you do get a bit of rest now there's such a long way to cart it,' he added reflectively.

Geoffrey had got to his feet.

'Tha'll mind who tha'rt nudging, I can tell thee,' he threatened heavily; adding, as Maurice continued to work, 'an' tha non ca's him a fool again, dost hear?'

'Not till next time,' sneered Maurice.

As he worked silently round the stack, he neared where his brother stood like a sullen statue, leaning on his fork-handle, looking out over the countryside. Maurice's heart quickened in its beat. He worked forward, until a point of his fork caught in the leather of Geoffrey's boot, and the metal rang sharply.

'Are ter going ta shift thysen?' asked Maurice threateningly. There was no reply from the great block. Maurice lifted his upper lip like a dog. Then he put out his elbow, and tried to push his brother into the stack, clear of his way.

'Who are ter shovin'?' came the deep, dangerous voice.

'Thaïgh,' replied Maurice, with a sneer, and straightway the two brothers set themselves against each other, like opposing bulls, Maurice trying his hardest to shift Geoffrey from his footing, Geoffrey leaning all his weight in resistance. Maurice, insecure in his footing, staggered a little, and Geoffrey's weight followed him. He went slithering over the edge of the stack.

Geoffrey turned white to the lips, and remained standing, listening. He heard the fall. Then a flush of darkness came over him, and he remained standing only because he was planted. He had not strength to move. He could hear no sound from below, was only faintly aware of a sharp shriek from a long way off. He listened again. Then he filled with sudden panic.

'Feyther!' he roared, in his tremendous voice: 'Feyther! Feyther!'

The valley re-echoed with the sound. Small cattle on the hill-side looked up. Men's figures came running from the bottom field, and much nearer a woman's figure was racing across the upper field. Geoffrey waited in terrible suspense.

'Ah-h!' he heard the strange, wild voice of the girl cry out. 'Ah-h!'—and then some foreign wailing speech. Then: 'Ah-h! Are you dea-ed!'

He stood sullenly erect on the stack, not daring to go down, longing to hide in the hay, but too sullen to stoop out of sight. He heard his eldest brother come up, panting:

'Whatever's amiss!' and then the labourer, and then his father.

'Whatever have you been doing?' he heard his father ask, while yet he had not come round the corner of the stack. And then, in a low, bitter tone:

'Eh, he's done for! I'd no business to ha' put it all on that stack.'

There was a moment or two of silence, then the voice of Henry, the eldest brother, said crisply:

'He's not dead—he's coming round.'

Geoffrey heard, but was not glad. He had as lief Maurice were dead. At least that would be final: better than meeting his brother's charges, and of seeing his mother pass to the sick-room. If Maurice was killed, he himself would not explain, no, not a word, and they could hang him if they liked. If Maurice were only hurt, then everybody would know, and Geoffrey could never lift his face again. What added torture, to pass along, everybody knowing. He wanted something that he could stand back to, something definite, if it were only the knowledge that he had killed his brother. He *must* have something firm to back up to, or he would go mad. He was so lonely, he who above all needed the support of sympathy.

'No, he's commin' to; I tell you he is,' said the labourer.

'He's not dea-ed, he's not dea-ed,' came the passionate, strange sing-song of the foreign girl. 'He's not dead—no-o.'

'He wants some brandy—look at the colour of his lips,' said the crisp, cold voice of Henry. 'Can you fetch some?'

'Wha-at? Fetch?' Fräulein did not understand.

'Brandy,' said Henry, very distinct.

'Brrandy!' she re-echoed.

'You go, Bill,' groaned the father.

'Aye, I'll go,' replied Bill, and he ran across the field.

Maurice was not dead, nor going to die. This Geoffrey now realized. He was glad after all that the extreme penalty was revoked. But he hated to think of himself going on. He would always shrink now. He had hoped and hoped for the time when he would be careless, bold as Maurice, when he would not wince and shrink. Now he would always be the same, coiling up in himself like a tortoise with no shell.

'Ah-h! He's getting better!' came the wild voice of the Fräulein, and she began to cry, a strange sound, that startled the men, made the animal bristle within them. Geoffrey shuddered as he heard, between her sobbing, the impatient moaning of his brother as the breath came back.

The labourer returned at a run, followed by the Vicar. After the brandy, Maurice made more moaning, hiccuping noise. Geoffrey listened in torture. He heard the Vicar asking for explanations. All the united, anxious voices replied in brief phrases.

'It was that other,' cried the Fräulein. 'He knocked him over—Ha!'

She was shrill and vindictive.

'I don't think so,' said the father to the Vicar, in a quite audible but private tone, speaking as if the Fräulein did not understand his English.

The Vicar addressed his children's governess in bad German. She replied in a torrent which he would not confess was too much for him. Maurice was making little moaning, sighing noises.

'Where's your pain, boy, eh?' the father asked, pathetically.

'Leave him alone a bit,' came the cool voice of Henry. 'He's winded, if no more.'

'You'd better see that no bones are broken,' said the anxious Vicar.

'It wor a blessing as he should a dropped on that heap of hay just there,' said the labourer. 'If he'd happened to ha' catched hisself on this nog o' wood 'e wouldna ha' stood much chance.'

Geoffrey wondered when he would have courage to venture down. He had wild notions of pitching himself head foremost from the stack: if he could only extinguish himself, he would be safe. Quite frantically, he longed not to be. The idea of going through life thus coiled up within himself in morbid self-consciousness, always lonely, surly, and a misery, was enough to make him cry out. What would they all think when they knew he had knocked Maurice off that high stack?

They were talking to Maurice down below. The lad had recovered in great measure, and was able to answer faintly.

'Whatever was you doin'?' the father asked gently. 'Was you playing about with our Geoffrey?—Aye, and where is he?'

Geoffrey's heart stood still.

'I dunno,' said Henry, in a curious, ironic tone.

'Go an' have a look,' pleaded the father, infinitely relieved over one son, anxious now concerning the other. Geoffrey could not bear that his eldest brother should climb up and question him in his high-pitched drawl of curiousity. The culprit doggedly set his feet on the ladder. His nailed boots slipped a rung.

'Mind yourself,' shouted the overwrought father.

Geoffrey stood like a criminal at the foot of the ladder, glancing furtively at the group. Maurice was lying, pale and slightly convulsed, upon a heap of hay. The Fräulein was kneeling beside his head. The Vicar had the lad's shirt full open down the breast, and was feeling for broken ribs. The father kneeled on the other side, the labourer and Henry stood aside.

'I can't find anything broken,' said the Vicar, and he sounded slightly disappointed.

'There's nowt broken to find,' murmured Maurice, smiling.

The father started, 'Eh?' he said. 'Eh?' and he bent over the invalid.

'I say it's not hurt me,' repeated Maurice.

'What were you doing?' asked the cold, ironic voice of Henry. Geoffrey turned his head away: he had not yet raised his face.

'Nowt as I know on,' he muttered in a surly tone.

'Why!' cried Fräulein in a reproachful tone. 'I see him—knock him over!' She made a fierce gesture with her elbow. Henry curled his long moustache sardonically.

'Nay lass, niver,' smiled the wan Maurice. 'He was fur enough away from me when I slipped.'

'Oh, ah!' cried the Fräulein, not understanding.

'Yi,' smiled Maurice indulgently.

'I think you're mistaken,' said the father, rather pathetically, smiling at the girl as if she were 'wanting'.

'Oh no,' she cried. 'I *see* him.'

'Nay, lass,' smiled Maurice quietly.

She was a Pole, named Paula Jablonowsky: young, only twenty years old, swift and light as a wild cat, with a strange, wild-cat way of grinning. Her hair was blonde and full of life, all crisped into many tendrils with vitality, shaking round her face. Her fine blue eyes were peculiarly lidded, and she seemed to look piercingly, then languorously, like a wild cat. She had somewhat Slavonic cheek-bones, and was very much freckled. It was evident that the Vicar, a pale, rather cold man, hated her.

Maurice lay pale and smiling in her lap, whilst she cleaved to him like a mate. One felt instinctively that they were mated. She was ready at any minute to fight with ferocity in his defence, now he was hurt. Her looks at Geoffrey were full of fierceness. She bowed over Maurice and caressed him with her foreign-sounding English.

'You say what you lai-ike,' she laughed, giving him lordship over her.

'Hadn't you better be going and looking what has become of Margery?' asked the Vicar in tones of reprimand.

'She is with her mother—I heared her. I will go in a whai-ile,' smiled the girl, coolly.

'Do you feel as if you could stand?' asked the father, still anxiously.

'Aye, in a bit,' smiled Maurice.

'You want to get up?' caressed the girl, bowing over him, till her face was not far from his.

'I'm in no hurry,' he replied, smiling brilliantly.

This accident had given him quite a strange new ease, an authority. He felt extraordinarily glad. New power had come to him all at once.

'You in no hurry,' she repeated, gathering his meaning. She smiled tenderly: she was in his service.

'She leaves us in another month—Mrs. Inwood could stand no more of her,' apologized the Vicar quietly to the father.

'Why, is she——?'

'Like a wild thing—disobedient, and insolent.'

'Ha!'

The father sounded abstract.

'No more foreign governesses for me.'

Maurice stirred, and looked up at the girl.

'You stand up?' she asked brightly. 'You well?'

He laughed again, showing his teeth winsomely. She lifted his head, sprung to her feet, her hands still holding his head, then she took him under the armpits and had him on his feet before anyone could help. He was much taller than she. He grasped her strong shoulders heavily, leaned against her, and, feeling her round, firm breast doubled up against his side, he smiled, catching his breath.

'You see I'm all right,' he gasped. 'I was only winded.'

'You all räight?' she cried, in great glee.

'Yes, I am.'

He walked a few steps after a moment.

'There's nowt ails me, Father,' he laughed.

'Quite well, you?' she cried in a pleading tone. He laughed outright, looked down at her, touching her cheek with his fingers.

'That's it—if tha likes.'

'If I lai-ike!' she repeated, radiant.

'She's going at the end of three weeks,' said the Vicar consolingly to the farmer.

II

While they were talking, they heard the far-off hooting of a pit.

'There goes th' loose 'a,' said Henry, coldly. 'We're *not* going to get that corner up to-day.'

The father looked round anxiously.

'Now, Maurice, are you sure you're all right?' he asked.

'Yes, I'm all right. Haven't I told you?'

'Then you sit down there, and in a bit you can be getting dinner out. Henry, you go on the stack. Wheer's Jim? Oh, he's minding the hosses. Bill, and you, Geoffrey, you can pick while Jim loads.'

Maurice sat down under the wych elm to recover. The Fräulein had fled back. He made up his mind to ask her to marry him. He had got fifty pounds of his own, and his mother would help him. For a long time he sat musing, thinking what he would do. Then, from the float he fetched a big basket covered with a cloth, and spread the dinner. There was an immense rabbit pie, a dish of cold potatoes, much bread, a great piece of cheese, and a solid rice pudding.

These two fields were four miles from the home farm. But they had been in the hands of the Wookeys for several generations, therefore the father kept them on, and everyone looked forward to the hay harvest at Greasley: it was a kind of picnic. They brought dinner and tea in the milk-float, which the father drove over in the morning. The lads and the labourers cycled. Off and on, the harvest lasted a fortnight. As the high road from Alfreton to Nottingham ran at the foot of the fields, someone usually slept in the hay under the shed to guard the tools. The sons took it in turns. They did not care for it much, and were for that reason anxious to finish the harvest on this day. But work went slack and disjointed after Maurice's accident.

When the load was teemed, they gathered round the white cloth, which was spread under a tree between the hedge and the stack, and, sitting on the ground, ate their meal. Mrs. Wookey sent always a clean cloth, and knives and forks and plates for everybody. Mr. Wookey was always rather proud of this spread: everything was so proper.

'There now,' he said, sitting down jovially. 'Doesn't this look nice now—eh?'

They all sat round the white spread, in the shadow of the tree and the stack, and looked out up the fields as they ate. From their shady coolness, the gold sward seemed liquid, molten with heat. The horse with the empty wagon wandered a few yards, then stood feeding. Everything was still as a trance. Now and again, the horse between the shafts of the load that stood propped beside the stack, jingled his loose bit as he ate. The men ate and drank in silence, the father reading the newspaper, Maurice leaning back on a saddle, Henry reading the *Nation,* the others eating busily.

Presently 'Helloa! 'Er's 'ere again!' exclaimed Bill. All looked up. Paula was coming across the field carrying a plate.

'She's bringing something to tempt your appetite, Maurice,' said the eldest brother ironically. Maurice was midway through a large wedge of rabbit pie, and some cold potatoes.

'Aye, bless me if she's not,' laughed the father. 'Put that away, Maurice, it's a shame to disappoint her.'

Maurice looked round very shamefaced, not knowing what to do with his plate.

'Give it over here,' said Bill. 'I'll polish him off.'

'Bringing something for the invalid?' laughed the father to the Fräulein. 'He's looking up nicely.'

'I bring him some chicken, him!' She nodded her head at Maurice childishly. He flushed and smiled.

'Tha doesna mean ter bust'im,' said Bill.

Everybody laughed aloud. The girl did not understand, so she laughed also. Maurice ate his portion very sheepishly.

The father pitied his son's shyness.

'Come here and sit by me,' he said. 'Eh, Fräulein! Is that what they call you?'

'I sit by you, Father,' she said innocently.

Henry threw his head back and laughed long and noiselessly.

She settled near to the big, handsome man.

'My name,' she said, 'is Paula Jablonowsky.'

'Is what?' said the father, and the other men went into roars of laughter.

'Tell me again,' said the father. 'Your name——?'

'Paula.'

'Paula? Oh—well, it's a rum sort of name, eh? His name——' he nodded at his son.

'Maurice—I know.' She pronounced it sweetly, then laughed into the father's eyes. Maurice blushed to the roots of his hair.

They questioned her concerning her history, and made out that she came from Hanover, that her father was a shop-keeper, and that she had run away from home because she did not like her father. She had gone to Paris.

'Oh,' said the father, now dubious. 'And what did you do there?'

'In school—in a young ladies' school.'

'Did you like it?'

'Oh no—no laïfe—no life!'

'What?'

'When we go out—two and two—all together—no more. Ah, no life, no life.'

'Well, that's a winder!' exclaimed the father. 'No life in Paris! And have you found much life in England?'

'No—ah no. I don't like it.' She made a grimace at the Vicarage.

'How long have you been in England?'

'Chreestmas—so.'

'And what will you do?'

'I will go to London, or to Paris. Ah, Paris!—Or get married!' She laughed into the father's eyes.

The father laughed heartily.

'Get married, eh? And who to?'

'I don't know. I am going away.'

'The country's too quiet for you?' asked the father.

'Too quiet—hm!' she nodded in assent.

'You wouldn't care for making butter and cheese?'

'Making butter—hm!' She turned to him with a glad, bright gesture. 'I like it.'

'Oh,' laughed the father, 'You would, would you?'

She nodded vehemently, with glowing eyes.

'She'd like anything in the shape of a change,' said Henry judicially.

'I think she would,' agreed the father. It did not occur to them that she fully understood what they said. She looked at them closely, then thought with bowed head.

'Hullo!' exclaimed Henry, the alert. A tramp was slouching towards them through the gap. He was a very seedy, slinking fellow, with a tang of horsey braggadocio about him. Small, thin, and ferrety, with a week's red beard bristling on his pointed chin, he came slouching forward.

'Have yer got a bit of a job goin'?' he asked.

'A bit of a job,' repeated the father. 'Why, can't you see as we've a'most done?'

'Aye—but I noticed you was a hand short, an' I thowt as 'appen you'd gie me half a day.'

'What, are *you* any good in a hay close?' asked Henry, with a sneer.

The man stood slouching against the haystack. All the others were seated on the floor. He had an advantage.

'I could work aside any on yer,' he bragged.

'Tha looks it,' laughed Bill.

'And what's your regular trade?' asked the father.

'I'm a jockey by rights. But I did a bit o'dirty work for a boss o'mine, an' I was landed. '*E* got the benefit, *I* got kicked out. '*E* axed me—an' then 'e looked as if 'e'd never seed me.'

'Did he, though!' exclaimed the father sympathetically.

''E did that!' asserted the man.

'But we've got nothing for you,' said Henry coldly.

'What does the boss say?' asked the man, impudent.

'No, we've no work you can do,' said the father. 'You can have a bit o'something to eat, if you like.'

'I should be glad of it,' said the man.

He was given the chunk of rabbit pie that remained. This he ate greedily. There was something debased, parasitic, about him, which disgusted Henry. The others regarded him as a curiosity.

'That was nice and tasty,' said the tramp, with gusto.

'Do you want a piece of bread 'n' cheese?' asked the father.

'It'll help to fill up,' was the reply.

The man ate this more slowly. The company was embarrassed by his presence, and could not talk. All the men lit their pipes, the meal over.

'So you dunna want any help?' said the tramp at last.

'No—we can manage what bit there is to do.'

'You don't happen to have a fill of bacca to spare, do you?'

The father gave him a good pinch.

'You're all right here,' he said, looking round. They resented this familiarity. However, he filled his clay pipe and smoked with the rest.

As they were sitting silent, another figure came through the gap in the hedge, and noiselessly approached. It was a woman. She was rather small and finely made. Her face was small, very ruddy, and comely, save for the look of bitterness and aloofness that it wore. Her hair was drawn tightly back under a sailor hat. She gave an impression of cleanness, of precision and directness.

'Have you got some work?' she asked of her man. She ignored the rest. He tucked his tail between his legs.

'No, they haven't got no work for me. They've just gave me a draw of bacca.' He was a mean crawl of a man.

'An' am I goin' to wait for you out there on the lane all day?'

'You needn't if you don't like. You could go on.'

'Well, are you coming?' she asked contemptuously. He rose to his feet in a rickety fashion.

'You needn't be in such a mighty hurry,' he said. 'If you'd wait a bit you might get summat.'

She glanced for the first time over the men. She was quite young, and would have been pretty, were she not so hard and callous-looking.

'Have you had your dinner?' asked the father.

She looked at him with a kind of anger, and turned away. Her face was so childish in its contours, contrasting strangely with her expression.

'Are you coming?' she said to the man.

'He's had his tuck-in. Have a bit, if you want it,' coaxed the father.

'What have you had?' she flashed to the man.

'He's had all what was left o' th' rabbit pie,' said Geoffrey, in an indignant, mocking tone, 'and a great hunk o' bread an' cheese.'

'Well, it was gave me,' said the man.

The young woman looked at Geoffrey, and he at her. There was a sort of kinship between them. Both were at odds with the world. Geoffrey smiled satirically. She was too grave, too deeply incensed even to smile.

'There's a cake here, though—you can have a bit o' that,' said Maurice blithely. She eyed him with scorn.

Again she looked at Geoffrey. He seemed to understand her. She turned, and in silence departed. The man remained obstinately sucking at his pipe. Everybody looked at him with hostility.

'We'll be getting to work,' said Henry, rising, pulling of his coat. Paula got to her feet. She was a little bit confused by the presence of the tramp.

'I go,' she said, smiling brilliantly. Maurice rose and followed her sheepishly.

'A good grind, eh?' said the tramp, nodding after the Fräulein. The men only half-understood him, but they hated him.

'Hadn't you better be getting off?' said Henry.

The man rose obediently. He was all slouching, parasitic insolence. Geoffrey loathed him, longed to exterminate him. He was exactly the worst foe of the hyper-sensitive: insolence without sensibility, preying on sensibility.

'Aren't you goin' to give me summat for her? It's nowt she's had all day, to my knowin'. She'll 'appen eat it if I take it 'er—though she gets more than I've any knowledge of—this with a lewd wink of jealous spite. 'And then tries to keep a tight hand on me,' he sneered, taking the bread and cheese, and stuffing it in his pocket.

III

Geoffrey worked sullenly all the afternoon, and Maurice did the horse-raking. It was exceedingly hot. So the day wore on, the atmosphere thickened, and the sunlight grew blurred. Geoffrey was picking with Bill—helping to load the wagons from the winrows. He was sulky, though extraordinarily relieved: Maurice would not tell. Since the quarrel neither brother had spoken to the other. But their silence was entirely amicable, almost affectionate. They had both been deeply moved, so much so that their ordinary intercourse was interrupted: but underneath, each felt a strong regard for the other. Maurice was peculiarly happy, his feeling of affection swimming over everything. But Geoffrey was still sullenly hostile to the most part of the world. He felt isolated. The free and easy intercommunication between the other workers left him distinctly alone. And he was a man who could not bear to stand alone, he was too much afraid of the vast confusion of life surrounding him, in which he was helpless. Geoffrey mistrusted himself with everybody.

The work went on slowly. It was unbearably hot, and everyone was disheartened.

'We s'll have getting-on-for another day of it,' said the father at tea-time, as they sat under the tree.

'Quite a day,' said Henry.

'Somebody'll have to stop, then,' said Geoffrey. 'It 'ud better be me.'

'Nay, lad, I'll stop,' said Maurice, and he hid his head in confusion.

'Stop again to-night!' exclaimed the father. 'I'd rather you went home.'

'Nay, I'm stoppin',' protested Maurice.

'He wants to do his courting,' Henry enlightened them.

The father thought seriously about it.

'I don't know . . .' he mused, rather perturbed.

But Maurice stayed. Towards eight o'clock, after sundown, the men mounted their bicycles, the father put the horse in the float, and all departed. Maurice stood in the gap of the hedge and watched them go, the cart rolling and swinging downhill, over the grass stubble, the cyclists dipping swiftly like shadows in front. All passed through the gate, there was a quick clatter of hoofs on the roadway under the lime trees, and they were gone. The young man was very much excited, almost afraid, at finding himself alone.

Darkness was rising from the valley. Already, up the steep hill the cart-lamps crept indecisively, and the cottage windows were lit. Everything looked strange to Maurice, as if he had not seen it before. Down the hedge a large lime-tree teemed with scent that seemed almost like a voice speaking. It startled him. He caught a breath of the over-sweet fragrance, then stood still, listening expectantly.

Up hill, a horse whinneyed. It was the young mare. The heavy horses went thundering across to the far hedge.

536

Maurice wondered what to do. He wandered round the deserted stacks restlessly. Heat came in wafts, in thick strands. The evening was a long time cooling. He thought he would go and wash himself. There was a trough of pure water in the hedge bottom. It was filled by a tiny spring that filtered over the brim of the trough down the lush hedge bottom of the lower field. All round the trough, in the upper field, the land was marshy, and there the meadow-sweet stood like clots of mist, very sickly-smelling in the twilight. The night did not darken, for the moon was in the sky, so that as the tawny colour drew off the heavens they remained pallid with a dimmed moon. The purple bell-flowers in the hedge went black, the ragged robin turned its pink to a faded white, the meadow-sweet gathered light as if it were phosphorescent, and it made the air ache with scent.

Maurice kneeled on the slab of stone bathing his hands and arms, then his face. The water was deliciously cool. He had still an hour before Paula would come: she was not due till nine. So he decided to take his bath at night instead of waiting till morning. Was he not sticky, and was not Paula coming to talk to him? He was delighted the thought had occurred to him. As he soused his head in the trough, he wondered what the little creatures that lived in the velvety silt at the bottom would think of the taste of soap. Laughing to himself, he squeezed his cloth into the water. He washed himself from head to foot, standing in the fresh, forsaken corner of the field, where no one could see him by daylight, so that now, in the veiled grey tinge of moonlight, he was no more noticeable than the crowded flowers. The night had on a new look: he never remembered to have seen the lustrous grey sheen of it before, nor to have noticed how vital the lights looked, like live folk inhabiting the silvery spaces. And the tall trees, wrapped obscurely in their mantles, would not have surprised him had they begun to move in converse. As he dried himself, he discovered little wanderings in the air, felt on his sides soft touches and caresses that were peculiarly delicious: sometimes they startled him, and he laughed as if he were not alone. The flowers, the meadow-sweet particularly, haunted him. He reached to put his hand over their fleeciness. They touched his thighs. Laughing, he gathered them and dusted himself all over with their cream dust and fragrance. For a moment he hesitated in wonder at himself: but the subtle glow in the hoary and black night reassured him. Things never had looked so personal and full of beauty, he had never known the wonder in himself before.

At nine o'clock he was waiting under the elderbush, in a state of high trepidation, but feeling that he was worthy, having a sense of his own wonder. She was late. At a quarter-past nine she came, flitting swiftly, in her own eager way.

'No, she would *not* go to sleep,' said Paula, with a world of wrath in her tone. He laughed bashfully. They wandered out into the dim, hillside field.

'I have sat—in that bedroom—for an hour, for hours,' she cried indignantly. She took a deep breath: 'Ah, breathe!' she smiled.

She was very intense, and full of energy.

'I want'—she was clumsy with the language—'I want—I should laike—to run—there!' She pointed across the field.

'Let's run, then,' he said, curiously.

'Yes!'

And in an instant she was gone. He raced after her. For all he was so young and limber, he had difficulty in catching her. At first he could scarcely see her, though he could hear the rustle of her dress. She sped with astonishing fleetness. He overtook her, caught her by the arm, and they stood panting, facing one another with laughter.

'I could win,' she asserted blithely.

'Tha couldna,' he replied, with a peculiar, excited laugh. They walked on, rather breathless. In front of them suddenly appeared the dark shapes of the three feeding horses.

'We ride a horse?' she said.

'What, bareback?' he asked.

'You say?' She did not understand.

'With no saddle?'

'No saddle—yes—no saddle.'

'Coop, lass!' he said to the mare, and in a minute he had her by the forelock, and was leading her down to the stacks, where he put a halter on her. She was a big, strong mare. Maurice seated the Fräulein, clambered himself in front of the girl, using the wheel of the wagon as a mount, and together they trotted uphill, she holding lightly round his waist. From the crest of the hill they looked round.

The sky was darkening with an awning of cloud. On the left the hill rose black and wooded, made cosy by a few lights from cottages along the highway. The hill spread to the right, and tufts of trees shut round. But in front was a great vista of night, a sprinkle of cottage candles, a twinkling cluster of lights, like an elfish fair in full swing, at the colliery, an encampment of light at a village, a red flare on the sky far off, above an iron-foundry, and in the farthest distance the dim breathing of town lights. As they watched the night stretch far out, her arms tightened round his waist, and he pressed his elbows to his side, pressing her arms closer still. The horse moved restlessly. They clung to each other.

'Tha doesna want to go right away?' he asked the girl behind him.

'I stay with you,' she answered softly, and he felt her crouching close against him. He laughed curiously. He was afraid to kiss her, though he was urged to do so. They remained still, on the restless horse, watching the small lights lead deep into the night, an infinite distance.

'I don't want to go,' he said, in a tone half pleading.

She did not answer. The horse stirred restlessly.

'Let him run,' cried Paula, 'fast!'

She broke the spell, startled him into a little fury. He kicked the mare, hit her, and away she plunged downhill. The girl clung tightly to the young man. They were riding bareback down a rough, steep hill. Maurice clung hard with hands and knees. Paula held him fast round the waist, leaning her head on his shoulders, and thrilling with excitement.

'We shall be off, we shall be off,' he cried, laughing with excitement; but she only crouched behind and pressed tight to him. The mare tore across the field.

Maurice expected every moment to be flung on to the grass. He gripped with all the strength of his knees. Paula tucked herself behind him, and often wrenched him almost from his hold. Man and girl were taut with effort.

At last the mare came to a standstill, blowing. Paula slid off, and in an instant Maurice was beside her. They were both highly excited. Before he knew what he was doing, he had her in his arms, fast, and was kissing her, and laughing. They did not move for some time. Then, in silence, they walked towards the stacks.

It had grown quite dark, the night was thick with cloud. He walked with his arm round Paula's waist, she with her arm round him. They were near the stacks when Maurice felt a spot of rain.

'It's going to rain,' he said.

'Rain!' she echoed, as if it were trivial.

'I s'll have to put the stack-cloth on,' he said gravely. She did not understand.

When they got to the stacks, he went round to the shed, to return staggering in the darkness under the burden of the immense and heavy cloth. It had not been used once during the hay harvest.

'What are you going to do?' asked Paula, coming close to him in the darkness.

'Cover the top of the stack with it,' he replied. 'Put it over the stack, to keep the rain out.'

'Ah!' she cried, 'up there!' He dropped his burden. 'Yes,' he answered.

Fumblingly he reared the long ladder up the side of the stack. He could not see the top.

'I hope it's solid,' he said, softly.

A few smart drops of rain sounded drumming on the cloth. They seemed like another presence. It was very dark indeed between the great buildings of hay. She looked up the black wall, and shrank to him.

'You carry it up there?' she asked.

'Yes,' he answered.

'I help you?' she said.

And she did. They opened the cloth. He clambered first up the steep ladder, bearing the upper part, she followed closely, carrying her full share. They mounted the shaky ladder in silence, stealthily.

IV

*A*s they climbed the stacks a light stopped at the gate on the high road. It was Geoffrey, come to help his brother with the cloth. Afraid of his own intrusion, he wheeled his bicycle silently towards the shed. This was a corrugated iron erection, on the opposite side of the hedge from the stacks. Geoffrey let his light go in front of him, but there was no sign from the lovers. He thought he saw a shadow slinking away. The light of the bicycle lamp sheered yellowly across the dark, catching a glint of raindrops, a mist of darkness, shadow of leaves and strokes of long grass. Geoffrey entered the shed—no one was there. He walked slowly and doggedly round to the stacks. He had passed the wagon, when he heard something sheering down upon him. Starting back under the wall of hay, he saw the long ladder slither across the side of the stack, and fall with a bruising ring.

'What wor that?' he heard Maurice, aloft, ask cautiously.

'Something fall,' came the curious, almost pleased voice of the Fräulein.

'It wor niver th' ladder,' said Maurice. He peered over the side of the stack. He lay down, looking.

'It is an' a'!' he exclaimed. 'We knocked it down with the cloth, dragging it over.'

'We fast up here?' she exclaimed with a thrill.

'We are that—without I shout and make 'em hear at the Vicarage.'

'Oh no,' she said quickly.

'I don't want to,' he replied, with a short laugh. There came a swift clatter of raindrops on the cloth. Geoffrey crouched under the wall of the other stack.

'Mind where you tread—here, let me straighten this end,' said Maurice, with a peculiar intimate tone—a command and an embrace. 'We s'll have to sit under it. At any rate, we shan't get wet.'

'Not get wet!' echoed the girl, pleased, but agitated.

Geoffrey heard the slide and rustle of the cloth over the top of the stack, heard Maurice telling her to 'Mind!'

'Mind!' she repeated. 'Mind! you say "Mind!"'

'Well, what if I do?' he laughed. 'I don't want you to fall over th' side, do I?' His tone was masterful, but he was not quite sure of himself.

There was silence a moment or two.

'Maurice!' she said, plaintively.

'I'm here,' he answered, tenderly, his voice shaky with excitement that was near to distress. 'There, I've done. Now should we—we'll sit under this corner.'

'Maurice!' she was rather pitiful.

'What? You'll be all right,' he remonstrated, tenderly indignant.

'I be all raïght,' she repeated, 'I be all raïght, Maurice?'

'Tha knows tha will—I canna ca' thee Powla. Should I ca' thee Minnie?'

It was the name of a dead sister.

'Minnie?' she exclaimed in surprise.

'Aye, should I?'

She answered in full-throated German. He laughed shakily.

'Come on—come on under. But do yer wish you was safe in th' Vicarage? Should I shout for somebody?' he asked.

'I don't wish, no!' She was vehement.

'Art sure?' he insisted, almost indignantly.

'Sure—I quite sure.' She laughed.

Geoffrey turned away at the last words. Then the rain beat heavily. The lonely brother slouched miserably to the hut, where the rain played a mad tattoo. He felt very miserable, and jealous of Maurice.

His bicycle lamp, downcast, shone a yellow light on the stark floor of the shed or hut with one wall open. It lit up the trodden earth, the shafts of tools lying piled under the beam, beside the dreary grey metal of the building. He took off the lamp, shone it round the hut. There were piles of harness, tools, a big sugar box, a deep bed of hay—then the beams across the corrugated iron, all very dreary and stark. He shone the lamp into the night: nothing but the furtive glitter of raindrops through the mist of darkness, and black shapes hovering round.

Geoffrey blew out the light and flung himself on to the hay. He would put the ladder up for them in a while, when they would be wanting it. Meanwhile he sat and gloated over Maurice's felicity. He was imaginative, and now he had something concrete to work upon. Nothing in the whole of life stirred him so profoundly, and so utterly, as the thought of this woman. For Paula was strange, foreign, different from the ordinary girls: the rousing, feminine quality seemed in her concentrated, brighter, more fascinating than in anyone he had known, so that he felt most like a moth near a candle. He would have loved her wildly—but Maurice had got her. His thoughts beat the same course, round and round. What was it like when you kissed her, when she held you tight round the waist, how did she feel towards Maurice, did she love to touch him, was he fine and attractive to her; what did she think of himself—she merely disregarded him, as she would disregard a horse in a field; why should she do so, why couldn't he make her regard himself, instead of Maurice: he would never command a woman's regard like that, he always gave in to her too soon; if only some woman would come and take him for what he was worth, though he was such a stumbler and showed to such disadvantage, ah, what a grand thing it would be; how he would kiss her. Then round he went again in the same course, brooding almost like a madman. Meanwhile the rain drummed deep on the shed, then grew lighter and softer. There came the drip, drip of the drops falling outside.

Geoffrey's heart leaped up his chest, and he clenched himself, as a black shape crept round the post of the shed and, bowing, entered silently. The young man's heart beat so heavily in plunges, he could not get his breath to speak. It was shock, rather than fear. The form felt towards him. He sprang up, gripped it with his great hands, panting 'Now, then!'

There was no resistance, only a little whimper of despair.

'Let me go,' said a woman's voice.

'What are you after?' he asked, in deep, gruff tones.

'I thought 'e was 'ere,' she wept despairingly, with little, stubborn sobs.

'An' you've found what you didn't expect, have you?'

At the sound of his bullying she tried to get away from him.

'Let me go,' she said.

'Who did you expect to find here?' he asked, but more his natural self.

'I expected my husband—him as you saw at dinner. Let me go.'

'Why, is it you?' exclaimed Geoffrey. 'Has he left you?'

'Let me go,' said the woman sullenly, trying to draw away. He realized that her sleeve was very wet, her arm slender under his grasp. Suddenly he grew ashamed of himself: he had no doubt hurt her, gripping her so hard. He relaxed, but did not let her go.

'An' are you searching round after that snipe as was here at dinner?' he asked. She did not answer.

'Where did he leave you?'

'I left him—here. I've seen nothing of him since.'

'I s'd think it's good riddance,' he said. She did not answer. He gave a short laugh, saying:

'I should ha' thought you wouldn't ha' wanted to clap eyes on him again.'

'He's my husband—an' he's not goin' to run off if I can stop him.'

Geoffrey was silent, not knowing what to say.

'Have you got a jacket on?' he asked at last.

'What do you think? You've got hold of it.'

'You're wet through, aren't you?'

'I shouldn't be dry, comin' through that teemin' rain. But 'e's not here, so I'll go.'

'I mean,' he said humbly, 'are you wet through?'

She did not answer. He felt her shiver.

'Are you cold?' he asked, in surprise and concern.

She did not answer. He did not know what to say.

'Stop a minute,' he said, and he fumbled in his pocket for his matches. He struck a light, holding it in the hollow of his large, hard palm. He was a big man, and he looked anxious. Shedding the light on her, he saw she was rather pale, and very weary looking. Her old sailor hat was sodden and drooping with rain. She wore a fawn-coloured jacket of smooth cloth. This jacket was black-wet where the rain had beaten, her skirt hung sodden, and dripped on to her boots. The match went out.

'Why, you're wet through!' he said.

She did not answer.

'Shall you stop in here while it gives over?' he asked. She did not answer.

' 'Cause if you will, you'd better take your things off, an' have the' rug. There's a horse-rug in the box.'

He waited, but she would not answer. So he lit his bicycle lamp, and rummaged in the box, pulling out a large brown blanket, striped with scarlet and yellow. She stood stock still. He shone the light on her. She was very pale, and trembling fitfully.

'Are you that cold?' he asked in concern. 'Take your jacket off, and your hat, and put this right over you.'

Mechanically, she undid the enormous fawn-coloured buttons, and unpinned her hat. With her black hair drawn back from her low, honest brow, she looked little more than a girl, like a girl driven hard with womanhood by stress of life. She was small, and natty, with neat little features. But she shivered convulsively.

'Is something a-matter with you?' he asked.

'I've walked to Bulwell and back,' she quivered, 'looking for him—an' I've not touched a thing since this morning.' She did not weep—she was too dreary-hardened to cry. He looked at her in dismay, his mouth half open: 'Gormin', as Maurice would have said.

' 'Aven't you had nothing to eat?' he said.

Then he turned aside to the box. There, the bread remaining was kept, and the great piece of cheese, and such things as sugar and salt, with all table utensils: there was some butter.

She sat down drearily on the bed of hay. He cut her a piece of bread and butter, and a piece of cheese. This she took, but ate listlessly.

'I want a drink,' she said.

'We 'aven't got no beer,' he answered. 'My father doesn't have it.'

'I want water,' she said.

He took a can and plunged through the wet darkness, under the great black hedge, down to the trough. As he came back he saw her in the half-lit little cave sitting bunched together. The soaked grass wet his feet—he thought of her. When he gave her a cup of water, her hand touched his and he felt her fingers hot and glossy. She trembled so she spilled the water.

'Do you feel badly?' he asked.

'I can't keep myself still—but it's only with being tired and having nothing to eat.'

He scratched his head contemplatively, waited while she ate her piece of bread and butter. Then he offered her another piece.

'I don't want it just now,' she said.

'You'll have to eat summat,' he said.

'I couldn't eat any more just now.'

He put the piece down undecidedly on the box. Then there was another long pause. He stood up with bent head. The bicycle, like a restful animal, glittered behind him, turning towards the wall. The woman sat hunched on the hay, shivering.

'Can't you get warm?' he asked.

'I shall by an' by—don't you bother. I'm taking your seat—are you stopping here all night?'

'Yes.'

'I'll be goin' in a bit,' she said.

'Nay, I non want you to go. I'm thinkin' how you could get warm.'

'Don't you bother about me,' she remonstrated, almost irritably.

'I just want to see as the stacks is all right. You take your shoes an' stockin's an' all your wet things off: you can easy wrap yourself all over in that rug, there's not so much of you.'

'It's raining—I s'll be all right—I s'll be going in a minute.'

'I've got to see as the stacks is safe. Take your wet things off.'

'Are you coming back?' she asked.

'I mightn't, not till morning.'

'Well, I s'll be gone in ten minutes, then. I've no rights to be here, an' I s'll not let anybody be turned out for me.'

'You won't be turning me out.'

'Whether or no, I shan't stop.'

'Well, shall you if I come back?' he asked. She did not answer.

He went. In a few moments, she blew the light out. The rain was falling steadily, and the night was a black gulf. All was intensely still. Geoffrey listened everywhere: no sound save the rain. He stood between the stacks, but only heard the trickle of water, and the light swish of rain. Everything was lost in blackness. He imagined death was like that, many things dissolved in silence and darkness, blotted out, but existing. In the dense blackness he felt himself almost extinguished. He was afraid he might not find things the same. Almost frantically, he stumbled, feeling his way, till his hand touched the wet metal. He had been looking for a gleam of light.

'Did you blow the lamp out?' he asked, fearful lest the silence should answer him.

'Yes,' she answered humbly. He was glad to hear her voice. Groping into the pitch-dark shed, he knocked against the box, part of whose cover served as table. There was a clatter and a fall.

'That's the lamp, an' the knife, an' the cup,' he said. He struck a match.

'Th' cup's not broke.' He put it into the box.

'But th' oil's spilled out o' th' lamp. It always was a rotten old thing.' He hastily blew out his match, which was burning his fingers. Then he struck another light.

'You don't want a lamp, you know you don't, and I s'll be going directly, so you come an' lie down an' get your night's rest. I'm not taking any of your place.'

He looked at her by the light of another match. She was a queer little bundle, all brown, with gaudy border folding in and out, and her little face peering at him. As the match went out she saw him beginning to smile.

'I can sit right at this end,' she said. 'You lie down.'

He came and sat on the hay, at some distance from her. After a spell of silence:

'Is he really your husband?' he asked.

'He is!' she answered grimly.

'Hm!' Then there was silence again.

After a while: 'Are you warm now?'

'Why do you bother yourself?'

'I don't bother myself—do you follow him because you like him?' He put it very timidly. He wanted to know.

'I don't—I wish he was dead,' this with bitter contempt. The doggedly: 'But he's my husband.'

He gave a short laugh.

'By Gad!' he said.

Again, after a while: 'Have you been married long?'

'Four years.'

'Four years—why, how old are you?'

'Twenty-three.'

'Are you turned twenty-three?'

'Last May.'

'Then you're four month older than me.' He mused over it. They were only two voices in the pitch-black night. It was eerie silence again.

'And do you just tramp about?' he asked.

'He reckons he's looking for a job. But he doesn't like work in any shape or form. He was a stableman when I married him, at Greenhalgh's, the horse-dealers, at Chesterfield, where I was housemaid. He left that job when the baby was only two month, and I've been badgered about from pillar to post ever sin'. They say a rolling stone gathers no moss. . . .'

'An' where's the baby?'

'It died when it was ten month old.'

Now the silence was clinched between them. It was quite a long time before Geoffrey ventured to say sympathetically: 'You haven't much to look forward to.'

'I've wished many a score time when I've started shiverin' an' shakin' at nights, as I was taken bad for death. But we're not that handy at dying.'

He was silent. 'But what ever shall you do?' he faltered.

'I s'll find him, if I drop by th' road.'

'Why?' he asked, wondering, looking her way, though he saw nothing but solid darkness.

'Because I shall. He's not going to have it all his own road.'

'But why don't you leave him?'

'Because he's *not goin' to have it all his own road.*'

She sounded very determined, even vindictive. He sat in wonder, feeling uneasy, and vaguely miserable on her behalf. She sat extraordinarily still. She seemed like a voice only, a presence.

'Are you warm now?' he asked, half afraid.

'A bit warmer—but my feet!' She sounded pitiful.

'Let me warm them with my hands,' he asked her. 'I'm hot enough.'

'No, thank you,' she said, coldly.

Then, in the darkness, she felt she had wounded him. He was writhing under her rebuff, for his offer had been pure kindness.

'They're 'appen dirty,' she said, half mocking.

'Well—mine is—an' I have a bath a'most every day,' he answered.

'I don't know when they'll get warm,' she moaned to herself.

'Well, then, put them in my hands.'

She heard him faintly rattling the match-box, and then a phosphorescent glare began to fume in his direction. Presently he was holding two smoking, blue-green blotches of light towards her feet. She was afraid. But her feet ached so, and the impulse drove her on, so she placed her soles lightly on the two blotches of smoke. His large hands clasped over her instep, warm and hard.

'They're like ice!' he said, in deep concern.

He warmed her feet as best he could, putting them close against him. Now and again convulsive tremors ran over her. She felt his warm breath on the balls of her toes, that were bunched up in his hands. Leaning forward, she touched his hair delicately with her fingers. He thrilled. She fell to gently stroking his hair, with timid, pleading finger-tips.

'Do they feel any better?' he asked, in a low voice, suddenly lifting his face to her. This sent her hand sliding softly over his face, and her finger-tips caught on his mouth. She drew quickly away. He put his hand out to find hers, in his other palm holding both her feet. His wandering hand met her face. He touched it curiously. It was wet. He put his big fingers cautiously on her eyes, into two little pools of tears.

'What's a matter?' he asked, in a low, choked voice.

She leaned down to him, and gripped him tightly round the neck, pressing him to her bosom in a little frenzy of pain. Her bitter disillusionment with life, her unalleviated shame and degradation during the last four years, had driven her into loneliness, and hardened her till a large part of her nature was caked and sterile. Now she softened again, and her spring might be beautiful. She had been in a fair way to make an ugly old woman.

She clasped the head of Geoffrey to her breast, which heaved and fell, and heaved again. He was bewildered, full of wonder. He allowed the woman to do as she would with him. Her tears fell on his hair, as she wept noiselessly; and he breathed deep as she did. At last she let go her clasp. He put his arms round her.

'Come and let me warm you,' he said, folding her up on his knee, and lapping her with his heavy arms against himself. She was small and *câline*. He held her very warm and close. Presently she stole her arms round him.

'You *are* big,' she whispered.

He gripped her hard, started, put his mouth down wanderingly, seeking her out. His lips met her temple. She slowly, deliberately turned her mouth to his, and with opened lips, met him in a kiss, his first love kiss.

V

*I*t was breaking cold dawn when Geoffrey woke. The woman was still sleeping in his arms. Her face in sleep moved all his tenderness: the tight shutting of her mouth, as if in resolution to bear what was very hard to bear, contrasted so pitifully with the small mould of her features. Geoffrey pressed her to his bosom: having her, he felt he could bruise the lips of the scornful, and pass on erect, unabateable. With her to complete him, to form the core of him, he was firm and whole. Needing her so much, he loved her fervently.

Meanwhile the dawn came like death, one of those slow, livid mornings that seem to come in a cold sweat. Slowly, and painfully, the air began to whiten. Geoffrey saw it was not raining. As he was watching the ghastly transformation outside, he felt aware of something. He glanced down: she was open-eyed, watching him; she had golden-brown, calm eyes, that immediately smiled into his. He also smiled, bowed softly down and kissed her. They did not speak for some time. Then:

'What's thy name?' he asked curiously.

'Lydia,' she said.

'Lydia!' he repeated, wonderingly. He felt rather shy.

'Mine's Geoffrey Wookey,' he said.

She merely smiled at him.

They were silent for a considerable time. By morning light, things look small. The huge trees of the evening were dwindled to hoary, small, uncertain things, trespassing in the sick pallor of the atmosphere. There was a dense mist, so that the light could scarcely breathe. Everything seemed to quiver with cold and sickliness.

'Have you often slept out?' he asked her.

'Not so very,' she answered.

'You won't go after *him?*' he asked.

'I s'll have to,' she replied, but she nestled in to Geoffrey. He felt a sudden panic.

'You musn't,' he exclaimed, and she saw he was afraid for himself. She let it be, was silent.

'We couldn't get married?' he asked, thoughtfully.

'No.'

He brooded deeply over this. At length:

'Would you go to Canada with me?'

'We'll see what you think in two months' time,' she replied quietly, without bitterness.

'I s'll think the same,' he protested, hurt.

She did not answer, only watched him steadily. She was there for him to do as he liked with; but she would not injure his fortunes; no, not to save his soul.

'Haven't you got no relations?' he asked.

'A married sister at Crick.'

'On a farm?'

'No—married a farm labourer—but she's very comfortable. I'll go there, if you want me to, just till I can get another place in service.'

He considered this.

'Could you get on a farm?' he asked wistfully.

'Greenhalgh's was a farm.'

He saw the future brighten: she would be a help to him. She agreed to go to her sister, and to get a place of service—until Spring, he said, when they would sail for Canada. He waited for her assent.

'You will come with me, then?' he asked.

'When the time comes,' she said.

Her want of faith made him bow his head: she had reason for it.

'Shall you walk to Crick, or go from Langley Mill to Ambergate? But it's only ten mile to walk. So we can go together up Hunt's Hill—you'd have to go past our lane-end, then I could easy nip down an' fetch you some money,' he said, humbly.

'I've got half a sovereign by me—it's more than I s'll want.'

'Let's see it,' he said.

After a while, fumbling under the blanket, she brought out the piece of money. He felt she was independent of him. Brooding rather bitterly, he told himself she'd forsake him. His anger gave him courage to ask:

'Shall you go in service in your maiden name?'

'No.'

He was bitterly wrathful with her—full of resentment.

'I bet I s'll niver see you again,' he said, with a short, hard laugh. She put her arms round him, pressed him to her bosom, while the tears rose to her eyes. He was reassured, but not satisfied.

'Shall you write to me to-night?'

'Yes, I will.'

'And can I write to you—who shall I write to?'

'Mrs. Bredon.'

' "Bredon"!' he repeated bitterly.

He was exceedingly uneasy.

The dawn had grown quite wan. He saw the hedges drooping wet down the grey mist. Then he told her about Maurice.

'Oh, you *shouldn't!*' she said. 'You should ha' put the ladder up for them, you *should.*'

'Well—I don't care.'

'Go and do it now—and I'll go.'

'No, don't you. Stop an' see our Maurice, go on, stop an' see him—then I s'll be able to tell him.'

She consented in silence. He had her promise she would not go before he returned. She adjusted her dress, found her way to the trough, where she performed her toilet.

Geoffrey wandered round to the upper field. The stacks looked wet in the mist, the hedge was drenched. Mist rose like steam from the grass, and the near hills were veiled almost to a shadow. In the valley, some peaks of black poplar showed fairly definite, jutting up. He shivered with chill.

There was no sound from the stacks, and he could see nothing. After all, he wondered, were they up there. But he reared the ladder to the place whence it had been swept, then went down the hedge to gather dry sticks. He was breaking

off thin dead twigs under a holly tree when he heard, on the perfectly still air:
'Well I'm dashed!'

He listened intently. Maurice was awake.

'Sithee here!' the lad's voice exclaimed. Then, after a while, the foreign sound of the girl:

'What—oh, thair!'

'Aye, th' ladder's there, right enough.'

'You said it had fall down.'

'Well, I heard it drop—an' I couldna feel it nor see it.'

'You said it had fall down—you lie, you liar.'

'Nay, as true as I'm here——'

'You tell me lies—make me stay here—you tell me lies——' She was passionately indignant.

'As true as I'm standing here——' he began.

'Lies!—lies!—lies!' she cried. 'I don't believe you, never. You *mean,* you *mean, mean, mean!*'

'A' raïght, then!' he was now incensed, in his turn.

'You are bad, mean, mean, mean.'

'Are yer commin' down?' asked Maurice, coldly.

'No—I will not come with you—mean, to tell me lies.'

'Are ter commin' down?'

'No, I don't want you.'

'A' raïght, then!'

Geoffrey, peering through the holly tree, saw Maurice negotiating the ladder. The top rung was below the brim of the stack, and rested on the cloth, so it was dangerous to approach. The Fräulein watched him from the end of the stack, where the cloth thrown back showed the light, dry hay. He slipped slightly, she screamed. When he had got on to the ladder, he pulled the cloth away, throwing it back, making it easy for her to descend.

'Now are ter comin'?' he asked.

'No!' she shook her head violently, in a pet.

Geoffrey felt slightly contemptuous of her. But Maurice waited.

'Are ter comin'?' he called again.

'No,' she flashed, like a wild cat.

'All right, then I'm going.'

He descended. At the bottom, he stood holding the ladder.

'Come on, while I hold it steady,' he said.

There was no reply. For some minutes he stood patiently with his foot on the bottom rung of the ladder. He was pale, rather washed-out in his appearance, and he drew himself together with cold.

'Are ter commin', or aren't ter?' he asked at length. Still there was no reply.

'Then stop up till tha'rt ready,' he muttered, and he went away. Round the other side of the stacks he met Geoffrey.

'What, are thaïgh here?' he exclaimed.

'Bin here a' naïght,' replied Geoffrey. 'I come to help thee wi' th' cloth, but I found it on, an' th' ladder down, so I thowt tha'd gone.'

'Did ter put th' ladder up?'

'I did a bit sin.'

Maurice brooded over this, Geoffrey struggled with himself to get out his own news. At last he blurted:

'Tha knows that woman as wor here yis'day dinner—'er come back, an' stopped i' th' shed a' night, out o' th' rain.'

'Oh—ah!' said Maurice, his eye kindling, and a smile crossing his pallor.

'An' I s'll gi'e her some breakfast.'

'Oh—ah!' repeated Maurice.

'It's th' man as is good-for-nowt, not her,' protested Geoffrey. Maurice did not feel in a position to cast stones.

'Tha pleases thysen,' he said, 'what ter does.' He was very quiet, unlike himself. He seemed bothered and anxious, as Geoffrey had not seen him before.

'What's up wi'thee?' asked the elder brother, who in his own heart was glad, and relieved.

'Nowt,' was the reply.

They went together to the hut. The woman was folding the blanket. She was fresh from washing, and looked very pretty. Her hair, instead of being screwed tightly back, was coiled in a knot low down, partly covering her ears. Before, she had deliberately made herself plain-looking: now she was neat and pretty, with a sweet, womanly gravity.

'Hello. I didn't think to find you here,' said Maurice, very awkwardly, smiling. She watched him gravely without reply. 'But it was better in shelter than outside, last night,' he added.

'Yes,' she replied.

'Shall you get a few more sticks?' Geoffrey asked him. It was a new thing for Geoffrey to be leader. Maurice obeyed. He wandered forth into the damp, raw morning. He did not go to the stack, as he shrank from meeting Paula.

At the mouth of the hut, Geoffrey was making the fire. The woman got out coffee from the box: Geoffrey set the tin to boil. They were arranging breakfast when Paula appeared. She was hatless. Bits of hay stuck in her hair, and she was white-faced—altogether, she did not show to advantage.

'Ah—you!' she exclaimed, seeing Geoffrey.

'Hello!' he answered. 'You're out early.'

'Where's Maurice?'

'I dunno, he should be back directly.'

Paula was silent.

'When have you come?' she asked.

'I come last night, but I could see nobody about. I got up half an hour sin', an' put th' ladder up ready to take the stack-cloth up.'

Paula understood, and was silent. When Maurice returned with the faggots, she was crouched warming her hands. She looked up at him, but he kept his eyes averted from her. Geoffrey met the eyes of Lydia, and smiled. Maurice put his hands to the fire.

'You cold?' asked Paula tenderly.

'A bit,' he answered, quite friendly, but reserved. And all the while the four sat round the fire, drinking their smoked coffee, eating each a small piece of toasted bacon, Paula watched eagerly for the eyes of Maurice, and he avoided her. He was gentle, but would not give his eyes to her looks. And Geoffrey smiled constantly to Lydia, who watched gravely.

The German girl succeeded in getting safely into the Vicarage, her escapade unknown to anyone save the housemaid. Before a week was out, she was openly engaged to Maurice, and when her month's notice expired, she went to live at the farm.

Geoffrey and Lydia kept faith one with the other.

Selected Poems

Moral Clothing

When I am clothed I am a moral man,
and unclothed, the word has no meaning for me.

When I put on my coat, my coat has pockets
and in the pockets are things I require,
so I wish no man to pick my pocket
and I will pick the pocket of no man.

A man's business is one of his pockets, his bank account too
his credit, his name, his wife even may be just another of his pockets.
And I loathe the thought of being a pilferer
a pick-pocket,
That is why business seems to me despicable,
and most love-affairs, just sneak-thief pocket-picking
of dressed-up people.

When I stand in my shirt I have no pockets
therefore no morality of pockets;
but still my nakedness is clothed with responsibility
towards those near and dear to me, my very next of kin.
I am not yet alone.

Only when I am stripped stark naked I am alone
and without morals, and without immorality.
The invisible gods have no moral truck with us.
And if stark naked I approach a fellow-man or fellow-woman
they must be naked too,

and none of us must expect morality of each other:
I am that I am, take it or leave it.
Offer me nothing but that which you are, stark and strange.
Let there be no accommodation at this issue.

Storm in the Black Forest

Now it is almost night, from the bronzey soft sky
jugful after jugful of pure white liquid fire, bright white
tipples over and spills down,
and is gone
and gold-bronze flutters beat through the thick upper air.

And as the electric liquid pours out, sometimes
a still brighter white snake wriggles among it, spilled
and tumbling wriggling down the sky:
and then the heavens cackle with uncouth sounds.

And the rain won't come, the rain refuses to come!

This is the electricity that man is supposed to have mastered
chained, subjugated to his use!
supposed to!

Desire

Ah, in the past, towards rare individuals
I have felt the pull of desire:
Oh come, come nearer, come into touch!
Come physically nearer, be flesh to my flesh—

But say little, oh say little,
and afterwards, leave me alone.
Keep your aloneness, leave me my aloneness,
I used to say this, in the past, but now no more.
It has always been a failure
They have always insisted on love
and on talking about it
and on the me-and-thee and what we meant to each other.

So now I have no desire any more
Except to be left, in the last resort, alone, quite alone.

For a Moment

For a moment, at evening, tired, as he stepped off the tram-car,
—the young tram-conductor in a blue uniform, to himself forgotten,—
and lifted his face up, with blue eyes looking at the electric rod which
   he was going to turn round,
for a moment, pure in the yellow evening light, he was Hyacinthus.

In the green garden darkened the shadow of coming rain
and a girl ran swiftly, laughing breathless, taking in her white washing
in rapid armfuls from the line, tossing in the basket,
and so rapidly, and so flashing, fleeing before the rain
for a moment she was Io, Io, who fled from Zeus, or the Danae.

When I was waiting and not thinking, sitting at a table on the hotel
   terrace
I saw suddenly coming towards me, lit up and uplifted with pleasure
advancing with the slow-swiftness of a ship backing her white sails into
   port
the woman who looks for me in the world
and for the moment she was Isis, gleaming, having found her Osiris.

For a moment, as he looked at me through his spectacles
pondering, yet eager, the broad and thick-set Italian who works in
   with me,
for a moment he was the Centaur, the wise yet horse-hoofed Centaur
in whom I can trust.

Forte dei Marmi

The evening sulks along the shore, the reddening sun
reddens still more on the blatant bodies of these all-but-naked, sea-
   bathing city people.

Let me tell you that the sun is alive, and can be angry,
and the sea is alive, and can sulk,
and the air is alive, and can deny us as a woman can.

But the blatant bathers don't know, they know nothing;
the vibration of the motor-car has bruised their insensitive bottoms
into rubber-like deadness, Dunlop inflated unconcern.

In a Spanish Tram-Car

She fanned herself with a violet fan
and looked sulky, under the thick straight brows.

The wisp of modern black mantilla
made her half Madonna, half Astarte.

Suddenly her yellow-brown eyes looked with a flare into mine;
—we could sin together!—

The spark fell and kindled instantly on my blood,
then died out almost as swiftly.

She can keep her sin
She can sin with some thick-set Spaniard.
Sin doesn't interest me.

Sea-Bathers

Oh the handsome bluey-brown bodies, they might just as well be gutta
   percha,
and the reddened limbs red indiarubber tubing, inflated,
and the half-hidden private parts just a little brass tap, rubinetto,
turned on for different purposes.

They call it health, it looks like nullity.

Only here and there a pair of eyes, haunted, looks out as if asking:
where then is life?

The Deadly Victorian

We hate the Victorians so much
because we are the third and fourth generation
expiating their sins
in the excruciating torment of hopelessness, helplessness, listlessness,
because they were such base and sordid optimists
successfully castrating the body politic,
and we are the gelded third and fourth generation.

Modern Problems

The worst of it is
When a woman can only love, flamily, those of her own sex
she has a secret, almost ecstasised hatred of maleness in any man
that she exudes like pearly white poison gas,
and men often succumb like white mice in a laboratory, around her,
specimens to be anatomised.

We Can't Be Too Careful

We can't be too careful
about the British Public.
It gets bigger and bigger
and its perambulator has to get bigger and bigger
and its dummy-teat has to be made bigger and bigger and bigger
and the job of changing its diapers gets bigger and bigger and bigger
    and bigger
and the sound of its howling gets bigger and bigger and bigger and
    bigger and bigger
and the feed of pap that we nurses and guardian angels of the press
    have to deal out to it
gets bigger and bigger and bigger and bigger and bigger and bigger
yet its belly ache seems to get bigger too
and soon even god won't be big enough to handle that infant.

Broadcasting to the G.B.P.

"Hushaby baby, on a tree top
when the wind blows, the cradle shall rock,
when the bough breaks—"

                                             Stop that at once!
You'll give the Great British Public a nervous shock!

"Goosey goosey gander
whither do you wander
upstairs, downstairs
in my lady's—"

                                    Stop! where's your education?
Don't you know that's obscene?
Remember the British Public!

"Baa—baa black sheep
have you any wool?
yes sir! yes sir!
three bags full!
One for the master, and one for the dame,
and one for the little boy, that lives down the—"

                                                 No!
You'd better omit that, too communistic!
Remember the state of mind of the British Public.

"Pussy-cat pussy-cat where have you been?
I've been up London to see the fine queen!
Pussy-cat pussy-cat what did you there?
I frightened a little mouse—"

                                      Thank you! thank you!
There are no mice in our Royal Palaces. Omit it!

"Gross, Coarse, Hideous"
(Police description of my pictures.)

Lately I saw a sight most quaint:
London's lily-like policemen faint
in virgin outrage as they viewed
the nudity of a Lawrence nude!

To Pino

O Pino
What a bean-o!
when we printed Lady C.!

Little Giuntina
couldn't have been a
better little bee!

When you told him
perhaps they'd scold him
for printing those naughty words
All he could say:
"But we do it every day!
like the pigeons and the other little birds!"

And dear old lady Jean
"I don't know what you mean
by publishing such a book.

We're all in it, all my family
me and Ekkerhart and Somers and Pamelie—
you're no better than a crook—!"

"Wait, dear Lady Jean, wait a minute!
What makes you think that you're all in it?
Did you ever open the book?

Is Ekke Sir Clifford? it's really funny!
And you, dear Lady Jean, are you Connie?
Do open the book and look!—"

But off she went, being really rattled
and there's a battle that's still to be battled
along with the others! what luck!

There Are No Gods

There are no gods, and you can please yourself
have a game of tennis, go out in the car, do some shopping, sit and talk,
   talk, talk
with a cigarette browning your fingers.

There are no gods, and you can please yourself—
go and please yourself—

But leave me alone, leave me alone, to myself!
and then in the room, whose is the presence
that makes the air so still and lovely to me?

Who is it that softly touches the sides of my breast
and touches me over the heart
so that my heart beats soothed, soothed, soothed and at peace?

Who is it smooths the bed-sheets like the cool
smooth ocean when the fishes rest on edge
in their own dream?

Who is it that clasps and kneads my naked feet, till they unfold,
till all is well, till all is utterly well? the lotus-lilies of the feet!

I tell you, it is no woman, it is no man, for I am alone.
And I fall asleep with the gods, the gods
that are not, or that are
according to the soul's desire,
like a pool into which we plunge, or do not plunge.